PENGUIN MODERN CLASSICS
Playground

Considered one of the greatest fiction writers in Hindi, PREMCHAND (1880–1936) was born Dhanpat Rai in Lamahi, a small village near Banaras. He wrote in Urdu under the name of Nawab Rai and changed it to Premchand when his collection of short stories, *Soz-e-Vatan*, was seized for sedition in 1909. In a prolific career, spanning three decades, Premchand wrote fourteen novels, two plays, almost three hundred short stories and several articles, reviews and editorials. He edited four journals, and also set up his own printing press. Though best known for his stories exposing the horrors of poverty and social injustice, he wrote on a variety of themes with equal facility—romance, satire, social dramas, nationalist tales, and yarns steeped in folklore.

MANJU JAIN retired as Professor from the Department of English, University of Delhi. She is the author of *T.S. Eliot and American Philosophy: The Harvard Years* and *A Critical Reading of the Selected Poems of T.S. Eliot*. She has also edited the collection *Narratives of Indian Cinema*.

PREMCHAND

Playground

RANGBHOOMI

Translated from the Hindi by Manju Jain

PENGUIN BOOKS

PENGUIN BOOKS
Published by the Penguin Group
Penguin Books India Pvt. Ltd, 11 Community Centre, Panchsheel Park,
New Delhi 110 017, India
Penguin Group (USA) Inc., 375 Hudson Street, New York, New York 10014, USA
Penguin Group (Canada), 90 Eglinton Avenue East, Suite 700, Toronto, Ontario,
M4P 2Y3, Canada (a division of Pearson Penguin Canada Inc.)
Penguin Books Ltd, 80 Strand, London WC2R 0RL, England
Penguin Ireland, 25 St Stephen's Green, Dublin 2, Ireland (a division of Penguin Books
Ltd)
Penguin Group (Australia), 250 Camberwell Road, Camberwell, Victoria 3124,
Australia (a division of Pearson Australia Group Pty Ltd)
Penguin Group (NZ), 67 Apollo Drive One, Rosedale, North Shore 0632,
New Zealand (a division of Pearson New Zealand Ltd)
Penguin Group (South Africa) (Pty) Ltd, 24 Sturdee Avenue, Rosebank,
Johannesburg 2196, South Africa

Penguin Books Ltd, Registered Offices: 80 Strand, London WC2R 0RL, England

First published in Penguin Modern Classics 2011
Translation copyright © Manju Jain 2011

ISBN 9780143102113

Typeset in AdobeGaramond by R. Ajith Kumar, New Delhi
Printed at Chaman Offset Printers, Delhi

My parents
For their gentle wisdom and loving care

Ashok
In memory of our shared childhood

Contents

Acknowledgements

My main intellectual and emotional debt is to my mother who has constantly stood by me as only a mother can. She meticulously read all the drafts of every chapter and provided nuances of meanings and idioms where dictionaries failed. The translation was begun when my father was still alive. He took keen interest in it, especially in Soordas's character. I have greatly missed his knowledge of Urdu and of Indian myth and history.

The prime mover behind this project is Harish Trivedi, whose impassioned lecture on Premchand and E.M. Forster several years ago inspired me to undertake the translation. He has given continuous cheerful support and much valuable information. Anand Prakash read an earlier draft, gave several suggestions, and prodded me into completing the work with his encouragement. Rukun Advani read an earlier draft of the first two chapters and gave detailed comments and suggestions which were of great help for the rest of the work as well. Rajiva Verma and Janet Fields read drafts of some of the chapters and gave useful comments. I am grateful to Alok Bhalla, Alok Rai, Arun Prabha Mukherjee, Bela Seth, Narayani Gupta, Rama Puri, Sumanyu Satpathy and Vanajam Ravindran for conversations, suggestions, encouragement and information, and to Christel Devadawson for assiduously tracing a reference. I should like also to thank the staff of the India International and the Sahitya Akademy Libraries for their help. At Penguin, I should like to thank Ravi Singh, Diya Kar Hazra, R. Sivapriya, Anupama Ramakrishnan, and Arundhati Nath.

Translator's Note

The main challenge in translating *Rangbhoomi* was to be faithful to the text while not being literal and doing justice to the multiple linguistic registers and discourses that Premchand deploys in the novel as well as to evoke the material culture in which it is embedded. To that end I have often translated metaphors and proverbs literally because these embody the nuances and the lived practices of a culture. I have included Hindi/Urdu words to suggest a flavour of the original and have given a glossary as well as annotations. The reader would otherwise either feel befuddled and ignore these or frequently have to look up dictionaries and encyclopedias to figure out meanings and references. Many Hindi/Urdu words have of course entered common usage and are to be found in the Oxford Dictionary of English. Perhaps such translations will enable more such words to be included and serve as bridges across different languages and cultures. I have not glossed culinary items which are now well-known thanks to the worldwide popularity of Indian cuisine and mostly found in the OED, except for a few that belong specifically to the rural milieu. Dialect is difficult to translate, especially when it is often a matter of pronunciation. I have therefore occasionally spelt a word to suggest the original pronunciation and have annotated it. It is of course impossible to capture the inflexions of dialect as well as of Dr Ganguly's Banglacized Hindi so I have not attempted to do that. I have also tried to be context-sensitive in translating words that can have different social and political meanings depending on the context, such as 'jaati', which can variously signify caste, community, race, nation, species, among others. I have attempted to capture the rhythms and the structure of Premchand's prose as well as the shifts in his use of tenses. He often uses short sentences which I have retained where possible to evoke the staccato effect that he probably wished to communicate. I have also retained the style that he uses for dialogues—the name of the person followed by a dash—for its clarity as well as for the dramatic counterpoint that it provides.

I have not used politically correct language in translating caste names and words for that would be to efface history as well as to negate Premchand's deep concern with caste oppression.

I have consulted the *Premchand Rachnavali* (vol. 3) edition of *Rangbhoomi* as well as the Diamond Pocket Books edition of 2000. Premchand's prefatory note is not included in the Rachnavali edition. The process of collating errors and misprints in both the editions gave me a heightened awareness of the instability of a text, where an alphabet or a syllabic mark can change the meaning of an entire sentence.

Finally, to quote T.S. Eliot on translating Shakespeare: 'What can be translated? A story, a dramatic plot, the impressions of a living character in action, an image, a proposition. What cannot be translated is the incantation, the music of the words, and that part of the meaning which is in the music.'* One may add that what cannot also be translated are the nuances of the lived realities of one culture in terms of another, as well as the multivalences of one language into those of another. Translation is yet another form of interpretation and not a mimetic rendition of the original text. All that a translator can hope to do is to make the novel accessible to readers who do not know the language.

---

* Eliot, 'Goethe as the Sage', *On Poetry and Poets*, p. 216.

Introduction

Premchand's oeuvre negotiates the wide-ranging transformations that were taking place in the country in the first three and a half decades of the twentieth century. It is germinated by the creative tensions in the development of his thinking as he witnessed and responded to the vast changes that were taking place around him, not only within the country, but in the international arena as well. In his journalism, letters, articles and speeches he commented upon and analysed practically every topic of contemporary importance, making him an exemplar of a writer and an intellectual who was cosmopolitan while remaining rooted in the local. It is my contention that a novel such as *Rangbhoomi* provides a radical alternative to colonial historiography as well as to colonial literary representations.

Looking back on his oeuvre towards the end of his life, Premchand wrote that *Rangbhoomi* was, in his opinion, his best work.[1] *Rangbhoomi* (which can variously be translated as playground/theatre/arena/stage/battlefield) is quite literally a veritable playground or battlefield of conflicting perspectives, ideological positions, discourses, genres, voices and linguistic registers that crisscross the novel. It constantly compels readers to engage with this plurality, evoking the fluidity and polyphony of the creative imagination at work, in a dialogic mode, through several, often contradictory, perspectives. This polyphony is heightened through the shifts and nuances of the narratorial voice—didactic, ironic, melodramatic, playful, disclaiming omniscient knowledge, eliciting the participation of the reader—much like the kathavaachak or storyteller in a village chaupaal.

Premchand had begun working on *Rangbhoomi* in October 1922. He completed the Urdu draft (as *Chaugan-e-Hasti*) on 1 April 1924 and was simultaneously turning it into Hindi. The manuscript of the Hindi version was completed within four months, on 12 August 1924, and published in January 1925. *Chaugan-e-Hasti* (Arena of Life) was

xiii

published later in 1928 (Rai 1982, 205-6, 390). The earlier Urdu draft was revised in the light of the Hindi version.[2]

Tracing back the temporal span of the novel on the basis of the internal evidence of Premchand's self-referential allusion to his own play *Karbala* (published in November 1924) in Chapter 41, just a short while before the final denouement, and Dr Ganguly's reference to the Bengal floods of 1922 (Ch. 32), makes it seem to cover a period of approximately five years, from about the end of 1919 to about the end of 1924.[3] Though completed in August 1924, the action of the novel is proleptically projected a few months into the future, or perhaps Premchand may have continued to write/revise it before its final publication. The eviction of Pandeypur begins on 1 May; the protest continues after that for about two months leading to Soordas's death; his statue is built about six months later, taking the action on to about the end of December 1924. This of course was a period in which there were vast upheavals in the country; *Rangbhoomi* dramatizes these changes as they were taking place. If, as Rai says, *Rangbhoomi* is the epic of Premchand's life up to this moment (Rai 1982, 197), it can also be regarded as an epic of the nation during this period, reflecting the turbulence of the times, with all the fissures and contradictions that were then prevalent. Since the novel is so deeply embedded in the history and politics of the time, it will be useful to trace the trajectory of Premchand's response to the events that were taking place and to see how they are mediated in *Rangbhoomi*.

It is worth recalling that the discourse of nationalism itself, at this stage in the formation of the nation, was undergoing radical modifications and was fraught with internal contradictions— between nation and community, loyalty to the country and loyalty to the community, whether of caste, region or religion. It was in the early 1920s that the nationalism of people like Gandhi changed, as Gyanendra Pandey writes, from the earlier stress on the 'possibility of a coexistence of loyalty to the country and loyalty to the (religious) Community' to the primacy of the one over the other (Pandey 1990, 237-38). 'Nationalism is greater than sectarianism', Gandhi wrote in January 1922, emphasizing that '[I]n that sense we are Indians first and Hindus, Mussulmans, Parsis, Christians afterwards' (in Pandey 1990, 238). It is important to remember, though, that there were several contending conceptions of nationhood, including the religious, resulting in compromises and vacillations among different kinds of nationalists (Pandey 1990, 255).[4]

The Early Political Context

The earliest political influences on Premchand were those of the Arya Samaj and the Social Reforms League led by Gopal Krishna Gokhale and Mahadev Govind Ranade who belonged to the moderate faction of the Congress as opposed to the militants led by Bal Gangadhar Tilak. Like the younger generation of revolutionaries, Premchand also admired Vivekananda, Mazzini and Garibaldi. However, the brutal repression of the militants within the Congress and the activities of the revolutionaries outside it by the government increasingly made Premchand more rebellious (Rai 1982, 65-68). This was especially so in the wake of the excesses of the British government in crushing the revolutionaries following the Partition of Bengal in October 1905. Premchand, in fact, wrote an article in support of the Swadeshi movement, started by Tilak, Aurobindo Ghosh, and Lala Lajpat Rai, which had been triggered off by this Partition, in November 1905 (*PR* 7, 39-40). Premchand's revolutionary ardour became even more intense when the fifteen-year-old Khudiram Bose was hanged for sedition by the British government on 11 August 1908. Premchand bought his portrait and hung it in his study even though he was employed in government service at the time (Rai 1982, 67-68). His own direct confrontation with the British colonial government occurred in 1909, when he was reprimanded by the district magistrate of Hamirpur, where he was posted as a deputy sub-inspector of schools, for the seditious content of his collection of short stories, *Soz-e-Vatan* (Dirge of the Nation), published in 1908. All the remaining copies of the book had to be surrendered and Premchand was informed that he could never again write anything without the government's permission (*PR* 7, 366-67). This led him to change his name from Nawab Rai, under which he had written so far, to Premchand.

The War and the immediate post-War years, as Sumit Sarkar writes, witnessed dramatic changes in Indian life, the three most crucial landmarks being constitutional reforms, the emergence of Gandhi as leader of 'a qualitatively new all-India mass nationalism', and important shifts in India's colonial economy (Sarkar 2002, 165). These years witnessed the traumatic events following the introduction of the Rowlatt Bill in the Legislative Assembly in February 1919. The Bill, which came into effect as the Rowlatt Act in March 1919, indefinitely extended the 'emergency measures' of the Defence of India Regulations Act enacted during the First World War for the purpose of controlling public unrest and eradicating sedition. Protests against the imposition of the Rowlatt Act led to Gandhi's Satyagraha movement, which roused massive nation-wide support. The Jallianwalla Bagh massacre took place on 13 April 1919 when soldiers of the British Indian Army, under the command of General Dyer, opened fire on an unarmed gathering of men, women, and children. In fact, there are repeated references in *Rangbhoomi* to the disturbances and brutal repressions in Punjab, and it is to Punjab that Rani Jahnavi, Indu and Dr Ganguly are headed at the end of the novel.

Constitutional Reforms

Meanwhile, in 1917, legislative autonomy had been promised to the country by the Lloyd George government through Edwin Montagu, Secretary of State for India. The Montagu-Chelmsford Report was prepared in 1918 and formed the basis of the Government of India Act of 1919. The principle of 'diarchy' was introduced by the setting up of Indian provincial and central legislative assemblies, in which authority was 'shared' between the British government and the Indians. Real power, however, remained in the hands of the viceroy and the provincial governors. Following widespread discontent with the Reforms, the Indian National Congress at its annual meeting in September 1920 supported Gandhi's proposal of 'swarajya' or self rule, which was to be implemented through a policy of non-cooperation with the British government. Gandhi had issued a manifesto on 10 March 1920 outlining his plan for non-cooperation.

Premchand was deeply sceptical about the Montgu-Chelmsford (Montford) Reforms. In a letter of 21 December 1919 to his friend Dayanarayan Nigam, editor of *Zamana*, he explained that, considering the moderate policy of *Zamana*, he did not think it appropriate to write on political issues for the paper. The moderate party, he wrote, was being unnecessarily arrogant at this time, because if there was any speciality about the Reforms it was only that the educated class would get more facilities, and given the way in which this class was sucking the blood of the people as lawyers, it would cut their throats in the same way on becoming officials in the future (*CP*, 94-95).

In *Rangbhoomi*, Dr Ganguly, who appears in part to be modelled on Gokhale, is made to reject any policy of appeasement by the British through such measures as the Montford Reforms thus going back on his earlier championing of a policy of cooperation and conciliation with the colonial government for the attainment of nationalist goals. Ganguly, in fact, now rejects the hypocrisy of the British liberal tradition as represented by Lord Ripon, the radical liberal Viceroy of India, A.O. Hume, one of the founders of the Indian National Congress, and even Annie Besant, on whom Premchand claimed to have based Sophia's character,[5] all of whom he had earlier constantly cited in support of his trust that the British wanted to rule India on the basis of justice (Ch. 50, 628-9). (Besant had by then become a moderate. She was shouted down for supporting the Montford reforms at the Delhi Congress of 1918 [Sarkar 2002, 188]). It may be noted here that Clark, the district magistrate, himself emphasizes that the British have only their imperialist goals in sight and are not inspired by noble and high principles, be they conservative or liberal, radical or labour, nationalist or socialist (Ch. 35, 450). This is what Premchand had to say about the Labour Party in an article of 13 April 1922, 'Systems that Nurture and Oppose Swarajya', even while praising it, corroborating Clark's assertion: 'There is no doubt that the leadership of the Labour Party is in the control of people who are "imperialists" at heart. These people want India's liberation, but by its remaining subject to England.... Their self-centredness has compelled India's well-wisher, Mr Andrews, to remark that we don't trust the justice of the English' (*PR* 7, 245). As Dayanarayan Nigam recounts: 'Premchand held in distrust the very idea of conciliation in an unequal fight.... He believed that there was no other way except direct confrontation with the government' (Rai 1982, 67). Prabhu Sevak is overwhelmed by the reception that he receives when he visits England and by the liberalism and enlightenment of English society. However, as Indradutt tells Vinay, 'the only difference is that he is preaching friendship without equality, we consider equality to be essential for friendship' (Ch. 41, 528). One cannot help recalling Aziz's rejoinder to Fielding in E.M. Forster's *A Passage to India* that there can be no friendship without equality.

Premchand had written a laudatory article on Gokhale in the November–December 1905 issue of *Zamana*, praising Gokhale for talking 'with great pride of the enormous benefits that have accrued to us due to the British rule' (Rai 1982, 66). Simultaneously, however, in an article of 16 November 1905, Premchand had also supported the Swadeshi movement that had begun as a result of the Partition of Bengal (*PR* 7, 39-40). In *Rangbhoomi*, Premchand no doubt had Gokhale's views in mind, as well as his own earlier admiration of them, when he has Kunwar Bharat Singh contradict Mrs Sevak's eulogy on the 'benefits' resulting from British rule (Ch. 14). Ganguly's political journey then may be seen to chart that of Premchand himself as well as that of the nation, torn between conflicting options for political action in the struggle for independence.

Ganguly also partially resembles Deshbandhu Chittaranjan Das in his moderate political stance (Rai 1982, 201). In his obituary on Das in 1925, Premchand wrote about the discussions and debates between the moderates and the militants concerning the Reforms and Das's proposal of joining the Councils to oppose the government in order to remove the passivity that had set in after Gandhi's imprisonment and to reawaken enthusiasm for nationalism. For Premchand, however, at this stage of the freedom struggle, there was an innate opposition between membership of Councils and non-cooperation. To join the Councils, he believed, was to support cooperation. Echoing Ganguly, however, Premchand writes of Das's desire that he should be reborn in this country and spend his life serving it. Other characteristics of Das that Premchand singles out, and that he shares with Ganguly, are his integrity, generosity, inability to save money, sociability, remaining firm on his principles, cheerfulness and simple-heartedness (*PR* 7, 310-13).

Premchand, however, later supported participation in the Councils and criticized their boycott by the Congress on the grounds that non-participation would only increase the autocracy of the government, allowing it to make whatever laws it wanted. He therefore welcomed Gandhi's later decision of supporting participation in the Councils, for 'the moves of an army should change according to new circumstances'.[6]

This may be seen less as a going back by Premchand on his earlier position than as a modification and a change in strategy in the light of the prevalent political circumstances.

Bolshevism

Premchand's revolutionary enthusiasm was also fuelled by the Bolshevik Revolution of 1917 which, for him, represented the rebellion of peasants after centuries of exploitation and oppression. On 21 Dec 1919, in the same letter in which he had criticized the moderate party for its acceptance of the Montford Reforms, Premchand wrote to Nigam, 'I am now more or less convinced by Bolshevist principles' (*CP*, 95). Before that, in his article of February 1919, 'Purana Zamana: Naya Zamana' (The Old Age: The New Age), Premchand prophetically proclaimed that the coming age would be that of the peasants and the labourers, and that India could not remain unaffected by these winds of change, for 'who knew before the Revolution that there was so much hidden strength in the oppressed people of Russia?' (*PR* 7, 197-98). Premchand continued to defend the Soviet Union as well as Stalin against rumours published against them as the propaganda of capitalist nations (*PR* 8, 165-66, 415; *PR* 9, 98). And in one of his last pieces, 'A Mercantile Civilization' (August 1936), in which he denounced capitalism, mercantilism, hereditary wealth and private property, he expressed his faith in the Soviet system whose basic principle was the recognition of individual merit and effort (*PR* 7, 515, 517).

The Russian Revolution caused widespread fear among the British authorities. 'In a panic reminiscent of that caused by the French Revolution', Sarkar writes, 'official reports from 1919-20 onwards and the Home Political Files of the 1920s were obsessed with the "Bolshevik Menace" and discovered Bolshevik ideas and Soviet agents everywhere, with even people like Gandhi or C.R. Das at times not above suspicion' (Sarkar 2002, 177, 249). *Rangbhoomi* reflects a pervasive fear among the authorities of the spread of communism and Bolshevism, which John Sevak also articulates in his conversation with Kunwar Bharat Singh (Ch 25, 301). Sophia is even thought to be a Bolshevik agent by Clark when she is with Veerpaal Singh and the dacoits in Rajputana.

And yet Premchand did not himself join the revolutionary

movement. He may at times have supported violence, advocated radical solutions and used Marxist rhetoric but like George Eliot, whose *Silas Marner* he had adapted in Hindi as *Sukhdas* (Devotee of Bliss), he too appears to have subscribed to an evolutionist and gradualist rather than a revolutionary path of social and political progress: 'I believe in social evolution', he wrote in his letter of 31 December 1934 in English, 'our object being to educate public opinion. Revolution is the failure of saner methods…. It may lead us to worse forms of dictatorship denying all personal liberty' (*CP,* 432). In *Rangbhoomi* too Sophia rejects the dacoits when she is confronted with the violence in which their terrorism has resulted. Her decision reflects Premchand's own fears of violence, despite his attraction towards revolutionary ideologies. Premchand was also critical of the hypocritical communism of the upper classes such as that of Mahendra Singh who is described as being inclined towards communism, despite being an affluent taluqdar, but is motivated only by his self-interest. For Prabhu Sevak, communism was merely a topic of entertainment, and Vinay's communism is comically transformed into selfishness as soon as he boards a train (Ch 35, 459).

The Impact of Gandhi and the National Movement

Premchand was simultaneously attracted to Gandhi's philosophy of non-violence. Like Gandhi, Premchand too was deeply influenced by Tolstoy's ideals of spirituality and non-violence, which he had imbibed before Gandhi's appearance on the Indian political horizon. He had already adapted twenty-three of Tolstoy's stories in Hindi, some of which Gandhi had also translated into Gujarati (Rai 1982, 43). The turning point in Premchand's life came on 8 February 1921 when Gandhi arrived in Gorakhpur, where Premchand had been teaching at the Normal School since August 1916, to enlist support for his Non-Cooperation movement. Responding to Gandhi's call for non-cooperation, Premchand resigned his government job on 15 February 1921 (Rai 1982, 154). Gandhi, however, called off the Non-Cooperation movement on 11 February 1922 at Bardoli, following the news of the burning alive of twenty-two policemen by angry peasants protesting against liquor sales and high food prices at Chauri Chaura, a village in Gorakhpur district (Sarkar 2002, 206,

224-25). He was arrested on 10 March 1922, tried for sedition, and sentenced to six years' imprisonment. He was released two years later on medical grounds in February 1924.

The Indian political scene, though, was by no means quiet even though the Non-Cooperation movement had been called off. It was volatile with widespread agrarian unrest, peasant and tribal movements, labour protests, railway and industrial strikes, strikes of the textile mills of Bombay in January–March 1924, and in September–December 1925, communal strife. There was a seething discontent with the Congress for having called off the Non-Cooperation movement, and the emergence of communism and revolutionary terrorism.[7]

Premchand did not see Gandhi's decision as an end to non-cooperation and the struggle for independence. In an article of May 1922, 'The Dividing Line', he wrote that it was wrong to conclude that Non-Cooperation had ended; the movement had to be given a form in which there would be no conflict with the bureaucracy because '[W]e do not wish to make our dear brothers the target of machine guns' (*PR* 7, 251-52). It has been conjectured that Premchand wrote *Rangbhoomi* in order to reawaken enthusiasm for the national movement, which was dormant during those years when the novel was being written, since the Non-Cooperation movement had been called off and its leaders were in prison. *Rangbhoomi* is a resounding proclamation of a resolve that the battle will continue, notwithstanding the absence of the prominent leaders, including of course, Gandhi himself (Sharma 1995, 80). As Soordas soliloquizes on his deathbed, they will continue to fight with renewed strength and unity and will recoup their forces even though they are defeated (Ch 46, 603). The very title of the novel is a metaphor taken from a song that Soordas sings in Ch 18 (234-5):

Bhai, why do you turn your face away from battle?
You have come to the rangbhoomi, to show your glory,
Why do you break the law of dharma?[8]

The metaphor of life as a playground that recurs throughout the novel, and the philosophy of disinterested action, central for an understanding of the conflict against oppression, may owe much to the Hindu philosophical tradition of the world as God's leela or play and to the *Gita*. One cannot help speculating too that Premchand was also deeply influenced in his use of the metaphor of Soordas as a player, 'the player had departed the field' (Ch. 46, 604), and of the struggle for independence as well as of life as a game to be played on the battlefield/ playground, by such popular and much anthologized poems as 'Vitai Lampada', by Henry Newbolt (1897) used for propaganda during World War I, with its emphasis on playing the game with stoicism and determination, on the cricket field as well as on the battlefield: 'Play up! Play up! and play the game'.[9] For Soordas's ruminations on his deathbed suggest that India had much to learn from the British when it came to the fight for independence. There may also be an ironic undercutting of the 'Great Game' of espionage in Rudyard Kipling's *Kim* in Premchand's use of the metaphor of the game.[9]

As Premchand himself claims in his prefatory note, Soordas, the blind protagonist, is an ideal Gandhian character. But even here, with his characteristic scepticism that refuses uncritically to accept any ideology, Premchand subjects Gandhi's philosophy and politics to a critical scrutiny. Soordas is by no means an idealized Gandhian figure—the metaphor of blindness and insight is apposite here. His defects and virtues alike are analysed by the narrator (Ch. 46, 604-5).[10] The artist who had crafted the statue to commemorate Soordas may have given it a sublime and spiritualized dimension, suggestive perhaps of Gandhi (Rai 1982, 201), but Premchand does not allow this idealization to remain. For the rebuilt statue, after it has been knocked down by Mahendra Singh, retains the distortions and blemishes that it had received as a result of the fall, suggesting perhaps the distortions and blemishes in Soordas, in Gandhi, and in human nature in general. Moreover, Soordas's prophecy on his deathbed that a mahatma will soon be born in this country (Ch. 44, 586) is surely a hope for the birth of a saviour other than Gandhi, who will lead the country forward.[11]

It has been suggested that Premchand's enthusiasm for Gandhi waned around 1931 after the Gandhi-Irwin Pact, calling off the Civil Disobedience movement (Sharma 1999, 43). However, in his letters and in his editorials for *Hans* and *Jagaran*, Premchand continued to express his veneration for Gandhi, although he did not support him and the Congress in their policy of non-participation in the Councils and pleaded that the Congress should participate in the elections (*PR* 8, 383, 395). Most significantly, he was scornful of Gandhi's attribution of the Bihar earthquake to 'previous sins' rather than to natural phenomena (*PR* 9, 17-25). Premchand, however, berated Gandhi's opponents who forgot that 'at this time only that old man can be India's leader' (*PR* 8, 342). He was often hyperbolic in his praise of Gandhi, raising him to the status of divinity and claiming that even Krishna 'can be proved to be higher than him only if he is considered to be a hero in the arena of the human mind' (*PR* 9, 394-95), and prophesying that if this was the epoch of Gandhi, in the end victory would be Gandhi's (Shivarani Devi 1944, 254).

To return to *Rangbhoomi*, the most striking instance of Premchand's endorsement of satyagraha and non-cooperation is the refusal of the sepoys to open fire when they are commanded to by the police superintendent, Mr Brown, an instance of non-cooperation that is seen as unique in the history of the army (Ch. 42, 555). This seems to be Premchand's assertion that the struggle against the colonial powers and their cohorts will continue at the ground level. Gandhi may have called off the Non-Cooperation movement in what was seen as a betrayal of the fight for independence. His lessons, though, had not been forgotten. History is here being made not by the elite leaders but by humble people at the grass roots level, who stood to lose their jobs and their lives. Premchand is also remarkably prescient here in pointing forward to the Peshawar incident of 23 April 1930. This was when the Royal Garhwal Rifles, led by Veer Chandra Singh Garhwal, refused to open fire on the unarmed Pashtoon satyagrahis, the Khudai Khidmatgar, demonstrating against the arrest of Ghaffar Khan, who had led the salt satyagraha movement in Peshawar. The entire platoon was arrested and many received heavy penalties including life imprisonment. Garhwal himself was tortured and sentenced to rigorous imprisonment. One cannot help wondering if Garhwal had been influenced by this incident in *Rangbhoomi*. Premchand paid tribute to those Garhwali heroes in his editorial of July 1930 in *Hans* (*PR* 8, 58-59).

The most significant aspect of *Rangbhoomi* is that Premchand should have chosen a blind, crippled beggar as his protagonist.[12] For Soordas is the epicentre of the struggle against the combined vested interests of the colonial state, its bureaucracy, the feudal landowning classes, the Indian bureaucracy, and the mercantile bourgeoisie. Premchand perceived the class interests at work within the national movement as well as the role of the British in consolidating those interests. In an article of 1919, he wrote: 'Among all our leaders for swarajya, the majority are advocates and landlords. These are the two groups that predominate in our elected councils as well....There is no reason why the people should prefer your rule to that of rulers from another country.... What is the guarantee that their condition will not actually worsen if they come into your clutches?' (*PR* 7, 196-98). And he wrote again in April 1922, 'Remember, we don't have to take swarajya from the British, we have to take it from our own compatriots' (*PR* 8, 21).

In *Rangbhoomi*, Premchand gives agency to Soordas and to the people of Pandeypur to articulate his conviction that resistance to oppression can come only from the oppressed, despite their own vested interests and the differences among them. Vinay is forced to realize how firm and resolute ordinary people could be, and the people of Pandeypur taunt him, 'Rajas and rais can't do what a helpless blind man can' (Ch. 43, 577). In fact, Premchand's analysis of the mechanics of power in *Rangbhoomi* is founded, like that of Michel Foucault, 'on the basis of daily struggles at grass roots level, among those whose fight was located in the fine meshes of the web of power' (Foucault 1980, 116). Power, for Premchand as for Foucault, is dispersed in a multiplicity of networks and indefinite fields of power relations or strategies of domination: 'Power is exercised from innumerable points, in the interplay of non-egalitarian and mobile relations' (Foucault, 1990, 94) and resistance can therefore be realized only through localized strategies. As Premchand proclaimed forcefully in 1918, 'India's liberation depends upon India's people' (*PR* 8, 19).

When discussing the issue of nationalism, it is also important to stress Soordas's insistence on dharma here. As Gyan Pandey points out, many of the ambiguities and inconsistencies of nationalist discourse in India can perhaps be explained in terms of an interaction and contrary pulls of two idioms: 'a "modernist" idiom deriving from the metropolitan culture of the colonizers', and 'a "dharmic" idiom which derived from the pre-colonial traditions of the colonized' (Pandey

1990, 208). Soordas insists throughout the novel that his fight is for dharma, and in making him do so, Premchand aligns himself with this aspect of nationalist discourse, which of course was the dimension that Gandhi had emphasized as well. Premchand lamented the role of Western modernity in destroying the foundation of dharma (*PR* 7, 220) and it was on this basis that he found communism to be inadequate, advocating instead the Gandhian way of karmayoga, ahimsa and love (*PR* 7, 360-62).

Premchand lauded the attempts of the Congress to mobilize the peasants in the nationalist cause, singling out the conflict of interests between the zamindars and capitalists on the one side and the peasants and labourers on the other. However, he gave credit to the political awakening among the peasants and workers for the democratization of the Congress rather than to its leaders (*PR* 7, 231). The peasant upsurge in south and south-east Avadh associated with Baba Ramchandra, who seemed to be a local variant of Gandhi and who claimed some religious inspiration, culminated in widespread agrarian riots between January and March 1921. There was renewed peasant violence in 1921 when Congress and Kisan Sabha workers sponsored a campaign called Eka (unity) (Dhanagare 1983, 118-19). Gandhi condemned these riots. In a speech at Faizabad after the UP agrarian riots of early 1921, he 'deprecated all attempts to create discord between landlords and tenants and advised the tenants to suffer rather than fight for they had to join all forces for fighting against the most powerful zamindar, namely the Government' (in Sarkar 2002, 209). As Sarkar says, 'the emphasis was always on unifying issues and on trying to cut across or reconcile class divisions' (Sarkar 2002, 209). A month later, Gandhi's *Instructions to U.P. Peasants* categorically ordered: 'We may not withhold taxes from the Government or rent from the landlord.... It should be borne in mind that we want to turn zamindars into friends' (in Sarkar 2002, 209-10).

Nehru's response in 1921 was no different. He recalls in his *Autobiography* that at a meeting in Faizabad he persuaded those who had indulged in violence to put up their hands, knowing full well that the police were present and the men would be jailed (Sarkar 2002, 223). By the summer of 1921, the kisan movement seems to have been swallowed up by Non-Cooperation, with specific peasant demands relegated to the background (Sarkar 2002, 224). Premchand elides the role that Gandhi, Nehru and the Congress played at this time in trying to reconcile class divisions and avoiding class-conflict and violence rather than foregrounding the demands and rights of the peasants and the workers, thus alienating them from the national movement.

However, while Premchand gives agency to the people of Pandeypur and the neighbouring villages and shows that violence is inevitable in the battle between the oppressors and the oppressed, *Rangbhoomi* is not really about peasants. Pandeypur is not a village but a muhalla, or a suburb on the peripheries of the city of Banaras. When they are dislocated, the residents of Pandeypur are very reluctant to move to the countryside. The text in fact charts the various spaces of the city as well as its varying hues of caste, class, religion and politics.

Premchand shared with Gandhi his critique of modern industrial civilization. He supported Gandhi's Swadeshi movement as well as his assertion of the need to preserve village economies. In 1921 Premchand wrote in a pamphlet entitled 'Swaraj and its Benefits': 'It should also be remembered that ours is predominantly an agricultural country. Craft and industry will always remain subservient to agriculture here.... There is no doubt that we won't be able to compete with foreign goods by this industrial policy. But when we stop foreign goods by taxing them, the question of competing with them won't arise' (*PR* 7, 223).

It is on this basis that John Sevak's veneer of patriotism and his tendentious arguments about encouraging indigenous industry are critiqued when he tries to persuade Kunwar Bharat Singh to invest in his cigarette factory, and Soordas's prophetic misgivings about the deleterious modernity that the setting up of the factory will bring to Pandeypur are fulfilled. *Rangbhoomi*, in fact, is a scathing denunciation of capitalism. In a later essay of 1936, 'Mahajani Sabhyata' (A Mercantile Civilization), written just before his death, Premchand condemned the evils of mercantile capitalism in terms that recall his denunciation of John Sevak and of the new business culture in *Rangbhoomi*: 'In this civilization the one motivation for all action is money.... (*PR* 7, 511-12). Premchand denounced capitalism even more forcefully when he wrote in 1933: 'To hope that the capitalists will desist from exploiting the destitute condition of the peasants is like expecting a dog to guard a hide. We'll have to arm ourselves in order to protect ourselves from this bloodthirsty beast' (*PR* 8, 466). John Sevak's predicament at the end is symptomatic of the emptiness at the heart of a capitalist society. His desire for wealth is insatiable and an end in itself, but it cannot fill the void within him.

Land Acquisition

Related to the question of industrialization is the issue of the diminution of grazing land for the cultivation of cash crops. At the time that Premchand wrote this novel, there was a controversy in Banaras over the acquisition of land by the government for the construction of a railway line and the industrial enterprises at Shivpur. This probably provided Premchand the theme of the uprooting of villagers by the incursion of industry into the areas surrounding big cities (Gopal 1964, 204-5). Premchand is here again remarkably prophetic in focusing on the negative effects of cultivating cash crops such as tobacco. He exposes the kind of rhetoric and reasoning that John Sevak deploys to persuade the residents of Pandeypur, which is similar to that which Lord Irwin would later use in addressing the landowners at Nagpur in 1926: 'You have referred to the great increase in cultivated area during recent years and the consequent diminution of grazing lands.... But I need hardly remind you of the service you are doing to your country by increasing the produce of your land. India today requires to import many things which she requires for the comfort of her people and the further development of her industries. For these she has to pay by her exports to the markets of the world, and therefore in increasing the quantity and improving the quality of your produce it is good to remember that there is patriotism to your great country as well as profit to yourselves' (in Fox 2008, 60).

Rangbhoomi is a narrative of homelessness, uprooting, and displacement in the name of development, progress, and industrialization, be they the victims of the Narmada project or of the Aswan dam. Soordas's declaration resounds almost a century later in the war cry of the villagers of Singur and Nandigram: 'We will give our blood, not our land.'[13] A central issue in *Rangbhoomi* is the politics of land acquisition, as brutal and oppressive then as they are now. Agricultural land was sought to be acquired in Singur in 2006 for the setting up of a car factory by Tata Motors under the archaic

1894 Land Acquisition Act, citing 'public purpose', when in fact it was for a private, profit-making project. It was under this very Land Acquisition Act, with the same 'public purpose' cited, that John Sevak had wanted to acquire Soordas's land for setting up his cigarette factory, with the connivance of the colonial administrative machinery. On 2 January 2007, the acquisition of 28,000 acres of land in Nandigram was announced for the setting up of a chemical hub and SEZ (Special Economic Zone), resulting in widespread protests and repressive state violence. As Shoma Anand writes, Singur and Nandigram are symptomatic of what is happening all over the country: 'Land takeover in the name of development or big industry. Summary eviction and displacement. Inadequate compensation. Lack of informed consent. Police action and state oppression.'[14] *Rangbhoomi*, then, makes us aware of how little things have changed over a century and how much more needs to be done when it comes to legislation and policies concerning land acquisition. Pandeypur, Singur, Nandigram belong to the same narrative of forced land acquisition in the name of progress, development and prosperity for the sake of personal profit, with the connivance of the state machinery, resulting in vociferous protests by the victims, repressed by brutal state violence.

'Untouchability' and Dalit Consciousness

It was from around this time, too, in the early 1920s, that Gandhi took up the issue of untouchability to include 'untouchables' within his vision of nationhood: 'Truthful relations between Hindus and Mussalmans, bread for the masses and removal of untouchability. That is how I would define swaraj at the present moment' (in Pandey 1990, 237). Even before that, in 1918, Premchand had rejected India's suitability for joining the League of Nations because of the existence of untouchability in Indian society: 'The idea of inequality still persists in our society. The chamaars are still untouchable and to touch doms is intense defilement' (*PR* 8, 18). He did not, however, support the government's attempt to try and segregate the 'untouchables' from the Hindus at the Second Round Table Conference. Nor did he support B.R. Ambedkar's demand for a separate electorate for the 'untouchables', seeing it as an attempt to divide Hindu society. When Gandhi undertook a fast unto death in the Yervada jail, which he had begun on 20 September 1932, Premchand made an eloquent appeal to Dr Ambedkar to heed the cry of the nation and not to let Gandhi's life be sacrificed (*PR* 8, 34-35).

Premchand's position on untouchability as well as his literary representations of the Dalits have been the subject of a great deal of contention and controversy among Dalit writers and intellectuals. On 31 July 2004, members of the Delhi-based Bhartiya Dalit Sahitya Akademi (Indian Dalit Literary Association or BDSA) burned copies of *Rangbhoomi* to protest against its inclusion by the National Council of Education Research and Training in the school syllabi because of Premchand's use of caste-specific terminology, specifically of the repeated naming of 'Soordas' as a 'chamaar' (Brueck 2010). The NCERT removed the word chamaar and replaced it by the less offensive Dalit. Interestingly, though, the word was not replaced in Dalit writings. For instance, in one of Om Prakash Valmiki's short stories, 'Khanabadosh', a footnote was added stating that 'the word is constitutionally banned and should not be practised in social behaviour' ('Dalit Atrocitities' 2006).

Several Dalit as well as non-Dalit writers and intellectuals protested against the burning of the book. The incident, however, crystallized issues related to Premchand's representations of Dalits as well as larger questions about Dalit identity, literary authenticity, and literary representations of the marginalized. Premchand has been criticized by Dalit writers for not being a follower of Ambedkar but of Gandhi, who is viewed by them as a traitor to Dalits in the cause of national unity, and for lacking the Dalit consciousness because he confuses caste and class oppression. A further question raised is that only the Dalits who have suffered caste oppression can represent Dalit identity.

The concept of identity, however, is itself problematic. Identity is not a unified entity but fluid, fragmented, multiple, shifting, replete with dissonances and contradictions. There are complex hermeneutical issues of representation and self-representation involved here that have been extensively debated in critical theory and philosophy and in areas such as gender studies, post-colonial studies and African-American studies. The authenticity of self-representations is questionable, given the evasions and contradictions that are involved in writing/presenting the self. Language and representations are not transparent upon reality and concepts such as 'pure experience', 'pure subjectivity' have been questioned and rejected. There are complex processes of mediation and interpretation involved in rendering subjectivity, whether one's own or that of others. Every marginalized and oppressed community will question its negative representations by those in power and will have its own narrative and history that will contest the dominant ones. It is also true that those who have not experienced the pain and injustice of oppression cannot express it with the same poignancy as those who have suffered it. But if it is contended that only I can represent myself, or that only a given group or community can represent itself, that would be to lapse into an untenable solipsism, precluding all attempts at understanding, 'each within a prison ... each confirms a prison'.[15]

It cannot be denied that Premchand is at times guilty of lumpenizing and stereotyping the Dalits in *Rangbhoomi*, as in the episode when Bhairo and his cohorts go around the muhalla lewdly dancing and singing. But it is Soordas who is the protagonist and the repository of the positive values in the novel. In fact, Soordas is probably the first Dalit hero in Hindi/Urdu fiction. Even before Gandhi went on a fast unto death at the Yervada prison on the question of the entry of untouchables in temples, an issue that Premchand took up in *Karmabhoomi*, in *Rangbhoomi*, Soordas is shown to be the life and soul of the singing of bhajans in the temple, and as the narrator sees it, the great achievement at the end has been that 'untouchable was eating with touchable'. Premchand's aesthetics are those of inclusion and not of exclusion, giving a voice and agency to the oppressed and the downtrodden who had hitherto been silenced and unrepresented. It would be apposite to quote Ambedkar in this context:

> It is usual to hear all those who feel moved by the deplorable condition of the Untouchables unburden themselves by uttering the cry, 'We must do something for the Untouchables.' One seldom hears any of the persons interested in the problem saying, 'Let us do something to change the Touchable Hindu' (in Anand 2006).

No writer could have done more than Premchand to change the 'Touchable Hindu' or to denounce brutalities and hierarchies of caste and class as well as to include the outcaste, the marginalized and the oppressed, within his vision of the nation. For Premchand, caste is not an essentialized, trans-temporal category, emptied of history and materiality. He is especially sensitive to power relations and gender oppression among the Dalits as well as to the extremities of degradation and poverty to which the social system has reduced them.

Communalism

The other issue with which Premchand is deeply concerned in *Rangbhoomi* is that of communalism. During the years when *Rangbhoomi* was being written, the entente between the Hindus and Muslims, that had been there during the years of the 'joint' Non-Cooperation-Khilafat movement, had broken down, following Gandhi's calling off of Non-Cooperation. Whereas only sixteen communal riots had occurred between 1900 and 1920, there were seventy-two between 1923 and 1926 (Pandey,1990, 117n.).

In order to emphasize Hindu-Muslim unity, Premchand highlighted the contribution of Islam to civilization at a time when communal violence was rife, especially in its emphasis on justice and egalitarianism (*PR* 7, 314-18). He deconstructed the received historiography of forced conversions to Islam, emphasizing that in fact the reason for the spread of Islam in India was the oppression of the lower castes by the higher castes of Hindus. There was no inequality in Islam; they were all Muslims not belonging to any particular caste. That was why the lower castes gladly welcomed Islam and entire villages converted to it, for in their eyes, Islam was not a victorious enemy but a liberator. Moreover, in wars between Hindus and Muslims, Hindu soldiers had often fought for Muslims and Muslims for Hindus and these wars had been waged on the basis of territory and economics rather than for religion (*PR* 8, 100-102).

In his editorials and articles, Premchand continued to oppose communalism and separatism. He claimed that the Nehru Report, with its ideal of 'dominion status', had alienated many Muslims and he criticized the Congress for not making as much effort as it should have done to win the cooperation of the Muslims. He opposed separate electorates for Hindus and Muslims and pleaded that India's liberation now lay 'not in our fighting for special rights but for equal ones', and that we should now 'move towards united progress as Indians, not as Hindu or Muslim, Untouchable or Christian, otherwise Hindus, Muslims, Untouchables and Sikhs will all go to the nether world', going on to prophesy, 'India will now tear into shreds the spider's web of separatism' (*PR* 8, 51, 75, 89, 96-97).

This concern for Hindu-Muslim unity also informs *Rangbhoomi*. While writing the novel, Premchand was simultaneously writing his play *Karbala*, in which Hindus are shown fighting alongside Muslims, to emphasize Hindu-Muslim unity and to dismantle received notions of centuries-old Hindu-Muslim animosity. In the conflict with the authorities at the end, Hindus and Muslims fight together in *Rangbhoomi*. For Rani Jahnavi, the Muslim who gave up his life for Vinay is a greater martyr than Vinay. The relationship between Tahir Ali's family and the people of Pandeypur is perhaps suggestive of the uneasy relationship between Hindus and Muslims at the time as well as of Premchand's plea for unity and tolerance. For Tahir Ali, there is no religion except Islam. It is, however, the chamaars who protect him even though they have been cheated by him. Subhagi quietly helps Kulsoom when Tahir is imprisoned, and Soordas pleads with John Sevak not to pull down Kulsoom's house. This is perhaps suggestive of class affiliations over communal and caste ones. There was a mixed reaction to *Rangbhoomi* among the Muslims. Abdul Majid, for instance, in his letter of 17 October 1928 to Premchand, brought to his notice that a section of Muslims looked upon *Rangbhoomi* as being anti-Islamist although he himself did not find 'anti-Islamism' or an 'aggressive' kind of 'Hinduiyat' in it anywhere (*CP*, 231).

The other community that Premchand deals with in *Rangbhoomi* is that of the Indian Christians, through the Sevak family. A history of forced conversions after the 1857 war is evoked through Ishvar Sevak's dim memories of going to bathe in the Ganga with his mother, her cremation, and soldiers entering their house and arresting his father. John Sevak articulates the predicament of the Indian Christians who are accepted neither by the British nor by the other Indians and have very little political power and representation. He thinks that they can attain special rights and status only by remaining separate from the other Indians or else they will lose their identity. Sophia's accident when she saves Vinay gives John Sevak an opportunity to gain an entry into the feudal aristocracy and thereby to expand his business interests. Mrs Sevak is represented as a pathetic caricature who disdains all Indians, including Indian Christians, and tries to mimic British ways. In fact, she is not given a name which has the effect of further dehumanizing and caricaturing her. Through the discussions in the Sevak household and Sophia's religious scepticism, Premchand shows his awareness of the religious controversies pertaining to Christianity, following the Higher Criticism of the Bible and evolutionary theory questioning the divinity of Christ and the status of Christianity as a divinely revealed religion. The text is as dismissive of the orthodoxies of Christianity as of Hinduism.

Christianity is regarded as alien by the people of Pandeypur and John Sevak as a contemptible representative of it. They are hostile to the conversion of the lower castes to Christianity who then attain upward social mobility, wear coats and pants, and become 'sahibs' (Ch 12). The padri is welcome in Pandeypur not for his religious message but because he brings sweets and books for the children.

It is through the younger generation, Sophia and Prabhu, however, who revolt against the patriarchal and religious oppression of their family, that the inclusion of Indian Christians in the national movement is depicted. Sophia's patriotic fervour is aroused when she hears the patriotic song in Vinay's palace after she leaves her home. Sophia, as has been noted earlier, is modelled on Annie Besant in her questioning of Christianity and her fascination with Hinduism.[16] Her turning to Hinduism is marked by the sartorial switch from gowns to saris during her stay with Vinay's family. A strong reason for her antipathy to Clark is his pious Christian religiosity. If Mrs Sevak is contemptuous of Hinduism, Rani Jahnavi is even more dismissive of Christianity and both are vehemently opposed to a marriage between Sophia and Vinay. *Rangbhoomi* is perhaps the first novel in Hindi that depicts the love between a Hindu boy and a Christian girl (Sharma 1995, 77). In the end, however, the obstacle is not religion so much as Sophia's and the narrator's scepticism about the fickleness of romantic love and the inconstancy of human nature. Love can transcend religious differences but social and religious obstacles do remain, as does the narrator's scepticism about ideal romantic love which, as John Sevak perceptively points out, can survive only in the sphere of idealism. Prabhu, an intellectual dilettante, proves his ability when he joins the society for social service and establishes his reputation in the arena of nationalist politics but has perforce to resign because of Kunwar Bharat Singh's timidity.

It would appear, then, that the text is more hostile to Christianity, which is regarded with suspicion as the religion of the rulers, than to Islam, which has been indigenized over the centuries. The overpowering message however, is that of unity and nationalism in the struggle for independence.

The Women's Question
Nowhere are the contradictions between orthodoxy and reformism in Premchand's thought more evident than in his views on women. Married at the age of fourteen, he abandoned his first wife on grounds of incompatibility. When it came to his second marriage, however, he insisted on marrying a child widow, not revealing the fact of his first marriage to the bride or to her family. Even as late as 1934, he maintained the fiction that he had married again only after his first wife's death (*CP*, 413). He deprived his daughter of an education but refused to perform her kanyadaan telling his wife: "'Among living things, only a cow can be donated. Then how can a girl be donated? … Should I then donate my daughter? I can't do it'" (Shivarani Devi 1944, 142). In 1905, in his novel *Prema*, under the influence of reformist movements, he had depicted the heroine, a widow, remarrying. But he revised the novel, and wrote in a letter of 7 may 1932: 'By making a widow marry I had made Hindu woman fall from the ideal. I was young then and the inclination for reform was strong. I did not want to see the book in that form' (*CP*, 341).

These contradictions are central to the relationship of the national movement to the 'women's question'. In the dichotomy between home and world, material and spiritual, Western and Indian, women were supposed to be the repositories of the values of spirituality as embodying a superior Indian culture even as they were encouraged to enter the public sphere and to participate in the national movement.[17]

Premchand was a staunch supporter of the reforms that were taking place in the women's movement. He championed the rights of women in his journalism and was vociferous in his critique of their patriarchal oppression. He lauded the forthcoming Sharada Bill in May 1931 for giving widows the right over their husbands' property, praised the achievements of women in the national arena and championed their rights (*PR* 8, 67, 70, 198).

And yet, even as late as 1935, he was prejudiced against educated girls and opposed to a Westernized modernity for them even while he was simultaneously supporting women's rights (*CP*, 475-76). He defined his ideal for a woman in his letter of 7 September 1934 in terms of prevailing stereotypes of ideal Indian womanhood: 'My ideal for a woman is sacrifice, service, purity, all of these blended together in one—sacrifice that has no end, constant service, such happiness and purity that nobody can ever raise a finger at her' (*CP*, 413).

These contradictions between Premchand's reformist ideals and his often reactionary views are dramatized in the depiction of the predicament of the women in *Rangbhoomi*. The text shows them challenging and rebelling against the constraints of their gender and yet they are not allowed emancipatory and liberating options.

Sophia, perhaps the first Indian Christian heroine in Urdu/Hindi fiction, rebels against the patriarchy of her family and the religious oppression inflicted on her and leaves home with the desire to find independence and an autonomous identity. She asserts her agency in her support of Veerpaal and the dacoits and in her rejection of Vinay when he becomes complicit in the brutal repressions of the riyasat. Her repressed sexuality is suggested but not fully explored. Sophia commits suicide at the end not so much because of the demands of the conventions of romantic tragedy but because of the ideological compulsions that dictate the end of a sati for her. As Dr Ganguly says, 'she was a sati, and this is the dharma of sati women' (Ch. 50, 631).

Rani Jahnavi is caught in the contradictions of her gender, caste, class and religion. An orthodox Hindu, she brings up Vinay to emulate the Rajput heroes, paradoxically feminizing him in the process by making him subservient to her maternal power. She is, of course, the Great Mother, the Magna Mater, compelling her son's love and submission as well as his rebellion and being an obstacle to his union with Sophia.[18] She enjoins the duties of a wife upon her daughter Indu, but is herself often scornful of her husband and appears to be deeply resentful of her position as his wife. Her surreptitious attraction to Dr

Ganguly is hinted at. Importantly, the text traces her development as she overcomes her prejudices to accept Sophia and to acknowledge that the Muslim who had died to save Vinay is a greater martyr than her son. More importantly, she donates her entire wealth to the Society, leaves the women's quarters, enters the arena of action and displays the zeal and conscientiousness that women are capable of in the public sphere.

Indu's development too is significant in showing the transition of women from the domestic sphere to that of politics. Docile to begin with, she accepts her gender role and an arranged marriage to Mahendra Kumar. But gradually she seethes with resentment and realizes that she is no better than a servant in her house. It is a radical gesture on her part when, despite her mother's sermonizing, she finally leaves her husband's home and establishes a trust for her riyasat with Dr Ganguly as its chairman, dissociating herself completely from it. Her action is in marked contrast to her father who had given control over his riyasat to the colonial government; she leaves for Punjab with Jahnavi and Ganguly, thus abjuring wealth and domesticity. Her attraction to Indradutt is delicately suggested but again not explored. It is as if women can be liberated from their traditional roles only if they participate in the larger political sphere of the national movement.

Subhagi is a victim of the oppression of her husband and of her mother-in-law, showing Premchand's concern for gender oppression irrespective of caste and class. She escapes from it to Soordas, who faces the ire of the muhalla and gives her shelter. She fights for her rights and returns on her own terms but she is co-opted back into domesticity. Kulsoom's steadfast patience in suffering the tyranny of her step mothers-in-law conforms to traditional gender stereotypes. But she too asserts her independence by eking out a living through her sewing when Tahir is in jail and refusing the money that the chamaars had collected for Tahir.

Princely States
Premchand extends the canvas of the novel to include the atrocities of the princely states in collusion with the British colonial state. Vinay is sent to Mewar in Rajputana along with the volunteers of the Society not only because of Jahnavi's pride in her Rajput ancestry but also

because Premchand wishes to dismantle the myth of Rajput valour that had been reinforced with the publication of James Tod's *Annals and Antiquities of Rajasthan* in 1829, with a second edition in 1873, glorifying the romantic past of the Rajputs. He also wishes to expose the exploitation of the peasants there by the riyasat and to show the interconnection of revolutionary movements in a remote corner of Mewar with the larger national movement.

Agro-economic unrest had prevailed in Rajputana against the traditional, exploitative feudal economic system under which the jagirdars and zamindars exploited the agricultural classes, especially the peasants, and had resulted in a series of uprisings since at least the late nineteenth century. However, it was only after 1914 that peasant disturbances in Mewar came to all-India notice (Ray 1978, 215). The central figure who linked the agrarian movements with the national movement in British India was Vijay Singh Pathik, who may have provided a prototype for Vinay's sojourn in Mewar. Pathik was a revolutionary nationalist from UP, whose real name was Bhoop Singh (Hooja 2006, 993). He had escaped from the British in 1915 and had taken refuge in Mewar where he played a leading role in organizing the peasant satyagraha movement in the thikana (jagir) of Bijolia which had its origins as far back as the Bijolia kisan movement in 1897. Bijolia led the rest of India in organizing a peaceful, organized peasant satyagraha, using the same techniques that Gandhi was to use a couple of years later (Ray 1978, 227). Pathik attended the Congress session of Amritsar in 1919 to persuade the Congress to extend its activities to Indian states. But the Congress was then following a policy of neutrality towards the political grievances of people in the princely states. Pathik was eventually arrested, like Vinay, produced before a court in Udaipur and jailed in 1924 (Ray 1978, 229). Newspapers and the printing press too played an important role in spreading opposition to British rule (Hooja 2006, 953). Simultaneously, the brutalities of the durbar and the jagirdars were widely publicized in British India, establishing a bond between the peasant unrest in the distant areas of Mewar and the larger national movement (Ray 1978, 229). The British government as well as the princely states of Rajputana felt increasingly threatened by these anti-feudal peasant movements and their links with the national movement. They looked upon literature pertaining to the national movement in India, political associations, and other activities considered to be 'disloyal' or treasonable, as being 'seditious' and took active measures to put them down (Hooja 2006, 989). The Chamber of Princes secured the passage of the Indian States Act in 1922 which prevented their subjects from publishing 'seditious' material in British Indian newspapers (Hooja, 957). This is the context in which the deewan, Sardar Neelkanth, accuses Vinay and his volunteers of sedition.

The British Resident at Mewar at this time was W.H.J. Wilkinson whose tenure, interestingly, coincides with Clark's in *Rangbhoomi*. It is tempting, therefore, to conjecture that he may have been a prototype for Clark. Wilkinson's Rajputana Agency Report of 1921 described Mewar as becoming 'a hotbed of lawlessness. Seditionist emissaries are teaching the people that all men are equal. The lands belong to the peasants and not to the state or landlords. It is significant that the people are being urged to use the vernacular equivalent of the word "comrade". The movement is mainly anti-maharana but it might soon become anti-British and spread to the adjoining British area' (Singh 1985, 32). Wilkinson also alleged that the Maharana was "'said to have been threatened to be meted the fate of [the] Czar'" (Sarkar 2002, 177). Hence Clark's allegation, made around the same time, of Sophia spreading Bolshevism among the peasants and the dacoits.

These fears of Bolshevism were greatly exaggerated in the attempt by the British to depose Maharana Fateh Singh, who was by no means subservient to the British and who consistently opposed their interference in the affairs of the state. Renowned for his piety and asceticism, he was aware of his position as the head of the Rajputs and virtually as the head of the Hindus. However, he was an obdurate traditionalist, out of touch with the peasant disaffection and social unrest in his state. He was formally deposed on 17 July 1921 but was permitted to retain his titular right to the throne. His son, Bhupal Singh, was much more amenable to British control. Although paralyzed from waist down because of tuberculosis of the bones, he loved hunting despite his handicap. He was very traditional concerning religious rites, like the maharaja whom Vinay meets.[19]

The text is silent about the transition from Fateh Singh's rule to Bhupal Singh's. To begin with, Vinay speaks of the Maharana with great veneration in response to Veerpaal Singh's account of the atrocities of the riyasat (Ch. 17, 225). This seems to be with reference to Fateh Singh. But when Vinay goes to meet the Maharana and is disgusted with his subservience to the British, it seems he would be Bhupal Singh in terms of the time scheme of the novel. Premchand deliberately caricatures the maharaja to emphasize the subservience of the riyasats to the British. In an interesting gesture, he highlights the 'orientalist' construction of the riyasats by the colonial state as 'harems' of the government. It may be noted here that Nehru, in fact, later reversed the orientalist metaphor to describe the British residents who 'exercised the harlot's privilege of exercising power without responsibility' (Nehru 1969, 311). The deewan too tells Vinay that they had deliberately used him in order to discredit the patriotism of the national movement in the eyes of the public. As for Vinay, his complicity in the reprisals and later repentance trace the trajectory of his decline and moral growth. As Premchand wrote, in English: 'Trials and troubles mould the human character, they make heroes of men. Power and authority is the curse of humanity. Even the noblest fall a victim to power and lose their character' (Rai 1982, 219).

Sophia and Vinay's interlude with the Bhils for a year reflects the growing concern of the national movement with the predicament of the tribals. In his call to make the Congress a mass movement, Gandhi could not neglect the tribals. He specifically referred to the Bhils: 'The Bhils have been long neglected by the States and reformers; if they are given a helping hand, they can become the pride of India. All they need is the spinning wheel in their homes and schools in which their children can receive simple education' (in Singh 1985, 32).

The Bhils of Mewar established links with the broader political movement in the state from 1920 onwards. They joined the peasant movement of Bijolia in 1920 and were part of the 'Eka' (unity) organization for tribals and non-tribals. The colonial administration reacted to their protests with brutal reprisals and unsuccessful attempts to break the Eka movement (Singh 1985, 32-39).

. Reverberations of this violence do not echo in the village where Sophia and Vinay live for a year. Premchand emphasizes the dignity, hospitality and peaceful nature of the Bhils. Unlike Gandhi, he is not condescending and patronizing towards them but shows respect for their traditional way of life. This idyllic representation is perhaps an attempt to negate colonial stereotypes of tribal violence.

Thus by a narrative strategy of intercutting across geographical locales Premchand evokes the crisscrossing and interweaving of plural histories as they are affected by colonial and indigenous oppression.

Aesthetics, Language and Politics

Premchand's politics and his aesthetics are inextricably intertwined to include within his concept of nationhood the voices of the poorest, the most downtrodden and the most oppressed. He developed his aesthetics to depict the predicament of a nation suffering under colonial oppression as well as from the burden of poverty, caste and class exploitation, and social injustice. For Premchand, indeed, as recorded by his wife, the relationship between literature, society and history was absolutely inviolable (Shivarani Devi 1944, 95). Moreover, 'the progress of literature', he asserted, 'is the progress of the nation' (*PR* 7, 384). Not for him the narrow aestheticism of 'art for art's sake'. 'It is time for art for art's sake when a country is prosperous and content', he asserted, shortly after completing *Rangbhoomi*, because 'wherever we look we see that we are fettered in various political and social bonds, there are scenes of dire grief and poverty' (*PR* 7, 296). Premchand defended his stories against the charge of didacticism on the grounds that didacticism is inevitable in the literature of a colonized country: 'India can never rise to the highest flights of Art, unless [*sic*] she is murmuring under a foreign yoke....The greater the feeling the more didactic the work' (*CP*, 250-51). He unequivocally declared that the value of art lies in its utility and that its basis is propaganda, thereby deconstructing the premises of literature as well as of all the arts (*PR* 7, 463).

Premchand's activist aesthetics are best articulated in 'The Aim of Literature', his presidential address to the first conference of the Progressive Writers Association in Lucknow on 10 April 1936, a few months before his death (*PR* 7, 499-511). He declares here that '[T]he duty of literature is to defend the downtrodden, the oppressed, the deprived, whether it is an individual or a group', and he rejects a narrow and limited aestheticism as well as the notion of art as the worship of 'beauty'. Beauty for him is to be found in 'the battle of life', 'in that poor, plain mother of children, who is sweating in toil after putting her child to sleep at the edge of the field'. The truths of life are not to be found in 'the best that has been thought and said in the world', as Matthew Arnold had claimed, nor in the sublimity of nature of the Romantics, but in the struggle and toil of the day-to-day lives of the poor and the downtrodden. Such literature 'generates movement, battle and restlessness', it awakens, disturbs and challenges, 'it does not put us to sleep because to sleep now is a sign of death'. Conflict, indeed, especially the conflict between truth and falsehood, is integral to Premchand's aesthetics. This, then, is Premchand's 'realist idealism' —realism in the depiction of the concrete struggles and conflicts of life and idealism in its power to disturb and challenge and to reform and change.

Premchand's views on language too are related to his nationalist vision. He underscored the need for a national language to shatter the yoke of colonialism (*PR* 7, 425) and insisted that it should be hybrid, plural and inclusive. As he told Shivarani Devi: 'When several races have come and mingled in the nation, even the nation has not remained pure, then how can there be a pure language?' (Shivarani Devi 1944, 129). He therefore dismissed the notion of 'pure Hindi': 'A living language, like a living body, is constantly evolving. Pure Hindi is a useless word. If India had been pure Hindu, its language would have been pure Hindi. As long as there are all the races here, Muslim, Christian, Parsee, Afghan, our language will also be broad-based' (*PR* 7, 426). Premchand's own creative use of language uses multiple registers, from the highly poetic to the colloquial. Dialect, for him, is the stuff and fibre of a living language and not merely a literary device.

Conclusion

Reading *Rangbhoomi* almost a century after it was written, one is struck by its disturbing contemporaneity and compelled to reflect not on how much has changed but on how little, as well as on the prescience of this modest writer from Lamahi who declined the offer of the title of Rai Sahib because he preferred to remain 'a humble servant of the people' and not become a lackey of the powers that be (Shivarani Devi, 1944, 159-61).

Endnotes

1 Letter of 26 December 1934 in English to Indranath Madan, *Chitthi-Patri*, 429. Hereafter cited in the text as *CP*. Translations from *CP* are mine.

2 Preface to *Chaugan-e-Hasti*, September 1928, *Premchand Rachnavali* 9, 449. Hereafter cited in the text as *PR*. Translations from *PR* are mine.

3 Although *Karbala* was first published in Hindi in November 1924, a few months after the Hindi draft of *Rangbhoomi* had been completed, Premchand obviously had the play in mind when he wrote the novel. The Urdu version was serialized in *Zamana* from July 1926 to April 1928 (Rai, 1982, 171-72).

4 For a discussion of these contradictions and vacillations in the nationalist views of Premchand as well as of other intellectuals and writers of the time, see Chandra 1981, 1982 and 1992.

5 Letter to Iqbal Varma 'Seher' Hitgami, possibly at the end of 1925, clarifying that the prototype for Sophia was Annie Besant and not Amelia of Thackeray's *Vanity Fair* as claimed by a critic, Avadh Upadhyaya (*CP*, 180).

6 Letter of January 1931 to Keshoram Sabbarwal (*CP*, 295); 11 September 1933, *Jagaran* (*PR* 8, 432); 16 April 1934, *Jagaran* (*PR* 9, 93).

7 For a detailed discussion of the history of these years, see Sarkar 2002, Ch V, 'Mass Nationalism: Emergence and Problems 1917-1927', 165-253.

8 Probably composed by Premchand himself. I owe this suggestion to Harish Trivedi. Premchand had used this metaphor of life as a game in a letter of 23 April 1923 to Dayanarayan Nigam to condole the death of Nigam's son when he was writing *Rangbhoomi* (*CP*, 145-46).

9 Premchand wrote an obituary on Kipling praising *The Jungle Book* and *Kim* 'He was an incomparable devotee of imperialism and in his view the West had come to the East to rule it forever, but even while disagreeing with this belief there is no doubt that he was an artist of a high order and perhaps he might have realized his mistake in the future' (*PR* 9, 225).

10 Premchand wrote in a letter of 26 December 1934 in English: 'I have in each of my novels an ideal character, with human weaknesses as well as virtues, but essentially ideal, such as ... Soordas in *Rangbhoomi*' (*CP*, 431).

11 In a letter of 25 March 1925, Premchand wrote that he had much to learn from a crippled, blind man such as Soordas (*CP*, 171). For an analysis of the differences and the similarities between Tolstoy, Gandhi and Premchand, see Sharma 1995, 152-63.

12 Premchand said that he got the idea for *Rangbhoomi* from a blind beggar who used to live in his village (*PR* 7, 300).

13 Shoma Anand, with Shantanu Guha Ray and Avinash Dutt, 'Bengal Shows the Way', *Tehelka*, vol. 4, 8 (3 March 2007), 10-16 (p. 16).

14 *Ibid.*, p. 11.

15 T. S. Eliot, *The Waste Land*, V. ll. 12-13. For a discussion of this issue, see Rai 2010, x-xiii.

16 Premchand wrote a tribute to Besant on her eighty-sixth birthday: 'Although she is Irish by birth, perhaps no one except Mahatma Gandhi has done as much for India as Dr Annie Besant has.... Her greatest achievement is that sentiment of universal brotherhood to which she has given a new life.... The encouragement that she has given Hindu culture and the shastras will remain forever' (*PR* 8, 146). And he paid his homage to her in his obituary, despite his own differences with her on a couple of principles, as 'the most renowned woman of this century', who provided 'an ideal for karmayoga' (*PR* 8, 443).

17 See Chatterjee 1994, 119-121 for a discussion of the women's question and nationalism; and Pandey, 1989, for a discussion of women in Premchand's fiction.

18 See Kakar 1982, 79-122 for a discussion of this deep attraction of the son to the mother in the Indian context.

19 Masters 1990, 140; Meininger 2000, 127-140.

Author's Note

Rangbhoomi's hero Soordas is a remarkable character in the history of the Indian novel. He has an extraordinary capacity to sacrifice himself for the public welfare. In brief, he is also an ideal Gandhian character.

Numerous coloured strands are entwined in the narrative of *Rangbhoomi*. The central thread is the life of village society in all its wretchedness and poverty. John Sevak's family is Christian. He is eager to build a cigarette factory on the grazing ground of the village. There are several wealthy people among whom there are innumerable internal dissensions—greed, lust for fame, many ambitions. There are maharajas. There are princely states for them to oppress. The wheel of events in the novel turns with immense speed. There is a swift flow in the narrative and abundant drama. The narrative is like a stormy river that emerges from vast mountainous caverns. It is not a river that flows gently on level land and makes it fertile.

— Premchand

1

A CITY IS A SITE WHERE THE RICH LIVE AND TRADE. THE AREA outside it is a space for their recreation and amusement. In the city's centre are located schools for their sons and their arenas for litigation, where the poor are strangled in the name of justice. On the peripheries of the city are to be found bastis, settlements of the poor. One such basti is Pandeypur in Banaras. The light of the city lamps doesn't reach there, nor do drops of water when the city is sprinkled, nor does the flow from the city's waterworks. There are small shops of halvais and banias on the roadside, behind which live several ikka-valas, carters, cowherds and labourers. There are also a few houses belonging to the depraved rich, which have been banished from the city because of their dilapidated condition. A poor, blind chamaar, whom people call Soordas, lives in one of these. Blind men need neither name nor work in India. Soordas is their ready-made name, begging for alms their ready-made vocation. Their qualities and temperament are also universally celebrated; special interest in music, exceptional love in the heart, distinctive passion for spirituality and religious devotion are their natural traits. The outer vision shut and the inner open.*

Soordas was extremely frail, weak and simple. Perhaps destiny had created him only to beg for alms. Every day, he would go tapping his stick to sit by the tarred road and implore the welfare of passers-by. 'Benefactor! May God make you prosperous' was his constant refrain. Perhaps he thought it a mantra to inspire compassion in people. He would remain seated while invoking blessings upon pedestrians. But if an ikka happened to pass by he would run after it, and his feet grew wings if they were buggies. Victorias, however, he considered to be beyond the scope of his good wishes. Experience had taught him that victorias don't listen to anybody. From morning to evening his time

---

* Soordas (1478/79–1581/1584), poet, saint and musician, was born blind and lived in Braj, near Mathura.

1

was spent only in invoking blessings. Neither the clouds and winds of winter nor the hot blasts of summer could keep him away.

It was an evening in the month of Kartik, and the breeze had become pleasantly cool. Soordas sat like a statue in his usual place, listening intently for the promising sound of an ikka or a buggy. The carters unfastened their carts under the trees which flanked the road and their bullocks, which were from the western region, began to chew oilcakes and straw on pieces of sacking. Some carters kneaded flour on a sheet while others made round baatis, which they baked on dried cow-dung cakes that they had burnt. Nobody needed utensils and mashed ghuiyen was adequate as curry. Not in the least worried by this destitution, they sang while baking baatis. The bells tied around the necks of the bullocks served as cymbals.

A carter, Ganes, asked Soordas – Listen, you bhagat, do you want to marry?

Soordas shook his head and asked – Is there a possibility?

Ganes – Yes, why not? There's a blind woman in a village from your caste and community. I'll settle the matter if you say so. It'll be fun having baatis for a couple of days in your baraat.

Soordas – You should have told me of a place from where I can get some wealth and get rid of this beggary. Right now I'm worried about my own belly, but then I'll have to think of a blind woman as well. I won't bind my feet with such a chain. If there has to be a chain, it should at least be one of gold.

Ganes – You won't get a woman worth a lakh of rupees. This one will press your feet at night and oil your hair so that you'll regain your youth. These bones won't show any more.

Soordas – Then I'll also lose my livelihood. People take pity on me only because of these bones. Who gives alms to fat men? Rather, they get only taunts.

Ganes – Oh no, she'll serve you and feed you too. She can earn four annas a day by winnowing oilseeds at Bechan Saah's.

Soordas – That will make it even more difficult. I won't be fit to show my face to anyone if I live off my wife's earnings.

Suddenly they heard a phaeton approaching. Soordas stood up with the help of his stick. This was the time when he could earn something since the wealthy and the illustrious of the city came here then to take the air. As soon as the phaeton approached, Soordas ran after it, crying, 'Benefactor! May God make you prosperous!'

Mr John Sevak was sitting with his wife on the front seat of the phaeton. Their son Prabhu and his younger sister Sophia were sitting on the other one. John Sevak was a stout, fair, attractive man. His face was ruddy even in old age. His hair and beard had turned to salt and pepper. His English apparel suited him very well. His face expressed arrogance and self-confidence. Mrs Sevak had been more persecuted by the passage of time. Her face was wrinkled and even her gold spectacles couldn't conceal the meanness that it exuded. Prabhu Sevak's moustache was beginning to appear. He was lean and slender, with a sombre, thoughtful expression on his lacklustre, bespectacled face, and eyes that seemed to glow with a compassionate light. He seemed to be enjoying the beauty of nature. Miss Sophia was a shy young woman with large, luminous eyes. She was extremely delicate, as if she had been created from flowers rather than from the five elements. Her appearance was so gentle that she seemed to be an incarnation of modesty and humility. Her whole being was vibrant with sensitivity and awareness, without the slightest inkling of insentience.

Soordas kept running behind the phaeton. Even an experienced player could not have run so fast and so far. Wrinkling her nose, Mrs Sevak said – This rascal's screams have burst my eardrums. Will he go on running?

John Sevak – When will the country get rid of this affliction? It will take centuries to liberate a country where begging is not a matter of shame, to the extent that even the highest castes make it their profession, and it's the sole support for mahatmas.

Prabhu Sevak – This custom has existed here since antiquity. In the Vedic age even princes used to beg for alms to support themselves and their gurus while they got their education in gurukuls. Nor was it thought to be humiliating for sages and rishis, but those people relied on clemency so that they could liberate themselves from illusions and attachments and attain knowledge. That custom is now being misused. I have even heard that several brahmans, who are zamindars, go to fight lawsuits with empty hands, ask for alms all day on the pretext of the marriage of a girl or the death of a relative, and sell the foodgrains in the evening, converting them into paise. Paise soon become rupees and eventually find their way into the pockets of the lawyers and officers of law courts.

Mrs Sevak – Syce, tell this blind man to run off, there are no paise.

Sophia – No mama, please give him some if you have them. The poor man has been running for half a mile. He'll be disappointed and his soul will be deeply hurt.

Mrs Sevak – Who told him to run? His feet must be aching.

Sophia – No, dear mama, give him something, the poor man is panting so hard.

Prabhu Sevak took out his case from his pocket but he couldn't find a copper or a nickel piece, and he was afraid of giving a silver coin for fear of annoying his mother. He said to his sister – Sophie, I'm sorry, I couldn't find any paise. Syce, tell the blind man to reach the godown slowly; there may be some there.

But where did Soordas have such patience? He knew that nobody would wait for him at the godown and that his efforts would be wasted if the phaeton moved on. So he continued following it for a full mile till they reached the godown and the phaeton stopped. All of them alighted. Soordas too stood aside like a stump among the trees. He was panting so hard that he was breathless.

John Sevak had opened a leather agency here. His accountant, Tahir Ali, was sitting in the veranda. As soon as he saw sahib, he got up and salaamed him.

John Sevak asked – Well, Khan sahib, how is the income from leather?

Tahir – Huzoor, not as much as it should be, but I hope that it will improve.

John Sevak – Make some effort, it won't do to keep sitting in one place. Make rounds in the surrounding countryside. I plan to meet the chairman sahib of the municipality and get an alcohol and toddy shop opened here. Then the chamaars living around will come here every day and you'll get a chance to get to know them. One can't succeed nowadays without these small tricks. Look at me, there's seldom a day when I don't meet a few wealthy and respected men of the city. We'll be saved several days of running around if we can get a policy of even ten thousand.

Tahir – Huzoor, even I'm worried. Don't I realize that it won't be worthwhile for maalik to do this work if he can't make some profit? However, the pay that huzoor has fixed for me isn't enough for me to subsist on. Twenty rupees aren't sufficient even for foodgrains, let alone other necessities. Though I don't have the courage to say anything to you right now, to whom else can I speak if not to you?

John Sevak – Work for a few days and you'll get a raise. Where are your accounts? Let me see them.

John Sevak sat down on a broken morha, while Mrs Sevak took a chair. Tahir Ali placed the ledger before him. Sahib began to examine it and, wrinkling his nose after turning a few pages, remarked, 'You don't yet know how to maintain accounts, and on top of that you want a raise. Accounts should be just like a mirror. It's difficult here to make out how much material you have bought and how much you have dispatched. Buyers are given a commission of an anna per hide; this hasn't been entered anywhere.'

Tahir – Do I have to enter that too?

John Sevak – Why, isn't it my income?

Tahir – I had thought that it was my right.

John Sevak – Never! I can file a case of embezzlement against you. (*Scowling*) Employees have a right! Splendid! You have a right on nothing else except your pay.

Tahir – Huzoor, there won't be such a mistake in future.

John Sevak – Show the amount that you have collected under this heading in the income. I don't make any allowances when it's a question of accounts.

Tahir – Huzoor, it's probably a very small amount.

John Sevak – That doesn't matter. You'll have to make it up even if it's only a pie. It may be a small sum right now but the numbers will increase to hundreds in a few days. I want to open a Sunday school here with that amount. Do you understand? It's memsahib's cherished desire. All right, where's the land that you had mentioned?

There was a large field behind the godown where animals from surrounding areas grazed. John Sevak wanted to acquire it to start a cigarette factory. Prabhu Sevak had been sent to America to be trained in this business. Prabhu and his mother also went along with John Sevak to see the land. Father and son together measured the area of the land and discussed for a long time such matters as the respective locations of the factory, the office, the bungalow of the manager, rooms for the labourers, the storehouse for the coal, and the water supply. Finally, Mr Sevak asked Tahir Ali – Whose land is it?

Tahir – Sahib, I don't know for sure, but I'll go and ask somebody here. Perhaps it belongs to Nayakram Panda.

John Sevak – For how much can you persuade him to sell it?

Tahir – I doubt very much that he'll sell it at all.

John Sevak – Aji, what's his status? Even his father will sell it. Offer seventeen annas for a rupee and get the stars from the sky.* Send him to me, I'll talk to him.

Prabhu – I'm afraid it may be difficult to obtain raw material here. People don't cultivate much tobacco in this area.

John Sevak – It will be your job to produce the raw material. A farmer has no love for sugarcane or for wheat and barley. He'll produce anything from which he can get a profit. This isn't anything to worry about. Khan sahib, you must send that panda to me tomorrow.

Tahir – Very well, I'll tell him.

John Sevak – Don't tell him, send him. I'll believe that you don't know anything about making a deal if you can't do even this much.

Mrs Sevak (*In English*) – You should have kept an experienced man in his place.

John Sevak (*In English*) – No, I'm afraid of experienced men. They use their experience for their own profit, not for ours. I stay miles away from such people.

The three of them reached the phaeton while discussing these matters, followed by Tahir Ali. Sophia was standing there, talking to Soordas. On seeing Prabhu, she exclaimed – Prabhu, this blind man seems to be a sage. He's a complete philosopher.

Mrs Sevak – You manage to find a sage wherever you go. Why, you blind man, why do you beg? Why don't you do some work?

Sophia (*In English*) – Mama, this blind man is not a mere rustic.

Soordas found these insults very hurtful after Sophia's respect. One's humiliation is much more unbearable in the presence of someone who has been respectful. He replied, raising his head – God created me, I serve only God. I can't serve anybody else.

---

* There were sixteen annas in a rupee.

Mrs Sevak – Why did your God make you blind, so that you can go on begging? Your God is very unjust.

Sophia (*In English*) – Mama, why are you humiliating him? I'm embarrassed.

Soordas – God is not unjust. Such was my earning from my previous birth. I'm suffering the results of my actions. All this is God's leela. He is a great player. He goes on building and destroying small, fragile playhouses. He bears no illwill towards anybody. Why would he be unjust to anyone?

Sophia – I would never have forgiven God had I been blind.

Soordas – Miss sahib, all of us have to suffer for our own sins. God is not to blame.

Sophia – Mama, I don't understand this mystery. Lord Jesus atoned for our sins with his blood, so why aren't Christians equal? There are all sorts of people in our community too, as in other religions – rich and poor, good and bad, maimed and crippled. Why is that so?

Before Mrs Sevak could reply, Soordas spoke up – Miss sahib, we have to atone for our own sins. There will be anarchy in the world if it gets to be known today that someone else has taken on the burden of our sins on his head.

Mrs Sevak – Sophie, it's a great pity that you can't understand something so obvious, although Reverend Pym himself has resolved your doubts so often.

Prabhu (*To Soordas*) – So you think that all of us should become ascetics?

Soordas – Yes, we can't escape sorrow until we become ascetics.

John Sevak – Begging with ashes smeared on one's body is itself the greatest affliction; how can he liberate us from sorrow?

Soordas – Sahib, it isn't necessary to smear ashes and beg to become an ascetic. In fact, our mahatmas say that it's hypocritical to smear ashes and to grow matted hair. Renunciation comes from the heart. To live in the world and not be of it—that's true renunciation.

Mrs Sevak – Hindus have learnt these things from the Stoics of Greece, but they don't understand how difficult it is to practise them. It's just not possible for human beings to remain unaffected by joy and sorrow. This very blind man will utter thousands of abuses in his heart this very minute if he doesn't get money.

John Sevak – Yes, don't give him anything, let's see what he says. I'll talk to him with my hunter if he fumes even slightly. He'll then forget all about renunciation. He begs and runs like a dog for miles to beg for each dhela, and on top of that he claims to be an ascetic. (*To the coachman*) Turn the phaeton, go to the club and then to the bungalow.

Sophia – Mama, do give him something. The poor man ran all this way with some hope.

Prabhu – Oho, I forgot to change some money.

John Sevak – Never, don't give anything. I want to teach him a lesson in renunciation.

The phaeton began to move. Soordas kept staring at it with his blind eyes like a statue of disappointment, as if he could still not believe that anybody could be so heartless. He walked several steps behind the phaeton in a semi-conscious state. Suddenly Sophia said – Soordas, I'm sorry, I don't have any paise right now. You won't have to be so disappointed when I come here again.

The blind are gifted with acute insight. Soordas understood the situation very well. Although he was resentful at heart, he said casually – Miss sahib, why worry about it? May God make you prosperous! I need your compassion, that's enough for me.

Sophia said to her mother – See mama, there's not the slightest malice in his heart.

Prabhu – Yes, he doesn't seem to be unhappy.

John Sevak – Ask his heart.

Mrs Sevak – He must be abusing.

The phaeton was still moving slowly. Meanwhile Tahir Ali called out – Huzoor, this land belongs to Soordas, not to Panda. So they say.

Sahib ordered the phaeton to stop. He looked at Mrs Sevak with embarrassment in his eyes, got down, and asked Soordas politely – Well, Soordas, is this land yours?

Soordas – Yes huzoor, it's mine. This is the only mark left of my ancestors.

John Sevak – Then my purpose is served. I was worried because I didn't know who the owner was and whether I could make a deal with him or not. There's no need to worry if it's yours. There won't be much difficulty with an ascetic and a good man like you. Why have you put on this garb when you own so much land?

Soordas – What can I do, huzoor? I'm only doing what God wishes.

John Sevak – So your troubles will be over now. Just give me this land. It will be a favour as well as a gain. I'll give you as much as you want.

Soordas – Sarkar, this is the only mark of my ancestors. How will I show my face to them if I sell it?

John Sevak – I'll get a well built on this road here. Your ancestors will continue to be remembered.

Soordas – Sahib, the muhalla-valas benefit a great deal from this land. There's not even a finger's worth of fodder anywhere. All the cattle around graze here. They'll have nowhere to go if I sell it.

John Sevak – How much a year do you get for the pasturage?

Soordas – Nothing. God gives me enough to eat anyhow, so why should I take any pasturage from anyone? I can at least do this much if I can't benefit anybody in any other way.

John Sevak (*Surprised*) – You have left so much land for grazing just like that? Sophia was right when she said that you are the incarnation of renunciation. I haven't come across such renunciation even among the great. You are blessed. But then how can you disappoint human beings if you feel so much compassion for animals? I won't let go of you without taking this land.

Soordas – Sarkar, although this land is mine I can't say anything until I ask the muhalla-valas. What will you do with it?

John Sevak – I'll open a factory from which the country and society will prosper, the poor will benefit, and thousands will get a living. You'll get the glory for all that.

Soordas – Huzoor, I can't say anything without consulting the muhalla-valas.

John Sevak – All right, ask them. I'll meet you again. You should realize that you won't be a loser if you make a deal with me. I'll make you happy in whatever way you want. Take this (*taking out five rupees from his pocket*), I thought you were just an ordinary beggar, forgive that insult.

Soordas – What will I do with the rupees? Just give a few paise in dharma's name, and I'll wish you well. I won't accept money on any other basis.

John Sevak – How can I give you just a few paise? Take this, assume that it's for dharma.

Soordas – No, sahib. Your dharma is tainted by your self-interest; it's no longer dharma.

John Sevak pleaded with him for a long time but Soordas didn't accept the money. He then sat down on the phaeton, defeated.

Mrs Sevak asked – What were you talking about?

John Sevak – He's only a beggar, but he's very arrogant. I offered him five rupees but he wouldn't take them.

Mrs Sevak – Is there any hope?

Mr Sevak – It's not as easy as I had thought it would be.

The phaeton began to move faster.

2

SOORDAS RETURNED HOME SLOWLY, TAPPING HIS STICK, THINKING as he walked along the way – Such is the selfishness of the wealthy! They were so overbearing at first, they thought that I was even lowlier than a dog, but look at their wheedling as soon as they found that the land belongs to me. I'll give them my land! They were showing me five rupees, as if I have never seen rupees in my life. I won't let them have my land for 500 rupees, let alone five. How will I show my face to the muhalla-valas? Why should the poor cows wander around wretchedly for the sake of their factory? Christians don't have the least compassion or dharma. They only want to go around making everybody Christians. They should have sent me packing at the very start if they didn't want to give me anything. But they shooed me away after making me run a whole mile. Only that girl seems to be good-natured. She is the only one among them with compassion and dharma. The old woman is a complete hag; she just can't speak straight. Such arrogance! As if she is Victoria! Rama-Rama! I'm so tired! I'm still out of breath. I have never before been bluntly refused after being made to run so far. This must be God's wish. O my heart! Don't grieve so much. Your task is to beg; it's for others to give. It's their wealth, why should you feel bad if they don't want to give it? Should I tell the others that sahib wants the land? No, they'll all feel alarmed. What's the use of telling them since I have already given my answer?

With these thoughts Soordas reached the doorway of his exceedingly humble hut. There was a neem tree at the doorway, and in the opening meant for doors, a detachable screen made of bamboo twigs. Soordas pushed away the screen and took out a tiny bundle containing a few paise from his waist. This was all that he had earned during the day. He then groped in the thatch of the hut and took out a bag, which was his sole possession in life. He put the bundle of paise into the bag quietly so that nobody could get an inkling of it. Then he hid it in the thatch and brought a flame from a neighbouring house. He lit the mud stove with a few dry twigs, which he had stored under the trees. There was a dim, flickering light in the hut. What frustration! How much hopeless destitution! There was no cot, no bedding, no utensils, no clay vessels. There was a clay pitcher in a corner, whose age could be estimated by the scum congealed on it, a small handi next to the mud stove, an old tawa that looked like a sieve, a small shallow wooden dish, and a small lota. These were the sole possessions of that home. What an epitome of human desires! Soordas put all the foodgrain that he had obtained during the day just as it was into the handi—a few grains of barley, wheat, gram and maize, and a fistful of rice—and sprinkled some salt over it. Who, indeed, has savoured the taste of such a khichri? It had the sweetness of contentment and nothing sweeter than that exists in the world. He put the handi on the mud stove and left the house, putting the screen in its place, to bring flour worth an anna from a bania's shop on the road. He kneaded the flour in the wooden dish, his feeble body and frayed cloth making a mockery of mankind's attachment to life in that dim light.

The handi boiled over several times, putting out the fire. Soordas's eyes began to water because he had to blow it up so often. Eyes can cry even though they can't see. That jelly comprising the six predominant tastes was finally ready. Soordas took it down. He then put on the tawa and began to make rotis, patting them with his hands and toasting them on the tawa with great precision. All the rotis were alike—neither small nor big, neither underdone nor burnt. He kept removing them from the tawa to puff them up on the burning coals and then put them down on the floor. When the rotis were ready, he stood at the doorway and called out loudly, 'Mitthu-Mitthu, come beta, the food is ready.' But when Mitthu didn't appear, he went to Nayakram's veranda after placing the screen on the door again, and called out 'Mitthu-Mitthu.' Mitthu, who was asleep there, got up startled when he heard the voice. He was Soordas's brother's son, a well-built, good-looking, cheerful child of twelve or thirteen. Both his parents had died in the plague, so his upbringing had become Soordas's responsibility since the last three years. This child was dearer to him than his own life. It didn't matter if he himself starved, but he made sure that Mitthu ate three times a day. He would be content with chewing peas himself but he'd be sure to feed Mitthu rotis, sometimes with sugar, sometimes with ghee and salt. If somebody gave him mithai or gur as alms, he would tie it with great care in a corner of his cloth and give it to Mitthu. He would tell everybody, 'This is an investment for my old age. Right now I can move about and can live by begging, but who will get me even a lota of water when I'm helpless?' Finding Mitthu asleep, Soordas picked him up in his lap and put him down at the doorway of the hut. Then he opened the door, helped the boy to wash his face, and put the rotis and gur before him. When Mitthu saw the rotis, he said, sulking, 'I won't eat rotis and gur,' and stood up.

Soordas – Beta, the gur is very good. Just eat it and see. And look, how soft the rotis are. They are made of wheat.

Mitthu – I won't eat.

Soordas – Then what will you eat, beta? What else can you get at this time of the night?

Mitthu – I want milk and rotis.

Soordas – Beta, eat this for the time being. I'll get you some milk in the morning.

Mitthu started crying. When Soordas failed to placate him, he got up, cursing his fate, picked up his stick, and went groping to Bajrangi the aheer's house, which was nearby. Bajrangi was sitting on a khaat, drinking coconut water. His wife Jamuni was cooking food. Three buffaloes and four or five cows were tied to the forage in the courtyard and were chewing fodder. Bajrangi asked, 'How does it go, Soorey? Who were the people in the buggy talking to you?'

Soordas – It was the sahib who owns the godown.

Bajrangi – You ran quite a distance after the buggy. Did you manage to get anything?

Soordas – Nothing at all. I got stones. Do Christians have any compassion or dharma? They want that land of mine.

Bajrangi – The one behind the godown?

Soordas – Yes. They tried their best to tempt me but I didn't agree.

Soordas had decided not to tell anyone about this for the time being, but flattery was necessary right now so that he could get some milk. He wanted to prove his nobility by displaying his sacrifice.

Bajrangi – Who would have let go of it even if you had agreed?

This is the only land between three or four villages. Where will our cows and buffaloes go if we lose it?

Jamuni – I would have tied them all at his doorway.

Soordas – Then I'll die before selling it. What do 500 or even 1000 rupees matter? Bhauji, please give me a mouthful of milk if you can spare it. Mitthua is waiting to eat, but he won't touch rotis and gur. He keeps asking only for milk. He always insists on getting whatever isn't there in the house. He'll go to sleep hungry if he doesn't get milk.

Bajrangi – Take it. There's no drought of milk. It has just been drawn. Gheesoo's mother, give Soorey a kulhiya of milk.

Jamuni – Sit down for a while, Soorey. I'll give it as soon as I'm free.

Bajrangi – Mitthua is waiting there to eat, and you say that you'll give it when you are free! I'll come if you can't get up.

Jamuni knew that the stupid fellow would give half a seer instead of a quarter. She hastened out of the kitchen and poured some milk into a kulhiya after filling half of it with water. Bringing it to Soordas, she said with malicious goodwill – Here you are. You have spoilt this brat's taste so much that he doesn't enjoy even a morsel without milk. He couldn't get enough gram to fill his belly when his father was alive and now he refuses to eat without milk.

Soordas – What can I do, bhabhi? I feel sorry for him when he starts crying.

Jamuni – You are bringing him up like this so that he will be useful some day. But wait and see if he'll give you even a sip of water. Mark my words. Somebody else's son can never be one's own. He'll kick you and go his own way as soon as he is grown up. You are nurturing a snake for yourself.

Soordas – I'm doing my dharma. For how long will he not give me credit when he becomes an adult? But of course what can anybody do if my own fate is wretched? Don't one's own sons turn away their faces when they grow up?

Jamuni – Why don't you tell him to take my buffaloes for grazing? Will he remain just a tiny tot all his life? He's a youth now; after all he's Gheesoo's age. Mark my words. He'll become mischievous if he's not made to do some work from now itself. He'll then lose interest in work and will eat phullauri all his life at your expense.

Soordas didn't reply. He picked up the kulhiya of milk and returned home, groping with his stick. Mitthu was asleep on the floor. Soordas woke him up again and fed him the rotis soaked in milk. Mitthu kept falling off to sleep but his mouth would open automatically whenever a morsel came his way. When he had eaten all the rotis, Soordas made him lie down on the straw mat and ate his khichri of assorted ingredients from the handi. Since he was still hungry he swirled some water in the handi and drank it. Then he picked up Mitthu in his lap, fixed the screen on the door, and went towards the temple.

The temple, at the other end of the basti, was that of Thakurji, the Supreme Deity. It had an elevated shrine. All around the temple there was a base three or four yards wide. This was the chaupaal of the basti where the inhabitants assembled. A few people would be sitting or lying there all day. There was also a brick well on which a hawker by the name of Jagdhar would sit selling, among other things, mithai cooked in oil, peanuts and ramdana laddoos. Wayfarers would come, buy mithai, draw water from the well and drink it, and go their way. The pujari of the temple, Dayagiri, lived in a hut nearby. He was a devotee of the sagun or personal deity, who believed that the path to liberation lay in bhajan-kirtan, in singing praises of God. He thought that nirvana was a fraud. He got a regular monthly allowance from the renowned rais, Kunwar Bharat Singh, who belonged to the old elite of the city. The bhog to Thakurji was made from this allowance, and something or the other was also obtained from the basti. The pujari was the image of contentment and patience, totally without desire or avarice. He would be immersed all day in singing bhajans to the Lord. There was a small group of devotees who would assemble in the temple at around 8 p.m. or 9 p.m. after their daily work to sing bhajans for an hour or two. Thakurdeen was an expert at playing the dhol, Bajrangi played the kartaal, Nayakram and Dayagiri the sarangi, while Jagdhar was skilled in playing the tambura. Those who couldn't do anything else played the cymbals, so their numbers fluctuated. Soordas was the life and soul of this group. He was equally skilled in playing all the musical instruments—dhol, cymbals, kartaal, sarangi, tambura—and there was nobody who could match his singing in several surrounding muhallas. He was not interested in thumris and ghazals but would sing the devotional songs of sants such as Kabir, Meera, Dadoo, Kamaal and Paltoo.* His blind face would then be radiant with joy. He became so enraptured while singing that he would lose all consciousness of his body and senses. All his worries and rancour would vanish in the bliss of devotion.

The meeting had already begun when Soordas reached there with Mitthu. All the members of the assembly were present, only the president was missing. On seeing Soordas, Nayakram said – You've taken a very long time to come, we have been waiting for you for half an hour. This brat is a heavy burden on you. Why don't you ask for something from our house to feed him?

Dayagiri – His belly will get filled with the prasad offered to Thakurji if he comes here.

Soordas – Doesn't he eat only what you people give? I'm there only to prepare it.

Jagdhar – It's not good to spoil boys so much. You carry him around in your lap as if he's a tiny child. My Vidyadhar is two years younger than Mitthu, but I never carry him in my lap.

Soordas – Orphans tend to become stubborn. All right then, what will it be?

Dayagiri – Let's begin with a chaupai from the Ramayana.

People picked up their instruments. Voices mingled and there was the chanting of the Ramayana for half an hour.

---

* Kabir: (1440–1518), brought up by childless Muslim weavers in Banaras, he distanced himself from fundamentalisms of all religions and sang of all humanity as one.

Meera: (c. 1498–1547), a Rajput princess and devotee of Lord Krishna since her childhood. Was married to Prince Bhoj, the eldest son of Rana Sanga of Chittor at the age of thirteen but she maintained that she was married only to Krishna. After her husband's death in battle, persecuted by her in-laws, she left the palace and began wandering throughout Rajasthan, singing and dancing ecstatically in praise of Krishna, gathering many followers. She eventually reached Vrindavan, near Mathura, where Krishna had spent his childhood.

Dadoo: Dadoo Dayal (1544–1603), a poet-saint from Gujarat. 'Dadoo' means brother and 'Dayal' means the 'compassionate one'. Was a Muslim by birth and a cotton-carder by profession. He later moved to Rajasthan.

Kamaal: Kabir's son, whose verses survive in oral traditions.

Paltoo: Paltoo Sahib (1710–80), lived in North India and earned his livelihood as a grocer. He fought the superstitions, rites and orthodoxies of his time.

Nayakram – Vaah, Soordas, vaah! You are the life and soul of the gathering.

Bajrangi – I'd give both my eyes for such talent.

Jagdhar – Bhairo isn't yet here. There's no sparkle without him.

Bajrangi – He must be selling toddy. Greed for money is a bad thing. He has a wife and an old mother at home, which means that there's wailing and grumbling day and night. But there's the whole day for work, so at night at least there can be some time for singing God's bhajans.

Jagdhar – Soordas gets breathless but Bhairo doesn't.

Bajrangi – You go and sell your khoncha. What do you know about breathing? Anybody else's heart would burst if he tried to hold his breath for as long as Soordas. It's not a joke.

Jagdhar – Very well, bhaiyya. Nobody else in the world can hold his breath for as long as Soordas. Are you happy now?

Soordas – Bhaiyya, what's there to quarrel about? When have I claimed that I can sing? I only try to sing as well as I can when you order me to.

Meanwhile, Bhairo too came and sat down. Bajrangi said sarcastically – Was there no one left to drink toddy? Why have you closed your shop so early?

Thakurdeen – We don't know if he has even washed his hands and feet, or if he has come straight from there to Thakurji's temple. There's no cleanliness left anywhere any longer.

Bhairo – Is my body smeared with toddy?

Thakurdeen – You shouldn't come like this to God's durbar. One's caste may be high or low, but there must be cleanliness.

Bhairo – Do you bathe every day before coming here?

Thakurdeen – Selling paan is not a low occupation.

Bhairo – As paan, so toddy. Selling paan is not a high occupation.

Thakurdeen – Paan is kept along with the bhog to God. Several illustrious janeudhaaris who wear the sacred thread eat the paan I make. Nobody accepts even water from your hands.

Nayakram – Thakurdeen, what you say is very true. Nobody allows a paasi to touch even a pitcher of water.

Bhairo – Come to my shop some day and I'll show you how many dharmatmas and tilakdhaaris come there. Has anybody ever come across ascetics eating paan? But you can see them drinking toddy, ganja, charas whenever you like. Several mahatmas come and fawn upon me.

Nayakram – Thakurdeen, answer Bhairo now. He would have outwitted lawyers had he been educated.

Bhairo – I'm only telling the truth. There's no difference between toddy and paan. In fact, people drink the toddy fermented in a paraat like medicine.

Jagdhar – Yaaron, let's have a bhajan or two. Thakurdeen, why don't you admit that Bhairo has won and you have lost? That's the end of it.

Nayakram – Vaah, why should he admit defeat? Is this sastraarth* or a joke? Yes, Thakurdeen, now think of a reply.

Thakurdeen – Your heart will be gladdened if you come to my shop. The fragrance of kevra and roses floats all around, but it's impossible to stand the stench at his shop. Even the gutter doesn't stink so much.

Bajrangi – If somebody gave me a kingdom for a day the first thing I'd do would be to have all the toddy shops in the city burned.

Nayakram – Well, Bhairo, answer this now. There really is a stink that wafts. Do you have a reply?

Bhairo – Not one but hundreds. A rotten paan is not even dirt cheap. But the price of toddy increases the more rotten it becomes. It sells for a rupee a bottle when it becomes vinegar, which is then consumed by the most prestigious janeudhaaris.

Nayakram – You have said something that has gladdened my heart. I'd give you a certificate for law this minute if I had the authority. Thakurdeen, admit defeat now. You can't get the better of Bhairo.

Jagdhar – Bhairo, why don't you be quiet now? You know Pandaji very well. His job is to make others fight and then to enjoy the show. You won't lose your honour merely by saying, baba, you win and I lose.

Bhairo – Why should I? Am I less than anyone when it comes to words?

Jagdhar – Thakurdeen, then why don't you be quiet?

Thakurdeen – Oh yes! What will I do if I keep quiet? We came here hoping that there would be some bhajan-kirtan, but we are only quarrelling uselessly. As for Pandaji, he gets imartis and laddoos to eat without making any effort. This is the kind of amusement that interests him. But I have to get back to the grind at the crack of dawn.

---

* A dialect variation of sastraarth: Meaning or interpretation of the Shastras; doctrinal debate.

Jagdhar – When I meet God next, I'll ask him to let me be born in a panda's home.

Nayakram – Bhaiyya, don't raise your hand at me, I'm a frail man. I'd prefer to buy mithai only from your khoncha but so many flies keep hovering over it and on top of that there's always so much dirt sticking on it, so I don't feel like eating.

Jagdhar (*Annoyed*) – My mithai won't rot and I won't starve if you don't buy it. I do manage to earn at least a rupee or twenty annas a day. Why would anybody buy my mithai if he can get free rasgullas?

Thakurdeen – There's no limit to Pandaji's income. What he can get daily is still not enough, and then there's the food into the bargain. And some foolish, wealthy person will be ready to give everything if he happens to get trapped—elephants, horses, land, property. Could anybody be luckier?

Dayagiri – Nobody, Thakurdeen. Money earned by the sweat of the brow is the best. Haven't you seen how pandas run after pilgrims?

Nayakram – Baba, if anybody's livelihood is earned by the sweat of the brow, it's mine. Ask Bajrangi.

Bajrangi – Other people may have earned their livelihoods by the sweat of the brow, but yours has been earned by bloodshed. Other people shed sweat, you shed blood. A river of blood is shed over each patron. What do people who only kill flies all day in front of their khoncha know about your livelihood? They won't find anywhere to run if they have to hold the front for even a day.

Jagdhar – Go on, you come pretending friendship. You convert a seer of milk into two and a half, and then you call yourself a devotee of God.

Bajrangi – If any mother's brat can extract even a drop of water from my milk I'll admit defeat. Mixing water in milk is equal to cow slaughter here. Unlike you, we don't deceive innocent children by selling mithai cooked in oil claiming that it has been cooked in ghee.

Jagdhar – All right, bhai, you win, I lose. You are true and your milk is pure. We are the ones who are bad and so is our mithai. That's the end of the matter.

Bajrangi – You don't know my temper, I'm warning you. I don't mind anybody beating me with a hundred shoes if he tells the truth, but my whole being seethes with rage if I hear a lie.

Bhairo – Bajrangi, don't boast so much. Nothing is gained by self-praise. Just don't make me open my mouth, I too have drunk the milk from your place. Even my toddy is better than that.

Thakurdeen – Bhai, anyone may claim to be honest but milk has now become a dream. All of it evaporates, there's no sign of cream. There was a time when a layer of cream as thick as a finger would form as soon as milk came to the boil.

Dayagiri – Bachcha, good or bad, at least you can still get some. The days are not far off when milk will be so scarce that there won't be enough even to soothe the eyes.

Bhairo – The fact is that the housewife converts one seer into three, and despite that they claim to sell genuine stuff. They'd become bankrupt if they really did so. This pomp wouldn't last even a day.

Bajrangi – People who become bankrupt are the ones who fatten themselves at others' expense, not those who sweat for their livelihood. Thank your stars that you are in a city; you would have been swallowing flies in a village. I think all those are sinners who buy here and sell there by haggling to make a living. Only people who tear their hearts out to extract wealth from the earth can earn an honest livelihood.

Bajrangi felt embarrassed after saying this because his remarks implicated all those present. He wanted to hint at Bhairo, Jagdhar and Thakurdeen but Soordas, Nayakram, Dayagiri, all of them got encompassed in the category of sinners.

Nayakram – In that case, bhaiyya, you have doomed me as well. I too am a sinner because I roam around all day and eat food that perhaps even the high and the mighty can't get.

Thakurdeen – I'm another sinner who earns rotis by selling something that people enjoy. Who will lose anything if there are no paan sellers in the world?

Jagdhar – I'm a third sinner who haggles all day. Will anybody die if they don't get sev and khurma to eat?

Bhairo – I'm a greater sinner than you because I earn a living by selling intoxicants. If you ask me, there's no work worse than this. The constant company of drunkards and drug addicts, listening to their conversation, living among them, is this any sort of life?

Dayagiri – Why, Bajrangi, sadhus and sants must be the greatest sinners because they don't do anything?

Bajrangi – No baba, what better vocation can there be than singing God's bhajans? The cultivation of Rama's name is the best work of all.

Nayakram – So Bajrangi is the only pious soul here, and everyone else is a sinner?

Bajrangi – If you really ask me, I'm the greatest sinner because I earn my living by depriving my cows and starving their calves.

Soordas – Bhai, cultivation is supreme; commerce is lower than that. That's the only difference. Why do you call commerce a sin? And why do you think that you are sinners? Yes, service is detestable and you can call it a sin if you like. God has been merciful so far; all of you do your own work. But such hard times are coming that you'll be forced to earn your living by serving and waiting upon others, when you'll no longer be your own servants but those of strangers. Then there'll be no trace of ethics and dharma left in you.

Soordas said all this very solemnly, as if a rishi were uttering a prophecy. Everybody was silent. Thakurdeen asked, anxiously – Why Soorey, is some disaster going to happen? Listening to you scares me. Will there be fresh trouble?

Soordas – Yes, those are the signs. The sahib who owns a leather godown here plans to open a tobacco factory and wants my land for that. That factory will be disaster for us.

Thakurdeen – Why are you giving your land when you know this?

Soordas – It doesn't depend on me, bhai. The land will be taken away whether I give it or not. People who have money can do everything.

Bajrangi – Sahib may be rich enough in his own house. Can he take our land by devouring it? He'll fall flat on his face. It's not a joke.

While this conversation was going on Sayyad Tahir Ali came there, and said to Nayakram – Pandaji, just come here. I want to speak with you.

Bajrangi – You want to talk about that land, don't you? It's not for sale.

Tahir – I'm not asking you. You are not its owner or agent.

Bajrangi – I've told you, that land is not for sale. It doesn't matter who the owner is or the agent.

Tahir – Come, Pandaji, come. Let them blabber.

Nayakram – Say what you want to here. They are all our own people, there are no secrets from anyone. Everyone will listen to what you have to say and a decision will be taken only after consulting everybody. Speak up, what do you want to say?

Tahir – I want to discuss that land.

Nayakram – In that case the owner is sitting before you. Why don't you speak to him? I don't want a commission by acting as a go-between. What's left for me to say when Soordas has already refused in sahib's presence?

Bajrangi – He must have thought that he can get the work done through Pandaji's mediation. Tell sahib that his lordliness won't work here.

Tahir – You are getting so worked up because you are an aheer and boasting so much because you don't know sahib yet. You won't be able to prevent him from taking the land once he is determined to. Don't you know how many contacts he has among the city officials? His daughter will soon be engaged to the district magistrate. Who can refuse him? You'll get a good price if you give your consent willingly, but you'll lose the land and not get even a kauri if you play any mischief. Did railway proprietors bring any land with them? Wasn't it our land that they took? Can this land not be taken over in the same way?

Bajrangi – You must be getting some commission; that's why you are currying so much favour.

Jagdhar – Take from us whatever you hope to get from them and tell them that they can't get the land. You are tricky customers. Hoodwink sahib so he loses his wits!

Tahir – I'm not trying to please him out of greed. I think it's immoral to take even a single kauri without my master's knowledge. I try to please him because I eat his salt.

Jagdhar – All right, sahib, forgive me, I made a mistake. I was only talking of the way of the world.

Tahir – So Soordas, what should I tell sahib?

Soordas – Just that the land is not for sale.

Tahir – I'm telling you again, you'll be deceived. Sahib is determined to get it.

Soordas – He won't get it as long as I'm alive. Yes, he may well get it if I die.

When Tahir Ali had left, Bhairo spoke up – The world thinks only of its own advantage. It doesn't matter if others live or die as long as one prospers oneself. Bajrangi, you have cows that graze; that's why it's in your interest that the land should remain as it is. I don't have cows that graze. My sales will increase fourfold with the opening of the factory. Why haven't you thought of that? Who are you to plead on everybody else's behalf? It is Soorey's land. It's for him to decide whether to sell it or to keep it. Who are you to jump into the fray?

Nayakram – Yes, Bajrangi, answer Bhairo. Who are you to interfere when it's none of your business?

Bajrangi – How is it not my business? Animals come here to graze from ten villages and muhallas. Where will they go—to sahib's house or to Bhairo's? He's concerned only about his shop. Why don't you burgle somebody's house? You'll get rich quick.

Bhairo – You go and burgle houses. We don't mix water in milk here.

Dayagiri – Bhairo, you really are very quarrelsome. Why don't you be quiet if you can't speak politely? It's a sign of foolishness, not intelligence, to talk so much.

Bhairo – You manage to get buttermilk every day in the name of Thakurji's bhog, don't you? Why won't you sing Bajrangi's praises?

Nayakram – The young man is so outspoken that nobody dares to open his mouth after getting an earful from him.

Thakurdeen – The devotional mood is now spoilt. Put your dhols and cymbals away.

Dayagiri – Bhairo, don't come here from tomorrow.

Bhairo – Why shouldn't I? It's God's temple; you haven't built it. Can you stop anyone from coming to God's durbar?

Nayakram – Take this babaji, aren't you satisfied yet or do you want some more?

Jagdhar – Babaji, why don't you withdraw? The glory of sadhus and sants won't be dimmed. Bhairo, you shouldn't mind what sadhus and sants say.

Bhairo – You can go and flatter, because that's how you get your rotis. We are not bullied by anyone here.

Bajrangi – All right, be quiet now, Bhairo, enough is enough. You are bragging too much.

Nayakram – Why are you threatening Bhairo? Do you think he's a coward? You may have won wrestling bouts in the past but you are no longer the same. It's Bhairo's word that counts now.

Bhairo laughed at Nayakram's sarcasm, not at all offended. It had the relish of wit and was enjoyable, not poisonous. Even toxic aconite becomes juice once crushed.

As soon as Bhairo started laughing, people picked up their instruments and began to sing. Soordas's sweet melody seemed to dance in the firmament as if it were the radiance of light shimmering in the depths of water:

> Delicate and fragile is woven the sheet
> What is the warp, what the woof, with what thread is woven the sheet?
> With the warp and the weft of two vessels and a contented heart is woven the sheet
> A spinning wheel of a cluster of eight lotuses that sways, five elements, three qualities, is the sheet
> It took the Lord ten months to stitch it, with great care is woven the sheet
> That sheet is worn by gods, men, and saints; wearing it, they have soiled the sheet
> The devotee Kabir wrapped it around carefully, and kept as it was the sheet.*

The conversation had continued far into the night. The clock struck 11 p.m. People collected the dhols and cymbals and the meeting ended. Soordas picked up Mitthu, took him to his hut and made him sleep on the mat. He then lay down on the floor.

---

* A poem by Kabir, translation mine.
 Two vessels: the left and the right of the three vessels of the body running from the loins to the head which, according to yoga, are the principal passages of breath (ingla-pingla).
 Eight lotuses: the eight chakras of the body.
 Three qualities: the three inherent constituents of nature—sattva (nobility, goodness), rajas (passion, action) and tamas (darkness, ignorance), also known as the pure, the subtle and the gross.

3

JOHN SEVAK'S BUNGALOW WAS IN SIGARA. HIS FATHER, ISHVAR SEVAK, had built it there on getting a pension from the army and was still its owner. There is no record of his ancestors before that, nor is there any great need for us to investigate it. However, this much is certain that the distinction of taking refuge in Lord Jesus did not belong to Ishvar Sevak but to his father. Ishvar Sevak still retained dim memories of his childhood when he used to accompany his mother to bathe in the Ganga. He had not yet forgotten her last rites. He recalled that several soldiers had entered the house after her death and had arrested his father. His memory became confused after that. But it could easily be inferred from his fair complexion and his appearance that he was well-born and that perhaps he belonged to this very province.

This bungalow had been built in the days when land was not that valuable in Sigara. There were vegetables and fruit trees instead of flowers in the compound. In fact, it was evident even from the flower-pots that more attention had been paid to utility than to aesthetics. Creepers of parval, pumpkin, kundru and beans yielded fruit and also enhanced the beauty of the bungalow. There was a tiled veranda on one side, where cows and buffaloes were reared, and a stable on the other. Neither father nor son was fond of cars. Keeping a phaeton was both economical and comfortable. Ishvar Sevak, in fact, disliked cars because their noise disturbed his peace. The phaeton's horse would be tied with a long rope in the compound and left there. The stable yielded manure for the garden and a syce alone sufficed for all the work that needed to be done. Ishvar Sevak was an expert at managing domestic affairs and his enthusiasm for household tasks had not diminished in the least. He would sit all day from morning to evening on his easy chair, which lay in the thatched veranda of the bungalow, bemoaning John Sevak's extravagance and the devastation of the house. He still lectured his son regularly for an hour or two and John Sevak's growing prestige and wealth were perhaps a result of his counsel. 'Economy' was the fundamental principle of his life and its violation intolerable to him. He could not bear to see money being wasted in his house, even if it was that of a guest. He was so devout that he went to church twice a day without fail. He had his own conveyance, an open litter, which a man would pull to the door of the church. Ishvar Sevak sent him back as soon as he reached there because there was no need for anyone to sit around in the compound of the church to guard the litter. The man could do some other work if he returned to the house. Ishvar Sevak often gave him instructions about the tasks that had to be done before sending him back. The man would return after a couple of hours to pull him back to the house. Ishvar Sevak seldom returned empty-handed, sometimes he would get a few papayas and sometimes oranges or a seer or half a seer of gooseberries. The padri respected him a great deal. No other man in his entire congregation was so old and so devout on top of that! The concentration with which he listened to the padri's sermons and the devotion with which he participated in the singing of hymns were exemplary.

It was morning. People had just got up from the table after taking some refreshments or finishing their chhoti haaziri. John Sevak ordered the gharry to be prepared. Ishvar Sevak had just finished drinking a cup of tea while sitting on his chair and was annoyed because there was too much sugar in it. 'Sugar isn't a boon that can be eaten until the belly bursts,' he grumbled, 'for one thing it's difficult to digest, and then it is expensive. Half the amount would have been enough to make the tea enjoyable. The right quantity should have been estimated; sugar isn't something with which to fill the stomach. I have said so hundreds of times, but who listens to me? Everyone thinks that I'm a dog. Who cares for his bark?'

Mrs Sevak had learnt well the lessons of religious zeal and frugality. She said, embarrassed – Papa, please forgive me. Sophie put in too much sugar today. You won't have this complaint from tomorrow, but what am I to do? Nobody likes light tea here.

Ishvar Sevak said indifferently – How does it concern me? I won't be here until doomsday, but these are signs of the devastation of the house. Jesus, hide me in your mantle.

Mrs Sevak – I admit my mistake. I should have given the sugar after estimating the quantity needed.

Ishvar Sevak – Well, this is nothing new. It's the same wailing every day. John thinks he's the master of the house and earns the money, so why shouldn't he spend it? But earning wealth is one thing, spending it wisely is another. A sensible man is one who knows the proper use of money. What's the point of getting it from somewhere and spending it elsewhere? It's better not to get any. He has bought a horse of such a high pedigree although I kept advising him against it. Where was the need? He doesn't have to go horse racing. A pony would have done. But of course, his pride would be hurt if other people's horses overtook his. He doesn't have to travel a long way. A pony would have eaten two seers of grain instead of six. After all, four seers are wasted, aren't they? But who listens to me? Jesus, hide me in your mantle. Sophie, come here, beti, and read the Holy Bible to me.

Sophie was in Prabhu's room, debating the Messiah's statement that the kingdom of heaven belongs to the poor, and that it is as difficult for a rich man to enter it as it is for a camel to go through a needle's eye. She doubted whether being poor was a virtue in itself and being wealthy a vice. Her reason couldn't grasp the purpose of this statement. 'Was the Messiah so critical of wealth only to please his followers? History says that to begin with only the meek, the wretched, the poor and the downtrodden sought refuge in his mantle. Surely that wasn't why he scorned wealth so much? There are so many poor people who are completely immersed in impiety and ignorance. Perhaps their wickedness is the cause of their poverty. Will their poverty alone atone for their sins? There are several wealthy people whose hearts are pure and as transparent as a mirror. Will their wealth wipe out all their good deeds?'

Sophia was always engrossed in investigating questions of truth and falsehood. It was her nature to test religious axioms against the touchstone of reason and she couldn't believe any principle on the basis of sacred texts alone until it was logically acceptable. She sought Prabhu's help whenever she tried to resolve her doubts.

Sophia – I've been thinking about this subject for a long time, but I can't understand it. Why did the Lord Messiah give so much importance to poverty and forbid wealth and pomp?

Prabhu – Go and ask the Messiah.

Sophia – What do you think?

Prabhu – I don't understand anything and nor do I want to. Food, sleep and entertainment, these are the three fundamentals of human life. Everything else is a maze. I think that religion is completely detached from reason. Reason is as unsuitable for assessing religion as a goldsmith's scales are for weighing a brinjal. Religion is religion and reason reason. Religion is either so brilliant that it dazzles reason with its light or so dreadfully dark that nothing is visible to reason. You are unnecessarily breaking your head over these disputes. Listen, do you know what papa said as he was leaving?

Sophia – No, I wasn't paying attention.

Prabhu – Just that I should soon place orders for the machinery. He has decided to get that land. He's very enthusiastic about this opportunity and wants the foundation to be laid as soon as possible. But I'm very nervous about this project. Although I've learned this business, if you really ask me, my heart was not in it even there. I used to spend my time rambling in philosophy, literature and poetry. How could I get the same pleasure in a factory that I could in discussions with the great scholars and literati? Actually, that's the reason why I went there. Now I'm in a deep dilemma. Papa will be unhappy if I don't help with this project. He'll think that thousands of rupees have gone down the drain and he might begin to hate the sight of me. But I'm afraid that if I do take on the work my discontent will result in making losses instead of profits. I'm not at all enthusiastic about this work. I need only a hut in which to live and a good library of philosophy and literature. I don't want anything else. But here you are, dada is calling you. Go, or he'll come here and waste several hours in useless chatter.

Sophia – This is my bad luck. He sends for me the moment I sit down for a while to read. He is making me read the story of Genesis these days. I doubt each and every word of it. He gets annoyed if I say anything. It's just unpaid labour.

Mrs Sevak came to call her daughter and overheard the last words. Furious, she said – No doubt it is useless to read the Holy Bible, it's a sin to take the name of the Messiah. You enjoy only the conversation of that blind beggar, you like to read the tall tales of Hindus and the Word of God is poisonous for you. Khuda knows how this obsession has possessed your mind. I always see you blaspheming against your true faith. You may think that the Word of God is a figment of the imagination, but it's not the sun's fault if its rays don't reach the eyes of a blind person, it's the blind person's. It's your misfortune and ignorance if your heart is turned against the mahatma to whom three-quarters of the people of the globe are devoted, the great soul whose eternal words are bestowing life on the whole world today. May Khuda have mercy on you!

Sophia – I have never uttered any improper words against Mahatma Jesus. I think he is the incarnation of righteousness, sacrifice and virtue. But reverence for him doesn't mean that I should believe the absurdities with which his disciples have filled his precepts or the miracles celebrated in his name. And this wrong has been done not only to the Messiah but to all the mahatmas of the world.

Mrs Sevak – You'll have to believe in every word of the Holy Bible, otherwise you can't count yourself among the Lord Messiah's disciples.

Sophia – Then I'll be forced to think that I don't belong to his congregation. It's impossible for me to believe in every word of the Bible.

Mrs Sevak – You are a heretic and you are depraved. The Lord Messiah will never forgive you.

Sophia – I have no objection to accepting these names if they are given for staying away from religious bigotry.

Mrs Sevak could no longer control herself. She had not struck a fatal blow so far. Her hands had been held back by maternal love. But Sophie's perverse arguments put an end to her patience. She said – There's no place in this house for anyone who opposes the Lord Messiah.

Prabhu – Mama, you are being very unfair. When has Sophie said that she doesn't believe in the Lord Messiah?

Mrs Sevak – Yes, this is just what she is saying. Your understanding is distorted. What else can disbelief in the Holy Bible mean? She doesn't believe in the miracles of the Lord Messiah and doubts his moral precepts. She doesn't believe in the truth of his atonement, nor does she accept his sacred creeds.

Prabhu – I have never seen her transgressing the creeds of the Messiah.

Sophia – I don't accept anybody else's instructions on religious matters except those of my own judgement.

Mrs Sevak – You are not my child and I don't want to see your face.

She entered Sophia's room, picked up several Buddhist and Vedanta texts, and threw them into the veranda. She trampled them under her feet in the same fit of anger and said to Ishvar Sevak – Papa, it's no use calling Sophie. She is blaspheming against the Lord Messiah.

Ishvar Sevak was so startled that it seemed as if a spark of fire had fallen on him. Staring in astonishment with his dull eyes, he asked – What did you say? Sophie is blaspheming against the Lord Messiah! Sophie?

Mrs Sevak – Yes, yes, Sophie. She says she doesn't believe in his miracles, his precepts and his creeds.

Ishvar Sevak (*Heaving a sad sigh*) – Lord Messiah, hide me in your mantle, lead your straying sheep on to the true path. Where is Sophie? Take me to her, hold my hands and raise me up. Khuda, illuminate my daughter's heart with your light. I'll fall at her feet and plead with her; I'll humbly make her understand. Just take me to her.

Mrs Sevak – I've given up after trying everything. Khuda's curse is on her. I don't want to see her face.

Ishvar Sevak – Don't talk like that. She is blood of my blood, life of my life, breath of my breath. I'll clasp her to my heart. The Lord Messiah took heretics into his bosom and gave shelter to the wicked in his mantle. He is sure to have mercy on my Sophie. Jesus, hide me in your mantle.

When Mrs Sevak still did not give him any support, Ishvar Sevak got up with the help of his stick. Tapping it, he went to Sophie's door and said – Beti Sophie, where are you? Come here, beti, let me embrace you. My Messiah was the beloved Son of Khuda—helper of the meek, protector of the weak, friend of the poor, supporter of the drowning, saviour of sinners, deliverer of the wretched! Beti, which other prophet's mantle is so ample that there's room for all the sins and vices of the world in its folds? He is the one and only prophet who gave the glad tidings of salvation to all sinners and heretics. How else could there have been any salvation for sinful souls like us? Who else was there to deliver us?

He then embraced Sophie. Her mother's harsh words had aroused her helpless anger. She was crying in her room, extremely upset. She thought, 'I should leave this house this very minute. Is there no place for me in this vast world? I can work hard and support myself. What's the use of being free of worldly cares if it's at the cost of sacrificing my independence? My soul is not such a trifling thing that it should be killed to make two ends meet.' Prabhu sympathized with his sister. He had far less faith than she did in religion but kept his independent views to himself. He went to church, participated in the family prayers, even sang hymns. He thought that religion was beyond the scope of serious reflection and went to church with the same attitude as going to the theatre. He first peeped into his room to make sure that his mother wasn't watching to avoid being struck by her thunderbolts. Then he went quietly to Sophie and said, 'Sophie, why are you being so foolish? What kind of wisdom is it to poke your finger into a snake's mouth? Think and believe what you like, don't believe what you don't want to; but where's the point in broadcasting it and being ridiculed by society? Who is going to peep into your heart?'

Sophia looked coldly at her brother and replied – I want my actions to match my words on religious matters. I want them both to be consonant. It's beyond me to pretend to be religious. I'm willing to suffer all the sorrows of the world for the sake of my soul. Even if there's no place for me in this house, there is at least this vast world created by God. I can subsist anywhere. I'll bear all the frustrations and am not worried about social disapproval, but I cannot live if I fall in my own eyes. I'll starve rather than sell my soul even if I realize that all doors are shut for me.

Prabhu – The world is much smaller than you think.

Sophia – There will be room enough for a grave.

Ishvar Sevak embraced her and tried to pacify her anguished heart with tears of ecstatic devotion. Sophia felt compassion for his piety. Who can be cruel enough to hurt an innocent child by ridiculing his wooden horse and shattering his beautiful dream?

Sophia said – Dada, come and sit on this chair. You are uncomfortable when you stand.

Ishvar Sevak – I'll stand here at your door like a beggar until you say with your own lips that you believe in the Lord Messiah.

Sophia – Dada, I've never said that I don't believe in Lord Jesus or that I don't venerate him. I believe, and will continue to believe, that he is a great man, an ideal, and the incarnation of forgiveness and compassion.

Ishvar Sevak kissed Sophia's cheeks and said – My heart is at peace now. Jesus, take me in your mantle. I'll go and sit down. Come and read the Word of God to me, bless my ears with the words of the Lord Messiah.

Sophia could not refuse. She opened a chapter from Genesis and began to read. Ishvar Sevak sat on the chair and closed his eyes, listening with rapt attention. Mrs Sevak left triumphantly when she saw this scene.

This problem was solved, but Ishvar Sevak's salve could not heal the wound in Sophia's soul. Religious doubts would arise daily in her mind and she found it increasingly intolerable to live in her house. Gradually even Prabhu's sympathy began to diminish. John Sevak had no time to spare from business affairs to quell her mental rebellion. Mrs Sevak ruled over her with complete autocracy. The most trying time for Sophia was when she had to read the Bible to Ishvar Sevak. She constantly tried to find excuses to escape this ordeal and began to hate her artificial life. She was often strongly inspired to leave the house and to go away somewhere so that she would be free to investigate questions of truth and falsehood, but she was too diffident to act on her desires. Earlier she could get some peace of mind by expressing her doubts to Prabhu, but with his growing indifference she began to lose her affection and respect for him too. She began to believe that he was devoted only to enjoyment and pleasure, and that he was not interested in principles. Even his poems, to which she used to listen with great pleasure, now seemed full of counterfeit feelings. She would often avoid listening to them by pretending to have a headache and would tell herself that he had no business to express such noble and pure emotions that had no basis in introspection and experience.

One day, when all the people in the house were leaving for church, Sophia pretended to have a headache. Until now she used to go to church every Sunday despite her doubts. Prabhu understood her mental state and said – Sophie, why do you object to going to church? It's not so difficult to sit there silently for half an hour.

Prabhu enjoyed going to church. It gave him an opportunity to collect material for the philosophical analysis and ridicule of affectation and pretence, hypocrisy and deception. For Sophia, worship was not a matter of amusement but of peace and fulfilment. She replied, 'It might be easy for you but not for me.'

Prabhu – Why are you putting your life in jeopardy? You know amma's nature.

Sophia – I don't need your advice. I'm willing to take the responsibility for my actions.

Mrs Sevak asked – Is your headache so bad that you can't even go to church?

Sophia – Of course I can, but I don't want to.

Mrs Sevak – Why?

Sophia – It's my wish. I haven't taken a vow to go to church.

Mrs Sevak – Do you want us to be ashamed of showing our faces anywhere?

Sophia – Never, I only want you not to force me to go to church.

Ishvar Sevak had already left on his litter. John Sevak only asked – Is the pain very bad? I'll get medicine on my way back. Try to read less and to go out every day.

He sat down in the phaeton with Prabhu. But Mrs Sevak was not going to let her off as easily as that. She said – Do you hate the name of Jesus so much?

Sophia – I venerate him with all my heart.

Mrs Sevak – You are lying.

Sophia – I would never have said so if I didn't venerate him in my heart.

Mrs Sevak – Do you consider the Lord Messiah to be your saviour? Do you believe that he will save you?

Sophia – Never. I believe that my deeds will save me, if there is any salvation to be had.

Mrs Sevak – Your deeds will blacken your face, not save you.

Mrs Sevak, too, then sat on the phaeton. It was evening. On the road, groups of Christians, some wearing overcoats, others shivering in the cold of Maagh, were happily going to church, but for Sophia even the dim light of the sun was becoming intolerable. She sat down with a sigh. 'Your deeds will blacken your face'—these words began to pierce her heart like a spear. She thought, 'This is the right punishment for my selfishness. I too am killing my soul and putting up with insults and disrespect only for my sustenance. Who wishes me well in this house? Who will shed any tears for me if I die? Perhaps my death will make them happy. I am so fallen in their eyes. Shame on such a life! I have seen how harmoniously people with different beliefs live together in Hindu families. The father is a follower of the Sanatan Dharma and the son of the Arya Samaj. The husband belongs to the Brahmo Samaj and the wife worships idols. They all follow their own beliefs. Nobody interferes with anyone else. Among us, our souls are crushed, but we still claim that our education and culture foster freedom of thought. There are some people with liberal views even among us, such as Prabhu, but actually their liberalism is undiscriminating. Those who are conservative are preferable to such liberals. They at least have some beliefs and are not mere dissemblers. And what makes mama think that she can go on hurting me with her cruel words? She probably thinks that I have nowhere else to go and that nobody is concerned about me. I'll show her I can stand on my own feet. Living in this house is now like being in hell. It's better to starve than to be so shamelessly dependent for one's sustenance. What do I care? Let people laugh, at least I'll be free. I won't have to listen to anybody's taunts and insults.'

Sophia got up and left the compound without deciding on a destination. The air of that house seemed polluted to her. As she walked on, she kept wondering where she would go. Hoodlums began to make innuendoes about her from various directions when she reached a thickly populated area. However, instead of hanging down her head in embarrassment, she walked on, answering the innuendoes and lecherous gazes with scornful eyes, like a forceful stream of water ignoring the stones and surging on. Eventually, she reached the open road that went towards Dashashvamedha Ghat.

She felt like walking by the river, hoping to meet some kind person. How could she get any sympathy unless she got to know a few people who would understand her plight? Who would know what was in her heart? One was lucky if one could find such compassionate people. How could one hope for kindness from others when one's own parents had become one's enemies?

She was walking along in this dejected state when suddenly she saw a huge palace with a very wide green field in front of it. There was a high gate at the entrance with a golden dome above it, in which a kettledrum was being beaten. A path of pounded brick, with beds of creepers and roses on both sides, led to the palace. Several men and women were sitting on the lush grass, enjoying the cool breeze of Maagh. Some were lying down, others sat on cushioned seats, smoking cigars.

Sophia had not seen such a beautiful place in the city. She was surprised that such entrancing places also existed in its centre. She sat on one of the seats and thought – They must have returned from church by now and will of course be taken aback when they don't find me at home, but they'll think that I have gone out somewhere. No one will worry about me even if I remain here all night; they'll eat and go to sleep comfortably. Yes, dada will surely feel sad, but that's only because there won't be anyone to read the Bible to him. Mama will be happy at heart because I'll be far away from her sight. I don't know anyone. That's why it's important to meet people; one doesn't know when somebody might be needed. I have been living here for years and I don't have even a formal acquaintance with anyone. The daughter of a rais here used to study with me in Nainital, she had an attractive name. Yes, Indu! She was so gentle! Her conversation was always very affectionate. We used to saunter together arm in arm; no other girl was so beautiful and refined. Our ideas were so similar! If only I could find her address I could stay as her guest for a few days. Her father had a nice name. Yes, Kunwar Bharat Singh. I could have dropped her a card if I had thought of it earlier. She couldn't have forgotten me; she didn't seem so callous. At least I'll get some experience of human nature.

We often remember people in times of trouble whose very appearance we may otherwise have forgotten. We embrace even a barber or a kahaar from our muhalla when we meet them in a foreign region, even though we may never have so much as spoken to them directly in our native land.

Just as Sophia was thinking of asking somebody for Kunwar Bharat Singh's address, a carpet was spread on the brick platform in front of the palace. Several men came and sat down with sitars, belas and mridangs, and several youths began to sing in a chorus in tune with these instruments:

You shall not lose your courage in the battle for peace, even by
mistake;
You shall not weep, even if thunderbolts strike you.
You shall not sow the seeds of revenge in your heart against
your foe;
You shall not again block your ears with cotton and sleep in
the house.
You shall gladly cleanse the nation's stain with waters of blood;
You shall shoulder the entire burden of service to the nation.
You shall not get enraged with bloodshot eyes and scowling
brows;
You shall gladly get slaughtered on the sacrificial altar.
You shall never fear death; mortal is the human body;
You shall not leave the way of truth and step on to the path of
selfishness.
You shall staunchly believe that victory will be that of dharma;
You shall live and die in this world for your motherland.

There was neither charm nor sweetness in the music but it was full
of the power and the inspiration that characterize a chorus. The sacred
message of self-sacrifice and elevation reverberated in the vast sky, in
the blue heavens, and in Sophia's restless heart. She had been engrossed
only in religious discussions until now and had never received an
opportunity to listen to the message of nationalism. That tune began
to emanate from every fibre of her being like the light of a lamp:
'You shall live and die in this world for your motherland.'

There was a ripple in her heart making her want to join the singers.
Various thoughts came to her mind, 'I should go to some other country
to speak of India's distress. I should stand here and declare that I
dedicate myself to serve India. I should give a lecture on the goal of
my life—we have not been created to lament the woes of fate and to
shed tears over our subjugated state.'

Time stood still as these thoughts seemed to dance before Sophia's
inward vision.

The sound of the music was still echoing, when suddenly a house
with a tiled roof inside the compound caught fire. By the time people
ran towards it the flames had begun to rage fiercely. The entire field

was illuminated. Trees and plants were bathed in a sea of blazing light. The singers immediately left their instruments where they were, tucked up their dhotis, rolled up their sleeves and ran to extinguish the fire. Several youths also came out of the palace. Some ran to fetch water from the well, others entered the fire and started throwing out things which they had picked up inside. But nowhere could be seen the haste, the confusion, the panic, the lamentation, the cries of 'run-run', the orders given to others without doing anything oneself, that are usually to be found during such accidental disasters. They were all going about their work so competently and systematically that not a drop of water was wasted and the advance of the fire gradually began to diminish. People were jumping into it as fearlessly as if it were a tank of water.

The ferocity of the fire had not yet abated when there was a cry from the other side – 'Run, run, a man is drowning.' A masonry tank was situated at the other end of the palace with steps leading down to the water. There were bushes on its edges and a tiny boat was tied to a hook at the bank. As soon as they heard the cry, several men who were busy extinguishing the fire left the group and jumped into the water to save the drowning man. Sophia heard the sound of their jumping, 'Splash! Splash!' What divine wrath had caused this simultaneous tumult in the two principal elements, that too in the same place? She got up to go towards the tank when suddenly she saw a man carrying a bucket of water slip and fall down. The fire had stopped raging all around but it was still burning fiercely where the man had fallen. The dreadful flames leapt towards that unfortunate man and would have consumed him but Sophia ran towards the fire with lightning speed and pulled him out. All this happened in a moment. The poor man's life was saved but Sophia's delicate body was scorched in the fire. She fell down unconscious as soon as she came out of the circle of flames.

Sophia did not open her eyes for three days. She didn't know in what worlds her mind travelled. She saw scenes that were sometimes strange and sometimes frightening. At times the gentle image of Jesus would come before her eyes and at others she would see a vision of the beautiful face of a cultured woman whom she thought to be Saint Mary.

When she opened her eyes on the morning of the fourth day, she found herself in an elegant room. There was a fragrance of roses and sandalwood. Sitting on a chair in front of her was the woman whom she had thought to be Saint Mary when she was unconscious. An old man with eyes full of compassion sat by the pillow. She had perhaps thought him to be Jesus when she was unconscious. Dreams are composed only of recurrent memories.

Sophia asked in a feeble voice – Where am I?

The old man replied – You are in Kunwar Bharat Singh's house. Rani sahiba is sitting before you. How are you feeling now?

Sophia – I'm well. I'm feeling thirsty. Where's mama? Where's papa? Who are you?

Rani – He is Dr Ganguly. He has been treating you for the past three days. Who are your parents?

Sophia – Papa's name is John Sevak. Our bungalow is in Sigara.

Dr Ganguly – Well, so you are John Sevak's daughter? I know him. I'll just send for him.

Rani – Shall I send somebody right now?

Sophia – There's no hurry. They'll come by and by. What happened to the man whom I had pulled out of the fire?

Rani – Beti, he is fine by God's grace. He hasn't received the slightest injury. He is my son Vinay and will soon be here. You were the one who saved his life. Goodness knows what would have happened if you had not hastened to reach there. I'll always be grateful to you. You are the devi who has saved my dynasty.

Sophia – Have all the people who were in the house that was on fire been saved?

Rani – That was only a performance. Vinay has formed a society for social service. Whenever there is a fair or a festival in the city, or news of any accident, the society reaches there to volunteer help. Kunwar sahib had staged this performance to test the society.

Doctor – Kunwar sahib is a devata who protects so many poor people. This society had gone to Bengal a few days ago. Lakhs of pilgrims will be coming here from afar to bathe during the solar eclipse. That's why these preparations are being made.

Just then a beautiful young woman came and stood there. Rays of light irradiated her face as if it were a glowing lamp. She wore no jewellery except a pearl necklace. She seemed an incarnation of the gleaming splendour of dawn.

Sophia looked at her for a moment and then exclaimed – Indu, how come you are here? I'm seeing you today after such a long time.

Indu was startled. She had been seeing Sophia continuously for three days and had thought that she had seen her somewhere before, but could not remember where. Her memory was awakened as soon as she heard Sophia speak, her eyes lit up, and she blossomed like a rose. She exclaimed – Oho! Sophie, it's you?

Both friends embraced each other. This was the same Indu who used to study with Sophie in Nainital. Sophia had not expected that she would greet her so affectionately. Indu would sometimes cry, remembering old times, and sometimes laugh or embrace Sophie. She began to sing Sophie's praises to her mother, who could not contain her happiness at seeing this love. Finally Sophia said with embarrassment, 'Indu, for God's sake, don't praise me any more, or I won't talk to you. You didn't write even one letter all these days and now you are pretending love.'

Rani – No, beti Sophie, Indu has spoken to me about you several times. She doesn't talk cheerfully to anyone here. I haven't heard her praise anyone except you.

Indu – Behen, your complaint is valid, but what can I do? I don't know how to write letters. I made a big mistake in not asking for your address but I couldn't have written anyway. I'm afraid that you'll laugh at me. My letter wouldn't have ended, and I don't know what I would have written in it.

When kunwar sahib came to know that Sophia was now well enough to talk, he too came to thank her. He was six feet tall, with large eyes, long hair, and a long beard. He wore a long kurta made of thick cloth. Sophia had never before seen such a charismatic being. He was just like the rishis of her imagination. The great soul in that magnificent body was reflected in his eyes. Sophie wanted to get up respectfully but kunwar sahib said in a soft, unaffected voice, 'Beti, keep lying down. It will be difficult for you to get up. Here, I'll sit down. I know your father, but I didn't know that you are Mr Sevak's daughter. I have sent for him but let me tell you that I won't let you go just yet. This room is now yours, and you'll have to come here once a day even after you leave. (*To the rani*) – Jahnavi, have the piano brought here. And ask Miss Sohrabji to come today and paint an oil portrait of Sophia. Sohrabji is more skilled but I don't want Sophia to sit before him. The portrait will remind us of the person who saved us when we were in great danger.'

Rani – Shall I also donate some foodgrain?

As she said this, the rani glanced coquettishly at Dr Ganguly. Kunwar sahib retorted – The same delusions again! If somebody is a pauper nowadays, he should remain one; if somebody is starving, he should starve. There's no reason for anyone to starve when two hours of toil can provide enough to eat. The number of lazy people that charity has produced in our country has perhaps not been produced by all the countries put together. I don't know why charity has been given so much importance.

Rani – The rishis made a mistake in not asking your advice.

Kunwar sahib – Yes, if I'd been there I would have said frankly, 'You people are sowing the seeds of inertia, vice and misfortune.' Charity is the root of inertia and inertia is the root of all evil. That's why charity is the root of all evil. At the very least it definitely fosters it. Not charity, but give a banquet for friends if you like.

Dr Ganguly – Sophia, did you hear what raja sahib said? Your Lord Messiah gives the greatest importance to charity. Don't you have anything to say to kunwar sahib?

Sophia turned towards Indu and looked down smiling, as if to say, I respect him, otherwise I'm not incapable of making a rejoinder.

Sophia was inwardly comparing the mutual love that these people had for each other with her own family – There's so much love among them. Mother and father would both give their lives for Indu. And I'm so unfortunate that nobody wants to see my face. I have been lying here for four days and no one has bothered to enquire about me or to look for me. Amma must have thought that I have drowned myself somewhere. She must be happy at heart to have got rid of this nuisance. I'm not worthy of living with such generous people. How can I compare myself with them?

Although there was no sign of pity in anybody's behaviour there, Sophia felt embarrassed by her wretched condition when she saw them giving her so much respect and hospitality. She became formal even with Indu. Indu would address her informally as 'tum' with affection but she would respond formally with 'aap'.

Kunwar sahib had said that he had informed Mr Sevak, who would soon be there. Sophia now began to fear his arrival and his insistence on her returning with him. 'The same misfortune will befall me again,' she thought. 'If I tell Indu about it she might sympathize with me. This maid is sitting here uselessly. How will I confide in Indu even if she comes here? How nice it would be if only I could speak with her alone before papa arrives. What shall I do? Should I send for Indu? I don't know what she's doing just now. If I play the piano perhaps she'll hear it and come.'

Even Indu had a lot to say to Sophia. There had been no opportunity to confide in her in raniji's presence. She was afraid of being lonely once again if Sophia's father took her away. Dr Ganguly had said that Sophia should not be allowed to speak too much and that there would be no need to worry if she could sleep comfortably for another day. That's why Indu had hesitated to go there. But she became impatient when it was getting on to nine. She came and asked the maid to leave on the pretext of wanting her room to be cleaned. Then she sat by Sophia's pillow and asked, 'Well, behen, are you feeling very weak?'

Sophia – Not at all. I think I'm well now.

Indu – I'll die if your papa takes you away with him. You too are waiting for him. You'll happily go back as soon as he comes here, and you'll probably forget all about us.

Indu's eyes became moist as she spoke. We often hide the improper surge of our emotions behind our smiles. Indu's eyes were full of tears but she was smiling.

Sophia said – You may forget me but how can I ever forget you?

She was about to confide her heartache but embarrassment made her tongue-tied. She changed the topic and said – I'll come and meet you sometimes.

Indu – I won't let you go from here for fifteen days. I would have never let you go if religion had not been an obstacle. Ammaji would have insisted on making you her bahu. She's completely enchanted by you. She keeps talking about you no matter where she is. Vinay too seems to have become your slave. He'll be the unhappiest person if you leave. I want to tell you a secret. If ammaji gives you a gift don't refuse it, she'll feel very hurt if you do.

This affectionate insistence removed the constraints of Sophia's embarrassment. That gentle sympathy was more than enough for somebody who was continuously used to hearing harsh words at home. Sophia now thought that she would be violating the rules of friendship if she concealed her feelings from Indu. She said tenderly, 'Indu, if I had my way I would never leave the rani's shelter. But what say do I have? Where else will I find this love?'

Indu could not understand these feelings. She asked with her natural simplicity – Is there any talk of marriage?

She thought that there could be no other reason, except marriage, for girls to be so unhappy.

Sophia – I have decided not to get married.

Indu – Why?

Sophia – Because I'll have to sacrifice my religious freedom after marriage. Religion strangles freedom of thought. I don't want to sell my soul to any doctrine. I can't hope to get a Christian who will be liberal enough to overlook my religious doubts. I cannot accept Jesus as the Son of God and as my saviour, nor can I be forced to go and pray in church just because of my helpless situation. I cannot accept Jesus as God.

Indu – I had thought that there's far more freedom among you people than among us. You can go alone wherever you like. It's difficult for us even to get out of the house.

Sophia – But at least there isn't so much religious bigotry?

Indu – Nobody is forced to worship and to pray. Babuji takes a bath in the Ganga every day and worships Shiva for hours. Ammaji never goes there to bathe, nor does she worship any God but babuji never insists. Devotion depends on one's faith and inclination. There's a difference of heaven and hell in the views of us brother and sister. I'm a devotee of Krishna and Vinay doesn't believe in the existence of God, but there's no argument or discussion on this subject between us, and babuji never says anything to us.

Sophia – Our freedom is temporal and therefore deceptive. Yours is spiritual and therefore genuine. Real freedom is not an obstacle to freedom of thought.

Indu – Don't you go to church?

Sophia – I used to go earlier because I was forced to by misguided zeal. I didn't go this time so my family was very angry and deeply insulted me.

Indu said with affectionate simplicity – You must have cried a lot when they were angry. Tears must have flown from these lovely eyes. I can't bear to see anyone crying.

Sophia – I used to cry at first, now I don't care.

Indu – If anybody says anything to me it's like an arrow piercing my heart. I cry the whole day. My tears don't stop flowing and those words go on hurting me. To tell you the truth, I don't cry at anyone else's anger; I cry at myself because I wonder why I have offended others and made such a mistake.

Sophia suspected that Indu wanted to embarrass her by showing off her forgiving nature. She frowned and said – You wouldn't have spoken like this if you had been in my place. After all, would you have given up your religious views?

Indu – I can't say what I might have done, but I'd have tried to please my family.

Sophia – Would you listen to your mataji if she forcibly prevented you from worshipping Krishna?

Indu – Yes, I would. I wouldn't offend amma. Krishna is omniscient. One doesn't need to worship him to please him. One worships only for one's own satisfaction.

Sophia (*Surprised*) – Wouldn't you feel the slightest mental agony?

Indu – Of course I would, but I'd bear it for her sake.

Sophia – All right, what if she wants to marry you off against your wishes?

Indu (*Shyly*) – That problem has been solved. I married the person my parents thought suitable. I didn't even open my mouth.

Sophia – Arey, when was this?

Indu – This happened two years ago. (*Looking down*) I'd never have married him if I could have had my way, even if it meant staying single. My husband loves me and there's no lack of wealth. But I have a right over only a quarter of his heart. Three-quarters of it is gifted to public work. Who can be content with one-fourth and not the whole? I prefer a millet puri to a quarter of a biscuit any day. At least one's appetite is satisfied, which is the real purpose of food.

Sophia – Does he put any obstacles in the way of your religious freedom?

Indu – No, where does he have the time?

Sophia – Then I must congratulate you.

Indu – You are welcome to, if it is appropriate to congratulate a prisoner.

Sophia – If the fetters are those of love?

Indu – I would have insisted on your congratulating me if that had been so. I have become imprisoned while he is free. I have been here for almost three months, but he hasn't come here more than three times, and that too for only an hour. He lives in this city and the car can reach here in ten minutes, but who has so much time? Yes, he wants to substitute his visits with letters, and what are those letters? They are full of his woes from beginning to end. There's this work to be done today, something else to be done the next day, he has to meet this person, welcome that one. Becoming the chairman of the municipality has made him think he has gained a kingdom. It's always the same obsession. There's time for everything else except for coming here. I'm warning you, never marry somebody who serves the country or you'll regret it. You'll be a mere object of amusement for his leisure.

Sophia – I have already decided my principles. I want to live by myself, where nobody will interfere with my independence. I want to be responsible for deciding whether to walk on the right path or the wrong one. I'm an adult and can take care of my own interests. I don't want to live under anybody's protection for the rest of my life, because the purpose of protection is only subjugation.

Indu – Don't you want to be obedient to your parents?

Sophia – No, there's only a difference of degree not of kind in subjugation.

Indu – Then why don't you stay in my house? It will be my good fortune. And you'll be the pupil of ammaji's eye. She feels anxious being alone when I'm not here. She won't let you go once she has you with her. Shall I speak to her? Nobody will interfere with your independence here. Tell me, shall I go and speak to amma?

Sophia – No, not yet, not even by mistake. I'll fall in your ammaji's eyes too when she comes to know that my parents don't care about me. If one has no respect in one's own house there's none outside.

Indu – No Sophie, ammaji's nature is very unusual. The reason why you fear disrespect is in fact a cause for winning her respect. She herself was offended with her mother about something and has not

returned to her maika since then. Nani died, but amma didn't forgive
her. She never went to see her mother even once although she was sent
for hundreds of times. Her respect for you will be doubled when she
gets to know your problem.

Sophie said with tearful eyes – Behen, my honour is now in your
hands.

Indu put Sophie's head on her lap and said – It's not less dear to
me than my own.

Over there, John Sevak said to his wife when he received kunwar
sahib's letter – See, didn't I tell you that Sophie is in some trouble?
Look at this, it's a letter from Kunwar Bharat Singh. She has been lying
there since the past three days. One of their huts caught fire. She too
tried to extinguish it and got caught in the flames.

Mrs Sevak – These are all excuses. I no longer believe anything she
says. Why will someone whose heart is turned away from Khuda be
afraid to tell lies? She went away offended from here, she must have
thought that she'll find a bed of flowers as soon as she leaves the house.
She had this letter sent when she couldn't find shelter anywhere. She
will now get to know the price of atta and daal. And Khuda has perhaps
punished her for her ignorance.

John Sevak – Be quiet now. I'm surprised at your callousness. I
haven't seen such a hard-hearted woman.

Mrs Sevak – I'm not going. You can go if you want to.

John Sevak – You can see for yourself that I don't have time even
to die. I'm negotiating for that land in Pandeypur. I have to deal with
such a scoundrel that I can't manage to get him into my clutches.
People who think that rustics are simple are mistaken. It's difficult
to find such cunning people. Since you are not doing anything right
now I'll call a car for you. Go in style and bring her back with you.

Ishvar Sevak was sitting there on the easy chair with eyes shut,
absorbed in prayer. Just as a deaf man becomes alert the moment he
hears something to his purpose, his concentration broke as soon as he
heard a car being mentioned. He said – What's the need for a car? Are
a few rupees hurting you? Even Kaaroon's treasure* won't be enough
if you spend like this. Will your dignity suffer if you don't go by car?

---

* Kaaroon: The cousin of Moses, known for his proverbial avarice.

Kunwar sahib won't be impressed by it; God has given him several. Lord, take your servant in your shelter; don't delay any longer. My poor Sophie is lying there among strangers; goodness knows how she must have spent so many days. May Khuda show her the true way! My eyes are searching for her. Who'll take care of the poor thing there? How can the poor subsist among the rich?

John Sevak – It's just as well. Wouldn't we have had to pay the doctor's fees here every day?

Ishvar Sevak – There would have been no need for a doctor. By God's grace, I too can practise a little medicine. The family's love is far more effective than medicines. I would have taken my child in my lap and read the Holy Bible to her and asked Khuda to bless her.

Mrs Sevak – Then why don't you go?

Ishvar Sevak – With all my heart! Get my tonga. All of us should go. Only love can bring wanderers back to the right path. I'll go too. One has to be humble before the wealthy and not claim to be their equal.

John Sevak – Please don't take me with you just now, I'll go another time. Right now nothing else will be possible except an exchange of civilities. I'll thank them; they'll thank me. I think this introduction is providential; I'll meet them at leisure. Kunwar sahib is very influential in the city; the chairman of the municipality is his son-in-law. I can easily get the land in Pandeypur with his help. He might perhaps buy some shares. But there won't be an opportunity today for such matters.

Ishvar Sevak – I feel amused at your intelligence. You are reluctant to meet the person from whose acquaintance you can get so much done. Your time is so precious that you can't spare even half an hour to go there. Do you want everything to be decided at the very first meeting? You don't know how to make use of such a golden opportunity.

John Sevak – Well, I'll go if you wish. I was doing something important but I'll finish it later. You don't need to take the trouble. (*To his wife*) You are coming, aren't you?

Mrs Sevak – There's no point in taking me but . . . all right . . . let's go.

It was decided that they would go after lunch which, according to English custom, was eaten there at 1 p.m. The intervening time was spent in preparations. Mrs Sevak took out her jewellery, from which she had not been able to detach herself even in old age, together with her best gown and blouse. She didn't dress up so much for any other festival except her birthday. She wanted to make Sophia jealous and to show her that she was not dying of grief without her. The coachman was given orders to wash and clean the phaeton. They decided to take Prabhu with them but didn't find him in his room. A philosophical text was lying open on his table. It seemed that he had gone out somewhere while reading it. Actually the text had been lying like that for three days. Prabhu hadn't had the time to shut it and to put it away. He would wander around the city from dawn until midnight, returning home only twice a day for his meals. There was no school left where he had not tried to find Sophie. Nor were there any acquaintances or friends at whose homes he had not searched for her. After running around the whole day he would return dejected in the evening and lie down on his bed crying and worrying for hours on end. Where could she have gone? He would go to the police station several times in a day to find out if there was any news of her. He had also informed the newspapers and would make frequent enquiries every day. He had gradually begun to believe that Sophia had left them forever. That day, too, he returned dejected and exhausted as usual at 1 p.m. when John Sevak gave him the good news that Sophia had been found.

Prabhu's face lit up. He exclaimed – Really! Where? Is there a letter from her?

John Sevak – She is at Kunwar Bharat Singh's house. Go and eat. You have to come with us too.

Prabhu Sevak – I'll eat after I return. My appetite has disappeared. Is she all right?

Mrs Sevak – Yes indeed. She's fine. Khuda has punished her for going away offended from here.

Prabhu Sevak – Mama, I don't know of what stone Khuda has made your heart. Did she leave the house in anger on her own? You made her leave and now you are not in the least sorry for her.

Mrs Sevak – It's a sin to have pity on heretics.

Prabhu Sevak – If Sophie is a heretic then so are ninety-nine out of a hundred Christians. Her fault is that she doesn't pretend to be religious; even those who would lay down their lives for Jesus don't venerate him as much as she does.

Mrs Sevak – Well, it's obvious that you can plead very well for her. I don't have time to listen to these arguments.

It was now time for lunch. They sat down at the table but Prabhu didn't join them despite their insistence. When the three of them sat down on the phaeton, Ishvar Sevak told John – You must bring Sophie back with you, and don't lose this opportunity. May the Lord Messiah give you wisdom and grant your cherished wish.

The phaeton reached kunwar sahib's house in a short while. Kunwar sahib welcomed them warmly. Mrs Sevak had thought that she wouldn't say a word to Sophia and would only see her from a distance. But her heart was wrenched with grief when she reached Sophia's room and saw her wan face. She couldn't contain her maternal love and eagerly rushed to embrace her, tears flowing from her eyes. The bitterness in Sophia's heart was washed away in this stream. She embraced her mother and for several moments both of them enjoyed the heavenly bliss of love. John Sevak kissed Sophia's forehead, but Prabhu kept standing before her with tears in his eyes. He was afraid that his heart would burst if he embraced her. At such moments, his gestures and speech usually became paralysed.

When John Sevak left the room with kunwar sahib after seeing Sophie, Mrs Sevak said – What came over you that day to make you come here? You must have felt nervous lying here among strangers. These people perhaps didn't even enquire about you because they are so arrogant about their wealth.

Sophia – No mama, that isn't so. There isn't the least arrogance in anybody here. They are all images of generosity and courtesy. Even the servants readily respond to every sign. I have regained consciousness on the fourth day today. But I would probably have had to stay in bed for several weeks if these people had not looked after me so affectionately. I couldn't have been more comfortable even at home.

Mrs Sevak – Well, how could they not have done even this much for you when you had risked your life?

Sophia – No mama, these people are extremely courteous and good. Raniji herself often sits with me and fans me with the pankha. Kunwar sahib looks me up several times a day, and Indu is like a sister. She is the same girl who used to study with me in Nainital.

Mrs Sevak (*Annoyed*) – You can see only good in others. All the faults fall to the lot of the family, so that even other religions are better than our own.

Prabhu – Mama, you flare up at the slightest excuse. Shouldn't one feel obliged to people if they have been good to us? There's nothing more dishonourable than ingratitude.

Mrs Sevak – This isn't anything new. It has become Sophie's habit to criticize the family. She wants to make me feel that these people care more for her than I do. Let me see what gift they'll give her when she leaves. Where is your rani sahiba? Let me thank her too. Take her permission and come home. Papa must be getting anxious alone.

Sophia – She was very keen to meet you. She would have come long ago but perhaps she thought it improper to intrude upon us without being asked.

Prabhu – Mama, let Sophie stay here comfortably for a few more days. It will be difficult for her to get up just now. Look, she has become so weak.

Sophia – Raniji too said that she wouldn't let me leave just now.

Mrs Sevak – Why don't you admit that you yourself don't want to leave? Who will give you so much love there?

Sophia – No mama, you are being unfair to me. I don't want to stay here another day. I won't give these people any more trouble. But I want to be sure of one thing. I won't be oppressed again, and there won't be any obstacles to my religious freedom?

Prabhu – Sophie, why are you discussing these things in vain? In what way are you oppressed? You make a mountain out of a molehill.

Mrs Sevak – No, it's very good that you have asked this. I too don't want any misunderstanding. There's no place in my house for those who rebel against the Lord Messiah.

Prabhu – You are unnecessarily getting entangled with her. Just assume that she's a crazy girl talking nonsense!

Mrs Sevak – What can I do? I haven't studied philosophy like you. I can't mistake illusion for reality. Only philosophers can. Don't think that I don't love my child. God knows how many difficulties I've faced because of you. Your father was then a clerk in an office. I had to do all the household chores—shop, cook, sweep. You were both frail as children, always ailing with one disease or another. I would have to go to the doctor whenever there was a moment's respite from household chores. Often enough, entire nights would be spent carrying you in my lap. I become mad with grief and anger when I see a child brought up with such self-sacrifice turning against God. I wanted to make you a true and righteous follower of the Messiah. Despite that when I see you turning your face against Jesus and doubting his message, his life and his miracles, my heart breaks and I don't want to see your face. My Messiah is dearer to me than the whole world and even my own life.

Sophia – If your Jesus is so dear to you, then my soul and my conscience are no less dear to me. I cannot stand any tyranny against them.

Mrs Sevak – God will punish you for this impiety. I only pray to him not to let me see your face again.

Mrs Sevak left the room. The rani and Indu were coming from the other side and they met at the door. Raniji embraced Mrs Sevak and let flow a stream of gratitude. Mrs Sevak thought that this guileless affection reeked of insincerity. But the rani didn't understand human nature. She said to Indu – Look, tell Miss Sophia not to get ready to leave yet. Mrs Sevak, I humbly request you to allow Sophia to stay here for a few more days for my sake. My heart is not yet satiated with her conversation, nor have I been able to look after her. I promise I'll send her back myself. We will of course meet at least once a day while she's here, won't we? You are indeed blessed to have such a refined daughter. She's the image of compassion and intelligence. There's self-sacrifice in every pore of her being.

Mrs Sevak – I won't force her to return with me. You are welcome to keep her for as long as you like.

Rani – Bas-bas! That's all I wanted. You've bought me over. This is what I expected from you. How could your daughter have possessed all these qualities if you hadn't been so refined? On the other hand there's my Indu who doesn't even know how to talk properly. She is the rani of a large riyasat, yet she doesn't know her annual income. There are ornaments worth lakhs lying in the coffer but she doesn't as much as touch them. But tell her to go for an outing and she'll wander around the whole day. Well, Indu, am I lying?

Indu – What am I to do? Should I sit loaded with a maund of gold? I don't like to imprison my body like that.

Rani – Did you hear what she said? Her body is imprisoned if she wears ornaments! Come and let me show you my house. Indu, tell them to prepare the tea.

Mrs Sevak – Mr Sevak must be waiting outside for me. It will get late.

Rani – Really, so soon? At least eat with us today. We'll go for an outing after lunch, and then chat for a while after returning. My car will take you home after dinner.

Mrs Sevak couldn't refuse. Raniji held her hand and showed her around the palace. For half an hour, Mrs Sevak felt that she was wandering around in Indra's paradise. It was not so much a palace as a playground of pleasure, luxury, taste and wealth. Priceless carpets were spread on marble floors into which the feet sank while walking. There were delightful mosaics and large, full-length mirrors on the walls, beautiful floral decorations to enchant the eyes, rare and priceless crystal objects, treasures crafted by ancient artists, unique china vases, excellent samples of artistic expertise from Japan, China, Greece and Iran, golden plant holders, lifelike statues from Lucknow, beds of ivory made in Italy, exquisite wooden arches, wall brackets and lamps, boats to tempt the eyes, and birds of different species chirping in cages. In the courtyard, there was a marble reservoir with marble apsaras at its edges. Mrs Sevak did not praise any of these objects, nor did she utter a word of wonder or joy. She felt not happy but jealous, and jealousy cannot appreciate excellence. She thought, 'Here's somebody so fortunate that God has given her several means for living a life of pleasure and luxury. And here am I, so unfortunate that I have to eke out my days in a hovel without the basic necessities, let alone decoration or display. And on top of that nobody here lifts a blade of grass while we tear out our hearts working from morning to evening. But why grieve over this? There's no place for the rich in the Kingdom of Heaven. That will be our inheritance. The rich will be cast out like dogs; they won't be able even to peep into it.'

Mrs Sevak felt somewhat reassured by this thought. The reason for the universal love of equality is the pervasiveness of jealousy. Rani sahiba was surprised that Mrs Sevak didn't like or praise anything. 'I've spent thousands on each painting and cup. Who else possesses such objects? They are rare now, unobtainable even for lakhs. Not that it matters. She is either pretending or so lacking in aesthetic appreciation that she doesn't know how to value such things.' The rani wasn't disappointed in spite of that. She took Mrs Sevak to see her gardens that had several varieties of flowers and plants. The gardener was very intelligent. He explained the qualities and history of each plant—where it had come from and when, how it was planted and protected—but Mrs Sevak still didn't open her mouth. Finally he showed her a tiny medicinal root that kunwar sahib himself had brought from Jerusalem with great care; each leaf that sprouted from it was no less significant than a good omen. Mrs Sevak promptly picked up the pot, touched it with her eyes, kissed the leaves, and said, 'I am blessed to have seen this rare object.'

The rani replied – Kunwar sahib himself venerates it a great deal. He wouldn't want to eat for two days if it withered today.

The tea was ready by then. Mrs Sevak sat down for lunch. Raniji didn't like tea, so she started talking about Vinay and Indu. She praised Vinay's conduct and his views, his devotion to service, and his love of philanthropy to such an extent that Mrs Sevak was bored. She couldn't respond by praising her own children in turn.

John Sevak and kunwar sahib were having lunch in the reception room. Kunwar sahib didn't like tea and eggs. Vinay too thought that both the things should be relinquished. John Sevak was one of those men whose personality soon attracted others. His conversation was so thoughtful that people would forget what they had to say and listen only to him. And it was not as if his speech was mere rhetoric. An experienced man, he was very knowledgeable about human nature. His intelligence was a gift of God, without which there can be no respect in any gathering. At this moment he was expressing his views on India's industrial and commercial weakness. Whenever there was an opportunity, he also described the methods that he had thought of for improving this disastrous state of affairs. Finally, he said, 'The salvation of our country lies in artistic expertise and industrial development. This cigarette factory will solve the problem of livelihood for at least a thousand people so that they won't be a burden on agriculture. It's futile for the entire household to be involved in ploughing and sowing a piece of land which one man alone can do well enough. My factory will give an opportunity to such unemployed people to earn a living.'

Kunwar sahib – But then tobacco will be cultivated in fields where foodgrain is now grown, with the result that foodgrain will become more expensive.

John Sevak – I think that the cultivation of tobacco will affect jute, cannabis, oilseeds and opium. Export crops will be somewhat reduced. Foodgrains will not be affected. And then we will also try to reclaim the land that's still lying uncultivated.

Kunwar sahib – But tobacco is not a good thing. It's counted among intoxicants and is bad for health.

John Sevak (*Laughing*) – These are all figments of doctors' imaginations. It's ridiculous to take them seriously. Life would come to an end if we tried to live it by the prescriptions of doctors. There are bacteria in milk, ghee has too much fat, tea and coffee are stimulants, and germs enter the body even when we breathe. According to their principles, the whole world is infested with germs that are bent on destroying our lives. Entrepreneurs don't get entangled in such mazes; they focus only on the conditions that exist in the present. We can see that cigars and cigarettes worth crores of rupees come into this country. It's our duty to prevent this flow of wealth from going abroad. Our economic life can never prosper otherwise.

He looked triumphantly at kunwar sahib, whose misgivings were laid to rest to an extent. We are often emboldened when we see that our opponent is nonplussed. Even a child fearlessly throws stones at a fleeing dog.

Unhesitatingly, John Sevak said – I've come to this conclusion after considering all these aspects, and I sent this servant of yours (*pointing at Prabhu Sevak*) to America to obtain scientific knowledge about this business. Most shares of my company have already been sold but the money has not accrued yet. It's not yet the practice to do collective business in this province. People don't have trust, so I have decided to begin the work by raising 10 per cent. Capital will flow in by itself after a year or two, when there will be an annual profit and success beyond expectations. A pigeon perched on the rooftop becomes suspicious and refuses to fly down when it hears the cry, 'come-come' but it will do so soon enough if you scatter grain. I'm fully confident that there will be a profit of 25 per cent in the first year itself. This is the prospectus, read it carefully. I have estimated the profits cautiously; they may increase but will certainly not be lower.

Kunwar sahib – You say 25 per cent in the very first year?

John Sevak – Oh yes, very easily. I'd have requested you to buy some shares but I can't insist until I show some profit for a year. I will, however, urge that then shares won't be available at par. Shares worth 100 rupees will then probably be available for 200 rupees.

Kunwar sahib – I have just one doubt. Why haven't similar companies been set up so far if there's so much profit in this business?

John Sevak (*Laughing*) – Because business acumen does not yet exist in educated society. Slavery is present in every fibre of people's being. Nobody looks in any other direction except law and government service. A few companies were set up but they didn't get an opportunity to benefit from the advice and experience of experts. These proved to be very expensive even when they were available. Twice as much had to be paid to obtain the machinery and satisfactory arrangements couldn't be made. Perforce, the companies had to shut down. This is the predicament of practically all companies here. Directors' bags are stuffed; lakhs are wasted in selling shares and advertising; agents are entertained lavishly; a large share of the capital is spent on buildings; managers are employed on high salaries . . . What's the result? Directors line their own pockets; managers enjoy their rewards; agents get their commissions—the entire capital is wasted on overheads. My principle is that of minimum expense and maximum profit. I haven't given even a kauri as commission, and I've eliminated the heading for advertisements. I've even decided on a salary of only 500 rupees for the manager, although he can easily get 1000 rupees at some other factory. Besides, he is a member of the family. I have also decided to give the director only a travel allowance.

Kunwar sahib was not a worldly man. Most of his time was spent in reading religious texts. He didn't want to participate in any work that would come in the way of his religious concentration. Deceitful people had made him a captious critic of human nature. He didn't trust anyone and was wary of giving donations to schools and orphanages. He would often cross the limits of propriety on this subject, so that he often disappointed even the deserving. But if restraint could exercise so much caution, the expectation of profit made it more credulous than is expedient. John Sevak's speech was replete with knowledge about business, but kunwar sahib was even more impressed by his personality. He now thought that Mr Sevak was not just a devotee of wealth but also a friend who wished him well. Such a man wouldn't deceive him. He said, 'There's no doubt that your business will prosper if you are so economical. Perhaps you don't know that I have started a society for social service here. This has now become an obsession. It has about 100 volunteers at present. Its task is to protect and serve people when there is hustle and bustle at fairs and festivals. I want to free it forever from financial difficulties. Organizations in our country are often short-lived because they don't have funds. I want to make this organization strong and it's my cherished ambition that it should benefit the country. I don't want to take help from anybody for this work. I want to arrange a permanent fund so that it can function smoothly. I'm asking you as my friend and well-wisher to tell me if my purpose will be served by buying shares in your factory. According to your estimate, how much money will have to be invested for a monthly income of 1000 rupees?'

John Sevak's professional greed had not yet deadened his better feelings. Kunwar sahib had put him in a dilemma by leaving the decision to him. He would have been more cautious in giving an estimate of the profits had he known that he would encounter this problem. Playing tricks on strangers is forgivable but there are few such devotees of self-interest who will deceive friends. Even perfidy is ashamed by honesty.

John Sevak wanted to give an answer that would be acceptable to both his conscience and his self-interest. He said – I have revealed the state of the company to you. I have also told you how it will be organized. I have taken into account all the factors for its success. Yet I may possibly have made a mistake, and the most important point is that man is a mere plaything in the hands of the Creator. All his conjectures, intelligence, good intentions are subject to natural phenomena. Farmers will have to be given money in advance to increase the cultivation of tobacco. One night's frost could be fatal for the company. One butt of a lighted cigarette could reduce the factory to ashes. Yes, as far as my limited intelligence goes, I haven't exaggerated anything. Keeping in view unexpected difficulties, you can slightly reduce the estimate of profit.

Kunwar sahib – By how much, finally?

John Sevak – Take it as 20 per cent.

Kunwar sahib – And in the first year?

John Sevak – At least 15 per cent.

Kunwar sahib – I'll be satisfied with 10 per cent in the first year and 15 per cent after that.

John Sevak – Then all I'll say to you is that you shouldn't delay in buying the shares. You won't be disappointed if Khuda so wills it.

The shares were worth 100 rupees each. Kunwar sahib promised to buy 500 and said – I'll send you an instalment of 10,000 rupees through the bank tomorrow.

John Sevak's imagination had not soared so high even in its wildest flights, but he wasn't happy at this success. His conscience reproached him – You have deceived an honest, good-hearted gentleman. You know you aren't striving for the country's industrial development but for your self-interest. By pretending to serve the country you want all your five fingers to be dipped in ghee. Your heart's desire is to consume the largest share of the profit by some stratagem. You have proved the proverb, 'A thief kills a stranger but a bania kills an acquaintance'!

John Sevak would have frankly told kunwar sahib that the company couldn't give him so many shares had he not been convinced that its credibility would be established among the public with kunwar sahib's collaboration. To jeopardize the existence of a philanthropic organization by investing its money in a business that was suspect was a bitter morsel for avarice to swallow. However, the god of wealth is not appeased without the sacrifice of the soul. Of course, this much was certain that until now John Sevak had been playing this game for his self-interest, that his intentions were not honest, and that he wanted to keep all the profits for himself under different designations. He now decided to act dispassionately and honourably. He said, 'As the founder of this company I'm sincerely obliged to you for this help. You'll never regret this decision if Khuda so wills it. I'd now like to make another request. Your kindness has made me presumptuous. The land I've chosen for my factory is situated beyond Pandeypur, by the tarred road. The railway station is nearby and there are several villages in the vicinity. The area is ten bighas. The land is lying uncultivated but the animals of the basti graze there. The owner is a blind beggar. You must have seen him if you have ever gone there to take the air.'

Kunwar sahib – Yes, of course. I went there just yesterday. Isn't it the same blind man, rather dark and thin, who runs after passengers?

John Sevak – Yes, indeed. That land is his but he doesn't want to part with it at any price. I offered him up to 5000 rupees but he didn't agree. He is somewhat crazy. He says he's going to build a dharmashala for travellers and pilgrims, a temple and a pool there. He subsists by begging all day yet he has such high aspirations. Perhaps he doesn't have the courage to make a deal because he is afraid of the muhalla-valas. I don't think it proper to take the government's help in a personal matter but I can't think of any other way in these circumstances. And this isn't just something personal. Both the municipality and the government will earn thousands of rupees a day because of this factory; thousands of educated as well as uneducated people will benefit. It is public work if you look at it from this angle, and I won't be violating propriety if I take the government's help.* The work can easily be accomplished if you could do a small favour.

Kunwar sahib – I don't have any power over that fakir and I wouldn't use it even if I did.

John Sevak – Raja Sahib of Chataari . . .

Kunwar sahib – No, I can't say anything to him. He is my son-in-law and it's improper for me to speak to him on this topic. Isn't he your shareholder?

John Sevak – Oh no, though he possesses untold wealth, he is contemptuous of the wealthy. He thinks that machines and factories harm the public by increasing the power of capitalists. He has become the chairman here because of these views.

Kunwar sahib – These are one's personal principles. We are living a divided existence and I believe that more followers of democracy can be found in the upper classes than in the lower. Well, at least go and meet him. What can I say, I don't own even an acre of land around the city, otherwise you wouldn't have faced this difficulty. Let me know if I can do anything else.

John Sevak – No, I don't want to give you any more trouble. I'll meet him myself and settle the matter.

Kunwar sahib – Miss Sophia will stay here until she is fully recovered, won't she? I hope you don't have any objection?

---

* Reference to the Land Acquisition Act of 1894 which allows the government to acquire any land in the country for public purposes after paying a compensation fixed by the government.

John Sevak left after discussing a few points on this topic. Mrs Sevak was already sitting on the phaeton, while Prabhu was strolling in the garden with Vinay. Vinay came and shook hands with John Sevak. Prabhu promised to come again the next day and left with his father. They began to talk on the way.

John Sevak – Even months of running around didn't accomplish as much as just this one meeting today. Kunwar sahib is a very decent man. He has bought shares worth 50,000 rupees. Our difficulties will be over if a few more such good people are found.

Prabhu – Everybody in that house is an image of compassion and dharma. I haven't met anyone as eloquent as Vinay. I have become very fond of him.

John Sevak – Did you discuss any business matters?

Prabhu – No, he's not in the least interested in the business affairs that are close to you. He has taken a vow of service and all this while he was discussing only his society.

John Sevak – Do you think that this acquaintance of yours can also influence the Raja Sahib of Chataari? Can Vinay get some work done for us through raja sahib?

Prabhu – Who'll speak to him? I don't have such courage. You should think of him as a patriotic ascetic. He tried very hard to persuade me to join his society.

John Sevak – You have joined it, haven't you?

Prabhu – No, I've said that I'll give an answer after thinking about it. How could I take such a difficult vow without thinking it over carefully?

John Sevak – But don't take months deliberating . . . Go and enter your name after a few days. Then you'll have a right to discuss a few business matters with him. (*To his wife*) How did you get on with raniji?

Mrs Sevak – I hate her. I haven't seen such arrogance in anybody.

Prabhu – Mama, you are very unfair to her.

Mrs Sevak – She may be a goddess for you but not for me.

John Sevak – I knew beforehand that you wouldn't get on with her. Neither of you can talk to the point. Your business is only to find fault with others. Why didn't you bring Sophie?

Mrs Sevak – If only she would come, or should I have forcibly dragged her away?

John Sevak – She didn't come or did the rani not let her?

Prabhu – She was prepared to come, but on the condition that there would be no religious tyranny over her.

John Sevak – How could this condition possibly be acceptable to her?

Mrs Sevak – Yes, I couldn't bring her back on this condition. She'll have to obey me if she lives in my house.

John Sevak – Neither of you has any sense. You are crazy and she is obstinate. She should be placated and brought back soon.

Prabhu – Perhaps she won't return home at all if mama remains obstinate.

John Sevak – After all, where will she go?

Prabhu – She doesn't need to go anywhere. The rani is devoted to her.

John Sevak – This creeper cannot flourish. One of the two will have to yield.

When they reached home, Ishvar Sevak eagerly asked with great tenderness as soon as he heard the gharry approaching – Sophie, you have come, haven't you? Come and let me embrace you. May Jesus take you in his mantle!

John Sevak – Papa, she's not in a condition to come here yet. She's very weak and will return after a few days.

Ishvar Sevak – The wrath of Khuda! This is her plight and all of you have left her to fend for herself! Isn't there the least thought of honour and dishonour left in you people? Has your blood turned so white that you lack all natural feelings?

Mrs Sevak – She'll come if you go and cajole her. She's not a child that I should have picked her up and brought her in my lap.

John Sevak – Papa, it's very comfortable there. Both the raja and the rani are very fond of her. If you want to know the truth, the rani didn't let her come.

Ishvar Sevak – Did you discuss any business affairs with kunwar sahib?

John Sevak – Yes indeed, congratulations! We have managed to get hold of a counter worth 50,000 rupees.

Ishvar Sevak – Thank God, thank God! Jesus, take me in your shelter.

He sat down again on the easy chair.

4

THE BLIND ARE OBJECTS OF AMUSEMENT FOR NAUGHTY CHILDREN.
Soordas was so distressed by their childish pranks that he would leave
the house at dawn when it was still dark and return only after the lamps
were lit at dusk. There would be trouble for him on the day that he
left late. He had no misgivings on the road where there were wayfarers
but he expected some mishap or the other at every step in the alleys
of the basti. Somebody would snatch his stick and run away with it,
somebody would say – Soordas, there's a ditch in front of you, turn
left. If Soordas did that, he would fall into the ditch. But Bajrangi's
son, Gheesoo, was so wicked that he would get up before dawn to
tease Soordas. He got a great deal of pleasure in snatching Soordas's
stick and running away with it.

One day when Soordas left the house before sunrise, Gheesoo was
hiding in a narrow alley. Soordas had some misgivings the moment he
reached there. He waited, listening. Gheesoo could no longer control
his laughter. He leapt and caught hold of Soordas's stick. Soordas held
on to it firmly. Gheesoo pulled with all his strength. His hand slipped,
he fell down with the force of his own strength, his head was injured
and began to bleed. He went home screaming and shouting when
he saw the blood. 'Why are you crying? What happened?' Bajrangi
asked. Gheesoo didn't reply. Boys know only too well in which law
court they'll win. He went to his mother and said, 'Soordas pushed
me.' His mother's eyes were ablaze with anger when she saw the head
injury. Holding the boy's hand, she said to Bajrangi, 'That blind man
has had it now. He pushed the boy so hard that he's bleeding all over.
How dare he? I'll make his pride in his money fall.'

Bajrangi said calmly – Gheesoo must have teased him. That poor
man keeps hiding for his life from him.

Jamuni – Even if he did, should he have pushed him so cruelly
that his head is now broken? All boys tease the blind but they don't
fight back with sticks.

Meanwhile, Soordas had also reached there, looking remorseful.

Jamuni rushed towards him and said, crackling like lightning – Why Soorey, you come with your pot every day as soon as it is evening, pestering us for milk and now, just because Gheesoo caught hold of your stick, you pushed him so hard that his head is broken. You make a hole in the very pattal in which you eat. Have you now become so proud of your wealth?

Soordas – God knows that I didn't recognize Gheesoo. I thought that it must be some brat, so I held on firmly to my stick. His hand slipped, so he fell down. Had I known that it was Gheesoo, I would have given it to him. So many days have gone by, but let anyone say that I have hit any boy without some good reason. I live on what you give, why would I hit your son?

Jamuni – No, you have become proud. You beg for alms but don't feel ashamed, you want to compete with everyone else. I have drunk a draught of blood today and put up with this suffering else I'd have set ablaze the hands with which you pushed him.

Bajrangi tried to stop Jamuni while other people also tried to make her see reason, but she wouldn't listen to anybody. Soordas stood there with his head lowered like a criminal, bearing the assault of these stinging words. He did not utter a word.

Bhairo, who was on his way to extract toddy, stopped and cast aspersions on Soordas – Such are the times, when begging for alms is the best way of earning a living. He was so poor until just a few days ago that there wasn't even parched grain in his house. Now he has a little money and pride comes with money, or else will you and I be the ones who are proud, when we earn a rupee and spend two?

Jagdhar was like a drenched cat in the company of others but he too stepped up to reproach Soordas. Soordas now regretted not having let go of the stick; how could he admit that he couldn't get another one? He became even more distressed at Jagdhar's and Bhairo's harsh words. He wanted to cry at his helplessness. Just then Mitthua reached there. He too was the image of mischief, in fact two fingers taller than Gheesoo. As soon as he saw Jagdhar, he began teasing him by singing this enchanting verse:

Laloo's face is red, Jagdhar's black
So Jagdhar becomes Laloo's saala.

He also recited a self-composed verse for Bhairo:

Bhairo, Bhairo, go sell toddy
Or sell your wife's sari.

Only psychologists can analyse why people get provoked. We have generally seen people getting provoked by expressions of love or devotion. Some are provoked by the names of Rama and Krishna so that people may at least take the name of God, if for no other reason than to annoy them. Somebody gets provoked so that he may be surrounded by flocks of children. Someone else gets provoked by brinjals or fish so that people may hate these inedible things. In brief, getting provoked is a philosophical activity. Its object is only the teaching of truth, but where did Bhairo and Jagdhar have this pious generosity? What did they know about enjoying the pranks of children? They both got provoked. Jagdhar began to abuse Mitthua but Bhairo was not content with that. He caught hold of Mitthua, gave him two or three tight slaps and pulled his ears hard. Mitthua began to whimper. Until now Soordas had been standing with his head humbly bowed. He scowled the moment he heard Mitthua crying and his face blazed with anger. Raising his head and staring with his blind eyes, he said, 'Bhairo, leave him if you know what's good for you. Has he shot a bullet at you that you want to take his life? Do you think he has nobody to protect him? No one can look askance at him as long as I am alive. I'd admire your courage if you shook hands with some big man. What valour have you shown by beating this child?'

Bhairo – Why don't you stop him if you dislike his being beaten so much? We'll beat him if he provokes us. Not once but a thousand times! Do what you like.

Jagdhar – Far from scolding the boy, you encourage him. He may be your darling, why should others . . .

Soordas – Be quiet now, you come here trying to do justice. Boys are like that but nobody kills them. You wouldn't have so much as opened your mouth if another boy had teased you. I've seen boys clapping their hands and teasing you wherever you go, but you go your way with your eyes shut. You know only too well that if you beat children who have parents they will pluck out your eyes. Even a potsherd is sharp enough for a banana.

Bhairo – Is there any comparison between him and the other boys? If we put up with darogaji's abuses should we also tolerate those of the domras? Right now I've given him only two slaps. If he provokes me again I'll pick him up and fling him down—let him live or die.

Soordas (*Holding Mitthu's hand*) – Mitthua, just tease him, let me see what they'll do. Let whatever has to happen today happen here.

But Mitthua's cheeks were still burning, his face was swollen and his sobs wouldn't subside. He lost whatever senses remained when he saw Bhairo's fierce appearance. When he didn't open his mouth even after so much encouragement, Soordas said irritably, 'All right, I'll tease you. Let me see what you'll do to me.'

He held on to his stick firmly and repeated the same couplet, like a child memorizing a lesson:

Bhairo, Bhairo, go sell toddy
Or sell your wife's sari.

He recited this several times in one breath. On the one hand, Bhairo was mad with rage but, on the other, he couldn't help laughing at Soordas's childish stubbornness. Other people began to laugh too. Soordas now became aware of his wretchedness and helplessness. 'This is the respect given to my anger,' he thought. 'They would have been trembling at my rage had I been strong. But they are just standing there and laughing, knowing that there's nothing that I can do to them.'

Bajrangi reproached both Bhairo and Jagdhar – Don't you feel ashamed bullying a blind man? For one thing, you have reddened the boy's face with slaps and on top of that you are bellowing at him. After all he's also a boy, so what if he is a poor man's? Even boys from well-to-do homes are not as pampered as he is. Just as other boys tease, so does he. What's there to be so annoyed about? (*Looking at Jamuni*) All this has happened because of you. You don't scold your own brat but you take out your anger on a helpless, blind man.

Jamuni was subdued when she saw Soordas crying; she knew how much power there was in a poor man's lament. Embarrassed, she said – How was I to know that such a small thing would cause so much trouble? Come, beta Mitthu, hold the calf so that I can draw some milk.

Pampered children can't bear to be hit even with a straw. When Mitthu did not stop crying despite the promise of milk, Jamuni wiped his tears, picked him up in her lap and took him home. She was short-tempered but was also quick to relent.

Mitthua went with her. Bhairo and Jagdhar too went their separate ways. But Soordas did not go towards the road. He returned to his hut and wept at his wretchedness. He had never felt as unhappy at his blindness as he did today – I'm so wretched because I'm blind and beg for alms. If only I could earn my living by hard work, I'd also have walked with my head held high, I'd also have been respected and not crushed underfoot like an ant. Would those two men have gone away laughing after beating my child if God hadn't made me a cripple? I'd have wrung each one's neck. Why doesn't anyone say anything to Bajrangi? Ghisooa broke Bhairo's pitcher of toddy, which meant a loss of several rupees, but Bhairo didn't so much as whimper. It's difficult for Jagdhar to leave the house because of him. His khoncha was overturned only a few days ago but Jagdhar too didn't so much as whimper. They know only too well that Bajrangi will catch hold of them by their necks at the slightest show of anger. I don't know what sins I committed in my last birth to deserve this punishment. But what will I eat if I don't beg? And then there's more to life than just filling one's belly. Something has to be done for the future. No, I'm blind in this birth but there'll be even greater suffering in the next one. The debt of my ancestors is on my head. How will they know that there's somebody in their dynasty if I don't perform their shraadh at Gayaji?* The family line will come to an end with me. Is there any boy here who will pay off this debt if I don't? What work can I take up? I could pull the pankha at some big man's house but that work is available only for four months in the year. What will I do for the rest? I've heard that the blind can weave

---

* Gaya: A city in Bihar, sacred to Hindus for performing the rituals of shraadh and pinda-daan for the salvation of the souls of their ancestors.

chairs, stools, durries, sacking but from whom can I learn this work? Come what may, I won't beg for alms now.

When Soordas felt complete despair on all sides, he thought – Why don't I sell this land? I don't have any support except this. For how long can I cry over my ancestors? Sahib has been eyeing it for so long. He's also giving a good price. I'll give it to him. Four or five thousand rupees are a lot. I'll sit at home like a seth and play the flute of contentment. There'll be people around me; I'll get respect in the muhalla. These very people who now bully me will then look up to me. All that will happen is that the cows of the muhalla will wander around wretchedly . . . Let them, what can I do about it? I've endured it for as long as I could. What should I do if I can't any longer? What do the people whose cows graze here care about me? Bhairo wouldn't have gone away twirling his moustache after making me cry if I had somebody's backing today. Why should I kill myself for others when I don't have even this much? The world is there because of the heart; fie on living if there's no respect!

After making this firm resolve, Soordas left his hut and went towards the godown, tapping his stick. He met Dayagiri in front of the godown. Dayagiri asked – Why have you come here, Soordas? You have left your adda behind.

Soordas – I want to discuss something with miyaan sahib.

Dayagiri – About this land?

Soordas – Yes, I'm thinking of selling it and going away somewhere on a pilgrimage. I can't live in this muhalla any longer.

Dayagiri – I hear that Bhairo threatened to beat you today . . .

Soordas – He'd have beaten me had I not turned a deaf ear. The entire muhalla sat there and laughed, nobody asked him why he was torturing a blind cripple. So why should I do anything for others if I don't have any well-wishers?

Dayagiri – No Soorey, I won't advise you to sell the land. You don't get the fruits of dharma in this birth. We should shut our eyes and keep walking on the path of dharma, trusting Narayana. If you ask me the truth, God has tested your dharma today. It's only in difficult times that patience and dharma are tested. Look, Gosainji said –

Test four things in times of adversity,
Patience, dharma, friend and woman.*

Let the land remain. Cows graze here; this is so meritorious. Who knows when some pious benefactor will come and build a dharmashala, a well or a temple so you'll become immortal. As for a pilgrimage, you don't need money for that. Sadhus and sants do that all their lives but they don't leave home with a bag of money. I'm also going to Badrinath after Shivaratri.** We'll have each other's company. You won't need to spend a kauri on the way; that's my responsibility.

Soordas – No baba, I can't bear this oppression any longer. How can I do dharmic work if it's not written in my destiny? Let these people realize that Soorey too is somebody to reckon with.

Dayagiri – Soorey, you can't understand anything even though your eyes are shut. This is pride. Get rid of it or you'll destroy this birth as well. Pride is the root of all sins.

Me and mine-thine are maya;
Life is spent in subjugating them.

Neither are you here, nor is your land; you have neither friend nor enemy; and wherever you look, there is only God –

Where there is no knowledge or pride,
Brahma's form can be seen everywhere.

Don't get into these wrangles.

Soordas – I won't be able to concentrate on either devotion or detachment until God has mercy. My heart is weeping at this moment; instruction and wisdom can't reach it. Damp wood can't be put on the lathe.

---

* Gosainji: Goswami Tulsidas, born in Rajpur, Uttar Pradesh, in 1554, lived in Banaras, and is the author of Ramcharitmanas, among other works. The following two stanzas are also by Tulsidas (translations mine).

**Shivaratri: a festival in honour of Shiva, held on the fourteenth of the dark half of the month of Phagun (twelfth lunar month of the Hindu calendar, i.e., February–March).

Dayagiri – You'll regret it.

Dayagiri went his way. It was his practice to bathe in the Ganga every day.

After he had left, Soordas said to himself – He, too, is preaching wisdom only to me. Even preaching has power only over the wretched; nobody preaches to the prosperous. He goes there to fawn upon them. He comes preaching wisdom to me! After all, he gets food from them twice a day. All his wisdom would vanish if he didn't get it for a day.

A speeding vehicle can jump over obstacles. Soordas became even more obstinate with this attempt to persuade him. He went straight to the veranda of the godown, where several chamaars were gathered. Hides were being bought. The chowdhary said – Come Soordas, what brings you here?

Soordas couldn't express his wish in front of so many people. He was tongue-tied with embarrassment. He replied – Nothing, I've just come by the way.

Tahir – Sahib wants his land that lies at the back and is willing to give him any price that he wants, but he refuses to be persuaded. Sahib himself has tried to persuade him; I have pleaded so hard, but nothing makes any impression on him.

Shame is extremely shameless. Even at the moment of death, when we think that it is gasping for breath, it suddenly becomes conscious and even more dutiful than before. We leave home and go to a friend to plead for help when we are in trouble but as soon as we are face to face, shame comes and stands before us and we return, talking of this and that. We don't let ourselves utter even a single word whose meaning will give an inkling of our inner pain.

Soordas's shame emerged mockingly as soon as he heard Tahir Ali. He said – Miyaan sahib, this land is a mark of my ancestors. How can I turn earnest money into a title deed? I have resolved to use it for dharmic work.

Tahir – How can dharmic work be done without money? You can go on a pilgrimage, serve sadhus and sants, get a temple built, only if you have money.

Chowdhary – Soorey, you'll get a good price right now. My advice is to give it; after all you don't get anything from it.

Soordas – The cows of the entire muhalla graze there. Isn't that meritorious? What better merit can there be than service to cows?

Tahir – You go around begging for alms to fill your own belly and you want to serve others. Those people whose cows graze here don't care in the least about you, let alone feeling obliged. This is your plight because of your dharma; otherwise you wouldn't be stumbling around all the time.

Tahir Ali himself was a very devout man but he didn't hesitate to scorn other religions. In fact, except Islam, he didn't consider any religion to be religion at all.

Soordas said excitedly – Miyaan sahib, dharma is not practised only as a favour. Good deeds should be done and then thrown into the river.

Tahir – You'll regret it. Sahib will do whatever you ask him to. He'll get a house built for you, give you a monthly allowance, send Mitthua to a madrasa, get your eyes treated; perhaps you'll be able to see. You'll become a man; otherwise you'll continue to be pushed around.

Nothing else tempted Soordas but the possibility of his vision being restored softened him a little. He asked – Can those who are blind from birth be cured?

Tahir – Are you blind from birth? Then it's hopeless. But he'll get you so many means for your comfort that you won't need your eyesight.

Soordas – Sahib, there'll be great dishonour. People all around will reproach.

Chowdhary – It's your property, give a guarantee or write a lease, how dare anyone else interfere?

Soordas – I can't bring dishonour to my ancestors.

The ignorant don't have any arguments. They respond to them by obstinacy. An argument can be convincing, moderate, or mistaken; who can convince obstinacy?

Tahir was angry at Soordas's stubbornness. He said – What can anybody do if you are fated to beg? You haven't yet had to deal with these big people. He's trying to please you now and is willing to compensate you but you are too proud. You'll be set right when he occupies your land by legal stratagems and gives you a few hundred rupees as compensation. You are depending on the people of your muhalla. Nobody will come near you then. Sahib is sure to take over this land, whether you are willing or unwilling.

Soordas proudly replied – Khan sahib, if the land goes, my life goes with it.

Having said this, he picked up his stick, went to his usual place, his adda, and sat down.

Meanwhile, Dayagiri told Nayakram that Soordas was selling the land. Bajrangi, who was also sitting there, was stunned. Both of them had been prancing around on Soordas's strength. 'Look at the way in which Soordas had talked to Tahir Ali the other day, and look how he has betrayed us today.' Bajrangi asked anxiously, 'Tell us, Pandaji, what should we do now?'

Nayakram – What can we do? You must reap as you have sown. Go and ask your wife. She's the one who kindled the fire today. You know that Soorey would give his life for Mitthua, then why didn't you beat up Bhairo? If I'd been there I wouldn't have let Bhairo go without telling him a harsh thing or two, if for no other reason than just for show. That poor man would also have realized then that he has some support. He was very resentful today, otherwise he would never have thought of selling the land.

Bajrangi – Arey, are you going to find a solution or should we just sit around crying over the past?

Nayakram – The only solution is to go and fall at Soorey's feet, reassure him, persuade him in whatever way you can, treat him as your dada-bhaiyya. If he agrees with you, well and good, otherwise get ready to fight with sahib. Don't let him occupy the land. If anyone comes near it, beat him up and make him run away. That's what I have thought. Today I'll give Soorey milk with my own hands and give Mitthua as much mithai as he wants. We'll see about it if he still doesn't agree.

Bajrangi – Why don't we go to miyaan sahib? We don't know what Soordas may have said to him. He will never change his mind if he has agreed to anything being put in writing, despite any amount of pleading.

Nayakram – I won't go to that munshi's doorstep. He will become even more swollen-headed.

Bajrangi – No, Pandaji. Please come with me for my sake.

Finally, Nayakram agreed. Both men went to Tahir Ali. It was silent there now. Buying and selling was over. The chamaars had left. Tahir was sitting alone, doing the accounts. There was some difference in the total. He'd add again and again but couldn't spot the error. Nayakram said, 'Munshiji, what did you discuss with Soorey today?'

Tahir – Aha! Come, Pandaji, forgive me, I was busy with calculations, take this morha. There will be no agreement with Soorey. He's in for trouble. He left today threatening that his life would go with the land. He's a poor man, I feel sorry for him. In the end, sahib will occupy the land through some legal loophole. Soorey may perhaps get some compensation, otherwise there's no hope even of that.

Nayakram – Can sahib take the land by devouring it if Soorey is unwilling? See, Bajrangi, what did I tell you? Soorey is not such a weak man.

Tahir – You don't yet know sahib.

Nayakram – I know sahib as well as sahib's father. They are strutting around like big men today by flattering officials.

Tahir – But these are the times for flattery. He won't rest without taking this land.

Nayakram – Then we, too, have decided not to let anyone occupy the land, even at the cost of our lives. We'll die for it. Several pilgrims come here. I make arrangements for all of them here in this field. Will I make arrangements for them on top of my head if the land is lost? Tell sahib that he won't succeed; his daal can't be cooked here. We too have some strength. We gamble openly all the year round. We make thousands in just a day. Everybody knows about it from the thanedar to the superintendent, but nobody dares raid us. We have even concealed murders.

Tahir – Why are you telling me all this? Don't I know about it? You must have heard of Sayyad Raza Ali Thanedar. I'm his son. There's no panda that I don't know.

Nayakram – Well, well, why should anyone die if there's a vaidya in the house? Then you are a family member. There's no officer like darogaji. He used to say, 'Beta, do whatever you like, but don't come into my clutches.' There used to be a gambling house at my doorstep, he'd sit on a chair and look on. There was complete informality. If I had any problem, I'd go and tell him the whole story. He'd say, stroking my back, 'Bas, go, I'll take care of it now.' Where can one find such men now? They were men of the satyuga. You have turned out to be our brother, why don't you drive sahib away? God has given you knowledge and intelligence and you can find several excuses—water collects during the rains; there will be lots of white ants; the soil will get saline and so on . . .

Tahir – Pandaji, now that there is a brotherly relationship between us, what's there to hide? Sahib is a wily old rascal of the first order. He is very friendly with the officials. He'll get the land free. Soorey may perhaps get a hundred or two hundred rupees but my reward will disappear. If you can persuade Soorey to settle the matter then he, you and I, all of us will gain.

Nayakram – We'll give you whatever reward you'll get from there. Then we'll also get an excuse to serve you. I feel the same way towards you as I did towards darogaji.

Tahir – May I be cursed, Pandaji, don't speak like that. I believe it's immoral to take even a kauri without maalik's knowledge. I'll gladly accept whatever he gives willingly but I won't hide anything from him. May Khuda save me from taking such a path! My vaalid earned so much but there wasn't a kauri for his shroud when he died.

Nayakram – Arey yaar, I'm not telling you to discredit yourself. Now that there's a brotherly relationship between us, our work will be done through you and yours through us. This is not dishonourable.

Tahir – No Pandaji, may Khuda keep my intentions pure. I can't be disloyal, I'm happy as I am. Some way will emerge for my welfare when He looks at me mercifully.

Nayakram – Bajrangi, did you hear what darogaji said? Go home and sit there quietly. Now we'll have to deal only with sahib.

Bajrangi thought that Nayakram had not cajoled and flattered enough. Had he come to get the work done or to show his bravado? Much more could be achieved by humility than by boasting. Nayakram put his cudgel on his shoulder and left. Bajrangi said, 'I'll just go and see to the cows and return.' He was otherwise a very stubborn man and wouldn't let a fly settle on his nose. The entire muhalla trembled at his rage, but he was afraid of legal proceedings. He was mortally afraid of the very name of the police and the court. Nayakram had to deal with the court daily, so he was experienced. Bajrangi had never had an occasion to testify in his entire life. Tahir Ali too went home after Nayakram had left but Bajrangi kept pacing up and down, hoping that Tahir would come out so that he could tell him his woes.

Tahir Ali's father had risen from the post of a constable to that of a thanedar in the police department. He had not left any property when he died; in fact, a loan had to be taken to pay for his last rites. But he had left Tahir with the responsibility of his two widows and their children. He had married three times. Tahir Ali was born from the first wife, Mahir Ali and Zahir Ali from the second and Zabir Ali from the third. Tahir was a patient and sensible man. After his father's death, he had hunted around for a job for a year. Sometimes he would get the position of a clerk in a cattle-pen or work as an agent for a chemist or as a munshi in a customs house. For some time now he had been working as Mr John Sevak's permanent employee. His ways were completely different from his father's. He strictly observed roza and namaaz and was honest in his intentions. He stayed miles away from ill-gained earnings. His mother was dead but both his stepmothers were alive. He was married and besides his wife, he had a son, Sabir Ali, and a daughter, Naseema. It was such a large household, with a monthly income of only thirty rupees. He had to face several difficulties in these times of high prices when it wasn't possible to live comfortably even with an income five times this amount. However, his intentions would not become fraudulent. The main quality of his character was that he was God-fearing. When he reached home, Mahir Ali was studying, Zakir and Zabir were crying for mithai and Sabir was jumping up and down, eating millet rotis. Tahir sat down on the wooden bed, picked up both brothers and tried to pacify them. His older stepmother, Zainab, had been standing at the door, listening to the conversation of Nayakram and Bajrangi. Bajrangi had just taken five or six steps when Mahir called out – Listen, man! Come here, amma is calling you.

Bajrangi returned with some hope and stood in the veranda again. Zainab was standing behind the bamboo screen. She asked – What was it about?

Bajrangi – It was about that land. Sahib wants to take it. We get our livelihood from it. I've been requesting munshiji somehow to get rid of this problem. I'm even willing to give a present but munshiji just won't listen.

Zainab – Why won't he listen? On whom will the curse of the poor fall if he doesn't listen? You are a rustic, what did you tell him? Such things shouldn't be discussed with men. You should have told me, I would have got it settled for you.

Zabir's mother was Raqiya. She too came and stood there. Both women stayed together like shadows. They felt and thought alike. There wasn't a trace of jealousy between them although they were co-wives. They loved each other like sisters.

Raqiya said – Of course, why should these things be discussed with men?

Bajrangi – Mataji, I'm a rustic. What do I know about this? You get this settled now. I'm a poor man; my children can then subsist.

Zainab – Tell the truth, how much will you give if this affair is suppressed?

Bajrangi – Begum sahib, I'm willing to give up to fifty rupees.

Zainab – You are very strange. You want to get such an important matter settled for only fifty rupees?

Raqiya (*Softly*) – Behen, he may shy away.

Bajrangi – What can I do, Begum sahib? I'm a poor man. I'll feed the boys with milk and curd, whatever you order, but I can't give more cash than this.

Raqiya – All right. Go ahead and arrange the money. It will all be settled if Khuda so wills it.

Zainab (*Softly*) – Raqiya, I'm baffled by your haste.

Bajrangi – Maaji, the entire muhalla will sing your praises if this work is done.

Zainab – But you don't want to give more than fifty rupees. Even sahib will give that much. And then the offence? Why displease him?

Bajrangi – Maaji, I'm not an outsider. I'll try and put together another five or ten rupees.

Zainab – So when will the money come?

Bajrangi – Give me two days. Until then please ask munshiji to speak to sahib.

Zainab – Well, well, mahto! You have turned out to be very shrewd. You want to get your work done for nothing. First get the money, after that it will be our responsibility if your work isn't done.

Bajrangi left happily, promising to bring the money the next day. Zainab said to Raqiya – You are too impatient. Just now you were ready to buy hides from the chamaars for two paise each. I'd have taken two annas, which they would have given gladly. This aheer would have given a full hundred. Impatience makes the needy cautious. He thinks that perhaps he's being fooled. Trust increases the more you delay and the greater the indifference that you show.

Raqiya – What can I do, behen, I'm afraid we may miss the mark if we are too hard.

Zainab – That aheer will definitely bring the money. Start filling Tahir's ears. He should be made to fear calamity. That's the only way of getting him into our clutches.

Raqiya – And if sahib doesn't agree?

Zainab – Then who'll go and complain against us?

Tahir had just gone to lie down after eating when Zainab went to him and said – Why does sahib want to take other people's land? The poor things are weeping.

Tahir – He doesn't want to take it for free. He's ready to compensate them.

Zainab – But this is tyranny against the poor.

Raqiya – Not merely tyranny but also a calamity! Bhaiyya, tell sahib frankly not to involve you in this calamity. Tell him, 'Khuda has also given me children. One doesn't know what may happen. I won't take this calamity on my head.'

Zainab – They are rustics; they may get after you. You should frankly say, 'I won't incur the enmity of the muhalla-valas, it will put my life in danger.'

Raqiya – Of course your life will be in danger. These rustics are loyal to nobody.

Tahir – Have you heard any rumours?

Raqiya – All these chamaars were saying among themselves that rivers of blood will flow if sahib occupies this land. I've lost my wits ever since I've heard this.

Zainab – Of course it's something to make one lose one's wits.

Tahir – Everyone is vilifying me for no reason. I'm not involved in any way. Sahib ordered me to discuss the land with that blind man. It was my duty to obey his order but these fools think that I incited sahib to buy the land, although Khuda knows that I never mentioned it to him.

Zainab – I'm not afraid of being vilified; yes, I am afraid of Khuda's wrath. Why take the lament of the helpless on your head?

Tahir – Why would calamity befall me?

Zainab – Who else will it fall on, beta? You are the one who's here, not sahib. He will set the hay on fire and watch the fun from a distance, you'll have to face the consequences. You'll have to occupy the land. If there are lawsuits, you'll have to prosecute them. I don't want to jump into this fire.

Raqiya – An agent at my maika had taken away a tenant farmer's land. His young son died the very next day. He did it on the orders of the zamindar but calamity fell on that poor man's head. Even calamity doesn't fall on the rich. Its blows fall only on the poor. Our children fall victim to the evil eye and demons every day, but we never hear of the children of the English being affected. They are not affected in the least by evil spirits.

This made sense. Tahir had also experienced this. All the children in his house were covered with charms and amulets and, on top of that, evil spirits had to be exorcized and cast out by throwing mustard seeds and salt into the fire every day.

The main pillar of religion is fear. Remove fear of misfortune and pilgrimages, prayers, ritual baths, meditations, roza-namaaz will vanish, there will be no sign left of any of these. Masjids will be empty, mandirs desolate.

Fear defeated Tahir. Devotion to the master and a sense of duty could not counteract the dread of divine wrath.

5

THE RAJA OF CHATAARI, MAHENDRA KUMAR SINGH, HAD BEEN ELECTED the municipality's chairman at a young age because of his ability and the prestige of his family. Thoughtfulness was the godlike quality of his character. There was no trace in his nature of the desire for luxury and the love of prestige common among the rais. He wore very simple clothes, hated pomp and splendour and was completely free of any vice. He had no use whatsoever for horse racing, cinema and theatre, music and entertainment, outings and shikar, chess or cards. If he was interested in anything, it was in gardening. He worked in his garden every day for an hour or two. He spent the rest of his time in inspecting the city and administering its organization. He very seldom met government officials unless there was reason to do so. Under his chairmanship, importance was given not only to those areas of the city where the bungalows of the officers were situated. The cleanliness of the dark alleys and smelly gutters of the city was considered no less important than that of wide streets and beautiful amusement spots. That was why the authorities were displeased with him and thought him to be arrogant and proud. But even the lowliest people of the city had no complaint about his pride or incivility. He always met everybody cheerfully. He very seldom needed to fine or prosecute people for violating laws. His influence and goodwill restrained the need for strict policies. His speech was precise. Silence is a sign of maturity in old age and of intellectual paucity in youth, but raja sahib's restrained speech proved this incorrect. Discernment and reflection embellished whatever he said. He was inclined towards communism despite being an affluent taluqdar. This could possibly be the result of his political principles because his education, power, situation and self-interest were opposed to this inclination but discipline and practice had now removed it from the level of intellect and made it intrinsic to his nature. He had played a leading role in cleaning up the constituencies of the city. That was why the rais were wary of him.

They thought his democracy was only a way of protecting his rights and that he had assumed this guise to make use of his public position for a long time to come. There were discussions about this from time to time even in the papers but raja sahib did not waste his intelligence and time in contradicting them. His main goal was to become famous. But he knew only too well that the only way of attaining this lofty position was service – and selfless service.

It was morning. After bathing and meditating, raja sahib was about to leave to inspect the city when he received John Sevak's visiting card. John Sevak mostly interacted with government officers; in fact they were the major shareholders of his cigarette company. Raja sahib had seen the company's prospectus but had not met John Sevak. There was distrust between them, the basis of which was rumour. Raja sahib thought him to be a sycophant and an opportunist. He seemed an enigma to John Sevak. But raja sahib had gone to see Indu the previous day and had met Sophie there. There had been some discussion about John Sevak. His opinion about Mr Sevak had changed to some extent after that. He came out as soon as he received the card and after shaking hands with John Sevak, took him to the reception room. It seemed like the hut of some yogi to John Sevak, where there was no trace of any ornamentation. It had only a few chairs and a table, on which were scattered papers and newspapers.

We can sense by our acute insight what other people think of us the moment we meet them. For a second, Mr Sevak did not have the courage to open his mouth; he couldn't think of a suitable opening. One was asking for help from the earth and the other from the sky in order to cross this impassable ocean. Raja sahib had thought of an opening – what better one than praise of Sophie's godlike sacrifice and service – but sometimes people feel as embarrassed when they praise somebody as they do when they hear themselves being praised. John Sevak did not feel this embarrassment. He was equally skilled in both praising and criticizing. He said, 'I have wanted to meet you for a long time, but I couldn't come because I didn't have an introduction. The fact is (*smiling*) that I had heard such things about you from the authorities that I couldn't express this desire. However, the sincere patriotism with which you have made the constituencies efficient has exposed their false allegations.'

John Sevak had proved his adroitness of speech by discussing the false allegations of the authorities. There wasn't a better way of winning raja sahib's sympathy. This was raja sahib's complaint against the authorities and the reason why he found it difficult to discharge his responsibilities and why there were delays and obstacles. He said – It's my misfortune that the authorities distrust me so much. My only fault is that I consider health and facilities to be as important for the public as for the authorities and the rais.

John Sevak – Sir, don't talk about the arrogance of these people. The world exists for their benefit. No one else has the right even to exist in it. Anyone who doesn't keep rubbing his forehead at their doorstep is a dissident, a traitor and uncivilized, and anyone with the slightest trace of nationalism – especially someone who wishes to revive artistic expertise and industry – is culpable. Service to the nation is the basest crime in their eyes. You must have seen the prospectus of my cigarette factory?

Mahendra – Yes, I have.

John – Ever since my prospectus came out, the authorities have withdrawn their goodwill from me. I used to be a recipient of their favours and was friendly with many officers. But from that very day I have been ostracized from their community and my social interaction with them has ceased. Following their example, Indian officers and the rais have also become indifferent. Now I'm more dangerous to them than the devil!

John Sevak came to the point after this long introduction. He expressed his objective with a great deal of embarrassment. Raja sahib understood human nature. He recognized the fake tilakdhaaris only too well. It wasn't easy to deceive him. But the problem was such that he was compelled to resort to injustice rather than to protect dharma. He wouldn't have so much as glanced at such a proposal on another occasion. It was against his principles to take away from the possession of a poor, weak, blind man the land that was the sole support of his life and give it to an industrialist. But for the first time he was forced to put his rules on the shelf. He could not ignore this proposal, knowing full well that Miss Sophia had saved the life of a close relative and that courtesy towards John Sevak would free Kunwar

Bharat Singh from a heavy debt. Gratitude can compel us to do all that ought to be rejected on principle. It is the grindstone that crushes all our principles and rules. The more a human being is without desire, the more intolerable is the burden of a favour. He promised to decide this matter according to John Sevak's wishes and Mr Sevak returned home happy with his success.

His wife asked – What have you managed to finalize?

John Sevak – What I went to finalize.

Mrs Sevak – Thank God! I didn't expect it.

Mr Sevak – All this is the blessing of Sophie's good deed or this gentleman wouldn't even have talked politely. It's the power of her self-sacrifice that has humbled such a proud and uncivil man as Mahendra Singh. He met me with such warmth, as if I were an old friend. This was an impossible task, and I'm indebted to Sophie for it.

Mrs Sevak (*Angrily*) – Then go and fetch her, I haven't prevented you. Why do you say these things to me again and again? As for myself, I won't ask her for water even if I'm dying of thirst. I don't know how to flatter. I speak my mind. Why should I flatter her if I'm firm in my belief and she turns away from Khuda and stays firm in her resolve?

Prabhu visited Sophia regularly every day. He was charmed by the courtesy and refinement of both kunwar sahib and Vinay. Kunwar sahib understood human nature. He had discerned on the very first day, at first sight, that Prabhu Sevak wasn't an ordinary youth. It was soon evident to him that Prabhu's natural inclination was towards literature and philosophy. Prabhu was as devoted to business and industry as Vinay was to zamindari. That's why kunwar sahib would often discuss such subjects as poetry and literature with Prabhu. He wanted to imbue Prabhu's interests with the sentiments of nationalism. Prabhu also realized that this gentleman was a connoisseur of poetry. That's why he began to feel the same affection for kunwar sahib that poets have for savants. He recited many of his poems to kunwar sahib, whose generous entreaties made him rather intoxicated. He would be absorbed in thinking about creativity all the time. The doubt and dejection, which new writers often experience about the dissemination and reception of their work, was transformed into confidence and enthusiasm because of kunwar sahib's encouragement.

The same Prabhu Sevak, who wouldn't pick up a pen for weeks on end, would now compose several poems in a day. The upsurge of his emotions emerged like the flow and abundance of a river. He was writing something when he saw John Sevak coming and went to find out what news he had brought. Prabhu had hoped that perhaps he wouldn't need to get caught in this bondage for a while because of the difficulties that had risen in the acquisition of the land. John Sevak's success destroyed that hope. In this state of mind, his mother's last words seemed very harsh. He said, 'Mama, you are making a big mistake if you think that Sophie has to put up with disrespect and insults there and will get bored and return of her own accord. Those people won't let go of her even if she stays there for years. I haven't come across such generous and refined people. Yes, Sophie's self-respect won't allow her to enjoy their hospitality and courtesy for an indefinite period. She wouldn't have become as weak as she has in these past two weeks even if she had been ill for months. She has all the comforts in the world, but her condition is like that of a plant that withers despite every effort when it is brought from a cold country to a hot one. Night and day she is consumed by the same anxiety, "Where shall I go? What shall I do?" You'll regret it if you don't call her soon. These days she is studying Buddhist and Jain texts, and I wouldn't be surprised if we lose her forever.'

John – You go there every day. Why don't you bring her with you?

Mrs Sevak – I'm not worried about this. A rebel against the Lord Messiah can't find refuge at my place.

Prabhu – If not going to church makes one a rebel against the Lord Messiah, all right, even I won't go to church from today. Turn me out too!

Mrs Sevak (*Crying*) – Then what do I have left in this house? Why don't I blacken my face and leave if I'm the knot of poison? You and Sophie can stay here comfortably; Khuda is my master too.

John – Prabhu, you can't insult your mother in my presence.

Prabhu – God forbid that I should insult my mother. But I won't let my soul be oppressed for the sake of religious pretence. I haven't opened my mouth on this subject so far for fear of your displeasure. But when I see that there's no concern for religion on any other matter, and that there's devoutness only for its outward appearance, I begin to suspect whether it has some other purpose.

John – In what way have you seen any violation of religion?

Prabhu – There are hundreds. If there was just one, I could speak of it.

John – No, mention just one.

Prabhu – Are the means that you are using to occupy the land of that helpless, blind man in conformity with religion? Religion ended when he said that he wouldn't give his land on any account. Getting your way by legal means, diplomacy and threats may seem to you to be in conformity with religion, but it seems irreligious and unjust to me.

John – You are not in your senses right now, so I don't want to discuss anything with you. Go and cool down first and then I'll give an answer.

Prabhu went to his room full of anger and wondered what he should do. Until then his satyagraha had been restricted to words, it was now time for it to become active; but the inability to act was the one shortcoming in his character. In this agitated state he would wear one coat, take it off and wear another, leave the room, and return. John Sevak then came and sat down. He said gravely, 'Prabhu, I'm more worried than sad at seeing your rage today. Until now I had confidence in your pragmatism, but now I have lost that trust. I was sure that you understood full well the relationship between life and religion, but now I've realized that you are deluded like Sophie and your mother. Do you think that thousands of men like me, who go to church every day, sing hymns, shut their eyes and pray to Jesus, are absorbed in religious devotion? If you haven't yet realized that religion is merely a selfish institution, you should do so now. It's possible that you believe in Jesus, perhaps you think him to be Khuda's Son, or at least a saint, but I don't believe even that. I have as much respect for him as for an ordinary fakir. The fakir too goes about singing the glory of charity and forgiveness and the melody of the joys of heaven in the same way. He is as much of an ascetic, as humble, and as devout. But despite so much disbelief, I still leave hundreds of tasks and go to church every Sunday. Not going will result in social disapproval, which will adversely affect my business. And then there'll be discord in the house. I inflict this punishment on myself only for your mother's sake, and I request you not to rebel unnecessarily. Your mother deserves pity, not anger. Do you have anything to say?

Prabhu – No.

John – So now you won't act in such an unrestrained way?

Prabhu smiled and said – No.

6

DEVOUTNESS HAS SEVERAL VIRTUES BUT IT ALSO HAS A FAULT—IT IS simple. It can easily be tricked by impostors. A devout person is not logical. His ability to discriminate becomes slow. There was deep turbulence in Tahir Ali's heart when he listened to his stepmothers. He would repeatedly invoke Khuda's blessings and try to resolve his doubts by consulting legal texts. The day passed somehow but as soon as it was evening he went to Mr John Sevak and said, very politely, 'Huzoor, I have come here at your service to make a special request. I'll speak if you permit me to.'

John Sevak – Yes, yes, speak. Is it something new?

Tahir – Huzoor, it would be well if you gave up the idea of taking that blind man's land. There are several problems. Not only Soordas, the entire muhalla is bent on fighting back. Nayakram Panda especially is very angry. He's a very dangerous man. Goodness knows how often he has breached the peace. Even if all these problems can be removed, I'll still urge you to think about some other land instead of this one.

John – Why?

Tahir – All this will be a calamity. Hundreds of men get their work done because of that land; their cows graze there; baraats stay there; several people put up huts when there's a plague. The entire population will suffer if that land goes and people will utter hundreds of curses for us in their hearts. There's sure to be a calamity because of this.

John (*Laughing*) – I'll be the one to bear the calamity, won't I? I can take on the burden.

Tahir – Huzoor, I too am under your protection. How can I escape that calamity? In fact, the muhalla-valas think that I'm a traitor. Huzoor comes here only sometimes, they see me all the time. I'll be an eyesore for them every day. Even the women passing by will abuse me. I have a family, Khuda knows what may happen. After all it's possible to get other pieces of land near the city.

Devoutness is ludicrous in the eyes of materialists. It is thought to be especially unforgivable in a young man. John Sevak pretended to be angry and said – Even I have children. Why are you afraid if I'm not? Do you think that my family is not dear to me or that I'm not afraid of Khuda?

Tahir – You are a prosperous sahib, you are not afraid of calamity. Even calamity is afraid of the prosperous. Khuda's wrath afflicts only the poor.

John – You must be the creator of this new religious principle because I haven't heard until today that even God's wrath is afraid of prosperity. In fact, according to our religious texts, the door of heaven is shut to the rich.

Tahir – Huzoor, it would be well if you kept me out of this conflict.

John – Today I'll keep you out of this conflict, tomorrow you may be apprehensive that Khuda disapproves of animal slaughter and say, please keep me away from purchasing animal hides. In that case from how many things will I keep you away, and in how many places will I protect you from God's wrath? It's much better that I should keep you away from myself. You'll have to face God's wrath if you stay with me.

Mrs Sevak – You can't work for us if you are so afraid of God's wrath.

Tahir – I don't object to serving huzoor, I only . . .

Mrs Sevak – You'll have to obey every order that we give, whether it pleases or displeases your Khuda. We won't allow your Khuda to interfere with our work.

Tahir was despondent. He tried to console himself, 'God is compassionate, can't He see that I'm imprisoned in these chains? What control do I have over all this? How will I take care of my family if I don't obey the orders of the master? I've managed to get this stable job after years of struggle. I'll have to face the same struggles if I leave it. If nothing else, at least there's enough to live on.' Domestic anxiety kills introspection.

Tahir was forced to remain speechless. The poor man had sold all the jewellery that his wife possessed and had spent the money. Not a single ring remained. Mahir studied English. Good clothes had to be made for him; the fees had to be paid every month. Zabir and Zahir studied in an Urdu madrasa but their mother clamoured every day to have them admitted in an English school. Should they end up working as peons by studying Urdu? They could enter some office or the other if they knew even a little English. Tahir's own needs were shoved aside in the upbringing of his brothers. He seemed so imprisoned in his pajamas that the cloth lost its actual shape. He had not been fortunate enough to possess new shoes for perhaps five years now and had to be content with Mahir's old ones. Fortunately, Mahir had big feet. As far as possible, Tahir didn't let his brothers face any difficulties. But, at times, because of his straitened circumstances, he couldn't get new clothes made for them, or there would be a delay in paying the fees or they wouldn't get breakfast, or else they wouldn't get money for refreshments at the madrasa. Both his stepmothers would then pierce his heart with their taunts. When he was unemployed, he would often send his wife and children to her maika to lighten his burden. He would call them back for a month or so to escape ridicule and then send them back again on some pretext or the other. In a way his good time had come ever since Mr John Sevak had employed him; he was no longer beset with anxiety about the next day. Mahir was now over fifteen. Tahir's hopes centred entirely on him. He'd think, 'When Mahir completes his matriculation, I'll get him to join the police with sahib's recommendation. His salary won't be less than fifty rupees. The combined salary of both us brothers will be eighty rupees. Then there'll be some joy in life. Zahir will grow up by then. After that there'll be peace and contentment. There'll be hardship only for three or four years.' There would often be quarrels with his wife. She'd say, 'None of these brothers and relatives will be of any use. They'll dust their wings and fly away at the first opportunity, you'll just stand there and stare.' Tahir would be offended by his wife's words. He'd make her cry by telling her that she was the one to have set the house on fire and was the knot of poison.

What reply could a human being so weighed down by hopes and worries give to Mrs Sevak's harsh words? Fear of the master defeated the wrath of God. He said in a pained voice – I eat huzoor's salt, your wish has the same importance as Khuda's command. It's written in books that there's the same reward for pleasing the master as there is for pleasing Khuda. How will I show my face to Khuda if I'm disloyal to you?

John – Yes, now you are on the right path. Go do your work. It's folly to weigh religion and business on the same scale. Religion is religion and business business; they are unrelated. One needs some business, not religion, to live in this world. Religion is the embellishment of business. It befits only the wealthy. If Khuda gives you a salary, and you have the opportunity and money to spare in the house, then offer namaaz, go on Haj, get mosques built and wells dug; religion means that it is a sin to take Khuda's name on an empty stomach.

Tahir bowed, salaamed, and returned home.

7

IT WAS EVENING. HOWEVER, DESPITE IT GETTING ON TO PHAGUN, ONE'S hands and feet would become stiff with cold. Chilly blasts pierced the bones. With Indra's support, winter was again collecting its scattered energies and desperately trying to reverse the wheel of time. There were clouds as well as raindrops, a cold wind and fog. The lord of the seasons couldn't succeed against so many different energies. People hid their faces in quilts like mice peeping from holes. Shopkeepers sat in front of mud stoves warming their hands, selling bargains not of money but of kindness. Pedestrians fell upon the open fires like moths falling on lamps. Women of prosperous houses hoped that the misrain would come today so that the meals could be cooked and they would get an opportunity to sit before the mud stove. There would be a crowd in front of the chai stall. Thakurdeen's paans were rotting in the khoncha but he didn't have the courage to hawk them. Soordas, however, sat at his usual place, he'd burnt a few twigs that he had collected from here and there and was warming his hands. How could there be any passengers today? But if a stray wayfarer happened to pass by, he would wish for his welfare while sitting. Ever since Sayyad Tahir Ali had threatened him, his heart was beset with the anxiety of losing the land. He thought, 'Was it for this day that I worked so hard for the land? My days won't always remain like this, after all some day Lacchmi* will be pleased. The eyes of the blind may not open but their fortune may turn. Who knows, I may get a benefactor or be able to collect a few rupees gradually. It doesn't take long to succeed. The only desire I had was to build a well and a small temple here, at least there would be some sign of me left behind after my death, otherwise who will remember this blind man? Pisanhaari had a well dug; he is remembered to this day. Jhakkar Saayin had a tank built; it's known even today as Jhakkar's tank. My name will be forgotten if the land goes. Of what use will a few rupees be then, even if I get them?

---

* Lacchmi or Lakshmi, the goddess of fortune and wealth, Vishnu's consort.

Nayakram reassured him, 'Don't worry at all. Which mother's son can take away your land as long as I'm there? I'll make a river of blood flow. How will that kirantey dare! I'll set the godown on fire. I'll stop him from coming here. What does he imagine? Don't give your consent—that's all.' But the solace that these words gave was wiped out by the jealous, bitter remarks of Bhairo and Jagdhar, and Soordas would just heave a long sigh.

While Soordas was absorbed in these thoughts, Nayakram came along, with a cudgel and thin towel on his shoulder and paans stuffed in his mouth, and said – Soordas, will you just keep sitting here and beating the ground? It's evening now; people who take the air won't come out in this cold. Did you get enough to eat or not?

Soordas – Where, maharaj? I haven't met a single fortunate person today.

Nayakram – You've got what was written in your destiny. Come, let's go home. Put this towel over your shoulder if you are feeling cold. I came here thinking that I'll have a few words with sahib if I happen to meet him. Let's confront him.

Just as Soordas got up to leave, he suddenly heard the sound of a gharry approaching. He stopped, full of hope. The phaeton reached in a moment. Soordas went forward and said – Benefactor, may God make you prosper, be mindful of a blind man.

The phaeton stopped and Raja Sahib of Chataari alighted. Nayakram was his panda and he got a little money every year from raja sahib's riyasat. Nayakram blessed raja sahib and asked – What brings sarkar here? It's very cold today.

Raja sahib – Is this Soordas, whose land lies ahead? Come, both of you, sit with me. I want to see that land.

Nayakram – Sarkar, you go ahead. We'll follow you.

Raja sahib – Aji, come and sit, you'll be slow and I haven't yet said my evening prayers.

Soordas – Pandaji, you sit, I'll come running and will reach along with the gharry.

Raja sahib – No, no, there's no harm in your sitting here too. Right now you are not the beggar Soordas but the zamindar Soordas.

Nayakram – Come and sit, Soorey, our master is divinity incarnate.

Soordas – Pandaji, I . . .

Raja sahib – Pandaji, hold his hand and make him sit, else he won't.

Nayakram picked up Soordas in his lap and made him sit on the cushioned seat. He too sat down and the phaeton began to move. This was the first time in his life that Soordas had got an opportunity to sit on a phaeton. It seemed to him that he was flying. He was surprised that they had reached so fast when, after a few minutes, the phaeton stopped at the godown and raja sahib got down.

Raja sahib – Well, the land is very suitable.

Soordas – Sarkar, it's a mark of my ancestors.

Several doubts arose in Soordas's mind. 'Has sahib sent him to see the land? It's said that he's a big dharmatma so why didn't he make sahib understand? Big men are all alike, be they Hindus or Turks; that's why he's giving me so much respect, just as a goat is given enough fodder to fill its belly before its throat is slit. But I won't be taken in.'

Raja sahib – Do you have any arrangements with customers?

Nayakram – No, sarkar, it remains fallow like this. All the cows of the muhalla graze here. There'll be a profit of at least 200 rupees if it's rented out but he says, 'Why should I give it on rent when God gives me enough to eat anyway?'

Raja sahib – Achcha! Soordas not only takes charity, he also gives it. One earns merit just by getting a darshan of such a being.

Nayakram had never before seen Soordas get so much respect. He said – Huzoor, he's a great mahatma from a previous birth.

Raja sahib – Not from a previous birth, he's a mahatma in this one.

A true benefactor doesn't desire fame. Soordas wasn't even aware of the import of his sacrifice and charity. Had he been, perhaps there wouldn't have been such humility in his nature. One's praise sounds sweet to the ears. This is the supreme reward of charity from a social point of view. Soordas's charity was that of the earth or the sky, which is not worried about fame or eulogy. He smelt deceit in raja sahib's generosity and was anxious to know his intentions.

Nayakram began to glorify Soordas's virtues to please raja sahib – Dharmavatar, he's not content even with this. He wants to build a dharmashala, a temple and a well here.

Raja sahib – Vaah! That settles the matter. Well, Soordas! Give six bighas of this land to Mr John Sevak. Use the money for dharmic work. Your desire will be fulfilled and sahib's work will also get done.

You won't get such a good price from others. Tell me, how much money shall I get for you?

Nayakram was afraid that he would lose face if Soordas refused. He said – Soorey, you know our maalik, don't you? He's the maharaj of Chataari. We are nurtured in his court. He's the highest official of the municipality. Nobody can even fix a stake at his own doorway without his permission. If he wants, he can get all the ikka drivers caught and stop the water supply in the entire city.

Soordas – Why don't you get some other land for sahib if you have such power?

Raja sahib – It's difficult to get any other land in the city that's so suitable. But why do you object to giving it? You don't know how long it will take to fulfil your wishes. This is a very good opportunity, take the money and use it for dharmic work.

Soordas – Maharaj, I'm not willing to sell the land.

Nayakram – Soorey, you haven't taken bhang, have you? Do you realize to whom you are speaking?

Soordas – Pandaji, I realize everything. Don't I have any sense even if I don't have eyes? But who am I to sell something if it doesn't belong to me?

Raja sahib – Isn't this land yours?

Soordas – No sarkar, it's my ancestors' land, not mine. I own only what I have earned with my own hands. I hold this land in trust. I'm not its owner.

Raja sahib – Soordas, this remark of yours has made a deep impression on me. Hundreds of homes wouldn't have been ruined today if all zamindars felt this way. People destroy large riyasats to live luxuriously. Pandaji, I have made this very proposal to the council that zamindars shouldn't have the right to sell their property, but I don't call it selling if it's done for dharmic work.

Soordas – Dharmavatar, the only relation that I have with this land is to protect it as long as I'm alive and to leave it as it is when I die.

Raja sahib – But remember that you are only giving a part of your land to others so that you can get money to build a temple.

Nayakram – Speak up, Soorey, how will you answer maharaj?

Soordas – Am I capable of giving an answer to sarkar? But sarkar knows at least this much, that if people can catch hold of a finger they seize the wrist. Sahib won't say anything at first but he'll gradually build a boundary wall, nobody will be able to go to the temple. Who will want to fight with him every day?

Nayakram – Deenbandhu! Soordas is right. Who will want to go around fighting with big men?

Raja sahib – What will sahib do? Will he dig up your temple and throw it away?

Nayakram – Speak up, Soorey, what do you have to say now?

Soordas – Sarkar! A poor man's wife is the bhaavaj of the entire village. Sahib is a Kirastaan, he'll make a godown for tobacco in the dharmashala; his labourers will sleep in the temple. The well will be an adda for his workers; betis and bahus won't be able to go there to draw water. If sahib doesn't do all this, his sons will. The good name of my ancestors will be destroyed. Sarkar, don't push me into this quicksand.

Nayakram – Dharmavatar, I can understand Soordas's point. There's no doubt that in a short while the temple, the dharmashala and the well will all become sahib's.

Raja sahib – Achcha, I agree, but also think of how much people will gain from this factory. Thousands of labourers, mechanics, clerks, accountants, blacksmiths and carpenters will settle down here. A good basti will come up, banias will open several new shops, local farmers won't have to take their vegetables to the city as they'll get a good price here. Hawkers, greengrocers, cowherds, dhobis, tailors will all benefit. Don't you want to be a part of this meritorious work?

Nayakram – Speak up Soorey, surely you don't have anything to say now? It's our sarkar's decency that he's arguing so much with you. You would have lost your entire land by just one order if it had been any other officer.

Soordas – Bhaiyya, isn't that why people want an officer to be a dharmatma, otherwise don't they know that officials don't so much as even speak without saying 'damn fool, sooar'? One doesn't have the courage even to stand in front of them, let alone speak. That's why we believe that if our rajas and maharajas had still been in power, they would have listened to our tales of woe. Sarkar is right, the muhalla will certainly prosper; workers on daily wages will also profit a lot. But if this prosperity increases so will the use of toddy and alcohol, prostitutes will also come and settle down, strangers will ogle at our betis and bahus . . . There'll be so much unrighteousness. Farmers from the countryside will leave their work and run away, tempted by wages; they'll pick up bad habits here and spread their bad behaviour in their villages. Girls and bahus from the countryside will come to work here and lose their dharma for money. This is the prosperity of the cities. There will be the same prosperity here. God forbid it! Sarkar, save me from such wickedness, such unrighteousness. All these sins will fall on my head.

Nayakram – Deenbandhu! Soordas is right. Calcutta, Bombay, Ahmedabad, Kanpur, I have travelled everywhere by your mercy. Patrons keep inviting me. I've seen the same conditions wherever there are factories.

Raja sahib – Aren't there vices in places of pilgrimage?

Soordas – Sarkar, their reform is also in the hands of big men. It isn't right to spread vices instead of removing them from places where they already exist.

Raja sahib – You are right, Soordas, you are very right. You win, I lose. I hadn't thought of these things when I promised sahib that I'd finalize this land. Don't worry, I'll tell sahib that Soordas won't give his land. Nayakram, see to it that Soordas doesn't have any trouble. I'll leave now. Take this, Soordas, your wages for coming so far.

He put a rupee in Soordas's hand and left. Nayakram said – Soordas, even raja sahib has acknowledged your intelligence today.

8

SOPHIA HAD BEEN AT INDU'S FOR FOUR MONTHS NOW. A SEARING PAIN would burn in her heart whenever she remembered her home and family. Prabhu came regularly to see her once a day but she never asked him about the welfare of the family. She didn't go out to take the air for fear of meeting her mother. Although Indu had kept her circumstances secret from everyone, they had all guessed her real plight. That's why everyone was careful to see that nothing happened to hurt her. Indu had become so fond of Sophie that she spent most of the time with her. Indu also became interested in religious and philosophical texts because of her company.

If a house leaks, one repairs it; if it falls, one abandons it. Sophie stopped trying to pretend when she realized that these people knew everything about her and became engrossed in the study of religious texts. Old resentments began to disappear. The wounds inflicted by her mother's harsh words began to heal. The narrowness that gives undue importance to personal feelings and worries now seemed trivial in the ambit of this care and kindness. She thought, 'It's not mama's fault but that of her religious intolerance. The sphere of her views is limited, she doesn't have the ability to respect freedom of thought, and I'm unnecessarily annoyed with her.' This was the one thorn that had kept rankling within her. Her mind was at peace when it was removed. Her life was now spent in perusing religious texts, and meditating and reflecting upon religious principles. Piety is the best medicine for inner pain.

However, it's not as if her mind was at peace as a result of this meditation and reflection. Several doubts arose daily—what's the purpose of life? Every religion gave various answers to this question but not a single one could be found which made an impression on the mind. What are these miracles? Are they figments of the imagination of devotees? The most knotty problem was the purpose of worship. Why does God want man to worship him? What is his intention? Does he feel happy listening to his eulogy by his own creation? She remained so absorbed in the investigation of these questions that she wouldn't leave her room for days on end. She was oblivious to the need to eat or drink. She even resented Indu's arrival at times.

She was reading a religious text one morning when Indu came in. Her face was sad. Sophia's attention wasn't drawn to her, as she was absorbed in her book. Indu said – Sophie, now I'm a guest here for just a few days, you won't forget me, will you?

Without raising her head, Sophie said – Yes.

Indu – Your mind will be diverted by your books, you won't even remember me but I won't be able to live without you for even a single day.

Sophie kept looking at her book and said – Yes.

Indu – I don't know when we'll meet again. I'll grieve the whole day.

Sophie turned the page of the book and said – Yes.

Indu could no longer bear Sophie's callousness. On another occasion, she would have felt offended and left, or seeing Sophie engrossed in self-study, wouldn't have set foot in the room. But at this moment her tender heart was full of the sorrow of parting. There was no room for pride in it. She said, crying, 'Behen! For God's sake, shut your book for a while. You can read to your heart's content after I leave. I won't come from there to tease you.'

Sophie looked at Indu. It was as if her deep meditation had been broken. Indu's eyes were full of tears, her face was somewhat wan and her hair dishevelled. She said – Arey Indu! What's the matter? Why are you crying?

Indu – You read your book, what do you care about anybody's crying and weeping? I don't know why God hasn't given me the kind of heart that you have.

Sophia – Behen, forgive me, I'm caught in a big tangle. I haven't yet been able to solve the puzzle. I had always believed that idol worship was false. I had thought that rishis have made this system for the spiritual peace of fools; today I've become an admirer of idol worship. The writer has proved scientifically that the form and dimensions of idols are based on scientific rules.

Indu – I've got my summons. I'll leave after three days.

Sophia – You've given me bad news. How can I stay here then?

There was only self-interest and no sympathy in this sentence. But

Indu interpreted it to mean that Sophie would find it unbearable to be separated from her. She said – Your mind will be diverted by books. But I'll be tormented by your memory. I'm telling you the truth, I won't forget your face for even a moment. This beautiful image will always hover before my eyes. Behen, if you don't mind, can I make a request? Would it be possible for you to stay with me for a few days? My life will be fulfilled in your noble company. I'll always be obliged to you for this.

Sophia – I'm bound by your love, take me wherever you wish. I'll go if I want to, and I'll go even if I don't want to. But tell me, have you asked raja sahib?

Indu – This is not something for which I need to ask his permission. He keeps telling me that I need a lady because I must be feeling uneasy alone. He'll be delighted when he hears this proposal.

Rani Jahnavi was making preparations for Indu's departure, and Indu kept bringing lace, clothes, etc. for Sophia. She filled several boxes with a variety of clothes. She wanted to take Sophia with her with such pomp and splendour that the maidservants would give her due respect. Prabhu didn't like Sophie's going with Indu. He still hoped that mama's anger would be pacified and that she would embrace Sophie. Ill-will was bound to increase if Sophie went. He tried to persuade Sophie but she didn't want to decline Indu's invitation. She had vowed not to return home.

When raja sahib came on the third day to fetch Indu, along with other matters, she mentioned taking Sophie with her. She said – I feel uneasy alone, my mind will be diverted if Miss Sophia is with me.

Mahendra – Is Miss Sevak still here?

Indu – The problem is that her religious views are independent, and her family can't tolerate them. That's why she doesn't want to return home.

Mahendra – But just think, what a scandal it will be for me if she stays in my house. Mr Sevak won't like it, and it's highly improper that I should keep his daughter in my house without his permission. There'll be a big scandal.

Indu – I don't see any cause for a scandal. Can't a friend be a guest of her friend? And Sophie's nature isn't so unrestrained that she'll wander around here and there.

Mahendra – She may be a devi but there are several reasons why I think that it will be improper for her to go with you. Your great fault is that you don't think of the propriety of an action before taking it. Do you think there's nothing wrong in ignoring the family honour? Her family only wants her to appear to follow the principles of her religion. I can only say that her independence of thought has gone far beyond the limits of propriety if she can't do even this much.

Indu – But I've promised her. I've been making preparations for her for several days now. I've even taken amma's permission. Everyone in the house, including the servants, knows that she's going with me. What will people think now if I don't take her with me? Think how humiliating it'll be for me. I won't be able to show my face to anyone.

Mahendra – It's possible to do anything to avoid scandal. Shall I speak to Miss Sevak if you feel embarrassed? She's not so innocent that she won't understand something so obvious.

Indu – I've become so fond of her while staying with her that it seems impossible for me to live without her for even a single day. That doesn't matter, because I know that some day I'll have to be separated from her. Right now I'm more worried about not keeping my word. People will say that I went back on it. Sophie had flatly refused at first. She agreed only after a lot of pleading. Accept my request for my sake this time. After this, I won't do anything without asking you first.

Mahendra Kumar couldn't be persuaded by any means. Indu cried and entreated, fell at his feet, used all the mantras that never fail, but her husband's hard heart didn't relent. His reputation mattered more to him than anything else in the world.

When Mahendra Kumar had left, Indu sat dejected for a long time. The same thought kept recurring – What will Sophie think? I've told her that my husband never refuses me anything. She'll now think that he doesn't bother to listen to me. But this is how it is, what does he care about me? He talks as if there's nobody in the world more generous than him, but that's utter nonsense. He just wants that I should sit alone all day crying over his name. He's probably jealous that I'll spend my days comfortably in Sophie's company. He wants to keep me like a prisoner. If he can be stubborn so can I. I'll also say, I won't go if you don't let Sophie come. What can he do to me? Nothing. He's probably afraid that the household expenses will increase if Sophie comes. He's a miser by nature. He's using the excuse of a scandal to hide his miserliness.

A suffering soul doubts another person's good intentions.

When Jahnavi and she went for an outing in the evening, Indu gave her this news and requested her to persuade Mahendra to take Sophie with them. Jahnavi said, 'Why don't you agree with him?'

Indu – Amma, I'm saying this sincerely, I'm not being stubborn. I wouldn't have felt at all unhappy if I hadn't already spoken with Sophia; but what will she think if I don't take her now after making all the preparations? I won't be able to show her my face. He wouldn't have refused such a small thing if he cared at all for me. How can you expect me implicitly to obey every order of his in such a situation?

Jahnavi – He's your husband. You have to accept whatever he says.

Indu – Even if he doesn't accept the small requests that I make?

Jahnavi – Yes, he has that right. I feel ashamed that my instructions haven't had the slightest influence on you. I want to see you as a devoted and virtuous sati who doesn't care in the least about her own prestige and respect before her husband's orders or wishes. Even if he wants you to walk on your head it's your dharma to do so, and you are dismayed by just this much?

Indu – You are asking me to do something impossible.

Jahnavi – Be quiet! I can't hear you saying such things. I'm afraid that perhaps you have also come under the spell of Sophie's independence of thought.

Indu didn't answer this. She was afraid to say anything that might increase this suspicion in amma's mind and make it difficult for poor Sophie to continue staying there. She sat silently all the way. When the gharry reached the house and Indu got down to go to her room, Jahnavi said – Beti, I request you with folded hands not to say another word about this to Mahendra, otherwise I'll feel very unhappy.

Indu looked at her mother, wounded to the quick, and went to her room. Fortunately, Mahendra Kumar had gone out straight after taking his meals otherwise it would have been very difficult for Indu to control her feelings. She wanted to go and ask Sophia to forgive her and to tell her frankly, 'Behen, I have no power. Although I'm a rani in name, I don't have as much freedom as the maidservants in my house.' But she stopped herself with the thought that criticism of her husband was against her dharma and traditions and that she would fall in Sophie's eyes. Sophie would think that she had no self-respect.

Vinay came to meet Indu at 9 p.m. She was in a mental turmoil, taking out from the boxes the clothes she had bought for Sophie and wondering how to send them to her. She didn't have the courage to go herself. When she saw Vinay, she asked, 'Why, Vinay, if your wife wanted to have a friend stay with her for a few days, would you refuse or be happy?'

Vinay – I'm not likely to face this problem, so I don't want to bother about it.

Indu –The problem is already there.

Vinay – Behen, I'm afraid of what you are saying.

Indu – Because you are deceiving yourself, but actually you are in deeper waters than you think. Do you imagine that the dreadful inner conflict, raging in the deepest recesses of your heart, can remain hidden by your not coming home for days on end, remaining busy with your society for social service, not raising your eyes to look at Miss Sophia, running away from her shadow? But just remember, don't let even a tinkle of this conflict be heard, or else there'll be disaster. Sophia respects you perhaps even more than a sati would her husband. She worships you. Your discipline, sacrifice and service have entranced her. But if I'm not mistaken, there's not a trace of love in her devotion. Although it's useless to give you any advice because you know only too well the difficulties that lie on this path, I request you to go away somewhere for a few days. By then perhaps Sophie will also have found some way out for herself. It's possible that caution now will prevent two lives from being destroyed.

Vinay – Behen, what can I hide from you when you know everything? I can't be cautious now. My heart alone knows the mental torment that I have suffered during these last four or five months. My discrimination has been destroyed; I'm falling into a ditch with my eyes wide open, I'm fully aware that I'm drinking a cup of poison. No obstacle, no difficulty, no doubt, can now save me from total destruction. Yes, I can assure you that not a single spark or flame from this fire will reach Sophie. My whole body may be consumed and my bones reduced to ashes but Sophie will not catch even a glimpse of this inferno. I too have decided to go away from here as soon as possible, to protect Sophie, not myself. Ah! It would have been far better if Sophie had let me get burnt in that fire, at least my secret would have remained concealed. What will amma's state be if she gets to know this? The very thought makes my hair stand on end. Now I have no choice except to blacken my face and drown myself somewhere.

Vinay then left, though Indu kept asking him to stay. He had told her more than he had wanted to in the heat of the moment. He didn't know what else he would have continued to say had he remained there any longer. Indu's condition was like that of someone whose feet were bound while her house was burning in front of her. She could see that this fire would consume the entire house—Vinay's high ambitions, their mother's lofty expectations, their father's plans, they would all be destroyed. She kept tossing and turning the whole night with these distressing thoughts. There was a palanquin waiting at the door for her when she got up in the morning. She embraced her mother and cried, washed her father's feet with her tears and went home. Sophie's room was on the way but she didn't so much as look towards it. Sophie got up and came to the door and shook her hand with tearful eyes. Indu quickly took it away and went ahead.

9

SOPHIA WAS IN THE KIND OF PREDICAMENT THESE DAYS WHEN ANY trivial joke, any ordinary glance, anybody's smiling at her, a moment's delay by a servant in obeying her orders—several such incidents that happen daily in homes, and to which no one pays attention—were enough to hurt her. Even a slight blow can be unbearable to a wounded part of the body. So how could Indu's going away without saying a word to her not have been painful? Although Indu had left, Sophie stood at her door like a statue, thinking, 'Why this disdain? What crime have I committed to deserve this punishment? Why wasn't she frank with me if she didn't want to take me with her? I didn't request her. Don't I know full well that one has no friends in times of trouble? She's a rani, it was enough of a favour that she would laugh and talk with me. Don't I know that I'm not fit to be her friend? But what kind of civility is it to turn away like this? It's only an excuse that raja sahib didn't agree. Raja sahib would never refuse such a small thing. Indu must have realized that important people would visit them there—why should she introduce me to them? Perhaps she suspected that her glory would be dimmed before me. That must be it. No doubt she would have taken me with her if I had been a fool, without beauty and talents; my inferiority would have enhanced her glory. It's my misfortune!'

She was still standing at the door when Jahnavi came to her room after seeing off her daughter and said – Beti, forgive me, I was the one who prevented you from going. Indu felt bad, but what could I do? She has left, but how would I have passed my time if you had also gone with her? Vinay is also ready to leave for Rajputana; I'd have died. My mind will be diverted if you stay here. To tell you the truth, beti, you have cast a magic mantra over me.

Sophia – It's your grace that makes you say this. I'm sorry that Indu didn't even shake hands with me when she left.

Jahnavi – Only out of embarrassment, beti, only out of

embarrassment! I'm telling you, she's the simplest girl in the world. I've been very unfair to her by preventing you from going with her. My child isn't at all happy there; her health deteriorates if she stays there for even a month. It's such a large riyasat and Mahendra puts the entire burden on her. He doesn't have any respite from the municipality. The poor child gets nervous trying to keep an account of the income and expenditure and, on top of that, each paisa must be accounted for. Mahendra is obsessed with keeping accounts. He harasses her if there's the slightest difference. Indu has the right to spend as much as she wants but she must keep the accounts. Raja sahib doesn't make concessions for anyone. A servant is dismissed if he misappropriates even a paisa even though he may have spent his entire life in his service. I never even look at Indu sternly here, no matter what the loss, even if she overturns a pitcher of ghee. And over there, she has to listen to raja sahib's rebukes for the slightest thing. The child can't bear it. She doesn't answer back—that's the dharma of a Hindu woman—but she starts crying. She's the image of compassion. Someone may take away everything from her but her heart melts the moment he cries in front of her. Sophie, God has given me two children, and my heart is soothed whenever I look at both of them. Vinay is as devout and courageous as Indu is sensitive and simple. He doesn't know how to chatter frivolously. It seems as if he has been born only to serve others. If a maidservant has a complaint, he leaves all his work and rushes to take care of her medical treatment. I had fever once and this boy didn't look at the door for three months. He sat with me daily, fanning me with the pankha or gently stroking my feet or reading to me from the Ramayana or the Mahabharata. No matter how much I'd say, son, go out, roam around, after all, what are these maids and servants for? The doctor comes every day, why are you becoming a sati along with me? But he would refuse to go. For the past few days now, he has been organizing the society for social service. Kunwar sahib's love for this society is the result of Vinay's beneficial company; otherwise three years ago there was nobody who loved pleasure more than he did in the entire city. He would get himself shaved twice a day. Dozens of dhobis and tailors were employed to wash and stitch his clothes. An expert launderer came from Paris to launder them. Cooks from Kashmir and Italy prepared the food. He had such a passion for paintings that he often travelled as far as Italy to get good ones. You were probably in Mussoorie in those days. A team of armed riders accompanied him whenever he went for an outing. He was addicted to shikar which he would play for months together. Sometimes in Kashmir or Bikaner or Nepal, he would go there only to play shikar. Vinay has completely transformed him. He's an ascetic from birth. He must have been a rishi in his previous life.

Sophia – How were such noble feelings of service and devotion awakened in you? Ranis here are usually engrossed in their luxurious lives.

Jahnavi – Beti, this is the result of Dr Ganguly's noble precepts. I fell ill when Indu was two years old. Dr Ganguly came to treat me. It was a heart disease; I'd feel restless, as if somebody had cast a mantra of distraction. The doctor began to read the Mahabharata to me. I found it so absorbing that sometimes I would stay awake reading it until midnight. I'd ask doctor sahib to read it to me when I'd get tired. Then I got so addicted to reading narratives of heroism that there's no story about the Rajputs that I didn't read. It was then that the sentiment of love for the community germinated in me. A new desire was awakened—that a son should be born from my womb, who would bring glory to the community, like Abhimanyu, Durgadas, Pratap.* I vowed that if I had a son, I'd sacrifice him for the welfare of the country and the community. In those days I'd sleep on the floor like

---

* Abimanyu: Arjuna's son and Krishna's nephew in the Mahabharata. He heard Arjuna tell his mother Subhadra the secret of penetrating a lotus-shaped formation of troops while in her womb but she fell asleep before Arjuna could reveal the way out. Though only a boy, Abhimanyu valiantly penetrated this formation in his father's absence during the battle of the Mahabharata between the Pandavas and the Kauravas, since he was the only one who knew the secret, but not knowing the way out, was brutally killed by the Kauravas.

Durgadas: (13 August 1638–22 November 1718); carried out a relentless struggle against the Mughals. After Aurangzeb's death in 1707, he seized Jodhpur and eventually evicted the Mughal forces. Premchand wrote a book for children on him, calling him 'the kohinoor among the Rajput heroes' for his self-sacrifice and patriotism and 'a sadhu' even while he was 'a lion'.

Pratap: Maharana Pratap (9 May 1540–29 January 1597); ruler of Mewar, fought Akbar all his life

a tapasvini and eat sparsely only once a day; I'd even wash my own utensils. On the one hand there were the devis who'd sacrifice even their lives for the honour of the community and here was I, so unfortunate that I had forgotten all the cares of this world as well as of the next one and was engrossed in worldly pleasures. Seeing the decline of the community, I'd feel ashamed of my luxurious living. God listened to my prayers. Vinay was born in the third year. From childhood itself, I made him get used to hardship. I never let him sleep on mattresses or be held in the laps of nursemaids and maidservants or eat dried fruits. He was educated only on religious narratives until the age of ten. After that I left him in Dr Ganguly's care. He was the only one whom I could completely trust and I'm proud that the person entrusted with the responsibility of Vinay's education was worthy of it in every respect. Vinay has travelled in most countries of the world. Besides Sanskrit and other Indian languages, he also knows the major European languages quite well. He is such an expert in music that even renowned musicians don't have the courage to open their mouths in front of him. He spreads a blanket on the floor daily to sleep on and also covers himself only with a blanket. He has won several prizes for walking. A fistful of gram for breakfast, rotis and vegetables for his meals—all other edibles of this world are taboo for him. Beti, what more can I tell you? He is a complete ascetic. The best result of his asceticism was that even his father was forced to become an ascetic. How could the old father of the young son remain a slave to luxury? I think that he was satiated by worldly pleasure, and that was a good thing. The pleasure-loving father of an ascetic son—what an extremely ridiculous scenario that would have been! He participates whole-heartedly in Vinay's noble activities and I can say that Vinay could never have been so successful without his devotion. There are a hundred youths in the society at present, many from wealthy families. Kunwar sahib wants the membership of the society to increase to 500. As its chairman, Dr Ganguly organizes this society with formidable enthusiasm even in this old age. He gives lectures on physical education to the youth for a couple of hours daily when he has time from administrative work. The curriculum is completed after three years and social service begins after that. Twenty youths will pass this year, and it has been decided that they will travel around India for two years but on the condition that they won't take with them any other possessions during their travels except a small lota, a string, a dhoti and a blanket. They won't even keep any money for their expenses. There'll be several gains because of this—the youth will get used to hardships; they'll get to know the real conditions of the country; their horizons will be widened; and, most importantly, their characters will be strengthened for they will develop qualities like patience, courage, industry and resolution. Vinay is going with them, and I feel very proud that my son is organizing all this for the welfare of the country. And I'm telling you the truth that I won't feel the slightest grief if an occasion should arise when he'll have to sacrifice his life to protect his country. I'll grieve when I see him bowing his head before prosperity or turning back from the arena of duty. God forbid that I should remain alive to see the day. I don't know what the state of my mind will be then. Perhaps I'll be thirsty for Vinay's blood. Perhaps these feeble hands may have the strength to strangle him.

As she said this, there was a strange radiance on the rani's face. The glow of self-esteem began to blaze in her tearful eyes. Sophia stared at her with astonishment. She could never have imagined that such a devoted and pure heart lay concealed in such a delicate frame.

A moment later, the rani said again – Beti, in my excitement I've told you so many things that are in my heart, but what can I do? There's a sweet simplicity on your face that attracts me. I've got to know you very well after all these days. You are not Sophie but Vinay in the guise of a woman. Kunwar sahib is charmed by you. He's always sure to talk about you when he comes home. Had it not been for the obstacle of religion (*smiling*), I'd have sent him long ago to Mr Sevak with the proposal of Vinay's marriage.

Sophia blushed with embarrassment, her long eyelashes drooped and there was a glimpse of an extremely subtle, calm, gentle smile on her lips. She covered her face with her hands and said – You are reviling me, I'll run away.

Jahnavi – All right, don't feel shy. Here, I won't talk about this. I only want to request you not to feel embarrassed by anything now. Indu was your friend, she knew your nature and understood your needs. I don't have such intelligence. Think of this house as your own and ask for whatever you need without embarrassment. Get the food cooked according to your taste. Ask for a gharry whenever you want to go out. Send any servant wherever you want to. There's no need to ask me anything. Come immediately if you want to speak with me, there's no need to let me know beforehand. If you don't like this room you can shift to the one next to mine in which Indu used to stay. I can talk to you there whenever I want. You can tell me what's happening around whenever you have the leisure. Just think of yourself as my private secretary.

Jahnavi left after saying this. Sophie felt relieved. She had been very worried about staying there after Indu's departure. Who would care about her? She'd be like an unwanted guest. Now she was no longer worried.

From that day onwards, she received even more hospitality. Maidservants were alert to every expression on her face and would ask, 'Miss sahib, is there any work?' The coachman came twice a day to ask if she wanted the gharry to be ready. Raniji also came to sit with her at least once a day. Sophie began to realize now the extent to which her heart was full of concern for women. She would be deeply grieved at the way in which women in India bowed their heads before bricks and stones. She thought that the main cause of India's decline was their materialism, false beliefs and selfishness. She would discuss these subjects with Sophie for hours on end.

This kindness and love gradually began to efface the desolation in Sophia's heart. Her behaviour began to change. She no longer felt embarrassed giving orders to the maidservants or going to any part of the palace. But as her worries diminished, her love of luxury began to grow. Her leisure time increased and she became interested in recreation. She would sometimes look at the paintings of ancient artists, or wander around in the garden, or play the piano. Sometimes she would even play chess with Jahnavi. She was not so indifferent to clothes and jewellery any longer. She started wearing silk saris instead of gowns. Sometimes raniji even persuaded her to chew paan. She became fond of combing and plaiting her hair. Worry is the cause of sacrifice. Freedom from care is allied with entertainment and pleasure.

She was sitting in her room one afternoon and reading. It was so hot that she was perspiring despite electric fans and khus screens. The hot blasts of the loo outside scorched the body. Suddenly Prabhu came in and said – Sophie, come and settle an argument. Vinay Singh has several doubts about a poem that I've written. I say something; he says something else. We've left the decision to you. Just come for a while.

Sophia – How can I make a decision on a debate concerning poetry? I don't know a word about prosody; I don't have the slightest knowledge about figures of speech. It's useless asking me to come.

Prabhu – You don't need to know prosody to decide that argument. There's a conflict between his ideals and mine. Just come.

A fire seemed to burn Sophie's body when she came out into the courtyard. She walked quickly to Vinay's room, which was on the other side of the palace. She had never gone there until then. There was no furniture in the room, just a blanket spread on the floor and a few books on the floor itself. There were no fans, khus screens, curtains, or pictures. The west wind blew directly into the room. The walls were burning like a griddle on fire. Vinay was sitting there on the blanket with his head bowed. He got up as soon as he saw Sophie and rushed to get her a chair.

Sophia – Where is he going?

Prabhu (*Smiling*) – To get you a chair.

Sophia – He'll get a chair and I'll sit down! How ridiculous!

Prabhu – He wouldn't have listened even if I had tried to stop him.

Sophia – How can he live in this room?

Prabhu – He's a complete yogi. I come here for love of him.

Meanwhile Vinay brought a cushioned chair for Sophie. Sophie was overcome with shyness and embarrassment. Vinay was in such a state that he seemed to be drenched in water. Sophia thought, 'What an ideal life!' Vinay thought, 'What incomparable beauty!' Both of them remained standing in their respective places. Finally, Vinay thought of a solution. He said, looking at Prabhu, 'We are both plaintiffs, so we can remain standing, but it's only proper that the judge's seat should be elevated.'

Sophie replied looking at Prabhu – A child doesn't forget himself while playing.

Finally, all three sat down on the blanket. Prabhu read out his poem, which was very melodious and full of noble and pure sentiments. The poet had made it replete with the sentiment of blessings given by a mother to her daughter who is leaving for her sasural, the home of her in-laws. The mother embraces her and says – Daughter, may you be a devoted wife, may your womb bear fruit and children as delicate as flowers play in your lap, may your home and your courtyard echo with the sound of their sweet laughter. May Lakshmi bless you. If you touch a stone, may it turn into gold. May your husband shelter you in the shadow of his love just as a roof shelters the walls under its shade.

The poet had painted such an attractive picture of married life with these sentiments that there was an abundance of light, flowers, and love; there were no dark valleys into which we fall, no thorns that pierce our feet, no mental agitation that makes us deviate from our path. After finishing the poem, Prabhu said to Vinay, 'Now say whatever you want to on this subject.'

Vinay replied with embarrassment – I've already said whatever I had to.

Prabhu – Say it again.

Vinay – Why should I keep repeating the same things?

Prabhu – Shall I summarize your views?

Vinay – Something came to my mind, so I expressed it; you are exaggerating it unnecessarily.

Prabhu – Why are you shying away from expressing those sentiments in front of Sophie?

Vinay – I'm not shy but I don't have any dispute with you. This ideal of human life seems best to you; it seems opposed to my present situation. There's nothing to quarrel about.

Prabhu (*Laughing*) – Exactly what I wanted you to admit! Why do you think it is opposed to your present situation? Do you believe that married life is always contemptible? Should everybody renounce the world and become a sanyasi?

Vinay – I've never implied that everybody should renounce the world and become a sanyasi. I only meant to say that married life nurtures selfishness. There's no need to prove this and it doesn't become an eminent poet lavishly to praise married life when selfishness permeates every pore of our being in this degraded state, when we don't do or say anything without being selfish, so that the relationship even of mother and son, guru and disciple, husband and wife is dominated by selfishness. We are becoming slaves to married life. We have made this our goal in life. What we need at present are people who will take vows, ascetics, worshippers of the highest truth who will sacrifice even their lives for the country's welfare. These are the lofty and pure sentiments that our poets should encourage. The population in our country has increased more than is necessary. Mother earth can no longer bear the burden of more offspring. One sees so many children in schools, on the streets, in the alleys that one doesn't know what they'll end up doing. There isn't enough produce in our country to provide one square meal a day for everyone. This lack of food is the main reason for the moral and economic downfall of our country. Your poem is untimely in every respect. I don't think it can benefit society. Right now it's the duty of our poets to show the importance of sacrifice, to generate devotion to celibacy, to preach self-restraint. Marriage is the source of bondage and this is not the right time to sing its praises.

Prabhu – Have you said what you wanted to?

Vinay – A lot more could be said, but this is enough for the time being.

Prabhu – I have already told you that I'm not criticizing the ideals of renunciation and sacrifice. That's the highest state for mankind and the person who attains it is blessed. However, just as the utility of food and water is not affected by the fasting of a few people who don't eat or drink, so married life can't be renounced because of the sacrifice of a few yogis. Marriage is the price of the social life of mankind. Renounce it and the binding of our social organization will fall apart; our condition will be like that of animals. Rishis have called domesticity the highest dharma, and if you think about it with a calm mind, it will be obvious that their pronouncement is not mere exaggeration. No other condition provides more favourable opportunities for the development of such godlike qualities as compassion, sympathy, tolerance, kindness and sacrifice than domestic life. In fact, I don't mind going so far as to say that this is the only condition that can be considered natural for human beings. The credit for the works that have brought glory to humanity does not belong to yogis but to those who enjoyed the bliss of married life. Harishchandra, Ramachandra, Krishna, Napoleon, Nelson were not yogis. Ascetics have definitely attained fame in the spheres of dharma and science but only those who participate in experience will wear the crown of glory in the arena of action. No proof can be found in history to show that the emancipation of a country has been attained through ascetics. Even today more than ten lakh ascetics dwell in India but who can say that society derives any benefit from them? It may be so imperceptibly but not visibly. Then why is it expected that the country will get some special advantage by scorning married life? Yes, there will certainly be some benefit if ignorance is considered to be a benefit.

Having completed this statement, Prabhu said to Sophia – You have heard the opinions of both sides and are now on the seat of justice. Decide between truth and falsehood.

Sophia – You can decide this yourself. Do you think that music is something very good?

Prabhu – Certainly.

Sophia – If someone's house is on fire, what will you say to the inhabitants who continue to sing and play?

Prabhu – I'll call them fools, what else?

Sophia – Why? Singing is not a bad thing.

Prabhu – Then why don't you admit frankly that you have given him the degree? I knew that you'd favour him.

Sophia – Why did you make me the judge if you feared this? Your poem is of a high standard. I'm willing to call it beautiful in every aspect. But it's your duty to use this rare gift of yours for the welfare of your countrymen. There's no need to sing the raga of beauty and love in this degraded condition. Even you will acknowledge this. There's no obligation or responsibility for ordinary poets. But your responsibility is greater in proportion to the important talent that God has given you.

After Sophia had left, Vinay said to Prabhu – I knew that this would be the verdict. I hope you didn't feel embarrassed?

Prabhu – She was being kind to you.

Vinay – Bhai, you are very unfair. You have accused her after all despite such a rational decision. I was of course already convinced about her intelligence, now I'm a devotee. This verdict has decided my fate. Prabhu, even in my dreams I didn't expect that I'd so easily become a slave to desire. I have strayed from my path. My self-restraint has deserted me like a treacherous friend at the first opportunity of being tested. I know full well that I'm going to pluck the stars from the sky; I'm going to eat the fruit that's forbidden to me. I know very well, Prabhu, that I'm going to sacrifice my life at the altar of despair. I'm going to wound my venerable mother's heart deeply. I'm going to drown the boat of my honour in the sea of shame. I'm going to renounce my high ambitions. But my inner being doesn't reproach me for this. Sophie can never be mine but I've become hers and will remain only hers all my life.

Prabhu – Vinay, Sophie will not stay here for even a moment if she gets to know about this. I hope she doesn't commit suicide. For God's sake, don't act in this destructive manner.

Vinay – No Prabhu, very soon I'll go away from here and never return. Let my heart burn to ashes but even the flames won't touch Sophie. I'll be in some country far away and worship this devi of knowledge, intelligence and purity. I tell you the truth, there's not a whit of lust in my love. This devotion is enough to give meaning to my life. Don't think that I'm abandoning my dharma of service. No, that won't happen. Even now I'll follow the path of service. The only difference will be that I'll worship the concrete instead of the abstract, the visible instead of the invisible.

Jahnavi came in suddenly and said – Vinay, could you go to Indu? There's been no news of her for several days. I fear she may be ill. She's never taken so long to send a letter.

Vinay got ready. He wore a kurta, took a stick and left. Prabhu wondered whether or not to tell Sophie about Vinay. When Sophie saw him looking worried she asked – Did kunwar sahib say anything?

Prabhu – He didn't say anything about that topic but I could never have imagined the feelings that he expressed for you.

Sophie looked down for a moment before replying – I understand. I should have understood earlier, but I'm not worried about it. This feeling germinated in my heart when on the fourth day after coming here I opened my eyes and in that semi-conscious state I found the figure of a god standing before me and looking affectionately at me. That look and that figure are imprinted on my heart to this day and will always remain so.

Prabhu – Sophie, don't you feel embarrassed saying this?

Sophia – No, I don't. It's nothing to feel embarrassed about. It's a matter of pride for me that he considers me worthy of his love. There's no embarrassment in being the recipient of the love of such a saintly, inspired man, who is the very incarnation of sacrifice. If any woman should feel pride on receiving the offering of love, I am that woman. This was the boon for which I was patiently doing tap in my mind all these days. I've received that boon today; for me it's something to rejoice in, not to feel embarrassed about.

Prabhu – Despite religious opposition?

Sophia – This thought is for those whose love is mingled with desire. There's the same difference between love and desire as between gold and glass. Love's boundary merges into devotion, there's only a difference of degree between the two. Devotion has more respect and love has a greater degree of the sentiment of service. Religious difference is not a fetter for love. Such obstacles are for the disposition whose goal is marriage, not for the love whose end is sacrifice.

Prabhu – I've warned you, be ready to leave this place.

Sophia – But there's no need to mention this to anybody at home.

Prabhu – Don't worry about it.

Sophia – Has anything been decided about when he intends to leave?

Prabhu – Preparations are being made. It won't be good for Vinay if raniji gets to know about this. I won't be surprised if she complains to mama.

Sophia proudly raised her head and replied – Prabhu, why are you speaking so childishly? Love is a mantra for fearlessness. The devotee of love is liberated from all worldly worries and obstacles.

When Prabhu had left, Sophia shut her book and went to the garden to lie on the green grass. Today she experienced a strange glory, an inexplicable beauty, a transcendental lustre in the swaying flowers, in the gentle breeze, in the chorus of the chirping birds on the trees, in the red glow of the sky. She had obtained the jewel of love.

A week went by but Vinay had still not left for Rajputana. He kept postponing his departure on some pretext or the other. There were no preparations to be made yet they had not been completed. It was now evident to both Vinay and Sophia that when there is love between man and woman it's not as easy to separate it from desire as they had thought. Sophia would go and sit in the garden every morning with a book tucked under her arm. In the evenings too, she would sit there and not go anywhere else. Vinay would also inevitably be seen at a little distance from her, reading or writing something, playing with the dog, or conversing with friends. Both of them would glance furtively at each other but were too embarrassed to start a conversation. Both felt shy but understood the implication of this language of silence, which they had not known earlier. There was only one longing, one restlessness, one flame in both their hearts. The language of silence did not comfort them but neither of them had the courage to start a conversation. Both would think up new speeches to express their love and forget them when they saw each other. Both held on to their vows and were idealistic but while one had no wish to look at doctrinal treatises, the other had no time to give a lecture to the society on his chosen topic. For both, the trial of love was in fact proving to be its stimulant.

One night, after dinner, Sophia was sitting next to Jahnavi and reading out from a newspaper when Vinay came and sat down. Sophia's condition became strange. She would forget the point up to which she had read and would stumble upon and repeat the sentences she had already read out. Her eyes couldn't focus on the words. She wanted to forget that there was somebody else in the room besides the rani but without even glancing at Vinay she knew, almost with a supernatural knowledge, that he was gazing at her and she immediately began to feel restless. Jahnavi interrupted her several times. 'Do you fall off to sleep? Why do you keep stopping? What's the matter with you today, beti?' Suddenly her gaze turned to Vinay at the very moment that he was staring at Sophie with ardent love. Jahnavi's cheerful, calm face flushed, as if a garden had been set on fire. With blazing eyes she turned to Vinay and asked, 'When are you leaving?'

Vinay – Very soon.

Jahnavi – My understanding of very soon is tomorrow morning.

Vinay – Several volunteers who are going with me are away right now.

Jahnavi – Don't worry. They'll go afterwards, you must leave tomorrow.

Vinay – As you wish.

Jahnavi – Go and inform everyone immediately. I want you to get a darshan of the sun at the station.

Vinay – I have to go and meet Indu.

Jahnavi – There's no need. The custom of meeting and embracing is for women, not for men, so just leave.

Vinay didn't have the courage to say anything after this; quietly, he got up and left. Sophie picked up the courage to say – It must be raining fire in Rajputana these days.

Jahnavi said decisively – Duty never cares about fire or water. Go, you should also sleep now, you have to get up in the morning.

Sophie stayed up the whole night. Her heart yearned to meet Vinay once. 'Ah! He'll go away tomorrow and I won't be able to say goodbye.' She would repeatedly peep out of the window hoping to get an inkling of Vinay's presence. She went to the roof to look; there was darkness, the stars laughed at her ardour. Time and again, she felt a strong impulse to jump down from the roof on to the garden, go to his room, and say, 'I'm yours.' 'Ah! Why would he have been so worried if religious doctrines hadn't placed obstacles in our way? Why would I feel so embarrassed? Why would the rani have rejected me? She would have happily accepted me if I'd been a Rajputani but I'm to be rejected because I'm a follower of Jesus. There's so much similarity between Jesus and Krishna, but so many differences among their followers! Who can tell how many atrocities have been inflicted on our souls by sectarian differences?'

As the night passed, Sophie became increasingly more despondent – Hai! If I remain sitting like this, it will soon be morning and Vinay will leave. There's no one through whom I can send him a letter. He has been given this punishment only because of me. A mother's heart is cruel. I thought only I was unfortunate, but now I realize that there are other mothers like mine!

She went down from the roof and lay down in her room. Despair took refuge in sleep but sleep is a mockery of desire—without peace and arid. She had just slept for a short while when she woke up with a start. Sunlight had spread in her room and Vinay was standing outside with several companions, ready to leave for the station. The garden was crowded with thousands of men.

She quickly reached the garden and, parting the crowd, stood in front of the travellers. The national anthem was being sung, the travellers were ready to leave, with bare heads, bare feet, wearing kurtas, bags slung around their necks and sticks in their hands. They were all happy, full of enthusiasm and intoxicated with the pride of nationalism. Jahnavi put saffron tilaks on their foreheads.

Kunwar Bharat Singh then garlanded them. Dr Ganguly gave them instructions in carefully chosen words. The travellers left after that. Cries of rejoicing uttered by thousands of voices reverberated in the atmosphere. A group of men and women followed them. Sophia stood still like a statue, watching. She was tormented by the desire to go along with these travellers to serve her fellow beings in distress. Her eyes were fixed on Vinay. Suddenly Vinay's eyes also turned towards her; there was so much despair in them, such heart-rending pain, so much helplessness, so much humility! He was walking behind all the travellers, very slowly, as if his feet were bound by chains. Sophia trailed the travellers, oblivious of her condition and reached the road. She came to the crossroads and then to some raja's huge palace but was still unaware that she had followed them. She could not see anything except Vinay. Some strong attraction kept drawing her on. So much so that she reached the crossroads near the station. Suddenly Prabhu's voice reached her ears; he was driving the phaeton very fast. He asked – Sophie, where are you going? You are not even wearing shoes, only slippers.

Sophia felt deeply embarrassed. She thought, 'Ah! Where have I come in this apparel? I wasn't even conscious.' She said, shyly – Nowhere really.

Prabhu – Do you want to go to the station with these people? Come, sit on the gharry. I'm going there too. I just came to know that these people are leaving and quickly got the gharry ready, else I wouldn't have been able to meet them.

Sophia – I've come so far, without the slightest inkling of where I was going.

Prabhu – Why don't you sit? Come to the station since you've come so far.

Sophia – I won't go to the station. I'll return from here.

Prabhu – I'll come on my way back from the station. You'll have to come home with me today.

Sophia – I won't go there.

Prabhu – Grandfather will be angry. He has been very insistent about your returning today.

Sophia – I won't step into that house until mama herself comes to fetch me.

She turned back and Prabhu went on towards the station. On reaching the station, Vinay looked all around eagerly but Sophie was not there. Prabhu whispered into his ear – She came up to the dharmashala wearing her nightclothes, but returned from there. Do write a letter when you reach, otherwise she'll land up in Rajputana!

Ecstatically, Vinay said – I'm taking only my body and leaving my heart here.

10

ENMITY HAS A PROFOUND EFFECT UPON CHILDREN AS DOES LOVE. Mitthua and Gheesoo had begun to think of Tahir Ali as an enemy ever since they had come to know that he was forcibly going to take away their field. They were unaware of the discussions between raja sahib and Soordas. Soordas himself was apprehensive that the problem would arise again despite raja sahib's assurance. John Sevak would not let go easily. Bajrangi, Nayakram and the others also discussed these matters. Mitthua and Gheesoo would listen to these discussions attentively and their enmity would become even more vehement. Gheesoo would shout loudly whenever he took the buffaloes to the field, 'Let's see who'll take away our land. I'll pick him up and fling him down so hard that he'll remember it. I'll break both his legs. Does he think that it's just a game?' Gheesoo was quite brave and he used to wrestle. Bajrangi himself had been a good wrestler in his youth. He wanted to make Gheesoo the leader of the city's wrestlers so that the Punjabi wrestlers wouldn't have the courage to slap their arms as a challenge; he would go far afield to fight and people would say, 'He's Bajrangi's son.' He had already begun to send Gheesoo to the wrestling ground to learn. Gheesoo became arrogant and thought that he could fell anyone with the tricks he knew. Mitthua didn't wrestle but sometimes sat near the wrestling ground; just that was enough for him to boast about his wrestling! Whenever they saw Tahir Ali anywhere, they would both chant, 'There goes the enemy, his face is black.' Mitthua would say, 'Jai Shankar, neither a thorn nor a pebble will hurt; harass the enemy.' Gheesoo would chime in, 'Bam Bhola,* the enemy has a swollen belly; he can't say anything.'

Tahir would listen to their frivolous comments and ignore them. 'Why bandy words with the boys?' he'd think. 'What can I do to them if they abuse me?' The lads would imagine that he was too afraid to speak and would become lion-like in their bravado. Gheesoo would

---

* Jai Shankar; Bam Bhola: Terms of address to Shiva.

practise with Mitthua the tricks with which to fling down Tahir. 'First catch hold of this hand and pull it towards me; then put the other one around his neck and trip his leg . . . And so, flat on the back!' Mitthua would immediately fall down, and Gheesoo would be convinced about the unique power of this trick.

One day, they decided to harass miyaanji's sons. They went to the field, called Zahir and Zabir to play and slapped them many times. Zabir was small so Mitthua pressed him down. Zahir and Gheesoo were equals but Gheesoo defeated Zahir in a moment with his wrestling tactics. Mitthua began to pinch Zabir; the poor thing started crying. Gheesoo gave Zahir several glancing blows. He too was stunned. He began to cry for help when he realized that Gheesoo was bent upon killing him. Hearing the wails of these two, the tiny Sabir came up brashly with a thin branch to help the afflicted ones and began to hit Gheesoo. When it had no effect, he used a weapon that was more hurtful—he began to spit on Gheesoo. Gheesoo let go of Zahir and gave Sabir a few slaps. Using this opportunity, but with more caution this time, Zahir clung to Gheesoo. There was a wrestling match between the two. Eventually Gheesoo again flung him down and tied his arms behind his back. Zahir now couldn't think of any other stratagem except to cry, which is the last resort of the weak. The distressed cries of all three boys reached Mahir Ali. He was getting ready to go to school. He immediately flung down his books and ran towards the field. He saw that Zabir and Zahir were lying down and wailing and Sabir was whining by himself. The blood of his noble family began to boil in his veins. 'I, a Sayyad, the son of a police officer, the brother of an excise clerk, a student of English in the eighth class! And this foolish, uncouth brat of an aheer . . . He has the guts to humiliate my brothers!' He gave Gheesoo a kick and several slaps to Mitthua. Mitthua began to cry but Gheesoo was tough. He left Zahir and got up. His morale was high since he had won two rounds; slapping his arms, he clung to Mahir. Mahir's white pajamas got dirty, there was dust on the shoes that he had polished just that day, his combed hair was dishevelled. Furious, he pushed Gheesoo so hard that Gheesoo staggered back a couple of steps and fell down. Sabir, Zabir and Zahir began to laugh. Boys' wounds disappear with revenge. Seeing them laugh, Gheesoo flared up even more. He got up again and clung to Mahir. Mahir caught hold of his throat and began to throttle him. Gheesoo thought, 'Now I'll die, he won't let me go until he kills me.' What won't a dying person do? He bit Mahir's hand, digging into it with three teeth; blood began to flow. Mahir screamed, and letting go of Gheesoo's neck, tried to free his hand. But Gheesoo refused to let go on any account. On seeing the blood flow, the three brothers started crying again. Zainab and Raqiya came to the door on hearing this din. When they saw that the battlefield was inundated with blood, they went to Tahir, hurling abuses. Zainab taunted him, 'You are sitting here clawing hides . . . Are you aware of what's going on around you? That aheer's lad is making our sons' blood flow. I would suck out that wretch's blood if only I could catch hold of him.'

Raqiya – Is that wretch a human being or the son of a demon? He has bitten Mahir's hand so hard that there are fountains of blood flowing. Any other man would have buried him alive.

Zainab – If only there had been somebody of our own, he would have chewed alive this fellow with a shaven head.

Tahir ran towards the field anxiously. He was beside himself when he saw Mahir's clothes soaked in blood. Catching hold of Gheesoo's ears, he pulled them hard and gave him several slaps. Mitthua saw that it was now his turn to be beaten, they had lost the field; he began to run, hurling abuses. Gheesoo also began to abuse. City lads are adept in the art of abusing. He kept shouting new, choice abuses to which Tahir responded with slaps. Mitthua went to Bajrangi and informed him of the battle. 'They have all got together and are beating Gheesoo, blood is flowing from his mouth. He had taken the buffaloes to graze, and all the three boys had come there and made the buffaloes run. When Gheesoo tried to stop them, they got together to beat him, and now burre miyaan has also joined them.' Bajrangi was furious when he heard this. He had given Tahir fifty rupees and had begun to think of the field as his own. He picked up his cudgel and ran. He saw that Tahir was binding Gheesoo's hands and feet. Infuriated, he said, 'Enough, munshiji! Go away if you want your welfare or I'll make you forget all your bravado. I'm not afraid of going to jail, I'll spend a year or two there but I won't leave you fit for anything. The land is not your father's. That's why I gave you fifty rupees. Were they unlawfully earned? Enough! Just go away now or I'll chew you alive . . . My name is Bajrangi.'

Before Tahir could reply Gheesoo, having gained courage on seeing his father, leapt forcefully, picked up a stone and threw it at Tahir. Tahir's head would have been split had he not ducked in time. Before Gheesoo could pick up another stone, Tahir leapt and caught hold of his hand, twisting it so hard that Gheesoo fell down wailing, 'Ah, I'm dying! Ah, I'm dying!' Bajrangi now lost his self-control. He sprang and hit Tahir so hard with his cudgel that Tahir was knocked down, quivering. Several chamaars who, until then, had thought this to be a fight among the boys, ran and caught hold of Bajrangi on seeing Tahir fall down. There was silence on the battlefield. Yes, Zainab and Raqiya were standing at the door letting forth a volley of words: 'This one with a shaven head has done something terrible, may Khuda's wrath fall upon him, may he not be fated to see another day, may his bier be carried away, why doesn't somebody go and inform sahib . . .? Arey-arey you chamaars, why are you just sitting and staring, why don't you go and inform sahib? Tell him to come at once. Bring him with you, tell him to bring the police, we are not here to give our lives . . .!'

Bajrangi took hold of himself on seeing Tahir fall down and didn't raise his hand again. He caught hold of Gheesoo's hand and went home. There was mayhem in the house here. Two chamaars went to John Sevak's bungalow. Some people picked up Tahir, put him on a cot and brought him into the room. His shoulder had been hit with the cudgel, so the bone was probably broken. He was still unconscious. The chamaars quickly ground some haldi, mixed it with gur and choona and applied the paste to his shoulder. One man leapt and plucked some castor-oil leaves from a tree; two of them began to foment the shoulder. Zainab and Raqiya began to dress and bandage Tahir's wounds but Kulsoom stood at the door crying; she couldn't bear to look at her husband. His head had been wounded because of the fall and blood had congealed on his forehead. His hair was matted, like dried paint on an artist's brush. There was a sharp pain in her heart. But as soon as she saw her husband's face, she almost fainted, so she stood at a distance, thinking, 'Perhaps all these people imagine that I don't love my husband at all and I'm just standing here, watching the spectacle. What can I do? I don't know what's happened to his face.' The same face whose misfortunes we would once have take upon ourselves becomes fearsome after death; we need to strengthen ourselves to look at it. Death too, like life, casts its most singular light on the face. All day long, Tahir was fomented and bandaged; the chamaars ran to and fro as if he were a close friend. Practical sympathy is a special trait of villagers. The chamaars sat by him all night to foment and bandage. Raqiya and Zainab kept taunting Kulsoom, 'Behen, you have a strange heart. Your husband's condition is so bad and you are sitting here comfortably. Our lives would be at the tips of our fingers if our husband had the slightest headache. Women these days have hearts of stone.' These arrows would pierce Kulsoom's heart, but she didn't have the courage to ask, 'Then why don't the two of you go? After all you too live off his earnings, much more than I do.' But where would she escape if she said as much? Both of them would be at her throat. She stayed awake the whole night, going to the door several times to get some inkling of Tahir's condition. Somehow, the night passed. Tahir woke up early in the morning; he was still groaning with pain but his condition was not that serious now. He sat up and rested against the pillow. Kulsoom heard him speaking with the chamaars. She felt that his voice was somewhat distorted. When the chamaars saw that he was conscious, they realized that they were no longer needed and it was now time for his wife to look after him. They left one by one. Kulsoom cautiously came and sat near her husband. On seeing her, Tahir said feebly, 'Khuda has punished us for ingratitude. The very people because of whom we thought ill of our aaka are now our enemies.'

Kulsoom – Why don't you leave this job? There will be some quarrel or the other until the land dispute is settled and people's enmity will increase. We are not here to give our lives. Khuda will give us a livelihood just as he has done all these days. At least our lives will be safe.

Tahir – Life will be safe but how will we live? Who else will give so much? You can see how good, educated people are wandering around wretchedly.

Kulsoom – It won't matter if we don't get so much; at least we'll get half the amount. We'll eat only once a day, not twice, but our lives won't be jeopardized.

Tahir – You may be happy if you eat only once a day but there are other people in the house as well. Who will listen to their complaints every day? I'm not my own enemy, but I'm helpless. Whatever Khuda wishes will happen.

Kulsoom – Will you give your life for the sake of the family?

Tahir – What are you saying? They are not strangers. They are our brothers and our mothers. Who else will take care of them if I don't?

Kulsoom – You perhaps imagine that they depend on you, but they don't care a bit about you. They think that there's no need for them to touch their own treasure as long as they can get everything free. My children hanker for every paisa while they get handis full of mithai which their boys enjoy. I can only look on and shut my eyes.

Tahir – I'm doing my duty. Why should I regret it if they have money? Let them enjoy what they eat and live comfortably. Your words stink of jealousy. For Khuda's sake, don't talk to me like this.

Kulsoom – You'll regret it. You get angry with me when I try to make you understand but you'll see, nobody will even ask how you are.

Tahir – All this is the fault of your motives.

Kulsoom – Yes, I'm a woman, so how can I have any intelligence? You are lying here and no one has even peeped in. They wouldn't have remained sitting peacefully had they really been anxious.

There was an unbearable pain in Tahir's shoulder when he turned over. He began to scream 'aah-aah' and there was sweat on his brow. Kulsoom asked anxiously – Why don't we send for the doctor? Perhaps your bone is injured.

Tahir – Yes, I'm also afraid of this. But how will I pay the doctor's fee?

Kulsoom – You have just received your salary. Has it been spent so fast?

Tahir – It hasn't been spent but there's no scope for the doctor's fee. This time, three months' fees will have to be paid for Mahir. Twelve rupees will be spent on the fees, leaving only eighteen rupees. And there's the whole month still left. Should we starve?

Kulsoom – The demand for Mahir's fees is always weighing on your mind. Wasn't it given just ten days ago?

Tahir – Not ten days but a month ago.

Kulsoom – The fees won't be given this time. The doctor's fee is more important. He won't bring prosperity to my house when he begins earning after completing his studies. I can depend only on you.

Tahir (*Changing the topic*) – These villains won't stop their mischief until they are strongly rebuked.

Kulsoom – Mahir was responsible for all the mischief; there's always fighting and quarrelling among boys. Would things have got so out of hand if he hadn't gone there? On top of that you flared up just because the aheer's lad bit him.

Tahir – It was as if I was possessed by a demon the moment I saw the blood.

Meanwhile Gheesoo's mother Jamuni arrived. Zainab called her as soon as she saw her and scolded her – It seems as if disaster is going to fall on you.

Jamuni – Begum sahib, it's not disaster but bad days, what else can I say? I heard about all this when I returned after selling yesterday's curd. I ran here straightaway to be at your service but finding several people gathered here, I returned, feeling embarrassed. I didn't go to sell curd today. I've come here feeling very scared. Forgive the wrong that's been done or we'll be ruined. We don't have anywhere to go.

Zainab – We can't do anything now. Sahib won't listen without filing a lawsuit and if he doesn't, we will. Are we dhuniyas and julahas? How will we maintain our honour if we let ourselves be oppressed by all and sundry? Miyaan's father was a thanedar; the whole area trembled at his name; eminent rais would stand before him with folded hands. Have his children become so worthless that inferior people can insult them? Your brat bit Mahir so hard that he was smeared with blood; he's lying bandaged. The misunderstanding could have been cleared if your husband had come and scolded the lad. But he gave a blow with his cudgel as soon as he arrived. We are respectable people; we can't be so lenient.

Raqiya – They'll come to their senses when the police beat them black and blue, besides the favours and bribes that they will have to give. Then they'll get to know the cost of atta and daal.

Jamuni too had her share of pragmatism from her husband. Undaunted by the threats, she replied – Begum sahib, where do we have so much money? We have managed to save five or ten rupees by mixing milk and water. That's our limit. What's left now in this livelihood? Three paseri of straw cost a rupee. A buffalo's belly can't be filled with just one rupee. Oilcakes, cotton seeds, bran, husk are all needed on top of that. Somehow we survive. I'll feed your children with milk for six months or a year.

Zainab realized that this aheeran was no novice. A different mantra would have to be used for her. Screwing up her nose, she said – Keep your milk at home, we don't need milk or ghee. This land will soon be ours; I can rear as many animals as I want. But I'm telling you that you won't be able to sit at home from tomorrow. The report is in sahib's hands. But Khuda has given us such knowledge that we have only to draw a magic picture and cast a spell over it and the demons will begin their work. Once when our husband was alive, there was an argument with an important English officer in the police. He said that he would throw us out. Miyaan said you won't rest in peace if you throw us out. Miyaan came and spoke to me. That very night I drew a horse with white eyes and cast a spell. His memsahib had a miscarriage with the foetus fully developed. He came running, fawned, fell at miyaan's feet, persuaded miyaan to forgive his mistake, only then was the mem's life saved. Why, Raqiya, don't you remember?

Raqiya – Of course I remember. I was the one who read the prayer. Sahib called at the door during the night.

Zainab – As far as we are concerned, we don't wish anybody ill but when our lives are at stake we teach such a lesson that it's never forgotten. Khuda knows what calamity may fall if we speak to our peer. Do you remember, Raqiya, when an aheer gave him milk mixed with water? All he said was – Go, may Khuda deal with you. When the aheer returned home, he saw that his buffalo worth 200 rupees had died.

Jamuni lost her wits on hearing this. Like other women, she was far more afraid of devils and demons than of prisons, police, courts and durbars. There were daily opportunities for witnessing the acts of demons in the neighbourhood. She believed also that the yantra and mantra of mullahs were far more effective. Zainab had revealed her intelligence in her subject by guessing Jamuni's fear of demons. Jamuni said fearfully, 'No begum sahib, God has given you children as well. Don't torture me or I'll die.'

Zainab – We shouldn't do this, we shouldn't do that, then how will we maintain our honour? Suppose your aheer arrives here with a cudgel again tomorrow, then? He won't be capable of carrying a cudgel if Khuda so wishes it.

Trembling, Jamuni fell at their feet and said – Bibi, I'm prepared to do anything you order.

Zainab gave one blow after another. After Jamuni's continuous crying and pleading, she agreed to take 425 rupees from her to give her the boon of protection from demons. Jamuni went home, brought the money and fell at her feet but she didn't tell Bajrangi about it. After she left, Zainab laughed and said, 'When Khuda gives, he gives miraculously. We hadn't thought of her at all. You get impatient otherwise I would have twisted some more. The rider should always keep a tight rein.'

Sabir then came and said to Zainab – Abba is calling you. When Zainab went there she found Tahir groaning. She said to Kulsoom – Bibi, you have a strange heart. Arey, good woman, go and cook some moong daal. The poor man didn't eat anything at night. What will his condition be if he doesn't eat even now?

Tahir – No, I don't want to eat anything. I've troubled you to ask if you could lend me some money if you have it. My shoulder is paining a lot, perhaps there's a broken bone. I want to show it to the doctor but I need money to pay his fees.

Zainab – Beta, just think, I swear on your head, from where will I get money? But why do you want to call the doctor? You should go straight to sahib. This uproar has happened only because of him, else why would anyone be concerned with us? Call an ikka and go to sahib. He'll write a note and you can be treated in a government hospital. You should realize this for yourself. Do we have the means to call a doctor?

Tahir took this to heart. He thanked his mother and wondered why he hadn't thought of this earlier. He called an ikka, sat on it with great difficulty with the help of his stick and reached sahib's bungalow.

After meeting Raja Mahendra Kumar, John Sevak had gone out of town to sell the shares of the company and had returned three days ago. He had met raja sahib again the day before and was very disappointed when he heard his decision. He argued for a long time but raja sahib didn't give a satisfactory answer. He returned disappointed and narrated the entire incident to Mrs Sevak.

Mrs Sevak was averse to Indians. Although she had been born and bred in this country, she thought that she had been liberated from all the vices of the Indians after taking shelter in Christ. In her opinion, God had completely deprived the inhabitants here of all the divine qualities such as decency, sensitivity, generosity and refinement. She was a devotee of European culture and lifestyle. Her modes of eating, dressing and living were all English. The one thing she couldn't do anything about was her dark complexion. She couldn't attain her wish despite the constant use of soap and other chemicals. Her one ambition was to move out of the category of Christians and to mix with the English; people should regard them as sahibs, their social interaction should be with the English, their sons should marry Anglo-Indians or at least Eurasians of a high class. Sophie had been given an English education but despite her mother's fervent pleas she wouldn't go to English parties and hated dancing. However, Mrs Sevak didn't miss these opportunities; if she didn't get her way, she would make a special effort to get invitations. If there were few dinners and parties at their house, it was because of Ishvar Sevak's miserliness.

On hearing this news, Mrs Sevak said – Have you now seen the 'decency' of Indians? You were beside yourself with happiness. Now you know how wicked and deceitful these people are. This is the respect you have compared to that given to a blind beggar! These people have imbibed partisanship from infancy and such is the state of these eminent people who are considered leaders of society and of whose liberalism people are proud. I had once talked to Mr Clark. He ordered all the tehseeldars to increase the cultivation of tobacco in their areas. This is the reward for Sophie's jumping into the fire! Just a little power in the municipality has turned their heads. Mr Clark had told me that if raja sahib doesn't settle the affair of the land, he'll get it for you legally.

Mr Joseph* Clark was a district officer. He had come here only a few days ago. Mrs Sevak had established social relations with him. Actually she had chosen him for Sophie and had invited him home a couple of times. Sophie had met him twice or three times before

---

* Clark's name is later changed to William. Premchand does not seem to have realized this error.

she had left home but wasn't particularly attracted to him. In spite of that, Mrs Sevak was not disappointed. She would say to Clark, 'Sophie has gone visiting.' This way she used every opportunity to fan the flame of his love.

John Sevak said with embarrassment – How was I to know that this gentleman would deceive me? He's very renowned here. He's known to be true to his word. Anyway, it doesn't matter. We'll have to think of another plan.

Mrs Sevak – I'll speak with Mr Clark. I'll also ask padri sahib to intercede.

John Sevak – Clark doesn't have the right to interfere in the municipality's affairs.

While John Sevak was worrying about this, he got news of the uproar. Stunned, he reported the matter to the police. The next day, he was just planning to go to the godown when Tahir Ali arrived, tapping his stick, and immediately sat down on a chair, half-dead because of the jolts from the ikka.

Mrs Sevak (*In English*) – Just look at his face, as if a mountain of misfortune has fallen on him.

John Sevak – Munshiji, it seems that you've been badly hurt. I'm sorry about it.

Tahir – Huzoor, just don't ask, the rascals left no stone unturned to kill me.

John Sevak – And you were interceding with me for these villains.

Tahir – Huzoor, I have been severely punished for my mistake. It seems that my neck-bone has been injured.

John Sevak – It's your fault. A broken bone is not a trivial thing; if it did break, you wouldn't have been able to come here. There's certainly some injury but it'll be all right if it's massaged for a few days. Why did this scuffle happen after all?

Tahir – Huzoor, it was all because of that devil Bajrangi the aheer.

John Sevak – But you can't be innocent just because you are hurt. It's because of your foolishness and carelessness. Why did you get involved with such people? Do you realize how much I have been humiliated because of this?

Tahir – But there was no excess on my part.

John Sevak – Of course there was. Villagers don't just come and provoke someone and fight. You should live in such a way that people are in awe of you, not as if any and everybody can have the guts to fight with you.

Mrs Sevak – It's nothing but his weakness. No one beats a passer-by.

Ishvar Sevak said from his chair – Son of Khuda, take me in your shelter; this is the punishment for not worshipping him with a true heart.

This conversation was like rubbing salt into the wound for Tahir Ali. He was so furious that he wanted to say then and there, 'To jahannum with your job!' But John Sevak thought of a way of making use of Tahir's misfortune. He got the phaeton prepared and took Tahir with him to Mahendra Kumar's house. Mahendra Kumar had just returned after taking a round of the city when John Sevak's card arrived. He was annoyed but he regained his composure and came out. Mr Sevak said, 'I'm sorry, you have been troubled at an inconvenient time, but the people of Pandeypur have raised such mayhem that I don't know to whom else I can turn. Yesterday all of them got together and attacked the godown. Perhaps they wanted to set it on fire. They couldn't do that but they attacked my agent here. They beat him and his brothers until they were unconscious. But they were still not satisfied and entered the women's quarters; there's no doubt that the women would have lost their honour, had they not bolted the door from inside. Tahir is so badly hurt that he probably won't be able to move for months. His shoulder bone is broken.'

Mahendra Kumar had a lot of respect for women. He would be furious if they were insulted. He asked fiercely – All of them entered the women's quarters?

John Sevak – They wanted to break open the door but they moved away when the chamaars threatened them.

Mahendra Kumar – These base people! They wanted to tyrannize women!

John Sevak – This is the most shameful aspect of this drama.

Mahendra Kumar – Not shameful sir, it's contemptible.

John Sevak – This poor man now says, accept my resignation or arrange security guards for the godown. The women are so afraid that they don't want to stay there even for a moment. This uproar has happened only because of that blind man.

Mahendra Kumar – He seems to be a very poor, straightforward man to me but he's crafty. I took pity on his poverty and decided to find some other land for you. But now that they have prepared themselves for mischief and want to remove you forcibly from there, they'll certainly be punished.

John Sevak – That's it, they want to throw me out. My godown will definitely be set on fire if there's leniency.

Mahendra Kumar – I understand very well. Although I believe in democracy and agree whole-heartedly with its principles, I'm a strong opponent of the unrest that has spread over the country in its name. Capitalism, dictatorship and all other isms are better than such democracy. Don't worry.

After some more conversation in a similar vein, John Sevak left, having poisoned raja sahib's mind to a great extent. On the way, Tahir thought – Sahib didn't feel at all embarrassed using my misfortune for his selfish ends. Can such wealthy, renowned, important, intellectual and learned people be so self-centred?

John Sevak guessed his feelings. He said – You must be wondering why I added so much colour to the events instead of narrating only the actual incident. But think of it this way, would I have got this result without exaggerating? Any good or ill in this world depends on the success of the work. One person may oppose the government. He's called a traitor if the officials defeat him but he's considered to be the nation's saviour if he attains his aim. Memorials are built to him. Success has an extraordinary power to erase crimes. You know what Mustafa Kemal was two years ago? A rebel, whose blood the country thirsted for. Now he's the soul of his country. Why? Because his cherished desire was fulfilled. But several years ago, he had run away to America, fearing for his life. Today he's the chief because his rebellion was successful. I brought raja sahib over to my side, so what's wrong if I exaggerated?

Meanwhile, the phaeton reached the bungalow. Ishvar Sevak immediately asked – Well, what have you achieved?

John proudly said – I've made the raja my disciple. Of course I had to add a little colour, but the effect was very positive.

Ishvar – God have mercy on me. Beta, can anything be done in this world without adding colour? This is the root mantra of success and it's essential for business. You may have the best possible object but no client will even look at it unless you eulogize it. It's not a bad thing to call your nice object invaluable, rare or unique. There's no harm in saying that your medicine is comparable to ambrosia, or that it is Ramabaan, an elixir, the boon of a rishi, sanjeevani, whatever you like. Ask any preacher, lawyer or writer, they'll all say that exaggeration and success are synonymous. It's a mistake to think that only artists need colour. You must be sure now that you'll get the land.

John – Yes, there's no doubt now. (*To Prabhu, tauntingly*) – Why are you just sitting there? Why don't you go to Pandeypur? How can I go on helping you if you continue like this?

Prabhu – I don't object to going but right now I have to go to Sophie.

John – You can easily go to Sophie on your way back from Pandeypur.

Prabhu – I think it's more important to meet Sophie.

John – What's the use of your meeting her every day when you still haven't been able to bring her back home?

Prabhu was on the verge of saying, 'I can't put out the fire that mama has lit.' He immediately went to his room, changed his clothes and was ready to set out at once to Pandeypur with Tahir. It was eleven o'clock, the earth was spitting fire, lunch was ready but he didn't stay for it despite his parents' pleas. Tahir was praying to Khuda that somehow the afternoon could be spent here. His pain was greatly soothed by the cool breeze blowing through the sieves of the screens under the fan but Prabhu's obstinacy deprived him of this pleasure.

11

BHAIRO PAASI WAS A DUTIFUL SON. AS FAR AS POSSIBLE, HE WOULD see to his mother's comfort. Fearing that his wife would starve her mother-in-law, he would have her food served in his presence and sit with her while she ate. The old woman was fond of smoking tobacco for which he brought her a beautiful coconut chillum gilded with brass. He would make her sleep on the khaat even if he himself had to sleep on the floor. He would say, 'Goodness knows how many difficulties she must have faced to bring me up; I can't repay my debt to her as long as I live.' If his mother had a headache he would anxiously call sorcerers and exorcists. The old woman was also fond of jewels and clothes. She wanted to enjoy under her son's rule the comforts of which she had been deprived under her husband's. Bhairo got several ornaments made for her such as heavy bangles and a collar-necklace. Instead of coarse cloth, he would get some printed fabric for her to wear. He had given strict instructions to his wife to see to it that amma suffered no discomfort. This was why the old woman felt emboldened. She would be offended if the most trivial thing went against her wishes and would rebuke her bahu, whose name was Subhagi [one who is lucky]. The old woman had named her Abhagi [one who is unlucky]. She would harass her bahu if there was the slightest delay in filling the chillum or if she forgot to make the bed, press her feet or pick the lice from her head as soon as she was ordered to do so. She would curse and defame her father and her brothers, and if she was not satisfied only with abuses, she would exaggerate everything a hundredfold as soon as Bhairo returned from the shop. Infuriated, Bhairo would sometimes sharply rebuke Subhagi or beat her with a stick. Jagdhar and he were close friends and, although Bhairo's house was on the western side of the basti and Jagdhar's on the eastern, Jagdhar visited him frequently. He got to drink for free the toddy that he couldn't afford. He had several dependants—a wife, five daughters and a son—but he was the only one who earned. How could there be enough profit from hawking to feed so many people and also to drink toddy and liquor? Subhagi resented him because he would always agree with everything that Bhairo said.

One winter night, two or three years ago, Bhairo and Jagdhar were sitting together drinking toddy. The old woman, having eaten, was warming herself before the mud stove. Bhairo said to Subhagi, 'Get some roasted peas, and also some salt, chillies and onions.' They needed to eat something spicy with the toddy. Subhagi roasted the peas but there were no onions in the house. She didn't have the courage to admit this. She ran to the greengrocer's shop but he had already shut it and wouldn't open it despite Subhagi's repeated pleas. Helplessly, she put the roasted peas in front of Bhairo. Bhairo was furious when he saw that there were no onions. He said, 'Do you think I'm a bullock that you have brought only roasted peas? Why haven't you brought onions?

Subhagi retorted – There are no onions in the house, so should I become one?

Jagdhar – Will the peas taste good without onions?

The old woman – A dhela's worth of onions had come only yesterday. Nothing remains in this house. Does this witch have a belly or an oven?

Subhagi – I can swear that I didn't so much as touch the onions. I couldn't have subsisted even for a day in this house if I had such an appetite.

Bhairo – If there were no onions, why didn't you bring some?

Jagdhar – If something isn't there in the house, you should take care of it.

Subhagi – How was I to know that you would hanker for onions today in the middle of the night?

Bhairo was drunk with the toddy. Intoxication is like anger. It's vented only on the weak. He picked up the stick that was lying nearby and hit Subhagi with it. All the bangles on her arm were broken. She ran from the house and Bhairo ran after her. Subhagi hid by the side of a shop. Bhairo tried very hard to find her but didn't succeed, so he returned home, bolted the door and didn't bother about her again throughout the night. Subhagi thought that if she now returned home she would lose her life. But where could she spend the night? She went to Bajrangi's house. He said, 'No, baba, I won't harbour this illness.

He's a spiteful man. Who wants to pick a fight with him?' Thakurdeen's doors were shut. Soordas was cooking. She entered his hut and said, 'Soorey, let me stay here the night. He keeps beating me and won't spare a single bone if I return now.'

Soordas replied – Come, lie down here. You can leave in the morning. He must be drunk right now.

The next day, when Bhairo got to know about this, he began abusing Soordas and threatened to kill him. Subhagi began to feel affection for Soordas from that day. She would come and sit with him whenever she got the opportunity. At times, she would sweep the floor or give him something stealthily, without her family's knowledge. She would call Mitthua to her house and give him gur and gram to eat.

Bhairo saw her coming out of Soordas's house several times. Jagdhar found them talking to each other. Bhairo began to suspect that there was a liaison between them. Ever since then, he was jealous of Soordas. He would provoke him and fight with him. He couldn't beat him up because he was afraid of Nayakram. His oppression of Subhagi increased day by day and Jagdhar, though peace-loving, would side with Bhairo.

On the day of the fight between Bajrangi and Tahir, there was also a squabble between Bhairo and Soordas. The old woman had taken her bath in the afternoon but Subhagi had forgotten to rinse out her dhoti. It was summer; the old woman began to feel hot again at nine in the night. She used to bathe twice a day during the summer and once in two months in the winter! Subhagi remembered the dhoti only when the old woman asked for it after her bath. She was pale with fear. With folded hands she said, 'Amma, I forgot to wash the dhoti today. Wear mine for a short while and I'll rinse it out and dry it.

The old woman was not that forgiving; she hurled abuses and sat there wearing the wet dhoti. Meanwhile Bhairo returned from the shop and said to Subhagi – Bring the food soon, there's going to be a gathering today. Amma, you also come and eat.

The old woman said – I'm sitting here wearing a wet dhoti after my bath. From now on I'll wash my dhoti myself.

Bhairo – Didn't she wash your dhoti?

The old woman – Why will she wash my dhoti now? She's the maalkin of the house. Isn't it enough that she gives me a roti to eat?

Subhagi made several apologies but Bhairo didn't listen. He picked up a stick and started beating her. Subhagi ran into Soordas's house. Bhairo also went after her, entered the hut, caught hold of Subhagi's hand and tried to pull her away but Soordas stood up and asked – What's the matter, Bhairo, why are you beating her?

Bhairo said angrily – Move away from the door or I'll break your bones first, and then all your hypocrisy will disappear. I've been watching your airs for quite some time. I'll get even with you today.

Soordas – What airs of mine have you seen? Just that I haven't turned Subhagi out of my house?

Bhairo – Bas, it'll be best if you just shut up. Why would God have made you blind if you had not been such a sinner? Move away if you know what's good for you.

Soordas – You can't beat her in my house. Beat her as much as you like after she leaves from here.

Bhairo – Will you move away or not?

Soordas – I won't let you make this din in my house.

Bhairo lost his temper and pushed Soordas. The poor man fell down since he was standing without any support. But he stood up and catching hold of Bhairo by the waist, said – Leave quietly now otherwise it won't be good for you.

Although Soordas looked frail, his bones were like iron. His body had become solid having borne the brunt of clouds and rain, cold and heat. Bhairo began to feel that it was an iron vice. No matter how hard he'd try, the vice wouldn't loosen. Subhagi took the opportunity to run away. Bhairo now began shouting abuses. The muhalla-valas came there on hearing the noise. Nayakram teased, 'So Soorey, your eyes open when they see a beautiful face . . . in the muhalla itself?'

Soordas – Pandaji, you're teasing me, and here I'm being defamed. I'm blind, a cripple, a beggar, a base man, but at least I was safe from accusations of thieving and badmashi. Today I'm also being accused of these.

Bajrangi – People see others as they want to.

Bhairo – As if you are a great sadhu. You've come here just after wielding your cudgel. For the past couple of years I've been observing that my wife comes and talks to him alone for hours on end. Jagdhar has also seen her leaving from here at night. Even today, right now, he was ready to fight with me because of her.

Nayakram – It's something to be suspicious about. A blind man is not necessarily a devata. And even devatas have not escaped the arrow of Kama. Soordas is just a human being and what's his age after all?

Thakurdeen – Maharaj! Why go after a blind man? Let's go and sing bhajans.

Nayakram – You are thinking of bhajans, and here it's a question of a decent man's respect. Bhairo, we'll speak if you listen to us. You beat Subhagi too much, that's why she can't get on with you. It happens once in two days now, but it shouldn't happen more than twice a month.

Bhairo realized that they were making a fool of him. He flared up – She's my woman, so what if I beat her? Does anyone else have a share in her? How can somebody who has never ridden a mare teach others to ride? What does he know about controlling a woman?

This sarcasm was directed at Nayakram, who was still unmarried. There was no dearth of wealth in the house and nothing to worry about, thanks to his patrons, but for some reason he was still a bachelor. He was willing to suffer a loss of 1000 to 500 rupees, but it didn't work out anywhere. Bhairo thought that Nayakram would feel deeply hurt but why would that seasoned city goonda pay heed to such taunts? He said, 'Tell us, Bajrangi, how is a woman controlled?'

Bajrangi – It isn't possible to control a tiny child by beating him, so how is it possible to control a woman thus?

Bhairo – Even the woman's father can be controlled! What price the woman? The fiend runs away only if it's beaten.

Bajrangi – Then even the woman will run away but she won't be controlled.

Nayakram – Well said, Bajrangi, you've said something very true, vaah-vaah! Even a fiend will run away if it's beaten, then so will a woman. So, haven't you now been proved wrong?

Bhairo – I proved wrong? Is it something to make fun of? The more you pound choona, the more it sticks.

Jagdhar – This is just talking for the sake of talking. A woman can be controlled only if that's what she wants and not in any other way.

Nayakram – Well, Bajrangi, do you have an answer?

Thakurdeen – Pandaji, you'll be satisfied only by making them fight. Why are you going after a poor crippled man?

Nayakram – What do you think of Soordas? He only looks so weak. Just shake his hand and you'll know. Bhairo, I'll give you a prize of five rupees if you can knock him down.

Bhairo – You'll slink out of it.

Nayakram – I'll have something to say to the person who'll slink away. See, I've put them in Thakurdeen's hand.

Jagdhar – What are you waiting for, Bhairo? Come on.

Soordas – I'm not going to fight.

Nayakram – Look here, Soordas, don't make a fool of yourself. Are you afraid to fight like a man? You'll merely lose, or is there something else?

Soordas – But bhai, I don't know any moves or tricks. Don't ask afterwards why I caught hold of his hand. I'll fight as I want to.

Jagdhar – Haan-haan, you fight as you want to.

Soordas – All right then, who wants to come?

Nayakram – Look at the blind man's boldness. Come on Bhairo, take the field.

Bhairo – What's the point of fighting a blind man?

Nayakram – Bas? Is this why you were being so insolent?

Jagdhar – Come on Bhairo, You can knock him down with one swoop.

Bhairo – Why don't you fight and take the prize?

Jagdhar was always worrying about money. Things never went well because of his large family; there was always a shortage of something or the other. He never lost an opportunity to make money. He said – Well Soorey, will you fight with me?

Soordas – Anyone will do, so come if you want to.

Jagdhar – Well, Pandaji, so you'll give the prize?

Nayakram – The prize was for Bhairo, but it doesn't matter. But the condition is that you'll knock him down with just one swoop.

Jagdhar tucked up his dhoti and clung on to Soordas. Soordas caught hold of one of his legs and pulled it so hard that Jagdhar fell with a thud. There was applause all around.

Bajrangi exclaimed – Vaah, Soordas, vaah! Nayakram ran to pat his back.

Bhairo – You told me that you could knock him down with just one swoop, then how come you got knocked down yourself?

Jagdhar – Soorey caught hold of my leg, otherwise how could he have knocked me down? If he had tripped me he would have fallen flat on his back.

Nayakram – Achcha, let's have another round.

Jagdhar – Haan-haan, you'll see this time.

There was a wrestling match once more between the two. This time Soordas twisted Jagdhar's hand so hard that he sat down on the ground groaning. Soordas immediately let go and caught hold of his neck, squeezing it so hard that Jagdhar's eyes nearly popped out. Nayakram ran to push Soordas away. Bajrangi picked up Jagdhar and making him sit down, began to fan him.

Annoyed, Bhairo said – What kind of a wrestling match is this that you squeeze whatever you can get hold of? This is a fight between the boorish, not a wrestling match!

Nayakram – This had been settled earlier.

Jagdhar got up carefully and quietly slipped away. Bhairo also followed him. There was a great deal of laughter and patting of Soordas's back afterwards. Everyone was surprised that someone as frail as Soordas could defeat someone as hefty and heavy as Jagdhar. Thakurdeen believed in yantra and mantra. He said, 'Soordas is favoured by a devata. Tell us also, Soorey, which mantra did you use?'

Soordas – Courage is the mantra of a hundred mantras. Give this money to Jagdhar, or I've had it.

Thakurdeen – Why should I give him the money? Has it been looted? You won, so you'll get it.

Nayakram – Achha Soordas, tell us honestly, with which mantra have you controlled Subhagi? There are only our own people here now. I'll also ensnare somebody!

Soordas said piteously, 'Pandaji, if you also talk like this, I'll blacken my face and go away somewhere. I think of another woman as my mata, beti, behen. You won't see me alive the day my heart becomes so fickle.' Soordas began to sob and continued after a while, controlling his voice, 'Bhairo beats her every day. The poor thing comes and sits with me sometimes. My only crime is that I don't rebuke her. You can accuse me of whatever you like, but I did only what I thought was my dharma. The man who turns his face away from dharma for fear of losing his reputation is not fit to be called a man.'

Bajrangi – You should have stayed away. She's his woman, it's not your business if he hits her or beats her.

Soordas – Bhaiyya, it's not possible to turn a blind eye! This is the way of the world but one should not be disgraced so severely for such a trivial thing. I'm telling you the truth. I didn't feel so much grief even when dada died. I'm crippled and live off other people's scraps, and this allegation?' He started to cry.

Nayakram – But why are you crying, good fellow? Aren't you a man even if you are blind? I would have been very happy if anyone had accused me of this. What do all these thousands of men do who go for a bath in the Ganga at the crack of dawn except to ogle? What happens in temples except all this? This is what happens in crowds and fairs. That's all that men do. There's no sign of sticks and swords now under sarkar's rule; there's manliness only in this ogling. Why worry about it! Come, let's go and sing to God, all these sorrows will vanish.

Bajrangi was worried about the outcome of the day's squabbles. 'The police will come tomorrow. Anger is a curse.' Nayakram assured him, 'Good fellow, why are you afraid of the police? Tell me, shall I call the thanedar and make him dance, or shall I call the inspector and have him slapped? Don't worry, nothing will happen. It's my responsibility to see to it that not a hair of your head is harmed.'

All three of them left. Dayagiri was already waiting for them. Several carters and banias were also there. The notes of the bhajan rose in a short while. Forgetting all his worries, Soordas sang with abandon. Delirious with devotion, he would sometimes dance or jump around or cry or laugh. Everyone was happy when the gathering dispersed, their hearts had become pure and the rancour had vanished, as if they had just visited a beautiful place. Soordas lay down on the base of the temple while the others returned home. However, after a short while the same worries began to plague him. 'How was I to know that there was so much resentment against me in Bhairo's heart? I wouldn't have allowed Subhagi to enter my hut in that case. Those who hear about this will spit on me. Nobody in this muhalla will now let me stand at his door. Oonh! God knows what's in their hearts. It's a man's dharma to console someone in grief. I give a damn if I'm disgraced because

I have followed my dharma. For how long can I cry because of this? Some day people will come to know what's in my heart.'

But the ulcer of jealousy was festering in the minds of both Jagdhar and Bhairo. Jagdhar would say – I had thought that we could easily win five rupees, otherwise was I bitten by a mad dog that I would get embroiled with him? He's made of iron.

Bhairo – I've tested his strength. Thakurdeen is right, he's favoured by a devata.

Jagdhar – Nothing of the sort, all this is because he's carefree. We are caught in the snare of domesticity, always worrying about salt, oil and wood, and concerned about profit and loss. What cares does he have? He happily eats what he gets and sleeps peacefully. You and I don't get even roti and daal twice a day. What does he lack? Someone gives him rice; he gets mithai from somewhere else, and ghee and milk from Bajrangi's house. Strength comes with eating.

Bhairo – No, that's not so. It's drinking that destroys strength.

Jagdhar – What perverse things are you saying? If that were so, why would the goras in the army be given brandy to drink? All the English drink—do they get weak?

Bhairo – I'll throttle Subhagi when she returns today.

Jagdhar – She must be hiding in someone's place.

Bhairo – That blind man has ruined my reputation. I'll become an outcaste if this affair spreads in the community; I'll have to give a feast.

Jagdhar – You're the one who's broadcasting it. You should have quietly gone home when you were knocked down. You could have spoken to Subhagi when she returned home, but you began complaining then and there.

Bhairo – I didn't think that this blind man was so deceitful, or else I would have taught him a lesson a long time ago. Now I'm not going to keep that witch in the house any longer. This disgrace at the hands of a chamaar!

Jagdhar – What greater disgrace can there be? It's enough for cutting his throat.

Bhairo – Bas, I just want to axe him and end the matter. But no, I'll first torment him and then kill him. It's not Subhagi's fault. It's that arrogant blind man who's responsible for this storm.

Jagdhar – Both are at fault.

Bhairo – But it's the man who begins the flirtation. I'll have nothing to do with her now, she can go where she likes and live as she likes. I have to deal with this blind man now. He seems so humble, as if he doesn't know anything, while his heart is full of deceit. His days are spent in begging but the unfortunate man's eyes don't open. Jagdhar, he has lowered my self-respect. I used to laugh at others, now everyone will laugh at me. My deepest resentment is that the unfortunate woman chose a chamaar to run away with. I wouldn't have resented it so much if she had run away with someone who was superior to me in caste, appearance and wealth. All those who get to know will think that I'm worse off than even this blind man.

Jagdhar – It's difficult to understand a woman's nature else where's the comparison between you and that blind man? Flies swarm over his face; he looks as if he has been beaten with shoes.

Bhairo – And yet he's so shameless. He begs and is blind but whenever you see him he's laughing. I've never seen him cry.

Jagdhar – He has money buried in his house. It's his evil spirit that'll cry. He begs only for the sake of appearances.

Bhairo – He'll cry now. I'll make him cry so hard that he'll be reduced to a state of complete helplessness; he'll remember chhatthi's milk.

Both returned home, talking thus. It was around two in the night when Soordas's hut was suddenly on fire. People were sleeping in their houses but the subconscious is awake even during sleep. Hundreds of people gathered immediately. There was a glow in the sky; the flames kept leaping towards it. Their shape would sometimes be like the golden cupola on the dome of a temple and sometimes they would tremble in the breeze like the reflection of the moon in the water. They tried to extinguish the fire but, like that of jealousy, the fire of a hut can never be extinguished. Somebody brought water, others unnecessarily made a racket but most stood silently, despondently watching the cremation as if it were the funeral pyre of a friend.

Suddenly Soordas came running and stood silently in the light of the blaze.

Bajrangi asked – How did this happen, Soorey, did you leave the fire burning in the stove by any chance?

Soordas – Is there any way of getting into the hut?

Bajrangi – The inside and the outside are now the same. The walls are burning.

Soordas – Is there no way that I can go in?

Bajrangi – How can you? Can't you see that the flames have reached here?

Jagdhar – Soorey, didn't you douse the stove today?

Nayakram – How would the hearts of the enemies have been doused if he had doused the stove?

Jagdhar – Pandaji, may my son be useless if I know anything about this. You are unnecessarily suspecting me.

Nayakram – I know who's responsible, you'll see if I don't ruin him.

Thakurdeen – What harm can you do? God himself will do it. Everything was consumed when there was a theft in my house.

Jagdhar – May God completely ruin the person who has so much wickedness in his heart.

Soordas – There are no flames now.

Bajrangi – Yes, the straw is burnt, now the beam is burning.

Soordas – Can I go in now?

Nayakram – You can go in but you can't come out. Now go and sleep peacefully. Whatever had to happen has happened. What's the use of regretting it?

Soordas – Haan, I'll go and sleep, what's the hurry?

The remnants of the fire also died down in a while. The saving grace was that nobody else's house was burnt. All of them left, criticizing this disaster. There was silence all around. But Soordas remained sitting. He did not grieve for the burning of his hut or his utensils and other belongings; he grieved for the bundle that was his lifelong earnings, the basis for all his hopes, and the substance for all his plans. The deliverance of his ancestors and of his heir was contained in that tiny bag. This was his lamp of hope for this world and the next, for his entire world. He thought, 'The money wouldn't have got burnt in the bundle. Where can the silver go even if the coins have melted? How was I to know that this disaster would happen today, otherwise wouldn't I have slept here? In the first place, nobody would have come near the hut, and even if he had set it on fire, I would have immediately removed the bundle. The truth is that I shouldn't have kept this money here. But where could I have kept it? Is there anyone in the muhalla with whom I could have kept it? Hai! There were all of 500 rupees and some paise over and above that. Did I save one paisa at a time for this day? At least I would have got some consolation if I had spent the money. What had I planned and what has happened! I had planned to go to Gaya and offer pinda to my ancestors. How will I be free of them now? I had hoped to get Mitthua engaged. I'll at least get a roti to eat if a bahu comes into the house. A lifetime has gone by flattening them with my own hands to eat them. I've made a big mistake. I should have completed one task at a time as and when I got the money. This is the result of wanting too much.'

The ashes had cooled by then. Soordas entered the hut, guessing the way to the door but after two or three steps he suddenly fell into the hot embers. There were ashes above but fire beneath. He quickly pulled his foot away and began to turn over the ashes with his stick so that the fire beneath could also be reduced to ashes. Within half an hour he had turned the ashes upside down and he then gingerly stepped on to them. They were hot but not unbearable. He began to grope in them in a straight line towards the place where he had kept the bundle in the thatch. His heart was beating. He was convinced that whether he found the money or not, the silver wouldn't have gone anywhere. He jumped suddenly; he had found something heavy. He picked it up but when he groped and felt it, he realized that it was only a piece of brick. He began fumbling again, like a man groping for fishes in water. Nothing came to hand. Then with the haste and impatience of despair, he began to search all the ashes. He scrutinized them fistful by fistful. He found his lota and tawa but not the bag. His foot, which was still on the ladder, slipped and he fell into an abyss. He screamed, and sitting there on the ashes, sobbed heartbrokenly. These were not ashes of straw but of his hopes. He had never before felt such grief at his helplessness.

It was dawn. Soordas was now gathering the ashes and putting them aside. Nothing is as long-lived as hope.

Jagdhar came just then and said – Soorey, tell the truth, you don't suspect me?

Soorey did suspect him, but hiding his suspicion he said – Why would I suspect you? What malice did I have towards you?

Jagdhar – The muhalla-valas will provoke you but I swear by God, I don't know anything about it.

Soordas – Whatever had to happen has happened. Who knows if somebody set the fire or if it was set by a spark that flew from someone's chillum? It's possible that there was fire remaining in the stove. Why should I suspect anyone without knowing anything?

Jagdhar – That's why I warned you, so that I'm not suspected.

Soordas – As far as you are concerned, I don't bear you any malice.

Jagdhar was convinced from Bhairo's talk that he was the culprit. He had talked about making Soordas cry and had carried out his threat in this way. He went straight to Bhairo, who was sitting silently smoking a huqqa from a coconut chillum but looking anxious. As soon as he saw Jagdhar he asked, 'Have you heard anything? What are people saying?'

Jagdhar – Everybody suspects you. You heard Nayakram's threat yourself.

Bhairo – I don't care about such threats. What's the proof that I lit the fire?

Jagdhar – Tell the truth, did you?

Bhairo – Yes, I stealthily lit a matchstick.

Jagdhar – I had already understood a bit but what you have done is wrong. What did you get by burning the hut? Another hut will be ready in a few days.

Bhairo – It doesn't matter, at least the burning in my heart has been soothed. Look at this . . .!

Bhairo showed a bag that had been blackened by smoke. Jagdhar eagerly asked – What's in it? Oh! It's full of money.

Bhairo – It's the fine for seducing Subhagi.

Jagdhar – Tell the truth, where did you get this money?

Bhairo – In that hut. It had been kept very carefully in the shelter of the beam. The scoundrel used to bring it by deceiving the wayfarers every day and put it in this bag. I've counted it. It's more than 500 rupees. How did he manage to collect so much? The rascal was conceited because of this money. Now that arrogance has gone. Let me see what he'll depend on now. I now have the means to invite the community for a feast. Where would the money have come from otherwise? You've seen how slack the sales are nowadays because of the volunteers in the army . . .

Jagdhar – I'll advise you to return his money. It's very hard-earned. You won't be able to digest it.

Jagdhar was not bad at heart but he had given this advice out of jealousy and not because he was well intentioned. It was unbearable for him that Bhairo should have got hold of so much money. He may have been satisfied if Bhairo had given him half of it, but it was too much to expect this of him. Bhairo said carelessly, 'I can digest it only too well. I can't return the money that I've got. He has collected it only by begging, not by weighing wheat.'

Jagdhar – The police will eat it all up.

Bhairo – Soorey won't go to the police. He'll just cry and wail, and then be quiet.

Jagdhar – A poor man's curse can be fatal.

Bhairo – He's poor! He's poor just because he's blind? A man who lures away another man's wife, who has saved hundreds of rupees, who can lend money to others—is he poor? If anyone is poor, it's you and I. Search the house and you won't find a whole rupee. Such sinners can't be called poor. It still rankles. The rancour will go when I see him cry. No matter what I do to somebody who has ruined my reputation, it won't be a sin.

Jagdhar was not content today making the rounds of the alleys with his khoncha. He was consumed with jealousy; a snake was writhing on his breast – He has got so much money so readily, now he'll enjoy himself. This is how fortune smiles. I have never come across even a single paisa lying around. It's not a question of sin and virtue. After all, even I don't do anything virtuous all day. I put my finger on the scales for worthless coins; I use counterfeit weights; and I sell mithai cooked in oil claiming that it has been cooked in ghee. It doesn't matter to me even if I'm dishonest. I know that it's wrong, but it's also important to bring up my children. He has at least gained something by being dishonest; his crime hasn't been without some relish. Now he'll get a contract for two or three more shops. My life would be successful if I too could get such riches.

The seeds of jealousy began to sprout in Jagdhar's heart. When he returned from Bhairo's house, he saw that Soordas was collecting the ashes and kneading them like dough. His whole body was besmeared with ashes and was streaming with perspiration. Jagdhar asked – Soorey, what are you looking for?

Soordas – Nothing. There was nothing here anyway. I was only looking for this lota and tawa.

Jagdhar – And whose bag does Bhairo have?

Soordas was startled, and thought to himself – Was this why Bhairo had come here? It must be so. He must have taken away the money before setting the house on fire.

But for a blind beggar poverty is not as much a matter of shame as wealth. Soordas wanted to hide his monetary loss from Jagdhar. He wanted to go to Gaya, get Mitthua married and have a well dug but in such a way that people would wonder how he had got so much money and they would believe that God helps the poor. For beggars, accumulating wealth is not less shameful than accumulating sin. He replied, 'Where do I have any bag? It must be someone else's. Would I have begged if I had a bag?'

Jagdhar – You are deceiving me. Bhairo himself told me that he had found the bag on top of the beam of the house. There are just a few more than 500 rupees.

Soordas – He must be teasing you. I have never been able to save even five and a half rupees, from where would I get five and a half hundred?

Meanwhile Subhagi reached there. She had hidden all night in the guava garden behind the temple. She knew that Bhairo had lit the fire. She was not that worried about Bhairo's allegation because she knew that nobody would believe him. But she was deeply grieved that Soordas had been completely ruined because of her and had come to console him. She thought of Jagdhar as another avatar of Bhairo. She had vowed never to return to Bhairo's house and to subsist by her own labour and hard work. 'There are no boys crying there, after all I'm the only burden on him. Now let him do the work and eat alone and drink the water with which he washes the old woman's feet. I can't do it. All these days he has probably not given me even a dhela's worth of sindoor of his own wish so why should I bother about him?'

Just when she was about to turn back, Jagdhar called out to her –

Subhagi, where are you going? Have you seen your khasam's trickery? He has destroyed poor Soordas.

Subhagi thought he was hoodwinking her and had thrown this net to know what was in her mind. She taunted – You are his guru, you must have given him the mantra.

Jagdhar – Yes, this is my work, how will I earn my living if I don't teach how to thieve and plunder?

Subhagi again taunted him – Why, didn't you get toddy to drink at night?

Jagdhar – Would I sell my honour for toddy? As long as I thought that he was a good fellow I used to sit with him, laugh and talk with him, and also drink toddy, I didn't go because I was greedy for toddy (how splendid, after all, you are such a dharmatma!).* But from today, you can pull my ears if you ever see me sitting with him. Someone who burns other people's houses and steals money from the poor—I wouldn't see his face even if he were my own son. Goodness knows how painstakingly Soordas must have collected 500 rupees. Bhairo has taken them all. He's ready to fight with me when I tell him to return them.

Soordas – You are going on repeating the same thing. I've already told you I didn't have any money; he must have stolen it from somewhere else. I would have been living in peace and playing the flute of contentment if I had 500 rupees. Why would I stretch out my hand before others?

Jagdhar – Soorey, I won't believe you even if you swear in the middle of the Ganga that it's not your money. I've seen that bag with my own eyes. Bhairo himself told me that he had found it in the hut on top of the beam. How can I believe you?

Subhagi – Have you seen the bag?

Jagdhar – Yes, would I tell a lie?

Subhagi – Soordas, tell the truth, is the money yours?

Soordas – Are you crazy? You are taken in by him! From where would I get the money?

Jagdhar – Ask him, if there was no money, what was he looking for, gathering ash at this time of the night?

Subhagi looked enquiringly at Soordas. He looked like a sick person

---

* The narrator's ironic comment on Jagdhar.

who was vainly trying to conceal his unbearable pain to reassure them. She went close to Jagdhar and said, 'The money was definitely there; his face shows it.'

Jagdhar – I saw the bag with my own eyes.

Subhagi – Now I don't care if he beats me or throws me out, but I'll stay only in his house. Where will he hide the bag? I'll find it sometime or the other. Soordas is in trouble because of me. I'm the one who has ruined him but I'll rehabilitate him. I won't be at peace until I can return his money.

She asked Soordas – Where will you stay now?

Soordas didn't hear this. He thought – I had earned the money. Can't I earn it again? All that will happen is that the work will be done later and not this year. It was not my money after all; perhaps I had stolen it from Bhairo in my last birth. I've been punished for that. But what will happen to poor Subhagi now? Bhairo will never keep her in his house. Where will the poor thing wander around wretchedly? Why do I have to bear this stigma? I'm left nowhere. Money, house, honour have all gone, only the land is left, and who knows if that will also go or remain. Was blindness not enough of a calamity that there's always one blow after another? Anyone feels free to taunt and rebuke me.

Soordas was so distressed by these thoughts that he began to weep. Subhagi went to Bhairo's house with Jagdhar while Soordas sat there alone and cried. All of a sudden, Soordas was startled on hearing a voice somewhere – You cry in a game! Mitthua was returning from Gheesoo's house crying, perhaps because Gheesoo had beaten him and was now taunting him – You cry in a game!

Whereas earlier Soordas had been drowning in the infinite waters of despair, shame, worry and anguish, as soon as he heard this warning it seemed as if someone had caught hold of his hand and had taken him to the shore – Vaah! I'm crying in a game. This is so wrong. Even boys think that it's wrong to cry in a game and taunt those who do, and I'm crying in a game! Genuine players never cry, they lose game after game, suffer wound upon wound, and are pushed time and again but they remain steadfast on the field without a frown. Courage doesn't desert them, not a trace of malice touches their hearts, they are not jealous of anybody, nor are they irritated. Why cry in a game? We play to laugh and enjoy, not to cry.

Soordas stood up and rapturously began to scatter with both hands the pile of ashes with the pride of victory. We go past our cherished goal in a fit of anger. Where's the restraint that can put away the sword in the scabbard after victory over an enemy?

In a moment Mitthua, Gheesoo, and several boys of the muhalla gathered around this stupa of ash and plagued Soordas with questions. Seeing him scatter the ashes they joined the game. It began to rain ash and it was all scattered in a trice, leaving only a black trace on the earth.

Mitthua asked – Dada, where will we live now?

Soordas – We'll build another house.

Mitthua – And if someone burns it again?

Soordas – Then we'll build it again.

Mitthua – And if it's burnt again?

Soordas – Then we'll build it again too.

Mitthua – And if someone burns it a thousand times?

Soordas – Then we'll build it a thousand times.

Children are very fond of numbers. Mitthua asked again – And if someone burns it 100 lakh times?

Soordas replied with that same childlike simplicity – Then we'll also build it 100 lakh times.

When there wasn't a pinch of ash left, the boys left in search of another game. The day was now well advanced. Soordas also picked up his stick and went towards the road. Meanwhile Jagdhar went to Nayakram and narrated the incident to him. Panda said, 'I'll get the money even from Bhairo's father! Where can he go? I'll rest only when I have extracted the money from his bones, whether the blind man says anything or not.'

Jagdhar then went to Bajrangi, Dayagiri, Thakurdeen as well as to all the people of the muhalla, big or small, and told them the story. He also spiced it up where necessary. The entire muhalla became Bhairo's enemy.

Soordas was at the roadside, invoking blessings on the wayfarers. Meanwhile the muhalla-valas had begun rebuilding his hut. Someone gave straw, someone else gave bamboos, somebody the beam . . . Several people were busy building the hut. Jagdhar was the prime minister of this group. Perhaps he had never before shown so much virtuous zeal. There isn't only darkness in jealousy but some virtue too. The hut was ready by the evening, larger and steadier than before. Jamuni brought two clay water pitchers and a few clay pots and put them there. She also made a mud stove. They had all decided that Soordas wouldn't get the slightest inkling about the building of the hut. They wanted to surprise him when he returned in the evening, so that when he asked who had built it, they could all say that it had got built by itself.

12

PRABHU SEVAK WAS FURIOUS WITH HIS FATHER WHEN HE LEFT WITH Tahir Ali. 'Does he want to make me a plodding ox tied to a mill? I should be intoxicated by tobacco for twenty-four hours of the day, rub my forehead at the doorsteps of officials, go around selling shares and getting advertisements published in papers, just become a box of cigarettes. I'm a human being, not a wealth-generating machine! The greed for wealth hasn't yet succeeded in crushing my feelings. It would be ingratitude if I were to use my God-given gift of creativity for this. Nature hasn't created me for producing wealth. Why else would it have endowed me with these sentiments? He says that there's no need for him to worry about wealth; he's just a guest for a few days, as if all these preparations are being made for me. But there would be mayhem if I were to tell him not to take all this trouble for me, I'm happy as I am. What a disaster to be trapped in; go and intimidate the villagers, scold them, abuse them. Why? They haven't done anything unusual. Naturally they'll be hell-bent on fighting if somebody forcibly tries to encroach on their property. How else can they protect their lives? I wouldn't sit quiet either if somebody tried to take possession of my house. Patience is the name for the final state of despair. We don't have recourse to it until we have no other remedy. This miyaanji came to complain just because he was slightly hurt. He's a sycophant who wants to win trust by flattery. Probably he too is obsessed about intimidating the poor. They can't live together on good terms. That's what papa also wants. I hope to God that they'll all revolt, set the godown on fire, and teach this gentleman such a lesson that he'll have to run away from here.' He angrily asked Tahir, 'What happened to make them all revolt?'

Tahir – Huzoor, absolutely nothing! I too have to protect myself from them.

Prabhu – There has to be a reason for any action but I've realized today that even this is a philosophical mystery, isn't it?

Tahir (*Not following*) – Oh yes, what else?

Prabhu – What's the meaning of 'oh yes, what else'? Don't you understand, or are you deaf? I say that there can be no fire without a spark; you reply, 'oh yes, what else'! What's your education?

Tahir (*Timidly*) – Huzoor, I've been educated up to middle school but unfortunately I couldn't pass. But I'll pay any fine you want me to if somebody who has passed middle school can do the work that I can. I've worked as a munshi in a customs house for quite a long time.

Prabhu – In that case who can doubt your scholarship and wisdom? Going by what you say, I should believe that you were sitting peacefully engrossed in perusing a book or possibly rapt in worshipping God, and an armed group of rebels attacked you.

Tahir – Huzoor is going there himself, what can I say? You can investigate for yourself.

Prabhu – One doesn't need a lamp to prove the existence of the sun. Villagers are generally very peace-loving. They don't fight or riot unless they are provoked. Unlike you, they don't earn their livelihood by worshipping God. They earn it by breaking their heads the whole day. It's surprising that you can't even tell the reason for what's happened to you. What else can this imply except that either your Khuda has made you very dense or that you put unwarranted pressure on people to intimidate them?

Tahir – Huzoor, the quarrel began with the boys. Several boys from the muhalla were beating my sons. I twisted their ears. Bas, there was an uproar because of such a trivial matter.

Prabhu – Congratulations! God hasn't been as unjust to you as I'd thought. There was a fight between your sons and the boys from the muhalla. You heard your sons crying and your blood began to boil. The sons of the villagers had the guts to beat your sons! Khuda's marvel! Your honour couldn't bear this oppression. You gathered your sense of propriety, far-sightedness and common sense, put them all on the shelf and ran to beat those foolhardy boys. So you shouldn't complain if others follow your example when they see such a civilized gentleman as you interfering in a fight among children. After living in the world for such a long time you should have learnt that the old shouldn't interfere with boys. The consequences are harmful. If you were inexperienced, you should be glad of this lesson that has given you such vital and important knowledge. There was no need to have complained.

The phaeton was flying and so were Tahir Ali's wits – I had thought that there'd be more humanity in this gentleman, but now I see that he's a couple of steps ahead of his father. He doesn't acknowledge either victory or defeat. I can't bear these taunts. They don't give me a salary for nothing. I work and get paid for my labour. He has made me appear base, foolish, uncouth, all these things, just by his taunts. He's so much younger than me! He must be just a few years older than Mahir but he's taking me on as if I'm an ignorant child! Does intelligence also increase with wealth? These things come to mind only when life is peaceful. He would have realized what experience is if he had to struggle for his livelihood. If aaka finds something objectionable, he has the right to explain it to me, I won't complain. But say what you have to gently and sympathetically. Don't spit poison and don't pierce my heart.

Meanwhile, they reached Pandeypur. Soordas looked very happy today. On other days, he would begin to run only after the passengers had gone ahead. But now, he began to run as soon as he heard the phaeton and welcomed it as it approached. Prabhu stopped the phaeton and asked harshly, 'Why, Soordas, you beg and pretend to be a sadhu but act like a badmash? You have dared to commit a criminal offence against me?'

Soordas – What criminal offence, huzoor? I'm a blind and crippled man, what criminal offence can I commit?

Prabhu – Wasn't it you who gathered the muhalla-valas to attack my munshiji and were prepared to set the godown on fire?

Soordas – Sarkar, I swear by God, it wasn't me. I beg from you people, I pray for the welfare of life and property, what criminal offence will I commit?

Prabhu – Why, munshiji, he was the leader, wasn't he?

Tahir – No huzoor, it was at his behest but he wasn't there.

Prabhu – I understand these tricks only too well. You probably realize that these people will be intimidated by these threats. But you'll see that I'll make each and every one of them sweat at the grindstone. What do you think sahib to be? Even if he were to lie to the officials, the entire muhalla would be arrested. I'm warning you.

They met Jagdhar when the phaeton moved on. He was walking with his khoncha balanced on his palm, swatting flies with his other hand. He stood and salaamed Prabhu as soon as he saw him. Prabhu asked, 'Were you also among those who were involved in the criminal offence yesterday?'

Jagdhar – Sarkar, I'm worth no more than a taka. How dare I commit a criminal offence? And how can poor Soordas have the guts to show any arrogance to sarkar? He has his own troubles. Somebody set fire to the poor man's hut during the night. His utensils and pots were all burned. Who knows with what difficulty he had saved some money; that was also looted. The poor man has spent the whole night crying. We have built his hut today. I've just got free, so I'm going out with my khoncha. Shall I give you something to eat if you let me? The kachaalu are very spicy.

Prabhu was tempted. He ordered him to put down the khoncha and began to eat kachaalu, dahi-bada and phullauri. He hungrily ate all these things with relish. He said, 'Soordas didn't tell me about this.'

Jagdhar – He'll never tell. He won't complain even if someone slits his throat.

Prabhu – Then he's surely a great man. Does anyone know who set the hut on fire?

Jagdhar – It's all clear, but huzoor, what can be done? He was told so often to report it to the police but the plaintiff says, 'Who wants to implicate anybody? What was fated to happen has happened.' Huzoor, it's all because of Bhairo the toddy-vala.

Prabhu – How do you know? Did anyone see him setting the fire?

Jagdhar – Huzoor! He told me himself. He showed me the bag of money. What better proof can there be?

Prabhu – Will you say this to Bhairo's face?

Jagdhar – No sarkar, there'll be bloodshed.

Just then Bhairo could be seen coming carrying a pitcher of toddy on his head. Jagdhar quickly picked up his khoncha and strode ahead in the opposite direction without taking any money. Bhairo came and salaamed. Glaring at him, Prabhu Sevak asked, 'You are Bhairo the toddy-vala, aren't you?'

Bhairo (*Trembling*) – Yes huzoor, my name is Bhairo.

Prabhu – You are the one who goes around setting fire to people's houses?

Bhairo – Huzoor, I swear by my youth, somebody has lied to huzoor.

Prabhu – You were involved in attacking my godown yesterday.

Bhairo – Huzoor, I'm your obedient servant, will I commit a criminal offence against you? Ask munshiji if I'm lying or telling the truth. Sarkar, I don't know why the whole muhalla is my enemy. I eat just one roti in my own house and people can't bear even that. This blind man, huzoor, is one badmash of a kind. He looks at other people's bahus and betis with bad intentions. He has saved money by begging and he also trades. The whole muhalla is under his influence. It's his disciple Bajrangi who has committed this criminal offence; he's intoxicated by his wealth, he has cows and buffaloes, he sells milk by mixing it with water. Who else would have the guts to commit a criminal offence against huzoor?

Prabhu – Achcha! This blind man also has money?

Bhairo – Huzoor, how could there be so much heat without money? It's only when the belly is full that one can think of looking at other people's bahus and betis with bad intentions.

Prabhu – What nonsense! How can a blind man look at anyone with bad intentions? I've heard that he's a very simple man.

Bhairo – Your own dog won't bite you, you stroke his back, but those whom he runs to bite won't think that he's so simple.

They had now reached Bhairo's shop where the customers were waiting for him. He entered the shop. Prabhu then said to Tahir, 'You say the whole muhalla had got together to beat you. I don't believe this. Such unity is impossible where there's so much enmity and conflict. We met two men, and they are both each other's enemies. Someone else in your place would have managed to gain as much as he wanted out of this enmity. He would have made them fight with each other and watched the fun from a distance. I feel sorry for these people instead of being angry with them.'

They found Bajrangi's house. It was now the third pahar. He was filling the buffaloes' troughs with water. When he saw Prabhu on the phaeton with Tahir, he realized that miyaanji had come with his master to intimidate him. 'He knows I'll be bullied in this way. I'm ready to pay whatever fine he wants me to if he can convince me but why should I be scared when it's entirely miyaanji's fault, not mine? He can browbeat me legally, or by his position, but I'm not afraid of threats.'

Tahir made a sign. 'This is Bajrangi.' Prabhu pretended to be angry and asked, 'Why, you wretch, were you also involved in yesterday's uproar?

Bajrangi – With whom was I involved? I was alone.

Prabhu – You're lying. Weren't Soordas and other people of the muhalla with you?

Bajrangi – I'm not lying. I'm not cowed down by anybody. Neither Soordas nor anyone else from the muhalla was with me. I was alone.

Gheesoo shouted – Padri! Padri!

Mitthua said – Padri has come! Padri has come!

Both ran to share this good news with their friends. Padri will sing, he'll show us pictures, give us books, distribute sweets and money . . . When they heard this, the other boys also ran to partake of this loot. Several children gathered there within moments. In the outlying muhallas of the city, any man wearing English clothes is synonymous with a padri. Nayakram was sitting after having drunk some bhang; he got up as soon as he heard the padri's name. He got special pleasure out of the padri's tuneless melodies. Thakurdeen also left his shop; he was addicted to religious debates with padris. He didn't miss these wonderful opportunities to show off his knowledge of religion. Dayagiri also reached there. However, the secret was revealed after they had all reached the phaeton. Prabhu was telling Bajrangi, 'May disaster not befall you, otherwise sahib will ruin you. You'll become useless. You had the guts!'

Bajrangi was about to answer when Nayakram stepped forward and said – Why are you getting angry with him? I committed the criminal offence; say what you want to me.

Surprised, Prabhu asked – What's your name?

Nayakram became reckless partly because of Raja Mahendra Kumar's assurance, partly because of the rapture of triumph and partly because of the awareness of his strength. Straightening his cudgel, he said – Pandey, the cudgel wielder.

This reply was more ludicrous than boastful. Prabhu's feigned anger disappeared. He laughed and said – Then it's not safe to stay here. I'll have to dig a hole somewhere.

Nayakram was a boorish man. He couldn't understand Prabhu's intentions. He thought suspiciously, 'He's laughing at me, as if to say that your nonsense doesn't matter, we are determined to take the land.' He flared up. 'Why are you laughing? Do you think you'll get the blind man's land so easily? Don't remain under this delusion.'

Prabhu was now angry. He had first thought that Nayakram was just joking but he now realized that he was really ready to fight. He said, 'I'm not under any delusion, I understand the problems only too well. I came here because I had believed until now that it could all be settled through negotiation. But if you want something else then let it be so. I had thought that you were weak, and I didn't want to use my strength on the weak. But I've now realized that you are overbearing and arrogant about your strength. So there'll be no injustice if we also show you our power.'

Good intentions were reflected in these words. Thakurdeen said – Huzoor, don't mind Pandaji's words. He blurts out whatever comes to his mind. We are your obedient servants.

Nayakram – You may rely upon other people's strength, here we only trust our own. Fulfil all your wishes. Don't say later that we attacked deceitfully. (*Softly*) All the Kirastaani will disappear with one blow.

Prabhu – What did you say? Why don't you say it loudly?

Nayakram (*A little frightened*) – I'm saying, fulfil all your wishes.

Prabhu – No, you said something else.

Nayakram – I'll repeat what I had said. I'm not afraid of anyone.

Prabhu – You abused me!

Prabhu got down from the phaeton, his eyes ablaze, his nostrils flaring, his whole body trembling, his heels taking off the ground as if they were the lids of a boiling pot. His expression was distorted. He was carrying only a thin stick. He got off the phaeton, leapt at Nayakram's throat, grabbed his cudgel and threw it away and gave him several blows with his stick in quick succession. Nayakram backed away shielding himself from the blows with both hands. It seemed that Prabhu was not in his senses. Nayakram knew that gentlemen may perhaps keep quiet if they are beaten but they can't bear to be abused. He didn't get a chance to attack since he was dazed partly because of regret, partly because of the promptness of the blows and partly because of fear of the consequences. He was somewhat dazed

by the continuous blows. There was no doubt that Prabhu was no
match for him but Prabhu had that courage of righteousness, that faith
in being on the side of justice which did not care about numbers, or
weapons and strength.

The others stood around dumbstruck; nobody intervened. Bajrangi
was among those who would shed Nayakram's blood rather than his
sweat. They had both played together and had fought on the same
wrestling ground. If Thakurdeen couldn't do anything else, he could
have stood in front of Prabhu, but they both kept staring mutely. All
this had happened within moments. Prabhu was still wielding his
stick. When he found that it was ineffective, he began to kick. This
blow was successful. After just two or three kicks, Nayakram's thigh
was wounded and he fell down. Bajrangi immediately ran and moved
Prabhu away from there and said, 'That's all, sahib, that's all! It's best
for you to go away now, otherwise there'll be bloodshed.'

Prabhu – Do you take me to be a chaffcutter, badmash? I'll drink
your blood . . . You dare abuse me!

Bajrangi – That's all, now don't go too far, it's only because of that
abuse that you are still standing here, otherwise who knows what
might have happened.

Prabhu had emerged from the frenzy of rage into a state of reflection.
He sat on the phaeton and whipped the horse. The horse vanished
like the wind.

Bajrangi went to Nayakram and picked him up. His knees were
severely wounded and he couldn't stand. It seemed as if a bone was
broken. He limped home slowly, supporting himself on Bajrangi's
shoulder.

Thakurdeen said – Nayakram, for good or ill, it was your fault.
These people can't tolerate abuses.

Nayakram – Arey, but when did I abuse him, bhai? All I said
was that the Kirastaani would disappear with one blow. Bas, he was
annoyed because of that.

Jamuni was standing at the door, watching this spectacle. She went
to Bajrangi and began scolding him – You just stood there staring,
and that lad battered and assaulted you and left. All your wrestling
was useless.

Bajrangi – I was nervous.

Jamuni – Be quiet. Don't you feel ashamed? A mere lad defeated everybody. This is a punishment to all of you for your arrogance.

Thakurdeen – You're right, Jamuni. After seeing this marvel, we can only say that God wanted to punish our arrogance, or else would such warriors have stood like puppets? God doesn't let anybody's pride remain.

Nayakram – That must be it, bhai. I didn't bother about anybody because of my pride.

Talking thus, they reached Nayakram's house. Somebody lit the fire; someone else ground the haldi. Soon, other people from the muhalla also gathered. They too were surprised that an incorrigible cudgel wielder could be so severely defeated. He could escape unscathed among hundreds of people but a mere lad had managed to besmear him. It was God's will.

Applying the haldi paste, Jagdhar said – It's Bhairo who has lit this fire. He poisoned sahib's ears on the way. I saw sahib. He even had a pistol in his pocket.

Nayakram – I'll take care of everything, pistol, rifle, and all; there's enmity now.

Thakurdeen – Some rite should be performed.

Jagdhar – Rites don't affect Kirastaans.

Nayakram – I'll stop the phaeton in the middle of the bazaar and beat him up, he won't be able to show his face anywhere after that. That's what I've decided now.

Bhairo came just then and stood there. Nayakram taunted him – You must be very happy, Bhairo.

Bhairo – Why, bhaiyya?

Nayakram – Haven't I been beaten up?

Bhairo – Am I your enemy, bhaiyya? I just heard about it at the shop. I lost my wits. Sahib seemed to be very simple and straightforward. He talked to me jovially. I don't know what demon possessed him when he came here.

Nayakram – I'll rid him of this demon, I'll rid him of it properly. Just let me get on to my feet. Yes, what's decided here shouldn't reach him else he'll be forewarned.

Bajrangi – There's no enemy of ours sitting here.

Jagdhar – Don't say this. It's the spy in the house that burns Lanka.

How does one know, somebody may well tell everything there to get praise, to get a reward, or to get importance.

Bhairo – You are suspecting me, aren't you? I'm not so base that I'll go around revealing the secrets of the house to others. There's bound to be friction where a few people live together but I'm not so mean that I'll get my brother's house burnt like Bhabhikan.* Don't I know that in life and death, in adversity and prosperity, it's only the people of the muhalla to whom one can turn? Have I ever betrayed anyone? Let Pandaji speak, have I ever disobeyed him? Without his protection, the police would have carted me off to jail a long time ago, but my name is not even in the register.

Nayakram – Bhairo, you have never let me down whenever the need has arisen, I have to admit this much.

Bhairo – Pandaji, I'll jump into the fire if you order me to.

Meanwhile Soordas reached there thinking, 'Why should I worry about where to cook today? Bas, I'll just make baatis under the neem tree. This is summer. There's no rain after all.' As soon as he reached Bajrangi's doorway, Jamuni narrated the entire events of the day. He lost his wits. He no longer thought of cow-dung cakes and fuel. He went straight to Nayakram's. Bajrangi said, 'Come Soorey, you've taken a long time to come, did you just set out? There was a lot of confusion here today.'

Soordas – Yes, Jamuni told me. I was taken aback when I heard about it.

Bajrangi – It was expected. He's just a lad, but he's very courageous. Before we could say 'haan-haan', he jumped off the phaeton and gave blow after blow.

Soordas – You people didn't even catch hold of him?

Bajrangi – You've just heard, he hit out before we could run to him.

Soordas – These big people lose their self-control if they are abused.

Jagdhar – He'll cry when he's beaten in the middle of the bazaar. Right now he must be delighted.

Bajrangi – We should stop his gharry and beat him with shoes when he enters the chowk.

---

* Vibhishan: Ravan's brother, whose betrayal resulted in the burning of Lanka by Hanuman in the Ramayana.

Soordas – Arey, what's happened has happened. What will we get now by humiliating him?

Nayakram – Should I let it go just like that? My name is not Nayakram if I don't beat him with shoes a hundred times for each blow of his stick. It's not my body that's been wounded but my heart. I have made several big people bow their heads; it won't take much time to ruin him. (*Snapping his fingers*) I'll get rid of him like this.

Soordas – Nothing will be gained by increasing enmity. You won't lose anything but all the people of the muhalla will be arrested.

Nayakram – What nonsense are you talking? Am I a dhuniya or chamaar that I'll stay quiet after being so humiliated? Why don't you people convince Soordas? Should I just remain sitting quietly? Speak, Bajrangi, are you people also scared that this Kirastaan will grind the entire muhalla and drink it up?

Bajrangi – I don't know about the others but if I had my way, I'd break his limbs even if I had to go to jail. This is not just your humiliation; the faces of everybody in the muhalla have been blackened.

Bhairo – You have taken the words from my mouth. What can I say, I wasn't there at the time otherwise I would have broken his bones.

Jagdhar – Pandaji, I'm not saying this just to flatter you. Even if you are persuaded by what the others say, I won't rest until I have given him a sound beating.

Several people then said – If the mukhia's respect is lost, so is everyone else's. These are the Kirastaans who go around all the lanes and alleys singing the songs of Isa Masih. Domras, chamaars, all those who go to church to eat, are the ones who become Kirastaans. Later on they wear coats and pants and become sahibs.

Thakurdeen – My advice is that we should perform some rite.

Nayakram – Soorey, now tell me if I should listen to you or to these people? You are perhaps scared that your land will be in danger, but don't worry about this. Raja sahib's words are like a line cut in stone. Even if sahib dies racking his head, he can't get the land.

Soordas – I'm not worried about the land. I won't carry it on my head and take it away with me when I die. But in the end this sin will be on my head. I'm the cause of this storm, it's because of me that there's all this wrangling and fighting; otherwise what enmity did sahib have towards you?

Nayakram – Friends, make Soorey understand.

Jagdhar – Soorey, just think, we have been so badly humiliated.

Soorey – It's God who maintains or destroys honour, not man. Honour should be maintained in his eyes alone. Where do men have the eyes to discriminate between honour and disgrace? When the bania who takes interest, the official who takes bribes, and the witness who tells lies are not considered dishonourable and people respect them, there's no one here to value true honour.

Bajrangi – It doesn't concern you, we'll do what we want to.

Soordas – I'll go and tell sahib everything if you don't listen to me.

Nayakram – Remember, if you step in there, that's where I'll bury you. I'm kind to you because you are crippled and blind, otherwise who are you? Should I lose my self-respect and blacken the faces of my forefathers because you are telling me to? Who do you think you are, pretending to be so wise? You are a beggar, you may not care about your self-respect, but my back has not bitten the dust until now.

Soordas did not reply. He got up quietly and lay down on the base of the temple. Mitthua was also sitting there waiting for the prasad. Soordas gave him some money to buy sattu and gur to eat. Mitthua was very happy and ran towards the bania's shop. Children prefer sattu and parched grain to rotis.

After Soordas had left, they sat silently for a while. His opposition had put them in a quandary. They were all afraid of his candour. They also knew that he always acted on his words. That's why it was necessary to deal with Soordas first. It was difficult to convince him. Threats too wouldn't work. Nayakram decided to support the allegation made against Soordas to defeat him. He said, 'It seems they've managed to win him over.'

Bhairo – Even I suspect this.

Jagdhar – Soordas is not the kind of man who's a traitor.

Bajrangi – Never!

Thakurdeen – That's not his nature, but who knows. One can't say anything about anybody. There was a theft in my house but were the thieves outsiders? It was the neighbours' doing. Goods worth a full 1000 rupees were stolen. And the very people who stole the goods are my friends even now. Who knows what the human heart may become from one moment to the next!

Nayakram – Soordas may have been prepared to make a deal about the land. But if sahib even looks this way, I'll set his bungalow on fire. (*Smiling*) Bhairo will help me, of course.

Bhairo – Pandaji, you people are suspecting me but I swear by my youth, I didn't go near his hut. Jagdhar comes to my house often, honestly, you can ask him.

Nayakram – There's nothing wrong in setting fire to the house of someone who looks at other people's bahus and betis with bad intentions. I didn't believe it at first but his temperament has changed colour now.

Bajrangi – Pandaji, you've known Soorey for thirty years now. Don't say this.

Jagdhar – Soorey may have many other faults, but this is not one of them.

Bhairo – I think we have accused him unjustly. Subhagi came this morning and fell at my feet and hasn't left the house since. She has been taking care of amma all day.

These were the discussions going on here—planning the reception to be given to Prabhu Sevak. As for Prabhu, when he went home, he did not have the satisfaction with the events of the day that is the greatest reward of righteous action. But there could be no doubt that his soul was at peace.

No decent man can tolerate abuses, nor should he. If someone is quiet after being abused, it can only mean that he lacks manliness and has no self-respect. If his blood does not boil after being abused, he is stupid, bestial, lifeless.

Prabhu regretted that he had let this situation arise. 'I should have been friendly with them and made them embrace Tahir Ali, but from whom can I learn this opportunism? Oonh! Let those whose ambition is to expand play these tricks, I just want to shrink. Papa will be furious when he hears this. He'll put the entire blame on me. I'm stupid, thoughtless, inexperienced. Of course I am. Someone who lives in this world but is not worldly-wise is dim-witted. Papa will be annoyed; I'll calmly bear his anger. I'll get my heartfelt desire if he abandons his plans for opening this factory because he's disappointed with me.'

But Prabhu was very surprised when John Sevak showed no sign of anger even after listening to the entire account. This silence was much more intolerable than ridicule or insult. Prabhu wanted his father to admonish him severely, so that he could get an opportunity to give an explanation, and to prove that he was not responsible for this incident. Anyone else in his place would have had to face the same disaster. He tried to incite his father's anger a couple of times but John Sevak looked at him sharply just once and left. A poet's desire for glory would perhaps not have been as wounded to the quick at the silence of the audience.

John Sevak was not one to cry over spilt milk. It was futile to criticize Prabhu's actions severely. He knew that self-respect pervaded every pore of Prabhu's being. John Sevak himself had nurtured that sentiment in him. He wondered how to solve this knotty problem. 'Nayakram is the leader of the muhalla,' he thought, 'and the whole muhalla is slave to his command. Soordas only adds his voice. And Nayakram is not only the leader but also a renowned goonda of the city. Thank goodness Prabhu has returned safe and sound. Raja sahib had come around with great difficulty. Nayakram is sure to go and complain to him; our excesses will be proved this time. As it is, raja sahib is hostile to capitalists, he'll be beside himself after listening to this story. It will be very difficult to bring him around after that.' John Sevak lay awake the whole night grappling with this dilemma. Suddenly he had an idea. There was the hint of a smile on his face. 'It's possible that this move may work and the damage be rectified.' After eating his haaziri in the morning, he ordered the phaeton to be prepared and left for Pandeypur.

Nayakram had bandaged his feet and had got his body massaged with haldi. He had called for a litter and was ready to go to see Mahendra Kumar. A few moments still remained for the muhurat, the auspicious moment. Bajrangi and Jagdhar were to accompany him. They were all taken aback when the phaeton arrived all of a sudden. In a moment, the whole muhalla gathered there wondering what would happen today.

John Sevak approached Nayakram and asked – Your name is Nayakram Panda, isn't it? I've come to apologize for what happened yesterday. I strongly rebuked the boy when he gave me the news, and I would have come to see you immediately had it not been too late in the night. The boy is misguided and foolish. I sincerely wish that he would become more humane, but he's so perverse that he doesn't pay heed to anything. I sent him to vilayat to be educated. He passed from there but didn't learn civility. What greater proof can there be of his ignorance than his insolence to you in the presence of so many people? If anyone throws a stone at a lion it's not his courage nor even his pride, but his foolishness. Such a person deserves pity because sooner or later he'll be a morsel in the lion's mouth. This is the exact plight of this lad. There's no knowing what may have happened if you had not been compassionate and forgiving. Please remove this resentment from your heart too since you have been so kind.

Nayakram lay down on the cot, as if it were difficult to stand, and said, 'Sahib, the resentment won't leave my heart, even if I were to lose my life. Call this our compassion or his luck that he escaped from here unscathed but the resentment is still there. It will go only when one of us is no longer alive. As for civility, he'll learn it soon enough if God so wills it. Bas, just let him fall into our clutches once again. We have taught several bigwigs to be courteous, what's his worth?

John Sevak – If you can teach him to be courteous so easily I'll send him to you, if you say so. I've tried everything unsuccessfully.

Nayakram – Speak up, bhai Bajrangi, answer sahib. I can't speak, I've spent the night groaning and moaning. Sahib says forgive him, don't keep any resentment in your heart. I don't know this kind of behaviour. I've only learnt to answer a brick with a stone.

Bajrangi – This is the custom among sahibs. First they beat up people and when they see that they too are likely to be beaten, they promptly ask people to forgive. They don't realize that those who have been beaten up won't be satisfied until they can also hit back.

John Sevak – You're right. But you should realize that forgiveness is not sought out of fear. A person hides from fear, he runs to seek help from others, he doesn't ask for forgiveness. He asks for forgiveness only when he's convinced of his injustice and faults. And when his soul shames him. Prabhu Sevak will never apologize if you ask him to. You can cut his throat with a sword but you won't be able to make him utter a word pleading for forgiveness. You can put this to the test if you don't believe me. This is because he believes that he hasn't done anything wrong. He claims that he was abused. But I can never believe that you could have abused him. A decent person neither abuses nor does he listen to abuses. I'm apologizing because I think he was entirely in the wrong. I'm ashamed of his bad behaviour, and I'm sorry that I let him come here. To tell you the truth, I now regret that I had ever thought of taking this land. You people beat up my agent; I didn't so much as report it to the police. I've now decided that I'll no longer mention the land. I don't want to trouble you people, I don't want to build my house by displacing you. I'll take it if you give it willingly, else I'll let it go. The greatest unrighteousness is to wound someone's heart. My soul won't be at peace until you people forgive me.

Insolence is only the extreme form of simplicity. Sahib's sweet words placated Nayakram's anger. Someone else could have as easily incited him to cut sahib's throat with a sword; possibly he would have been hell-bent on murder at the sight of Prabhu Sevak but right now it was as if sahib's words had him spellbound. He said, 'Well, Bajrangi, what do you say?'

Bajrangi – What's there to say? If someone bows his head before you, you also have to bow yours. Sahib also says that now he won't have anything to do with this land, so now what's the quarrel between him and us?

Jagdhar – Haan, it's best now to put an end to the quarrel. Nobody gains anything by illwill and conflict.

Bhairo – Chhotey sahib should now ask Pandaji to forgive him. He's not a child any longer that you should plead for him. It would have been different if he had been a child, then we would have blamed you. He's an educated man, his beard and moustache have now grown; he should come himself and settle the matter with Pandaji.

Nayakram – Yes, this is for sure. The resentment in my heart won't go away until he takes back his words.

John Sevak – So you think that intelligence comes with beard and moustache? Haven't you seen people with grey hair and broken teeth but no sense? Had he not been stupid, Prabhu Sevak would not have raised his hand against a wrestler like Pandaji amid so many people. He won't apologize, no matter how much you pressurize him. As for the land, if you people want me to suppress the matter, let it be so. But perhaps you haven't yet thought over it, otherwise you wouldn't have opposed it. Tell me, Pandaji, what are your doubts?

Nayakram – Bhairo, give an answer. Sahib has now convinced you.

Bhairo – Where has he convinced me? Sahib is only saying that chhotey sahib has no sense, so why doesn't he jump into a well or bite his hand with his own teeth? How can anyone believe that such people are mad?

John Sevak – Of course a person is mad if he doesn't understand what to say or do when.

Nayakram – Sahib, I can't believe on any account that he's mad. But yes, I won't increase my enmity with him because of my regard for you. Your courtesy has humbled me. I'm telling the truth, your civility and decency have calmed my anger; otherwise I didn't realize how much resentment there was in my heart. Chhotey sahib would have been in the hospital by this evening if you had delayed coming here even for a short while. My back has not bitten the dust until today. It's the first time in my life that I have been so humiliated, and it's the first time that I have also learnt to forgive. This is the benefit of your wisdom. I respect your intelligence. Now, Bajrangi, answer sahib's second point.

Bajrangi – What's there to discuss now? Sahib has said that he won't mention it. So the quarrel is over.

John Sevak – But you won't let me take that land even if my getting it means that the benefit will be entirely yours?

Bajrangi – How will we gain anything? We'll be completely ruined.

John Sevak – I'll show you that these are your illusions. Tell me, what is your objection?

Bajrangi – Pandaji has thousands of pilgrims who come here. They stay in this field for ten or twenty days at a time. They cook and sleep here. How can people from the countryside find comfort in the city's dharmashalas? No pilgrim will even peep in here if the land doesn't remain.

John Sevak – How will it be if houses with tiled roofs are built on the roadside for the pilgrims?

Bajrangi – Who'll build so many houses?

John Sevak – That's my responsibility. I promise I'll get a dharmashala built here.

Bajrangi – Where will my cattle and those of the muhalla-valas graze?

John Sevak – You'll have the right to the pasturage in the compound.

Also, now you have to take all your milk to the city. The halvai takes the milk from you and makes cream, butter and curd, and is much more prosperous than you. After all, he makes this profit from your milk! If you make cream and butter here, who'll buy it now? When the factory is opened here, a basti of thousands of people will come up, you'll sell the cream from the milk, and the milk will be sold separately. That way there'll be a double profit. You can sell your cow-dung cakes from your house. There's only profit for you if the factory is opened.

Nayakram – You've understood, Bajrangi, haven't you?

Bajrangi – Of course I understand, but I'll be the only one who'll make cream from milk, there are other people who rear animals so that they can consume milk. They'll have problems.

Thakurdeen – I too have a cow. The thieves would have taken her away as well if they had their way. She grazes all day long. I let her go after milking her in the mornings and evenings. I don't have to get even a dhela's worth of fodder. Even eight annas worth of straw daily won't be enough then.

John Sevak – You have a paan shop, don't you? You probably earn about ten to twelve annas now. Your sales will then increase fourfold. The loss here will be made up there. Labourers don't know how to hold on to money; if they have a moment's leisure somebody will fall for a paan, somebody else for a cigarette. Khoncha-valas' sales will be particularly good, and as for alcohol made from toddy, if you want you can sell water as alcohol. Carters' rates will go up too. This muhalla will flourish like the chowk. Your sons go to the city to study now but then a madrasa will be opened right here.

Jagdhar – Will a madrasa also be opened here?

John Sevak – Yes, after all where will the sons of the factory people go to study? English will also be taught.

Jagdhar – Will the fees also be lower?

John Sevak – There'll be no fees at all. There's no question of less or more.

Jagdhar – In that case it will be very convenient.

Nayakram – What will the owner get?

John Sevak – Whatever you people decide. You are the panch for me. Bas, it's your job to persuade him.

Nayakram – He is willing. You have persuaded everyone in an

instant. Otherwise people had assumed all kinds of things here. It's true, knowledge is a great thing.

Bhairo – Will I have to give anything there for the toddy shop?

Nayakram – There'll obviously be competition if someone else also makes a claim.

John Sevak – No, your right will be considered greater than anyone else's.

Nayakram – Then you'll flourish, Bhairo!

John Sevak – So shall I leave, Pandaji, now that there's no resentment in your heart?

Nayakram – Now don't make me say anything, I have seldom seen anyone as decent as you.

After John Sevak had left, Bajrangi said – What if Soorey doesn't agree?

Nayakram – We'll make him agree. We'll get him 4000 rupees. There's benefit now only in this compromise. The land can't be retained. This man is so clever that we can't get the better of him. Who else will treat us like this if we let it go? We shouldn't spurn unasked for glory if we get it.

Dinner was ready when John Sevak reached home. Prabhu asked, 'Where did you go?' Wiping his face with his handkerchief, John replied, 'One needs discernment for every task. Writing a poem is one thing, accomplishing something is another. You went to perform a task and came away determined to fight the entire muhalla. They had all gathered at Nayakram's door when I reached there. He was perhaps ready to go to see Raja Mahendra Singh on a litter. All of them looked at me as if they would tear me to pieces. But I acted with such patience and humility, and brought them around with such arguments and smooth talk, that they were all singing my praises by the time I left. The matter of the land was also settled. There's no obstacle now in our getting it.'

Prabhu – Earlier they were all prepared to die and kill for that land.

John – And if there was anything missing, you went and completed it. But remember, you always have to be on the lookout for some crucial opportunity in such matters. This is the root mantra of success. The hunter knows when to take aim at the deer. The lawyer knows when his arguments will be most effective in the court. A month earlier, even a day earlier, my words would not have had the least effect on these people. Your insolence yesterday gave me that opportunity. I went to them requesting forgiveness. I got the opportunity of presenting my problem to them by being submissive, by yielding, with humility and courtesy. If there had been anything unwarranted on their part I too would have acted sternly. Being submissive in that situation would have been imprudent and improper. The excess was on our part, and that was my victory.

Ishvar Sevak said – God, take this sinner in your shelter. Ice has become very expensive these days. I don't understand why it's being used so callously. The water in the surahi is quite cold.

John – Papa, I'm sorry, thirst can't be quenched without ice.

Ishvar – If God wills it, beta, the matter of that land will be settled. You acted with great intelligence today.

Mrs Sevak – I don't trust these Indians. People should learn treachery from them! They are all saying haan-haan now, but they'll all slink away when the opportunity arises. Didn't Mahendra Singh deceive you? It's this race that's our enemy. Not a single Christian would remain in this country if they had their way.

Prabhu – Mama, you are being unfair. No matter how hostile Indians were to Christians earlier, things have changed now. We ourselves imitate the English and provoke them; we try to oppress them at every opportunity with the help of the English. But this is our political delusion. Our salvation lies in brotherly feelings for our compatriots, not in being domineering. After all we too are children of the same mother. It's impossible that the white races should have friendly relations with us only because of religion. The Negroes in America are also Christians but the behaviour of the white Americans towards them is bestial and oppressive. Our liberation is with the Indians.

Mrs Sevak – May God not bring the day when we'll have to make the friendship of these infidels the means of our salvation. We belong to the same religion as the rulers. Our religion, our traditions and customs, our food and manners are like those of the English. We bow our heads with them in the same church before one God. We want to live in this country like rulers, not like the ruled. It's probably Kunwar Bharat Singh who has given you these ideas. A few more days in his company and perhaps you'll also become hostile to Jesus.

Prabhu – I don't see any special signs of awakening among the Christians.

John – Prabhu, you have started a very profound topic. I believe that our welfare lies in interacting with the English. Right now the English are worried about the united strength of the Indians. We can impress them with our patriotism through our friendship with them and get whatever rights we want. It's regrettable that our community has not yet stepped into the political arena. Although we are way ahead of other communities in education, we have no political power. We'll be lost if we mingle with the Indians; we'll vanish. We can get special privileges and prestige if we remain separate from them.

While this conversation was going on, a chaprasi came with a letter from the district magistrate, Mr Clark. Several guests had come to his place from England. Mr Clark was giving a dinner in their honour to which he had also invited Miss Sophia. He had also made a special request to Mrs Sevak to ask Sophia to return for a week.

After the chaprasi had left, Mrs Sevak said – This is a golden opportunity for Sophie.

John – Yes it is, but how will she come?

Mrs Sevak – Shall I send her this letter?

John – Sophie won't even open this letter. Why don't you go and fetch her?

Mrs Sevak – She refuses to come.

John – You've never asked her, why will she come?

Mrs Sevak – She has laid down such a condition for coming.

John – Break your conditions if you want her welfare.

Mrs Sevak – Shouldn't I open my mouth even if she refuses to go to church?

John – Thousands of Christians don't go to church, and the English go there very seldom.

Mrs Sevak – Should I keep quiet even if she criticizes the Lord Messiah?

John – She doesn't criticize the Messiah and nor can she do so. Anyone to whom God has given the slightest intelligence will sincerely respect the Lord Messiah. Even the Hindus take Jesus' name with respect. If Sophie doesn't believe that the Messiah is her saviour, or the Son of God, or God, why should she be forced? Several Christians have doubts on this topic although they may be afraid to express them. I believe that someone who does good deeds and has pure thoughts is far superior to the devotee of the Messiah who chants his name but whose intentions are bad.

Ishvar – Ya Khuda! Take this family under your protection. Beta, don't utter such words. The servant of the Messiah can never stray from the true path. The Lord Messiah has mercy on him.

John (*To his wife*) – Go tomorrow morning, you can meet the rani and also bring Sophie back.

Mrs Sevak – I'll have to now. I don't want to but I will. Let her have her way!

When Soordas returned home in the evening and heard the news, he said to Nayakram – You've given my land to sahib?

Nayakram – Why would I give it? What do I have to do with it?

Soordas – I had thought you to be all in all, and I used to jump around because of your might, but you too have deserted me today. It's all right. I was wrong to be so puffed up because of your strength. I've been punished for that. Now I'll fight on the strength of justice and trust only in God.

Nayakram – Bajrangi, just go and call Bhairo so that he can explain everything. For how long can I rack my brains with him?

Bajrangi – Why should I call Bhairo? Can't I do even this much? Bhairo has been given so much importance, that's why he has become so arrogant.

Bajrangi then recounted all the schemes of John Sevak, exaggerating some and minimizing others and said – Tell us, why should we fight with sahib if everybody gains from the factory?

Soordas – Are you convinced that everybody will gain?

Bajrangi – Yes, we are. If something is worth accepting, it will be accepted.

Soordas – All of you were ready to lay down your lives for the land until yesterday. You even suspected me of joining sahib. Today you have weakened with just one move made by sahib?

Bajrangi – Nobody had explained all this so clearly until now. The factory will benefit the whole muhalla, the whole city. The wages of the labourers will go up, the sales of the shopkeepers will increase. So we don't have any quarrel now. We advise you to give away the land. You are getting a good price. If you don't give it this way, it will be taken away from you legally. What's the use of that?

Soordas – Unrighteousness and ignorance have increased so much. Do you know that too?

Bajrangi – Unrighteousness comes with wealth, but nobody lets go of wealth.

Soordas – So now you people won't support me? Don't. Help isn't needed where there's justice. It's my property, the earning of my forefathers; no one else has a claim over it. If the land goes, so will my life along with it.

Soordas then stood up and after reaching the door of his hut, lay down under the neem tree.

13

AFTER VINAY'S DEPARTURE, IT SEEMED TO SOPHIA THAT RANI JAHNAVI stayed aloof. She called her very seldom to read books and papers or write letters, and observed Sophia's behaviour with suspicion. Although, as far as possible, she didn't show her indifference, it seemed to Sophie that she was not trusted any more. Whenever she went to the garden for a stroll or out elsewhere, it appeared, when she returned, that her books had been disarranged. The aloofness became even more unbearable when, on the postman's arrival, raniji would herself receive the letters and examine them carefully to see if there was one for Sophia. Very often, Sophia found that the envelopes of her letters were torn. She understood the secret of this diplomacy only too well. All these checks and restraints were meant only to prevent any correspondence between her and Vinay. Earlier raniji would often discuss Vinay and Indu with her. Now she didn't mention Vinay's name even by mistake. This was the first test of love.

However, it was surprising that Sophia no longer had the self-respect that would not allow even a fly to settle on her nose; she was extremely tolerant now. Instead of being annoyed with raniji, she looked for opportunities to allay her mistrust. She always considered raniji's conduct to be just. She'd think, 'Her supreme desire is that Vinay's life should be ideal, and that I should not be an obstacle to his self-discipline. How can I convince her that her ambition won't suffer even by a whiff because of me? I have sacrificed my own life for an ideal for which he alone is not sufficient. I myself won't let anyone else's desire become an impediment in the way of my goal.' However, Sophie didn't get this opportunity. There's never an opportunity for matters that cannot be expressed.

Sophie would often be annoyed by the restlessness of her mind. She would try to divert her attention by being engrossed in reading a book, but she would shut it with irritation when it remained open before her and her mind wandered elsewhere. 'What kind of a predicament am I in?' she'd think. 'Does maya want to lure me away from the right path by assuming this deceitful guise? Why do I consciously pretend to be ignorant? I vow now that I'll remove this thorn from my heart.'

However, the vow of those possessed by love is the coward's desire for war, which disappears at the opponent's challenge. Sophia wanted to forget Vinay but, at the same time, she was also convinced that he wouldn't forget her. When she didn't get news of him for several days, she thought, 'He must have forgotten me, surely he has forgotten. If I knew his address I'd have written to him every day, I'd have sent several letters but he doesn't have the time to write even one! He's trying to forget me. That's good. Why should he love a Christian? Aren't there any number of beautiful, educated, devoted princesses available for him?'

She was so distressed by these thoughts that one day she went to the rani's room and began to read Vinay's letters. In a trice, she had read all those that she could find. 'Let me see, is there any hint about me, any sentence with the fragrance of love?' However, she couldn't find a single word from which she could extract some hidden meaning. Yes, there was an elaborate description of the difficulties they were facing in that mountainous terrain. Youth loves to exaggerate. We try to increase our importance not by being victorious over difficulties but by describing them vividly. An ordinary fever is called a collapse. Walking in the mountains for just one day is described as constantly breaking one's head against them. Vinay's letters were full of such tales of heroism. Sophia was distraught at reading of these conditions. 'He is facing so many difficulties,' she thought, 'and here am I, living in such comfort.' She entered her room in this agitated state and wrote Vinay a long letter in which every word was saturated with love. She ended with a loving and humble plea requesting his permission to join him, since she could no longer stay where she was. Her style became strangely poetic. After completing the letter, she immediately posted it in a letter box nearby.

After posting the letter, when her agitation had subsided, she realized that it was highly improper for her to have gone secretly to raniji's room and read the letters. She was worried about this all day and repeatedly rebuked herself, 'God! I'm so unfortunate. I sacrificed my life in quest of the true dharma and for years I have been absorbed in the quest for truth, but I succumbed at the very first blow of desire. Why have I become so weak? Will my sacred ideal get drowned in the whirlpool of desires? I never thought I'd become so debased that I'll steal someone's things. I've betrayed the person who has so much love for me, so much trust, faith and respect. If this is my predicament now, God alone knows what it will be like later. It is better that my life should now come to an end! Ah! That letter which I have just posted, I would tear it up if I could get it back.'

She was sitting there worried and remorseful when raniji came into the room. Sophia stood up and began staring at the floor to hide her eyes. But it's not easy to stop one's tears. The rani asked harshly, 'Sophie, why are you crying?'

The truth automatically comes out when we are ashamed of our mistakes. Sophia said hesitatingly, 'It's nothing . . . I've committed a crime and ask your forgiveness.'

The rani asked even more sharply – What is it?

Sophia – I went to your room today when you had gone out for a stroll.

Rani – What for?

Sophie, full of embarrassment, said – I haven't touched anything of yours.

Rani – I didn't think you to be so debased.

Sophia – I wanted to see a letter.

Rani – Vinay's?

Sophia bowed her head. She was so degraded in her own eyes that she wished the earth would part and swallow her. The rani said contemptuously, 'Sophie, you perhaps think that I am ungrateful but I've made a big mistake by keeping you in my house. I've never before made such a mistake. I didn't know that you would turn out to be a snake in the grass. It would have been far better if Vinay had been burnt in the fire that day. I wouldn't have felt so much sorrow. I didn't understand your behaviour earlier. There was a veil before my eyes. Do you know why I sent Vinay away from here so soon? Because of you. To save him from the wounds inflicted by your love. But even now, like fate, you are not letting go of him. After all, what do you want from him? You know that you can't marry him. Even if I don't consider status and family honour, there is the wall of religion between us. What else can be the result of this love except that you will destroy him along with yourself and reduce my long-cherished desires to dust? I want to make Vinay the kind of human being of whom society will be proud, in whose heart there will be love, courage and endurance, who won't turn his face away from dangers, who will always be ready to sacrifice his life for the sake of service, in whom there won't be a trace of sensuality, who will annihilate himself for the sake of dharma. I want to make him a good son, a faithful friend and a selfless worker. I don't hanker for his marriage and I don't wish to play with my grandsons. There's no dearth of self-serving men and devoted mothers in the world. The earth is being crushed under their burden. I want to make my son a Rajput. I would be the most fortunate mother in the world if he were to sacrifice his life to protect someone today. You are shattering this golden dream of mine. I'm telling you the truth, Sophie, in this situation I would have thought it my duty to poison you to get rid of you had I not been weighed down by your favour. I am a Rajputani, I know how to die as well as how to kill. I'll strangle you before I see you correspond with Vinay. I beg of you, don't try to ensnare Vinay in your love, or the consequences will be disastrous. God has given you intelligence and prudence. Act prudently. Don't destroy my family.'

Sophia (*Crying*) – Give me your permission. I'll leave today.

The rani softened somewhat and said – I'm not telling you to leave. You are most welcome to stay here. (*Feeling embarrassed*) Forgive me for the harsh words I just uttered. Old age is very brusque. This is your home. Stay here with pleasure. Vinay will probably not return. He can face a tiger but not my anger. He'll pluck the leaves in forest after forest but he won't return home. If you love him then be prepared to sacrifice yourself for his welfare. There's now only one way of saving his life. Do you know what that is?

Sophie shook her head and said – No.

Rani – Do you want to know?

Sophie shook her head and said – Yes.

Rani – Get married to some eligible man. Show Vinay that you have forgotten him and that you don't care about him. It's only this disappointment that can save him. It's possible that it may alienate him from life so that he'll seek shelter in attaining knowledge, which is the sole refuge of dejection. However, despite that possibility, there's no other way except this solution. Do you agree?

Sophie fell down at the rani's feet and said, weeping – For his welfare . . . I can.

The rani raised Sophie, embraced her and said tenderly – I know you can do anything for him. May God give you the strength to fulfil this vow!

Jahnavi left after that. Sophie sat down on a couch, hid her face with both hands and sobbed bitterly. Every pore of her body ached with remorse. She was not angry with Jahnavi; she had boundless faith in her. 'What a noble and sacred ideal! In fact I'm the fly in the milk, I should leave,' she thought. But the rani's last order was the bitterest morsel for her. She could become a yogini but the very thought of besmirching love abhorred her. Her condition was like that of the patient who goes to a garden for a stroll and is caught for the crime of plucking fruit. Vinay's sacrifice had made her his devotee, worship soon took on the guise of love, and that love was forcibly dragging her towards the darkness of hell. If she were to free herself then the danger was . . . She couldn't think beyond this. Her thoughts were paralysed. In the end all the worries, remorse, disappointment, frustration, disappeared in a long sigh.

It was evening. Dejected and sad, Sophia sat staring towards the garden like a widow mourning for her husband when Prabhu entered the room.

Sophia did not speak to him. She sat quietly, like a statue. She had reached the condition when even sympathy is unwelcome. The last state of disappointment is detachment.

But Prabhu was so eager to recite his new creation that he did not notice Sophie's face. As he came in, he said – Sophie, look, I wrote this poem tonight. Listen to it attentively. I have just recited it to kunwar sahib. He enjoyed it immensely.

Prabhu then began to recite his poem in a melodious voice. The poet had expressed the emotions of a distressed being in the world of the dead on seeing the constellations of the stars. He would recite each line swaying with great delight, repeating it twice or three times but Sophia did not praise them even once, as if she were devoid of any taste for poetry. When the poem came to an end, Prabhu asked, 'What do you think of it?'

Sophia said – It's good.

Prabhu – You didn't pay attention to my beautiful verses. No poet until now has compared the constellations of the stars to divine souls. I'm sure there will be a sensation among the poets as soon as it is published.

Sophia – I seem to remember that Shelley and Wordsworth have already used this simile. Poets here have also given a similar description. Perhaps it's also the title of one of Hugo's poems. It's possible that your imagination has been influenced by them.

Prabhu – I know more about poetry than you but I haven't found this simile anywhere.

Sophia – Well, perhaps I'm the one who doesn't remember. The poem is not bad.

Prabhu – If any other poet can achieve this miracle, I'll become his slave.

Sophia – Then I'll say that you don't value your independence too much.

Prabhu – Then I'll also say that you need much more practice to appreciate poetry.

Sophia – I have far more important things to do in my life. What news of home?

Prabhu – It's the same old situation. I'm frustrated now. Papa is obsessed with the factory and I hate that work. Papa and mama are always fuming. No one talks with a straight face. I can't find a place, else I wouldn't stay a day in this nest of illusions. I don't know where to go.

Sophia – It's very surprising that someone as qualified and scholarly as you can't find a way to subsist. Is there no place for self-respect in the world of the imagination?

Prabhu – Sophie, I can do everything else but I can't carry the burden of domestic worries. I want to remain free, without cares, detached. To remain in a beautiful garden, under a dense tree, listening to the sweet chirping of birds, meditating on poetry, this is my life's ideal.

Sophia – Your life will be spent in these dreams.

Prabhu – Be that as it may, at least I don't have any worries, and I'm free.

Sophia – Freedom runs miles away when the soul and principles are murdered. I call this shamelessness, not freedom. The cruelty of parents is not less painful; in fact, the tyranny of others is not as unbearable as that of parents.

Prabhu – Oh, we'll see. I'll bear it when I have to. Why cry before it's time to die?

He then narrated the Pandeypur incident and boasted so much that Sophie said, annoyed – Come on, what great feat have you accomplished by beating up a villager? You are the god of non-violence in your poems but lose self-control over something so trivial.

Prabhu – Should I have tolerated abuses?

Sophia – When will you follow non-violence if you too beat those who beat and abuse? No one beats somebody walking on the road. Actually, no youth should have the right to preach, no matter how remarkable his poetic talent may be. Preaching is only for those men who have proved themselves. Preaching peace and non-violence is not for just anyone who can put together a few verses. You should first learn for yourself what you want to teach others.

Prabhu – This is just what Vinay has written in his letter. I've remembered now. This is your letter. I forgot all about it. I would have carried it back in my pocket if this topic had not come up.

He handed Sophia an envelope.

Sophia – Where is he nowadays?

Prabhu – He's wandering around in the mountainous regions of Udaipur. He has written clearly in his letter to me that he's totally unfit for social service. He says he doesn't have the endurance it needs. Youth is the time for gaining experience. It's only in old age that one should do social service. To send a young man to do social service is like sending a child vaidya to heal patients.

After Prabhu had left, Sophia wondered if she should read the letter. 'Vinay wants to keep it a secret from raniji, otherwise he'd have sent it to this address. I have just promised raniji that I won't correspond with him. It's not proper to open this letter. I should show it to raniji. That will remove her suspicion of me. But I don't know what's written. Perhaps there's something that may excite her anger even more. No, I should keep this letter a secret. It isn't possible to show it to the rani.'

Then she thought – What's the use of reading it? I don't know what my predicament will be. I don't trust myself any longer. Why should

I nurture this sprout of love when it has to be rooted out anyway? It's better to hand over this letter to the rani.

Sophia didn't deliberate any longer. She thought she might waver. Water doesn't remain in a sieve. She went immediately and gave the letter to the rani.

Rani – Whose letter is it? This seems like Vinay's handwriting. It's in your name, isn't it? You haven't opened the envelope?

Sophia – No.

The rani said, pleased – I give you permission, read it. I'm very happy that you have kept your promise.

Sophia – Forgive me.

Rani – I'm saying this gladly, read it. See what he has written.

Sophia – No.

The rani put away the letter in the box as it was. She too didn't read it because it would have been unethical. She then said to Sophia – Beti, now I have another request. Write a letter to Vinay and explain to him clearly that it's best for both of you to retain only the relationship of brother and sister. Your letter should make it evident that you care for his patriotic views more than for his love. This letter of yours will be far more effective than thousands of instructions from his father or me. I'm sure that his goals will change as soon as he gets your letter and he will be determined to follow the path of duty. I shall be obliged to you till the end of my life for this favour.

Sophie said timidly – I'll obey you.

Rani – No, it's not enough to obey me. It won't be effective if he realizes that the letter has been written at someone's instigation.

Sophia – Shall I show you the letter when I have written it?

Rani – No, just send it.

Sophia didn't know what to write when she began the letter. She thought – He'll think that I'm callous. He'll feel so distressed if I let him know that I didn't even read his letter. How can I tell him that I don't love him?

She got up from the table and decided that she'd write the next day. She began to read a book. It was 9 p.m. and time to eat. She had just finished washing her face and hands when she saw the rani peeping through the door. Sophie thought that perhaps she had come for some work and began to read her book. Before fifteen minutes had passed, the rani returned from the other side and peeped into the room.

Sophie thought her hovering around like this to be very offensive. 'She just wants to make me a puppet,' she thought. 'I should go on dancing to her tune, that's all. She couldn't bring herself to read out the letter to me when I handed her the unopened envelope. After all, what should I write? I don't know what he has written in his letter.' She realized then that her letter may turn out to be a sermon and that Vinay would feel offended on reading it. We want to listen to matters of love and pleasure from our lovers, not sermons and instructions. 'It was just as well or goodness knows what he would have thought on reading my sermon. He would have thought that listening to sermons in church has made me devoid of the feelings of love. I would have felt awful had he written me such a letter. Ah! I have been terribly deceived. I had first thought that I would only love him spiritually. It's evident now that spiritual love belongs only to the world of religion. It's impossible for pure love to exist between a man and a woman. Love first catches hold of the finger and is then quick to seize the wrist. I know that this love is making me fall from the high ideal of wisdom. We have been given this life to elevate it by noble thoughts and virtuous deeds and then one day to merge into the eternal light. I also know that life is perishable and impermanent, just like the joys of the world. I know all this yet I'm like the moth falling on the lamp. That's because in love there's the forgetfulness that veils restraint, knowledge and determination. Even devotees who experience spiritual bliss are not liberated from desires. To tell someone who is being forcibly dragged to desist is such great injustice.'

The night is a difficult tapasya for those who suffer. Sophie's agitation increased with its passing. After helplessly battling with her emotions until midnight, she allowed herself to indulge in the play of love, as if the manager of a theatre, fed up of the jostling of the spectators, opens the doors for the general public since the noise outside would obstruct the melodious flow of sounds inside. Sophie surrendered herself to thoughts of love and began to enjoy them uninhibitedly.

'Well, Vinay, what difficulties will you face for me? Insults, disdain, anger, the opposition of parents, will you bear all these obstacles for me? But religion? See, you are looking sad now. You can do anything except give up your religion. I'm in the same situation. I can fast with you, I can suffer disdain, contempt, criticism but how can I give up my religion? How can I leave the refuge of Jesus? I don't care about Christianity, for that's only an institution of self-interest, but why should I turn away from that pure soul who was the incarnation of forgiveness and compassion? Isn't it possible for me to remain enfolded in Christ's shelter and also satisfy my desires for love? Is there anyone who can't get shelter in the generous shade of Hinduism? Believers and non-believers alike are Hindus, so are those who believe in thirty-three crore gods. Is there no place for worshippers of Christ where there is room for devotees of Mahavira and Buddhadev? You have invited me to love you, how can I refuse? I'll also get engrossed in social service; I'll roam the forests with you and live in huts.

'Ah, I made a big mistake. I unnecessarily gave that letter to raniji. It was my letter and I had every right to read it. The relationship between us is that of love, which is purer and greater than any other in the world. I'm being unfair to Vinay by sacrificing my right. No, I'm betraying him and besmirching love. I'm ridiculing his feelings. I'd have felt so distressed had he torn up my letter without reading it that I'd never have forgiven him. What should I do? Should I ask raniji for the letter? She shouldn't object. No matter how annoyed she may feel, she will surely return what belongs to me. She's not ungenerous like mama. But why should I ask her? It's my property; no one else has a claim to it. Why should I ask anyone else's favour to take what belongs to me?'

It was 11 p.m. There was silence all around the palace. All the servants had gone to sleep. When Sophia looked out into the garden from the window, it seemed as if the sky were raining milk. Moonlight was generously splattered. The two marble fairies standing at the edge of the reservoir seemed as if they were illuminated images of silent music, enrapturing all of nature.

Sophia experienced a strong desire to go and get her letter that very moment. With strong determination, she fearlessly went towards raniji's reception room. She kept explaining to herself – Why should I be afraid, I want to get back my own thing. I can say that frankly to anyone who asks. It's not a sin to take Vinay's name.

However, despite this repeated reassurance, she walked so carefully that there was no sound of her footsteps even on the cemented floor of the veranda. Her face reflected the turbulence that is a sign of inner anxiety. She would keep looking apprehensively right and left, back and front. Her feet would automatically stop at the slightest sound and she would hide behind the pillars of the veranda. There were several rooms on the way. Although they were dark and the lights had been extinguished, she would stop for a moment at each door in case anyone was sitting there. She suddenly saw a terrier whom raniji loved very much coming towards her. Sophie's hair stood on end. There would be a commotion in the house if he were to open his mouth. The dog looked at her suspiciously and was just about to signal his decision, when Sophie softly called him by his name, and picking him up in her lap, began to stroke his back. The dog began to wag his tail, but instead of going his way, he went along with Sophie. Perhaps his animal instincts had sensed that there was something wrong. She found raniji's reception room after five rooms. The doors were open but there was darkness inside. There were electric switches inside, so there could be light in the room with the slightest touch of the finger. But at this moment pressing the switch was no less dangerous than putting a match to a heap of gunpowder. She had never before been so afraid of the light. The problem, however, was that she couldn't attain her objective without it. It was ambrosia as well as poison. She was annoyed that there were glasspanes in the windows. The curtains were so fine that anyone's face would be visible. It was less a house, more a decorated shop—a complete imitation of the English. And where was the point in extinguishing the lights? After all it wasn't all that economical.

When we walk down a narrow road, we find the coming and going of vehicles very troublesome. We wish that there could be some way of stopping them from moving on these roads. If we had our way, we wouldn't allow any vehicles on them, especially cars. But when we ourselves travel on a vehicle on these roads, we feel irritated when we have to stop at every step for pedestrians because they don't walk on the pavement and unnecessarily get in the way. It's human nature to be annoyed at circumstances when we ourselves are in difficulty.

Sophia stood near the switch for several minutes. She didn't have the courage to press it. The whole courtyard would be illuminated. Even someone who is asleep in the dark wakes up as soon there is light. Helplessly, she began to grope on the table. The inkpot turned over, spilling the ink and staining her clothes. She was sure that the rani had kept the letter in her handbag. That was where she kept important letters. She found the bag with great difficulty and began to take out all the letters one by one to examine them in the dark. Most of the envelopes were of the same shape; her eyesight failed her. When she found that she couldn't attain her objective this way, she picked up the handbag and left the room. She thought that since there was still light in her room, she could easily find the letter there and then put the handbag back. While returning she was not as cautious as she had been on her way there. She had then looked around at every step. Now she walked so fast that she had no time to look around. There was scope for an excuse when she was empty-handed, but there can be no apologies, no excuse when one is caught red-handed.

As soon as she reached her room, Sophie shut the door and pulled the curtains. She was perspiring heavily because of the heat and her hands were trembling as if they were paralysed. She pulled out the letters and began to examine them. Not only did she have to examine them, she had to put them back carefully in their place. There was a post office in front of her. Letters several years old were enjoying nirvana there. Sophia spent several hours searching those letters; she came to the end of the post office but didn't find what she was looking for. She began to feel somewhat disappointed and even put away the last letter after turning it this way and that. Sophia then took a deep breath. Her condition was like that of a man who looks for his friend in a fair. He looks all around and loudly calls his name, thinking that the friend is standing there, he rushes towards him and then returns embarrassed. In the end he sits down on the ground disappointed and starts crying.

Sophia also began to cry. 'Where was that letter? The rani had put it in this bag in my presence. All her other letters are here. Has she kept it somewhere else?' But hope is like the grass that gets burnt in the heat of the summer, there's no sign of it on the earth that becomes as bright as a newly minted coin but the burnt roots begin to flourish again as soon as it begins to rain and greenery begins to sway in that arid space.

Sophia's hope was reawakened. Perhaps she had overlooked a letter. She began to read the letters again more attentively. She opened each and every envelope to check if the rani had put the letter in some other envelope. When she realized that the night would pass this way, she began to open the envelopes that seemed heavy. Finally even this doubt was settled. There was no sign of that envelope. Now the roots of hope withered and there were no raindrops.

Sophia lay down on the bed, tired. There is a great deal of vivacity in success and unbearable turmoil in failure. Hope is intoxication; disappointment is sobriety. We run towards the battlefield when we are intoxicated; we rest at home when we are sober. Hope takes us towards senselessness, disappointment towards consciousness. Hope shuts our eyes; disappointment opens them. Hope is the pat that puts us to sleep, disappointment the whip that awakens.

Sophie was angry with herself for her moral weakness. 'I unnecessarily burdened my soul with this crime. Couldn't I have asked the rani for my letter? She wouldn't have hesitated even for a moment to give it to me. And then why did I give her the letter at all? What will raniji think of me if she gets to know of this deceitful behaviour of mine, and she is sure to get to know of it? Surely there's no creature more debased and vile than I.'

All of a sudden, Sophia heard the sound of sweeping. She was startled, was it morning? When she raised the curtain and opened the door, she saw that the day had dawned. There was darkness before her eyes. She looked at the bag, really frightened, and stood there like a statue. Her consciousness was paralysed. She was so annoyed at her action and her predicament that she wanted to slit her throat. 'How will I face her? The rani gets up very early, she's sure to see me. But what else can happen now? God! You are the pillar of support for the meek; my honour is now in your hands. God, don't let the rani awaken just now.' There was so much humility, helplessness, pain, faith and such shame in her prayer! Perhaps she had never before prayed with such a pure heart!

There was not a moment to be lost. She picked up the bag and went outside. Self-respect had never before been so demeaned. She would perhaps not have gone so stealthily had her face been blackened! Even a gentleman in chains in the guise of a criminal would not have felt so deeply ashamed. When she reached the door of the reception room, her heart began to beat as if it were being pounded by a hammer. She hesitated awhile and peeped into the room; the rani was sitting there. Sophia's predicament at that moment can only be imagined. She felt deeply humiliated. If lightning had struck her, or if the ground beneath her had parted, she would probably have thought it to be as pleasant as a shower of flowers or a water sport compared to this great calamity. Looking down at the floor, she quietly put the handbag on the table. The rani gave her the kind of piercing look that feels like an arrow deep within. It was deeply contemptuous; there was no anger, no pity, no rage, just pure, living, eloquent contempt.

Sophia was about to return when the rani asked – Were you looking for Vinay's letter?

Sophia was stunned. It seemed as if she had been pierced with a javelin.

The rani said again – I have kept it separately. Shall I send for it?

Sophia didn't reply. She began to feel dizzy, as if the room were spinning.

The rani shot the third arrow – Is this the investigation of truth?

Sophia fainted and fell down on the floor.

14

WHEN SOPHIA REGAINED CONSCIOUSNESS, SHE FOUND HERSELF lying on her bed. The rani's last words echoed in her ears – Is this the investigation of truth? She thought herself to be so debased at this moment that even if the sweeper of the household had abused her she would probably not have raised her head. She was so defeated by desire that she couldn't see any hope of taking hold of herself. She was apprehensive that her heart could make her act in such ways that make human beings bow down their heads with shame at their very thought. 'I used to laugh so much at others, I was so proud of my religious disposition, I used to reflect deeply on such profound topics as rebirth and liberation, man and nature, and I used to disdain others for being enslaved by desire and selfishness. I thought I'd reached close to God, that having rejected the world, I was liberated from life, but my devotion has been exposed today! What will Vinay think when he gets to know all this? I'll perhaps fall so low in his eyes that he won't even want to talk to me. I'm unfortunate, I have disgraced him; I have besmirched my family, murdered my soul, defiled the generosity of those who have sheltered me. I have even disgraced religion, otherwise would I have been asked – 'Is this the investigation of truth?'

She looked towards the head of her bed. Sacred texts were arranged in the cabinets. She didn't have the courage to glance at them. 'Is this the result of my self-study?' she thought. 'I had set out to investigate truth but I've fallen so badly that it's difficult to get up now.'

There was a picture of Lord Buddha on the wall in front. His face was so radiant. Sophia lowered her eyes. She was ashamed to look towards him. She had never before believed so fully in the Buddha's immortality. Even a wooden log becomes alive in the dark. There was a similar darkness in Sophie's heart.

It was 9 a.m. but Sophia thought that evening was approaching. She wondered – Have I been asleep the whole day? Nobody even woke me up! Why would anyone wake me up? Who cares for me here now, and why should they? I'm a sinner, nobody will gain anything from me,

I'll set fire wherever I am. I set foot in this house at an inauspicious moment. It will be desolated because of me, I'll ruin Vinay along with myself. Mata's curse will surely fall on me. God, why are such thoughts coming to my mind today?

At that point, Mrs Sevak entered the room. As soon as Sophia saw her, she felt as if a fountain had welled up in her heart. She ran and clung to her mother. This was now her last refuge where she could get the sympathy without which it was difficult for her to live. This was where she could get the rest, the peace, the shade for which her tormented soul yearned. Where else could this blissful heaven be found except in her mother's lap? Who else except her mother would embrace her and apply balm to her heart? Her mother's harsh words and her cruel behaviour, all vanished in the surge of this desire for comfort. She felt as if God had taken mercy on her suffering and had sent mama. When she put her troubled head on her mother's lap she once again experienced the strength and courage that she had not yet forgotten. She began to sob, but there were no tears in her mother's eyes. She was impatient to give the good news of Mr Clark's invitation. The moment Sophia's tears abated, Mrs Sevak said, 'You'll have to come with me today. Mr Clark has invited you to his place.'

Sophia didn't reply. Her mother's words seemed very distasteful.

Mrs Sevak again said, 'He has asked about your welfare several times ever since you came here. He always talks about you whenever we meet. I have not seen such a courteous civilian. He could easily marry into an English family, and it's your good luck that he still remembers you.'

Sophia turned her face away contemptuously. Her mother's craving for status was intolerable. There was no talk of love, no words of consolation, no welling up of tenderness. She would probably not have been so happy even if the Lord Messiah had invited her.

Mrs Sevak said, 'You shouldn't refuse now. Delay cools the ardour of love and then no blow can affect it. Such a golden opportunity won't come again; a wise man has said that "every being gets only one opportunity in his life to test his fate, and that decides the future". This is the opportunity of your life. You'll always regret it if you let it go.'

Sophia said, distressed, 'You would probably not have remembered me at all if Mr Clark had not invited me?'

Mrs Sevak replied in a restrained voice, 'God only knows what's in my heart but not a day goes by when I don't pray to Him for Prabhu and you. It's the auspicious result of those prayers that you have got this opportunity.'

Mrs Sevak then went to meet Jahnavi. The rani didn't show her any special respect. She kept sitting where she was and said, 'I'm seeing you here after a long time.'

Mrs Sevak said with a dry laugh, 'Your return visit is still due.'

Rani – But when did you come to see me? Earlier too you had come to meet Sophia, and that's why you have come even now. I was about to write you a letter today. If you don't mind, can I ask you something?

Mrs Sevak – Go ahead, why should I mind?

Rani – Miss Sophia is quite old now. Have you thought about her marriage or not? Because the sooner she gets married, the better it will be. Girls among you people get married when they are very mature.

Mrs Sevak – She could have got married long ago, several Englishmen were excessively eager, but she doesn't agree. She's so interested in religious texts that she thinks of marriage as a snare. Proposals are coming now from Mr Clark, the district magistrate. Let me see whether she agrees. I've come with the intention of taking her away today. I don't want to form ties with Indian Christians. I don't like their way of living and it shouldn't be difficult to find an English husband for a well-educated girl like Sophie.

Rani – In my opinion, marriages should always take place within one's community. Europeans don't have much respect for Indian Christians and the consequences of incompatible marriages are not good.

Mrs Sevak (*With pride*) – There's no European who would consider it beneath his dignity to marry into my family. We are the same as them. We believe in the same God, we pray in the same church and are followers of the same prophet. Our lifestyles, eating and drinking habits, customs and traditions are the same. We get the same respect here in the society of the English, in clubs, at parties. Just three or four days ago, there was a function for awarding prizes to girls. Mr Clark himself made me the chief guest of that function and I distributed the prizes. A Hindu or a Muslim lady could not have received this honour.

Rani – Hindus or Muslims who have any pride in their community don't think it prestigious to interact with the English, to the extent that among the Hindus, those who eat and drink with the English are disdained by the others, not to speak of marriage! Political power is a different matter. A gang of dacoits can easily defeat an assembly of scholars. But that doesn't diminish the importance of the scholars. Every Hindu knows that the Messiah had come here during the Buddhist era, he was educated here, and he preached in the West the knowledge he had attained here. Then how can Hindus consider the English to be superior?

This squabbling continued between the two women. They both wanted to demean each other; both understood each other's thoughts. Nobody uttered words of gratitude or thanks. In fact when Mrs Sevak took her leave, Jahnavi didn't so much as see her to the door. She just held out her hand from where she was sitting and began reading the newspaper while Mrs Sevak was still in the room.

Sophia was ready when Mrs Sevak came to fetch her. Books were tied up in bundles. Several maids were standing around hoping to get tips. They were glad at heart to get rid of this nuisance at last. Sophia was very dejected. She felt sad at leaving this house. She didn't know what her destination was. She had no idea where destiny would take her, what difficulties she would have to face, on which bank the ship of her life would come to rest. It seemed to her that she wouldn't meet Vinay again and that she was being separated from him forever. She forgot the rani's contemptuous words, her rebukes and her suspicions. There was only one sound emanating from each string of her heart— she would not meet Vinay again.

Mrs Sevak said – I'll go and meet kunwar sahib too.

Sophia was afraid that her mother might get to know of the previous night's incident; kunwar sahib might jokingly mention it. She said – It will get late. Meet him some other time.

Mrs Sevak – Who'll have the time then?

They reached kunwar sahib's reception room where there was a crowd of volunteers. There was a famine in Garhwal; there was no food or water there. The animals were dying but even death did not come to human beings; they could only suffer helplessly and weep. A group of fifty volunteers was to leave to allay the sufferings of the afflicted. Kunwar sahib was selecting them and explaining important matters to them. Dr Ganguly had accepted the leadership of this group even in this old age. Both men were so busy that they didn't notice Mrs Sevak. She said at last, 'Doctor sahib, when do you intend to leave?'

Kunwar sahib turned towards Mrs Sevak. Going forward, he shook her hand with great alacrity, asked after her welfare, and made her sit on a chair. Sophia stood behind her mother.

Kunwar sahib – These people are going to Garhwal. You must have read about it in the papers, the people there are suffering from such a dire calamity.

Mrs Sevak – May God grant success to the efforts of these people. No praise is enough for their sacrifice. I see that they are here in large numbers.

Kunwar sahib – I didn't have so much hope, I didn't believe Vinay. I'd wonder from where to get so many volunteers. I'd see everybody lamenting the lack of enthusiasm among the youth—they don't have zeal, or the spirit of sacrifice, or vigour, they are all engrossed in taking care of their own interests. So many organizations for social service were established but not a single one flourished. But now I can see how misled people were about our youth. We already have 300 names registered. Some people have vowed to dedicate themselves to lifelong social service. Several among them have spurned salaries worth thousands of rupees to come here. I have become very optimistic on seeing their enthusiasm.

Mrs Sevak – Mr Clark was full of praise for you yesterday. If God so wills it, you will soon be C.I.E.* and I'll get the opportunity to congratulate you.*

Kunwar sahib (*Embarrassed*) – I'm not worthy of such respect. It's Mr Clark's generosity that he thinks me to be so worthy. Miss Sevak, be ready, these people will depart by the 3 p.m. mail train tomorrow. Prabhu has also promised to come.

Mrs Sevak – Sophie is going home today. (*Smiling*) Perhaps you'll

---

* C.I.E.: Companion of the Order of the Indian Empire. A title awarded from 1878 to 1947 to any British or Indian citizen who had rendered meritorious service to India. Rulers of princely states not entitled to a gun salute usually received this honour.

soon have to perform her kanyadaan. (*Softly*) Mr Clark is casting his net.

Sophie was deeply embarrassed. She was furious at her mother's shallowness – 'Where's the need to boast about these things? Does she think that kunwar sahib will be impressed if she mentions Mr Clark's name?'

Kunwar sahib – That's very good. Look, Sophie, don't forget us, and especially your poor brothers. God has given you so much compassion and you are also getting a good opportunity. Our good wishes will always be with you. We will always be obliged to you for the favour you have done us. Do remember us sometimes. I didn't know earlier, otherwise I would have definitely sent for Indu. Anyway, you know the state of the country. Mr Clark is a very promising man. Some day he's sure to be the ruler of some province of this country. I'm confidently prophesying this. You can then greatly benefit the country by your influence, ability and position. You have seen the condition of your compatriots; you have full experience of their poverty. Make good use of this experience in their service and for their improvement.

Sophia was so embarrassed she couldn't speak. Her mother said – You must bring raniji with you. I'll send a card.

Kunwar sahib – No, Mrs Sevak, please excuse me. I'm sorry but I can't attend that function. I have vowed not to have any contact with government officials. The favours of officials, in apparent or inapparent ways, make us self-serving and unrestrained. I don't want to put myself through this test because I don't trust myself. I don't want to differentiate between raja and subjects, high and low, among my people. All are subjects, king as well as beggar. I don't want my head to be turned by the pride of false power.

Mrs Sevak – God has made you a raja. A raja can interact only with other rajas. The English are not familiar with babus because it would be insulting to the rajas here.

Dr Ganguly – Mrs Sevak, he has been a raja for a long time, now he's fed up. I'm his childhood friend. We studied together. He seems younger than me but he's several years older than he looks.

Mrs Sevak (*Laughing*) – This is not something to be proud of for a doctor.

Dr Ganguly – We know how to cure others but not ourselves. Kunwar sahib is a *pessimist** from those days. That pessimism was an impediment in his education. He's in the same predicament even now. But there's some change. Earlier he was a *pessimist* in words as well as actions. Now there's no congruity between his words and his actions. He's still a *pessimist* when it comes to words, but he does the kind of work that only a confirmed *optimist* can.

Kunwar sahib – Ganguly, you are being unfair to me. I don't have the qualities of an optimist. An optimist is a devotee of the Supreme Being, a complete sage, a complete rishi. He sees the light of the Supreme Being everywhere. That's why he doesn't distrust the future. I have been a devotee of pleasure from the beginning; I couldn't attain that divine knowledge which is the key to optimism. There's no other way for me except *pessimism*. Mrs Sevak, the essence of life for doctor mahodaya is self-sacrifice. He has faced so many calamities that any rishi would have become an atheist. It would be rare to find an example of a man whose seven sons betrayed him when they grew up, but who did not waver at all from the path of duty. His endurance doesn't know how to give way; the blows of misfortune give him even greater strength. I lack courage and manliness. I can't believe that any ruling nation can treat its subjects with justice and equality. I haven't found human nature to be so disinterested in any country or age. The nation that has lost its independence once cannot regain it. Slavery becomes its destiny. But our doctor babu doesn't think that human nature is so selfish. He believes there are infinite rays of light even in the hearts of beasts of prey; all that's needed is to remove the veil. I have despaired of the English; he believes that India's salvation will happen only through them.

Mrs Sevak (*Coldly*) – So you don't believe that perhaps no nation has done as much for another nation or country as the English have for India?

Kunwar sahib – No, I don't believe this.

Mrs Sevak (*Surprised*) – Has there been such widespread education at any other time?

---

* The italicized words are in English in the original.

Kunwar sahib – I don't consider that to be education at all which makes human beings puppets of self-interest.

Mrs Sevak – Railways, telegraphs, ships, the post—all these glories have come with the English!

Kunwar sahib – They could have also come without the English, and even if they have come, it's mostly for their benefit.

Mrs Sevak – There has never before been such a just Constitution.

Kunwar sahib – That's right, when was there such a just Constitution that can prove injustice to be justice and lies to be truth! This is not law but a legal maze.

Jahnavi entered the room. Sophia's face fell the moment she saw her. She left the room, she couldn't face the rani. Mrs Sevak was also apprehensive of the possibility of another discussion with the rani. So she too came out. Kunwar sahib helped them both on to the phaeton. With tearful eyes, Sophia folded her hands to do pranaam to him. The phaeton started. There were black clouds in the sky, the phaeton was moving fast on the road, and Sophia was crying. Her predicament was like that of a child who, while eating a roti, hears the cry of a mithai-vala and runs after him. He stumbles and falls, loses his money, and returns home crying.

15

ALTHOUGH MAHENDRA SINGH DID NOT IN THE LEAST YIELD TO THE authorities on matters of principle, he thought it was not only futile but also inappropriate for the country to oppose them on minor matters. He believed in a policy of pacifism rather than extremism, especially because in the present circumstances he could render whatever service was possible only by winning the confidence of the rulers. Consequently, he was often compelled to adopt a policy that gave an opportunity to the extremists to point a finger at him. If he had a weakness, it was that he craved esteem, and like several other men of the same kind, he decided his course of action not on the basis of what was proper but with a view to attaining greater fame. To begin with, he had sided with justice and had refused to get Soordas's land for John Sevak but he was now compelled to act differently. To conciliate those of his own class, it was sufficient to have taken action when the people of Pandeypur had been incited to force their way into Tahir Ali's house. But actually it was the reciprocal friendship between John Sevak and Mr Clark that had prompted him to change his decision. However, he had not yet presented this proposal to the board. He was apprehensive of being accused of siding with a rich businessman. It was his habit to consult Indu, or his close friends in Indu's absence, before presenting a proposal. He'd satisfy himself by trying to resolve their doubts and getting their support for his point of view. Although these discussions made no difference and he would remain entrenched in his position, an exchange of ideas for an hour or two gave him much reassurance.

It was the third pahar. The volunteers of the society were gathering at the station to leave for Garhwal. Indu ordered the gharry to be prepared. Although it was very cloudy and the sky was darkening every moment, it was necessary to go to the station to see off the volunteers. Jahnavi had pleaded earnestly with her to come. Indu was just about to leave when raja sahib came in. Seeing that she was about to leave, he asked, 'Where are you going? It's very cloudy.'

Indu – The volunteers of the society are going to Garhwal. I'm going to the station to see them off. Ammaji has also asked me to come.

Raja sahib – It's sure to rain.

Indu – I'll drop the curtain, and so what if I get wet? After all, those who are going so far for social service are also human beings.

Raja sahib – Will it matter if you don't go? The station will be very crowded.

Indu – Why should it matter? They'll leave anyway, whether I go or not, but I can't help myself. Those people are leaving their homes, goodness knows what difficulties they will have to face and when they will return. Can't I at least see them off? Why don't you also come along?

Raja sahib (*Surprised*) – I?

Indu – Yes, will there be any problem if you come?

Raja sahib – I don't join such organizations.

Indu – What kinds of organizations?

Raja sahib – These kinds of organizations.

Indu – Is it objectionable even to sympathize with societies for social service? I don't think that there can be anything embarrassing or objectionable about participating in such noble activities.

Raja sahib – There's a vast difference between your understanding and mine. Had I not been chairman of the board, a part of the administration and ruler of the riyasat, I would have participated freely in every kind of social work. In the present situation, my participation in such an organization will be taken as proof that the government authorities are sympathetic to it. I don't want to spread this illusion. The society for social service comprises the youth and, although at present it believes in the ideal of social service and wants to tread only that path, experience has proved that service and philanthropy often take forms that are unacceptable to any government, and visible as well as invisible efforts have to be made to extirpate them. I don't want to take on such a great responsibility.

Indu – Then why don't you resign? Why sacrifice your freedom?

Raja sahib – Only because I know that no one else can administer the city as well as I can. I don't care at all about my freedom since I have such a rare opportunity to serve the city. I'm the ruler of a state so naturally my sympathies are with the government. Democracy and communism are hostile to wealth. I won't support communism until I decide to sacrifice my wealth. I can't be a follower of communism in words and oppose it by my actions. Such a deep opposition between words and actions is intolerable for me. Those who proclaim equality while enjoying their wealth are deceitful and hypocritical. I don't understand with what face they can be worshippers of communism and also live in grand palaces, cruise on motorboats, and uninhibitedly enjoy the pleasures of the world. Removing the carpets from your room and wearing simple clothes isn't communism. This is shameless deception, blatant hypocrisy. To throw the leftover morsels from your kitchen to the poor is to mock communism, to discredit it.

This was an aspersion against kunwar sahib. Indu understood. She frowned, but controlled herself, and to close this unpleasant topic, she said – I'm getting late, it's almost 3 p.m., and the train leaves at 3.30 p.m. I'll meet ammaji and also get news of Vinay's welfare. So it will be killing two birds with one stone.

Raja sahib – The reasons for which it's improper for me to go apply to you too. Whether you go or I, it's the same.

Indu immediately returned to her room. 'If this is not injustice, what else is it?' she thought. 'It's insufferable tyranny! I'm supposed to be a rani but I don't have the right to go out of the house. Even the maids are better off than I.' She felt depressed and her eyes filled with tears. She rang the bell and told the maid, 'Tell them to unfasten the gharry. I'm not going to the station.'

Mahendra Kumar followed her in and said – Why don't you go out somewhere?

Indu – No, it's cloudy, I'll get drenched.

Raja sahib – Are you angry?

Indu – Why should I be angry! I'm a slave to your orders. You told me not to go, so I won't.

Raja sahib – I don't want to pressurize you. If you don't see any objection to going there even after knowing my apprehensions, then go with pleasure. My purpose was merely to awaken your good sense. I want to prevent you on the strength of justice, not by ordering you. Suppose I'm disgraced by your going, would you still want to go?

This was like letting a bird fly by clipping its wings. Indu didn't even attempt to fly. There could only be one answer to this question, 'Never!

This would be against my dharma.' But Indu resented her dependence so much that she didn't even hear this question, or if she heard it, she didn't heed it. It seemed to her that he was sprinkling salt on her wounds. 'What will amma think? "I called her but she didn't come. How wealth has affected her!" How will I plead for her forgiveness? If I write that I'm unwell, she'll come here immediately and I'll be embarrassed. Ah! I would have reached there by now. Prabhu Sevak must have written a very powerful poem. Dadaji's instructions will also be momentous. Each word will be saturated with devotion and love. The group of volunteers must be looking so handsome in uniform.'

These fantasies fuelled Indu to such an extent that she was provoked into being disobedient. 'I will go. So much for disgrace! These are excuses for preventing me. You are afraid, so suffer the consequences of your actions. Why should I be afraid?' Having made up her mind, she said decisively, 'You gave me permission to go, so I'm going.'

Raja sahib said, defeated – It's your wish; go with pleasure if you want to.

After Indu had left raja sahib thought – Women are so cruel, so fond of independence, so capricious. She's going as if I'm nothing. She's not at all concerned about what the authorities will say to me if they hear about this. The correspondents of newspapers are sure to write about this event, and the Rani of Chataari's name will appear in bold letters among the women who were present. Had I known that she'd be so stubborn I wouldn't have refused but would have gone along with her. If I were disgraced on the one hand, I would have been praised on the other. But now I've lost both ways. I'm at fault on both sides. I've realized today that frankness doesn't work with women, they are persuaded only by flattery and cajoling.

Indu proceeded towards the station with a heavy heart. What we term victory on the battlefield is seen as expertise in acting, cruelty and incivility at home. Indu was not proud of this victory. She regretted her obstinacy. 'He must think me to be so arrogant. Perhaps he believes that if she can be indifferent over trivial things and is ready to fight over small differences of opinion, what hope can there be of any sympathy from her during a crisis? Ammaji will think that I'm in the wrong if she hears of this. No doubt I've made a mistake. I'll return and ask his forgiveness. I don't know what demon possesses me. I got embroiled unnecessarily! God, when will I have the sense to learn to obey his wishes?'

When Indu looked out the signal of the station was visible. Crowds of men and women were running towards the station. There was an uninterrupted line of vehicles. She told the coachman, 'Turn the gharry, I won't go to the station, go home.'

The coachman said – Sarkar! We have reached now. Just look, several men are signalling to me to make the horses move, they have recognized the gharry.

Indu – I don't care, turn the horses immediately.

The coachman – Is sarkar feeling unwell?

Indu – Don't talk rubbish. Turn the gharry back.

The coachman turned the gharry. Indu sighed deeply and thought, 'People must be waiting for me. They recognized the gharry as soon as they saw it. Amma must have been so happy, but she as well as the others must have been so surprised to see the gharry turning back!' She told the coachman, 'Just look back . . . Is someone coming?'

The coachman – Huzoor, there is a gharry approaching.

Indu – Make the horses go faster. Let go of the leash.

The coachman – Huzoor, it's not a gharry, it's a car, definitely a car.

Indu – Whip the horses.

The coachman – Huzoor, it seems to be our car. Heengan Singh is driving it. I've recognized it very well; it's our car.

Indu – You are crazy. Why would our car come here?

The coachman – Huzoor, if it's not our car, then the punishment due to a thief is mine. I can see it clearly, it's the same colour, there's no other car like this in the city.

Indu – Just look carefully.

The coachman – What should I see, huzoor? It's here. Sarkar is sitting inside.

Indu – Are you dreaming?

The coachman – Here, huzoor, it's alongside us now.

Indu looked out anxiously and saw that indeed it was their car. It stopped next to the gharry and raja sahib got down. The coachman stopped the gharry. Indu asked surprised, 'When did you come?'

Raja sahib – I left five minutes after you.

Indu – But I didn't see you anywhere on the way.

Raja sahib – I came from the way of the railway line. The road this way is bad. I thought it would be a rather roundabout way but I'll reach sooner. Why have you returned from the station? What's the matter? Are you well? I was worried. Come, sit in the car. The train is at the station; it will leave in ten minutes. People are getting excited.

Indu – I won't go now. You had gone there after all.

Raja sahib – You'll have to come.

Indu – Don't force me, I won't go.

Raja sahib – You were so keen to come here, why are you refusing now?

Indu – I came against your wishes. You have violated your principles because of me, so with what face can I go there? You have taught me a lesson in modesty forever.

Raja sahib – I have promised those people that I'll bring you. I'll be so embarrassed if you don't come.

Indu – You are unnecessarily pleading so much. This was the last occasion for you to be annoyed with me. I won't be so presumptuous again.

Raja sahib – The engine is blowing the whistle.

Indu – For God's sake, let me go.

Raja sahib (*Disappointed*) – As you wish. It seems there's some basic opposition between our planets that keeps showing its results at every step.

He sat in the car and went at great speed to the station. The buggy also moved forward. The coachman asked – Huzoor, why didn't you go? Sarkar was offended.

Indu didn't reply. She wondered – Have I made another mistake? Is it proper for me to go? Was he sincere in his plea or did he want to slap me again? God alone knows! He alone is omniscient. How do I know what's in someone else's heart?

The gharry moved forward slowly. The clouds had begun to disperse. Indu thought – Ah! Is there really some basic opposition between our planets which crushes my expectations at every step . . .? I try so hard not to take even one step against his wishes but this innate opposition always makes me feel humiliated. If his request was sincere, then my refusal was totally absurd. Ah! I have hurt him again. He forgave my mistake with his characteristic courtesy and didn't care about his principles for the sake of my self-respect. He must have realized that if she goes alone people will think that she has come against her husband's wishes, otherwise would he also not have come? He inflicted this punishment on himself to save me humiliation. He must have despaired of my stupidity; otherwise he would never have uttered this sentence. I'm really unfortunate.

Engrossed in these melancholy thoughts, Indu reached Chandra Bhavan and went straightaway to raja sahib's reception room. She tried to avoid meeting any of the servants. She felt as if there was a blemish on her face. She wished that raja sahib would be furious with her the moment he returned, strongly rebuke her, pierce her heart with taunts; this would be proof of his sincerity. If he spoke affectionately, she would understand that he was not sincere and that all this was only civility. At this moment she wanted her husband's severity. During summer, a farmer craves not rain but heat.

Indu didn't have to wait long. Raja sahib reached around 5 p.m. Indu's heart began to beat fast; she got up and stood at the door. As soon as he saw her, raja sahib said very gently – Today you missed the opportunity of witnessing a unique spectacle of patriotic fervour. It was such a beautiful scene. The entire earth was covered with flowers when thousands of people showered them on the travellers. The national anthem of the volunteers was so emotional and moving that the assembled spectators were enthralled. My heart leapt with patriotic pride. There's the constant regret that you weren't there. You should understand that I can't express that joy. All the doubts that I had about the society have been allayed. I wished that I could also leave all this to accompany that group. I used to think Dr Ganguly to be a mere babbler. I was taken aback today when I saw his enthusiasm and courage. You made a big mistake. Your mother also kept regretting it.

Indu's suspicions were confirmed. She thought, 'All this is dissembling. He's not sincere. He thinks I'm a fool and he's making a fool of me. There's so much bitterness concealed in his sweet talk.' She said, annoyed, 'You would have resented it if I had gone.'

Raja sahib (*Laughing*) – Only because I stopped you from going? Why would I have gone myself if I resented it?

Indu – I don't know why you went. Perhaps you wanted to humiliate me!

Raja sahib – Indu! Don't be so distrustful. I'm telling you the truth. I wouldn't have minded your going at all. I admit that I first resented your obstinacy but when I thought it over, my behaviour seemed very unjust. I realized it was completely wrong to suppress your wishes. I went to the station to atone for this injustice. Your rebuke convinced me when you said that I shouldn't sacrifice my freedom to remain a confidant of the rulers; it's a good thing to have a good reputation, but to let oneself be suppressed because of it for the right causes is to murder one's soul. Do you believe me now?

Indu – I can't counter your arguments but I beg of you, punish me and scold me severely if I make a mistake. The relationship between crime and punishment is that of cause and action, that's all I understand. I have never seen anyone massaging a criminal's head with oil. This seems unnatural to me. It arouses all kinds of suspicions in my mind.

Raja sahib – People try to placate the devi when she's offended. What's wrong with that?

This altercation went on for a long time. Like a fowler, Mahendra wanted to throw grain before the bird to trap it but the bird would be suspicious and fly away. Deceit begets deceit. He couldn't reassure Indu. So he left it to time to alleviate her distress and began to read a paper, and Indu went inside with a heavy heart.

The next day when raja sahib opened the daily newspaper, he found that a detailed description of the volunteers' journey had been published in it. The author had also commented on raja sahib's presence in this context – 'The presence of the chairman of the municipality, Raja Mahendra Singh, on this occasion is a matter of great importance. It is surprising why somebody as circumspect as raja sahib thought it necessary to go there. Raja sahib cannot separate his person from his position, and his presence can be the cause of putting the government in a quandary. Experience has proved that no matter how well intentioned societies for social service may be when they are initially formed, in the course of time they become centres of rebellion and unrest. Can raja sahib take the responsibility that this society will not follow its preceding organizations in the future?'

Raja sahib put away the paper and became thoughtful. He said involuntarily – I was afraid that this would happen. As soon as I reach the club today, suspicious looks will be cast on me from all sides. I have to meet commissioner sahib tomorrow, what will I say if he questions me? This wicked editor has tricked me badly. Like the police, this profession too is very callous. They don't make any allowances. I try so hard to keep his mouth shut and to make him happy, I warm his fists by getting essential and inessential advertisements published, he's the first one to whom I send an invitation whenever there's a party or a function, I even got him a prize from the municipality last year. This is the return for all those favours! A dog's tail remains as crooked as ever even if it's buried for a hundred years. How do I salvage my honour now? It wouldn't be proper to go to him. Should I think of an excuse?

Raja sahib stood there in a dilemma for a long time. He wanted to think of a way out by which the dignity of the authorities would be retained and at the same time he wouldn't have to be discredited before the public, but his mind wouldn't work. Several times he thought of asking Indu's help in solving this problem. But he didn't have the courage to say anything to her, since he was apprehensive that she would say, 'Let the authorities be annoyed, what do you have to do with them? Give your resignation letter immediately if they pressurize you.' In that case there would be no way out for him. He didn't have the courage to say anything to her.

He fretted about this through the night. Indu was also rather quiet. A few friends came in the morning and discussed that article. One of them said – When I went to meet the commissioner, he was reading this article and repeatedly stamping his feet on the floor.

Raja sahib lost his wits even more. He immediately thought of a plan. He ordered the car and went to the commissioner's bungalow. This gentleman usually sent for raja sahib as soon as he received his card but today the orderly said – Sahib is busy with some important work. Memsahib is with him. Wait for an hour.

Raja sahib understood that the signs were not favourable. He sat down and began looking at the pictures in an English magazine – Vaah! What clear and beautiful pictures. Those in our magazines are so crude; the paper is unnecessarily spoilt by being smeared and glossed over. At the most, somebody will use Biharilal's sentiments to paint a picture of a beautiful woman and write a doha below it expressing them or someone else will illustrate Padmakar's poems.* That's all, their imagination doesn't go any further.

An hour passed somehow and sahib sent for him. When raja sahib went in, he saw that sahib was frowning. Raja sahib, furious after waiting for an hour, remained standing and said – I'll speak if you have the time, otherwise I'll return later.

Commissioner sahib asked coldly – First, I want to know if you have happened to see the criticism about you in this paper?

Raja sahib – Yes, I've seen it.

Commissioner – Do you want to give an explanation?

Raja sahib – I don't think it's necessary. If I'm not trusted because of something so trivial, and if years of loyalty don't matter, I'll be forced to resign from my position. Would this paper have had the courage to criticize you if you had gone there? Never! This is my punishment for being an Indian. I don't know how I can perform my duties as long as such hostile criticism continues to be made about us.

The commissioner softened a little and said – It's the duty of every government officer not to give an opportunity for such allegations to be made about him.

Raja sahib – I know that you people can't forget that I'm an Indian. Similarly, it's impossible for my colleagues on the board to forget that I'm a part of the administration. You know that I'm going to place before the board the proposal of giving Mr John Sevak the Pandeypur land. But until I can prove by my conduct that I have presented this

---

* Bihari Lal Chaube or Bihari (1596–1663) was born in Govindpur, Madhya Pradesh, and lived in Mathura. He is famous for his *Satsai* (Seven Hundred Verses), written in Brajbhasha, which is a collection of approximately 700 distichs. These are not arranged in any narrative sequence but according to the technical classification of the sentiments that they convey as set out in the treatises on Indian rhetoric. They are inspired by Krishna worship and the love of Krishna and Radha.

Padmakar Bhatt (1753–1833) was born in Sagar, Madhya Pradesh. He wrote on bravery, love and devotion. Like Bihari, his dohas or couplets were inspired by the love of Krishna and Radha.

Both Bihari and Padmakar belonged to ritikaal, a period in Hindi literature characterized by a great deal of technical poetic innovations.

proposal of my own accord, without any pressure, only for the good of the people, there's no hope of its being accepted. That's why I went to the station yesterday.

The commissioner was delighted. He began to converse jovially.

Raja sahib – Do you think it's necessary for me to give an explanation?

Commissioner – No, no, not at all!

Raja sahib – I should get your full support.

Commissioner – I'll help to the best of my ability.

Raja sahib – Even if the board consents, there's danger of a riot by the people of the muhalla.

Commissioner – It doesn't matter. I'll instruct the police superintendent to help you.

When raja sahib left, he felt that he was walking on the sky. He then went to Mr Clark and used the same strategy before returning home in the afternoon. However, he was plagued by the thought that although he had managed to accomplish his work on this pretext, he had perhaps done an injustice to Soordas and that in the end he would be discredited before the citizens. He went to Indu to discuss this topic and asked, 'Are you doing something important? I want your advice on something.'

Indu was afraid that the process of taking advice could result in an altercation. She said – I'm not doing anything. God hasn't given me so much intelligence. He has made me only to eat, sleep and pester you.

Raja sahib – It's your pestering that's so enjoyable. Tell me, what's your opinion about Soordas's land? What would you have done in my place?

Indu – What have you decided finally?

Raja sahib – You tell me first, then I'll tell you.

Indu – I think that it would be unjust to seize Soordas's ancestral property.

Raja sahib – Don't you know that Soordas doesn't profit from this property? It's only stray cattle that graze on it.

Indu – At least he has the satisfaction that the land is his. The muhalla-valas must feel obliged to him. His dharmic nature will be satisfied if he does something meritorious.

Raja sahib – But as the chief administrator of the city, I can't let it lose thousands of rupees for the actual or imagined welfare of one man. With the opening of the factory, thousands of people will earn a livelihood, the city's income will increase and, most important, that immeasurable amount of wealth, which has to be given to other countries for cigarettes, will remain in the country.

Indu looked sharply at the raja. She wondered, 'What does he mean? He's not particularly fond of capitalists. This is not asking for advice but a discussion. Has he decided to give the land in Mr Sevak's favour under the pressure of the authorities and does he now want me to support his decision? It seems so from his behaviour.' She said – From this point of view, it does seem just to seize Soordas's land.

Raja sahib – Bhai, you don't have the licence to change sides so soon. Stay firm on that earlier argument of yours. I don't want just advice, I want to know your doubts on this topic and whether I can answer them satisfactorily. I've done whatever I could. Now I want to reassure myself by discussing it with you.

Indu – You won't be angry if I happen to say something that you may not like?

Raja sahib – Don't worry. The second name for the service of the country is shamelessness. I'll have to go to the mental asylum if I get annoyed over trivial things.

Indu – If you don't want to harm the city because of one person, is Soordas the only one who has ten bighas? There are people in the city who have much more land. There are so many bungalows with a circumference of more than ten bighas. The area of our bungalow is not less than fifteen bighas. The circumference of Mr Sevak's bungalow too is not less than five bighas, and dadaji's palace is an entire village. You can take any of these for this factory. The cattle of the muhalla graze on Soordas's land. It's not much, but at least one muhalla profits by this. Nobody profits from these places except one person, so much so that even an animal will be shot immediately if it enters them.

Raja sahib (*Smiling*) – It's a very impressive argument. I'm convinced. I don't have an answer. But perhaps you don't know that the blind man is not as abject and helpless as you think. The whole muhalla is ready to support him, to the extent that people entered Mr Sevak's agent's house, set it on fire, beat up his sons and even dishonoured the women.

Indu – This is one more proof that the land should not be taken.
Its occupation will not reduce such incidents; they will increase. I'm
afraid there'll be bloodshed.

Raja sahib – Those who dishonour women don't deserve pity.

Indu – People are not going to stroke your feet if you seize their land.

Raja sahib – It's surprising you think dishonouring women is an
ordinary matter.

Indu – The goras of the army and the officers of the railways daily
dishonour our sisters; no one says anything to them. That's because
you can't harm them in any way. Register a case against the criminals
if people have rebelled and punish them. Why seize their property?

Raja sahib – You know that there's a great deal of social interaction
between Mr Sevak and the authorities here. Mr Clark is like a durbaan
at his door. The government will lose its trust in me if I can't do this
much for him.

Indu said in a worried tone – I didn't know the chairman's situation
is so pitiable.

Raja sahib – Now you know. Tell me, what should I do now?

Indu – Resign.

Raja sahib – Will my resignation save the land?

Indu – You'll at least be saved from crime and sin.

Raja sahib – Resignation over such trivial matters is ridiculous.

Indu was very proud of her husband being the chairman. She had
thought this position to be very high and respectable. She had believed
that raja sahib was completely independent, that the board was under
him, that he could do whatever he wanted. But now it was evident
that this was an illusion. Her pride was shattered. She realized now
that the chairman was only a toy in the hands of the government
authorities. He could do whatever he wanted with their permission
but nothing without it. He was the zero of numbers, whose value
depended only on the cooperation of the other numbers. Raja sahib's
craving for position seemed to her like the blow of a hatchet. She said,
'Ridicule isn't as contemptible as injustice. I don't understand why you
accepted this position when you knew its problems. I wouldn't have
had any complaint against you if you had appropriated Soordas's land
thinking it to be just; but it's highly contemptible to turn your face
away from the path of justice because you are afraid of the authorities,

or to escape ignominy. You should protect the rights of the citizens, especially of those who are poor. You should support those who are oppressed by the rulers. You should oppose the rulers without thinking of your personal loss or gain and create a pandemonium in the whole city—in the whole country—even if you have to resign or to face the greatest difficulties. I'm not familiar with the principles of politics; I'm only talking about your duty as a human being. I'm warning you that I won't remain silent if you appropriate Soordas's land because of the pressure brought by the rulers. So what if I'm a woman, I'll show you that even the most powerful being can't easily crush a poor man under his feet.'

Indu stopped after saying all this. She realized that she was crossing the limits of propriety in her rage. Raja sahib was so ashamed that he was speechless. At last he said, embarrassed – You don't know what difficulties the servants of the nation have to face. They won't be able to serve even as much as they can now if they perform their duty fearlessly. The intimacy between Mr Clark and Mr Sevak has completely changed the situation. Mr Clark is constantly with Miss Sevak ever since she left your house. He doesn't go to the sessions of the court, or do any official work, or even meet anyone. Miss Sevak seems to have cast a magic spell on him. They both go for outings and to the theatre together. I think that Mr Sevak has given his word. . .

Indu – So soon! It's not even a week since she left our place.

Raja sahib – Mrs Sevak had already settled everything. The love affair started as soon as Miss Sevak went there.

Until now, Indu had thought Sophia to be an ordinary Christian girl. Although she acted like a sister to her, respected her abilities and loved her, she still considered Sophia to be beneath her. But her innermost feelings were shaken when she heard about her marriage to Mr Clark. She thought, 'Sophia will consider me to be inferior to her when she'll meet me as Mrs Clark; there'll be a false humility in her behaviour, her words and her manners; no matter how much she bends before me, she'll make me feel even smaller. I won't be able to bear this insult. I can't be inferior to her. Couldn't this unfortunate Clark have found a European lady that he had to fall for Sophia? He must be from a low family; probably no Englishman is willing to let his daughter marry him. Vinay gives his life for this shallow woman.

God alone knows what that poor thing's condition will be like now. She's a loose woman. What else can the influence of community and family be, after all? She may be beautiful, educated, intelligent and thoughtful but after all she's a Christian. The father has earned some wealth and status by deceiving people. But so what? I'm still going to behave in the same way towards her. I won't extend my hand until she comes forward. But no matter what I do, or how much I assert my superiority, she's sure to be proud of the fact that one stern look of hers can reduce my husband's status and position to dust. She may possibly present herself with even greater humility. The awareness of our power makes us modest. It will seem ridiculous if I'm stiff or if I sulk. Her shallowness is better than her humility. I hope to God that she won't talk politely to me, for onlookers can then reproach her in their hearts, this is how my pride can be salvaged, but she's not so thoughtless.'

In the end, Indu decided that she wouldn't meet Sophia – I won't meet Sophia at all. I can't assert my pride as a rani before her. Yes, I can at least scorn her by being the wife of a servant of the country and displaying my pride at the prestige of my lineage.

All these thoughts flashed in Indu's mind in a second. She said – I won't advise you to be pressurized.

Raja sahib – And if I have to give in to the pressure?

Indu – Then I'll think that I'm unfortunate.

Raja sahib – So far there's no harm done but I hope you won't start a rebellion. I'm asking because you have just threatened me with this.

Indu – I won't remain silent. You may be pressurized but why should I be?

Raja sahib – No matter how much I'm disgraced?

Indu – I don't think it to be disgrace.

Raja sahib – Think it over. It's an accepted fact that Mr Sevak will get that land. I can't prevent that even if I want to, and this is also an accepted fact that you will have to take a vow of silence on this topic.

Raja sahib was famous for his forbearance and congenial behaviour in public life but he was not so tolerant in his personal relations. Indu's face blazed with anger. She said sharply – If your esteem is dear to you, my dharma is dear to me too.

Raja sahib left enraged and Indu was left alone.

Neither of them spoke to each other for seven or eight days, as if curd had set in their mouths. Whenever raja sahib came home he would exchange a few words and then escape as if he were being drenched in water. He wouldn't sit down and Indu wouldn't ask him to. He was distressed because she didn't care for him at all. 'She puts obstacles at every step of my way. She'll be content when I resign. She wants that I should reject the world forever and sever all relations with it, sit at home and chant Rama-naam, stop interacting with the authorities, fall in their eyes, be degraded. All my ambitions and desires are worthless for her, she laughs in her heart at my worship of esteem. Perhaps she thinks me to be base, selfish and self-serving. Even after living with me for so long she doesn't love me, she doesn't understand me. A wife is her husband's well-wisher, she shouldn't ridicule his work or criticize him. She has said clearly that she won't remain silent. I wonder what she intends to do. I'll be finished if she writes even a very short letter to the newspapers! I won't be left anywhere. It will be time to drown myself. Let me see how this boat comes ashore.'

Indu was unhappy and thought, 'God has given him everything, so why is he so intimidated by the officers and why does he fawn upon them so much, why doesn't he remain firm on his principles instead of placing them below his self-interest and making a pretence of service to the country? What kind of a man is someone who has sacrificed dharma and justice for the sake of his reputation? There used to be those warriors who didn't bow down their heads before emperors and who would sacrifice their lives for the sake of their vows and their honour. What must people think of him? It's not easy to deceive the world. He may suffer from the illusion that people think him to be a sincere servant of the country, but actually everyone knows him for what he is. They must all think, what a hypocrite he is.'

Gradually her views began to change. 'This is not his fault but mine. Why do I want him to conform to my ideal? Nowadays, most men are like this. It doesn't matter what the world says or thinks of them but at least no one is hypercritical of them at home. It's the duty of a wife to be a companion to her husband. But the question is does a woman have no identity apart from her husband? One's intelligence can't accept this. They both have to suffer the consequences of their sins as well as their meritorious acts. Actually it's the fault of our destiny, otherwise why would there be such a great difference in our views? I try so hard to prevent any differences between us but there's some problem or the other every day. Before one wound can be healed, another opens. Will it be like this all my life? We desire peace in our lives, we give our lives for love and friendship. But how can there be any peace for somebody who has a naked sword hanging over her head all the time? The tyranny is that I'm not even allowed to remain silent. I pleaded so much with him not to drag me into this discussion, not to haul me over these thorns but he wouldn't listen. Now when the thorns pierce my feet and I groan with pain, he blocks his ears with his fingers. I don't have the freedom even to cry. "Hit violently and don't allow to cry." Eight days have passed and he hasn't bothered to ask if I'm alive or dead. I'm lying here as if I'm in a sarai. It would have been far better if I'd died. I've lost happiness and comfort, what's left? Crying and fretting! For how long can this continue? For how long can the mother goat ensure her kid's welfare? Both of us will become indifferent to each other and not want to see the other's face.'

It was evening. Indu felt very agitated. She thought, 'Let me go and see amma,' when raja sahib came in and stood before her. His face was lifeless, as if the house were on fire. He said, in a voice trembling with fear – Indu, Mr Clark has come to see me. It must be to discuss that land. What's your advice? I have come here on the pretext of getting a paper.

He looked at Indu terrified, as if the troubles of the whole world had fallen on him, or a farmer from the countryside had been caught in the clutches of the police. After taking a short breath, he spoke again – I'll be in trouble if I oppose him. You don't know how much power these English officers have. I can keep him as a servant if I want to, but one complaint from him will reduce my prestige to dust. The higher officials won't listen to a word of mine against him. The rais don't have the freedom even of an ordinary farmer. All of us are toys in their hands; they can fling us down on the floor whenever they want and shatter us to smithereens. I can't disobey him. Have pity on me, have pity on me!

Indu looked at him forgivingly and asked – What do you want me to do?

Raja sahib – Just this, either watch the spectacle of this tyranny silently or give me a little poison with your own hands.

Indu was moved by compassion because of raja sahib's cowardice and helplessness, his face distorted by fear, his pitiable meekness, his plea for forgiveness. There was no sympathy in this compassion, no respect. It was the pity aroused in the heart of a generous person when he sees a beggar. She thought, 'Ha! Is there a limit to this fear? Even children are probably not so afraid of a bogeyman. After all, what can Clark do even if he's annoyed? He can't remove him from his post, that's beyond his capacity; he can't seize the riyasat, there'll be chaos. At the most he can write a complaint to the officers. But right now it's useless to argue with him. He's not in his senses.' She said, 'Do whatever pleases Clark if his displeasure is unbearable for you. I promise you I won't open my mouth. Go, it must be getting late for sahib, he may be offended by this.'

Raja sahib cringed inwardly at this ridicule. He got up and left with a small face, just as a client obsessed by need gets up dejected at the moneylender's refusal. He wasn't satisfied by Indu's reassurance. He thought, 'I have fallen in her eyes. I was so afraid of disrepute, but now I can't show my face in my own house.'

As soon as raja sahib had left, Indu sighed deeply and lay down on the floor. She spontaneously uttered these words, 'How can I respect him from my heart? How can I think of him as my god worthy of being worshipped? I don't know what punishment I'll get for this impiety. I want to worship my husband, but God, I can't control my heart! Why are you putting me through this difficult test?'

16

VINAY SINGH IS SITTING UNDER A BANYAN TREE IN THE HILLS OF Aravalli. The rain has adorned that uninhabited, harsh, dull, stony landscape with love, joy and radiance, as if a desolate house has become prosperous. But Vinay is oblivious of this natural beauty, he is in that state of anxiety when the eyes and ears are open but one can't think of anything or hear anything; the external consciousness is paralysed. His face has become lifeless and his body so emaciated that each rib can be counted.

Our desires are the source of life; how then can the flow of life not come to a standstill if there is snowfall over them?

A fierce conflict rages continuously within Vinay's innermost being. The path of service was his aim. The thorns of love have become obstacles in the way. They are constantly trying to turn him away from his path. Overcome with mortification, he sometimes wonders why Sophia had pulled him out of that cauldron of fire. External fire can only destroy the body which itself is perishable, inner fire destroys the immortal soul.

It is several months since Vinay has arrived here but his restlessness increases with time. He had come here out of embarrassment, but each moment seems an age. To begin with, he had greatly exaggerated his difficulties in his letters to his mother. He was convinced that ammaji would call him back, but that desire was not fulfilled. Meanwhile he received Sophia's letter, which extinguished the wavering lamp of his fortitude. There was now darkness all around him. He would grope all around in it but couldn't find a way. There is no aim in his life now, no definite path. He is like a boat without a helmsman, dependent only on the mercy of the waves.

However, he unwaveringly fulfils his duty even in this state of worry and remorse. There is not a single child in the region of Jaswantnagar who doesn't recognize him. The people of the countryside are so devoted to him that the entire village gathers for his darshan the moment he reaches. He has taught them to help themselves. The people of this region no longer run to the police to drive away the animals of the forest, they unite and do that themselves, they don't knock at the doors of law courts for every trivial matter but settle it themselves in the panchayat. There are brick wells where there had never been any wells at all; people have also begun to pay attention to cleanliness; there are no longer heaps of garbage at doorsteps. In short, now each person is not only for himself but for others as well. He thinks himself to be surrounded not by opponents but by friends and companions. Collective life has been regenerated.

Vinay is quite knowledgeable about medicine as well. Several patients have been cured by him. So many homes that had been destroyed because of persistent strife are again prosperous. In these circumstances it is not difficult to imagine how eager people are to welcome and to serve him. But how can there be any comfort in the lot of social workers? Vinay has no need of anything except dry roti and the shade of a tree. This sacrifice and detachment have made him the most esteemed and loved person in that region.

However, the state authorities have become progressively more suspicious of him with the increasing devotion of the people and his growing influence over them. They think that the public is becoming more rebellious day by day. Darogaji's fists are no longer warmed; lawsuits no longer come to the managers and the other officers; nothing comes into their clutches; what else are these if not signs of rebellion among the people? These are the sprouts of rebellion, and it would be best to uproot them.

Several new reports from Jaswantnagar are daily sent to the durbar, some factual, others imagined, and plans are being made to draw Vinay Singh into the clutches of the law. These reports arouse the suspicions of the durbar and several spies are appointed to investigate Vinay's conduct but his selfless service does not give anyone an opportunity to harm him.

Vinay found it difficult to walk because his heels were cracked. He dozed off in the cool shade of the banyan tree. It was afternoon when he awoke. He got up quickly, picked up his stick, and walked on. He had planned to rest in Jaswantnagar today. The day was speeding by, the movement of the sun quickens after the third pahar. Evening was approaching and there was no sign yet of Jaswantnagar. His cracked heels made it difficult for him to take even one step. He didn't know what to do. Not even a farmer's hut was visible nearby where he could spend the night. The voices of beasts of prey can be heard in the mountains as soon as it is sunset. While in this dilemma, he saw a man approaching from a distance. Vinay was so happy when he saw the man that he left his path and took several steps towards him. When he came close, Vinay realized it was the postman. The postman knew Vinay. Greeting Vinay, he said, 'At this pace you won't reach Jaswantnagar even by midnight.'

Vinay – My heels are cracked and I can't walk. I'm so glad to see you. I was very nervous wondering how I'd go alone. Now that there are two of us, there's nothing to worry about. Is there any letter for me?

The postman gave Vinay a letter. It was from raniji. Although it was getting dark, Vinay was so excited that he opened the envelope immediately and began reading the letter. He finished it in a moment and then, sighing deeply, put it back in the envelope. He was so dizzy that he almost fell. He sat down on the ground. The postman asked anxiously – Is there some bad news? Your face has become pale.

Vinay – No, there's no such news. My feet hurt; I probably won't be able to go on.

Postman – Will you stay alone in this wilderness?

Vinay – What's there to be afraid of?

Postman – There are many animals here, only yesterday they took away a cow.

Vinay – Even the animals won't bother about me. You go on, leave me here.

Postman – That can't be, I'll also stay here.

Vinay – Why are you putting your life in danger because of me? You go on, you'll reach soon, by nightfall.

Postman – I'll go only if you come too. What's my life worth? I don't do anything else except earn a living. Thousands benefit because of you. If you are not worried about yourself why should I be worried about myself?

Vinay – Bhai, I'm helpless. I can't walk.

Postman – I'll carry you on my shoulders but I won't leave you here.

Vinay – Bhai, you are taking too much trouble. Come, but I'll walk very slowly. I would have remained lying here today if it hadn't been for you.

Postman – My life wouldn't have been safe had it not been for you. Don't think that I'm insisting so much because of you; I'm not such a noble soul. I'm taking you with me for my own safety. (*Softly*) Right now, I have 250 rupees with me. I've been delayed because I dozed off somewhere. It was my good luck that I met you; otherwise my life wouldn't have been safe from the dacoits.

Vinay – This is very dangerous. Do you have a weapon?

Postman – You are my weapon. There's no danger to me if you are with me. No dacoit would dare to raise his hand at me if he sees you. You have managed to control even the dacoits.

Suddenly they heard the sound of horses' hooves. The postman looked back nervously. Five riders were approaching, carrying spears and speeding up their horses. He lost his wits and became pale with fear. He said – See, they have all come. It has become difficult to come this way because of them. They are murderers. They don't know how to spare government servants. My life can now be saved only if you save me.

Meanwhile, the five riders crowded around. One of them called out – Abey, you postman, come here, what's in your bag?

Vinay was sitting on the ground. As he got up with the help of his stick, one of the riders attacked the postman with his spear. The postman had been in the army. He stopped the attack with his bag and the spear went through it. The rider was about to attack a second time when Vinay came forward and said – Bhaiyyon! Why are you creating so much anarchy? Will you take a poor man's life for the sake of a few rupees?

Rider – Why doesn't he give the money if his life is so dear to him?

Vinay – Life is dear and so is money. He can't give either.

Rider – Then he'll have to give both.

Vinay – Then first put an end to me. Your wish can't be fulfilled as long as I'm here.

Rider – We don't raise our hands at sadhus and sants. Get out of the way.

Vinay – I won't get out of the way until your horses trample my bones under their hooves.

Rider – We are telling you to get out of the way. Why do you want to burden us with the sin of murder?

Vinay – I do what's my dharma; you do what's yours. I have bowed my head.

The second rider – Who are you?

The third rider – He's already wounded. Give him a blow and he'll fall down. We'll do penance.

The first rider – Who are you after all?

Vinay – Whoever I may be, how does it concern you?

The second rider – You don't seem to belong here. Why, you postman, who is he?

Postman – That I don't know, but his name is Vinay Singh. He's a dharmatma and a social worker. He has been staying in this region for several months.

All the five riders jumped down from their horses the moment they heard Vinay's name and stood before him with their hands folded. The sardar said – Maharaj, please forgive our crime. We have heard your name. Now that we have got your darshan, our lives have been fulfilled. Your fame is being sung in every home in this region. My son fell from his horse; his rib broke. There was no hope that he would live. There's a maharaj with you, Indradutt. He came to see the boy and immediately dressed and bandaged him. After that he came every day for a month to treat him. The boy became well. I can't be free of my debt to you even if I give my life. Liberate us sinners. Give us leave to rub the dust from your feet on our foreheads. We are not worthy even of this.

Vinay smiled and said – So now you won't take the postman's life? I'm afraid of you.

Sardar – Maharaj, now don't embarrass us. Postman mahashaya, you must have seen a good man's face when you woke up today or else your life would have been a bird flying in the sky. You've heard my name, haven't you? I'm Veerpaal Singh, whom the servants of the state have vowed to destroy.

Vinay – Why do you tyrannize the servants of the state so much?

Veerpaal – Maharaj, you have been here in this region for several months, don't you know about their misdeeds? They are looting the people with both hands. They have no mercy or dharma. They are our own kin but it's our throats that they slit. If anyone wears clothes that are slightly clean, they'll be after him. If you don't give a bribe to somebody, he's your enemy. Thieve, plunder, burn houses, slit the throats of the poor, no one will say anything. Bas, keep warming the fists of the officers. Murder in broad daylight but worship the police and you'll get away untainted, for an innocent person will be hanged in your place. No one listens to any complaints. Who'll listen, they are all of a kind. Just imagine that there's a circle of beasts of prey; they hunt and eat together. The raja is a blockhead. He's obsessed with going to vilayat and making grand speeches before scholars. I did this and I did that. His only job is to boast, that's all. He'll either travel around in vilayat or he'll go on shikar with the English here, he'll just keep bootlicking them all day. He has no other work except this. The people may live or die for all he cares. It's best only to do what the officers tell you, don't complain, don't move your tongue, if you want to cry, do so with your mouth shut. We have taken to this path of murder because we are helpless. The eyes of these villains should be opened somehow. They should be made to realize that there's someone to punish them. They'll be transformed into human beings from animals.

Vinay – I knew something about the conditions here but I didn't know that things were so lamentable. I'll now meet raja sahib myself and tell him about all this.

Veerpaal – Maharaj, don't ever make this mistake or we'll be past all hope. This is a benighted place. Why would the state be in this condition if the raja had so much sense? In fact he'll be after you.

Vinay – I'm not worried about that. At least I'll be satisfied that I've done my duty. I want to say something to you too. Your thinking that the authorities will become devoted to the public by these murderous actions of yours is baseless and illusory in my opinion. To end a disease by putting an end to the patient is neither sensible nor just. Fire doesn't pacify fire, only water can.

Veerpaal – Maharaj, we can't argue with you but we also know that poison counteracts poison. When man reaches the pinnacle of cruelty, he loses all mercy and dharma; when his humanity is destroyed, when he begins to act like animals, when the light of his soul is tarnished, there's only one way out for him and that's the death sentence.

Murderous beasts such as tigers may be subjugated if they are tended. But no divine power can defeat self-interest.

Vinay – There is such a power but it has to be used properly.

Vinay had not finished what he was saying when suddenly there was the sound of a rifle shot. The riders looked at each other surprised and, taking the horses aside, let them go. The horses disappeared into the mountains in a flash. Vinay couldn't understand from where the sound of the rifle shot had come and why the five riders had run away. He asked the postman – Where are they all going?

Postman – The sound of the rifle shot must have alerted them to a victim, they have gone in that direction. Some government servant's life is sure to be in danger today.

Vinay – If the state of the officials here is what they have claimed it to be then I'll have to go and see Maharaj as soon as possible.

Postman – Maharaj, why should I hide anything from you? This is how things really are. We are employees worth only a taka, how will we bring up our children if we don't earn a few paise over and above what we get? We don't get our wages for a year on end, but here, the higher the post, the larger the belly.

Both men reached Jaswantnagar around ten o'clock. Vinay sat down under a tree outside the basti and told the postman to go ahead. The postman pleaded earnestly with Vinay to accompany him to his house. When Vinay couldn't be persuaded, he went home and returned with some food. After eating, they lay down there. The postman did not leave him alone to return home. He was tired, so he slept immediately, but how could Vinay sleep? Each word of raniji's letter pierced him like a thorn. The rani had written – You have deceived me as well as your friends. I'll never forgive you. You have reduced my hopes to dust. I never suspected in the least that you would so easily become a slave to your senses. It's useless, your staying on there. Return home, get married and blissfully enjoy a life of luxury. You have neither attained, nor will you be able to attain, the conduct and the psychological strength that are essential for the service of the nation. We entertain grand illusions about our abilities when we are young. You have also fallen into the same delusion. I'm not criticizing you. Return with pleasure, everybody in the world is engrossed in his own self-interest; you too can be absorbed in it. But I can now no longer feel the pride in you that had elated me. Your father doesn't yet know about this incident. One doesn't know what his plight will be when he hears about it. But if you don't already know, I'm informing you that now you'll have to find another sphere for your love affairs because Miss Sophia is engaged to Mr Clark and they will get married in a few days. I'm writing this so that you won't have any illusions about Sophia and you can realize what you mean for someone for whom you have murdered your lifelong ambitions as well as those of your parents.

There was such turmoil in Vinay's heart that if Sophia had been there with him at that moment, he would have reproached her – Is this the gift for my infinite love? I had trusted you so much, but I have realized now that for you it was merely a game of love. You were the goddess of the sky for me. I had imagined you to be a heavenly vision, a divine light. Ah! I was ready to sacrifice even my dharma at your feet. Was it for this that you saved me from the mouths of the flames? Well, whatever has happened is for the best. God has saved my dharma; this agony will also be pacified. I'm unnecessarily rebuking you. You did what other women would have done in this situation. I'm distressed because I had different hopes from you. That was my mistake. I know that I'm not worthy of you. Where do I have the qualities that you could respect? But I also know that no one can have the devotion that I had and still have for you. Clark may be learned, intelligent, able, a receptacle of virtues, but if I'm not mistaken in you, you can never be happy with him.

However, at this moment, more than this disappointment, he was anguished at the thought of having fallen in his mother's eyes – How did she come to know? Did Sophie show her my letter? She couldn't have hurt me more cruelly if this is what she had done. Does love also become malicious after it has become cruel? No, I won't wrong Sophie by suspecting her of this. Now I understand, Indu's simplicity must have lit this fire. She must have mentioned it light-heartedly. Will she ever have any sense? It was an amusement for her but I know what I'm going through here.

Brooding over all this provoked Vinay into wanting revenge. Disappointment makes even love take on the guise of rancour. He felt a strong desire to write a long letter to Sophia rebuking her to his heart's content. He thought of the letter that he would write – I had read several stories in books about the artful character of women but I could never believe them. I could never imagine that woman, whom the Supreme Being has made a receptacle of pure, delicate and divine sentiments, could be so heartless and base, but this is not your fault, it's that of your religion, in which there is no ideal of taking a vow of fidelity. If you have studied Hindu religious texts, you must have come across not one but several examples of devis who never even thought of another man all their lives after taking the vow of fidelity. Yes, and you will also have come across those devis who took this vow and lived all their lives in a state of inviolable widowhood. By becoming Mr Clark's companion you'll reach the category of the conquerors from that of the conquered in one leap, and it's quite possible that it's this desire for glory that has made you determined to hurl this thunderbolt but your eyes will soon open and you'll realize that you have lost your respect, not enhanced it.

Vinay thus gave full vent to his animosity by indulging in these rancorous thoughts. It's difficult to imagine what the predicament of that woman suffering the pangs of separation would have been if he could have splashed even one drop of these poisonous feelings on Sophia. Perhaps her life would have been jeopardized. But Vinay himself was ashamed of his malice. 'How could such evil thoughts come to my mind? Her extremely tender heart can't bear such cruel blows. She loved me. My heart tells me that she is sympathetic to me even now. But like me, she too is bound by the chains of religion, duty, society and custom. Perhaps her parents have coerced her and she has sacrificed herself for their wishes. It's also possible that mataji has thought of this plan to remove her from the path of my love. Mataji is as wrathful as she is compassionate. I'm displaying my impetuosity by blaming Sophia without knowing anything.'

Tossing and turning agitatedly, Vinay dozed off. The nights are very pleasant in the mountainous regions. It was dawn in the blink of an eye. One doesn't know for how long Vinay may have continued to sleep but he woke up with a start when raindrops fell on his face. It was cloudy and there was a light drizzle. He got up, thinking of going to Jaswantnagar, when he saw several men galloping on horses coming towards him. He thought that they were perhaps Veerpaal Singh and his companions but when they approached, he realized that they belonged to the police of the riyasat. The postman had been sleeping next to him but he was nowhere to be seen; he had left earlier.

The officer asked – Are you Vinay Singh?

'Yes.'

'Several men had camped here with you last night?'

'No, there was only a postman from the post office with me.'

'Do you know Veerpaal Singh?'

'I only know that I met him on the way, I don't know where he went after that.'

'Did you know that he was a dacoit?'

'This was the very word that he had used for the officials of the state.'

'I gather from this that you knew about it.'

'You can gather anything you like.'

'He has looted the government treasury's gharry three miles from here and murdered a sepoy. The police suspects that this serious incident happened at your behest. That's why we are arresting you.'

'This is a grave injustice to me. I don't know anything about that dacoity and murder.'

'The court will decide this.'

'At least I have the right to ask why the police is suspicious of me.'

'That's the report given by the postman who had slept here next to you.'

Vinay exclaimed, surprised, 'It's the report of that postman?'

'Yes, he gave this information just before the night was over. It must be obvious to you now how cautious the police is about gentlemen like you.'

This was Vinay's first experience that human nature could be so complicated and difficult to understand. Such villainy and diabolism hidden behind such veneration and devotion!

Two policemen handcuffed Vinay's hands, seated him on a horse, and proceeded towards Jaswantnagar.

17

VINAY SINGH HAS BEEN LYING IN PRISON FOR SIX MONTHS. THERE
is no information about the dacoits nor is there any case against him.
The authorities still suspect that the dacoity took place at his behest.
That's why they torture him in several ways. When they find that this
strategy does not work, they try temptation and then revert to their
old tactics. At first, Vinay had been kept with the other prisoners but
when they found the criminals getting very attracted to him, they
locked him in solitary confinement, fearing that there would be a
rebellion in the prison. The cell was very cramped, there was not a
single window, it would be dark in the afternoon and there was an
intolerable stink. The door would open only once a day; the guard
would bring the food and shut the door again. Vinay had become
accustomed to suffering hardships, he could bear hunger and thirst;
he didn't need bed and bedding, he didn't suffer much without them
but the darkness and the stink were a severe punishment for him. He
felt suffocated and yearned to breathe pure, clean air. He now had
perceptible experience of the priceless value of fresh air. But he was
not distressed or heartbroken while suffering this maltreatment. He
could envisage the liberation of the country in these difficult tests. He
would tell himself, 'This difficult vow can't be futile. We can't serve
the country unless we learn to cope with difficulties and to sacrifice
luxury and pleasure.' This thought would fortify him.

But all his fortitude, zeal and self-sacrifice would vanish in despair
when he remembered Sophia's betrayal. No matter how hard he'd try
to persuade himself that Sophia must have been helpless, this argument
wouldn't satisfy him. 'Couldn't Sophia have said frankly that she didn't
want to get married? The wishes of our parents are decisive among us
in matters concerning marriage, but it's the wishes of the woman that
are paramount among Christians. Couldn't Sophia have flatly refused
Clark if she didn't love him? Actually the ties of love in the weaker
sex are also weak; they snap at the slightest wrench. When a woman

as thoughtful, principled and progressive as Sophia, who would give her life for her honour, can be so inconstant, what can be expected from other women? It's futile to trust this sex. Sophia has cautioned me forever, the lesson that she has taught me is so deep-rooted in my heart that I'll never forget it. If Sophia can be deceptive, which woman can be trusted? Ah! How could I have known that such sacrifice and simplicity, so many noble intentions, would finally submit to self-interest? Now I won't look at a woman all my life. I'll avoid her like a black she-snake. I'll stay clear of her as I would from a thorn. It's against civility and propriety to hate anyone, but now I'll hate this sex.'

He would become so agitated in this state of despair, grief and anxiety that he'd wish, 'Let me go and bang my head against the wall and give up my life before that stone-hearted woman so that she's also mortified. I'm burning here in this cauldron of fire, there are blisters in my heart, and nobody there is even aware of this, they are engrossed in amusement and pleasure. She too would have felt ashamed of her deviousness and cruelty if I had rubbed my heels and had given up my life in front of her. God, forgive me for these depraved thoughts. I'm miserable, if only she would also burn before me in the fire of despair! If only Clark would deceive her just as she has betrayed me! If there's any power in ill will and any punishment for turning away from the path of love, then some day I'll also see her weeping tears of grief and anguish. It's impossible that gratuitous bloodshed won't be effective.'

But this despair was not always a cause of anguish; the sprouts of self-purification were also hidden in it. The goodwill that had been killed by the fantasies of love was reawakened. Despair destroyed egotism.

One night, Vinay lay wondering what had happened to his companions. 'Are they also in trouble like me? There's no news of anyone.' Suddenly he heard a loud bang near his pillow. Startled, he listened attentively. He realized that some people were digging the wall. It was of stone, but very old. There were salt encrustations at the joints of the stones. The stone slabs fell easily from their places. Vinay was surprised. 'Who are these people? If they are thieves, what will they get out of breaking the prison wall? They perhaps think that this is the house of the daroga of the prison.' He was in this dilemma when there was a glimpse of light inside. He realized that the thieves had completed their work. He went to the hole and asked, 'Who are you? Why are you digging this wall?'

A voice came from outside – I'm your old servant; my name is Veerpaal Singh.

Vinay said scornfully – Don't you have the walls of any treasury, is that why you are digging those of a prison? Go away from here or I'll create a din.

Veerpaal Singh – Maharaj, we were guilty of a great crime the other day, forgive us. We didn't realize that you would have to bear this suffering for spending a few moments with us; otherwise we wouldn't have looted the state treasury. We were worried day and night because we wanted to have your darshan and to free you from danger. Come, there's a horse ready for you.

Vinay – No, I don't want to be saved by those who are unrighteous. You are deceived if you think that I'll escape from the prison and save my life with such a serious crime on my head. My life is not so dear to me.

Veerpaal – It's we who are the criminals, you are absolutely innocent, the authorities have done you this grave injustice. You shouldn't have any qualms about escaping from here in such a situation.

Vinay – I can't go from here on any account until the court releases me.

Veerpaal – To expect justice from the courts here is like milking a bird. We are all victims of these courts. I hadn't committed any crime; I was the village headman, but all my property was seized only because I saved a helpless woman from the landlord. There was nobody in her family except her old mother, who had recently been widowed. The landlord's evil eye fell on her and he tried to abduct her from her house. I got to know of it. As soon as the landlord's men tried to enter the old woman's house at night, I reached there with several friends, beat up the villains, and threw them out. Bas, the landlord became my sworn enemy from that day. He accused me of theft and imprisoned me. The court was blind; the judge did what the landlord told him to. You are uselessly hoping for justice from such courts.

Vinay – While talking with me the other day, you people ran away so fast the moment you heard the rifle shot that I still don't trust you.

Veerpaal – Maharaj, don't ask, it was as if we were frenzied the moment we heard the rifle shot. We forget ourselves whenever we get a chance to take revenge against the riyasat, it's as if we are possessed by a demon. The riyasat has completely ruined us. Our ancestors had built its foundations with their blood, today it is thirsty for our blood. When we ran away from you we found, at a short distance, several men from our group fighting the sepoys of the riyasat. We attacked the official employees as soon as we reached, snatched their rifles, killed one man and ran away, piling the bags of money on to the horses. We have been running to and fro trying to get you out of here from the moment we heard that you had been arrested on the suspicion of helping us. This place is not right for men as devout, fearless and independent as you. Only rascals, dissemblers, hypocrites and villains of the first order can subsist here, who won't hesitate to do the worst possible things for their own ends.

Vinay answered with great pride – Even if what you say is true word for word, I'll still not do anything that will give the riyasat a bad name. I'll gladly drink poison with my brothers but I can't complain against them and put them in danger. We have always regarded this riyasat with pride. Even today we look upon Maharaja Sahib with the same veneration. He is the descendant of the same Sanga and Pratap* who had sacrificed their lives for the Hindus. We think of him as our guardian, our well-wisher, the tilak of the kshatriya clan. All his employees are our kin. Then why shouldn't we trust the court here? We won't open our mouths even if they are unjust to us. By accusing the riyasat, we'll prove ourselves to be unworthy of that great objective which is the cherished aim of our lives.

'You'll be deceived.'

'I'm not worried.'

'How will I get rid of this stigma on my head?'

'By your good deeds.'

---

* Sanga: Maharana Sangram Singh (12 April 1484–17 March 1527); ruler of Mewar; renowned for his valour, chivalry and generosity. He united several Rajput states to fight against the invasions of the Muslim rulers, but he lost to Babur in the battle of Khanwa in 1527 owing to the betrayal of a traitor. Maharana Pratap was his descendant.

Veerpaal understood that Vinay would not waver from his principles. All five men rode away on their horses and, in a flash, the dense fog of winter hid them in its veil. The sound of their horses' hooves could be heard for a while, then that too vanished.

Vinay began to wonder, 'What will people think when they see this hole in the morning? They'll be sure that I'm mixed up with the dacoits and am trying to escape secretively. But no, when they'll see that I didn't escape even when I had the chance, they'll be on my side.' He then began to pick up the pieces of stone and to fill up the hole. He had only a light blanket, and the frosty wind of the winter kept whistling in through the hole. He had probably never felt so cold even in the open field. The wind was piercing every pore like a needle. He lay down after filling up the hole.

There was a hue and cry in the prison in the morning. The naazim, the landlord, all of them reached the scene of the incident. Enquiries began. Vinay narrated the entire incident. The authorities were worried that those dacoits would manage to take him away. They handcuffed him and chained his feet. It was decided that his trial would be held that very day. Armed police took him towards the court. A crowd of thousands of people accompanied him. They were all saying: 'The rulers are prosecuting such a courteous, kind man who does so much good for others. What they are doing is wrong. Goodness knows at what inauspicious moment the poor man set foot here. We of course are unfortunate; we are bearing the results of our karma in our previous birth. He should have left us to our fate, he jumped into this fire unnecessarily.' Several people were crying. It was certain that the judge would give him a severe punishment. The spectators were increasing every moment and the police were afraid that the people would get out of hand. All of a sudden a car arrived and the chauffeur got down and handed the police officer a letter. They were all watching closely to see what would happen next. Meanwhile, Vinay was made to sit in the car, which then sped away. They were all astonished.

When the car had traversed some distance, Vinay asked the chauffeur, 'Where are you taking me?' The chauffeur replied, 'Deewan sahib has sent for you.' Vinay didn't question him any further. He was happy rather than afraid because of this opportunity of meeting deewan sahib. He would now be able to discuss the condition of this place with him. 'He is known to be a learned man. Let me see why he supports this policy.'

All of a sudden the chauffeur said – This deewan is one rascal of a kind. He doesn't know how to be merciful. Some day I'll make the fellow fall from this very car in such a way that there'll be no sign of his bones and ribs.

Vinay – Certainly, do make him fall. That's the punishment for such tyrants.

The chauffeur looked suspiciously at Vinay. He couldn't believe his ears. He hadn't expected to hear such words from Vinay. He had heard that Vinay was a receptacle of divine qualities, with a pure heart. He said, 'Is this your wish too?'

Vinay – What's to be done? Nothing else affects such men.

Chauffeur – I was afraid until now that people would call me a murderer but why should I be afraid if this is what such a godly man as you also desire? The fellow goes out very late at night; one stumble will do the job.

Vinay was startled when he heard this, as if he had seen a frightening dream. He realized now what great harm he had done by supporting one vengeful thought. He also realized that eminent people should be careful about opening their mouths, because each word of theirs can be replete with the power to incite. He was regretting having spoken those words and was wondering how to turn back the arrow that had been shot from the bow, when they reached deewan sahib's palace. Two armed sepoys were standing at the huge gate, and there were two brass cannons a little further away. The car stopped at the gate and the two sepoys escorted Vinay inside. Deewan sahib was ensconced in the reception room. He sent for Vinay as soon as he was told of his arrival.

Deewan sahib was tall, well-built and fair. Although he was middle-aged, the glow on his face was like a full-blown flower. His moustache was taut; he was wearing a colourful Udaipuri turban, Udaipuri pajamas, a smart hunting coat and a heavy overcoat. Several medals and signs of honour were visible on his chest. He had participated in the European Great War with the Udaipur cavalry and had surprised the leaders of the army with his extraordinary valour on several occasions. He had been appointed to this position because of that fame. His name was Sardar Neelkanth Singh. Vinay Singh had never before seen such a distinguished man.

As soon as deewan sahib saw Vinay, he smiled and gestured to him to take a chair and said – These ornaments don't become you very well, but they command the respect in the eyes of the public that my medals and stripes can never have. Am I wrong, then, in being envious of you when I see this?

Vinay had thought that deewan sahib would shout at him and be furious the moment he entered. He had been prepared for that treatment. He was now embarrassed when he heard deewan sahib's kind words. There was no scope for the harsh reply that he had thought of. He said, 'This is not such a rare object that you should be envious.'

Deewan sahib – (*Laughing*) It may not be rare for you but it is for me. I don't have the noble courage and enthusiasm by which all these things are obtained as gifts. I came to know today that you are Kunwar Bharat Singh's son. He's an old acquaintance. He may have forgotten me now. I have special affection and respect for you, partly because you are my old friend's son and partly because you have sacrificed sensual pleasure in youth and taken a vow of social service. Personally, I accept your services and am grateful to you for what you have done for the welfare of the riyasat in this short time. I know very well that you are innocent and that you can't be associated with the dacoits. I don't have any doubts about this. There was a discussion about you for an hour with Maharaja Sahib too. He too was full of praise for you but circumstances compel us to plead with you that it would be best if you stayed away from the public. I deeply regret to tell you that this riyasat can no longer enjoy the privilege of extending its hospitality to you.

Suppressing his rising anger, Vinay said – I'm grateful to you for your kind words about me. But I regret that I can't obey your orders. Social service is the main aim of my life and I can't break my vow by dissociating myself from society.

Deewan sahib – You shouldn't have come to a riyasat if this is the main goal of your life. Riyasats are like the harems of the government where even sunlight can't enter. All of us are the habshi eunuchs of the harem. We don't let anyone cast his lovelorn gaze here, no flirtatious youth dare step this way. Should this happen we'll be considered unfit for our posts. Our licentious badshah occasionally sets foot here for his pleasure according to his wishes. The sleeping fortunes of the harem wake up on that day. You know that all the ambitions of the begums depend on their beauty, blandishments and adornment, otherwise the licentious badshah will not so much as look at them. Our licentious badshah is a lover of Eastern melodies and flavours; his orders are that the clothes and the ornaments of the begums should be Eastern, their adornment should be Eastern, their customs and traditions should be Eastern, their eyes should be full of modesty, they should not have the vivacity of the West, their pace should be as slow as that of geese, they shouldn't prance around like Western women. They should be the maidservants, the daroga, of the harem, the habshi slaves, the high four walls within which even a bird can't beat its wings. You have had the temerity to enter this harem, our licentious badshah finds this intolerable, and what's more, you are not alone, there's a gang of social workers with you. There are several suspicions about this gang. It's a Nadirshahi order that it should be removed far away from the harem. Look at this, the Political Resident has written a ballad about the deeds of your companions. Somebody forms associations of farmers in the court; somebody is eager to remove the roots of unemployment in Bikaner; somebody is opposing taxes in Marwar that have been collected traditionally. You people go around beating the drum of communism. You say that everyone has an equal right to food and clothing and to live peacefully. By preaching these principles and ideas in this harem you will make our government suspicious of us, and we'll have nowhere to go in this world if it withdraws its favours from us. We won't let you set our garden of love on fire.

We take refuge in irony to hide our weaknesses. Deewan sahib tried to win Vinay's sympathy by being ironic but Vinay was not that ignorant of psychology. He understood his ploy and said – We had thought that we would win your sympathy by our selfless service.

Deewan sahib – You have been fully successful in that. Our heartfelt sympathies are with you, but you know that we can't move even a straw against the wishes of Resident sahib. Have mercy on us, leave us in this predicament; you'll get infamy not fame by trying to uplift degraded people like us.

Vinay – Why don't you oppose the Resident's unwarranted interference?

Deewan sahib – Because we are not as selfless and detached as you. We collect whatever taxes we want under the protection of the government, we make whatever laws we want, and give whatever punishment we want; no one says a thing. This is considered our expertise, we get prestigious titles as a reward for this, we get promotions. Why should we oppose it in these circumstances?

Flaring up at deewan sahib's shamelessness, Vinay retorted – It would have been far better if there were no traces left of riyasats.

Deewan sahib – That's why we are pleading with you to turn your merciful gaze on some other province.

Vinay – Suppose I refuse to go?

Deewan sahib – Then with deep regret I'll have to entrust you to the same court where justice is murdered.

Vinay – Innocent?

Deewan sahib – You have been charged with the crime of helping the dacoits.

Vinay – But you just said that you have no such suspicion about me.

Deewan sahib – That was my personal view, this is my official assent.

Vinay – You have the authority.

Vinay sat in the car again. He thought – Only God can save the boat that has such shameless helmsmen who blow their own trumpets about their infamy. So, take me away, it's for the best. Mataji will be satisfied if I'm in prison. She would have been completely disappointed in me if I had escaped from here and had saved my life. She'll know now that her letter was not futile. Let me now go and witness the farce of the court of law.

18

WHEN SOPHIA RETURNED HOME, HER SELF-RESPECT HAD BEEN completely shattered; she had fallen in her own eyes. Now she was angry neither with the rani nor with her parents but only with her own soul, which had made her suffer so much and had entangled her in thorns. She decided that she would trample her feelings so that no sign of them remained. She didn't want to be ruled by her heart when she was in a dilemma; she staunchly vowed to silence it forever. She knew that it was very difficult to silence the heart but she wanted it to be ashamed of its indiscretion if it wavered from the path of duty. Just as a Vaishnava tilakdhaari hesitates when he goes to a liquor shop and is too embarrassed to look up, she wanted her heart to be bound by her upbringing so that it would shy away from base desires. She was prepared to take on the stigma of being devious and despicable for this self-sacrifice and to burn all her life in the fire of despair and separation. She wanted to take revenge on her soul for the humiliation that she had suffered at the rani's hands. Her heart craved liquor; she wanted to quench its thirst with poison. She decided to surrender herself to Mr Clark. There was no other means available for self-sacrifice.

However, no matter how much her self-respect had been degraded, the outward respect shown to her was at its most resplendent. She had never before received so much attention and care at home or been so dear to Mrs Sevak, nor had she heard such loving words from her, to the extent that Mrs Sevak even began to sympathize with her religious investigations. Sophia was no longer tormented on the subject of the worship of God. She was now the mistress of her own wishes and Mrs Sevak was delighted to see that Sophia would be the first to reach the church. She thought that this improvement had happened because of Mr Clark's salutary company.

But who else except Sophia could know what she was going through? She had to pretend to be in love every day, which she found psychologically contemptible. Against her desires, she had to mimic insincere feelings and was forced to listen attentively to expressions of love and devotion that were like the blows of a sledgehammer on her heart. She had to let herself become the object of those rapt looks before which she would want to shut her eyes. Mr Clark's conversation would sometimes be so charming that Sophia wanted to reveal her secret and put an end to this insincere life but, at the same time, the suffering and anguish of her soul gave her a malicious satisfaction. 'Sinner, this is your punishment, this is what you are worth. You have humiliated me so much, now you'll have to do penance for it.'

This was the predicament of that woman, weeping and suffering the pangs of separation, and the problem was that there seemed to be no end to this agony. Unwittingly, Sophia was somewhat distant from Mr Clark; no matter how hard she tried, she couldn't relate to him. This indifference fuelled Mr Clark's passion even more. Despite this, if Sophia didn't encourage him, it was mainly because of Mr Clark's religious nature. She thought there was no greater vice than religiosity. It was, for her, a sign of conservatism, hatred, arrogance and bigotry. Mr Clark realized inwardly that he had not yet been able to win Sophia and that was why, despite his zeal, he didn't have the courage to propose to her. He didn't have the confidence that his proposal would be accepted. But hope kept him tied to Sophia's skirts.

More than a year went by in this manner and Mrs Sevak began to suspect that Sophia was perhaps deluding them with false hopes. Eventually, she said to Sophia – I don't understand what you are up to, sitting with Mr Clark day and night. What's the matter? He hasn't proposed, or are you running away from him?

Sophia blushed with embarrassment and said – He doesn't want to propose, so should I become his mouthpiece?

Mrs Sevak – It's not possible that a man won't propose if the woman wants him to. Mr Clark waits for an opportunity all the time. You must be the one who doesn't encourage him.

Sophia – Mama, don't embarrass me by talking like this.

Mrs Sevak – It's your fault, and if you don't give Mr Clark a chance to propose within a few days, I'll send you to rani sahiba and never call you back.

Sophia began to tremble. It was far better to die than to return to the rani. She made a firm decision – Today I'll do something that perhaps no other woman has ever done. I'll say frankly, 'The doors of my home are shut for me. Give me shelter if you want to, otherwise I'll find another way out for myself. Don't expect love from me. You can be my husband but not my lover. If, knowing this, you can accept me, do so; otherwise don't show me your face again.'

It was an evening in the month of Maagh, on top of that it was windy and cloudy; the limbs would stiffen because of the cold. The sky was not visible, nor was the earth. There was a fog all around. It was Sunday. Dressed immaculately and wearing heavy overcoats, Christian men and women were entering the church one by one. In a moment John Sevak, Mrs Sevak, Prabhu Sevak and Ishvar Sevak alighted from the phaeton. The others quickly went in, only Sophia stayed outside. Prabhu came out and asked her, 'Well, Sophie, has Mr Clark gone in?'

Sophie – Yes, he has just gone in.

Prabhu – And you?

Sophia said meekly – I'll also go.

Prabhu – You look very sad today.

Sophia's eyes filled with tears. She said – Yes, Prabhu, I'm very sad today. It's the day of the greatest crisis in my life because I'll force Mr Clark to propose to me today. I'm devastated morally and psychologically. I'm no longer the Sophia who would give her life for her principles, who considered maintaining her honour to be God's will, who would test the truths of religion on the touchstone of debate. That Sophia no longer exists in the world. I'm now ashamed of revealing who I am.

Despite being a poet, Prabhu did not have the sensitivity to understand someone else's deepest feelings. He wandered constantly in the world of his imagination and thought it absurd to get involved in worldly joys and sorrows. These were merely the affairs of the world, why bother with them? Human beings should just eat and be merry. He had heard Sophia repeating the same words several times. He said, irritated, 'What's there to cry and moan about? Tell amma frankly. Has she forced you?'

She said, reproaching him – Prabhu, don't hurt me by talking like that. How would you know what I'm going through? Nobody willingly drinks a cup of poison. There's hardly a day when I don't repeat to you my story that I have told you hundreds of times. And you still ask if I have been forced by anyone? You are a poet, how can you be so insensitive? What else could have dragged me here except helplessness? I didn't want to come here today but here I am. I'm telling you the truth, I don't care at all about religion. Fools don't feel ashamed to say that religion is God's blessing. I say it is God's wrath, a divine calamity that has descended to destroy mankind. It's because of this wrath that I have to drink poison today. Why else would someone as kind as Rani Jahnavi have become hostile to me? Why would I have deceived that godly man whom I still worship in my heart and will always worship? If that had not been the reason, I wouldn't have had to punish my soul so cruelly. The more I think about this subject the more I lose faith in religion. Ah! Vinay must have been so anguished by my cruelty. I get paralysed when I think of it. Look, Mr Clark is calling me. Perhaps the sermon is about to begin. I'll have to go or mama won't let me live.

Prabhu went ahead but Sophia had taken just a few steps when she heard someone singing on the road. When she looked over the wall, she saw a blind man with a small khanjari in his hand walking along and singing—

Bhai, why do you turn your face away from battle?
The duty of the brave is to fight, to make a name in the world,
Why do you give up your honour?
Bhai, why do you turn your face away from battle?
Why do you want victory, why do you worry about defeat?
Why do you make ties with sorrow?
Bhai, why do you turn your face away from battle?
You have come to the rangbhoomi, to show your glory,
Why do you break the law of dharma?
Bhai, why do you turn your face away from battle?

Sophia recognized the blind man: it was Soordas. He was singing this song so rapturously that it ached the hearts of those who heard it. People passing by would stop and listen. Sophia listened to this song, totally absorbed. It seemed to her that this verse was saturated with the whole mystery of life—

You have come to the rangbhoomi, to show your glory,
Why do you break the law of dharma?
Bhai, why do you turn your face away from battle?

The raga was so melodious, sweet and stirring that it evoked an ambience. The beat of the khanjari made it even more devastating. All those who heard the song were enthralled.

Sophia forgot that she had to go to church; she didn't remember the sermon at all. She stood at the gate for a long time listening to this 'sermon'. In fact, the sermon was over and the devotees came out and left. She was startled when Mr Clark lightly touched her shoulder.

Clark – Lord Bishop's sermon is over and you are still standing here.

Sophia – So soon? I was just listening to this blind man's song. How long was the sermon?

Clark – Not less than half an hour. Lord Bishop's sermons are brief but delightful. I have never before heard such a divine sermon, replete with knowledge, not even in England. It's a pity you didn't come.

Sophia – I'm surprised that I've been standing here for half an hour.

Meanwhile, Ishvar Sevak arrived with his family. Mrs Sevak looked at Mr Clark with maternal affection and said – Well, William, what does Sophie have to say about today's sermon?

Clark – She didn't even go in.

Mrs Sevak looked disapprovingly at Sophia and said – Sophie, this is shameful.

Sophia said, embarrassed – Mama, I've committed a great crime. I just stopped for a while to listen to this blind man's song and, meanwhile, the sermon was over.

Ishvar Sevak – Beti, today's sermon was like nectar, which gratified the soul. Those who didn't hear it will regret it all their lives. Lord, hide me in your mantle. I had not heard such a sermon until now.

Mrs Sevak – It's surprising that you preferred that rustic song to the heavenly rain of nectar.

Prabhu – Mama, don't say that. The music of the villagers is sometimes so melodious that it's rare even in the compositions of the greatest poets.

Mrs Sevak – Arey, it's the same blind man whose land we have taken. How has he come here today? The unfortunate man didn't take money, now he goes around everywhere begging.

Just then Soordas said loudly – Have mercy, panch! Have mercy! Sevak sahib and raja sahib have grabbed my land by force. No one listens to the complaints of miserable people like us. Have mercy!

Don't torment the one who is weak, his deep lament,
In one breath will turn the cursed one's skin to ashes.*

Clark asked Mr Sevak – He was given compensation for his land, wasn't he? What's the problem now?

Mr Sevak – He didn't take the compensation. The money has been put into the treasury. He's a badmash.

A Christian barrister, who was the Raja Sahib of Chataari's rival, asked Soordas – Why, you blind man, what was this land? How did raja sahib take it?

Soordas – Huzoor! It was the land of my forefathers. Sevak sahib wants to open a factory for making cheroots there. Raja sahib has grabbed that land from me because he told him to. Sarkar have mercy! Panch have mercy! No one listens to the poor.

The Christian barrister said to Clark – I think it's wrong to occupy someone's land for personal profit.

Clark – He has been given very good compensation.

Barrister – You can't force someone to take compensation until you can prove that you are taking the land for some public work.

Mr John Bird, the owner of Kashi Iron Works and John Sevak's old competitor, said – Barrister sahib, don't you know that opening a cigarette factory is the supreme good? Someone who smokes cigarettes doesn't have the slightest difficulty in reaching heaven.

Professor Charles Simeon, who had written a pamphlet opposing cigarettes, said – If the government can acquire land for cigarettes, why not for brothels? To occupy the land for a cigarette factory is to misuse that article of the law. I've cited the views of the greatest scholars and doctors of the world in my pamphlet. The main cause of bad health is the widespread consumption of cigarettes. It's a pity the public didn't heed that pamphlet.

---

* A verse by Kabir. Translation mine.

The minister for the Kashi Railway Union, Mr Neelmani, said – All these rules have been made for the benefit of capitalists, who have been given the right to decide where to use them. A dog has been given the responsibility of guarding the hide. Why, you blind man, how much land do you have?

Soordas – It must be a little more than ten bighas. Sarkar, this is the only sign of my forefathers. Raja sahib first wanted to give a price for it but when I didn't give it, he took it by force. Huzoor, I'm blind and crippled, who else can I complain to if not to you? Whether anyone listens or not, God will listen.

John Sevak couldn't stay there now even for a moment. He was afraid of an altercation and, coincidentally, all his rivals were gathered there. Mr Clark too sat in his car with Sophia. John Sevak said on the way, 'Raja sahib will be distraught if he hears this blind man's complaint.'

Mrs Sevak – He's a rascal. Why don't you hand him over to the police?

Ishvar Sevak – No beta, don't ever make this mistake or the journalists will exaggerate the matter and defame you. Lord, hide my face in your mantle and make this villain hold his tongue.

Mrs Sevak – He'll calm down in a few days. You have briefed the contractors, haven't you?

John Sevak – Yes, the work will begin soon, but it's not easy to silence this wretch. I have split the muhalla-valas—they won't help him—but I had hoped that he would be discouraged when he loses their support. That hope hasn't been fulfilled. It seems he's a very spirited man; it won't be easy to control him. Raja sahib doesn't have so much power in the municipal board; otherwise there would have been nothing to worry about. He had to plead with the board members for a whole year to get the proposal approved. I hope that they won't play some trick again.

Meanwhile, Raja Mahendra Kumar's car stopped in front of them. Raja sahib said – Well met! I've just come from your bungalow. Come, let's go for an outing. I want to discuss some important matters with you.

John Sevak sat in the car and they began their conversation. Raja sahib said – Your Soordas has turned out to be a rascal. He has been wandering around the entire city since yesterday, singing and defaming both of us. The blind are adept at singing. His voice is very melodious. Thousands of people surround him in no time. When there's a big crowd, he makes this lament and defames us.

John Sevak – He had come to the church just now. He kept making this lament. Professor Simeon, Mr Neelmani and other eminent men whom you know were encouraging him even more. He's perhaps still standing there.

Mahendra Kumar – Have you discussed this with Mr Clark?

John Sevak – He was also there. His advice is that the blind man should be sent to a mental asylum. He would have immediately written to the thanedar had I not prevented him.

Mahendra Kumar – You did very well to prevent him. It's easy to send him to a mental asylum or a jail but it's difficult to make the public believe that there has been no injustice done to him. I wouldn't have bothered about his laments and complaints, but you know how many enemies we have. If he continues like this, we'll be objects of ridicule in the whole city within a few days.

John Sevak – Power and infamy are intimately related. Don't worry about that. I'm sorry that I made big promises to the muhalla-valas to control them. My promises are now useless since nobody could influence the blind man.

Mahendra Kumar – Aji, you have won on all sides. I'm the one who's left nowhere. You couldn't have got so much land for less than 10,000 rupees. This is what you'll need to build a dharmashala. It's my reputation that's been ruined. This is perhaps the first time in my life that I seem to have fallen in the eyes of the public. Come, let's go to Pandeypur. We may perhaps be able to persuade the muhalla-valas.

The car turned towards Pandeypur. The road was bad; raja sahib had ordered the engineer to get it repaired but not a pebble could be seen yet. He made an entry in his notebook that this should be looked into. When they reached the toll gate they saw that the munshi was comfortably lying down on a cot and several gharries were waiting for permits. Munshiji had decided that he would charge one rupee per gharry for the permits, otherwise he would let them stand there the whole night. Raja sahib got the permits for the gharry-valas as he went by and entered the account in munshiji's register. It was dark when they reached Pandeypur. The car stopped. Both the gentlemen got down and went to the temple. Nayakram, with a lungi tied around him, was grinding bhang. He came running. Bajrangi, who was filling water in the trough, also came there promptly. After salaams and greetings John Sevak said to Nayakram – That blind man is very angry.

Nayakram – Sarkar, he's so angry that he hasn't returned home since the proclamation about the land. He roams around in the city all day, singing bhajans and lamenting.

Raja sahib – You people didn't try to make him understand?

Nayakram – Deenbandhu! He thinks no end of himself. Another man can be set right if he's threatened but it's as if he knows no fear. He hasn't returned home since that day.

Raja sahib – You people should persuade and cajole him to return. You've sifted the whole world, can't you control a fool?

Nayakram – Sarkar! I don't know how to persuade and cajole, if you allow me, I'll break his limbs—that will silence him.

Raja sahib – Chhee, chhee! What are you saying? I see there's no water pipe here. It must be very difficult for you people. Mr Sevak, take the contract for bringing a pipe here.

Nayakram – That's very kind of you, deenbandhu. It will be splendid if there's a pipe here.

Raja sahib – You people never applied for it.

Nayakram – Sarkar, this basti is outside the limits.

Raja sahib – It doesn't matter. There'll be a pipe here.

Thakurdeen then said – Sarkar, let me also show some hospitality. He then offered beedas of paan wrapped in silver leaf to the two eminent men. Despite his English lifestyle Mr Sevak didn't dislike paan; he ate it with pleasure. Putting the paan into his mouth, raja sahib said – Are there no lamps here? It must be very troublesome in the dark.

Thakurdeen gave Nayakram a piercing look as if to say 'it's my paan that's effective'. He said – Sarkar, who listens to us? It will surely be there now that it has come to huzoor's attention. Bas, have a lamp put only on this temple, nowhere else. When sadhus and mahatmas come here it's troublesome for them in the dark. The lamp will increase the glory of the temple. They will all bless you.

Raja sahib – You people should send in an application.

Thakurdeen – Thanks to the glory of huzoor, one or two sadhus and sants come here every day. I do whatever I can to look after them, otherwise who else will bother about them here? Sarkar, I've lost my courage ever since the theft.

Both the men were about to sit in the car when Subhagi, wearing a red sari, with her head and face covered, came and stood a short distance away, as if she wanted to say something. Raja sahib asked – Who is she? What does she want to say?

Nayakram – She's a paasin. What is it, Subhagi? Do you want to say something?

Subhagi (*Softly*) – Will anyone listen?

Raja sahib – Haan-haan, what do you want to say?

Subhagi – Nothing, maalik, I just came to say that a great injustice has been done to Soordas. He'll die if his complaint is not heard.

John Sevak – Should sarkar stop his work for fear of his dying?

Subhagi – Huzoor! Is sarkar's work to look after the public or to ruin it? The poor man can neither eat nor drink ever since that land was taken away. He is the only support of us poor women, otherwise the men of the muhalla won't let us live, and the men are all united. If a man wants, he can chop off each part and each joint of a woman's body, nobody will stop him. Thieves become cousins. That poor man was the only one who stood by us.

Meanwhile, Bhairo had also arrived. He said – Huzoor, she wouldn't have been standing in front of you if it had not been for Soorey. He was the one who risked his life to save her.

Raja sahib – He seems to be a very bold man.

Nayakram – What's bold about it, sarkar? Bas, he lives by murder.

Raja sahib – That's it. You are right. He lives only by murder. I can have him arrested today if I want, but then I remember that he's blind, why should I be angry with him? You people are his neighbours. He's sure to listen to you. You should try to make him understand. Nayakram, I'm telling you this strongly.

It was an hour into the night. The fog was thickening even more. It seemed as if there was a thick sheet of paper all around the lamps of the shops. Both the gentlemen left, but they were both deeply worried. Raja sahib wondered if the lamps and the water pipe would have any effect. John Sevak was worried about losing a game that he had almost won.

19

SO ENGROSSED WAS SOPHIA IN HER OWN WORRIES THAT SHE HAD completely forgotten Soordas. Her heart trembled when she heard his complaint. Such terrible tyranny on this humble being! Her compassionate nature could not tolerate this injustice. She wondered, 'How can I free Soordas from this difficulty? How can I save him? Papa will never listen to me. He's so obsessed with his factory that he won't hear a word on this subject.'

After a great deal of thought, she decided, 'I'll plead with Indu. It's possible that raja sahib may listen to her if she speaks to him forcefully.' She was very distressed whenever she had to oppose her father but compassion occupied such a high place in her religious outlook that his profit and loss were inconsequential compared to it. She knew that raja sahib cared about the poor and that he had struck this thunderbolt on Soordas only because of Mr Clark. 'When raja sahib comes to know that I'm not in the least grateful to him for this, he may be prepared to rethink his decision. They will all become my enemies at home when they come to know about it, but why should I worry? I can't forsake my duty because of this fear.'

Three days went by in this dilemma. On the fourth day, she went to meet Indu in the morning. It was a hired vehicle. She thought – Indu will come running and hug me as soon as I enter; she'll complain that I've come after so many days. She may not let me return today. She's sure to persuade raja sahib. Goodness knows how papa has managed to trick him.

Absorbed in these thoughts, she reached raja sahib's house and informed Indu about her arrival. She believed that Indu would come out herself to receive her but, after fifteen minutes, a maidservant came and took her in.

Sophia saw that Indu was sitting on a chair in front of the stove in her sitting room, wearing a shawl. She entered the room, but Indu did not get up even then. In fact when Sophia extended her hand, Indu merely extended hers indifferently and didn't say anything. Sophia thought she wasn't well. She asked, 'Do you have a headache?' She had no idea that there could be any other reason except illness for this indifference.

Indu said in a feeble voice – No, I'm quite well. It must have been very troublesome for you in this cold and frost.

Sophia was a self-respecting woman. Hurt by Indu's callousness, she first thought of returning but then she realized that this would be ridiculous, so she presumptuously pulled up a chair and sat down.

'It's a year since I met you.'

'Yes, I don't have much time to move around. The rani sahib of Madiyahu has come here three times this month, but I haven't been able to go even once.'

Sophia, amused inwardly, said sarcastically – What am I, if even ranis are not so fortunate? Do you also have to look after the affairs of the riyasat?

'Nothing and everything. Raja sahib has no respite from public work, so somebody is needed to take care of the business of the house. I too don't trouble him too much when I see that because of this work he enjoys the respect that even the highest officers don't have.'

Sophia could still not fathom the reason for Indu's displeasure. She said – You are very fortunate that you can help him like this in his noble work. Raja sahib's fame today has spread in the entire city. But don't mind, sometimes he too can be calculating and he ignores the humble people for the important ones.

'This is probably the first complaint that I have heard about him.'

'Yes, unfortunately, this task has fallen to me. You know Soordas. Raja sahib has given his land to papa. The poor man wanders around in every lane and alley these days asking for justice. I know that it's shameful for me to utter a single word against my father. But I can't help saying that raja sahib should have had more pity on a poor man.'

Indu looked questioningly at Sophia and asked – Are there differences with your father too nowadays?

Sophia said proudly – Not supporting father, son, or husband for the sake of justice and duty isn't anything to be ashamed of.

'Then you should have first brought your father to the right path. Whatever raja sahib did was for you, and you are blaming him? It's such a pity! He doesn't need to submit to Mr Sevak, Mr Clark, or anybody else in the world. But perhaps you would have been the first to accuse him of ingratitude if he had not supported your father. This injustice has been done to Soordas because you saved Vinay from danger and you are your father's daughter.'

Sophia was furious when she heard these harsh words. She said – Had I known that this would be the reaction to my trifling service, I'd probably not have gone near Vinay. Pardon me, I made a mistake in bringing this complaint to you. I'd heard that there was no constancy in the rich. I have got proof of that today. I'm leaving. But I'm telling you that I won't remain silent about this issue even if papa thinks it a sin to see my face.

Indu said, more gently – What do you want from raja sahib?

'Why does wisdom wane with wealth?'

'I haven't become the vazir from being a pawn.'

'It's a pity that you haven't yet understood my meaning.'

'Pity's not going to make me understand.'

'I want Soordas's land to be returned to him.'

'Do you realize how much raja sahib will be humiliated because of this?'

'Humiliation is better than injustice.'

'You're also aware that whatever has happened is because of your . . . Mr Clark's instigation?'

'I'm not aware of it because I haven't discussed this subject with Mr Clark. But even if I had been aware I'd have thought it proper to entreat raja sahib first, thinking of the damage to his honour. It's far better to correct one's own mistakes than to let others rectify them.'

Indu was hurt. She thought she was being threatened. So much pride at Mr Clark's power! She said stiffly – I don't think that a government officer has the authority to interfere in the decision of the board, and even if it means that atrocities may have to be committed on the blind man some day, raja sahib will not raise any issue to change his decision. A raja's honour is far more important than some trifling justice.

Sophia said, anguished – Truthful men have been beheaded for this trifling justice.

Indu slapped her hand on the arm of her chair and said – We are no longer living in times when we can make a farce of justice.

Sophia didn't reply. She got up and said – Pardon me for this trouble.

Indu began to fan the fire of the stove. She didn't so much as look at Sophia.

Sophia was heartbroken at Indu's curt behaviour. She kept wondering – Where is that cheerful, happy-go-lucky, fun-loving Indu? Does wealth taint human nature? I have never said anything to hurt her. Have I changed, or has she? She didn't even talk to me properly. Let alone talk, she abused me instead. I trusted her so much. I thought her to be a devi. I've seen her true self today. But why should I bow down before her wealth? She has insulted me without rhyme or reason. Perhaps raniji has filled her ears but there's such a thing as courtesy.

Sophia decided then and there fully to avenge this insult, in fact more than fully.

It didn't occur to her that perhaps Indu was disturbed for some reason or that some calamity had put her in this dilemma. She just thought, 'The most terrible mental torment, the worst economic harm, the most acute physical pain are inadequate as retaliation for such incivility, such villainy. She has challenged me; I accept it. She's proud of her riyasat, I'll show her that she herself is not the light of the sun; she is merely the reflected light of the moon. She'll get to know that rajas and rais are all toys in the hands of the rulers, who make or destroy them according to their whims.'

Sophia began her deception from the very next day. Her love for Mr Clark began to increase. She became a puppet of her own resentment. Now she would listen to his sweet talk with her head bowed. She would put her arms round his neck and say, 'Who has taught you how to love?' Both of them would constantly be seen together. Sophia wouldn't let go of sahib even in the office. She would repeatedly write to him, 'Come soon, I'm waiting for you.' All this pretence of love was only to take her revenge on Indu. She was not in the least concerned about protecting justice; she only wanted to shatter Indu's arrogance.

One day, Sophia took Mr Clark towards Pandeypur for an outing. When the car passed the godown, she said, pointing to the heaps of bricks and rubble – Papa is working with great enthusiasm.

Clark – Yes, he's a dynamic man. I'm jealous of his capacity to work.

Sophia – Papa didn't consider questions of right and wrong.

Whether anyone agrees or not, I can only say that an injustice has been done to the blind man.

Clark – Yes, there has been an injustice. I didn't want it at all.

Sophia – Then why did you give your permission?

Clark – What else could I do?

Sophia – You could have rejected it. You should have clearly written that someone's land can't be acquired.

Clark – Wouldn't you have been angry?

Sophia – Never! Perhaps you don't know me yet.

Clark – Your papa would surely have been angry.

Sophia – Papa and I aren't the same. There's a world of difference in our values and actions.

Clark – I'd have won you a long time ago if I'd been so intelligent. I didn't know your nature and views. I thought that perhaps this permission would be in my interest.

Sophie – To sum it up, I'm the root of this injustice. Raja sahib placed this proposal before the board to please me. You also gave your permission to make me happy. You people have ruined my honour.

Clark – You know my principles. I had to exercise great self-control to accept this proposal.

Sophia – You exercised control not over yourself but over me, and now you'll have to atone for this.

Clark – I didn't know that you cared so much about justice.

Sophia – Praising me will not atone for this injustice.

Clark – I'll get the blind man land of the same size in some other village.

Sophia – Can't his own land be returned to him?

Clark – It's difficult.

Sophia – But not impossible.

Clark – It's just short of impossible.

Sophia – Now I've understood that it's not impossible. You'll have to atone for this. Revoke that proposal tomorrow.

Clark – Dearest, don't you know what the result will be?

Sophia – I'm not worried about that. If papa feels bad, let him. If raja sahib is humiliated, let him be so. Why should I bear this sin for someone else's profit or honour? Why should I be a participant in God's punishment? You people have burdened me with a great sin against my wishes. I can't bear it. You'll have to return the blind man's land.

While this conversation was going on, Sayyad Tahir Ali saw Sophia in the car. He immediately came and greeted her. Sophia stopped the car and asked – Well, munshiji, has work on the building begun?

Tahir – Yes, the line for the foundation will be marked tomorrow. But I don't see it being completed.

Sophia – Why? Has anything happened?

Tahir – Huzoor! Ever since this blind man has begun his wailing and complaining in the city, there have been strange problems. The people of the muhalla now don't say anything but the rogues and scoundrels of the city come and threaten me daily. Somebody wants to set the house on fire, someone else comes to loot, someone threatens to murder me. Hundreds of people came this morning with sticks and surrounded the godown. Some people began to scatter the heaps of cement and lime, some began to break the stone slabs. What could I do alone? The labourers were so frightened that they ran for their lives. It was like facing the end of the world. It seemed that in a moment it would be the Day of Judgement. I shut the door and was chanting 'Allah-Allah' so that somehow the turmoil would end. Finally, my prayer was accepted. Just in time, I don't know from where that blind man came and said, crackling like lightning, 'Why are you people raising an uproar and putting this shame on my head? Setting fire will not put out the fire in my heart; bloodshed won't give me peace of mind. This fire and burning will go away with your good wishes. Ask Parmatma to take away my sorrow. Pray to God to take away my trouble. Let mercy and dharma awaken in the hearts of those who have done me this injustice; that's all, I don't want anything else from you people.' When they heard this, some people moved away but many others were angry and said, 'You may be a god, so be one; we are not gods; we'll give tit for tat. Let them also taste the result of oppressing the poor.' They started picking up stones and hurling them. Then that man did something that only an aulia can. Huzoor, I was absolutely sure that he's an angel. His words are still echoing in my ears. His picture is still there in front of my eyes. He picked up a biggish piece of stone from the ground and putting it to his forehead said, 'If you people still don't listen to my request, I'll beat my head with this stone and give up my life. I'm willing to die, but I can't see this anarchy.' He just had to utter these words and there was silence all around. All those present remained where they were like statues. In a short while people gradually began to leave and the entire crowd disappeared in half an hour. Huzoor! I'm fully convinced that he's not a human being but an angel.

Sophia – Somebody must have informed him of these rascals having come here.

Tahir – Huzoor, I think he has knowledge of the invisible.

Sophia (*Smiling*) – Haven't you informed papa?

Tahir – Huzoor, I haven't had a chance since then. I can't leave my family alone. All the men ran away earlier. I was standing here, worried, when I saw huzoor's car.

Mr Clark – This blind man is definitely an extraordinary man.

Sophia – Just exchange a few words with him. You'll be surprised when you listen to his spiritual and philosophical views. He's a sadhu, a philosopher. Worldly life would surely be blissful if only we could act on his views. He's ignorant, completely illiterate, but each sentence of his is profounder than the great texts of scholars.

When the car started, Sophie said – You people don't scruple to be unjust to such saints, who don't throw a pebble even at their enemies. This was also the supreme virtue of the Lord Messiah.

Mr Clark – Dearest, don't embarrass me. There'll definitely be a penance for this.

Sophia – Raja sahib will strongly oppose this.

Mr Clark – Thooh! He doesn't have the moral courage. He looks at our disposition before doing anything. That's why he's never unsuccessful. Yes, he has this special ability of transforming our proposals to get his work done and presenting them so cleverly to people that his prestige is enhanced in their eyes. There's a great lack of self-confidence among the Indian elite and politicians. They can accomplish what we can't with our help. But they can't do anything without it.

The car reached Sigara and Sophia got down. Clark looked at her fondly, shook hands, and left.

20

AS SOON AS MR CLARK GOT DOWN FROM THE CAR, HE COMMANDED the orderly, 'Give my salaam immediately to deputy sahib.' The bailiff, the record keeper and the other staff were also summoned. They were all anxious. 'Why this untimely summons today, has some mistake been found? Has somebody complained about a bribe?' The poor things were very flustered.

Deputy sahib was annoyed. 'I'm not sahib's personal servant that he can summon me whenever he likes. He can summon me as often as he wants during court hours but what's the meaning of sending me his salaam at his whim?' He decided not to go but he didn't have the courage to refuse openly. He wanted to make an excuse of being ill but the orderly said, 'Huzoor, sahib will be very angry if you don't come now. It's something very urgent, that's why he sent his salaam as soon as he got down from the car.'

Eventually deputy sahib was forced to go. The junior staff didn't make the slightest squeak; as soon as they saw the orderly, they left their huqqas, quietly changed their clothes, reassured their children, and regarding the officer's order as untimely death, scrambled to reach the bungalow. As soon as deputy sahib saw sahib, all his anger disappeared and he scurried around to carry out his orders. Mr Clark sent for the file on Soordas's land; he had it read out to him and listened attentively, after that he made deputy sahib write an order in Mahendra Kumar's name, the gist of which was – The land that has been acquired in Pandeypur for the cigarette factory is opposed to the objective of that particular article of the law, I therefore withdraw my permission. I have been deceived in this matter and the law has been misused for personal gain.

Deputy sahib expressed his misgiving in a subdued voice – Huzoor, you don't have the right to revoke that order now, because the government has approved it.

Mr Clark said harshly – I'm the government, I have made that law, I have every right. Write the order to raja sahib immediately and send a copy to the local government tomorrow. I'm the one who is the master of the district, not the government of the province. If there's an uprising here, I'll have to deal with it, the government of the province won't come here.

The clerks trembled and cursed deputy sahib – Why does he interfere? He's English. One never knows, he may hit out in anger. He's the badshah of the district, he can do what he likes, how does it concern us?

Deputy sahib's heart also began to beat faster; he didn't open his mouth again. The order was ready, sahib signed it, and an orderly took it to raja sahib immediately.

Deputy sahib informed Mr Sevak about the order.

John Sevak was eating; his appetite disappeared when he heard the news. He said – What's this that Mr Clark has thought of?

Mrs Sevak looked sharply at Sophie and asked – You haven't refused, have you? There's definitely some rigmarole.

Sophie looked down and said – That's all, you are always angry with me, I'm responsible for whatever happens.

Ishvar Sevak – Lord Messiah, hide this sinner in your mantle. I kept saying until the very end, don't take away the old man's land, but who listens? They must be thinking in their hearts that he's senile, but I have seen the world. The raja must have gone to Mr Clark because he was afraid.

Prabhu – That's what I also think. Raja sahib himself must have spoken to Mr Clark. Nowadays it's difficult for him to venture out in the city. The blind man has raised a hue and cry in the whole city.

John – I had thought that I would ask for policemen to maintain law and order tomorrow and now this has come to light. I can't imagine what could have happened.

Prabhu – I think it would be best for us to give up this land. The godown wouldn't have been safe today if Soordas had not reached there, goods worth thousands of rupees would have been destroyed. This uprising won't calm down.

John Sevak, ridiculing him, said – Yes, that's excellent. We should all get together and go to the blind man and bow our heads at his feet. Today I should be afraid of him and give up the land, tomorrow I should break the contract for the leather agency, the day after I should leave this bungalow, and after that I should hide my face and go away somewhere. Why, isn't this your advice? Then there'll be peace all around and no fight or quarrel with anybody. You are welcome to this advice. The world is not an arena of peace but of battle. It's the brave and the courageous that win here, the weak and the cowards are killed. What are Mr Clark and Raja Mahendra Singh worth? The entire universe now can't take that land away from me. I'll raise a hue and cry in the whole city; I'll shake the whole of India. The example of this arbitrary functioning of the authorities will be published in all the papers of the country, it will be proclaimed not by one but by thousands of voices in the councils and assemblies, and its echo will reach the British Parliament. This is a question of private industry and enterprise. All the businessmen of India, whether Indian or English, will support me on this issue, and the government is not so unintelligent that it will shut its ears to the collective voice of businessmen. This is the age of business rule. In Europe large, powerful empires are made and destroyed at the behest of capitalists; no government has the courage to oppose their wishes. What do you think of me? I'm not soft fodder that can be eaten by Clark and Mahendra.

Prabhu was so disconcerted that he didn't speak again. He got up and left quietly. Sophia was also astounded for a moment. Then she thought, 'Even if papa starts a movement, it will take years for it to have a result, and who knows what the outcome will be? Why worry about it now?' There was a smile of triumph on her pink lips. At this moment, she could have sacrificed everything to see the colour waning from Indu's face. 'If only I could have been there! I could have seen the embarrassment on Indu's face. Even if our relationship were to end forever, I would certainly have said this much, "Have you now seen your raja sahib's power and strength? Is this what you were so proud of?"' But how was she to know that Clark would act so fast.

She went to her room after she had eaten and began to enjoy Indu's mental anguish in her imagination – raja sahib, pale and distraught, will come and sit by Indu. Indu devi will see the envelope; she won't believe her eyes, then she'll turn up the light and look at it, after that she'll wipe raja sahib's tears. 'You are unnecessarily so disturbed, you should get a drum beaten in the city and proclaim that you have fought with the government and have got back the land for Soordas. Your justice will become famous throughout the city. People will think that you have respected public opinion.' What a fawning ass! He fooled William by tricking him. He has suffered such a setback that he'll always remember it. Anyway, if not today, then tomorrow, or the day after, some day I'll meet Indu devi. For how long will she hide her face?

Sophia then sat down at her table and began to write a farce on this incident. Jealousy fuels the imagination. Sophia had never before written a farce. But now, carried away by jealousy, she wrote an amusing play of four scenes within an hour. She penned such hurtful quotations and rib-tickling witticisms that she was surprised at her own talent. She momentarily thought that she was being foolish. To taunt a defeated enemy after victory is the worst kind of meanness but in her jealousy she found an argument to resolve the problem. 'This is the punishment for such dissembling, prestige-hungry, deceitful, flattering rais who betray the people by pretending to be their friends. The only way to reform them and bring them to the right path is to make them afraid of falling in the eyes of the public. They'll become lions without the fear of ridicule and will think everybody else to be beneath them.'

Prabhu was sleeping soundly. It was past midnight. He got up startled when Sophia woke him up; thinking that a thief had entered her room, he ran towards the door. The incident of the godown came to his mind. Sophia caught hold of his hand and asked, 'Where are you running away?'

Prabhu – Are there any thieves here? Should I light the lantern?

Sophia – There aren't any thieves. Just come to my room. I'll read something to you. I have just written it.

Prabhu – Vaah-vaah! You've spoilt my sleep for such a small thing. Couldn't it have waited till the morning? What have you written?

Sophia – It's a farce.

Prabhu – Farce! What farce? Since when have you begun to practise writing farces?

Sophia – Today! I tried very hard to control myself till the morning, but I couldn't resist.

Prabhu went to Sophia's room and in a moment they both began to guffaw loudly. Sophia couldn't stop laughing when she read the sentences that had not amused her at all when she had written them. When anything amusing was to come, Sophia would begin laughing. Prabhu would look at her with his mouth open, not understanding what the matter was, but he would join her laughter and its sound would become louder as soon as he understood. Their faces reddened, water began to flow from their eyes and their stomachs began to writhe, even their jaws started paining. By the time the farce was over, they were coughing instead of guffawing. It was just as well that the doors were closed on both sides or the noise would have shaken the entire bungalow.

Prabhu – What a name you have given, Raja Mucchendra Singh! Mahendra and Mucchendra are so alike. Mucchendra Singh's bowing down again and again to salaam Pilpili sahib on being lashed by his hunter is really splendid.* One hopes that raja sahib won't eat poison.

Sophia – He doesn't have so much shame.

After a while they both went to sleep in their rooms. Sophia got up in the morning and began to wait for Mr Clark. She was sure that he would come and the entire matter would become clear, right now there were only rumours. It was possible that raja sahib, distraught, had gone to him with his lament but it was 8 a.m. and there was no sign of Clark. He too had been ready to come early in the morning but had hesitated in case Sophia thought that he had gone to assert an obligation for something so trivial. More than that, he was afraid to face the people there, for they might feel resentful at heart when they saw him or openly accuse him. The greatest fear was from Ishvar Sevak, who might call him a rascal, a sinner, a devil, an infidel. He was an old man, what could one say to him? That was why he had been reluctant to go and had hoped that Sophia would come herself.

Sophia was impatient after having waited for Clark until 9 a.m. She decided to go herself when John Sevak came and sat down and, looking at Sophia with blazing eyes, said – Sophie, I didn't expect this from you. You have reduced all my ambitions to dust.

---

* Mucchendra: Somebody with a long moustache; a buffoon; a keeper and trainer of monkeys.
  Pilpili: Flaccid; slippery; smooth. The reference is obviously to Clark.

Sophia – What have I done? I don't understand what you mean.

John – I mean that Mr Clark has revoked his earlier order at your instigation.

Sophia – You are mistaken.

John – I have never accused anyone without proof. I have just met Indu devi. She gave me proof that this is your doing.

Sophia – Are you sure that Indu's allegation about me is correct?

John – I don't have any proof to think that it's false.

Sophia – If Indu's word is sufficient to think that it's true, why is my word not enough to think that it's untrue?

John – Truth generates trust.

Sophia – I'm unfortunate that I can't add salt and spice to what I say, but I can assure you that Indu has enacted this farce to create differences between William and me.

John Sevak, in a quandary, said – Sophie, look at me. Are you telling the truth?

Sophia tried very hard to look candidly at her father but her eyes lowered themselves of their own accord. One's proclivity may taint one's speech but it has no power over the body. The tongue may be silent, but the eyes are expressive. John Sevak saw her eyes pained with shame and asked, stunned, 'Why, after all, have you sown these thorns?'

Sophia – You are being very unfair to me. You should get a clarification about this from William. Yes, I'll say this much, instead of becoming notorious in the whole city, it would be far better for you to give up your claim to that land.

John – Well! So you have played this trick for the sake of my good name? I'm deeply obliged. But this thought has come to you very late. The Christian community is already so notorious because of its religion that it's difficult for it to become more so. All our churches would be reduced to heaps of dust if the public had its way. People are not so hostile to the English. They think that the customs and traditions of the English are their own, in consonance with their country and society. But when an Indian, no matter what his sect, adopts English ways, the public thinks him to be absolutely worthless; he's liberated from the bonds of good and evil, there's no hope of any good deed from him, nobody is surprised at his wicked actions. I'll never believe that you have made this effort to protect my reputation. Your aim is only the destruction of my business objectives. Religious debates have unsettled your common sense. You don't understand that sacrifice and philanthropy are ideals—for poets, for the entertainment of devotees, for the ornamentation of the speeches of preachers. These are not the times for the birth of the Messiah, the Buddha, or Moses; wealth and glory, despite being despised, are the heaven of human desires and will always remain so. For Khuda's sake, don't test your religious principles on me; I don't want lessons from you on morality and religion. You think that Khuda has made you the monopolist of justice, truth and mercy, and all the rich and famous men are unjust, selfish and cruel. But if, despite believing in God's design, you think that the cause of inequality and conflict is only man's selfishness, I can only say that you have followed religious texts with your eyes shut, you haven't understood their meaning. I don't have words to express my sorrow at your bad behaviour, and although I'm not a vali or a fakir, just remember that sometime or the other you will have to reap the bitter fruit for rebelling against your father.

The climax of anger is the desire to harm. 'God will punish you for this'—this sentence is more wounding than a dagger or a spear. When we realize that physical power is not enough to punish wicked deeds, we invoke spiritual punishment. Anything less is inadequate for our gratification.

John Sevak left after uttering these curses. But they didn't make Sophia at all unhappy. She entered this debt too in Indu's account and her desire for revenge became more intense. She decided, 'I'll publish this farce today. If the editor doesn't publish it, I'll have it published myself as a book and distribute it free. Her face will be so blackened that she won't be able to show it to anyone again.'

Ishvar Sevak was very angry when he heard John's harsh words. Mrs Sevak too didn't like this behaviour. Ishvar Sevak said – When will you learn to distinguish between your profit and loss? It's not difficult to carry out something that has been accomplished. You should have acted with such patience and maturity on this occasion that the harm that has been done could have been offset. It's not wise to pull down the whole house if a corner falls. If you have lost the land think of a way of acquiring it again, rather than losing your reputation and respect along with it. Go and persuade raja sahib to appeal against

Mr Clark's decision and maintain your interaction with Mr Clark as if you haven't been harmed at all because of him. You are unnecessarily making Clark your enemy by antagonizing Sophie. Contact with the officers will help you to get many more pieces of land like this one. Lord Messiah, hide me in your mantle and remove this misfortune.

Mrs Sevak – I had to persuade her so hard to come here and you have spoilt everything.

Ishvar – Lord, give me the kingdom of heaven. Even if we believe that this has happened because of Sophie, we shouldn't have any complaint against her, in fact my respect for her has increased. Khuda has given her the true light; she has the blessing of devotion and trust. Not to praise her for what she has done is to strangle justice. The Lord Messiah sacrificed himself for the meek and the suffering; unfortunately we don't have such faith. We should be ashamed of our selfishness. It isn't right to scorn Sophie's feelings. A sinner feels ashamed when he sees a sadhu, he doesn't become his enemy.

John – This is neither worship nor love of religion, it's merely rebellion and resentment.

Ishvar Sevak didn't reply. He went to Sophie's room tapping his stick and said – Beti, do you mind if I come in?

Sophia – No, no, come. Sit down.

Ishvar – Jesus, show this sinner the light of faith. John reproached you just now; forgive him. Beti, one's father has the place of Khuda in this life, you shouldn't mind what he says. Khuda's hand is over you; you have his blessing. Your father's entire life has been spent in furthering his own interest and he is still its devotee. Pray to God to take away the darkness of his heart with the divine light of knowledge. Our Lord Messiah had said of those who had tortured him—Khuda, forgive them, for they know not what they do.

Sophia – I'm telling you the truth, I don't mind what papa has said at all, but he's making a false accusation against me. He doesn't give any importance to what I say compared to what Indu says.

Ishvar – Beti, that's his mistake. But you should forgive him in your heart. Social beings have been criticized so much, but if you look at it fairly, they are such objects of compassion. After all, whatever man does is for his children, for their happiness and peace, he gladly bears criticism, humiliation, everything, to protect them from the malevolent gaze of the world; he even sacrifices his soul and his religion for their sakes. In these circumstances, he flares up when he sees that he's giving his blood and sweat for the welfare of the very people who are opposing him. Then he can't distinguish between right and wrong. Look, don't make the mistake of telling Mr Clark about all this; it will only increase the rancour between us. Do you promise?

When Ishvar Sevak had left, Prabhu came and asked – Where have you sent that farce?

Sophia – I haven't sent it anywhere yet; should I send it?

Prabhu – Of course, it will be great fun. There'll be a hue and cry in the whole city.

Sophia – Let me wait for a couple of days.

Prabhu – There shouldn't be any delay in a good deed, send it today. I have also completed my story today. Shall I read it?

Sophia – Yes, of course, do read it.

Prabhu began to read his poem. Each word was saturated with the sentiment of compassion. The story was so tragic that Sophie's tears began to flow. Prabhu was also crying. The emotions of love and forgiveness dripped like tears from every word. When the poem was over, Sophie said, 'I had never imagined that you could evoke this sentiment so skilfully. I want to kiss your pen. Oof! It's such a divine gift. Don't mind, but your composition is far superior to you. How can such pure, delicate and powerful sentiments flow from your pen?'

Prabhu – Just as such humorous, libellous sentiments flowed from yours. Is your composition inferior to you?

Sophia – What am I or my composition? Each verse of yours is delightful. Actually forgiveness is the highest human sentiment. Compassion doesn't have such a high place. Compassion is the seed that sprouts on porous earth. In contrast forgiveness is the seed that sprouts among thorns. Compassion is the stream that flows on level land, forgiveness the stream that flows over pebbles and rocks. The path of compassion is simple and straight, that of forgiveness is crooked and difficult. Each word of yours pierces the heart. It's surprising that there's not a jot of forgiveness in you.

Prabhu – Sophie, actions have no importance compared to sentiments. The poet's arena of action is limited, but that of his sentiments is eternal and infinite. Don't think that a being is inferior if he professes sacrifice and detachment himself but gives his life for kauris. Perhaps his voice may reach some great sinner's heart.

Sophia – There's a different name for somebody whose words and actions are so opposed.

Prabhu – No Sophie, that's not it. A poet's sentiments reveal what he could have become if he had had the opportunity. If he couldn't attain the greatness of his sentiments it's because circumstances were unfavourable.

It was time to eat. After that Sophie began to read the Bible to Ishvar Sevak. She had never before been so humble and polite. Ishvar Sevak's thirst for knowledge overcame his consciousness. In fact the condition of sleep was his inner consciousness. He would listen to the sacred text while lying on his chair and snoring. But the wonder was that as soon as the reader stopped, thinking him to be fast asleep, he would immediately speak up, 'Yes, yes, read, why have you stopped? I'm listening.'

Sophia kept reading the Bible until the evening and then she was free. Ishvar Sevak went to the garden for a stroll and Prabhu got a chance to chat with Sophie.

Sophia – Grandfather doesn't let one go once he catches hold of you.

Prabhu – He doesn't ask me to read the Bible. I couldn't sit there even for a moment. I don't know how you can keep sitting there and reading.

Sophia – What to do, I feel sorry for him.

Prabhu – He only pretends. He never misses out on anything when it suits him. All this devotion is only for show.

Sophia – You are being unfair. Whatever his faults, he has firm faith in the Lord Messiah. Come, let's go out somewhere.

Prabhu – Where do you want to go? Let's sit by the side of this tank and discuss poetry. I don't enjoy anything else so much.

Sophia – Let's go towards Pandeypur. We can give this news to Soordas if we meet him.

Prabhu – He'll jump with joy.

Sophia – Given a little encouragement, he'll drive this raja out of the city.

They went to the road, hired a tonga and left for Pandeypur. The sun had set. The clerks of the court, their satchels under their arms, were leaving, looking the pictures of timidity and selfishness. Tennis was being played in the bungalows. The hooligans of the city were gathered at the paan shops, oblivious of the world around. Labourers' wives were buying ingredients for food at banias' shops. The tonga reached the bridge on the Barna river when suddenly a crowd of people was seen. Soordas was playing the khanjari and singing. Sophie stopped the tonga and told the tonga-vala, 'Go and call that blind man.' Soordas came there in a moment tapping his stick and stood with his head bowed.

Sophia – Do you recognize me, Soordas?

Soordas – Yes, how can I not recognize huzoor?

Sophia – You have defamed us in the whole city.

Soordas – What else could I do except complain?

Sophia – What was the result of that complaint?

Soordas – My desire has been fulfilled. The officers have returned my land. It isn't possible that someone should work with all his being and there's no reward. You can get God with tapasya. Burra sahib's orderly came and told me this last night. I have to feed five brahmans today. I'll go home tomorrow.

Prabhu – It's miss sahib who has persuaded burra sahib and got back your land for you. Her father and raja sahib are both very angry with her. She has a lot of compassion for you.

Sophia – Prabhu, you can't keep anything in your stomach. What's the point in telling him that miss sahib got the land for him? It's not such a great thing.

Soordas – Sahib, I have known this from the day I first spoke to miss sahib. I knew then that there's compassion and dharma in her heart. God will reward her for this.

Sophia – Soordas, this is not the result of my recommendation but of your tapasya. You have really harassed raja sahib. There's just a little bit left. Malign him such that he won't be able to show his face in the city, so that he resigns and goes back to his estate.

Soordas – No, miss sahib, this is not the ethic of players. The player doesn't laugh at the one who loses after winning; he embraces him and tells him, with folded hands, 'Bhaiyya! Please forgive me if I have said or done anything wrong during the game.' This way both the players laugh and separate from each other, they become friends as soon as the game ends, and there's no ill-will between them. I went to see raja sahib today with folded hands. He gave me some food. When I was leaving, he said, 'I don't have any ill-will for you, don't have any fear.'

Sophia – He's not that sincere. He's sure to deceive you whenever he gets the chance, I'm telling you.

Soordas – No, miss sahib, don't say that. Doubting someone taints one's own heart. He's a scholar, a dharmatma; he'll never deceive anyone. And even if he does, he'll be the one to lose his dharma; how does it matter to me? I'll go on complaining in the same way. The God who has heard me now will hear me again.

Prabhu– And if he files a case and has you imprisoned?

Soordas (*Laughing*) – He'll get the result of that from God. My dharma is to catch hold of a person's hand if he stretches it towards something that belongs to me. I'll fight if he fights, and I'll give my life for it. I'm not bothered about getting it; my job is to fight and that too, to fight for dharma. Even if raja sahib betrays me, I won't betray him.

Sophia – But I won't let raja sahib off that cheaply.

Soordas – Miss sahib, you are so learned yet you talk like this. I'm surprised. It doesn't become you. No, you are only joking. You can never do anything like this.

Meanwhile, somebody called out – Soordas, come, the brahmans are here.

Soordas went towards the bank tapping his stick. The tonga also started.

Prabhu asked – Shall we go to Mr Clark?

Sophia said – No, let's go home.

There was no conversation on the way. Sophia was lost in thought. The lamps had been lit when they reached Sigara. Sophie went straight to her room, pulled out the drawer of her table, took out the script of her farce, tore it to bits and threw it on the floor.

21

SOORDAS'S CRY OF SUFFERING SHOOK THE FOUNDATIONS OF Mahendra Kumar's renown and esteem. That mansion of fame which used to touch the sky fell to the ground in just a moment. People in the city seemed to have forgotten his services. No one remembered how much the city had profited by his industry. Its drains and roads, gardens and alleys were so deeply indebted to his untiring efforts! No one paid any attention to the improvements that he had brought to the education and the hygiene of the city from such poor conditions. There was a change in the times before one's eyes. People would criticize raja sahib – No longer are the names of rajas and rais taken with respect, no longer does the public have innate devotion to them. Those days are gone. Worship of prosperity was a part of the worship of royalty in ancient times. People would give their lives for their rajas, jagirdars and even zamindars. The universally honoured moral principle was that the raja was the consumer and the public the consumed. These were the laws of creation but now the relationship of raja and public is not that of consumer and consumed, but of servant and served. If a raja is respected now, it is because of his desire to serve, otherwise his plight is like that of a tongue caught between the teeth. The public also doesn't trust him. It respects and gives its life only for someone who has sacrificed everything for it, who is rich in the wealth of sacrifice. No one can win over the public until he has learnt to tread the path of service.

Raja sahib now realized that fame is like a white cloth on which not a single stain can be concealed. People would jeer at him wherever his car went; sometimes they would even clap. The poor man was in great trouble. He had wanted to win fame but had lost even his honour. On other occasions he would have consulted Indu, which would have given him some peace of mind, but now even that door was closed. There was no hope of any sympathy from her.

It was 9 p.m. Raja sahib was in his reception room thinking over this very problem – People are so ungrateful. I spent seven years of my life in their constant service, I gifted them so much of my time, experience and comfort! The gift that I have got for that in return today is that a blind man goes around abusing me in the whole city and nobody catches hold of his tongue, rather they provoke and encourage him even more. Had I made such good arrangements for my own estate, the profit would have increased by lakhs of rupees. There was a time when people used to stand and greet me wherever I went, they would be eager to listen to my speeches at gatherings and I would be given a chance to speak at the end, and today they mock me and enact farces on me. The blind man still has some sense; otherwise the hooligans of Banaras would have looted my house in broad daylight.

Meanwhile, the orderly came and placed Mr Clark's order before him. Raja sahib was startled. He was astounded when he opened the envelope. Disaster upon disaster! Whatever little remained of his respect was also reduced to dust.

Chaprasi – Huzoor, will you give a reply?

Raja sahib – There's no need.

Chaprasi – I haven't been given a tip. If huzoor . . .

Raja sahib didn't let him say anything else. He took out a rupee from his pocket and flung it. The orderly left.

Raja sahib thought – The rascal had no shame asking for a tip, as if he'd brought me a letter of thanks. They are dogs. They run to bite you if you don't give anything and make false complaints. I can't understand why Clark has revoked his order. Has there been some misunderstanding with John Sevak? Perhaps Sophia has rejected Clark. Well, it's for the best. People will of course say that the blind man has humiliated raja sahib, but at least I'll be rid of this lamentation.

His predicament at this moment was like that of a man who is glad that his headstrong horse has run away. 'At least there's no longer the fear of my bones being broken. I haven't suffered a loss. Now the offended rani will also be happy. I'll tell Indu that I had urged Mr Clark to revoke his decision.'

He had not met Indu for several days. He was afraid to go in because he didn't know how he would answer Indu's taunts. Indu too avoided him for fear of uttering hostile words. After every marital discord, when she reflected with a calm mind, she realized that she was to blame and would be deeply distressed at her obstinacy. Since her childhood, her mother had placed before her the very high ideal of a devoted wife. She would be vexed at heart and would reproach herself whenever she fell from that ideal – My dharma is to obey his orders. I should serve him with all my being. My prime duty is towards him, the place of the country and of the community is secondary. But my misfortune makes me waver from the path of duty again and again. I unnecessarily got entangled with him because of that blind man. He's learned and thoughtful. It's my insolence that I challenge him and try to assert my superiority over him. How can I expect him to be impartial on every subject when I keep thinking of my respect and disrespect over small things?

She had become averse to Soordas because she had been mulling over all this for several days. She thought – I'm suffering from this remorse because of that unfortunate man. He's the one who has caused this resentment. After all, that land is the salvation of the muhalla-valas, so if they don't have any objections, why is he complaining as if his nani is dying? Why should anyone forcibly occupy somebody else's land? This is nothing else but hypocrisy. The weak have been oppressed from time immemorial and will continue to be oppressed. When this is a widespread custom, then one more or one less, how does it matter?

When Soordas began to malign raja sahib in the city around this time, the balance of Indu's sympathy had tilted the other way very fast. She became averse to Soordas's name – This man worth a taka has the courage to be so impudent! If this is the meaning of communism, then God save us from it. These are changing times or he wouldn't have dared to bespatter us.

Indu could feel pity for the downtrodden—the awareness of power is concealed in pity—but she couldn't do justice, for the foundation of justice is equality. She thought – Why doesn't he hand over that rascal to the police? I couldn't have tolerated this humiliation. Whatever the outcome, at least for the time being the police would have been so brutal that the onlookers' hair would have stood on end.

It was while she was engrossed in these base thoughts that Sophia had arrived.

She had blamed raja sahib for being unjust to Soordas and had given an open threat. Indu was so furious that she would have clawed

Soordas's face if she could have found him. After Sophia had left, she went to meet raja sahib, full of anger but she came to know that he had gone to the estate for a few days. She passed these days restlessly. She was sorry that he had left without even asking her.

Raja sahib received Mr Clark's order after returning from the estate. He was thinking about it when Indu came and said – You went to the estate and I had no idea about it, as if I'm not in the house.

Raja (*Embarrassed*) – There was some urgent work. There would have been a breach of peace on the estate if there had been even a day's delay. I've realized now how much the people suffer if the taluqdars don't stay on their estates.

'At least we wouldn't have been so maligned if we'd stayed on the estate.'

'Oh! So you have also come to know about it. I made a big mistake by not listening to you. This blind man has created such a problem for me that I don't know what to do. He is maligning me in the whole city. I don't know how the people of the city have become so sympathetic to him. I hadn't been in the least apprehensive that he would incite them against me.'

'I'm so furious ever since I've heard that the blind man is maligning you that if I had my way I would have him buried alive.'

Raja sahib said, delighted – So after circling round and round, we have reached the same objective.

'This villain should be given such a punishment that he'll remember it all his life.'

'Mr Clark took the decision. Soordas's land has been returned to him.'

Indu felt that the ground was subsiding and she was sinking into it. She would have fallen if she had not held on to the wall – This is how Sophia has humiliated me! This diplomacy has been used against me. She wants to reduce our honour to dust so that I should kiss her feet. Never!

She asked raja sahib – What will you do now?

'Nothing. What's there to be done? If you ask me, I'm not at all unhappy about it. I've been liberated.'

'But there has been so much humiliation.'

'It's certainly humiliating. But it's better than this disgrace.'

Indu's face blazed with pride. She said, 'This doesn't become you. It's not a question of a good name or a bad name but of protecting our honour. It's a blow to the honour of your dynasty; it's your supreme duty to protect it, even if the principles of justice have to be sacrificed for it. What's Mr Clark's status? I won't let my honour suffer even at the hands of an emperor, although I may have to give up all that I have, even my life. You should immediately inform the Governor of Mr Clark's interference against justice. Our ancestors had protected the lives of the English at a time when they were in grave danger. The government can't efface those obligations. No, you should go yourself and meet the Governor, tell him that Mr Clark's interference is an insult to you, that you'll fall in the eyes of the public, and that the educated class will not have an iota of trust in the government. Prove that insulting a rais is not a joke.'

Raja sahib said, worried – There'll be hostility against Mr Clark forever. I don't expect the Governor to take my side against him. You don't know these people. Their officer–subordinate relationship is only apparent; actually they are all united. Everyone supports what one of them does. There'll be unnecessary harassment.

'Appeal to the Viceroy if the Governor doesn't listen. Go to England and meet the leaders there. This is not a small matter; there's the burden of a great responsibility on your shoulders, submitting even a jot will disgrace you forever.'

Raja sahib thought it over for a minute and said – You don't know the state of the educated people here. You probably think that they'll help me, or at least sympathize with me, but the day I openly complain against Mr Clark, they'll stop coming to my house. They won't show their faces. They'll avoid me and go the other way. Not just this, they'll secretly complain to Clark against me and won't scruple to harm me. The moral condition of our educated society is extremely shameful. They are all, in apparent and inapparent ways, dependent on the government. They will extend their hospitality to me only as long as they know that I'm friendly with the authorities. The day they come to know that the district magistrate is no longer favourably inclined towards me, it will be the end of my esteem and respect. It's this weakness of our friends and their devious greed for furthering their self-interest that frustrates our fearless, honest and courageous leaders.

Raja sahib tried several excuses and stratagems. He drew a very negative picture of the situation but Indu didn't budge a jot from her aim. She wanted to awaken that dormant sentiment in his heart that used to be enraptured by the names of Pratap and Sanga, Tipu and Nana.* She knew that this sentiment was not dead but was immersed in the deep stupor of the love of power. She said, 'Suppose all your apprehensions are realized, you lose your esteem, the whole city becomes your enemy, the authorities look at you suspiciously, to the extent that there's the possibility of your estate being seized, I will still tell you to remain firm in your position. This is our kshatriya dharma. This news will be published in the newspapers today and, if not the whole world, at least the whole of India will look expectantly at you to see with what fortitude, courage and sacrifice you'll protect the prestige of your country. Our defeat will occupy the place of a great victory in this battle, because it's not the fight of brutal strength but of spiritual power. But I'm quite sure that your misgivings will prove to be baseless. By complaining against the injustice of an officer to the government, you'll show that staunch loyalty to the rulers, you'll proclaim your complete trust in that policy of justice of the government, which is the foundation of empire. A child may cry before his mother, be stubborn or restive, but the mother's love doesn't diminish even for a moment. I'm sure that the government will respect you even more to establish awe at its justice. The leaders of the nationalist movement are often decorated with prestigious titles, there's no reason why you shouldn't receive the same honour.'

This argument seemed worth considering to raja sahib. He said, 'All right, I'll think about it.' He left after that.

---

* For Pratap and Sanga, see Chapters 9 and 17 footnotes.

Tipu Sultan (November 1750–May 1799); de facto ruler of the kingdom of Mysore. Was defeated in the Fourth Anglo–Mysore War by the combined forces of the East India Company, the Nizam of Hyderabad, Travancore, and the Marathas. He died defending his capital Srirangapatnam on 4 May 1799.

Nana Sahib (b. 1824); adopted son of the exiled Peshwa Baji Rao II. He played a prominent role in the 1857 War of Independence. He disappeared after the British recapture of Kanpur in July 1857 and was supposed to have escaped to Nepal. His ultimate fate remains unknown.

The next morning John Sevak came to meet raja sahib. He too advised raja sahib not to be at all pressurized on this issue, saying that he would do the fighting, all that raja sahib needed to do was to keep slapping his back. Raja sahib was somewhat encouraged; now there were two of them. In the evening, he went to consult kunwar sahib, who gave him the same advice. Dr Ganguly was sent a telegram asking him to return. Kunwar sahib went so far as to say, 'Even if you remain quiet, I'll raise this issue in the Legislative Assembly. The government can't remain so indifferent to our commerce and industry. This is not a question of justice or injustice, of respect or disrespect; it's only a question of business competition.'

Raja sahib said to Indu – Well, I'm following your advice. I'm playing with my life.

Indu looked at him respectfully and said – If God wills it, you'll win.

22

SAYYAD TAHIR ALI WAS CONFIDENT THAT HE WOULD GET A
promotion when work began on the cigarette factory. Mr Sevak had
promised him that. Apart from this hope, for the time being, he
couldn't see any other way of paying his debts, which were growing
by the day like grass during the rains. He himself lived thriftily. Milk
perhaps never went down his throat except on Eid. Mithai was taboo
for him. He was not at all fond of paan and tobacco. But no matter
how much he himself economized, he thought it unjust to cut corners
when it came to the needs of his family. He'd say, 'This is the time for
boys to eat and drink, it's at this age that their bones become broad
and smooth, their minds and hearts develop. Their entire lives are
ruined if boys don't get nourishing food at this age.'

Whether this view was true or not for the boys, the truth of the
argument used by Tahir Ali's stepmothers on the subject of paan and
tobacco was self-evident – Women can't subsist without them. People
will say, can't these people afford even paan? This is the one sign of
gentility left now; no maidservants, no attendants and now we can't
even get paan. Men don't need paan that much. They have to meet
officers and salute strangers, why would they need paan?

The problem was that Mahir and Zabir would eat mithai and
drink milk as well while Naseema and Sabir would just stand and
stare. Zainab would say – The father of their gur mill is alive by the
grace of Khuda. He should eat after providing for everyone; only then
can it be called providing. He controls everything; he can feed them
whatever he wants and keep them as he likes; who's to prevent him?

The two of them would chew paan all day like goats while Kulsoom
would get just a beeda after a meal with great difficulty. They didn't
think it necessary to ask Tahir Ali for these needs or to live within
their means.

It was early morning. Leather was being bought. Hundreds of
chamaars were sitting and smoking chillums. This was the only time
when Tahir Ali got some joy from his prestige. He would then get

slightly intoxicated by his importance. One chamaar would sweep the doorway, another would clean his seat, another would fill water, somebody would be sent to the bazaar to buy saag and vegetables, someone else would be made to split wood. He would believe that he too was somebody when he saw so many men eager to serve him. Zainab and Raqiya, sitting in purda, would collect the expenses for the paandaan. Sahib had prohibited Tahir from taking a commission but he had not forbidden the women from taking the expenses for paan leaves. They had both got jewellery made for themselves from this income. Tahir Ali thought it to be too trivial a matter to ask for an account for this amount.

Jagdhar arrived just then and said – Munshiji, when will you settle the account? I'm not a lakhpati that I can go on providing mithai whether I get paid or not. I'll be bankrupt if I get a few more customers like you. Get me the money and don't make excuses now, I've been very generous to the village and the muhalla. I too have outstanding debts to the mahajan. Have a look at this paper and settle the account.

For debtors, an accounts sheet is an order from Yamraj. They don't have the courage to look at it; looking at it means having to give the money. The debtor has only to take the accounts sheet in his hand for the creditor to be full of hope because there can be no excuse after that. That's why debtors don't have the courage even to look at it.

Tahir Ali said with great humility – Bhai, I know all the accounts; your debt will be cleared very soon now. Have patience for a few more days.

Jagdhar – For how long? A few days have now become several months. Mithai tastes sweet when eaten but why is there a bitter taste when the price has to be paid?

Tahir – Biraadar, I'm rather hard up these days but work on the factory will begin soon and I'll also be promoted. Bas, I'll pay back each and every kauri.

Jagdhar – No sahib, I'll go back today with the money. I won't get a chhataank worth of goods if I don't return the mahajan's money. God alone knows if I have even a taka at home. You should realize that you are giving what you owe, not what's mine. Let my youth be useless if I'm lying to you, let my children sleep hungry. I raised a cry in the whole muhalla but nobody gave me even four annas.

The chowdhary of the chamaars took pity on Jagdhar. He said to Tahir – Munshiji, give him the sum that's due to me, you can give it to me in a few days.

Tahir – Jagdhar, Khuda is my witness, I don't have any money! Wait a few days for Khuda's sake.

Jagdhar – Munshiji, telling lies is like eating a cow. I won't be anywhere if the mahajan's money doesn't reach him today.

Tahir Ali went home and asked Kulsoom – The mithai-vala is clamouring, he won't be put off on any account. What should I do? Should I take out ten rupees from the cash and give them?

Kulsoom said, annoyed – It's obvious that the person who is owed money will be on top of one's head! Why don't you go and ask ammajaan? My children didn't get any mithai. Why are those who were so eager to eat and to feed sitting there like drenched cats when it comes to paying?

Tahir – This is why I don't tell you anything. What's the harm in taking it from the cash? I'll return it as soon as I get my salary.

Kulsoom – For Khuda's sake, don't do something so disastrous. Think of the cash as a black snake. Suppose sahib examines the amount today, then what?

Tahir – No way. Where does sahib have the time to balance the cash?

Kulsoom – I won't tell you to touch the amount in the deposit. If that's the case, remove Naseema's tauk and pawn it, there's nothing else that I can do.

Tahir Ali was very upset, but what could he do? He wept and removed Naseema's tauk. Kulsoom consoled her lovingly and coaxed her, telling her that they were getting a new one made for her. Naseema was overjoyed at the thought of getting a new tauk.

Tahir went out with the tauk in a handkerchief, took Jagdhar aside and said – Bhai, take this and make do by pawning it somewhere. There's no money in the house.

Jagdhar – It's a sin to sell borrowed goods, but what can I do? I'll just keep wandering around if I sell for cash.

He took the tauk with embarrassment and was regretful as he left. Another man would not have got back his money by pestering his customer so much. He would have felt pity for the girl, who asked smiling, when will you make my tauk and bring it? But the unbearable burden of domesticity had forced Jagdhar to be more callous than he really was.

It was barely half an hour since Jagdhar had left that Bajrangi came frowning and said – Munshiji, give the money if you mean to, otherwise just say, baba I can't do it. Bas, I'll be patient. I'll console myself that one cow didn't yield milk. Why do you make me run around every day?

Tahir – Biraadar, wait a few more days since you have been patient for so long. If Khuda wills it, not a pie of yours will remain this time.

Bajrangi – You have made these promises several times.

Tahir – I'm making a firm promise this time.

Bajrangi – When will you settle the accounts?

Tahir was in a dilemma. Which day should he specify? Debtors are as afraid of the day of reckoning as sinners. They take refuge in such indecisive words as 'a few', 'very soon' and 'today or tomorrow'. Such promises are not made to be kept but only to evade the creditors. Tahir was an honest person by nature. He would be very distressed because of the creditors and was as afraid of them as of the devil. He would begin to tremble for his life as soon as he saw them from afar. For several minutes, he wondered how to reply – 'Such is the state of my expenses, and I get a blunt response when I ask for a promotion.' Finally, he said, 'Which day can I specify? The accounts will be settled when you come after a few days.'

Bajrangi – Munshiji, don't play tricks with me. I too have to deal with all kinds of customers. If I come after ten days, you'll say why did you take so long? The money is spent now. If I come after four or five days, you'll say, I haven't yet got the money. That's why give me a specific day so that I don't lose anything and it's convenient for you.

Tahir – I wouldn't have had any objection to giving you a specific day but the problem is that there's no fixed date for getting my salary; there can be a difference of a few days. Send a boy after a week and you'll get the money.

Bajrangi – All right, what you say is true. But I won't come again to ask if you don't keep your promise this time.

Tahir began to boast after Bajrangi had left – You people probably think that we get such high salaries, so we save them and keep them at home but the expenses are such that the money disappears before half the month is over. Gentility is nothing but a disease.

A chamaar said – Huzoor, the expenses of the high and mighty are also high. The poor subsist only because of you. Only a horse can put up with the kick of another horse.

Tahir – Aji, so much is spent on paan alone that two people can live well enough on it.

Chamaar – Huzoor, don't we know that the ways of the high and mighty are also high and mighty?

Tahir Ali's tears had not yet properly dried when Thakurdeen arrived. The poor man tried to prepare an excuse. Meanwhile, Thakurdeen said salaam to him and asked, 'Munshiji, when will the work begin on the factory?'

Tahir – The material is being assembled. The engineer hasn't yet made the plan, that's why the delay.

Thakurdeen – The engineer too must have taken something? They are a very dishonest community, huzoor! I too have been a contractor for some time; I had to give the engineers whatever I earned. Finally I was afraid and left. The brothers of engineers are doctors. The patient may be dying but they won't talk before taking a fee. Even if they make some concession in the fees, they'll make up for it by medicines and the fare for the gharry. (*Showing the accounts sheet*) Just have a look at this.

Tahir – I know everything, you won't have written it incorrectly.

Thakurdeen – Huzoor! If there's honesty, there's everything. Nobody accompanies you when you die. So what are my orders?

Tahir – Give me time for a few days.

Thakurdeen – As you wish. Huzoor, I was helpless because of the theft, otherwise why would a few rupees matter? I was ruined by that theft. There's not even a broken lota left in the house. I was deprived even of a few grains, huzoor. I saw the thieves running away in front of my eyes, I ran after them up to the mental asylum. It was a dark night; it wasn't possible to make out the high ground from the low. I fell into a ditch. One's possessions are very dear but the thieves escaped. I informed the thana. I pleaded with the thanedars. The point is does the Lachchmi who has gone ever return? So when should I come?

Tahir – There's no need for you to come, I'll send it myself.

Thakurdeen – As you wish, I have no objection. I would have felt embarrassed making the claim. A good man doesn't postpone and make excuses if he has the money in hand; he immediately takes it out and flings it. I had to get paan today so I came here. At least give a little if not the whole sum. There was no other way so I came to you. I can recognize a man, huzoor, but such is the situation that has arisen.

Thakurdeen's humility and cheerful generosity charmed Tahir. He opened the box, took out five rupees, and put them in front of Thakurdeen. Thakurdeen did not pick up the money. He thought for a moment and then asked – Is this your money or the official cash?

Tahir – Take it. Are you interested in eating the mangoes or in counting the trees?

Thakurdeen – No, munshiji, this won't do. Give it if it's your money, if it's maalik's cash then let it be, I'll come back and take it. Since I get a few paise from you, I won't see you falling into a ditch in front of my eyes. If you don't mind, then listen to me, I'm not worried about this, I'm notorious for being frank, some day you'll be deceived if you spend your money so extravagantly. Gentility doesn't lie in increasing pomp and splendour but in protecting one's honour.

Tahir said tearfully – Take the money.

Thakurdeen stood up and said – Give it when you have it.

Until now, Tahir had been hopeful that the factory would be built. He would return the money as soon as his income increased but he found it difficult to explain to his creditors when Mr Clark had ordered work on the factory to be stopped for an indefinite period. The creditors began to trouble him even more. Tahir was very worried; his mind wouldn't work. Kulsoom would say, 'All the extra expenses should be stopped. People won't suffer without milk, paan and mithai. How many people can afford these things during these times? What can I say about others, my own children are deprived of them. I've explained this before, and I'm explaining it again, that those for whom you are shedding your blood and sweat won't even ask after you. You'll see; they'll fly away the moment they sprout their wings. I can see their tendency even now. They lend money to others on interest but one just gets a blunt reply if they are asked to give something for the household expenses, "I don't have it." They should have some mercy on you. It would be difficult to live in the house if milk and mithai were to be stopped today.'

It was the third pahar. Tahir Ali was sitting despondently in the veranda. All of a sudden Bhairo came, sat there and said – Why, munshiji, will the factory really not be built here now?

Tahir – Why won't it be built? It has been stopped only for a few days.

Bhairo – I was very hopeful that my sales would go up if the factory gets built; the sale at the shop is very slow. I want to sit here for a while in the mornings. I hope that you'll approve. I can make a few sales then. I'll gift you something too for your paan.

On another occasion, Tahir would have severely scolded Bhairo. It was against his religion to give permission to open a toddy shop. But at this moment he was in a dilemma because he was worried about money. Even earlier, before this anxiety, there had been a conflict several times between his principles and his religion, and on every occasion it was his principles that he had murdered. Today there was the same conflict and again principles gave way to circumstances. 'What can I do? How am I to blame? I'm not breaking shara for some extravagant expenses. Circumstances have made me helpless.' He said, somewhat abashed, 'Toddy won't sell here.'

Bhairo – Huzoor, the smell of toddy will make it sell. Alcoholics are so addicted that they may not drink liquor for years if they don't see it, but they can't resist when it's there before them.

Tahir – But how can I give permission without sahib's orders?

Bhairo – As you wish! I think there's no need to ask sahib. I'm not going to set up my shop here. I'll bring a pitcher in the morning, sell it within a moment, and go my way. He won't have any idea that somebody is selling toddy here.

Tahir – You are teaching me to be disloyal, are you?

Bhairo – Huzoor, where's the disloyalty? Who doesn't make use of an opportunity on the side?

The deal was made. Bhairo agreed to pay a lump sum of fifteen rupees. He told Subhagi – See, I've made the deal! You said he'll never agree. He's Islam – toddy and liquor are prohibited among them, but I told you that Islam or baamhan, there's no dharma or karma left in anyone. They all jump at money. These miyaan only appear to be in bright clothes from the outside. They don't have even parched bhang at home. Miyaan at first shilly-shallied just for show and then agreed to fifteen rupees. Fifteen rupees will be made up in fifteen days.

Subhagi had earlier wanted to become the mistress of the house, that's why she was beaten with a stick every day. Now she is the mistress of the house by being a slave for the entire household. She controls the money. Her mother-in-law, who couldn't stand the sight of her, blesses her several times a day. Subhagi quickly took out the money and gave it to Bhairo. Perhaps two separated friends would not have embraced each other with such eagerness as the fervour with which Tahir Ali fell upon this money. It was a small amount but he had been forced to murder his religion for it. The creditors took the money owed them. The burden on Tahir Ali's mind was lighter but he couldn't sleep for a long time. The soul has a long life. Its throat may be slit, but life doesn't depart it.

23

AS LONG AS SOORDAS LAMENTED THE TYRANNY OF THE CITY'S officers, the people of his muhalla sympathized with him despite being John Sevak's well-wishers. People inevitably pity the weak. But their pity turned to envy the moment Soordas was victorious. People suspected that Soordas would consider them to be inferior; he would probably think that if he could humiliate someone like Raja Mahendra Kumar Singh and shatter his prestige, then what were these people worth? All the muhalla-valas were jealous of him in their hearts. Thakurdeen was the only one who continued to visit him. He was now convinced that Soordas was favoured by some devata, he must have obtained some mantra; otherwise how would he have dared to make such eminent people bow their heads? People say that yantra-mantra are all delusion. Their eyes don't open even by this wonder.

Soordas's nature also changed somewhat now. He had been patient even earlier but sometimes he'd lose his temper on matters of justice and dharma. Now there was not even a spark of fire left in him; he was just a heap of rubbish on to which everyone throws trash. The muhalla-valas would tease and taunt him as they passed by but he wouldn't retort; he would merely continue to beg with his head bowed and quietly return to his hut and lie there. But Mitthua was not like him; he wouldn't talk properly to anybody. He'd say, 'No one should think that the blind man merely begs, he makes the high and mighty bite the dust.' He'd pointlessly tease people and wrangle with decent men. He'd tell his companions, 'I can get the whole muhalla imprisoned if I want to.' He would unabashedly pluck gram, peas, radish and carrots from farmers' fields and be all set to fight if anyone dared stop him. Soordas began to get complaints every day. He would try and make Mitthua see sense when they were alone but to no effect. It was unfortunate that nobody saw Soordas's humility and tolerance but they all noticed Mitthua's bragging and mischief. People, in fact, went to the extent of saying that Soordas had spoilt him; the calf leaps only as far as the stake will allow. Jealousy regards even children's play as devious diplomacy.

Sophia would often meet Soordas along with Mr Clark. She would always give him something and sympathize with him. She would ask, 'Are the muhalla-valas or raja sahib's men troubling you?' Soordas would reply, 'All of them have pity on me, I don't have complaints against anybody.' The muhalla-valas would think, 'He complains against us to burra sahib.' They would also express their feelings through adages: 'What's there to be afraid of, now that the beloved is the kotwal?' and 'If you become the farzi from being a pawn, you can walk crookedly.' On one occasion, Nayakram's house was searched in connection with some theft. Nayakram suspected that Soordas had shot this arrow. Similarly, on another occasion, the daroga of the excise department demanded an explanation from Bhairo, who had perhaps kept his shop open until midnight, which was against the law. Bhairo too suspected that Soordas had lit this spark. Soordas didn't mind their suspicions but he was deeply pained when Subhagi began to malign him openly. He had believed that at least Subhagi understood him. 'She should have saved me from these people but she too has turned against me.'

Several months went by in this way. One night, Soordas was lying down after having eaten when someone quietly caught hold of his hand. Soordas was startled, but recognizing Subhagi's voice, he asked, 'What do you want?'

Subhagi – Nothing. Come to the hut, I want to tell you something.

Soordas got up and went to the hut with Subhagi. He asked – Speak, what do you want to say? Even you are against me now. You abuse and vilify me everywhere. Tell me, what wrong have I done you that you are bent upon maligning me? I wouldn't have minded if other people had criticized me but I want to cry and my heart aches when I hear your taunts. You cursed me so much when there was an enquiry against Bhairo. Tell me the truth, did you also suspect that I was the one who had complained to darogaji? Do you think that I'm so mean? Tell me.

Subhagi replied tenderly – I don't respect anyone as much as I respect you. I would have worshipped you with the same devotion if you had been a devata.

Soordas – Am I proud? Do I complain to sahib against anyone? People weren't jealous of me when I lost the land. Why have they all become my enemies now that I've got it back? Tell me, how am I proud? Have I got a badshahi to make me proud now that my land has been returned?

Subhagi – God alone knows the state of my mind.

Soordas – Then why do you torment me?

Subhagi – That's why.

She gave Soordas a small, heavy bag. Soordas recognized it when he groped it. It was his bag that had been stolen. It seemed at a guess that the amount of money was also the same. Surprised, he asked – Where did you find it?

Subhagi – It's your hard-earned money so it has come back to you. Keep it carefully now.

Soordas – I won't keep it. Take it away.

Subhagi – Why? What's wrong with taking your own thing?

Soordas – It's Bhairo's now, not mine. He sold his soul for it, he made an expensive bargain. How can I take it?

Subhagi – I don't know about all that. It's yours, so you must take it. I have deceived my family because of it. That's why I've been playacting all these days. What will I do with it if you don't take it?

Soordas – Bhairo won't let you live if he comes to know.

Subhagi – He won't get to know. I've thought of a way.

Subhagi left. Soordas didn't get a chance to argue any more. He was in a deep dilemma – Should I keep this money or not? Is it my bag or not? Can I take my money in exchange for his? Subhagi has so much pity for me. She used to taunt me so that this secret wouldn't come out into the open.

While he was in this dilemma, there was a sudden cry, 'Thief! Thief!' It was the first stage of sleep, so people had become negligent. The cry came again, 'Thief! Thief!'

It was Bhairo's voice. Soordas understood that Subhagi had planned this stratagem. He stood at his door. Meanwhile, Bajrangi's cry could be heard – 'Where has he gone, where?' He took a stick and ran in the dark. Nayakram also emerged from his house and ran crying, 'Where, where?' There was a clash with Bajrangi on the way. Each thought the other to be the thief. They attacked each other and fell down, hurt.

A crowd gathered in a while. Thakurdeen asked, 'What has he taken? Look carefully; he could be stuck to the roof. Thieves stick to the wall in such a way that they can't be seen.'

Subhagi – Hai! I've been robbed. I was sitting here just now massaging amma's feet. Meanwhile, I don't know when the rascal came.

Bhairo (*Searching with a lamp*) – All the savings have been looted. Hai Rama!

Subhagi – Hai, I saw his shadow and thought it must be him [Bhairo]. When he stretched out his hand to the box, then too I thought it must be him.

Thakurdeen – He must have climbed on to the roof and come from there. All the thieves had climbed on to the roof when there was a theft in my house.

Meanwhile, Bajrangi arrived with his head bleeding. He said – I saw him running. I hit out with my stick. He also attacked. I was dizzy and fell down. But he received such a blow that his head too must have been split.

Nayakram then arrived, moaning, and fell down. His entire body was soaked in blood.

Thakurdeen – Pandaji, did you also collide with him?

Nayakram's gaze fell upon Bajrangi. Bajrangi looked at Nayakram. Nayakram said to himself, 'You mix water with milk and sell it; now you have found this way.' Bajrangi said to himself, 'You loot pilgrims, now you are robbing the muhalla-valas.'

Nayakram – Yes, bhai, I met him here in the alley. He was a very hefty youth.

Thakurdeen – That's why he could wound two men alone. The thieves who broke into my house looked like demons. I have never before seen such well-built men. It seems that you have received a heavy blow from him.

Nayakram – My blow was also heavy. I saw him fall. I'm sure his head was split.

Bajrangi – I also gave him such a blow that the rascal must have felt completely helpless and remembered chhatthi's milk. He fell down flat.

Thakurdeen – It seems to be the work of a known person. There can never be a theft without a spy in the house. Didn't they give mithai to my younger daughter to find out the secrets of the house?

Bajrangi – You must report it to the thana.

Bhairo – I won't be satisfied only to report it. I'll make the rascal grind the millstone. Even if I have to sell myself I'll grind them as well. I know everything.

Thakurdeen – Not only did he take the goods but he also wounded two men. That's why I didn't go near the thieves. I just kept shouting, 'Catch them, catch them.' If life remains safe, the goods will return.

Bhairo did not suspect Bajrangi or Nayakram, he suspected Jagdhar. In fact, not only did he suspect Jagdhar, he fully believed that Jagdhar was the culprit. Only Jagdhar knew where the money had been kept. Jagdhar was also good at wielding the cudgel. And, despite being a neighbour, he had been the last to reach the scene of the incident. All these reasons strengthened his suspicion.

People began to talk as they left. Thakurdeen said – They were not his earnings; it was Soordas's money.

Nayakram – Another's goods become one's own once they are in the house.

Thakurdeen – One has to face the punishment for one's sins, sooner or later.

Bajrangi – Did your thieves get any punishment?

Thakurdeen – Where do I have the favour of any devata? Soordas has it. Not a kauri of his can be digested by anyone, no matter how much chooran he may eat. I'm saying this with a curse; all the goods will be recovered if his house is searched right now.

The next day, as soon as it was dawn, Bhairo informed the police station. Darogaji arrived by afternoon to make enquiries. Jagdhar's house was searched but nothing was found. Bhairo thought he had hidden the goods somewhere. From that day onwards, it was as if Bhairo were possessed by a demon. He would reach darogaji's house in the morning and serve him the whole day, fill his chillum, massage his feet, cut grass for his horse, flatter the chowkidars. He would discuss this theft all day in his shop. 'What can I say, I have never slept like this before, I don't know how I went off to sleep that day. But my name is not Bhairo if I don't get him imprisoned. Darogaji is on the lookout. There are not only rupees but also asharfis. The seller will immediately be caught when they are sold.'

Gradually, Bhairo began to suspect the whole muhalla. People had been jealous of him even earlier but now the entire muhalla became his enemy. He began to vent his anger on his own family. Subhagi would again be beaten. 'You have ruined me. How could the thief have entered the house if you had not been so careless? I have to go around with a basket the whole day to sell, so I got tired and went off to sleep. What do you do lying around at home all day? Get my money somehow or the other or I won't let you live!' He had always respected his mother until now, but he would be at her too. 'You say that you can't sleep at night; you stay awake the whole night. How did you go off to sleep that day?' The gist of it was that he had no respect, no trust, no love left for anyone. Virtuous sentiments had also departed from his heart along with wealth. He would see blood when he saw Jagdhar and would frequently taunt him to make him lose his temper so that he could get even with him but Jagdhar avoided him. He was more adept at stabbing behind the back than at hitting out openly.

One evening, Jagdhar went to meet Tahir Ali. Tahir asked – What brings you here?

Jagdhar – I've come to tell you something. The daroga of the excise department just met me. He asked, 'Does Bhairo put up his shop at the godown?' I said, 'Sahib, I don't know.' He left then, but he's sure to return in a few days to make enquiries. I thought he may perhaps also make a complaint against you, that's why I came running.

The very next day Tahir Ali made Bhairo leave.

Several days after this, Soordas was cooking one night when Jagdhar came and asked – Well, Soorey! Have you got back what belonged to you?

Soordas asked innocently – What belonged to me?

Jagdhar – That money which was stolen from your hut.

Soordas – Where did I have the money?

Jagdhar – Now don't deceive me! I know everything and am happy that you've got back what was yours from the clutches of that sinner. Subhagi is a very determined woman.

Soordas – Jagdhar, don't drag me into this wrangle. I'm a poor man. If Bhairo gets any inkling of this, he'll take my life later but he'll throttle Subhagi first.

Jagdhar – I'm not going to tell him but what's happened is after my heart. The rascal read dada's fatiha with such relish all these days at the halvai's shop, his feet wouldn't touch the ground, now he has come to his senses.

Soordas – You are needlessly after my life.

Jagdhar – Just laugh heartily once, and I'll go. People are delighted when they get back what they have lost. Had I been in your place, I would have danced and frolicked, sang and played, and gone crazy for a while. I would have laughed so much that there would have been a ball of wind in my tummy, and you are so glum! Come, laugh now!

Soordas – I don't feel like laughing just now.

Jagdhar – Why don't you feel like laughing? I'll make you laugh.

He began to tickle Soordas. Soordas was a fun-loving person, he began to guffaw. It was a strange spectacle of jealous banter. They were both laughing like actors on a stage, unaware of the consequences of this laughter. The unfortunate Subhagi was returning after buying goods at the bania's shop. She was surprised when she heard the sky-piercing laughter at Soordas's house. How could there be water in an empty well? She stood at the door and asked Soordas, 'What have you got today, Soordas, that you are so bloated with happiness?'

Soordas said, controlling his laughter – I've got back my bag; a thief broke into the house of the thief.

Subhagi – So will you digest all the goods alone?

Soordas – No, I'll bring a kanthi of small gold beads for you, then you can sing bhajans for Thakurji.

Subhagi – Keep your kanthi at home. Get me a kantha with large gold beads!

Soordas – Then your feet won't touch the ground!

Jagdhar – Whether you get a kantha made or not, you must get a nosering made for her old woman. It will suit her flabby face very well, as if a she-monkey is wearing it.

All three of them burst out laughing. By a coincidence, Bhairo was also returning from the thana. He looked into the hut on hearing the sound of laughter. 'What was this revelry going on today?' He saw blood at this merrymaking, as if somebody had put hot iron on his heart. He was insane with rage and used the harshest and most obscene abuses, like a warrior using his weapons to inflict the most fatal wounds. 'You are a loose woman, you laugh with my enemies, you lewd woman, you sell your self-respect for a taka. Khabardaar, I'm warning you, I'll suck your blood if you set foot into my house. Tell this blind man not to show his face again if you care for your well-being or I'll cut off your necks with the same sickle. I have to wander around helplessly and this cursed woman makes merry here with her yaars. The blind sinner doesn't even die so that the muhalla can be cleansed. Who knows what misfortunes he is fated to suffer because of his karma? Perhaps he'll die grinding the millstone of the jail.'

He left after this. Subhagi was numb, as if lightning had struck her. Jagdhar was inwardly happy at Soordas's agitation like a hunter when he sees a deer. 'He's so upset!' But Soordas? Ah! His condition was like that of a sati, who has lost her satitva, her chastity. All three stood there, stunned. Finally, Jagdhar asked, 'Subhagi, where will you go now?'

Subhagi looked at him despairingly – I'll go home, where else?

Jagdhar – He's fuming, he won't rest unless he takes your life.

Subhagi – Let him beat me or burn me, after all that's my house.

Jagdhar – Why don't you stay somewhere else for a while? You can go when his anger has cooled down.

Subhagi – I'll go to your house, will you let me stay?

Jagdhar – My house! He's jealous of me anyway, he'll kill me then.

Subhagi – If your life is so dear to you, why should anyone else take on his enmity?

Subhagi immediately went to her house after that. Jagdhar didn't say anything, neither yes nor no. He said to Soordas – Soorey, come and sleep at my house tonight. I'm afraid that Bhairo may create some uproar today. He's a rascal, he may start a fight.

Soordas – Bhairo is not as foolish as you think. He won't say anything to you but he'll beat Subhagi to his heart's content.

Jagdhar – He's not in his senses when he's drunk.

Soordas – I'm telling you, he won't say anything to you. You haven't hidden anything from him. He won't have the courage to fight with you.

Jagdhar's fear did not subside. He gave up on Soordas and left. Soordas stayed awake the whole night. He thought it was shameful to stay here after such a grave accusation. He couldn't think of any other way except to leave with his face blackened – I have not harmed anyone, so why is God punishing me? For which sins do I have to atone? Perhaps this sin can be removed by a pilgrimage. I should leave tomorrow. Bhairo had accused me of this sin even earlier. But then all the people of the muhalla respected me, and what he had said was ridiculed and dismissed. In fact, people had scolded him. Now the whole muhalla is my enemy and people will easily believe him; my face will be blackened. No, it's best to run away from here now. I'll take the shelter of the devatas, only they can protect me. But what about Subhagi? Bhairo is sure to turn her out now. How will the poor thing live if I also leave? There's nobody in her naihar. She's a young woman; she can't labour and work hard. Who knows what may happen? I'll go and explain everything frankly to Bhairo when we are alone. I have never had a frank talk with him. There's resentment in his heart. That's why he suspects me. It's not right for me to leave until his doubts are cleared. People will say, Soorey was guilty and ran away because he was afraid! I'll also return this money to him. But I won't take Subhagi's name if he asks me from where I had got it; I'll say I found it in the hut. Subhagi's life won't be safe if I don't hide this. But how can there be frankness if I keep it secret? It won't do to hide it. I'll tell everything truthfully from beginning to end. Only then will his misunderstanding be removed.

This thought gave him great solace, like that of a poet who has solved a complex problem.

He got up at the crack of dawn and called out at Bhairo's door. Bhairo was asleep. Subhagi was sitting there crying, for Bhairo had given her the customary beating as soon as she had reached home. She recognized Soordas's voice and was surprised that he had come this early in the morning. She was apprehensive that there would be a fight between the two. She knew just how strong Soordas was. She was afraid that Soordas had come to take his revenge for what had happened the previous night. 'He's usually very tolerant, but he's a man after all, so he must be angry. It's natural to be angry at a false allegation. Soorey may kill him in a fit of anger. He'll surely take his life if he can catch hold of him.' Subhagi would be beaten by Bhairo and be turned out of the house, but no outsider could dare to say anything to him and get away with it. She'd claw his face. She didn't wake up Bhairo but opened the door and asked, 'What is it, Soorey? What do you want?'

Soordas was strongly tempted to ask, 'What happened to you last night?' But he controlled himself. 'How does it concern me? She's his woman, let him beat her or love her. Who am I to ask?' He asked, 'Is Bhairo asleep? Wake him; I want to talk to him.'

Subhagi – What about? I also want to know.

Soordas – It's just something. Wake him.

Subhagi – Go away now. You can come back and talk later.

Soordas – When will there be time later? Don't I have to go and sit at the roadside? It won't take long.

Subhagi – You have never before come this early in the morning. What's the matter today?

Soordas said, annoyed – I'll tell him, it's not something I can tell you.

Subhagi was convinced that he was not in control of himself and would surely start a brawl. She said – He didn't beat me. He just repeated the same things that he had said there, that's all.

Soordas – Come on, I heard your screams with my own ears.

Subhagi – He threatened to beat. Bas, I began to scream loudly.

Soordas – He may not have beaten you. How does it concern me even he did? You are his wife, he can do what he wants. Go and send him. I have to tell him something.

When Subhagi still did not go, Soordas began to call out Bhairo's name loudly. Bhairo's voice could be heard after several calls – Who is it? Sit down, I'm coming.

As soon as Subhagi heard this she went inside and said – Take a stick with you if you are going. It's Soordas, he may have come to fight.

Bhairo – Come and sit here. He has come to fight! Don't play the artful tricks of a woman with me.

Subhagi – I think he's angry, that's why I'm telling you.

Bhairo – Why don't you say that you have encouraged him to come? He doesn't have so much malice. He doesn't keep anything in his heart.

Bhairo picked up his stick and went outside, thinking, 'What's there to fear even if the blind man is behaving like a tiger? Even a child can knock him down.'

Soordas said to Bhairo – Is there anyone else here? I want to tell you a secret.

Bhairo – There's no one else. Tell me what you want to.

Soordas – I've found out who your thief is.

Bhairo – Really, you swear by your youth?

Soordas – Yes, I'm telling the truth. He came and left your money with me. Is anything else missing?

Bhairo – You've come to make me jealous, aren't you satisfied yet?

Soordas – No, by God, your bag was found as it was in my house.

Bhairo – He must have been crazy. Then why did he steal?

Soordas – Yes, he was crazy, what else?

Bhairo – Where is it? Just let me see.

Soordas removed the bag from his waist and showed it to Bhairo. Bhairo leapt and took it. It was tied up just as it had been.

Soordas – Count it, is it all there or not?

Bhairo – Yes, it's all there. Tell the truth, who stole it?

Bhairo was less happy to get the money than he was eager to know the name of the thief. He wanted to know if the thief was the person he had suspected or whether it was someone else.

Soordas – What will you do by finding out the name? Are you concerned with your goods or with the thief's name?

Bhairo – No, I put you under oath. . . Tell me, he's from this muhalla, isn't he?

Soordas – Yes, he's from the muhalla, but I won't tell his name.

Bhairo – I swear by my youth, I won't say anything to him.

Soordas – I've promised him that I won't tell his name. What if I tell his name and you then create a din?

Bhairo – Believe me, I won't tell anyone. I'll take whatever oath you want. If I open my mouth you can believe that there's a doubt about my legitimacy. One's word and one's father are the same. Now what oath do you want me to take?

Soordas – If you change I'll beat my head at your door and give up my life.

Bhairo – Why should you give up your life? Take mine, I won't make the slightest squeak.

Soordas – There was a theft in my house once, you remember, don't you? The thief must have suspected that you had taken my money. That's why the thief stole from your house and returned my money. The thief took pity on my poverty, that's all. It was nothing else. I have no other relationship with the thief.

Bhairo – Achcha, I've heard all this, now tell me the name.

Soordas – Look, you have taken an oath.

Bhairo – Yes, bhai, I'm not going back on my oath.

Soordas – Your wife and my sister Subhagi.

Bhairo went insane as soon as he heard this. He ran into the house and said to his mother – Amma, this witch stole my money. Soordas says so himself. This is how the hag fills the houses of her wicked friends by robbing me. She deceives me on top of that. Just wait and see the plight to which I'll reduce you. Speak, is Soordas telling the truth or is he lying?

Subhagi bowed her head and said – Soordas is lying.

Before she could complete what she was saying, Bhairo hit out hard with the stick. The blow missed the mark. This enraged Bhairo even more. He ran after Subhagi. Subhagi went into one of the rooms and bolted the door. Bhairo began to beat the door. There was a din in the whole muhalla – Bhairo is killing Subhagi! People came running. Thakurdeen went in and asked, 'What's this, Bhairo, why are you breaking the door? Good man, does one get so angry with a family member?'

Bhairo – What family member? Such a family member who makes merry with other people should be beheaded. Am I deaf, crippled, maimed, lame? What defect do I have that she should make merry with others? I'll let go of her only after cutting off her nose. This hag was responsible for the theft in my house. She stole the money and gave it to Soordas.

Thakurdeen – To Soordas?

Bhairo – Haan-haan, to Soordas. He's standing outside, why don't you ask him? When he realized he wouldn't be able to digest the theft, he brought all the money and gave it to me.

Bajrangi – Achcha, so Subhagi stole the money!

People calmed Bhairo and pulled him outside. There were comments on Soordas. Nobody dared to say anything openly. They were afraid that he would complain to memsahib but they expressed their feelings through quotations. Soordas realized today that nobody had been afraid of him earlier but they had all respected him in their hearts; now they were all afraid of him but no one had any genuine respect for him. He felt so ashamed that he wished a thunderbolt would strike him there and then and reduce him to cinders and ashes.

Thakurdeen said softly – Soorey was never like this. We've known him not just from today but since he was a boy.

Nayakram – He was not like this earlier but he has become so now. He doesn't care about anybody now.

Thakurdeen – They all get intoxicated when they get power, but I haven't seen any such thing in Soorey.

Nayakram – He's a chhipa Rustam!* Bajrangi, I had suspected you.

Bajrangi (*Laughing*) – Pandaji, I swear by God, I had suspected you!

Bhairo – And if you ask me the truth, I had suspected Jagdhar.

Soordas listened to these taunts and insults on all sides with his head bowed. He was full of regret – Why did I tell this to such a mean man? I had thought that frankness would clear the doubts in his heart. This is the result. My face has of course been blackened; I don't know what the plight of that poor thing will be. God! Where are you now? Did you come to deliver your servants only in stories and Puranas; why doesn't a messenger come from the sky now and say that the blind man is innocent?

The cup of Soordas's patience spilled over after this playacting had gone on for more than half an hour at Bhairo's doorway. He thought that to remain silent now was not only cowardly but also base. 'Such a serious allegation is being made on a sati and I am standing here listening quietly. This is a great sin.' He stood up straight and said, looking steadily and wrathfully, 'Yaaron, why are you throwing mud on those afflicted people who are already suffering and using these knives? Have some fear of God. Is there no justice left in the world? I was being decent in returning Bhairo's money. This is what I get in return! I won't tell you why Subhagi did this and why she returned the money to me but may God make me even more miserable if I have thought Subhagi to be anything else but my younger sister. My only fault is that she came to my hut at night. Jagdhar was also there. Ask him what we were talking about. A blind, crippled man can't subsist in this muhalla now. I'm leaving but before I go I want to say that it won't be well for anyone who slanders Subhagi. She is a sati, and

---

* One who hides his light under a bushel. Rustam: the Persian warrior who concealed his identity and killed Sohrab, unaware that Sohrab was his long lost son.

no one can be happy if he maligns a sati. After all, who's there to cry for me? Anyone will give me a pinch of atta if I go and stand at his doorstep. I don't have any support for my livelihood here now. But a day will come when all of you will get to know everything and then you'll realize that the blind man was innocent.'

Soordas then went towards his hut.

24

AFTER GETTING SOORDAS'S LAND RETURNED, SOPHIA AGAIN BECAME aloof towards Mr Clark. As the days went by, she became increasingly distant. She now found it far more intolerable to pretend insincere love than to bear insults, embarrassment and contempt. She thought, 'I've jumped into the fire to escape water.' Nature cannot tolerate the use of force. She had forcibly tried to draw her heart away from Vinay and now it was swiftly racing back towards him. Meanwhile, she had begun to read several texts on bhakti and as a result there was a transformation in her thoughts. She began to lose her fear of contempt and social criticism. Now there was the supreme ideal of love before her, where the voice of the ego cannot reach. The ascetic engrossed in renunciation had tasted somrasa, and worldly pleasures as well as honour and esteem seemed meaningless to her now. The views that had inspired her to reject Vinay and decide to marry Clark now seemed extremely unnatural to her. She had inflicted this torture upon herself to suppress her emotions because Rani Jahnavi had scorned her. But she had not realized then that she was actually reacting strongly against that decision, for she hadn't thought that there was anything wrong with her behaviour. Now her soul was rebelling strongly against that base decision. She was surprised that she had decided to install Clark in Vinay's place. 'Mr Clark does not lack good qualities; he is capable, decent, generous, sensitive. He can please any woman who craves worldly comforts. But where does he have that renunciation, that desire to serve, that high ideal of life, that vow of bravery, that self-sacrifice?' Sophia now found the stories of devoted love and poetry in which the bhakti rasa was prominent more attractive than discussions of such profound topics as creature and soul, the finite and the infinite, reincarnation and moksha. She also read Krishna's biography, which shook the foundations of her devotion to the Lord Messiah. She would mentally compare both the great men. She found more solace in Krishna's love than in the Messiah's compassion. Until now, she had only known about the Krishna of the Gita and, compared to the Messiah's compassion, selfless service and holiness she had found Krishna's enigmatic life to be even more obscure than the complex philosophical discussions of the Gita. Her mind would bow down before the uplifting thoughts of the Gita but the feeling of devotion would not be awakened in her heart. She had thought Krishna's childhood to be a figment of the imagination of his devotees and had considered it futile to dwell upon it. But now the compassion of Jesus seemed arid before this childhood play. There was spirituality in the compassion of Jesus but emotion in Krishna's love; the compassion of Jesus was infinite like the sky, Krishna's love was as enticing as a flourishing garden of fresh blossoms; the compassion of Jesus was the melodious sound of the flow of water, Krishna's love the yearning call of the flute; one was a god, the other a man; one was an ascetic, the other a poet; in one there was enlightenment and self-knowledge, in the other love and ecstasy; one was a businessman, thinking of profit and loss, the other an amorist who would unstintingly surrender all he had; one was self-restrained, the other an epicure. Sophia was now continuously absorbed in this erotic play, she was infatuated with Krishna; he had played his flute for her.

Mr Clark's social manners now seemed ridiculous to Sophia. She knew that this romantic play would not pass even one test. She would often be indifferent to him. He would come smiling, pull a chair by her side and sit down but she wouldn't so much as glance at him. She even went to the extent of often deeply hurting Mr Clark's pious nature by her religious impiety. She seemed to him to be a mystery that he couldn't unveil. He was as strongly attracted by her incomparable beauty, her bewitching personality and her strange pensiveness as he was afraid of her pride, independence and incivility. He had a feeling of inferiority before her and was aware at every step that he was not worthy of her. That was why, despite so much intimacy, he did not have the courage to bind her to a promise. Mrs Sevak added fuel to the fire; on the one hand, she would incite Clark and, on the other, she would try and make Sophia understand. 'You are mistaken if you think that such opportunities come again and again in life. Human beings get only one chance, and that determines their destinies.'

John Sevak also began playing a double game on his father's orders.

He would secretly try to manipulate Mahendra Kumar but outwardly he left no stone unturned in entertaining Mr Clark. As for Ishvar Sevak, he thought that Khuda had made Sophia only for Mr Clark. He would often go to Mr Clark's house and also eat there. Just as a salesman follows a customer and doesn't let him visit another shop, Ishvar Sevak would stick to Mr Clark to prevent him from being attracted to a better shop. But despite having so many well-wishers, Mr Clark thought that it would be difficult for him to succeed.

Sophia had become very fond of dressing up these days. She had never cared about her hair or clothes and jewellery until now. She had wanted to abstain from indulging in pleasure. Religious texts had taught her that the body is mortal, the world is a void, life is a mirage, that's why it was unnecessary to adorn oneself. Real adornment is something else; one should focus only on that. But now life didn't seem to be so worthless. She had never before looked so radiant. Her craving to look beautiful had never before been so acute.

It was evening. The cool rays of the sun, like the benediction of some god, were making the trees laugh gently. Sophia was standing in an arbour smiling to herself when Mr Clark's car arrived. Seeing Sophia in the garden, he went straight to her and held out his hand, looking pleadingly at her. Sophia turned her face away, as if she had not even seen his outstretched hand.

After a moment, she joked – How many criminals have you sentenced today?

Mr Clark was abashed. Embarrassed, he said – Dearest, these are everyday affairs, what should I discuss about them?

Sophia – How do you decide whether somebody is really a criminal or not? Do you have a yantra?

Clark – There are witnesses.

Sophia – Are the witnesses always truthful?

Clark – Never! Witnesses often tell lies and are tutored.

Sophia – And you decide on the basis of their testimony?

Clark – Is there any other way?

Sophia – Why should your incompetence take away someone's life? So you can have a car, a bungalow, khansamas, several kinds of liquor, and various forms of entertainment?

At a loss, Clark said – So should I resign from my job?

Sophia – When you know that there are so many shortcomings in the present system of administration, why do you become a part of it and murder innocent people?

Clark – Dearest, I have never thought about this subject.

Sophia – And you daily murder justice without giving it a thought. You are so cruel.

Clark – We are merely cogs in the machine, what do we have to do with such thoughts?

Sophia – Are you sure that you haven't committed any crime?

Clark – No human being can claim that.

Sophia – So you have escaped punishment because your crimes are hidden?

Clark – I don't want to admit it, but I'm forced to.

Sophia – It's surprising that you don't have any shame punishing criminals when you are one yourself.

Clark – Sophie, you can reproach me about this some other time. Right now I want your advice about something urgent. Think it over carefully before giving your opinion. I have already told you that Raja Mahendra Kumar has petitioned the Governor about my decision. I had thought then that the Governor would ignore the petition. It is against our procedure to help any rais against a district officer because this hampers the administration. But this is what the situation has become during the last six or seven months. Raja sahib has used the prestige of his dynasty, his determination, and his skill in arguing so well that now the decision may be against me. The Governor has very little importance in the council now that Indians have the majority. Although he can dismiss the decision of the council, he can use this right only on rare occasions. There'll be mayhem in the country the very next day if raja sahib's petition is rejected, and newspapers will get the opportunity that they look for daily to make a noise about a new atrocity of the foreign government. That's why the Governor has asked me whether I'd be unhappy if raja sahib's tears are wiped. I don't know how to reply. I haven't yet been able to make a decision.

Sophia – Is it difficult to decide this?

Clark – Yes, it's difficult because it will look bad if we crush the arrangement that we ourselves have made for ruling with the assent of the people. No matter how strong the king may be, sometimes even he has to bend to maintain the prestige of justice. It doesn't matter to me whether the decision is in my favour or against me, it won't affect me, rather the public will be in greater awe of our justice. (*Smiling*) The Governor has even punished me for this crime. He wants to remove me from here.

Sophia – Will you have to submit so much?

Clark – Yes, I'll be made the Political Agent of a riyasat. It's a very enjoyable position. The raja is there only in name; all the power is in the hands of the Agent. Only those among us who are very lucky are given this position.

Sophia – In that case you are very lucky.

Mr Clark was cut to the quick by this sarcasm. He had thought that Sophie would be delighted when she heard this news and he would then get the opportunity to tell her that it would be necessary for them to get married before leaving this place. 'In that case, you are very lucky'—this cruel sarcasm threw water on all his hopes. The cruelty, scorn and indifference in this sentence crossed the limits of civility. He thought, 'I expressed my wish without her consent, did she mind this? Perhaps she thinks that he's so happy because of his selfish ambitions and is not at all bothered about what will happen to that helpless blind man. Why did he begin this melody if this is what he was going to do?' He said, 'That depends on your decision.'

Sophia answered indifferently – You are more intelligent than I am on these subjects.

Clark – I'm worried about that blind man.

Sophia said callously – You are not the only Khuda of that blind man.

Clark – I'm asking your advice and you are leaving everything to me.

Sophia – Suppose my advice harms you?

Clark answered with great courage – Sophie, how can I convince you that I can do anything for you?

Sophia (*Laughing*) – I'm much obliged to you for this.

Meanwhile, Mrs Sevak came and began to talk jovially with Clark. Sophie returned to her room when she realized that there was no longer any scope for mocking Mr Clark. She saw Prabhu sitting there and said – This gentleman will now have to pack his bags. He'll be the Agent of some riyasat.

Prabhu (*Surprised*) – When?

Sophia – Very soon. Raja Mahendra Kumar has got the better of him.

Prabhu – Then you are a guest here for just a few days.

Sophia – I won't marry him.

Prabhu – Really?

Sophia – Yes, I made this decision several days ago but I didn't get a chance to tell you.

Prabhu – Were you afraid that I'd raise a hue and cry?

Sophia – Actually, yes.

Prabhu – I can't understand why you mistrust me so much. As far as I can remember, I have never betrayed your trust.

Sophia – Forgive me, Prabhu! I don't know why I can't trust you. You are still so immature and such an open, carefree person that I'm as afraid of telling you anything as somebody who's afraid of stepping on the delicate branch of a tree.

Prabhu – That's good, be afraid of me! Mice start running in my belly if I hear anything and I'm not comfortable until I tell someone. Anyway, I congratulate you on this decision. I've never told you this frankly but I have often hinted that I wouldn't like Mr Clark as my brother-in-law in any circumstance. I don't know why I'm averse to him. The poor man respects me a lot but I can't get along with him. I had once recited my poem to him. I've become averse to him since that day. He just sat there listening with a poker face as if I were talking to somebody else. He doesn't know anything about poetry. I feel like having him on whenever I see him. I must have recited my compositions to any number of people but I haven't found such a connoisseur as Vinay. If he writes, he'll write splendidly. Every pore of his being is poetic.

Sohpia – Have you been to kunwar sahib's?

Prabhu – I have just returned from there. Vinay is in deep trouble. The authorities at Udaipur have imprisoned him.

Sophia's face didn't show any sign of anger or grief. She didn't ask why he had been arrested or what the crime was. She guessed all these things. She only asked – Is raniji going there?

Prabhu – No. Kunwar sahib and Dr Ganguly are both ready to go but the rani won't let them. She says Vinay can take care of himself. He doesn't need anyone's help.

Sophia sat still in deep thought for a while. Vinay's brave image kept moving in front of her eyes. She suddenly looked up and said decisively – I'm going to Udaipur.

Prabhu – What will you do there?

Sophia – I don't know what I'll do by going there. If nothing else, at least I can stay in the jail and take care of Vinay, I'll sacrifice my life for him. My betrayal of him, for whatever reason, continuously pierces my heart like a thorn. I feel distressed whenever I imagine the pain it must have given him. I now want to atone for that betrayal, with my life if there's no other way.

Sophia looked out of the window and saw that Clark was still standing there talking to Mrs Sevak. The car was also parked there. She promptly came out and said to Clark – William, will you spend the night just talking to mama? I'm waiting to go out with you.

It was such a melodious voice! This loving appeal was made by such a bewitching figure, with lotus-eyes filled with the magic of such sweet laughter! Clark looked repentantly at Sophia and thought, 'This is the same Sophia who was making fun of me a moment ago. Then there was the dark reflection of the sky on the water, and now the golden ray of the moon is dancing on it, and the radiance of its trembling, joyful, lively ripples is in her eyes.' He said, embarrassed, 'Forgive me, dearest, I forgot. I got delayed while talking.'

Sophia looked guilelessly at her mother and said – Mama, have you seen his cruelty? He's already tired of me. He's so oblivious of me that he didn't even pretend to ask if I wanted to go out.

Mrs Sevak – Yes, William, this is very wrong of you. Sophie has caught you red-handed today. I used to think that you were innocent and I'd put all the blame on Sophie.

Clark smiled slightly to get rid of his embarrassment and, taking Sophia's hand, went towards the car. But he still doubted whether the delicate wrist in his hand was an object or only imagination and a dream. The enigma was becoming even more difficult to unravel. Is this a conjuror who makes a monkey dance, or a child who is happy when he sees a monkey from afar and gives it mithai, but screams with fear when it comes close?

When the car started, Sophia said – The Agent has a lot of power; he can interfere in the internal affairs of a riyasat if he wants to, isn't it?

Clark said, delighted – He has supreme power even within the raja's palace. Not just the riyasat, he even decides when the raja should eat and sleep, when he should rest, whom he should meet, from whom he should keep a distance, whom he should respect and whom ignore—all these matters are under the Agent. He can decide the cups that should be there on the raja's table, what and how many clothes he requires, and even his marriage. In fact, he is the Khuda of the riyasat.

Sophia – In that case there'll be a lot of scope for outings and recreation? You won't have to sit all day in the office as you do here?

Clark – What office? The Agent's job is not to sit in an office. He's in the position of a badshah there.

Sophia – Well, you can go to any riyasat you want?

Clark – Yes, I'll have to do some correspondence first. Which riyasat would you like?

Sophia – I like mountainous regions. The villages dwelling on the lower slopes of the mountains, the sheep grazing in their laps, and the waterfalls cascading from there, these scenes seem poetic to me. It seems to me that it's a different world, far more peaceful and radiant. Mountains are a captivating dream for me. Which riyasats are in the mountains?

Clark – Bharatpur, Jodhpur, Kashmir, Udaipur . . .

Sophia – That's it. Apply for Udaipur. I've read Udaipur's stories of valour in history, and have longed to see that region ever since. The Rajputs there are so brave, so freedom-loving, so willing to give their lives for their honour. It's written that the janeus of the Rajputs who died in battle in Chittor were worth seventy-five maunds when they were weighed. Thousands of Rajput women sat together on the funeral pyre and were burnt to ashes.* Such men who are so true to their oath perhaps don't exist anywhere else in the world.

Clark – Yes, I've also come across these episodes in history. No respect is too high for such a brave community. That's why the raja of Udaipur is regarded as supreme among the Hindu rajas. Hyperbole

---

* Chittor was conquered by Akbar in 1568. The women of the fort burnt themselves on a collective funeral pyre to escape dishonour at the hands of the enemy.

has been used extensively in stories about his valour but it must be acknowledged that no other community in this country is so dauntless.

Sophia – Apply today for Udaipur, and we'll leave within a month if it's possible.

Clark – But . . . I'm afraid to say this . . . You understand what I mean . . . Before leaving, I want to ask you that long-nurtured . . . My life . . .

Sophia said smiling – I've understood, don't take the trouble of expressing it. I'm not so dim-witted but my decision-making ability is very weak, so it takes me hours of deliberation even to decide whether to go for an outing. I can't make such a quick decision on such an important issue concerning my whole life. In fact, to be frank, I haven't been able to decide whether such an unfettered woman like me with independent views is suitable for married life or not. William, I'm telling you frankly, I'm afraid of domestic life. That's why, until you know my temperament well, I don't want to deceive you by awakening false hopes in you. We have known each other only for a year. So far I'm an enigma for you. Am I or am I not?

Clark – Yes, Sophie! Actually I don't know you very well.

Sophia – In that case you should realize how foolish it would be for us to get married. If you ask me, I'm as content to be the friend of a sensitive, courteous, thoughtful and good-natured man as being his wife. I don't know what you feel, but I think sympathy and being together to be far more important than a passionate relationship.

Clark – But for social and religious customs, such relationships . . .

Sophia – Yes, such relationships are unnatural. And ordinarily they can't be followed. Even I don't want to make it a lifelong custom but I think such a relationship is necessary until we get to know each other well, until our inner beings become mirrors for each other.

Clark – I'm a slave to your desires. I can only say that without you my life is a house with no one to live in it, a lamp without light, a poem without feeling.

Sophia – All right! All right! This language of lovers is appropriate only for love stories. Here, we have reached Pandeypur. It's dark. Soordas must have left. That poor man will be heartbroken when he gets to know this.

Clark – Shall I make some other arrangement for his livelihood?

Sophia – He didn't earn his livelihood from this land. It was only the animals of the muhalla that grazed here. He's poor, a beggar but he's not greedy. He seems to be a sadhu to me.

Clark – The blind are acutely intelligent and religious.

Sophia – I have come to respect him a great deal. Just see, papa has got the work started. He would never have had the courage to oppose you if he had not stroked the raja's back.

Clark – Your papa is a very intelligent man. It's such people who are successful in this world. At least I couldn't have played this double game.

Sophia – You'll see, only the houses of the factory labourers will be here in this muhalla in a few years. Not a single person who belongs to this place will be able to live here.

Clark – The blind man had raised a hue and cry earlier. Let's see what he does now.

Sophia – I'm sure he won't stay quiet, even if he has to give his life for this land.

Clark – No, dearest, that will never happen. The day it does, I'll be the first to raise a cry of victory for him; my hands will be the first to shower flowers on him.

Sophia looked at Mr Clark with respectful affection for the first time today.

25

THE SALVOS BETWEEN RAJA MAHENDRA KUMAR AND MR CLARK
continued for a year. The page of the letter was the battlefield; instead
of ranks of warriors there were arguments that were far more powerful.
Maunds of ink flowed; several pens were used. Arguments would be
beheaded and come alive again like Ravana's army. Raja sahib would
be repeatedly disheartened because opposing the government was like
an ant opposing an elephant. But Mr John Sevak and, even more,
Indu would encourage him. The rais of the city acted less with courage
than with self-interest. When it was time to sign the petition that
Dr Ganguly had written on behalf of the citizens to send to the
Governor, several gentlemen fell ill with such an incurable disease that
they didn't have the strength to hold a pen in their hands. Somebody
went on a pilgrimage; someone else went away somewhere on urgent
work; the few who couldn't make any excuses went to Mr Clark
to apologize for having signed. 'Huzoor! We didn't know what was
written in it, we just received a blank paper. We were merely told that
it was a request for a reduction in the water tax. We would never have
picked up our pens had we known that a complaint against huzoor
would be written afterwards in that letter.' But the worthies who had
bought shares in the cigarette company were forced to sign. Although
there weren't many signatures, Dr Ganguly got an excuse to raise
questions in the Legislative Assembly. With irrepressible enthusiasm and
patience, he kept firing a volley of questions. He was greatly respected
in the Assembly; several members supported his questions. In fact, the
authorities were even defeated by a majority on one of his proposals.
People had very high hopes from this proposal but when it had no effect,
meetings were held at several places to express lack of confidence in the
government. The rais and the zamindars were silent out of fear but people
from the middle class began openly to oppose this autocracy. Kunwar
Bharat Singh was appointed their leader and they began to say openly,
'Now we should stand on our own feet. Our liberation will come only

from ourselves.' Mahendra Kumar also began to encourage this group secretly. The rulers lost faith in Dr Ganguly despite his reassurances. Despair springs from weakness but strength is born from its womb.

It was nine o'clock at night. On getting news of Vinay Singh's imprisonment, kunwar sahib had invited some of his well-wishers to discuss the situation. Dr Ganguly, John Sevak, Prabhu Sevak, Mahendra Kumar and several other gentlemen had come. Indu had also come with raja sahib and was talking to her mother. Kunwar sahib had sent for Nayakram, who was sitting at the doorway of the room, smoking tobacco.

Mahendra Kumar said – The government has a lot of power over the riyasats. They are crippled and are forced to dance to its tune.

Bharat Singh contradicted raja sahib – It's best that the traces of somebody who doesn't do anyone any good and the basis of whose existence is destruction should be effaced as soon as possible. It's far better to die than to live as the instrument of the injustice of foreigners.

Dr Ganguly – The authorities there are themselves degraded. They are afraid that they won't be able to loot the public if there's a propagation of independent views in the riyasat. The raja just sits there, reclining on a cushion, and his servants rule at their own will.

John Sevak said, taking a neutral position – The government doesn't force any riyasat to be unjust. But yes, because they are powerless and can't protect themselves, they are more than eager to act in ways that they think will please the government.

Bharat Singh – You people are not unaware of how humble, courteous and patient Vinay is. I can't believe that he can harm anyone.

Prabhu was intimate with kunwar sahib. He had not spoken so far for fear of John Sevak, but he couldn't stop himself now. He said – Why, aren't thieves harmed by the police? Aren't the wicked harmed by sadhus? And aren't there people in the world who kill such an animal as a cow? Vinay had wanted to serve the oppressed farmers. This is the reward that he has got for it. There should be a limit to the tolerance of the public, and there is. The law itself can't exist if that's ignored. To break the law in that situation is the duty of every thinking person. If today the government orders that everyone should go out with blackened faces, it will be our dharma to defy that order. The durbar of Udaipur has no right to force anyone to leave the riyasat.

Dr Ganguly – Udaipur can give such an order. It has the right.

Prabhu – I don't agree. It's not necessary to obey an order that's based on brute strength. It would have been a different matter if there had been a responsible government in Udaipur and if this order had been given on the basis of a majority. But when the public has never expressed this desire to the durbar but rather dotes on Vinay Singh, the mere wishes of the authorities can't force us to obey their orders.

Raja sahib looked around apprehensively to see if there was any enemy of his in the room. John Sevak also began to frown.

Dr Ganguly – We can't fight with the durbar.

Prabhu – We can at least incite the public to fight for its rights.

Bharat Singh – What can the consequence of this be but revolt? And the durbar will take the government's help to quell it. Thousands of helpless people will be killed.

Prabhu – As long as we are afraid of bloodshed, our rights will also be afraid to come to us. After all, they can be protected only by bloodshed. The political arena is no less dreadful than the battlefield. It's cowardice to be afraid of bloodshed after entering it.

John Sevak could no longer control himself. He said – Such impulsive young men like you should weigh your words carefully before expressing any views on complex political issues. This situation calls for calm and cool reflection.

Prabhu said, in a muted voice, as if talking to himself – Cool reflection is another name for cowardice.

Dr Ganguly – I think a deputation should go to the Indian government.

Bharat Singh – The government will say that it doesn't have the right to interfere in the internal affairs of the riyasat.

Mahendra Kumar – Why don't we send a deputation to the riyasat?

John Sevak – Yes, this is my advice too. To rebel against the state is to weaken it and to make the public rebellious. It's essential for the power of the state to remain indestructible in every situation; otherwise the consequence will be the widespread form that communism has assumed today. The world has tested democracy for three centuries and has been frustrated in the end. Today, the whole world is distressed by the terror of democracy. It's our greatest good fortune that its flames haven't yet reached our country, and we should make every effort to see to it that we don't have to fear it in the future as well.

Kunwar Bharat Singh was a great champion of democracy. Seeing his principles contradicted, he said – If you build a straw hut you can't remain unafraid of the fire flames. It's quite possible that the fire may not come from outside, but a mere spark inside the house itself may fall on it. Why should you want a hut at all? Democracy may not be an ideal system, but has the world yet found a better system of governance? Anyway, what else can we do except be patient since it is evident that we can't exert any influence on the durbar? I want to stay away from political issues because it's not worth it. The price of independence is blood. Since we don't have the will to shed it, why should we tighten our belts, change our stance, slap our arms? Our welfare is in detachment.

Prabhu – It's difficult not to open my mouth if I see my house being looted in front of my eyes.

Bharat Singh – Yes, it's very difficult, but we'll have to restrain our inclinations. The only solution is not to become the handle of the hatchet. Even if the hatchet is hard and sharp, it can't do us much harm if the handle doesn't help it. It's something to be deeply ashamed of that we should become the right hands of the rulers and cut the throats of the public on the strength of our education, prestige and wealth, and feel proud that we are masters.

John Sevak – The educated class has always been dependent on the state and will remain so. It can't destroy its entity by opposing the state.

Bharat Singh – That's the greatest calamity. As long as the educated class remains dependent on the rulers, we won't be nearer our objective even by a jot. It will have to find some other support for itself for a short, a very short while.

Mahendra Singh was looking sideways for an opportunity to slip away. To end the discussion, he said – So what have you people decided? Will a deputation be sent to the durbar?

Dr Ganguly – I'll go myself to free Vinay.

Bharat Singh – It's better to remain silent than to plead with the executioner for mercy. At least the status quo will remain.

Dr Ganguly – That *pessimism** again! I'll explain to Vinay and persuade him to return.

---

* In English in the original.

Rani Jahnavi heard these last words as she came. She said proudly – No, Dr Ganguly, don't do Vinay this favour. This is his first examination. To help him in it would be to destroy his future. He's on the side of justice; he doesn't have to submit to anybody. I'll be the first to put a black teeka of disgrace on his forehead if he accepts this injustice for fear of his life.

People were stunned by the rani's fervent words. It seemed as if a goddess had descended from the sky to deliver this message.

After a moment, Bharat Singh interpreted the rani's words – I think Vinay should be left to his plight for the time being. This is his examination. The supreme act that a man can perform is to sacrifice himself for self-protection. This is the highest aim of human life. It's only by succeeding in such tests that we can obtain the glory that will win us the confidence of the nation.

Dr Ganguly – The rani is our devi. I can't say anything in front of her. But what devis say may not be suitable for the conduct of human beings who live in the world. I'm fully confident that our government will intervene.

Rani – The example of the government's justice is before you. If you can still have confidence in it, I can only say that you need to take some medicine for a few days.

Dr Ganguly – We'll know in a few days. The government is also concerned about its reputation.

After a long time, Mahendra Kumar said – We have waited so long that our eyes have been blinded. Our hope isn't that eternal.

All of a sudden, the telephone rang. Kunwar sahib asked – Who is it?

'I'm Pran Nath. Mr Clark has been transferred.'

'Where?'

'He's going to the political department in a lower grade.'

Dr Ganguly – Well now, haven't I been proved right? You people said that the government's intentions were malicious. But I said that it will have to listen to us.

Mahendra Kumar – Pran Nath is a prankster, he must be playing a prank on you.

Bharat Singh – No, he has never played pranks on me.

Rani – The government has acted with such ethical courage for the first time.

Dr Ganguly – Those times have gone now when the government could ignore the opinion of the public. Now it will have to accept the proposal of the Council.

Bharat Singh – The times are the same, and there's not much change in the government's policy. There's definitely some political secret about this.

John Sevak – The business community took the wind out of the sails of the government by supporting my proposal.

Mahendra Kumar – My deputation reached at a very apt time.

Dr Ganguly – I united the Council to such an extent that we have never before got such a large majority.

Indu was standing behind the rani. She said – There were so many signatures on the petition because of my efforts. I'm sure the miracle is a result of that.

Nayakram had been sitting silently until now. He couldn't make out what was happening here. He hadn't understood the conversation on the phone. But he realized now that they were all tying the sehra of success on their own heads. He was not one to lag behind on such an occasion. He said, 'Sarkar, here too people have not been sitting around negligently. The civil sergeant had been given hints that a thousand cudgel-wielding youths are ready on raja sahib's side. There'll be bloodshed if his orders are not upheld, there'll be turmoil in the city. He must have definitely conveyed this to Laat sahib.'

Mahendra Kumar – I'm sure this miracle has happened because of your threats.

Nayakram – Dharmavatar, what threats? A river of blood would have flown. Your prestige is so great that I can get the city looted if I want to. These people with red turbans will be left just standing and staring.

Prabhu joked – If you ask me, it's the result of that poem that I had written in the *Hindustan Review*.

Rani – Prabhu, that's a good hit. Dr Ganguly is stroking his head. Well, doctor, did it go home or not? You people are so delighted by a trivial success. Don't think that it's a victory; actually it's a defeat that distances you miles away from your goal and strengthens the noose around your necks. The musicians warm their instruments with fire when it's cold so that sounds sweet to the ear emerge from them. You people are also being warmed; strengthen your backs for the blows.

Jahnavi went inside, and the effect of this taunt also diminished the moment she had left. People began to sing the same tune again.

Mahendra Kumar – Clark mahodaya will also remember that he had somebody to reckon with.

Dr Ganguly – How can anyone deny now that these people are so just?

John Sevak – Now we should take care of that blind man as well.

Nayakram – Sahib! He doesn't care about defeat or victory. He'll remain the same even if he gets ten times that land.

John Sevak – I'll begin work at the mill tomorrow. Let me also see to Mr Clark.

Mahendra Kumar – I won't give him a ceremonial address. They'll try to put pressure but the majority on the board is with me.

Dr Ganguly – There's no need to give a ceremonial address to such officers.

Mice were running in Mahendra Kumar's belly because he was impatient to discuss this good news with Indu. Although he was a very solemn man, this victory had made him rapturous with a childlike joy and he seemed to be rather intoxicated. A short while after the rani had left, he came in somewhat pompously with a smile on his face, a cheerful heart, and head held high with pride. Indu was sitting with the rani. She got up and said, 'Sahib bahadur had to pack his bags finally, didn't he?'

Mahendra Kumar couldn't express his malicious joy in front of the rani. He said – Yes, now he'll have to move.

Indu – Tomorrow I'll go and enquire about the welfare of the lady sahib whose feet wouldn't touch the ground, who had thought herself to be superior to everyone else. Shall I invite her for a party?

Mahendra Kumar – She'll never come, and where's the need?

Indu – Why isn't there any need? She'll at least feel embarrassed and humiliated. It doesn't matter if she doesn't come. Amma, you've seen how humble and friendly she used to be, but she has become so swollen-headed as soon as there was talk of marriage with Mr Clark.

Rani (*Gravely*) – Beti, you are mistaken. Sophia will never marry Mr Clark. If I know anything about human nature, you'll see that I'll be proved right.

Indu – Amma, she's engaged to Clark. It's also possible that they are also married secretly. Can't you see how intimate they are?

Rani – It doesn't matter how intimate they are but they are not married nor will they be. No matter how much I may scorn Sophia because of my narrow-mindedness but she is a sati; there's not an iota of doubt about that. You'll regret it if you embarrass her.

Indu – If she's that generous, she's sure to come if you ask her.

Rani – Yes, I'm sure.

Indu – Then send for her, why should I arrange a party?

Rani – You want to humiliate her by calling her here. I'm confiding my innermost thoughts in you; if she had not been a Christian I would marry Vinay to her five years from now and consider it to be my good fortune.

Indu didn't like this conversation. She got up and went to her room. Mahendra Kumar also followed her in a moment and they both began to boast. A boy who wins a game would not have been so intoxicated.

The gathering in the reception room also dispersed and people went home. After they had all left kunwar sahib called Nayakram and said – Pandaji, I want you to do something for me, will you?

Nayakram – Sarkar, I'll give my life if you order me to. What is it?

Kunwar – Look, don't be diplomatic. What I want done is not easy. You'll have to spend a great deal of time and use your intelligence and strength. Your life may also be in danger. Say yes if your heart is strong enough or refuse frankly, I'm not a pilgrim that you should try to impress me. We know each other so we should be frank with each other.

Nayakram – Sarkar, how will I show my face to God if I'm diplomatic with you? Your salt is mingled in every pore of my being. I'll do the work if it's in my power, even if I have to risk my life. You just have to order me.

Kunwar – Can you get Vinay freed and bring him here?

Nayakram – Deenbandhu, I won't hesitate even if I have to give my life to bring him.

Kunwar – Do you know why I asked you this question? I have hundreds of men here. Dr Ganguly himself is prepared to go. Mahendra will also go if I send him. But I don't want to express my wishes before these people. I don't want to be accused of saying something and doing something else. I'm in a dharmic dilemma. But love for my son won't consent. After all I'm human, I don't have a heart of stone. How can I be patient? I have brought him up with such high hopes; he's the one support of my life. Bring him with you at any cost. The staff and officials of Udaipur are not gods; you can get into the jail by tempting them and meet Vinay, you can bring him out with the help of the staff, it's not difficult. What's difficult is to persuade Vinay to come here. I'll leave that to your intelligence and cunning. I'm sure he'll agree to come if you can make him aware of my plight. Tell me, can you do this work? I'll give you whatever you want for your efforts together with an old father's blessings.

Nayakram – Maharaj, I'll leave tomorrow. God willing, I'll bring him with me or I won't show my face.

Kunwar – No, Pandaji, he's sure to come when he gets to know how distraught I am. He won't sacrifice his father's life for the sake of a principle. I transformed my life for his sake and donned the garb of a fakir; won't he do this much for me? Pandaji, just imagine, can somebody who has always rested on velvet beds get any comfort on this wooden plank? Vinay's love is the mantra that has compelled me to do this difficult tapasya. How could I have remained engrossed in luxury in this old age when Vinay has taken a vow of sacrifice? Ah! These thorns have been sown by Jahnavi. I can't get my way before her. It's because of her that the heaven of my happiness, my beloved Vinay, is eluding my grasp. The world will be hell for me if I lose such a jewel of a son. Will you go tomorrow? Take as much money as you want from the muneem.

Nayakram – There's no lack of anything because of your mercy. I only need your blessings. People would have been wonderstruck if somebody else had made the sacrifice that you have made despite being so illustrious. Is it a joke to make a sacrifice? I don't have even parched bhang at home, I don't know from where the food would come if I didn't take care of the pilgrims but I've become so addicted to the plant that I go crazy the day I don't get it. How can anyone make sacrifices like you?

Kunwar – I'm sure that you'll bring Vinay back if you go. Now tell me what dakshina can I give you? What's your greatest desire?

Nayakram – Sarkar should remain happy with me, that's enough for me.

Kunwar – So that means you don't want to do my work?

Nayakram – Sarkar, don't say that. You provide for me, what face will I show God if I don't obey your orders? And then, how is it your work, after all it's also mine.

Kunwar – No, bhai, I can't trouble you so much for nothing. You have treated me in the best way possible. I also want to treat you in the way that you think the best. How many sons do you have?

Nayakram bowed his head and said – Dharmavatar, I'm not even married yet.

Kunwar – So that's it! Half your life is over and you are still a bachelor!

Nayakram – Sarkar, what can I call it except destiny?

There was such anguish in these words that they expressed Nayakram's lifelong desire to kunwar sahib. He asked, 'So you live alone in the house?'

Nayakram – Yes, Dharmavatar! I remain lying there alone like a ghost. By your mercy, I have a house with two floors; I have gardens, cows and buffaloes, but nobody to live there, nobody to enjoy it all. Only those who are very fortunate in our community get married.

Kunwar (*Smiling*) – So, shall I arrange your marriage somewhere?

Nayakram – Maharaj, where do I have such a destiny?

Kunwar – I'll make your destiny. But is it necessary that the girl should belong to a very high family?

Nayakram – Deenbandhu! One doesn't look at high or low families for girls. Girls and cows are sacred. They become even more sacred after coming to a brahman's house. And then, whoever accepts a sacred offering, let alone a woman, digests all the sins of the world. A man's life is worth two kauris, sarkar, if he's not married.

Kunwar – That's good then, you'll become a bridegroom as soon as you return, if God wills it. You have never mentioned this earlier.

Nayakram – Sarkar, how could I tell you? I've told only my close friends. I feel embarrassed. Whoever gets to know of it will say there's definitely some defect in him. I have been taken in several times by impostors and have lost hundreds of rupees. What could I tell anyone? I'm just depending on God.

Kunwar – So which train will you take tomorrow?

Nayakram – Huzoor, I'll go by the Mail.

Kunwar – I hope to God that you'll return soon. I'll be waiting for you. Here, take this for your expenses.

Kunwar sahib called the muneem and whispered something in his ear. The muneem signalled to Nayakram to accompany him and, sitting on his cushion, asked – Say, how much is yours and how much mine?

Nayakram – This is not a dakshina.

Muneem – You'll get the amount.

Nayakram – I won't get it, it's being sent to Vinay Singh. Rascal, you betray your master even when he's in trouble? A calamity has fallen upon him and all you can think of is filling your house. Greedy people like you should be beaten up where even water isn't available.

The muneem was embarrassed and gave Nayakram a bundle of notes. Nayakram counted them, tied them to his waist, and said – Will you get me some dakshina?

Muneem – What dakshina?

Nayakram – Ready cash. Do you value your job or not? You know that you won't even get alms anywhere if you are dismissed from here. Push a wad of fifty rupees with your left hand if you know what's good for you or I'll complain to kunwar sahib. You'll be dismissed there and then. You'll be beaten so mercilessly that you'll turn bald.

Muneem – Guru, this bluster with friends! You've got so much money. Kunwar Vinay Singh is not going to write receipts.

Nayakram – Are you giving the money or not? Hurry up!

Muneem – Guru, you . . .

Nayakram – Are you giving the money or not? I don't have time to waste in talking. Think about it quickly. I'm leaving. Remember, you won't get even alms anywhere.

Muneem – I don't have it with me. This is official money.

Nayakram – Achcha, then write a hand note.

Muneem – Guru, just look here, I'm a poor man.

Nayakram – You are poor? Rascal! You are getting fat on ill-begotten kauris, and you pretend to be poor? Hurry up and write! Kunwar sahib won't have any mercy. Has he given me so much money for nothing? All I need to do is to tell him, that's all. There'll be a case of embezzlement against you. Beta, have you understood? Come, do pooja for your father. It's not every day that wily old rascals like you get caught.

The muneem sensed by Nayakram's behaviour that he wouldn't now let go without taking dakshina. He quietly took out twenty-five rupees and put them in his hand saying, 'Pandit, now have mercy and don't torment me so much.'

Nayakram took the money in his fist and said – All right, rascal, now don't torment anybody. I'll be on the lookout for you.

After Nayakram had left, the muneem said to himself – Take it, I'll think I've given charity.

Kunwar sahib was standing at the door of the reception room. There was no pleasure in the coolness of the breeze today. The sparkling constellations of the stars in the sky pierced his heart like a mocking gaze. In the groves of the trees in front, the memory of Vinay's image, cloudy, quivering like a tender voice, as ephemeral as smoke, seemed to emanate like a sigh from an anguished heart.

Kunwar Sahib stood there crying for several minutes. Blessings for Vinay emerged from his innermost being like the tender, sweet, gentle, cool rays of the rising sun of the dawn.

26

JASWANTNAGAR IS NESTLED ON THE LOWER SLOPES OF THE VERDANT hills of Aravalli like a child sleeping in his mother's lap. Streams of milk from the mother's breast, oozing restlessly with love, overflowing, singing sweetly, fill the tiny mouth of the child and flow down. The mother's tender and beautiful body is purified after bathing in the golden rays of the dawn and the child keeps peeping out of her aanchal to gaze at her loving face, leaping forward and smiling. But the mother keeps covering him with her aanchal to protect him from the evil eye.

Suddenly there was the piercing sound of cannon shots. The mother's heart trembled; the child clung to her lap.

That dreadful sound again! The mother was terrified; the child clung to her. There were continuous cannon shots after that. The mother's face clouded with fear. The new Political Agent of the riyasat is expected there today. These salutes are being fired in his honour.

Mr Clark and Sophia had arrived there a month ago. They had been so busy with parties, receiving gifts, meeting jagirdars that there had been no time to discuss anything with each other. Time and again, Sophia had wanted to talk about Vinay Singh, but she didn't get the opportunity, nor did she know how to start the topic. Finally, when a whole month had gone by, she said to Clark one day, 'This succession of parties will go on and the rains will soon be over. I'm bored here now. We should visit the mountainous regions. The hills will be in full glory.' Clark agreed with her.

They have both been visiting the riyasat since a week, accompanied by the riyasat's deewan, Sardar Neelkanth Raav. They are welcomed with pomp and splendour wherever they go, they are saluted, addresses are given in their honour, they are taken around the prominent places. Schools, hospitals and other public institutions are inspected. Sophia is very fond of inspecting prisons. She scrutinizes the prisoners, their dining rooms, and the rules of the jails with great interest and pleads earnestly with the officials for the reform of the prisons.

No other Agent until now had taken any notice of these unfortunate beings. Their plight was pitiable, human beings were treated in such a way that the very thought of it makes the hair stand on end. But their condition improved because of Sophia's untiring efforts. Today Jaswantnagar has the good fortune of extending its hospitality to the guests and the entire qasba, that is, all the state officials of the qasba, are running around hither and thither with turbans tied. Nobody is in his senses; it is as if somebody has dreamt of wolves in his sleep. The officers have got the bazaars decorated; the prisoners of the jail and the chowkidars of the town have been used as coolies and labourers, nobody from the basti is allowed on to the streets without identifying himself. No inhabitant of the town has participated in this welcome and this is how the riyasat has responded to their indifference. Armed sepoys are lined on both sides of the street so that no sign of any public unrest would be visible. Meetings have been banned.

It was evening. The procession started. The pedestrians and the riders were in front. The army bands were playing. The roads were illuminated but there was darkness in the houses and on the roofs. Flowers were being showered but from the hands of the sepoys, not from the roofs. Sophie understood everything but there seemed to be a veil in front of Clark's eyes. Unlimited power has made him lose his wits. Officials can do everything but they have no control over devotion. There is no sign of rejoicing in the town, rather there is an atmosphere of mourning; there are no triumphal cries at every step, no beautiful woman comes to perform the aarti, nor is there any music. It is as if there is a celebration going on before a mother absorbed in grief for her son.

After going around the township, Sophie, Clark, Sardar Neelkanth and a few high officials went to the palace while the rest left. Tea was served. When Mr Clark poured a drink from the bottle, sardar sahib, who hated its smell, slipped away and sat next to Sophia. He asked, 'How do you like Jaswantnagar?'

Sophia – It's a beautiful place. The view of the hills is very enticing. Except Kashmir, perhaps such natural beauty doesn't exist anywhere. I'm delighted by the cleanliness of the town. I'd like to stay here for a few days.

Neelkanth was afraid. Peace could be maintained in the town for a day or two with the strength of the police and the army, but not for a month or two at any cost. It was impossible. The town's real situation would be evident to these people if they remained ensconced here. It was difficult to know what the consequences would be. He said, 'Don't be taken in by the outward appearance of this place. The climate is very bad. You'll find many places that are more beautiful further on.'

Sophia – I don't care, I'm going to stay here for two weeks. Why, William, you are not in a hurry to leave this place, are you?

Clark – I'm ready to be buried here if you want to stay.

Sophia – See, sardar sahib, William doesn't have any objection.

Sophia was enjoying harassing sardar sahib.

Neelkanth – I'll still urge that Jaswantnagar is not a very nice place. Besides the polluted climate, seeds of unrest have sprouted among the public here.

Sophia – In that case, it's even more necessary for us to stay here. I haven't heard this complaint in any other riyasat. The government has given internal independence to the riyasats but that doesn't mean that the germs of anarchy should be allowed to spread. This is the responsibility of the authorities, and the government has the right to ask for a satisfactory explanation for this negligence.

Sardar sahib was very nervous. He had spoken to Sophia quite unsuspectingly. Her humility had convinced him that the gift he had given her had worked, so he had become rather informal. He was taken aback when he heard this rebuke. He said timidly, 'I can assure you that although this situation is the riyasat's responsibility we have done and are still doing everything possible to control it. This seed has come from an unexpected direction or you can say that the drops of poison were brought in gold vessels. The volunteers of the rais of Banaras, Kunwar Bharat Singh, acted so skilfully that we had no information. Wealth can be protected from dacoits but not from sadhus. The volunteers have cast such mantras on the foolish public here in the guise of service that the riyasat has had to face the greatest difficulties to dispel them. Kunwar sahib's son especially is a very devious youth. He spread his rebellious views in this region to such an extent that he made it an arena for rebels. There was such magic in the way he spoke that the public would flock to him as if they were all thirsty. His garb of a sadhu, his simple, ascetic life, his gentle sensitivity, and above all his godlike appearance, seemed to have cast a spell on everybody, big and small. The riyasat was very worried. We lost our sleep. There was the fear of a revolt flaring up every moment. We even had to send armed help from the cantonment. Vinay Singh was arrested somehow but his companions are still hiding in the region and inciting the public. The state treasury has been looted here several times. There have been several misguided attempts to free Vinay Singh from the jail, and the officials are in constant fear of their lives. I have been compelled to narrate these events to you. I'll never advise you to stay here. You can now realize for yourself that we couldn't have done anything else.'

Sophia said, very worried – The situation is far worse than I had thought it to be. William will not be doing his duty if he leaves in these circumstances. He has come here as the representative of the government, not merely for sightseeing. Why, William, you don't object to staying here, do you? You'll also have to give a report about this place.

Taking a sip, Clark said – I can enjoy the bliss of heaven even in hell if you wish it. As for the report, it's your job to write it.

Neelkanth – It's my humble request to you to give a little more time to manage the riyasat. To give a report now will be very harmful for us.

This was the playacting going on here; Sophia was ensconced on the throne of power while supremacy was whisking away the flies and the ashtsidhi were waiting upon her with folded hands.

Vinay, however, was lamenting the cruelty and callousness of women in his dark cell, dejected and silent. The other prisoners were cleaning their rooms; they had been given new blankets and kurtas, which was a novel incident in the riyasat. The officials of the jail were tutoring the prisoners, 'If memsahib asks, what are your complaints, all of you should answer with one voice, we are very happy by the glory of huzoor, and we pray for the welfare of huzoor's life and property. If she asks, what do you want, say, huzoor should prosper every day; we don't want anything else. Beware if anybody raises his head or opens his mouth; he'll be skinned alive.' The prisoners were delighted. Mithai would be distributed to celebrate memsahib's arrival. There would be a holiday. May God always keep her happy because she has been so merciful to such unfortunate beings.

But Vinay's room had not yet been cleaned. The new blanket was lying there, but it was untouched. The kurta was lying folded just as it was; he was wearing his old one. There was just this voice emanating from each pore of his body, from each atom of his mind, from each beat of his heart, 'Sophia! Why should I go before her?' He thought, 'Why is Sophia coming here? Does she want to insult me? Sophie, who was the living image of compassion and love, does she want to summon me in front of Clark and trample me underfoot? Such cruelty, and on someone so unfortunate as I, who is himself crying out his days! No, she's not so hard hearted and cruel. This is Mr Clark's mischief; he wants to embarrass me in front of Sophia but I won't give him this opportunity. I won't go before him. Whoever wants to can take me there by force. Why should I pretend that I'm sick? I'll say frankly that I won't go there. If this is the rule of the jail, let it be so, I don't care about such rules that are completely meaningless. I've heard that they want to stay here for a week. Will they totally crush the public? Even now, there must be just half the people left. Hundreds were turned out, hundreds crammed into the jail. Do they want to reduce this qasba to dust?'

The daroga of the jail came just then and said harshly – You haven't yet cleaned your room! Arey, you haven't even changed your kurta or spread your blanket, haven't you been given orders?

Vinay – I did get the order but I didn't think it necessary to obey it.

The daroga said more heatedly – The consequence will be that you'll also be treated like the other prisoners. We have treated you decently until now because you are the son of an esteemed rais and have come to this foreign country. But I won't tolerate any mischief.

Vinay – Tell me if I'll have to go before the Political Agent.

Daroga – Why else have this blanket and kurta been given? Has anyone else ever got a new blanket here? You people are very lucky.

Vinay – I'm willing to obey you if you can do me the kindness of not forcing me to go in front of sahib.

Daroga – What nonsense! Do I have any authority? You'll have to go.

Vinay said humbly – I'll never forget this favour.

Darogaji would probably have lost his self-control on another occasion, but today it was necessary to keep the prisoners happy. He said – But, bhai, making this concession is beyond my power. I don't know what calamity I may have to face. Sardar sahib will eat me alive. Memsahib is obsessed with seeing jails. Burra sahib is the enemy of the officials and memsahib is even ahead of him. If you want to know the truth, it's memsahib who is all in all. Sahib is a slave to her wishes. If she happens to get annoyed, your term will be doubled; we'll also be crushed.

Vinay – It seems that memsahib has a lot of power.

Daroga – Power! You can say that memsahib is the Political Agent. Sahib is there only to sign. All the gifts and offerings go into memsahib's hands.

Vinay – Just do me the kindness of not forcing me to go in front of her. One man less among so many prisoners won't be noticed. Yes, I'll go if she calls me by name.

Daroga – Sardar sahib will swallow me alive.

Vinay – But this is what you'll have to do. I'll never go of my own will.

Daroga – I'm a bad man, don't harass me. I have unstiffened the necks of several high and mighty people in this very jail.

Vinay – You have the right to scold me but you know that I'm not one to submit to force.

Daroga – Bhai, you're a strange being. The entire town is being vacated by her orders, and you're still being stubborn. You may not value your life but I value mine.

Vinay – What? Is the town being vacated? Why?

Daroga – It's memsahib's orders. Her wrath has fallen on Jaswantnagar. She is furious ever since she has heard about the incidents here. She would have it dug up and thrown away if she had her way. Orders have been given that for a week no young man should be allowed to remain in the qasba. There's fear of a revolt, the cantonment has been asked for help.

The daroga exaggerated the situation to impress Vinay Singh and he succeeded. Vinay was apprehensive that his disobedience could anger the authorities and make them inflict more atrocities on him. 'The public may revolt if they come to know about it. In that situation I will also become a participant in the crimes of those murderers. Who knows, perhaps my companions have incited the people even more in my absence; there is no lack of rebellious youths among them. No,

the situation is very delicate. I'll have to act with restraint.' He asked
the daroga, 'When will memsahib come here?'

Daroga – There's no fixed time for her arrival. She can trick us and
come at a time when we are lax. That's why I'm telling you to clean
the room and change your clothes. Who knows, she could come even
today.

Vinay – All right, I'll do whatever you want me to. You can relax
now.

Daroga – You won't refuse to come when it's time to salaam?

Vinay – No, you'll find me the first to be there in the courtyard.

Daroga – You won't complain against me?

Vinay – It's not my habit to complain; you know that very well.

The daroga left. It was beginning to get dark. Vinay swept his
room, changed his clothes and spread the blanket. He didn't want to
do anything that would attract attention to him; he wanted to remove
the suspicions of the rulers by his indifference. It was time to eat but
Mr Clark had not arrived. Finally, the daroga, disappointed, had the
gates of the jail shut and ordered the prisoners to rest. When Vinay lay
down, he thought, 'Why has Sophie been transformed like this? That
image of modesty and humility, that idol of service and sacrifice, has
today become the goddess of autocracy. She used to be so sensitive,
so compassionate; her thoughts were so lofty and pure; her nature
was so simple; each glance used to wound the heart like a simile of
Kalidasa;* the words she uttered illuminated the mind like the light
of a lamp. It seemed that she had been created with the fragrance of
flowers; it was such abiding, pensive, charming beauty! That Sophie
has now become so cruel!'

There was silence everywhere, as if a storm was about to break. The
daroga's animals were not tied in the courtyard prison today, nor were
there any heaps of grass in the verandas. No prisoner had to clean the
dirty eating utensils of the jail staff, no one had to massage the soldiers'
heads. The old maidservant of the jail's doctor was not abusing the

---

* Kalidasa: Renowned Sanskrit poet and dramatist; probably lived in the period
370–450, during the reign of the Gupta dynasty. Author of *Shakuntala*, among
the first Sanskrit works to be translated into English, and *Meghadoot* ('Cloud
Messenger').

prisoners today and the gifts of the relatives of the prisoners were not being distributed and shared in the office. There were lamps in the rooms; the doors were open. Vinay thought, 'Why don't I escape? People will perhaps calm down if I explain to them. The army from the cantonment will be arriving; there may be a revolt over the most trivial thing. If I'm successful in establishing peace it will be the atonement for my crime.' He looked stealthily at the high wall of the jail but didn't dare to come out of the room. Suppose someone saw him? 'People will think that I tried to escape to incite the public.'

The night passed in this dilemma. The officials were not fully awake when the sound of the car announced the arrival of the visitors. The daroga, the doctor, the warder, the chowkidar, all came out in a flurry. The first bell rang, the prisoners came to the field, they were ordered to stand in rows, and at that very moment Sophia, Mr Clark and Sardar Neelkanth entered the jail.

Sophia looked over the prisoners as soon as she arrived. There was no expectation in that look, no eagerness; there was fear, anxiety, restlessness. The desire that had made her weep for years and had drawn her here, and for which she had sacrificed her cherished principles, made her timid when she was face to face with it, like a stranger returning to his village after a long time, afraid to enter, apprehensive of hearing some bad news. Suddenly, she saw Vinay standing with his head bowed. There was a violent surge of love in her heart and darkness before her eyes. The house was the same but in ruins, covered with leaves and grass, difficult to recognize. Where was that cheerful face which had reflected the simplicity of poetry? Where was that broad, manly chest? Sophie felt a compelling desire to fall at Vinay's feet, to wash him with her tears, to embrace him. Suddenly Vinay fainted, there was an anguished cry that swelled for a moment and then became silent in the surge of grief. Sophie immediately went to Vinay. There was chaos everywhere. The jail's doctor came running. The daroga bustled around like a madman. 'The servants are in for it now. Memsahib will ask why he wasn't kept in the clinic if he is in such a delicate state . . . I'm in deep trouble. This good man had to choose just this moment to faint. It's nothing; he's just holding his breath and pretending; he's bent on ruining me. Rascal! Let memsahib leave, I'll take such good care of you that all your fainting will disappear and you'll never think of fainting again. What's happened to him today? I have never before seen a prisoner faint like this. Yes, I've read about people fainting over the smallest thing in stories. He probably has epilepsy.'

The daroga was thinking of ways of escaping while sardar sahib was telling Mr Clark, 'This is the youth who is creating turmoil in the riyasat.' Sophie brusquely told the doctor to get out of the way, helped Vinay up and took him into the office. Invaluable carpets were spread there today; there were silver chairs, a brocade tablecloth and beautiful vases on the table, as well as ingredients for refreshments. It had been planned that sahib would have refreshments here after the inspection. Sophie made Vinay lie on the carpet and gestured to everybody to leave. Nobody was surprised; her compassion and pity were famous. When there was nobody else in the room, Sophie drew the window curtains, put Vinay's head on her thigh, and began to fan him with her handkerchief. Warm teardrops from her eyes began to fall on Vinay's face. There was such life-giving power in those drops of water! Her entire mental and spiritual strength was contained in them. Each drop of water was a drop of her life. Vinay opened his eyes. An imperishable flower of heaven, bathed in infinite fragrance, moving like the gentle swaying of the breeze, was ensconced before him. The most enticing and charming image of beauty is that which is drenched in tearful grief. That is its spiritual form. Vinay did not get up startled; this is the accomplishment of lovers who are yogis, this is their heaven, their golden empire, the end of their desires, how can there be any satiation in this heavenly bliss? A tender feeling was awakened in Vinay. 'If only my eyes would close forever lying like this on the bed of love! All desires would end. What better opportunity can there be to die?'

He remembered suddenly that he was forbidden even to touch Sophie. He promptly pulled away his head from her thigh and said, his voice choking – Mrs Clark, you have been very kind to me, I'm obliged to you for this.

Sophie said, looking at him scornfully – Obligation is not expressed through abuses.

Vinay said, surprised – I have never committed such a grave crime.

Sophia – If connecting me unnecessarily with a man isn't an abuse, what is it?

Vinay – Mr Clark?

Sophia – I don't think Clark to be worthy of untying your shoelaces.

Vinay – But ammaji . . .

Sophia – Your ammaji wrote lies and you did me a great injustice by believing her. The koyal doesn't fall upon the berries of the neem tree if it can't get mangoes.

Meanwhile, Clark came in and asked – How is this prisoner? The doctor is coming. He'll treat him. Let's go, it's getting late.

Sophia said coldly – You go, I don't have the time.

Clark – For how long should I wait for you?

Sophia – I don't know. I think it's more important to take care of a human being than to go for outings.

Clark – Well, I'll stay a little longer.

When Clark left, Sophie said to Vinay, wiping the perspiration from his forehead – Vinay, I'm drowning, save me. I enacted this farce to allay raniji's suspicions.

Vinay said unbelievingly – Why have you come here with Clark, and how are you staying with him?

Sophia blushed with embarrassment and said – Vinay, don't ask this, but God is my witness that whatever I have done is for you. I couldn't think of any other way of freeing you from this imprisonment. I have intoxicated Clark. I have assumed this deceptive guise only for you. I'll stay with you if you tell me now to live here in the jail with you. I'll go with you today if you catch hold of my hand and tell me to. I have taken refuge in you and now I can't leave it on any account, even if you reject me. I have even surrendered my self-respect to you. Vinay, this has been ordained by God, it's at his inspiration or you wouldn't have found me alive after so much insult and ridicule.

Vinay asked, wanting to gauge Sophie's innermost feelings – If this has been ordained by God, why has he built this wall between us?

Sophia – This wall has not been built by God but by human beings.

Vinay – Is it so strong?

Sophia – Yes, but it's not impregnable.

Vinay – Can you break it?

Sophia – This very moment, at one sign from you. There was a time when I had thought that this wall had been created by God and I had respected it, but now I have seen its real form. Love doesn't care for these obstacles; this is not a physical relationship but a spiritual one.

Vinay took Sophie's hand in his and said, his eyes distraught with love – So from today you are mine and I'm yours.

Sophie's forehead rested on Vinay's heart; tears rained from her eyes, like black clouds bending over the earth and satiating it in a moment. She was silent and did not utter a word. The limit of grief is speechlessness, but arid and smouldering; the limit of bliss is also speechlessness, but saturated and cool. Sophie now experienced an inner strength in each part of her body and in each beat of her pulse. The boat had found the support of the helmsman. Now her goal was fixed. She wouldn't waver now with the swaying of the breeze or the flow of the waves, but would walk resolutely on her path.

Vinay was also soaring in the sky of bliss that had opened for both of them. There was fragrance in the breeze there, and sparkle in the light; no object seemed unpleasant to the sight, harsh to the ear, hard to the touch, or bitter to the taste. The flowers didn't have thorns, the sun didn't have so much heat, the earth didn't have afflictions, there was no poverty, no worry, no strife, but an empire of pervasive peace. Sophia was the queen of this empire and he himself was sporting in the lake of her love. This life of sacrifice and asceticism seemed so arid and depressing, this dark cell so frightening, compared with this dream of bliss.

Clark came in again and said – Darling, don't delay now, it's getting very late, Sardar Neelkanth is entreating. The doctor will take care of this patient.

Sophie stood up and turning away her face from Vinay, said with a voice quivering with tenderness – Don't worry, I'll come again tomorrow.

It seemed to Vinay that the blood in his vessels was drying up. He remained lying there like a wounded bird. Sophie came to the door and making an excuse to get her handkerchief, returned and whispered in Vinay's ear – I'll come again tomorrow and then we'll both go away from here. I'll apologize to Sardar Neelkanth on your behalf.

These impatient, eager, loving words kept echoing in Vinay's ears even after Sophie had left like the last notes of some melodious music. But he was soon forced to return to this world. The doctor of the jail came and made him lie down on a bed in the office itself and gave him nutritious medicines. There was soft bedding on the bed as well as pillows, and a pankha was being swayed. The daroga came every second to ask about his welfare, and the doctor wouldn't think of leaving. Vinay got fed up of these attentions and said to the doctor, 'I'm absolutely fine; you can go now and return in the evening.'

Doctor sahib said rather apprehensively – I'll leave when you have fallen asleep.

Vinay reassured the doctor that he would fall asleep as soon as he had left. The doctor went, apologizing for his crimes. Vinay made the daroga, who had become the image of decency and compassion, also leave on this pretext. He had thought, 'I'll see to him after memsahib leaves' but that desire had remained unfulfilled. Sardar sahib had emphasized to him before leaving that there should be no shortcoming in Vinay's care and hospitality, otherwise memsahib would send him to hell.

Concentration is as necessary for calm reflection as it is for meditation. The movement of the wind doesn't allow the scales to be evenly balanced. Vinay now reflected – What will ammaji think when she gets to know about this? So many of her desires are focused on me. She exiled me to save me from Sophie's love and she also maligned Sophie for this. She will be heartbroken. Pitaji will also be distressed, but he'll forgive me, he's sensitive to human weaknesses. Ammaji has only the mind, pitaji has both mind and heart. But why should I call this a weakness? I'm not doing anything exceptional. How many people in the world have sacrificed themselves for the country? It's only a few worthies who have done whatever they could for the country while also taking care of their self-interest. Those who have sacrificed everything for the country can be counted on one's fingers. And then the authorities of the country don't have justice and discrimination. The public doesn't have zeal and endeavour. No, it's futile to die for it. What can one get by crying before the blind except losing one's own sight?

Gradually, desires began to assemble the ingredients of happiness in life – I'll go and live in the countryside. I'll build a small house there, clean, open, airy. There's no need for much pomp and show. Both of us will go and live there peacefully, away from everyone. What's the use of ostentation? I'll work in the garden, lay the beds for flowers and vegetables, plant seedlings and surprise Sophie with my skill. I'll make bouquets and present them to her and ask with folded hands, 'Sarkar, some reward, please.' I'll send baskets of fruits to raniji and say, 'Raniji, some consideration, please.' Sophie will also water the plants sometimes. I'll fill water from the pond. She'll water the beds with it. Her delicate body will be wet with perspiration and her beautiful clothes with water. Then I'll make her sit down under a tree and sway the pankha. Sometimes we'll go for boat rides. There'll be a rustic canoe, one with oars. A motorboat doesn't give the same pleasure or the same rapture. Its speed makes one's head spin; its noise pierces the ears. I'll row the canoe; Sophia will pluck lotuses. We won't be separated even for a moment. Prabhu will come sometimes. Oh! It'll be such a blissful life. We'll both go home tomorrow, where Mangal awaits us with outstretched arms.

Sophie and Clark had been invited to a party by a jagirdar in the evening. When the tables had been laid and the conjuror from Hyderabad began to show his skills, Sophie took the opportunity of saying to Sardar Neelkanth – That prisoner's condition seems to be very serious to me. His heartbeat has become very slow. Why, William, did you see, his face had become so pale?

For the first time today Clark replied contrary to expectations – The face often becomes pale in a faint.

Sophie – That's what I was also saying, that his condition isn't good, why would he have fainted otherwise? You should hand him over to a good doctor. I think he has been punished enough for his crime and should be released now.

Neelkanth – Memsahib, don't go by his looks. You don't know how much influence he has over the public here. He can cause such a raging turmoil in the riyasat that it will be difficult to suppress it. He's very stubborn and not willing to leave the riyasat.

Clark – It's better to keep such a rebel imprisoned.

Sophie said excitedly – I think this is a grave injustice. And I've come to know for the first time today that you are so heartless.

Clark – I don't claim to be as kind-hearted as you.

Sophia looked at Clark's face with curiosity. From where did this arrogance and self-grandeur come? She said scornfully – A man's life is not such a trivial thing.

Clark – An individual's life has no significance for the protection of the empire. I believe in the compassion and generosity that fills the belly of a poor being, that removes his physical suffering and gives consolation to a distressed creature, and I'm proud that I'm not deprived of that wealth. But I consider the sympathy that will weaken the foundation of empire, encourage rebels, propagate anarchy among the public, to be not merely short-sightedness but madness.

The light of an inhuman energy could be seen on Sophie's face, but she controlled herself. Perhaps she had never before acted with such restraint. Devoutness and forbearance are antagonistic but one unrestrained word from her at this moment could ruin her entire life. She said mildly, 'Yes, from this point of view individual life undoubtedly has no value. I didn't think of this aspect. But I can still say that he won't step into this riyasat if he is released, and I can confidently vouch for it that he'll be true to his word.'

Neelkanth – Has he promised you?

Sophie – Yes, you can think of it as a promise. I can give a surety for him.

Neelkanth – I can also say this much that he won't go back on his promise.

Clark – I can't do anything until I get a written petition from him.

Neelkanth – Yes, that's essential.

Sophie – What will be the subject of the petition?

Clark – First he should admit his crime and give an assurance about his patriotism and then take an oath that he won't step into this riyasat again. There should be a surety with it too, either in cash or the guarantee of prestigious people. No matter how important your surety may be for me it has no value for the law.

Sophie thought, when she returned to the palace from the party – How can this problem be solved? I can persuade Vinay to leave the riyasat if I plead with him, but he'll never give a written oath. Even if I were somehow to make him consent to this by pleading and entreating, which prestigious person here will give a surety for him? Yes, cash can be sent from his home. But rani sahiba will never agree to this. She won't have mercy on Vinay no matter how much he may suffer. It would be best if there's no condition of a written petition or surety and he's freed illegally. There's no other way.

The palace was illuminated by electric lights. The black clouds of Saavan were lowering all around outside the palace and there was an impenetrable darkness outside. In that black ocean the illuminated palace seemed as if the moon had arisen in the blue sky. In her decorated room, sitting in front of the mirror, Sophie was awakening all the accomplishments whose powers are infinite. After ages today, she had braided flowers in her hair, she was wearing a turquoise silk sari, and there were bangles on her wrists. For the first time today, she was using those seductive arts at which women are accomplished. Only they know the mantra by which a toss of the hair, a wave of the aanchal can make the mind restless. She was determined to conquer Mr Clark's imperialism today; today she was going to test the power of her beauty.

The pitter-patter of raindrops was like flowers falling from the maulsiri tree.

There was a melodious sound in the raindrops. The palace on the mountain peak appeared as if the gods had decorated an assembly for a festival of joy. Sophia sat at the piano and began to sing a heart-rending raga. Just as the golden aura of dawn awakens every aspect of nature the moment it bursts forth, Sophie's first notes twisted the heart. Mr Clark came and sat down on a couch and began to listen enraptured, it was as if he were transported to another world. Sometimes he would imagine a boat rocking on the swelling ocean, over which tiny, beautiful birds hovered. And sometimes he would see a mendicant in an unending forest, with his bag on his shoulder, tapping his stick. Music makes the imagination picturesque.

Clark was engrossed as long as Sophie sang. When she stopped, he went to her and putting his hands on the arms of her chair, bringing his face close to hers, said – I'll keep these fingers in my heart.

Sophia – Where's the heart?

Clark put his hand on his chest and said – It's beating restlessly here.

Sophia – Perhaps, but I don't believe it. I think God hasn't given you a heart.

Clark – That's possible. But God's lack has been made up by your melodious voice. Perhaps it has the power to create.

Sophia – If I had that power, I wouldn't have felt humiliated before a stranger today.

Clark said impatiently – Did I humiliate you? I?

Sophia – Yes, you! I have perhaps never felt so distressed by your cruelty as I have been today. I have been taught since childhood that one should be compassionate towards every creature; I have been told that this is the greatest dharma of human beings. Even according to religious texts, compassion and sympathy are the special virtues of human beings. But it's clear today that cruelty is much more important than compassion. The greatest sorrow for me is that I was insulted in front of a stranger.

Clark – God knows, Sophie, how much I respect you. Yes, I do regret that I was forced to oppose you. You know the reason for this. Our empire can remain invincible only as long as the public is terrified of us and considers us to be its well-wishers, its protectors, its refuge, and has implicit trust in our justice. Our empire will end the day the public loses its confidence in us. If it's our aim to maintain the empire, then individual emotions and thoughts have no significance. We can suffer the greatest losses for the empire and practise the greatest austerities. Our rule is dearer to us than our lives, and we'll crush the person from whom we expect the slightest harm, we'll destroy him, we cannot show him any mercy or sympathy or even justice.

Sophia – If you imagine that I don't care for the empire as much as you do, and I can't make so many sacrifices for it, you haven't understood me at all. I can confidently claim that I'm not lagging behind anybody by even a jot on this issue. But I could never have imagined that there could have been so many differences between two lovers that there's no room for sympathy and tolerance, and especially in such a situation when there are other ears listening besides those of the wall. The deewan is devoid of the feelings of patriotism; he's not in the least familiar with its depth and extent. He must have thought that if there can be so much wrangling between these two in my presence, then who knows what the situation must be at home. Perhaps he has lost his respect for me from today. He must have narrated this incident to others as well. I have felt demeaned. You think that I'm singing, but this is not singing, it's crying. If this is the situation at the threshold of our wedding, when I should have been greeted with flowers, joyful music, loving embraces, gentle laughter, how can I have the courage to enter? You have broken my heart into

pieces. Perhaps you think that I'm being *sentimental** but I don't have
the power to change my nature. I congratulate myself that I have acted
with so much foresight on the subject of marriage.

Tears began to drip from Sophie's eyes. The sensation of actual grief
is aroused even when it is merely enacted. Mr Clark began to sing
the tune of regret and inability but he could find neither appropriate
words nor thoughts. The flow of tears doesn't allow a way out for
arguments or words. With great difficulty he said, 'Sophie, forgive
me; actually I hadn't thought that something so trivial would give
you so much mental pain.'

Sophia – I don't have any complaint about that. You are not my
slave that you should obey my wishes. I don't have the qualities that
can attract men's hearts, nor that beauty or appearance, nor the art of
arousing passion. I don't know how to flirt, or how to retire wrathfully
to my boudoir. I only regret that whereas that man heeded just one
sign from me, you go on refusing despite so much pleading. He's
also a man of principles; he suffered insults and the torture of the
authorities, he accepted imprisonment in a dark cell, but he resolutely
kept his promise. It didn't matter whether his insistence was right or
wrong but for him it was right. Fear or temptation or punishment
couldn't make him waver from what he thought to be just. But when
I gently explained to him that his condition was serious, he uttered
these pitiable words, 'Memsahib, I don't care about my life, it's not
a creditable thing to go on living after being degraded in the eyes of
one's friends and companions, but I don't want to refuse you. Your
words are sensitive, not harsh, and I have not yet become void of
feelings.' But no mantra of mine worked on you. Perhaps you are
more principled than he is, although this has not yet been tested.
Well, I don't want to act the jealous co-wife with your principles.
Please arrange a conveyance for me; I'll leave tomorrow and won't be
a thorn in your way with my follies.

Mr Clark said with deep anguish – Darling, you don't know what
a dangerous man he is. We are not so afraid of rebellion, conspiracies,
or battles, as of such resoluteness and perseverance. I'm also a human
being, Sophie, although this claim seems inappropriate coming from

---

* In English in the original.

me at this time, but at least in the name of that pure soul, whose extremely humble devotee I am, I have the right to say this—I respect that youth from the bottom of my heart. I admire his firm resolution, his courage, his truthfulness. I know that he's the son of a wealthy father and that he can live like a prince engrossed in revelry but it's these fine qualities that have made him so invincible. It's not so difficult to face an army as it is to face a few such people who take vows and don't fear anything in the world. My patriotism has tied my hands.

Sophie realized that her threat had not been entirely unsuccessful. The tongue had uttered words of helplessness, the heart had felt regret, and the first goal of consent had been attained. She also realized that her blandishments wouldn't be as effective at this moment as strong insistence. A man of principles can strengthen his heart and resist blandishments, he can't acknowledge his weakness before his inner being, but he becomes powerless when confronted with obstinacy. Then he can't get his way. Giving him a sidelong glace, Sophie said, 'If your duty to your country is dear to you, my self-respect is dear to me. Nobody has yet defined patriotism but protecting the honour of women is a prominent aspect of it, and so it should be, you can't deny this.'

She went to the table as if she were the mistress and took out a docket letter on which the Agent wrote his orders.

Clark – What are you doing, Sophie? For God's sake, don't be stubborn.

Sophia – I'll write an order in the name of the jail's daroga.

She then sat down in front of the typewriter.

Clark – Don't make this mistake, Sophie, there'll be disaster.

Sophia – I'm not afraid of a calamity, let alone a disaster.

Sophie pronounced each word as she typed the order. At one place she deliberately typed an inappropriate word that should not have been there in an official letter. Clark prompted her – Don't type this word.

Sophia – Why, I shouldn't 'express my gratitude?

Clark –Where's the need to mention gratitude in an order? It's not personal.

Sophia – Yes, that's right, I'll remove this word. What should I write below?

Clark – There's no need to write anything below, there'll only be my signature.

Sophia read out the entire order.

Clark – Dearest, what you are doing is wrong.

Sophie – It doesn't matter, I want to do wrong. Should I type the signature as well? No (*taking out the stamp*), I'll stamp it.

Clark – Do whatever you want. What can I say when you're so obstinate that you can't distinguish between right and wrong?

Sophia – Will this be copied anywhere else?

Clark – I don't know anything.

Mr Clark then went towards his bedroom. Sophie said – You are feeling sleepy so soon today?

Clark – Yes, I'm tired. I want to sleep now. There'll be chaos in the riyasat because of your letter.

Sophia – I'll tear the letter if you are so afraid. I don't want to tickle so much that it stimulates tears instead of laughter. Come and sit or I'll tear this envelope.

Clark sat down on the chair indifferently and said – All right, I've sat down, what do you want to say?

Sophia – I don't want to say anything. Listen to a song of gratitude before you go.

Clark – There's no need for gratitude.

Sophie began to sing again and Clark sat listening quietly. There was a tender desire for love reflected on his face. For how much longer this scrutiny and examination? Is there any end to this play? This desire liberated him from anxiety about empire. 'Ah! If only I knew whether you are happy at getting such a big present!' Sophia greatly fuelled his passion and then she suddenly shut the piano, and without saying anything, went to her bedroom. Clark remained sitting there, like a tired traveller sitting alone under a tree.

Sophie spent the whole night drawing pictures of her future life but she couldn't paint it as she wanted to. She would first paint a picture and then stand back a little to view it, it would seem that there was shade where there should have been sunlight, and sunlight where there should have been shade, there was too much red, an unnatural beauty in the garden, too much greenery on the mountains, transcendental peace in the rivers. When she'd take up her brush again to rectify these deficiencies, the entire scene would seem too arid, melancholy and tarnished. Because of her piety she now regarded her life as God's design. Now God was her helmsman; she was free from the sins and virtues of her good and bad deeds.

Mr Clark was still asleep when she got up in the morning. It was raining heavily. She called the chauffeur and ordered him to get the car and promptly left for the jail, like a child running home from school.

There was turmoil in the jail when she arrived. The chowkidars scurried to wear their uniforms. Darogaji wore his achkan inside out in his haste and ran out swiftly. Doctor sahib came running barefoot, he couldn't remember where he had kept his shoes at night and he didn't have the time to look for them now. Vinay had gone to sleep very late and was still sleeping soundly. There was a breeze in the room, moist with dew. A soft carpet had been spread. The night lamp had not been switched off, as if it was testifying to Vinay's restlessness. Sophie's handkerchief was still lying on Vinay's pillow and a fragrant perfume was emanating from it. The daroga salaamed Sophie and she went with him to Vinay's room. She saw that he was still asleep. His face had blossomed like a flower in his deep sleep. There was a slight smile on his lips like rays shining on a flower. Vinay had never before seemed so beautiful to Sophie.

Sophie asked the doctor – How was he during the night?

Doctor – Huzoor, he fainted several times, but I didn't leave him even for a moment. I went to eat only after he had fallen asleep. He seems to be very well now.

Sophie – Yes, I think so too. That pallor isn't there today. I want to ask him now if I should have him sent to another jail. The climate here doesn't suit him. But he won't speak openly in your presence. If you people could leave for a moment, I'll wake him up and ask him and also take his temperature. (*Smiling*) Doctor sahib, I'm also familiar with this knowledge. I'm a quack, but I'm not a risk to life.

When there was solitude in the room, Sophie put Vinay's head on her thigh and began gently to stroke his forehead. Vinay opened his eyes. He got up startled as if he had slipped into a river in his sleep. Seldom perhaps had anyone's dreams been realized so promptly.

Sophie said smiling – You are still asleep. Look at my eyes; they didn't blink all night.

Vinay – Who can be more unfortunate than I if I don't sleep soundly after obtaining the brightest jewel in the world?

Sophia – I've got ensnared in even more worries after getting an even brighter jewel. I'm afraid of losing it. There's the comfort of sleep only in the absence of worries. All right, now get ready.

Vinay – What for?

Sophia – Have you forgotten? To come into the light from this darkness. To leave this cell. I've brought the car and the order for your release is in my pocket. There's no dishonourable condition. There's only an oath not to enter the state of Udaipur without permission. Let's go. I'll drop you at the railway station and then return. Wait for me after you reach Delhi. I'll meet you there within a week and then even God won't be able to separate us.

Vinay's plight was like that of a child who sees a hamper of mithai but is afraid to open his mouth for fear of being beaten by amma. His mouth begins to water at the memory of the taste of the mithai. 'The rasgullas are so juicy, it seems as if the teeth have slipped into a pool of juice. The imartis are so crisp; they must also be very juicy. The gulab jamuns are so fragrant that one can go on eating them. One can't have enough of mithai. Amma won't give me money. She probably doesn't have it, whom will she ask? She'll start crying if I sulk too much.' With tearful eyes, Vinay said, 'Sophie, I'm an unfortunate man, leave me to my plight. Don't ruin your life along with me. God has made me only to suffer. I'm not worthy enough that you . . .'

Sophia cut him short and said – Vinay, I'm hungry only for difficulties. I would have turned away from you if you had been replete with happiness, if your life had been luxurious, if you had been a slave of desires. Your truthful courage and sacrifice have attracted me to you.

Vinay – You know ammaji, she'll never forgive me.

Sophia – I'll calm her anger if I get the shelter of your love. Her heart will melt when she sees that I'm not a chain binding your feet but the dust flying behind you.

Vinay looked lovingly at Sophie and said – You don't know her nature. She gives her life for the Hindu dharma.

Sophia – I also give my life for the Hindu dharma. I have found the spiritual peace that I couldn't get anywhere else in the love stories of the gopis. Where's the true Hindu who'll scorn me if I go as the servant of that avatar of love who made the gopis drink the nectar of love, who rowed Kubja's boat to the shore,* who sanctified the earth with his feet only to reveal the mysteries of love?

Vinay said smiling – So that trickster has also cast his spell on you? I think that Krishna's love story is only the imagination of devotees.

Sophia – That's possible. But the Lord Messiah is often said to be imaginary too. Shakespeare is also mere imagination. How can anyone assert that Kalidasa was created by the five elements? But we are devotees of the sacred glory of these men despite their being imaginary, more than we are of the glory of actual men. Perhaps because they have been created not by gross atoms but by subtle imagination. These may or may not be the names of human beings; they are definitely the names of ideals. All these men embody an ideal of human life.

Vinay – Sophie, I can't get the better of you in an argument. But I feel that I'm taking undue advantage of your simple warm-heartedness. I'm telling you from my heart, Sophie, you are not seeing my real self. You may not even want to look at me if you happen to see it. You may not be the chains binding my feet, but you are sure to become the breeze that will awaken the fire suppressed in me. Mataji has thought carefully about putting me under this vow. I'm afraid that once I'm released from this bond, desire will sweep me away so fast that there may be no trace of my existence. Sophie, don't put me through this difficult test. Actually I am a very weak, sensual person. Your ethical greatness is making me fearful. Yes, at least do me the favour of going somewhere far away from here today.

Sophie – Do you want to run away so far from me?

Vinay – No, no, there's another reason for it. For some reason, an order has been passed that Jaswantnagar will be vacated for a week. No young man will be allowed to remain in the qasba. I think sardar sahib has made this arrangement for your safety, but people are vilifying you.

---

* Kubja: Reference to Krishna's encounter on his way from Vrindavan to Mathura with Kubja, a hunchback girl, who prepared perfumes for Kansa, Krishna's uncle who had usurped the throne of Mathura. Krishna healed Kubja's deformity.

Neelkanth had immediately passed this order on hearing the continuous arguments between Sophie and Clark. He was sure that sahib would never get his way before memsahib and Vinay would have to be released. That's why it was essential to take measures to maintain the peace. Sophie asked, surprised, 'Has such an order been given?'

Vinay – Yes, I have this information. A chaprasi mentioned it.

Sophie – I have no information at all about this. I'll go and find out about it right now and get this order repealed. Such excesses don't happen anywhere else except in riyasats. All this will get done but you have to come with me right now.

Vinay – No, Sophie, forgive me. The beautiful scene at a distance becomes a desert when it comes close. You are an ideal for me. I can enjoy the bliss of your love only in my imagination. I'm afraid of falling in your eyes. For how long can I live secretively? My life will again become arid if I attain you, I won't have anything to worship or to strive for. Sophie, I don't know what nonsensical things I'm saying. I myself doubt whether I'm in my senses or not. It's not surprising if a mendicant's mind begins to waver after ascending the throne. Let me remain here. My last request to you is to forget me.

Sophie – My memory is not so inert.

Vinay – At least don't force me to go away from here because I have decided not to. Seeing the situation in the qasba, I'm not sure that I can control the public.

Sophie said gravely – As you wish. You are far more diplomatic than I had thought you to be with your simplicity. I understand what you mean, and that's why I'm saying, as you wish. But perhaps you don't know that a young woman's heart is like that of a child. It will leap towards whatever is denied it. I may have become disinterested in you if you had praised yourself or if you had subtly boasted about your work. You have conquered me even more by revealing your faults and defects. You are afraid of me, that's why I won't come before you, but I'll still stay with you. I'll accompany you like a shadow wherever you go. Love is emotional, it's nurtured only by emotions, it lives only by emotions, and it vanishes only by emotions. It's not something physical. You are mine; this confidence is enough to keep my love alive and satisfied. This life will come to an end the day the roots of this confidence are shaken. If you have decided that you can achieve the goal of your life more successfully by staying in this prison, I bow my head before your decision. This asceticism has greatly increased my respect for you. I'll go now but I'll return tomorrow evening. You'll be surprised when I tell you what womanly wiles I have used to get this order. One 'no' from you has thrown water over all my efforts. Clark will say, 'I told you, he'll never agree,' he'll perhaps make fun, but it doesn't matter, I'll make some excuse.

Sophie's lips, tormented with desire, bent towards Vinay but she controlled herself from falling like somebody whose foot had slipped on scum. She softly pressed his hand and went towards the door but she returned and said humbly – Vinay, I want to ask you something. I hope you'll tell me frankly. I came here with Clark, I deceived him, I gave him false hopes and I'm still keeping him under an illusion. Do you think that this is improper, am I tainted in your eyes?

Vinay had only one possible answer to this question. Sophie's conduct seemed objectionable to him. He had also communicated this by his surprise as soon as he had seen her. But he couldn't express this feeling at this moment. That would have been a grave injustice and such great cruelty! He knew that Sophie had done all this under the influence of a religious belief. She thought it to be divine inspiration. She would probably have despaired by now if that had not been so. In such a situation the bitter truth would be like a thunderbolt. He said promptly, with deep respect, 'Sophie, you are doing yourself, and me even more, an injustice. So far you have made only sacrifices for me, without caring about respect, prosperity, principles. I would be the most ungrateful person in the world if I were to disdain this love.'

He stopped while he was speaking. Sophie said – Do you want to say anything else, why have you stopped? Isn't it because you don't like my being with Clark? I'll kick Clark away the day I despair that I can't do anything for you through deception. After this you'll see me in the guise of a yogini of love whose only aim in life will be to dedicate herself to you.

27

NAYAKRAM LEFT FOR UDAIPUR AFTER TAKING LEAVE OF THE muhalla-valas. The passengers on the train soon began to respect him a great deal. He'd rub tobacco for someone, or fondly take somebody's child on his lap. If he saw that a passenger couldn't find a place and was wandering around, being pushed in every compartment, he would call him and make him sit by his side. And then he would soon begin to ask question after question – Where is your house? Where are you going? How many sons do you have? What is your business? These questions would end with the request, 'My name is Nayakram Panda. Mention my name whenever you go to Kashi, every child there knows it. You can stay there comfortably for a few days or months, for as long as you like; you'll find everything, a house as well as servants; you'll get all the comforts of home; give whatever you wish when you leave, don't give if you don't have anything. There's nothing to worry about, send it when you return home. Don't ever think that there's no money now so we'll go later. One shouldn't wait for an auspicious time for good work; just take the train fare and leave. I'm there in Kashi; you won't face any difficulties. We are prepared to risk our lives when there's some work to be done; so don't put off a pilgrimage. Nobody knows when he'll have to make the long journey; the problems of the world are never-ending.'

Several new passengers boarded the train when they reached Delhi. They were going to an Arya Samaj function. Nayakram began to ask them the same questions. One of them said angrily – Why do you want to know about our forefathers? We won't be trapped in your net. We don't believe in Gangaji, nor do we think that Kashi is the city of heaven.

Nayakram was not in the least put off. He said smiling – Babuji, you are an Arya and you are talking like this. It's the Aryas who have maintained the honour of the Hindu dharma otherwise the whole country would have become Musalmaan-Kirastaan. You are the saviours of the Hindu dharma so how can you not believe in Kashi? Raja Harishchand had to go through his ordeals in that city,* it was there that Buddha bhagwan preached his dharma-chakra, it was there that Shankara bhagwan debated the Shastras with Mandana Misir;** Jains, Bauddhs, Vaishnavas go there. It's not the city of Hindus alone, but of the whole world. The pilgrimage of people who come from afar is not successful unless they have a darshan of Kashi. Gangaji liberates and removes sins—all that is only for the diversion of the ignorant. They won't know what you are talking about if you tell them to go and see that sacred city where the marks of the Aryas can be found at every step, whose name recalls the memories of countless mahatmas, rishis and munis. But this is actually the fact. The importance of Kashi is in its being the living ancient city of the Aryas.

These men didn't have the courage to criticize Kashi again. They felt embarrassed and became convinced about Nayakram's knowledge of dharma, although Nayakram had mugged up these few sentences from somebody's speech only for such occasions.

He would be sure to get down at the railway stations and get to know the railway staff. Somebody would give him paan to eat; someone else would give him refreshments. The entire journey was over but he didn't lie down at all or sleep a wink. If he saw two travellers fighting,

---

* Raja Harishchandra: The twenty-eighth king of the lunar dynasty in Hindu religious texts. Renowned for his truthfulness and for keeping his promise, for which he had to suffer several ordeals and had to go through various tests, including penury, separation from his family and bondage. These finally ended in Banaras.

**Adi Shankara (788–820 CE), whose teachings are based on the non-dualism or advaita of the Vedanta, propagating the unity of the atman (the soul) and the brahman (the Supreme Being without attributes).

Mandana Mishra (c. eighth century CE) a contemporary of Shankara, best known as the author of *Brahmasiddhi*, who believed in the importance of the stage of the householder and the value of karma, denouncing the value of sanyas or renunciation. The reference is to the debate between Shankara and Mandana Mishra over several days on several philosophical subjects, in which Shankara won and, according to some accounts, Mandana then became one of his four main disciples.

he would promptly become the mediator and reconcile them. He reached Udaipur on the third day and, after meeting the authorities of the riyasat and wandering around, he entered Jaswantnagar. He saw that Mr Clark was encamped there. Outsiders were being thoroughly investigated, the doorway of the town seemed to be shut, but who can stop a panda? On reaching the qasba he wondered how to meet Vinay. He stayed in a dharmashala at night and reached the house of the jail's daroga as soon as it was morning. Darogaji had just seen Sophie off and was scolding the servants for not filling his huqqa. Meanwhile, he heard Pandaji's footsteps in the veranda and came out. Nayakram promptly took out a bottle of Gangajal as soon as he saw him and sprinkled his head with the water.

Darogaji asked absent-mindedly – Where have you come from?

Nayakram – Maharaj, I'm from Paraagraj* but I have come from very far. I wanted to give my blessings to the patrons here too.

Darogaji's son, about fourteen-fifteen years old, came out. Nayakram scrutinized him from head to toe, as if he was very happy to see him, and said to darogaji – He's your son, isn't he? May he live long! Father and son are so alike that he can be recognized from afar. Chhote thakur sahib, what are you studying?

The boy said – I'm studying English.

Nayakram – I had already realized this. Nowadays there's a craze for this subject; after all it's the language of the rulers. In which class are you studying, bhaiyya?

Daroga – He has just begun learning English, but he's not interested even in that, he has studied very little so far.

The boy thought he was being insulted. He said – At least I've studied more than you.

Nayakram – That's nothing to worry about, he'll get to know everything. What's his age after all? With God's blessings, he'll bring honour to the family's name. Do you have any land as well with your house?

Darogaji understood now. His intellect was not very sharp. He sat stiffly on a chair and said – Yes, I have several villages in the region of Chittor. It's an old jagir. My father was a courtier with the maharana.

---

* Prayag (Allahabad).

Rana Pratap gave this jagir to my ancestors during the battle of Haldighat.* Even now I get a seat in the durbar and I'm welcomed with paan-ilaichi. A messenger comes from the maharana if there's any function. The maharana sent a condolence letter when my older son died.

Nayakram – What can one say of a jagirdar? A jagirdar is a raja. The difference is only in the name. The real rajas are the jagirdars, the rajas are there only in name.

Daroga – There's constant interaction with the royal family.

Nayakram – Are there negotiations going on anywhere about him?

Daroga – Aji, people are after my life. There's a message from somewhere or the other every day but I give them all a blunt answer. It's folly to marry off the boy until he completes his studies.

Nayakram – You are right. Actually this is how it should be. The intellects of big people are also big. But customs have to be followed. All right, give me permission to leave now; I have to go to several places. But don't give your word to anybody until I return. You won't find such a girl or such a good family.

Daroga – Vaah-vaah! You'll leave so soon? At least eat something. We would like to know whose message you have brought. Who are they? Where do they live?

Nayakram – You'll get to know everything, but I don't have permission to say anything just now.

The daroga told the boy – Tilak, go and get a paan made for pandit-ji and also bring some refreshments.

He followed Tilak inside and said to his wife – There's a message from somewhere for Tilak's marriage. Send the paan on a plate. Aren't there any refreshments? I knew that. No matter how many things come into the house, there's no sign of them again. From where have all these famished people come? Only yesterday a whole thaal of mithai had come from a prisoner's house, what happened to it?

Wife – Ask these boys what happened. I vow that I didn't even touch it. This is not something to be locked in a box. They just take

---

* The battle of Haldighati (June 1576) between Maharana Pratap of Mewar and the Mughal army of Akbar.

it out and eat it when they want to. Nobody has even looked at rotis since yesterday.

Daroga – What are you there for? When something comes to the house you can't even put it away carefully and use it properly. Where has that lad gone?

Wife – You are the one who had scolded him just now, so he has left. He says that he can't put up with this constant scolding.

Daroga – This is another problem. These small people become insolent day by day, for how long can one go on pacifying them? Now who'll bring mithai from the bazaar? I can't even send a sepoy today; I don't know when I'll be rid of this nuisance. Tilak, you go.

Tilak – Why don't you give him sharbat?

Wife – There's no sugar. Why don't you go?

Tilak – Yes, why don't you go? People will see that hazrat is carrying mithai.

Daroga – So how's that an abuse? You are not stealing from anybody's house. You should feel ashamed of doing something wrong. Where's the shame in doing your own work?

Tilak would normally not have gone to the bazaar despite repeated pleas, but he went now because he was happy about his marriage. Darogaji put some paan on a plate and took it to Nayakram.

Nayakram – Sarkar! I won't eat paan at your house.

Daroga – Aji, where's the harm? Nothing has been settled yet.

Nayakram – Everything will be all right if I'm satisfied.

Daroga – This is a big problem that you have created. It isn't possible that you should come to our door and we'll let you leave without fitting hospitality. I may agree, but Tilak's mother won't on any account.

Nayakram – That's why I had refused to bring this message. If you go to any good person's door, he won't let you go without food and dachhina. That's why some impostors have made finding a groom into a business, and I feel even more embarrassed doing this work.

Daroga – Such villains come here daily but I don't offer them even water. A person gets a beeda according to his face. I can gauge the pulse of every person at a glance. You can't go like this.

Nayakram – I would have talked like an impostor if I had known that you would be after me like this. At least I could have escaped.

Daroga – I'm not such a novice, I can recognize a flying bird.

Nayakram made himself comfortable. By afternoon, he had become friendly with everybody. The darogain also sent her respectful greetings. Blessings were sent in return. The daroga had left for the office at 10 a.m. Puris, kachauris, raita, dahi, chutney, halva were made in the house with great care for Nayakram. Panditji went in to eat. The mistress of the house herself swayed the pankha. Then he established his influence even more. He began to read the palms of the boys and girls. The darogain also shyly showed her palm. Panditji gave a good account of his knowledge of palmistry. His authority increased. When darogaji returned from the office in the evening, panditji was ensconced in style, resting on a cushion, surrounded by several people from the neighbourhood.

The daroga settled down on a chair and said – This position is not so high, and the pay is not much either but the work calls for so much responsibility that it's given only to those who are trustworthy. Important people come here when they are sentenced for a crime. I can collect thousands of rupees from their relations for each visit if I want to, but that's not my way. What I get from sarkar is enough for me. A coward couldn't last here a moment. One murderer after another, dacoits and rascals, keep coming here; they have several companions; they can get the jail looted in broad daylight if they want to but I put them in awe of me in such a way that I don't lose my reputation and I don't have to suffer any loss. In fact, right now, there's a crorepati raja from Kashi, Maharaja Bharat Singh, whose son has been accused of rebelling against the state. Even the rulers respect him so much that burra sahib's memsahib comes here twice a day to ask about his welfare and Sardar Neelkanth regularly writes letters to enquire about his well-being. If I want, I can get lakhs from Maharaja Bharat Singh for just one meeting, but that's not my dharma.

Nayakram – Achcha? Is Raja Bharat Singh's son imprisoned here?

Daroga – Who else does sarkar trust so much?

Nayakram – It's difficult to get a darshan of such mahatmas as you. But if you don't mind, I'll say that you should take care of your family as well. A man leaves the house only to earn a few paise.

Daroga – Arey! I haven't taken a vow but I don't throttle anyone. Come, I'll take you around the jail. It's a very clean place. When I have guests, that's where I put them up. What else can you get if you are friendly with the jail's daroga except the air of the jail?

The daroga smiled when he said this. He wanted some excuse to put him off. The servant had run away; it was not an occasion for using prisoners and chaprasis. He thought, 'I'll have to fill the chillum myself, draw the water and also make the bed. It will be difficult to maintain our status and the real situation of the house will be revealed. If I put him up there and also send food, the curtain will remain.

Nayakram – Come, who knows, some day I may have to come here in your service. Let me see the place of residence beforehand. What was the crime of the maharaja sahib's son?

Daroga – There was no crime, it was just the stubbornness of the authorities. He would go around preaching in the villages; bas, that was enough to make the authorities suspect that he was spreading rebellion against the state. He was brought here and imprisoned. But you'll see him soon. I've never before seen such a grave, calm, thoughtful man. Yes, he doesn't submit to anyone. He may fill water for someone if he's requested, but he won't submit a jot if he's forced.

Nayakram was delighted inwardly because he had left at such an auspicious moment that God was himself opening all the doors for him. 'Let me see now what the conversation will be like with Vinay Singh. As it is, he won't leave; I'll have to make an excuse of raniji's illness. If he agrees, then it's my job to take him away from here. If God has mercy I'll get my wish, I'll settle down, my life will be fulfilled.'

28

AFTER SOPHIA HAD LEFT, SEVERAL DOUBTS AROSE IN VINAY'S MIND. The mind has a timid enemy who always attacks from behind. So long as Sophie was there, it didn't have the courage to come out in the open. As soon as Sophie turned her back, it began to hammer its beat – I don't know how my words have affected Sophia. I hope she didn't think that I've taken a vow of service for my entire life. I'm so dim-witted, I made her afraid of mataji's displeasure, like innocent children who have the habit of always threatening to tell amma. It's highly unethical of me to dissemble about my vow of service and duty when she is making so many sacrifices for me and is even prepared to break the sacred bond of religion. She probably thinks that I'm cruel, timid and heartless. It's true that philanthropy is the ideal way of life, but it's not always possible to sacrifice self-interest. Even the greatest patriot is inclined towards it. It's enough to efface just a part of self-interest for the sake of patriotism. This is the law of nature. Ah! I've cut my feet with my own hatchet! She's so self-respecting yet she has suffered so many insults for my sake. If her mother had insulted her as much as mine has, she wouldn't have seen her face again. What was I thinking of? I'm definitely not worthy of her, her strong determination makes me afraid. But can't my devotion make up for my faults? If a self-serving, dim-witted man like Jahangir could make Noorjahan happy, can't I make her content with my self-sacrifice and love? I hope she doesn't become indifferent to me forever because of my coldness. Life will be unbearable if this is the result of my vow of service, of my mother worship and of my diffidence.

Ah! What unique beauty! There's such spiritual gravity on her face because of her high education and thoughts. It seems as if a devi has descended from Indralok, who has nothing to do with the external world, and who inhabits only the inner world. Contemplation makes natural beauty so charming. The real adornment of beauty is elevated thoughts. Clothes and jewellery destroy its natural charm and make it artificial and carnal. Only *vulgar** words can express this distinction. The difference between ornamental and refined beauty is that between laughter and a smile, sunlight and moonlight, music and poetry. Her smile is so attractive, like the cool breeze of spring or a poet's inviolable vision. One often feels dejected if one talks to a beautiful woman, either her sheen-kaaf are incorrect or she doesn't know anything about gender difference.** To scorn vows, customs and principles for Sophie is not only forgivable but also admirable. This is a question of life and death for me. Without her, my life will be like a withered tree, which can't flourish again even if it is watered with continuous rain. The validity and purpose of my life will vanish. Life will go on but joyless, loveless, aimless.

Vinay was absorbed in these thoughts when darogaji came, sat down and said – It seems that this nuisance will soon go away. Agent sahib is about to depart. Sardar sahib has made a proclamation in the town that it isn't necessary for anybody to leave the qasba now. It seems memsahib has given this order.

Vinay – Memsahib is a very thoughtful woman.

Daroga – It's very good that this happened or there would have been a revolt and hundreds of lives would have been lost. As you say, she's very thoughtful though she's so young.

Vinay – Are you sure that she'll leave?

Daroga – Yes of course. I don't go by hearsay. I keep track of the officers, hour by hour. Provisions and unpaid labour that were to be requisitioned for a week have been stopped.

Vinay – Won't she come here again?

Daroga – You are very impatient, as if you are infatuated with her.

Vinay (*Embarrassed*) – She had told me that she'd come to see me tomorrow.

Daroga – She may have said so but now she's getting ready to leave. I'm glad that I have escaped untarnished, because jailors everywhere else have been penalized.

After darogaji had left, Vinay thought – Sophia had promised to come tomorrow. Has she forgotten? Won't she come now? If only

---

* In English in the original.
**Sheen-kaaf: the Urdu alphabet; Urdu and Hindi are gendered languages.

she'd come once, I'd fall at her feet and say, 'Sophie, I'm not in my senses. Surely the devi isn't displeased with her devotee because he hesitates to touch her feet. This is not a sign of his disrespect but of infinite devotion.'

Vinay's agitation increased as the day went by. But there was nobody in whom he could confide his anguish. He thought – I'll somehow escape at night and go to Sophie. How unfortunate! She had even brought the order for my release; I don't know what demon possessed me then.

It was sunset. Vinay was walking in front of the office with his head bowed. All of a sudden he thought – Why don't I pretend to faint again? People here will be anxious and Sophie is sure to get news of me. She'll come to see me even if her car is ready. But I don't know how to pretend. I'll begin to laugh at myself and I'll be humiliated if I can't control myself. People will realize that I'm pretending. If only it would rain so heavily that she can't leave the house. But perhaps even Indra is my enemy, there's no sign of clouds in the sky, as if it's the cruel heart of a murderer. She'd be prevented from leaving even if something were to happen to Clark.

When it was dark, he felt angry with Sophie – Why did she promise to come tomorrow if she was to leave today, why did she deliberately lie to me? Will I never meet her again? If I do, I'll ask her then. She should have realized for herself that I was unstable. The state of my mind was not hidden from her. She knows of the inner conflict that rages so fiercely in my heart. On the one hand, there's love and devotion and, on the other, there's my vow, fear of my mother's disapproval and the embarrassment of social criticism. What's so surprising if somebody talks nonsense because of the combination of so many conflicting emotions? She shouldn't be annoyed with me in such a situation. She should have soothed my anguish with her love and sympathy. If she wants me to die wretchedly in this state, so be it. This fire in my heart will be pacified only when I die. Ah! These two days were so blissful! It's night now, I'll be locked up again in that dark, smelly cell. Who'll be there to ask if I'm living or dying? Even when I glimpsed the light of the lamp in this darkness, it vanished by the time I reached it.

Darogaji returned again but this time he was not alone, a pandit was with him. It seemed to Vinay that he had seen this pandit somewhere but he couldn't remember where. Darogaji stood talking to panditji for a long time. No one spoke to Vinay. He thought he must be mistaken. The prisoners lay down at night after eating. All the doors were shut. Vinay was trembling at the thought of returning to his cell but for some reason he was allowed to stay where he was.

The lights were extinguished. There was silence all around. Vinay stood there in the same agitated state, wondering how to escape. He knew that all the doors were shut; there was no rope, nor any friend. Despite that he waited at the door, hoping that he could think of a strategy. Expectation is the stick of the blind in despair.

A man could be seen coming from the front. Vinay thought it must be a chowkidar. He was afraid the man would be suspicious of him if he saw him standing there. Softly, he went towards his room. He had never before felt so afraid. Even a sepoy standing in front of a cannon is apprehensive when he sees a scorpion.

Vinay had just reached his room when that man also entered behind him. Startled, Vinay asked – Who is it?

Nayakram – I'm your slave, Nayakram Panda.

Vinay – How are you here? Now I remember, you were the one who was standing with the daroga with a turban tied. Your appearance was such that I couldn't recognize you. How did you come here?

Nayakram – It's you I have come to see.

Vinay – You're a liar! Do you have any patrons here?

Nayakram – Patrons, where? There's only my master here.

Vinay – When did you come? Is everything all right there?

Nayakram – Yes, everything is more or less all right. Kunwar sahib is very anxious ever since he heard about your plight, and raniji is also ill.

Vinay – Since when has ammaji been ill?

Nayakram – Since a month or so. She's wasting away. She neither eats nor drinks anything, she doesn't talk to anybody. One doesn't know what kind of a disease it is that no baid, hakim or doctor can understand it. Doctors have been called from afar but they can't diagnose the disease. They all say different things. A kaviraj has come from Calcutta; he says she can't be saved now. It's frightening to see how much she has wasted away. When she saw me, she said softly, 'Pandaji, now it's time for me to die.' I stood there and cried.

Vinay (*Sobbing*) – Oh God! Won't I ever see my mother again?

Nayakram – When I kept asking, does sarkar wish to see anyone, her eyes filled with tears and she said, I want to see Vinay once but it's not destined, I don't know what his plight must be.

Vinay wept so much that he began to hiccup. When he could control his voice somewhat, he said – Nobody has ever seen ammaji cry. I'm very anxious now. How will I get her darshan? I don't know for which sins God is punishing me.

Nayakram – I asked her, if you so order, should I go and bring him? As soon as she heard this, she quickly sat up and holding my hand, said, 'Will you bring him? No, he won't come; he's annoyed with me. He'll never come. If you can bring him it will be a great favour.' I left promptly on hearing this. Now don't delay, you'll regret it all your life if your mother's desire remains unfulfilled.

Vinay – How can I leave?

Nayakram – Don't worry about that, I'll take you. Since I have managed to come so far, it won't be difficult to escape.

Vinay thought a little and said – Panda, I'm prepared to leave but I'm afraid that ammaji will be annoyed; you don't know her nature.

Nayakram – Bhaiyya, there's no fear of that. She told me to bring you somehow. She even said that if necessary, even forgiveness should be asked for on this occasion.

Vinay – All right, then let's go, but how?

Nayakram – We'll jump over the wall, that's not difficult.

Vinay was apprehensive that someone would see them. 'What will Sophie say if she gets to know? All the authorities will mock me. Sophie will think, he claimed to be so truthful; where's that truthfulness now? If Sophie could somehow be given this information, she'd be sure to send the order for my release. But how can I tell Nayakram about this?' He said, 'Suppose we are caught?'

Nayakram – We'll be caught! Who'll catch us? I'm not a novice. I've already fixed everyone.

Vinay – Think it over carefully. There'll be no escape if we are caught.

Nayakram – Don't talk about getting caught. Just look, there are bricks against the wall. I have already fixed all this. I'll stand on several bricks. You can get on to my shoulder and climb on to the wall with this rope. Throw the rope on the other side. I'll hold it fast here while you get down slowly. Then hold the rope fast on your side so that I can also escape. The rope is very strong; it won't break. But yes, don't let go of it or my bones will break.

Nayakram took the bundle of rope and stood near the bricks. Vinay too began to walk slowly. Suddenly, something rattled. Vinay said, startled – Bhai, I'm not going. Let me stay here. I'm not fated to see mataji.

Nayakram – Don't be afraid, it's nothing.

Vinay – My legs are trembling.

Nayakram – So it was with this resolve that you had come to poke your finger into the snake's mouth? One doesn't think of position and prestige in the face of danger.

Vinay – You are sure to get me caught.

Nayakram – You are a man and you are so afraid of being caught? Even if we are caught, we are not wearing bangles that they'll get soiled. To escape from the prison of the enemy is not something to be ashamed of.

He stood on the bricks and said to Vinay – Climb on to my shoulder.

Vinay – What if you fall?

Nayakram – Even if there are five riders like you, I can carry them and run with them. There's strength in the earnings from dharma.

He caught hold of Vinay's hand and hauled him up on to his shoulder as easily as if he were a child.

Vinay – Someone is coming.

Nayakram – Let him. Tie this rope around your waist and climb up with the help of the wall.

Now Vinay strengthened his resolve. This was the decisive moment. It needed only one leap. If he could reach the top, there'd be safety else there would be dishonour, shame, punishment. Heaven above and hell below, moksha above and a web of illusions below. He had no other help except his hands for climbing the wall. He was strong despite being thin. He leapt and reached his goal; he was on top of the wall and he then climbed down holding the rope. Unfortunately there was a deep ditch full of rainwater adjoining the wall. The moment Vinay let go of the rope, he was neckdeep in water and managed to emerge with great difficulty. Then he caught hold of the rope and signalled to Nayakram, who was an experienced player. He was down in a moment.

It seemed that he had been sitting on top of the wall, ready to jump.

Vinay – Be careful, there's a ditch.

Nayakram – I had seen it earlier. I forgot to tell you.

Vinay – You are an expert. I could never have escaped. Where shall we go now?

Nayakram – I'll first go to Devi's* temple and then take a car to the station. If God wills it, we'll reach home on the third day. This work couldn't have been done so quickly and so easily without Devi's help. She has removed this danger. I'll offer her my blood.

They were both free now. Vinay felt so light that it seemed to him as if his feet were moving of their own volition. In a short while, both of them reached the road.

Vinay – The bustle will begin as soon as it is morning.

Nayakram – We'll be miles away from here by then.

Vinay – They can also send a warrant home and arrest us.

Nayakram – Don't worry about that. It's our rule there.

There was a great deal of turmoil on the road today. Hundreds of men with lanterns were going towards the cantonment from the town. One group would come from one direction and another from somewhere else. Practically all of them were carrying sticks. Vinay was curious because there was such a crowd there today. There was a silent purposefulness among the people, which is a sign of a fierce agitation, but he couldn't question anybody for fear of being recognized.

Nayakram – We'll have to go on foot to Devi's temple.

Vinay – First ask these people where they are running to. I think there's trouble somewhere.

Nayakram – So what? How does it concern us? Come, let's go our way.

Vinay – No, no, just ask what it is.

When Nayakram asked somebody, he came to know that Agent sahib had come with memsahib in his car towards the bazaar around nine. The car was going very fast. When it reached the crossroads, it ran over a man who was coming from the left. Sahib saw the man being run over but didn't stop the car. Several men ran after it. By the time the car reached this side of the bazaar, several men had

---

* The goddess Durga, Shiva's consort.

surrounded it. Sahib scolded the people and told them to get out of the way immediately. When they didn't move, he fired his pistol. One of the men immediately fell down. Now, crazed with anger, the men were going to sahib's bungalow.

Vinay asked – Where's the need to go there?

One man – Whatever has to happen will happen. We'll get killed, isn't that all? We are being killed anyway. We have to die one day. The world won't be empty if a few men die.

Vinay lost his wits. He was convinced there would be an uprising today. An enraged public is like an unstoppable flow of water. 'These people are furious. It's futile to talk to them about patience and forgiveness at this time. They might surround the bungalow. Sophia is also there. They might attack her. Decency is destroyed in rage.' He said to Nayakram, 'Let's go to the bungalow.'

Nayakram – Whose bungalow?

Vinay – The Political Agent's.

Nayakram – What will you do by going there? Aren't you tired of philanthropy? It's their business, how does it concern us?

Vinay – No, it's a delicate situation. We must go there!

Nayakram – You are unnecessarily risking your life. What if there's a riot there? After all I'm also a man, I won't be able to look on silently. I'll also hit out. I'll be imprisoned, that's all. What's the use?

Vinay – It doesn't matter. I can't go to the station after seeing this turmoil.

Nayakram – Raniji will be asking about you every moment.

Vinay – But it's not as if we'll be staying here for a few days. You stay, I'll return soon.

Nayakram – If you are not afraid, then who's there to cry for me? I'll go ahead of you. Look, don't leave me. Take this, it's a dangerous affair. This stick is enough for me.

Nayakram took out a double-barrel pistol from his waist and put it in Vinay's hand. Vinay took the pistol and went ahead. When he approached the palace, there was such a throng there that it was difficult to take a step; he was forced to stop when a shot ricocheted off the palace wall. Only heads were visible. An electric lamp was burning in front of the palace and the swaying, restive, faltering, hesitating flow of people was moving towards the palace in its bright light as if it would swallow it. In front of the palace, a row of uniformed sepoys, with bayonets mounted, were standing silently to stop this flow, and Sophie was standing on a high platform, saying something but her voice couldn't be heard in this uproar. It seemed as if she was the image of a wise woman making a gesture of wanting to say something.

Suddenly Sophie raised both hands. There was silence all around. Sophie said in a loud and quivering voice – I'm warning you for the last time to leave peacefully, otherwise the soldiers will be forced to fire. This field should be cleared immediately.

Veerpaal came forward and said – The public can't put up with these atrocities any longer.

Sophia – Why would such accidents happen if people walked carefully?

Veerpaal – Isn't there any law for people who have cars?

Sophia – You don't have the right to make laws for them.

Veerpaal – We can't make laws but surely we can protect our lives?

Sophia – If you want to rebel, you will have to bear the evil consequences.

Veerpaal – We are not rebels but we can't remain silent if a brother of ours is run over by a car, even if it is the maharana's.

Sophia – That was a coincidence.

Veerpaal – Caution could have prevented that coincidence. We won't leave now until we get a promise that in future the criminal will get appropriate punishment for such accidents, no matter who he may be.

Sophia – Promises can't be given for coincidences. But . . .

Sophie wanted to say something when somebody threw a stone, which hit her head so hard that she sat down clutching it. Had Vinay instantly stood at some high point and reassured the public, perhaps there wouldn't have been a revolt and people would have gone home peacefully. Sophie being injured by a stone would have been enough to calm the public. But the stone that had wounded Sophie wounded Vinay's heart even more severely. He saw blood and lost control over himself. Forcefully parting the crowd, pushing and crushing people, he reached Sophie's side, took out the pistol from his waist, and shot Veerpaal Singh. And after that, it was as if the soldiers had been given orders. They began to fire. There was pandemonium but despite that, for several minutes, people stayed on, responding to the bullets with bricks and stones. A few shots were fired from the other side too. Veerpaal escaped by the skin of his teeth and, recognizing Vinay, said, 'You are among them too?'

Vinay – Murderer!

Veerpaal – Parmatma has turned away from us.

Vinay – Don't you feel ashamed raising your hand at a woman?

There were cries all around – It's Vinay Singh. From where has he come? He has also joined them; he's the one who had fired the pistol.

–He was just dissembling. The spy in the house burns Lanka.

–Perhaps he has been let off on a condition.

–He's obsessed with the lust for wealth.

–Throw a stone at him and break his head; he too is our enemy.

–He's a traitor.

–Such a big man and he has sold his honour for just a little money.

For how long could unarmed men resist the rifles? There was a stampede when several men from their side began to fall continuously and they began to run helter-skelter. But Veerpaal Singh and his five riders who held rifles closed in on Vinay from behind the palace. Nobody noticed them in the dark. Vinay was startled when he heard the sound of the horses' hooves behind him. He fired his pistol, but it was empty.

Veerpaal said sarcastically – You were supposed to be a friend of the public.

Vinay – It's against my principles to help murderers like you.

Veerpaal – But we are better than those who side with the authorities to cut the throats of the public.

Enraged, Vinay swooped like a hawk to snatch the rifles from their hands but a companion of Veerpaal pounced on Vinay so that he fell down, and another one was about to spring upon him with his sword when Sophie, who had been lying unconscious on the ground, screamed and got up and clung to Vinay. The sword didn't reach its goal but fell on Sophie. Meanwhile, Nayakram arrived with his cudgel and began to attack with it. Two of the rebels fell down, wounded. Veerpaal had been standing there at a loss until now. He didn't know who had thrown the stone at Sophie nor had he told his companions to attack Vinay. All this was happening before his eyes, but against his wishes. But he couldn't stand there indifferently when he saw his companions fall. He balanced the stock of his rifle and hit Nayakram's head so hard that it split and, in a moment, all his three companions took their wounded companions with them and escaped. Vinay got up carefully and saw that Nayakram was lying unconscious by his side, soaked in blood. There was no sign of Sophie. He had no idea who had taken her or why or where.

There was not a single man on the field, although a few corpses were scattered here and there. Where was Mr Clark? The storm came and was over, the fire was lit and had died out but he was nowhere to be seen. He was lying in his bedroom, intoxicated with liquor, oblivious to the world. Sophie had come out of the palace on hearing the rebels' noise. She didn't try to wake up Clark because she was afraid that his presence would cause bloodshed. She had wanted to maintain the peace by peaceful methods and this was the result. The situation may not have become so terrible if she had taken precautions.

Vinay looked at Nayakram. His pulse couldn't be found. His eyes were glazed. Vinay was so distressed by worry, grief and regret that he began to weep. He was worried about his mother whom he had not been able to meet. There was grief for Sophia; he didn't know who had taken her away. There was regret at his anger, which was the cause of this rebellion and bloodshed. This revolt could have been quelled if he had not fired at Veerpaal.

There were heavy, dark clouds in the sky, but the clouds of grief in Vinay's heart were far denser, more impenetrable and indiscernible.

29

LIKE HIS COMPATRIOTS, MR WILLIAM CLARK WAS A DEVOTEE OF liquor but not its slave. Unlike Indians, he didn't get intoxicated when he drank. He knew how to ride a horse without letting it get out of control. But today Sophie had deliberately made him drink too much; she would repeatedly instigate him, 'Vaah! Only so much, have at least one more glass, all right, this is for my sake. Vaah! You have not yet drunk to my health.' Sophie had promised to meet Vinay tomorrow but she didn't get a moment's peace because of what he had said. She thought, 'Why did Vinay find these new excuses today? I didn't even care about religion for his sake but he's still trying to run away from me. What can I do now? Is the god of love so hard-hearted that he's not pleased by the highest worship? He had never been so afraid of his mother's disapproval. His love has cooled now, that's all. This is yet another proof that men's hearts are fickle. His confession of his unworthiness seems so unnatural coming from him; he's so generous, detached, truthful, dutiful, and he tells me that he's not worthy of me! He doesn't know how devoted I am to him; I'm not fit even to touch his feet. What a pure soul, what brilliant thoughts, what spiritual self-sacrifice! No, he's making these excuses to distance himself from me. He's afraid that I'll be the chain binding his feet, I'll take him away from his path of duty, I'll turn him away from his ideal. How can I resolve his doubts?'

Having been absorbed in these thoughts all day, she was so agitated by evening that she decided to meet Vinay again at night. She had made Clark unconscious with liquor so that he wouldn't suspect anything. She had nothing to fear from the jail authorities. She had wanted to use this opportunity to entreat with Vinay, to awaken his love, to resolve his doubts but her attempt proved to be harmful for her. The situation may not have become so dangerous if Mr Clark had reached there in time and at least Sophie would not have had to suffer so much. Clark would have protected her with his life. Sophie had destroyed herself by deceiving him. No one knew her whereabouts or her plight. People generally thought that the rebels had killed her and had taken away her body with them because of their greed for her jewellery. Only Vinay Singh did not accept this view. He was convinced that Sophie was still alive and that the rebels had imprisoned her for ransom so that advantageous terms could be negotiated for a treaty. Sophie was a tool in their hands for pressurizing the riyasat.

This incident caused panic in the riyasat; the authorities as well as the public feared for themselves. It wouldn't have been a matter of great concern had it been confined among the officials of the riyasat. The riyasat would have been content with taking blood for blood, at the most it would have killed four people instead of merely one, but the problem had become complex because of Sophie. The matter was now outside its sphere of authority; in fact, people feared that some calamity might now befall the riyasat. That was why there was an unusual alacrity in capturing the criminals. People were imprisoned on the slightest suspicion and were subjected to the most dreadful torture. Witnesses and proofs no longer had any validity. A separate court had been set up to decide the fates of these criminals. The most experienced tyrants were selected and appointed on it. This court did not know how to acquit anyone. The testimony of a sepoy was sufficient to sentence an accused to death. Sardar Neelkanth was busy searching for the rebels day after day, without anything to eat or drink. In fact, His Highness the Maharaja Sahib himself was coordinating between Shimla, Delhi and Udaipur. Strict instructions were sent daily to the police officials. A succession of injunctions was sent from Shimla, followed by threats. Oppression increased here in the same proportion in response. Mr Clark was convinced that the riyasat also had a hand in this revolt. The rebels would not have dared to raise their heads if the riyasat had made life difficult for them from the start. Even the highest authorities of the riyasat trembled if they had to confront the rebels. They took a unit of the English cavalry with them when they went on tour and devastated region after region and ruined village after village. Even the women were tyrannized. The most regrettable fact was that Vinay was cooperating whole-heartedly with the riyasat and with Clark with his mind, words and actions in this tyranny. He was actually in a state of intoxication. The sentiments of service and philanthropy were completely obliterated from his heart. He was concerned only with finding the whereabouts of Sophie and her enemies. He didn't give a thought to what the world said about him, to the goal of his life, or to mataji's predicament. He had now become the riyasat's right hand. The authorities would incite him even more from time to time. No police officer or servant of the riyasat could have been so ruthless, thoughtless and unjust in repressing the rebels! There were no limits to his loyalty to the riyasat; rather it can be said that he was now its steersman, to the extent that even Sardar Neelkanth would submit to him. Maharana sahib began to trust him so much that he wouldn't do anything without his advice. There were no restrictions on his movements; Mr Clark and he were now close friends. They lived in the same bungalow and there was talk in the inner circles of Vinay replacing sardar sahib.

This free-for-all continued in the riyasat for about a year. When Jaswantnagar had been cleansed of the rebels, that is to say, when there were no young men left there, Vinay decided to search for Sophie himself. Several experienced men from the secret police were appointed to help him. Preparations were being made for their departure. Nayakram was still weak. In fact there had been no hope of his survival, but he was fated to live longer, so he survived. When he saw that Vinay was ready to leave, he decided to accompany him. He said, 'Bhaiyya, take me with you, I won't stay here alone.'

Vinay – I'm not going to a foreign country. I'll come here every seventh day, so I'll keep meeting you.

Sardar Neelkanth said – You are not fit to leave just now.

Nayakram – Sardar sahib, you are also talking like him. How will I show my face to raniji if I don't go with him?

Vinay – You'll be more comfortable here. I'm saying this for your good.

Nayakram – Sardar sahib, please explain to bhaiyya. Man doesn't control even a moment, let alone seven days. And then we have to overcome Veerpaal, whose power even I acknowledge. He fenced several such blows from my cudgel that if one of them had landed on him, that would have been the end. He's a seasoned cudgel player. Is my life dearer than yours?

Neelkanth – Yes, Veerpaal is one devil of a kind. No one knows when he'll attack, from where, and with how many men. His spies are spread all over the riyasat.

Nayakram – Then how can I leave him alone in this danger? How does it matter if I lose my life in the service of my master, and what's this life for, after all?

Vinay – Bhai, the fact is that I don't want to risk a stranger's life along with mine.

Nayakram – Yes, if you think that I'm a stranger it's a different matter. Of course, I'm a stranger. If I had not been a stranger, why would I have come running here at raniji's behest? How would I have brought him out of the jail? Why would I have been bedridden for a year? Sardar sahib, huzoor, now you should give justice. Am I a stranger? The person for whom I carry my life in my hands thinks that I'm a stranger.

Neelkanth – Vinay Singh, you are being unjust. Why do you call him a stranger? One's well-wishers feel distressed if you call them strangers.

Nayakram – Bas, sardar sahib, huzoor has said something worth a lakh of rupees. I'm a stranger but the policemen are not.

Vinay – If it makes you unhappy to be called a stranger, I take it back. I used it because I'm answerable to your family for you; I'm not answerable to anybody for the policemen.

Nayakram – Sardar sahib, now you answer this. How can I say that if anything happens to me, kunwar sahib won't make enquiries? After all, I have been sent by him. Bhaiyya will surely be answerable.

Neelkanth – He may have sent you, but you are not so innocent that Vinay Singh should be responsible for your welfare. You can take care of yourself. Won't kunwar sahib understand even this much?

Nayakram – Dharmavatar, now you'll have to take me with you, sardar sahib has given me a degree. I'm not a child that you are answerable to sarkar for me.

Finally, Vinay agreed to take Nayakram with him. After a few days, a group of ten people, disguised and fully equipped with search dogs, entered the inaccessible mountains. The mountains were breathing fire. There was often not a drop of water for miles on end; the paths were stony, there was no sign of trees. They rested in caves in the afternoons, and at night they lay down in a chaupaal or a temple away from the basti. The men were paired in twos. All of them had to gather together once after twenty-four hours. They would disperse again after deciding the programme for the next day. Nayakram and Vinay were paired. Nayakram was still too weak to move about, he would get tired and sit down when climbing the mountains, he also ate very little and had become so thin that it was difficult to recognize him, but he was ready to sacrifice his life for Vinay. He knew how to interact with the villagers and was acquainted with people of different temperaments and classes. There would be a hue and cry in every village where he went that the Pandaji from Kashi had arrived. Devotees would flock there, barbers and kahaars would reach there, there would be an abundance of milk and ghee, flowers and fruits, greens and vegetables, a khaat would be placed on the base of a temple, young and old, men and women, would go unabashed to Pandaji and give as much dakshina as they could. While conversing with them, Pandaji would get all the news of the village. Vinay now realized how many difficulties he would have had to face had Nayakram not been with him. Vinay was a man of few words by nature, shy and serious. He didn't have that aptitude for ruling that can terrorize the public, nor that melodious speech that can attract the heart. Nayakram's company was no less than divine help for him in this situation.

They would sometimes encounter beasts of prey. Nayakram would be a shield on such occasions. One afternoon, they walked along a path without a sign of habitation. It was difficult to take a step because of the dazzling sunshine. No well or pond was visible either. Suddenly they saw a high hillock. Nayakram climbed it, hoping that a village or a well may be visible. When he reached the top and looked around, he saw a man going into the distance. He was carrying a stick in his hand and a bag on his back. He seemed to be a sepoy without a uniform. He turned his head to look when Nayakram called out to him loudly several times. Nayakram recognized him. He was a volunteer who had accompanied Vinay. His name was Indradutt.

Indradutt asked – How have you been trapped here? Where is your kunwar?

Nayakram – First tell me if there's a village here where we can get something to eat and drink.

Indradutt – What can a person lack if his Rama is wealthy? Didn't the royal durbar supply any food? It's like marrying an oil miller and crying for oil.

Nayakram – What can I do, bhai, I've been badly trapped, I can neither stay nor leave.

Indradutt – You are defiling your honour as well along with him. Where is he these days?

Nayakram – What will you do?

Indradutt – Nothing, I just want to meet him.

Nayakram – He's here too. You can meet him here. Is there anything in your bag?

As they talked, they reached Vinay. On seeing Indradutt, Vinay said with hostility – Indradutt, why are you here? Why haven't you returned home?

Indradutt – I was very keen to meet you. There's so much that I want to talk to you about. First tell me, why have you changed your garb?

Nayakram – Take out something from your bag first and then we'll talk.

Vinay was always eager to justify his transformation. He said – Because I realized my mistake. I used to think that the public was very tolerant and peace-loving. Now I know that it is base and wicked. It misuses its power as soon as it becomes aware of it. It's better for a person to remain powerless and oppressed if he gets intoxicated as soon as he gets power. The present revolt is a shining example of this. In this situation whatever I have done and am doing is entirely just and natural.

Indradutt – Do you think that the public shouldn't protest, no matter how many atrocities are inflicted on it?

Vinay – Yes, that's its dharma in the present situation.

Indradutt – Should its leaders follow the same ideal as an example?

Vinay – Certainly!

Indradutt – In that case when you saw the public ready to rebel, why didn't you stand before it and preach patience and peace?

Vinay – It would have been futile. Nobody would have listened to me then.

Indradutt – If nobody would have listened, wasn't it your dharma to stand between the two sides and be a target for a bullet yourself first?

Vinay – I don't consider my life to be so worthless.

Indradutt – What better death could there have been for a life that has been dedicated to service and philanthropy?

Vinay – Jumping into the fire is not service. Subjugating it is service.

Indradutt – If that's not service, sacrificing the humble public to your amorous desires isn't service either. It was quite possible that Sophie could have silenced Veerpaal Singh with her arguments but you were overpowered by your passion and fired the first shot from your pistol. That's why you are entirely responsible for this bloody episode, and sooner or later you'll have to repent. Do you know how much the public hates your name? If anyone here recognizes you, the first thing he'll do will be to shoot an arrow at you. The stigma of your heinous betrayal of the public of this place, of your companions, of your country and, above all, of your respected mataji will never be effaced from your forehead. Raniji may stab you in the neck with her own hands when she sees you. What I've learnt from your life is how morally degraded a man can become.

Vinay said, a little more humbly – Indradutt, you are being very unfair to me if you think I helped the authorities for my self-interest. It's far easier to get notoriety for supporting the authorities than to win fame for supporting the public. I knew that. The dharma of a servant, however, is not to think of fame or notoriety but to walk on the right path. I have taken a vow of service, and I hope to God that I don't live to see the day when there is a mixture of self-interest in my desire to serve. But that doesn't mean that I should support the public when I see its impropriety. My vow can't kill my discrimination.

Indradutt – At least you do believe that the public shouldn't be harmed for the sake of self-interest.

Vinay – Somebody who doesn't believe this much is not fit to be called a human being.

Indradutt – Haven't you created difficulties for the entire public of the riyasat only for Sophia, and aren't you even now obsessed with its destruction?

Vinay – You are making a false accusation against me. I can't turn away from the truth for the sake of the public. Truth is dearer to me than both the country and the community. As long as I had believed that the public is on the side of the truth, I protected it. When it became evident to me that it had turned away from the truth, I also turned away from it. I don't have any internal differences with the authorities of the riyasat. I'm not the kind of person who'll unnecessarily oppose the rulers even when I see them being just, and nor can I support the public even when I see it bent on revolt and misguided zeal. If a man was run over by Miss Sophia's car, it was an accident. Sophia didn't deliberately run him over. For the public to have been excited like that in such a situation is living proof that it wants to control the authorities by force. By making allegations about my behaviour towards Sophia, you are not only being unfair to me but also tainting your own soul.

Indradutt – Why have these thousands of innocent men been killed? Was this also the public's fault?

Vinay – You would never have asked me this question if you had any idea about the difficulties faced by the authorities. You deserve forgiveness for this. Perhaps I had also thought this way a year ago when I had no relationship with the authorities. But now I have realized how many difficulties they have to face in order to be just on some occasions. I don't agree that a man is transformed as soon as he gets authority. Man is just by nature. He doesn't get pleasure by unnecessarily giving pain to others, but is as unhappy and distressed as a social worker. The only difference is that the social worker consoles himself by blaming someone else, that's where his duty ends; the authorities don't get that opportunity. They can't give explanations for themselves for their actions. You have no idea how many difficulties the rulers had to face in searching for the criminals. The public would hide the criminals and no political strategy had any effect on it. So it was quite possible for the innocent to be caught with the guilty. And then you don't know in what grave danger this revolt has placed the riyasat. The British government suspects that the durbar had created this entire conspiracy. Now it's the duty of the durbar to exonerate itself from this allegation and the riyasat's predicament is extremely disturbing as long as there's no clue about Miss Sophia. As an Indian it's my duty to remove this stigma from the riyasat, no matter how many insults, allegations and harsh words I have to bear, even if I lose my life. The situation of a patriot doesn't remain constant; it changes with circumstances. Yesterday I was the sworn enemy of the riyasat, today I'm its whole-hearted devotee, and this doesn't embarrass me at all.

Indradutt – God has given you the intelligence to argue and you can use it to prove that day is night, but no argument of yours can remove this belief from the heart of the public that you have betrayed it, and your eyes will be opened by the torment that you'll get from Sophia for this betrayal.

Vinay leapt and caught hold of Indradutt's hand as if he were going to run away and said – Do you know where Sophia is?

Indradutt – No.

Vinay – You are lying.

Indradutt – Possibly.

Vinay – You'll have to tell me.

Indradutt – You no longer have the right to ask me. I don't want to risk the lives of others to serve your purpose or the durbar's. You have betrayed once, you can do so again.

Nayakram – He'll tell us, why are you so anxious? Bhaiyya Indradutt, at least tell us if memsahib is all right.

Indradutt – Yes, she's very well and happy. At least she's never agitated about Vinay Singh. If you really want to know, she now hates his name.

Vinay – Indradutt, we are childhood friends. I'll give my life for you if the need arises, and you refuse to tell me such a small thing? Is this friendship?

Indradutt – Why should I endanger other people's lives for the sake of friendship?

Vinay – I swear by mataji's feet, I'll keep it secret. I want to meet Sophia just once.

Indradutt – A wooden pot can't be put on the fire again and again.

Vinay – I'll be obliged to you all my life.

Indradutt – Oh no! Even a docked cock is fine if the cat will let go of it.

Vinay – Take any oath from me that you want.

Indradutt – You are unnecessarily pleading with me to tell you something I don't have a right to.

Vinay – You have a heart of stone.

Indradutt – I'm even harder than that. You can reproach me as much as you like, but don't ask me anything about Sophia.

Nayakram – Yes, bhaiyya, now this refrain will go on. This is all that men can do. There's just a blunt answer that I know but I won't tell, whether anybody likes it or not.

Indradutt – So now the veneer has been removed, hasn't it? Why, kunwar sahib, now you won't talk big?

Vinay – Indradutt, now don't sprinkle salt on the wound. Tell me what I want to know otherwise you'll have to cry for my life. I have never before entreated anyone as much as I'm pleading with you, but it has no effect on you.

Indradutt – I've said that there's no way I can tell you something I don't have the right to. Your entreaties are futile. Here, I'm going my way. You go where you want to.

Nayakram – Sethji, don't run away. You can't leave before telling us where miss sahib is.

Indradutt – Will you force me?

Nayakram – Yes, I'll force you. I'm a brahman asking for alms and you are refusing, and then you pretend to be a dharmatma, a devotee, a servant. You should understand that a brahman doesn't go away from the door without alms; he remains sitting there if he doesn't get them and gets up only after getting them.

Indradutt – Don't use these tricks of pandas with me, do you understand? Those who give such alms are different kinds of people.

Nayakram – Why do you want to taint the names of your forefathers, bhaiyya? I'm telling you, you can't escape without giving these alms.

Nayakram then promptly sat down on the ground, clutched Indradutt's feet, put his head on them and said – Now do whatever is your dharma. I'm a fool, I'm a boor, but I'm a brahman. You are an intelligent person, do what you think is proper.

Indradutt still didn't relent, he tried to free his feet and to leave but it was evident from his face that he was in a great dilemma and that he was very embarrassed at having to reject this humility. He was a strong man; no other youth among the volunteers was as huge as he was. Nayakram was still weak. Indradutt was about to free his feet and escape when Nayakram said to Vinay, 'Bhaiyya, why are you standing there looking on? Catch hold of his feet; let me see how he won't tell.'

Vinay thought it improper to plead to attain his ends, let alone falling at anybody's feet. He wasn't embarrassed to express his humility before a sant or a mahatma if he respected him from his heart. He had not learnt to bow his head only to achieve his purpose. But there was no room for self-respect when he saw Nayakram falling at Indradutt's feet. He thought, 'If being a brahman, Nayakram can suffer this humiliation for my sake, it isn't right for me to stand on my dignity.' Although just a moment ago he had spoken rudely to Indradutt and was now embarrassed to entreat him ingratiatingly, there seemed to be no other way of getting news of Sophia. He surrendered his self-respect too to Sophie. 'I had only this one thing left that I had not yet given you. Now I hand over even that to you.' His soul did not wish to bow down even now, but his back was bent. His hands reached Indradutt's feet in a moment. Indradutt immediately pulled them away, tried to raise Vinay and said, 'Vinay, what's this absurdity?'

Vinay's plight was that of a servant whose master had given him the punishment of licking his spit. He wept at his humiliation.

Nayakram (*To Indradutt*) – Bhaiyya, you could shoo me away, thinking me to be a mendicant, but speak now.

Indradutt (*Embarrassed*) – Vinay, why are you embarrassing me so much? I have promised not to tell anyone this secret.

Nayakram – No one is forcing you. Do what you think is your dharma. You are intelligent enough.

Indradutt (*Annoyed*) – What's this if not force? Self-interest is crazy but today I have realized that it's also blind. Vinay, you are unnecessarily being unfair to your soul. Good man, have you dissolved your self-respect as well and drunk it? You should have given your life to protect your soul. You must have realized now how selfish desire can degrade a human being. I know that a year ago the whole world united could not have made you bow your head; today this is the extent of your moral degradation. Get up now and don't drown me in sin.

Vinay was so furious that he wanted to pull Indradutt's feet and climb on to his chest. The villain didn't stoop to sting even in this situation. But then realizing that what had happened had happened, he said remorsefully, 'Indradutt, I'm not as vile as you think but I can do anything for Sophie. My self-respect, my intelligence, my manly strength, my dharma have all been consumed in the havan-kund of love. If you still don't have pity on me, take my pistol from my waist and end it all with one aim.'

Vinay's eyes filled with tears. Indradutt raised him and embraced him, and said compassionately – Vinay, forgive me. Although you have harmed the country, I know that you only did what perhaps I or anyone else in your place would have done. I don't have the right to scorn you. If you have performed the final rites for your self-respect for the sake of your love, I'll also go back on my promise for the sake of friendship and decency. I'll tell you what you want to know. But it won't do you any good, because you have fallen in Miss Sophia's eyes, she now hates your name. You'll feel distressed if you meet her.

Nayakram – Bhaiyya, if you agree, it's his job to persuade miss sahib. Lovers are very shrewd operators, they are out and out scoundrels; they only look simple. They can win over the beloved with a snap of the fingers. They only have to look with eyes filled with tears for the beloved to melt.

Indradutt – Miss Sophia will never forgive me but from where can I get a heart like hers? Yes, tell me something. I can't tell you anything without getting an answer.

Vinay – Ask.

Indradutt – You'll have to go there alone. Promise that nobody from the secret police will accompany you.

Vinay – Don't worry about that.

Indradutt – If you go with the police, you won't find anything except Sophia's corpse.

Vinay – Why would I do something so stupid?

Indradutt – You should realize that by telling you where Sophia is, I'm putting the lives of those people in your hands in whose search you have abjured food and drink.

Nayakram – Bhaiyya, they won't be harmed even if we have to lose our lives. But tell us also if our lives are in danger there.

Indradutt (*To Vinay*) – You wouldn't be alive till now if those people had wanted to harbour any enmity against you. All the powers of the riyasat couldn't have protected you. They have information about each and every thing concerning you. You must realize that your life is in their hands. If you are still alive after oppressing the public so much, it's only because of Miss Sophia. It would not have been difficult for Miss Sophia to meet you if she had wanted to, but she detests even your name. Come with me if you still want to meet her.

Vinay was confident about his ability to change views. He didn't have the least doubt that Sophie wouldn't talk to him. Yes, but it was regrettable that this was the result of the help that he had given the authorities for Sophia's sake. 'Why would I have resorted to this injustice if I had known that Sophia doesn't like my course of action, and that she's with friends and is comfortable? I didn't have any enmity against the public. Sophia is also partly responsible for this. She knew my proclivities. Couldn't she have sent me a letter to inform me about her situation? Since she didn't do so, what right does she have to be annoyed with me?'

With these thoughts, he began to walk behind Indradutt. Hunger and thirst had vanished.

30

IT WAS EVENING AS THEY WALKED ON. EVENING IN THE MOUNTAINS is much more dangerous than the night in the plains. The three men walked on but they had no idea of their destination. The shadows of the hills lengthened. The day was over even before sunset. They couldn't discern the way. Both men would repeatedly ask Indradutt, 'How far is it now?' But the only answer they got was, 'Keep going, we'll reach soon.' Vinay Singh was provoked into asking angrily, 'Indradutt, if you are thirsty for our blood, why don't you admit it frankly? Why are you killing us by torturing us like this?' To this too, Indradutt merely said, 'Keep going, it's not far now, but be careful, the way is difficult.'

Vinay now regretted that he had come with Indradutt and had not instead sent Sophia a letter through him. He would have gone without worrying if he had recognized Sophia's handwriting on receiving a reply. 'Sophie is not so hard-hearted that she wouldn't have replied to my letter. I have made a big mistake in my haste. Indradutt's intentions don't seem to be genuine.' These suspicions made his path even more difficult. As they went forward, the way became increasingly rough and uneven. Sometimes they would have to climb mounds, or they would have to descend so much that it would seem as if they were walking towards rasaatal, the lowest of the seven hells. Sometimes they'd find a narrow footpath flanked by deep ravines. They couldn't see at all; they could only depend on conjecture, which is actually insight. Vinay's pistol was pointed; he had decided to fire the first shot at Indradutt on the slightest suspicion.

Indradutt stopped suddenly and said – Well, we have reached. That's all, stay here. I'll go and inform those people.

Vinay said surprised – There's no one here, there's just a tree.

Indradutt – Political rebels need such secret places where even the messengers of Yamraj can't reach

Vinay – Bhai! Don't leave us alone like this. Why don't you call out from here? Or come, I'll also go with you.

Indradutt – Even the sound of a conch may perhaps not reach from here, and I don't have permission to take anybody with me because it's not my house and how can I take you to someone else's? These poor people don't have an army or a fort; it's only the inaccessibility of the path that protects them. I won't be long.

He left swiftly and after taking several steps, disappeared below that tree. For some time Vinay apprehensively waited for him, then he said to Nayakram – This rascal has trapped us. He has brought us to this desolate place where we'll meet an untimely death. He has still not returned.

Nayakram – Why should you worry? Lovers carry their lives on the palms of their hands. I'm the one who'll die without gaining anything!

Vinay – I had guessed his intentions.

Nayakram – Then why did you come without shaking your ears or tail? You have drowned me along with you. Does the mind go astray in love?

Vinay – It's half an hour and there's no sign of anyone. Where can we go even if we want to run away? He has definitely betrayed us. We had only this long to live.

Nayakram – You are a lover and you are afraid to die! All of us have to die one day, so why not today? What's there to be afraid of? Why worry about the pestle when you have put your head into the mortar? Let it pound as much as it wants to.

Vinay – Suppose Sophia really comes?

Nayakram – What could be better, grab her immediately! It will be such fun if you begin to wail and cry, and she wipes your tears with her aanchal.

Vinay – Bhai, look, don't laugh if I cry when I see her. I'll run and hold her so tight that she won't be able to free herself.

Nayakram – Here, take my towel and promptly tie her feet with it.

Vinay – You are making fun of me and my heart is beating at the thought of what might happen. Ah! I've understood now. I've come this way before. We are somewhere near Jaswantnagar. Indradutt has made us wander around so much to mislead us.

Nayakram – What's it to us if Jaswantnagar is here? Who'll hear us if we scream?

Vinay – Has he really deceived us? I want to go away from here. My heart will break if Sophie begins to speak harshly. How will I bear the cruelty of somebody for whose welfare I have done so many impious and wrong things? This is how one's heart becomes bitter, when the one for whom one has become a thief cries out 'thief'!

Nayakram – This is how women are.

Vinay – Yes, now one can actually see what one had heard about.

Nayakram – I'll spread the towel here, the stone is cold now, lie down comfortably. If miss sahib comes, it's God's will else we'll leave at dawn. We'll find the way somehow. I'll sit here with the pistol, if there's any sound, we'll see about it. I'm fed up of being here. When will the day come when I'll see my home again?

Vinay – My ties with my home are broken now. I won't be able to enter if I return with Sophie; I won't return at all if I can't find her. I'll light a dhooni here.*

Nayakram – Bhaiyya, I'm being brash in saying this but I've become bold being with you. Miss sahib doesn't seem to me to be such a great apsara. By God's grace, there are such beauties to be seen every day that miss sahib is nothing in front of them. Their faces are like diamonds sparkling. And you are willing to sacrifice your throne for her! I'm telling you the truth; raniji will be very distressed. It's a great sin to pain a mother's heart. We haven't got any news either, we don't know if she's alive or dead.

Vinay – Pandaji, I'm not a devotee of Sophie's beauty. I myself don't know what it is about her that attracts me so much. I can sacrifice not just my throne but also my religion for her. If I controlled the world, I'd gift it to Sophia. If I come to know today that Sophia is no more, you won't find me alive. The source of my life is the hope of finding her. The first and last ambition of my life is to die at her feet.

They could see the light of a lantern near the tree. Two men were approaching. One held a lantern and the other a jaajam, a sheet of cloth to spread on the floor. Vinay recognized them both. One was Veerpaal Singh and the other his companion. Veerpaal put down the lantern when he came close, and after greeting Vinay, both the men quietly began to spread the jaajam. After they had spread it, Veerpaal said,

---

* Smoke-fire of an ascetic who sits beside it as a penance; to light a dhooni or a smoke-fire is to become a yogi.

'Come, sit down, you have suffered a lot. Miss sahib will be here soon.'

Vinay's heart was sinking between the dual waves of hope and disappointment. He felt ashamed because he had to become a mendicant at the door of the very men whom he had attempted to wipe out with the help of the authorities. 'It would have been a joy if all these people had come before me handcuffed and I had obtained forgiveness for them. Actually the sehra of glory has remained on their heads. Ah! Those whom I had thought to be vile murderers are the arbiters of my destiny today.'

When he sat down on the jaajam, and Nayakram began cautiously to pace up and down, Veerpaal said – Kunwar sahib, it's my great good fortune that today I'm not seeing you in a court of law but at my door, otherwise my throat too would have been cut along with those unfortunate people who had committed no crime except to cry when they were beaten.

Vinay – Veerpaal, don't make me feel ashamed by mentioning those crimes. I'm willing to atone for them if that's possible.

Veerpaal – With a sincere heart?

Vinay – Yes, if you have protected Miss Sophia.

Veerpaal – You'll see her for yourself soon.

Vinay – Then I'll also try my best to have you forgiven.

Veerpaal – Do you know why I brought miss sahib here? Because we hoped to protect ourselves by taking care of her and getting her recommendation. We hoped to save our lives through her but, unfortunately, her wound was deeper than we had thought and took full nine months to heal. I don't want to say it myself but only I know the devotion with which I've taken care of her. You can just imagine that I couldn't leave the house for six months. All those days there was a brisk market for manslaughter in Jaswantnagar; I'd hear the news daily and beat my head helplessly. I had brought miss sahib here to protect myself. The entire region was devastated because of her. Anyway, what happened was Parmatma's will. My plea to you now is that we should be treated with mercy. Parmatma has given you power. Our lives will be saved at one sign from you.

Vinay said, uninhibitedly – I'm fully convinced that the durbar will forgive your crimes. But you'll have to promise that from now you won't have rebellious intentions against the riyasat.

Veerpaal – I'm prepared to take a vow. Kunwar sahib, the truth is that you have made us completely powerless. It's your oppression that has made us so weak. All those men whom we had trusted have betrayed us. It's difficult to differentiate between friend and enemy. They have all become snakes in our sleeves to save their lives, to prove their innocence, or to win the trust of the authorities. I'm the same person who had looted Jaswantnagar's official treasury and who is now hiding like a mouse in a hole. There's the fear of the police coming every moment.

Vinay – Does Miss Sophia ever remember me?

Veerpaal – You can't imagine how much miss sahib loves you. It was she who had saved you from his blow (*pointing to his companion*) and it's because of her that you have been saved from us. We didn't have the opportunity to meet you, but our rifles did. Miss sahib would cry for hours remembering you but now she has become so hostile to you that she flares up even if somebody mentions your name. She says, 'God has punished me for giving up my religion.' But I think that she is still infinitely devoted to you. Like love, respect also grows with intimacy. Don't be disappointed in her. You are a raja; everything is forgiven you. The bonds of dharma are for small people.

The light of another lantern was suddenly seen near that tree. An old woman was coming with a lota. Sophie was behind her carrying a thaali with a lamp of ghee burning on it. It was the same Sophia, that same image of radiant beauty. The gentle lustre gave her an indescribable, gleaming white ethereal allure as if she was created not from the five elements but from atoms of pure moonlight. As soon as he saw her, there was such an upsurge in Vinay's heart that he wanted to run and fall at her feet. The image of beauty doesn't merely attract; it captivates. The old woman put down the lota and left with the lantern. Veerpaal and his companions also moved away, together with Nayakram.

Vinay said – Sophia, it's my lucky day today. I had begun to despair.

Sophia – It was my supreme good fortune that I have got your darshan today. Your darshan was destined, otherwise there was nothing wanting for death.

Vinay's doubts began to appear baseless. He thought that Indradutt and Veerpaal had unnecessarily made him apprehensive. Reunion awakens love. His simple understanding was flowing in this current of rapture like a garland of flowers. He didn't understand the acerbic sarcasm in this sentence.

Sophie took some rice and curd from the thaali and put a tilak on Vinay's forehead. She said smiling – Now I'll perform the aarti.

Vinay (*Delighted*) – Dearest, what's this nonsense? Have you also got trapped in these customs?

Sophia – Vaah! How can I not welcome you? You are my saviour, you are liberating me from the clutches of these dacoits and murderers; how can I not greet you? You created chaos in the riyasat for my sake, killed hundreds of innocent people, extinguished the lights of so many homes, made mothers savour what it is to grieve for their sons, made young women sit in the lap of widowhood and, above all, destroyed your soul, your principles, your ideals. Shouldn't I greet you even after you have attained so much glory? I'm not so ungrateful. You are no longer a humble volunteer but the right hand of the riyasat. Rajas and maharajas respect you, so how can I not?

Vinay's eyes were opened now. Each word of sarcasm was like an arrow. He said – Sophie, I'm still your devotee and the old social worker. You are being unfair to me by ridiculing me like this. It's possible that people may have been mistakenly harmed because of me, but my aim was only to protect you.

Sophia (*Excited*) – That's a complete lie. All this was for your sake not mine. Your purpose was only to satiate that base tyranny that's in your inner being in the guise of service. I didn't dedicate myself to you because of your love of power but because of your service, compassion and patriotism. I made you the god I worshipped because of the high ideal of your life; there was a glimpse in you of the Lord Messiah's compassion, Lord Buddha's detachment, and Luther's steadfast truthfulness. Was there a dearth of merciless, selfish authorities in the world that tyrannized the miserable? Your ideal made me bow down at your feet. When I had begun to hate the world, seeing all creatures engrossed in selfishness, your selflessness made me your devotee. But just one turn in the course of time revealed your true self. You even sacrificed all thought of righteousness and unrighteousness to search for me. Someone who can be such a tyrant to attain his selfish ends can also commit the most heinous crimes. You were degraded from your ideal the moment you thought it proper to use cruelty and oppression rather than peaceful methods to subjugate the revolt. The devil had attacked you for the first time, and after that you didn't take hold of yourself, you kept falling. You have become so degraded now with stumble after stumble that there's not the least decency, discrimination and humanity left in you. My forehead would bow down of its own accord whenever I saw you. The basis of my love was devotion. That basis has been shaken at the very roots. You have destroyed my entire life. Ah! Nobody could ever have been as deluded as I have been. The person for whom I opposed my parents, left my country, sacrificed my long-preserved principles, suffered insults, censure, harm, turned out to be so selfish, self-serving, undiscriminating! Some other woman may be enchanted by these qualities of yours, women don't think of ideals and sacrifices when it comes to love. But my education, my associations, my studies and, more than anything else, my temperament have not taught me to respect these qualities. If you had come before me suffering, oppressed, insulted and punished by the riyasat, I would have taken your misfortunes on myself, I would have put the dust from your feet on my forehead and considered myself to be very fortunate. But I have contempt for the thing that people call a successful life. A successful life implies flattery, oppression and deceit. The lives of the mahatmas whom I think to be supreme in the world were not successful. From the worldly point of view, they were even more worthless than ordinary people. They suffered difficulties, they were exiled, stoned, rejected, and finally the world said farewell to them without shedding a tear and sent them to the abode of the gods. You have set out to search for me with a group of policemen. The purpose of that is only to terrorize the public! In my view, the sooner the traces of a kingdom whose entity rests on injustice vanish, the better. Anyway, what's the use of all this now? You are welcome to your prestige and power; I'm satisfied with this situation. The people I am with are generous; they can protect a humble creature with their lives, they have the sentiments of service and philanthropy far more than you do.

Vinay (*Annoyed*) – Sophie, for God's sake, don't be so unfair to me. My plight would not have been so wretched if I had wanted power and prestige. I only did what I thought was just. As far as possible, I have not for a moment turned away from justice.

Sophia – This is what's so regrettable, that something so unjust seemed just to you! This shows your inner inclinations, you are selfish by nature. Man doesn't value all things equally. There are so many people who spurn wealth for the sake of fame. They can't call themselves selfless. Seeking one's own advantage does not conform to high ideals. I at least can't respect somebody whose temperament is so weak, and love without respect becomes a stigma.

Vinay was not one of those people who are not affected by adverse circumstances. He would soon be conquered by despair. He said, agitated – Sophie, I didn't expect this from you. Whatever I have done has been because I thought it to be just or because circumstances made me helpless.

Sophia – All the wrong deeds of the world happen only because of error or circumstance. I haven't yet heard of a third reason.

Vinay – Sophie, had I known that you have become so hard-hearted towards me, I wouldn't have shown my face to you.

Sophia – I wasn't keen for your darshan.

Vinay – I didn't know this. But even if I have been unjust, should I get this punishment from you? I had feared this from mataji, not from you. Ah Sophie! Don't let our love end like this. Don't destroy my life like this. For the sake of the love you once had for me, don't be unfair to me. This pain is unbearable for me. You won't believe me because at the moment your heart has turned to stone as far as I'm concerned, but this blow will be fatal for me. And if there's life after death this pain will continue to torment me in that life as well. Sophie, I'm not afraid of death, I can bear the point of a spear on my heart, but this cruel look of yours, this merciless blow, they pierce my innermost being. It would be far better if you gave me poison. I'll shut my eyes and drink that cup like a devotee drinking charnamrit. I'll be satisfied that this life that I have gifted you has been useful to you.

Vinay would perhaps never have uttered such unrestrained words of love on any other occasion, and perhaps he would have been surprised that he had uttered them when he recalled them again, but at this moment the upsurge of emotions had made him reckless. Sophie stood indifferently, her head bowed. Then she said, callously, 'Vinay, I entreat you not to talk like this. Don't trample whatever respect I still have for you, because I know that these words are not being uttered from your innermost being. On the contrary, at this moment you are thinking of ways of getting your revenge for this scorn. I'll be surprised if this place doesn't become the recreation ground of the secret police by sunrise, and if the inhabitants here are not arrested and sentenced to death. You must have thought of some other plan to punish me. I can't imagine what it might be, but I know that you won't hesitate at all if you can make me suffer physical or mental pain by criticizing me or by making allegations against my conduct. It's possible that this assumption of mine may be unfair, but I can't get rid of it. There's no superhuman power, no supernatural accomplishment that can make you worthy of my respect. There's no place in my heart for somebody whose hands are soaked in blood. Don't imagine that these words don't pain me. Each word cuts my heart like a saw. And don't think that I'll remove you from my heart and ensconce some other image here again, although I won't be surprised if this is the evil thought in your mind. No, this is my first and last circumambulation in love. This life will now follow a different path. Who knows, perhaps God has punished me at your hands for wavering from the path of duty. I did everything that I should not have done for your sake. Trickery, cunning, craft, deceit, womanly wiles, I didn't scruple to use any of these because from my simple viewpoint you were a divine, disinterested, pure soul! You can have no idea how mortified I felt accompanying Mr Clark. I had thought that you would be the lamp for the path of my life, and that you would uplift my life and make it successful. After all, what quality do I have that you are infatuated with me? If you desire beauty, there's no dearth of it in the world, you can get a much more beautiful girl than me. If my words sound sweet to your ears, you can get women whose speech is much more melodious than mine. There's no need to despair. Sooner or later, you'll find a beautiful young woman to suit your taste and temperament, with whom you can enjoy your glory and prestige, because you don't have the ability to serve and you never will. My heart will not even look at love now, even by mistake. I won't nurture this disease again. You have made me detached from the world; you have extinguished my thirst for pleasure. Despair has shown me the path that I couldn't find by a constant study of the sacred texts. I'm obliged to you for this.

What jewel did I find by serving dharma and truth? Unrighteousness!
Now I'll serve unrighteousness. Do you know what I'll do? I'll revenge
myself with the blood of those sinners who have cut the throats of the
public. I'll throw each and every one of them into the fire of hell, only
then will my soul be satiated. I'll burn those people in the cauldron
of hell who are now enjoying prestige and fame after killing innocent
people, and I won't rest until I extirpate this band of tyrants, even if
I lose my life in this enterprise, even if there's a revolt in the riyasat,
even if all traces of the riyasat vanish. You are the one who has fuelled
this misguided zeal in my heart, and you are to blame for it. Even
the immortal fame of the forgiveness and mercy of Jesus, Buddha's
patience and restraint, Krishna's love and asceticism cannot quench
this thirst for blood. Years of meditation and reflection, thought and
self-study have failed because of your crimes. Bas, go now. I've told
you what I'm going to do. I'm going to join the revolutionaries from
today; you can take the shelter of the secret police. Go, I hope God
won't let us meet again.

Sophie picked up the thaali and left, like hope leaving the heart.
Vinay took a deep breath, no less pitiful than a lament, and sat down
on the ground, like an unfortunate widow who sits down with a sigh
after her husband's corpse has been taken away.

All the three men who had been standing at a distance came and
stood near Vinay. Nayakram said – Bhaiyya, there was a lot of talking
today! You made up for all these days once you found her. So she has
now come into your clutches, hasn't she? I had already said that lovers
are big tricksters. First she performed the aarti and put a teeka with
curd and rice. She's a mem but so what, she knows our ways. When
have you decided to leave? Let's go soon, so that I can also settle down.

Vinay's eyes were filled with tears, but he laughed at this sentence. He
said – It'll be soon now. Write a letter home to begin the preparations.

Nayakram – Bhaiyya, it'll be great fun if both the baraats leave
together.

Vinay – Of course, they'll leave together, first yours, and mine
behind it.

Nayakram – Thakur sahib, now make arrangements for some
conveyance, so that we can leave in the morning while it's still cool.
We can get a palanquin here, can't we?

Veerpaal – All the arrangements will be made. Now eat some food and rest, it's late.

Vinay – How far is Jaswantnagar from here?

Veerpaal – Why do you want to know this?

Vinay – I have to reach there immediately.

Veerpaal (*Suspiciously*) – You are tired after the whole day, the way is bad.

Vinay – It doesn't matter, I'll go.

Nayakram – Bhaiyya, miss sahib will also be with us, how can you leave at night?

Vinay – You have become senile, what is miss sahib to me and why would she go with me? If I were to die today, perhaps no one would be happier than her. You can rest if you are tired, but I can't stay here even for a moment. A path of thorns will be more comfortable for me than a bed here. Can anyone of you show me the way?

Veerpaal – I'm ready to go myself, but the way is very dangerous.

Vinay – It doesn't matter. Make arrangements for me to go there immediately and, if possible, blindfold me. I no longer trust myself.

Veerpaal – At least eat something, accept this much hospitality.

Vinay – If you want to give me hospitality, shoot me. You can't give me better hospitality than that. If you had done me one per cent of the harm that I have done you, I wouldn't have needed any instigation. I'm a fiend, a murderer and the sooner the earth is rid of my burden, the better it will be.

Nayakram – It seems that miss sahib is really angry. But I'm telling you, she'll come running after you within a few days. A lover's lament is dreadful.

Veerpaal – Kunwar sahib, listen to me. Don't go now. I'm afraid miss sahib will be anxious if you go away like this. I promise you that you'll reach Jaswantnagar by sunset tomorrow. Eat something now.

Vinay – Even the water here is forbidden for me. Don't come if you don't want to, I don't have the right to so much hospitality. I'll go alone.

Veerpaal helplessly agreed to go with him. Nayakram was dying of hunger but what could he do, he stood up when he saw Vinay leaving. The three went on their way.

They walked on silently for half an hour. Vinay didn't remember anything else that Sophia had said, but each word of the allegations that she had made on his intentions and her bitter prophecy about him echoed in his ears. 'Sophia thinks that I'm so base. She doesn't want to consider the circumstances at all. She doesn't want to make any allowances for one's state of mind.'

He suddenly asked Veerpaal – Do you think that I did this injustice in a fit of frenzy, or am I base by nature as Miss Sophia thinks?

Veerpaal – Kunwar sahib, don't at all mind what Miss Sophia said just now. Just as you had lost your senses in a fit of frenzy, she too must have said nonsensical things in her rage. You have given up your kingdom for social service and philanthropy, so with what face can anybody call you selfish?

Vinay – I don't know from where she has learnt such harsh words! Even a beggar should be answered politely. She reproved me as if I were a dog.

Nayakram – She'll marry an Englishman, what else? What do the black men have here? From where will the hen's egg come?

Vinay – You're an utter fool. You are concerned about the hen's egg.

Nayakram – I want to say something. Where can she have the same freedom with you? You'll make her a rani and put her in purda. You won't let her ride a mare and take her for shikar. You won't put your arm around her waist and help her to sit on the tamtam. You won't take off your hat and cry hurray-hurray.

Vinay – The same refrain again. Listen, ponga maharaj, what do you take Sophia to be? Even a pandit probably doesn't have as much knowledge about our religion as she does. She is in no way inferior to our ladies here. She should have been born in a raja's house. Goodness knows why she was born in a Christian family. She can't ever be close to anybody else after rejecting me. I'm as sure about this as about my own eyes. She won't get married at all now.

Veerpaal – You are very right. She's a devi.

Vinay – Tell me the truth, did she ever discuss me?

Veerpaal – She didn't talk about anything else. The wound was deep, so she would remain lying unconscious, but she would often call out to you, startled. She'd say, 'Call Vinay, I'll die only after seeing him.' Sometimes she'd be obsessed with you for days on end. Whenever she saw anybody she'd only ask, 'Has Vinay come? Where is he? Bring him to me. Where are his feet?' We'd weep at her helplessness. I can't tell you the way in which the surgeon dissected her, my hair stand on end when I remember. She would shrink as soon as she saw him but the moment he'd say that there's news of Vinay Singh coming today, she would strengthen herself and get the dressing done. She'd tell the surgeon, 'Hurry up, he's coming, don't delay or he'll reach here.' You should realize that your name pulled her out of the jaws of death.

Vinay (*Choking*) – Stop it, don't say more. I can't listen to this pitiful story. My heart comes to my mouth.

Veerpaal – One day she was ready to go to you in that condition. She said, crying, 'People have arrested him, I'm going to free him . . .'

Vinay – Stop it Veerpaal, or my heart will burst. Help me lie down somewhere, I don't know why my heart is sinking. Ah! This is the right punishment for somebody as unfortunate as I. The gods couldn't bear my happiness. Nobody has ever benefited from them. Come, let's go on, I won't lie down. I have to reach Jaswantnagar immediately.

They began to walk silently. Vinay was walking so fast that it seemed as if he was running. There was a strange energy in his aching limbs. Poor Nayakram was huffing and puffing as he ran. It must have been around two at night. There was an invigorating coolness in the breeze now. The beautiful night had now become old, when its restless image takes on a mellow garb and its captivating power is irresistible. Nayakram dozed off several times and escaped falling down. Vinay also wanted to rest when Veerpaal said, 'Here, we have reached Jaswantnagar.'

Vinay – So soon! We must have been walking only for four hours.

Veerpaal – We came straight today.

Vinay – Come, today I'll get you cleared by the authorities here.

Veerpaal – You have cleared me, so now I don't care about anyone else. Now say goodbye to me here.

Vinay – Be my guest at least for one day.

Veerpaal – We'll soon meet again if God wills. Be merciful to me.

Vinay – Don't say anything about me to Sophia.

Veerpaal – I won't, until she herself does.

Vinay – This anxiety of mine, this craziness, don't mention them even by mistake. I don't know what nonsense I'm blabbering. I no longer trust my words or thoughts, it's as if I'm unconscious. Just tell her that I didn't say anything to you. Promise me this.

Veerpaal – I won't say anything if she doesn't ask me.

Vinay – For my sake, at least tell her that I hadn't mentioned her at all.

Veerpaal – I can't tell a lie.

Vinay – As you wish.

31

SOORDAS RETURNED TO HIS HUT FROM BHAIRO'S HOUSE WONDERING what to do when Dayagiri suddenly arrived and said – Soordas, people are very angry with you today because they think that you have become arrogant. Why are you caught in this web of maya, why don't you come with me on a pilgrimage?

Soordas – That's what I was also thinking. If you go, I'll also leave with you.

Dayagiri – Yes, let's go, I'll make some arrangements for the temple. There's no one here who'll light the lamp when I'm away, let alone make the bhog.

Soordas – You'll never get leave from the temple.

Dayagiri – Bhai, I can't just leave the temple without any support. I don't know when I'll return, and the grass will have grown tall here by then.

Soordas – So if you are trapped in maya yourself, how will you liberate me?

Dayagiri – No, I'll leave soon now. I'll just go and get some flowers for pooja.

After Dayagiri had left, Soordas again began to wonder – What is this play of the world that your hands get burnt when you do something good? I had gone to do a good deed and this is the result. The muhalla-valas believed. People believe so soon in bad things. But good deeds can never remain hidden. The reality will be known sometime or the other. Defeat and victory are a part of life, I'll win sometimes and lose at others, why worry about it? I had won against the high and mighty yesterday; today I have lost even in victory. This is part of the game. Where will poor Subhagi go now? The muhalla-valas won't let her stay here. Who will support her? There's no one in her maika. A young woman can't stay alone anywhere. These are bad times, how will she protect her honour? She loves Bhairo so much. She thought I had gone to beat him; she was trying so hard to tell him to be careful! She loves him so much, but Bhairo is never nice to her, she's unfortunate. Another man would have worshipped her, but Bhairo always has his sword hanging over her. She'll have no well-wisher if I also go away. The muhalla-valas will see her in trouble and laugh at her! For how long will she bear it? She'll go and drown herself somewhere. This blind man Bhairo who has eyes isn't at all concerned about where she'll go if he turns her out. There'll be a hue and cry in the city if she becomes a Musalman or a Kirastaan; but right now there's no one who can make her husband see reason. No one will even know where she has gone if she comes into the clutches of the recruiters. They are all knowingly pretending to be ignorant.

He was going towards the road reflecting about this when Subhagi arrived and said – Soorey, where will I live?

Soordas (*Feigning indifference*) – How do I know where you'll live? You were the one who told Bhairo to bring his stick with him. Did you think I'd gone to beat Bhairo?

Subhagi – Yes, Soorey, why should I lie? I did suspect this.

Soordas – Why do you speak to me if you think that I'm so bad? You would have just stood and watched the fun if he had come with his stick and had beaten me, isn't it? Even Bhairo is better than you because he didn't come with sticks and cudgels. When you are determined to have ill-will for me, why shouldn't I also have ill-will for you?

Subhagi (*Crying*) – Soorey, if you also talk like this who else will give me shelter even for a moment? He has beaten me just now, but his belly isn't filled, he says that he'll make a complaint to the police. He has thrown out all my clothes and belongings. I don't have any other refuge except this hut.

Soordas – Will you have me also thrown out of the muhalla with you?

Subhagi – I'll go with you wherever you go.

Soordas – Then you won't let me show my face anywhere. Everyone will say that the blind man has eloped with her.

Subhagi – You'll escape being disgraced but how will I save my honour? Is there anyone in the muhalla who'll protect somebody's respect and honour when it's in danger? I won't get a morsel of roti here if I ask for it. I don't have anyone else now except you. I used to think that you are a man, now I think that you are a devata. Let me stay here if you wish, otherwise tell me to blacken my face and die somewhere.

Soordas said, after being engrossed in worry for a long time – Subhagi, you are sensible. Do what you want. It's not difficult for me to support you. I still have enough respect in the city so that I won't be refused if I go and stand at anyone's door. But my heart says that it won't be good for us if you stay here. Both of us will be disgraced. I think of you as my sister but this blind world doesn't see anybody's intentions. You heard just now the kinds of things that people were saying. There have been abuses earlier too. There'll be chaos if you openly stay with me. People will be bent on cutting our throats. Tell me, what should I do?

Subhagi – Do what you want. But I won't leave you and go anywhere else.

Soordas – If that's what you want then let it be so. I was thinking of going away somewhere. There'll be no pain if I'm not here to see for myself, but seeing you in trouble I don't want to go now. Come, stay here. We'll see when the time comes. It's better to be disgraced than to leave you midstream.

Soordas then left to beg for alms. Subhagi sat down in the hut. She saw that the tiny household of that tiny house was scattered here and there. A lutiya was overturned somewhere, pitchers were toppled elsewhere. The hut had not been cleaned for months, as if the dust had settled there. Spiders had woven their webs in the straw thatch. There was even a bird's nest. Subhagi spent the whole day cleaning the hut. The same hut that had characterized the saying that 'a house without a housewife is the abode of ghosts' looked so clean and whitewashed that even the gods would have yearned to stay in it. Bhairo had left for his shop, so Subhagi went home and brought her bundle. When Soordas returned in the evening, she gave him some parched grain to eat, brought water in a lutiya, and began to fan him with her aanchal. Soordas had never before in his life enjoyed this comfort and peace. He experienced the rare joy of domesticity for the first time. After burning in the hot wind and blast by the roadside all day, this comfort seemed like heaven to him. For a moment, a new desire germinated in his heart. He thought, 'I'm so unfortunate. If only she were my wife, how blissful life would be. Now that Bhairo has turned her out of the house, what's the harm if I keep her? How should I ask her? I don't know what she'll think. I'm blind, but am I not a man? Will she mind it? Why would she look after me so well if she didn't care for me?'

Every human being, every creature yearns for love. It takes the form of desire in voluptuaries and of the enjoyment of peace in simple-hearted, humble people.

Subhagi opened Soordas's bundle and took out some wheatflour, a little rice, some gram and three annas. She brought some daal from the bania, made rotis and called Soordas to eat.

Soordas – Where's Mitthua?

Subhagi – How do I know? He must be playing somewhere. He came in once during the day to drink water and went away when he saw me.

Soordas – He must be feeling shy of you. I'll go and call him.

Soordas went out and called out to Mitthua. On other days, Mitthua would go home to get some grain, get it roasted, and eat it; today he starved the whole day. He was sitting in the temple at this moment hoping to get prasad. He ran as soon as he heard Soordas's voice. Both of them sat down to eat. Subhagi put rice and rotis in front of Soordas and only rice in front of Mitthua. There was very little atta so only two rotis could be made.

Soordas asked – Mitthu, do you want another roti?

Mitthu – I didn't get a roti.

Soordas – Then take it from me. I'll eat only rice.

Soordas gave both the rotis to Mitthu. Subhagi said angrily to Mitthu – You just roam around all day like a wandering bull, why don't you work somewhere? You can get five or six annas a day if you work at the mill here.

Soordas – He's not ready to work yet. His strength will be worn out if he begins to work at this age.

Subhagi – Labourers' sons are not so weak. They all go to work; nobody's strength is worn out.

Soordas – He'll work when he wants to.

Subhagi – If somebody can get food without making any effort, it's his evil spirit that goes to work.

Soordas – Oonh, I'm not worried about any debts or wealth. I eat what I get by begging. I'll see about it the day I lose my vigour. Why should I worry about it now?

Subhagi – I'll send him to work. I'll see how he won't go. It's arrogance that the blind should beg and the louts who can see should sit around and eat. Have you heard, Mitthu? You'll have to work from tomorrow.

Mitthu – I won't go if you tell me to. I'll go if dada tells me to.

Subhagi – You like roaming around like an uncouth lout. You don't realize that the blind man has to beg while you eat comfortably. Will you remain a boy all your life?

Mitthu – What does it have to do with you? I'll go if I want to, I won't if I don't want to.

This argument continued between the two of them for a long time. Eventually Mitthua got up angrily from the chauka. Soordas tried very hard to persuade him but he didn't sit down to eat again. Finally, Soordas also got up without finishing his food.

When he lay down, there was a different picture of domesticity before him. There was neither that peace, nor that splendour, nor that rapture. This quarrel had begun on the very first day, if the bismillah, the beginning, was wrong then who could tell what would happen in the future? Subhagi's harshness seemed inappropriate to him. 'Why should I burden the boy with domesticity as long as I'm willing to earn? He'll have to suffer whatever may happen to him after I die.'

That sprout, that tiny desire that had sprung up in his heart in the evening, was burnt in the blast of this heat and the sprout withered.

Subhagi was obsessed with a new worry – How can I make Mitthua work? I'm not his servant that I should wash his utensils and cook for him while he loafs around. There's nobody to provide for me either. Why should I be provided for anyway? Why should he roam around like a dandy when everyone else has to work?

When she left the hut at dawn to fill the pitcher with water, Gheesoo's mother put her hand on her breast and said – Well, did you spend the night here?

Subhagi said – Yes I did. So?

Jamuni – Don't you have your own home?

Subhagi – I no longer have the strength to put up with kicks.

Jamuni – You'll be at peace only after getting a few heads chopped off. This blind man has also lost his wits so that he's deliberately poking his finger into the snake's mouth. Bhairo is a man who'll slit a man's throat. Nothing has been lost even now! Go home.

Subhagi – I won't set foot in that house now, even if I'm killed. Soorey at least has enough pity to catch hold of the arm of somebody who is drowning. Who else is there?

Jamuni – It's not good for you to stay in a house where there's no woman.

Subhagi – I know, but to whose house can I go? Will you let me stay if I come to your house? I'll do whatever you tell me to—make cow-dung cakes and set them out to dry, give fodder to the buffaloes, fill the water, grind your atta. Will you keep me?

Jamuni – No baba! Who wants to take on a quarrel unnecessarily? I should provide for you and on top of that also be thought immoral!

Subhagi – Should I put up with abuses and beatings every day?

Jamuni – He's your man, even if he beats you does it mean that you should leave your home and go away?

Subhagi – Why are you boasting, Jamuni? You have an ox that sits wherever you want him to. I would have seen how you'd remain in the house if he had been after you with a stick day and night. Only the other day when he wanted to beat you because you had mixed water in the milk, you picked up your chaadar to run to your maika. It's easy to preach to others. One's eyes are opened only when one suffers oneself.

Subhagi then went to the well to fill water. Here too she gave the same truculent reply to the critics. After bringing the water, she washed the utensils, set up the chauka and went with Soordas to help him reach the road. Until now, he used to go alone, groping with his stick but Subhagi couldn't bear to see this. 'He's a blind man; the boys will harass him if he falls down. After all, I'm just sitting here.' Nobody questioned her after that. It was established that Soordas had set up house with her. Now there was no room for sarcasm, criticism or ridicule. Yes, Soordas had fallen in everybody's eyes. People said, 'What could he have done except return the money? He must have been afraid that Subhagi would be sure to tell Bhairo one day, so why shouldn't I be prepared beforehand? But why did Subhagi steal the money from her own house? Vaah! What's there to be surprised about this? Bhairo didn't give her money. The mistress of the house is old. Subhagi must have thought, I don't have any wealth; if I steal the money I'll also have some. Who knows, both of them may have planned this earlier. She may have thought Soorey to be a good man and so had kept the money with him. Or Soordas may have taken the money and then returned it so that he wouldn't be exposed. The blind are very secretive and far-sighted.'

This gossip continued for several days.

But people are not accustomed to discussing a topic for too long. They don't have the time to bother about such things nor the intelligence to solve these puzzles. Human beings are active by nature, where do they have the ability to analyse? Nobody had any objection to speaking and interacting with Subhagi, nobody asked her any questions or taunted her. Yes, Soordas's respect and prestige vanished. Earlier, the whole muhalla had been in awe of him; the trust that people had in him far exceeded his status. His name used to be taken with respect. Now he too began to be counted among ordinary people, there was nothing special about him any more.

But this was a thorn in Bhairo's flesh. He wanted to avenge this living insult somehow. He would go very seldom to the shop. There was a complaint to the officers that this contractor doesn't open the shop so the customers for toddy have to return disappointed. The staff of the narcotics department had threatened to dismiss Bhairo, but he said, 'I'm not worried about the shop, you can keep anybody you want.' But they couldn't find another paasi and the officers didn't think it appropriate to be strict for fear of the shop being shut.

Gradually, Bhairo became hostile not only to Soordas but to the whole muhalla. He thought that it was the duty of the muhalla-valas to have supported him and given Soorey such a punishment that he would have remembered it all his life. 'Why should anybody live in such a muhalla where justice and injustice are sold at the same price? No one says anything to the wrongdoers. Soordas goes by arrogantly. This witch roams around with kaajal in her eyes. Nobody blackens their faces. Such a village should be burnt.' But for some reason his ability to act was paralysed. He would avoid Subhagi when he saw her on the way and merely chew his lips when he saw Soordas. He didn't have the courage to attack. Now he never went to the temple to sing bhajans; he also lost interest in fairs and spectacles, the taste for intoxicants disappeared on its own. The sharp pain of insult was persistent. He had thought that Subhagi would blacken her face and go away somewhere and his stigma would be wiped out. But not only was she still here, deliberately causing him pain and vexation, grinding moong on his chest, she was enjoying herself with the man who was his enemy. His greatest sorrow was that the people of the muhalla continued to behave with both of them just as they had done earlier, nobody went after them or reviled them. His affront seemed to be sitting in front of him, making faces. Now he did not get solace from abuses and curses. He was only concerned about finishing the two of them. 'I want to beat them in such a way that they'll die rubbing their heels and won't get even a drop of water.' But what can a lone man do? He would look all around but there didn't seem to be any hope of help. There was nobody bold enough in the muhalla. After reflecting for a long time, he remembered that the blind man had greatly maligned the Raja Sahib of Chataari. He had also gone around vilifying the sahib of the factory. 'I'll go and complain to them. Both of them must be annoyed with the blind man, they probably kept quiet because they thought it beneath their dignity to engage with somebody so low. If I stand in front, they are sure to take an aim behind me. They are big people, it's difficult to reach them. But if I can approach them and they listen to me, they'll straighten this rascal so that all his blindness will disappear. What else does he have except his blindness?'

For several days, he wondered how to approach those people. He didn't have the courage. 'Suppose they beat me instead and throw me out, it will be even more humiliating.' Finally, one day, he strengthened his resolve and went to raja sahib's house and stood at the syce's door. On seeing him, the syce asked harshly, 'Who are you? Why are you peeping here like a thief?'

Bhairo (*Meekly*) – Bhaiyya, don't scold me. I'm a poor, suffering man.

Syce – If you are poor and suffering, you should have gone to a seth or a moneylender's house. There's nothing here.

Bhairo – I'm poor but not a beggar. Everyone has his respect and honour. If somebody in your community were to seduce your bahu or beti and escape, would the panchayat let him off scot-free? It will surely give some punishment. If the panchayat doesn't, the court will do something about it.

The syce was a chamaar by caste where such misfortunes occur daily and the community gets intoxicants because of them. There was a discussion every day in his house about this. He was more interested in these issues than in anything else. He said – Come and sit, smoke a chillum . . . Who are you, bhai?

Bhairo – I'm a paasi. I live here in Pandeypur.

He sat next to the syce and they both began to talk in whispers as if somebody could eavesdrop on them. Bhairo narrated the entire incident, and taking out a rupee from his waist, said – Bhai, think of a way by which raja sahib can get to know about this. After that I'll tell him everything myself. By your mercy, I'm not a fool in my talk and bearing. I have never been afraid of the daroga.

When the syce saw the rupee coin, he was ecstatic. It was an auspicious start to the morning. He said – I'll inform raja sahib about you. Go if he sends for you. Raja sahib doesn't have a trace of arrogance. But be careful, don't take too long or maalik will be annoyed. Tell him everything frankly, that's all. Big people don't have time to talk. They are not like me that they can gossip all day.

He left after that. Raja sahib was getting his hair dressed, which was his daily habit. The syce salaamed him.

Raja – What is it? Don't come to me for your wages.

Syce – No huzoor, I haven't come for wages. That Soordas who lives in Pandeypur . . .

Raja – Well, that blind rascal.

Syce – Yes huzoor, he has seduced a woman.

Raja – Really? People said that he was a very good man. He has now started practising this deceit!

Syce – Yes huzoor, her husband has come here to complain. Shall I bring him with your permission?

Raja sahib shook his head to give permission and, in a moment, Bhairo came there skulking.

Raja – She's your woman?

Bhairo – Yes huzoor, she was mine until a few days ago.

Raja – Was she inclined to trafficking even earlier?

Bhairo – She may have been, sarkar, I don't know.

Raja – Where has he taken her?

Bhairo – He hasn't gone anywhere, sarkar, he's in his own house.

Raja – He's very insolent. Don't the villagers say anything?

Bhairo – Nobody says anything, huzoor.

Raja – Do you beat your woman a lot?

Bhairo – Who doesn't give a beating if the woman makes mistakes?

Raja – Do you beat her a lot or a little?

Bhairo – Huzoor, where does one think of this when one is angry?

Raja – What kind of a woman is she, beautiful?

Bhairo – Yes huzoor, she's not bad-looking.

Raja – I can't understand why a beautiful woman should like that blind man! You didn't by any chance beat your woman and turn her out of the house because she had put too much salt in the daal and so the blind man kept her?

Bhairo – Sarkar, the woman stole my money and gave it to Soordas. Soordas returned it in the morning. When I tricked him, he even told me who the thief was. What else could I have done except beat her?

Raja – Whatever else there may be, the blind man is at least honest at heart.

Bhairo – Huzoor, he doesn't have good intentions.

Mahendra Kumar Singh was very just and also very cautious about revealing his base thoughts. People who love fame have full control over their speech but he was so annoyed by Soordas and had suffered so much mental torment because of him, that he couldn't hide his feelings. He said – Aji, he maligned me so much here that it was tough for me to go out of the house. He has become so arrogant just because of a little encouragement from Clark sahib. I don't like to torment a poor man but I can't see him clawing the hair of good men either. It's my bench; file a case against him. You'll get witnesses, won't you?

Bhairo – Huzoor, the whole muhalla knows.

Raja – Present them all. People here have become his devotees. They think that he is a rishi. I want to expose his veneer. This opportunity has come to me after so long. If I have ever been humiliated it's by this blind man. He couldn't be suppressed by either the police or the court. His humility and weakness were his armour. This case will be the deep ditch from which he won't be able to escape. I was apprehensive about him, but I'll be at peace once he's unmasked. Who's afraid of a snake once his poisonous teeth are broken? File this case as soon as possible.

We become fond of an eminent man when we see him crying. When we see him gilded with power, we forget for a while that he's also a human being. We imagine that he doesn't have the ordinary human failings. He is a subject of curiosity for us. We wonder what he eats, what he drinks, what he thinks, there must always be elevated thoughts in his mind, he's not concerned about trivial things—respect is just the apparent form of curiosity. Bhairo had been afraid of meeting raja sahib but he now realized that he was also human like anybody else. It was as if he had realized something new today. He said somewhat boldly, 'Huzoor, he may be blind but he's very arrogant. He thinks himself to be superior to everyone else. The muhalla-valas only have to say Soordas-Soordas for him to be puffed up. He thinks he's the only one who matters in the world. Huzoor, give him such a punishment that he'll spend his days grinding the millstone. Only then will his bravado be humbled.'

Raja sahib now frowned. He saw that this villager was letting himself go too far. He said – All right, leave now.

Bhairo thought that he now had raja sahib in his clutches. Had he not been given orders to leave, in a moment he would have addressed him less formally, his 'huzoor' would have become 'aap'. He would have continued to talk non-stop until evening. He would have made up any number of lies. The criticism of others never has so much power over the tongue as it does in the presence of the wealthy. Why do we yearn so much for their good opinion? We even begin to cast aspersions on people for whom we don't have the least malice. We want the respect of these wealthy people even if we don't have anything to gain for ourselves. There's a compulsive inner desire to win their trust. Our speech is then unrestrained.

Bhairo left, feeling rather humiliated, but now he didn't doubt that he had achieved his ambition. He returned home and told Bajrangi – You'll have to be a witness. Don't refuse.

Bajrangi – What witness?

Bhairo – About that affair of mine. I can't bear this blind man's arrogance any longer. I was quiet all these days waiting for him to turn out Subhagi; she could go where she wanted as long as she was out of my sight. But I see that he's swinging higher and higher every day. The blind man is becoming more and more of a dandy. He wouldn't wash himself for months together, but now he bathes daily. She brings the water, rinses his dhoti, massages his hair with oil. I can't see this immorality.

Bajrangi – It is immoral, I'm seeing it for myself. I didn't think that Soorey was so base. But I'm not giving any testimony.

Jamuni – Why? Will somebody slit your ears in the court?

Bajrangi – It's my wish, I won't go.

Jamuni – So much for your wish! Bhairo, you get my name written as a witness. I'll go and testify. What does truth have to fear?

Bajrangi (*Laughing*) – You'll go to the court?

Jamuni – What can I do? If the men's bangles are soiled by going there, it's the woman who'll have to go. At least that prostitute's face should be blackened somehow.

Bajrangi – Bhairo, the fact is that Soorey has definitely done something wrong but you also took the wrong path. Nobody beats a member of the family so heartlessly. And not only did you beat her you also turned her out of the house. When there's no rope to tether the cow, of course it will go to other people's fields. How is it her fault?

Jamuni – Let him blabber, Bhairo, I'll be your witness.

Bajrangi – You probably think that I'll go to the court because of this threat; there are no such fools here. And the truth is that no matter how bad Soorey may be, he's still better than all of us. Returning the bag of money was not a small thing.

Jamuni – Bas, be quiet. I understand you only too well. You also go there and exchange a few jokes, so how can you not be faithful to this friendship? You won't be able to exchange glances with anybody if Subhagi is punished.

Bajrangi flared up on hearing this allegation. Jamuni knew where he camped. He said – There'll be worms in your mouth.

Jamuni – Then why are you being influenced when it comes to testifying?

Bajrangi – Include my name, Bhairo, this wretch won't let me live. If I'm defeated by anybody, it's by her. If anybody rubs dust on my back, it's she. Otherwise I have never been cowed down by anybody here. Go, get it written.

Bhairo went to Thakurdeen after that and made the same proposal. Thakurdeen said – Haan-haan, I'm prepared to be a witness. Get my name written on top. I can't bear the sight of that blind man. Now I'm convinced that he has definitely attained some siddhi, otherwise why would Subhagi go running after him?

Bhairo – The rascal will understand when he'll have to grind the millstone.

Thakurdeen – No bhaiyya, he has a lot of influence, he'll never grind the millstone, he'll return untainted. Yes, it's my dharma to give my testimony, so I'll give it. If a man uses some siddhi to harm others his throat should be cut. Why on earth does God create thieves and sinners? You should realize that I haven't slept since the theft in my house. I'm constantly worried about it. I'm always afraid that I'll be in the same plight again. In one way, you are well off because you got back all your money. I'm left with nothing.

Bhairo – Then your testimony is certain?

Thakurdeen – Yes, not once but a hundred times certain. If I had my way, I'd have buried him alive. Nobody is as straightforward as I am but there's nobody as crooked when it comes to villains. I'm ready to give a false testimony so that they are punished. I'm surprised at what has happened to this blind man. He was so concerned about dharma and karma, he did so much good for others, he was so well behaved, and now this villainy.

From there Bhairo went to Jagdhar, who had just returned after selling his khoncha and was about to go for a bath, taking his dhoti with him.

Bhairo – You are also a witness, aren't you?

Jagdhar – You are fighting a case against Soorey without cause. He's innocent.

Bhairo – Will you swear to it?

Jagdhar – Yes, I'll swear by anything you tell me to. You turned Subhagi out of your house; Soorey took her into his. Otherwise no one knows where she would have been by now. She's a young, beautiful woman; there are several customers for her. Soorey, in fact, was good to her because he didn't let her go astray. I'll say that it's his fault if you want to bring her back to your house to stay with you but he won't let her go and is ready to fight with you. I have heard him reasoning with Subhagi with my own ears. What can the poor man do if she doesn't want to return?

Bhairo understood that he wasn't a devata to be satisfied with merely a lota of water; it would be necessary to give him a gift. He was familiar with his greedy nature.

He said – Bhai, it's a question of honour. Don't use such blandishments. A neighbour can claim a lot but it's not beyond me, whatever you want, ten or twenty rupees, is at your disposal. But you'll have to testify.

Jagdhar – Bhairo, I'm very base, but not so much that I'll knowingly get an innocent person caught.

Bhairo (*Annoyed*) – Do you think the enquiry depends only on you? What difference will it make if the whole village says something and you don't? A grasshopper can't stop a storm.

Jagdhar – Then, bhai, grind her and drink her up. When have I said that I'll save her? But I won't help you to grind her.

Bhairo went away but the selfish, greedy, jealous, devious Jagdhar began to try and split his witnesses. He was not so devoted to Soordas as he was jealous of Bhairo. Even if Bhairo had asked his help for a good deed, he'd have scorned it as promptly.

He went to Bajrangi and said – Why, Bajrangi, are you also testifying for Bhairo?

Bajrangi – Yes, I'm going.

Jagdhar – Have you seen anything with your own eyes?

Bajrangi – What are you saying? I see it every day, there's nothing hidden.

Jagdhar – What do you see? That Subhagi lives in Soordas's hut? Is it wrong to take care of an orphaned woman? You won't talk about the courage of the blind man that he managed to do what nobody else could; rather you are being his enemy. Do you know what her plight will be if Soordas turns her out of the house? The honour of the muhalla will be sold at the hands of the factory labourers. You'll see. Listen to me, don't get into this business of testifying, wrong will be done instead of right. Bhairo is resentful of Subhagi because she returned the money that he had stolen to Soorey. Bas, that's why there's all this resentment. Why should we criticize anybody without knowing anything? Yes, if you are going to testify, find out carefully how both of them live . . .

Bajrangi (*Pointing to Jamuni*) – Ask her, she's the one who knows everything; she's the one who has forced me.

Jamuni – Yes, I did, is your heart still trembling?

Jagdhar – Do you think it's a joke to go and testify in court? You have to hold Gangajal, take tulsi leaves, put your hand on your son's head. That's why those with children are afraid.

Jamuni – Tell the truth, do we have to take all these vows?

Jagdhar – There cannot be a testimony without vows.

Jamuni – Then, bhaiyya, I'm damned if I'll give such testimony. Let Soora go into the stove and Bhairo into the oven, there'll be nobody to help in bad times. Let it be!

Bajrangi – We've known Soordas since he was a boy, he didn't have such a habit.

Jagdhar – It wasn't there and it won't be there. I'm not praising him but he won't get involved in anything wrong even if you give him a lakh of rupees. Someone else would have quietly kept the money that he had lost, nobody would have known anything about it, but he returned it all. This is enough to clear him.

After winning over Bajrangi, Jagdhar tackled Thakurdeen, who was about to eat after performing pooja. On hearing Jagdhar's voice, he said – Sit down, I'll eat and come.

Jagdhar – Sit down to eat after listening to me. The food won't run away. Are you also going to testify for Bhairo?

Thakurdeen – Yes, I'm going. I would have gone on my own even if Bhairo had not asked me. I can't see this immorality. These are different times; such a man would have been beheaded during the nawabi. Is it a joke to seduce somebody's bahu or beti?

Jagdhar – It seems that worshipping the gods you have also become all-knowing. I ask you, what are you going to testify to?

Thakurdeen – It's not a secret, the whole place knows.

Jagdhar – Soordas is a budding youth, that's why the beauty is infatuated with him. Isn't it? Or he has heaps of wealth and jewellery, that's why the woman became greedy. You haven't seen God but you know him with your intelligence. After all, what did Subhagi see in him that she left Bhairo to live in Soorey's house?

Thakurdeen – No one knows what's in somebody else's mind, and even God doesn't know what's in a woman's mind. Even the gods cry out for mercy to be saved from her.

Jagdhar – All right then, go, but I'm telling you that you'll have to bear the consequences. There's no greater sin than to make a false allegation against a poor man.

Thakurdeen – Is it a false allegation?

Jagdhar – It's false, completely false. There's not a grain of truth in it. You'll remember the lament of a helpless man all your life. A man who can return his lost wealth can't be so base.

Thakurdeen (*Laughing*) – This is the blind man's trick. He's so far-sighted that anybody who hears about it will be baffled.

Jagdhar – I've warned you, now you know best. Will you keep Subhagi in your house? I'll bring her here from Soorey's. If you ever see Soorey talking to her again then do what you want to. Will you keep her?

Thakurdeen – Why should I keep her?

Jagdhar – So what wrong did Shivji do when he took the poison of the whole world on his head?* Soorey gave shelter to somebody who had nowhere else to go. Should he get such a punishment for doing this good deed? Is this justice? If Soorey turns Subhagi out of the house because of the pressure put by all of you and she's dishonoured, the sin for that will be on your head. Remember this.

Thakurdeen was a God-fearing soul. He was in a dilemma. Jagdhar understood his plight and said a few more things in this vein. Eventually Thakurdeen refused to testify. Jagdhar's jealousy worked like the sermon of a sadhu. Bhairo realized that he wouldn't find any witnesses. He could only gnash his teeth. The lamps had been lit. The other shops in the bazaar were closing. It was time to open the toddy shop. The customers were gathering. The old woman was making daal-motth with peas, and spicy pakoras for the savouries, and Bhairo was sitting at the door reciting the woes of the whole world to Jagdhar and the muhalla-valas. 'They are all impotent and blind, that's why there's so much misery. People ask why there's a famine or a plague, why does cholera spread? What else can happen where such dishonest people, sinners and villains live? It's surprising that God doesn't devastate this country. Anyway, if life is still there, Jagdhar and I both live here, we'll see.'

One is quick to recall one's good deeds in a fit of anger. Bhairo began

---

* Reference to the myth of the churning of the ocean of milk by the gods for the nectar of immortality. Shiva drank the poison that emerged from the ocean to save the universe from destruction.

to describe the favours that he had done Jagdhar – His wife was dying. Someone said she could be saved if she drank fresh toddy. I'd climb the tree at the crack of dawn to bring fresh toddy for her. Nobody else would have climbed a tree that early in the morning, not even for five rupees. I must have brought pitchers of toddy for her. He comes here whenever he wants tobacco, I'm the one to help him whenever he needs money and he deceives me like this! Such are the times.

Jagdhar's house adjoined his. He heard everything but didn't open his mouth. He was an expert at stabbing from behind, not at attacking from the front.

Meanwhile, a mechanic from the factory, wearing half-sleeves, smeared with coal ash and as dark as coal, carrying a sledgehammer, and flaunting leather shoes, came and said – Are you coming to the shop or will you go on wrangling about this? It's getting late and we also have to go to sahib's bungalow.

Bhairo – Go away, you are worried about the shop. Here my heart is burning so fiercely that I want to set the village on fire.

Mechanic –What is it? What are you so angry about? Tell me.

Bhairo narrated the entire tale in brief and began to lament the cowardice and rudeness of the villagers.

Mechanic – Forget the villagers. How many witnesses do you need? I'll get you as many as you want—one, two, ten, twenty? Good man, why didn't you tell me earlier? I'll fix them today; just let them all drink to their heart's content.

Delighted, Bhairo said – It doesn't matter about the toddy, it's your shop, drink as much as you want but get some reliable witnesses.

Mechanic – If you want, I can even bring the babus. Just make them drink so much that all of them will go home drunk from here.

Bhairo – Aji, I'll make them drink so much that a few corpses will be carried away from here.

Talking in this vein, both of them reached the shop. Twenty to twenty-five people who worked in the factory were waiting eagerly for Bhairo. Bhairo began to measure the toddy as soon as he reached and the mechanic began to fix the witnesses. They talked in whispers.

One of them – It's a good chance. Where will she go after leaving the blind man's house? Bhairo won't keep her now.

The second – After all, we also need something to entertain us.

The third – God has sent her himself. The hanging basket of food has dropped down for the cat.

While this intriguing was going on, Subhagi was telling Soordas – Legal action is being taken against you.

Soordas asked anxiously – What legal action?

Subhagi – For running away with me. Witnesses are being fixed. Nobody could be found from the village, but several factory labourers are ready. Jagdhar just told me that all the men of the village had been ready to testify at first.

Soordas – Then why did they stop?

Subhagi – Jagdhar persuaded them and stopped them.

Soordas – Jagdhar is a very good man, he's very kind to me.

Subhagi – So what will happen now?

Soordas – Let them take legal action, there's nothing to be afraid of. Just tell them that you won't live with Bhairo. If they ask why, tell them frankly that he beats you.

Subhagi – But you will be so disgraced.

Soordas – I'm not afraid of the disgrace, I won't let you go until he's willing to keep you.

Subhagi – I won't go to his house even if he agrees. He's a very foul man, he's sure to take revenge for this. I'll go away from your house as well.

Soordas – Why will you go away from my house? I'm not throwing you out.

Subhagi – You'll be a laughing stock because of me. I was not afraid of the muhalla-valas. I knew that nobody would doubt you and, even if they did, the suspicion would be removed in a moment. But what do these uncouth factory labourers know about you? All of them drink toddy at Bhairo's. He'll make them drunk and ruin your honour. He'll calm down if I don't stay here. After all, I'm the knot of poison.

Soordas – Where will you go?

Subhagi – Where I can blacken his face, where I can grind moong on his chest and give him a hard time.

Soordas – If his face is blackened, won't mine be blackened first? After all, you are my sister.

Subhagi – No, I'm nothing to you. Don't make me a beti-behen.

Soordas – I'm telling you, don't leave this house.

Subhagi – I won't disgrace you now by living with you.

Soordas – I'll accept disgrace but I won't let you go until I know where you'll go.

Bhairo passed the night somehow. He rushed to the court early in the morning. The doors were still shut, sweepers were sweeping the floor, so he sat under a tree, meditating. From 9 a.m. onwards, the clerks began to arrive, briefcases pressed to their sides, and Bhairo rushed to greet them. Raja sahib arrived at the bench at 11 a.m. and Bhairo got his complaint written by the clerk and filed it. When he returned home in the evening, he boasted, 'Now I'll see which bold lad will support them. I'm not my father's son if I don't blacken their faces and throw them out from here.'

There were summons on the fifth day for Soordas and Subhagi. The date was fixed. Subhagi became increasingly nervous as the date of the hearing approached. She would repeatedly argue with Soordas – You are responsible for all this, you are ruining your honour and you are dragging me along with you. Why would anybody have had any enmity against you if you had let me go? To appear in the full court, to stand before everybody, is like poison for me. I won't see his face, even if the court kills me.

Eventually the date of the hearing arrived. There was so much interest in this case in the muhalla that people stopped their work and reached the court. The labourers of the mill came in hundreds. Several people in the city had come to know Soordas. They thought him to be innocent. Thousands of people came to the court out of curiosity. Prabhu Sevak had reached there earlier; Indu rani and Indradutt also arrived by the time the hearing began. There's always a crowd in court but for a woman to come there was like a bride coming to the mandap. It was as if a bazaar had been set up in the court. Two gentlemen were ensconced on the bench – Raja Sahib of Chataari and a Muslim who had been very enthusiastic about enrolling recruits during the European Great War. There was also a lawyer to plead for Bhairo.

Bhairo gave his testimony. The witnesses gave theirs. After that, Bhairo's lawyer questioned them to argue his case. Then Soordas gave his testimony. He said – Bhairo's wife has been staying with me since a few days. Who am I to provide for anyone? It's God who provides for us. She stays in my house; she can leave today if Bhairo wants to keep her and if she wants to stay with him, in fact that's what I want. That's why I have let her stay with me otherwise nobody knows where she would have gone.

Bhairo's lawyer (*Smiling*) – Soordas, you seem to be very generous but generosity towards beautiful young women has no importance.

Soordas – Isn't that why this case is being fought? I haven't done anything wrong. Yes, the world can think whatever it wants to. I care only about God. He's the one who watches over everybody's actions. I won't let this woman leave my house if Bhairo doesn't keep her and if sarkar doesn't send her to a place where she can live with respect and honour. I won't let her leave even if she wants to. Ever since she has heard about this case she keeps saying, let me go, but I don't let her.

Lawyer – Why don't you say frankly that you have kept her?

Soordas – Yes, I have kept her, as a brother keeps his sister, as a father keeps his daughter. Sarkar will be responsible for her honour if she is forced to leave my house.

Subhagi gave her testimony – I was innocent but Bhairo would beat and abuse me. I won't live with him. Soordas is a good man, that's why I'm staying with him. Bhairo can't see this and he wants me to be turned out of Soordas's house.

Lawyer – Did you go to Soordas's house earlier as well?

Subhagi – Whenever I was beaten at my house, I would save my life and run to his house. He used to protect me. His house was burnt because of me, he was beaten, what troubles didn't he have to suffer? The only thing missing was a court case and now even that has happened.

Raja – Bhairo, will you keep your woman?

Bhairo – Yes sarkar, I'll keep her.

Raja – You won't beat her?

Bhairo – Why should I beat her if she doesn't go astray?

Raja – Subhagi, why don't you go to your husband's house? He says he won't beat you.

Subhagi – I don't trust him. He'll beat me even today till I'm senseless.

Lawyer – Huzoor, the case is clear, there's no need now for elaborate proofs. Soordas's crime has been proved.

The court gave its judgement – A penalty of 200 rupees for Soordas and rigorous imprisonment for six months if he couldn't pay it. A penalty of 100 rupees for Subhagi and rigorous imprisonment for three months if she couldn't pay it. The money, if collected, would be given to Bhairo.

The spectators began to discuss this judgement.

One of them – Soordas seems innocent to me.

A second – All this is raja sahib's doing. Soordas had maligned him about the land. It's revenge for that. These are the deeds of our prestigious–respected–voluptuous leaders.

A third – The woman doesn't seem wanton to me.

A fourth – She's talking in the full court, what else is she if not wanton?

A fifth – She says she won't stay with Bhairo.

Suddenly Soordas said loudly – I'll appeal against this judgement.

Lawyer – There can't be an appeal against it.

Soordas – I'll appeal to the panch. I can't be guilty because of what one man says; it doesn't matter how great he may be. The judge has punished me, so I'll bear it but I also want to hear the judgement of the panch.

He then turned to the spectators and addressed them with heart-rending words – Panch, this is a lament; so many of you are gathered here. You heard the testimonies of Bhairo and his witnesses, Subhagi's testimony and mine, and also the decision of the judge. I appeal to you—do you also think that I'm guilty? Do you believe that I seduced Subhagi and am keeping her with me as my wife? If you believe this, I'll sit down with my head bowed on this very field and all of you can kick me five times each. I won't regret it if I die being kicked. This is the right punishment for such a sinner. How does imprisonment matter? And if you think I'm innocent, proclaim loudly, 'We think you are innocent.' Then I'll happily go through the most rigorous punishment.

There was silence in the courtroom. Raja sahib, the lawyers, the clerks, the spectators were all startled. Nobody knew what to do. There were dozens of sepoys but they stood like statues. The situation had taken a strange turn for which there was no precedent in the history of the court. The enemy had attacked in such a way that the predetermined plan of the opposing army was destroyed.

The first to compose himself was raja sahib. He ordered, 'Take him out.' The sepoys surrounded both the accused and took them out of the court. Thousands of spectators followed them.

After walking a short distance, Soordas sat down on the ground and said – I'll go on only after hearing the orders of the panch.

There was no fear of contempt of court outside. Several thousand voices cried – You are innocent; we think you are innocent.

Indradutt – The court is dishonest.

Several thousand voices repeated – Yes, the court is dishonest.

Indradutt – It's not a court but an altar for sacrificing the poor.

Several thousand voices echoed – It's a tool of oppression in the hands of the rich.

When the chowkidars saw that the crowd was increasing every moment and people were getting excited, they rushed to catch hold of a buggy-vala and took both of them away. People followed the gharry for some distance, then returned to their homes.

The orderly of the court stopped Bhairo as he returned home with his witnesses. Bhairo gave him two rupees. As soon as they reached the shop, the pitchers were opened and rounds of toddy began. The old woman began to cook pakoris and puris.

One of them said – Bhairo, this isn't right. Come and sit down, drink and give us drink. Let's drink doggedly today.

A second – I'll drink so much today even if I collapse here. Why are you filling up this kulhar again and again? Bring the handi.

Bhairo – Aji, put your mouth into the pitcher, what's the capacity of a handi or a kulhar? The plaintiff has been humiliated today.

A third – Both of them must be lying there in custody and crying. But bhai, so what if Soordas has been punished? He's innocent after all.

Bhairo – So you are also taken in by him! He lives by this deceit. Just see how he managed to change the minds of thousands of people by his talk.

A fourth – He has the blessings of a devata.

Bhairo – We'll know about that if he manages to come out of the jail.

The first – I bet that he'll come out of the jail tomorrow.

The second – Old woman, bring the pakoris.

The third – Abey, don't drink too much or you'll die. Isn't there anyone to cry for you at home?

The fourth – Let's have some music. Bring the dhol and the cymbals.

All of them took up the dhol and the cymbals and began to sing – Chhattisi,* how she flashes her eyes!

In a short while, an old mechanic got up and began to dance. The old woman couldn't stop herself now. She also covered her face and began dancing. Dancing and singing are natural talents among the shudras, they don't need to learn them. The old man and the old woman both danced, swaying their waists obscenely. The suppleness of their limbs was amazing.

Bhairo – The muhalla-valas thought I wouldn't get any witnesses.

One of them – They are all jackals, jackals!

Bhairo – Come, let's go and blacken their faces.

All of them shouted, haan-haan, let the dancing go on. The procession left in a moment, stumbling, dancing and singing, beating the dhol, blabbering stupidly, shouting and creating a din. They first found Bajrangi's house. They stopped there and sang –

The milkmaid's cow has fled, so she mixes water in milk.

The night had become very damp and Bajrangi's door was shut.

They went to Thakurdeen's door and sang –

The tamolin's** eyes are beautiful, she exchanges glances with her yaars.

Thakurdeen was eating but he was too afraid to come out. The procession went ahead and came to Soordas's hut.

Bhairo said – Bas, now just stay fixed here.

'The dhol has become slack.'

'Warm it, warm it; take straw from the hut.'

One man took out a little straw, another took out some more, and a third pulled out a bunch. The frenzy of intoxication is well known. Somebody threw the burning straw on to the hut and said – It's Holi, it's Holi. Several men echoed – It's Holi, it's Holi.

Bhairo said – Yaaron, what you've done is wrong. Run or you'll be caught.

---

* A lewd woman who pretends to be chaste
** Paan-seller's wife; a woman who sells paan

Fear doesn't leave us even when we are intoxicated. All of them ran. When the fire began to rage, the people of the muhalla rushed there. But who could control a fire of straw? The hut was burning and people stood by talking with anger and pain.

Thakurdeen – I was eating when I saw all of them coming.

Bajrangi – I want to beat Bhairo until he's lifeless.

Jagdhar – He won't be rid of this obsession until he gets a sound beating.

Bajrangi – Yes, this is what's going to happen now. Gheesoo, just bring out the stick. The fire will be put out only after a few murders today.

Jamuni – It's not your business, come and lie down. He'll get the fruit of his actions from God.

Bajrangi – Whether God gives him the fruit or not, I won't listen now! It's as if my body is burning.

Jagdhar – It's enough to make it burn. It won't be a sin to behead such a sinner.

Thakurdeen – Jagdhar, it's not good to sprinkle oil on fire. If you have any enmity against Bhairo, why don't you go and challenge him yourself, why do you provoke others? You only want the two of them to die fighting while you watch the fun. You are very base.

Jagdhar – If saying something is to provoke, all right, I'll keep quiet.

Thakurdeen – Yes, it's best to be quiet. You should go and sleep. Bajrangi! God himself will punish the sinner. He didn't let off somebody as mighty as Ravana, what's he worth? God will not tolerate this anarchy.

Bajrangi – He's mad with pride. Come, Jagdhar, why don't we go and have a talk with these people?

Jagdhar – No, bhaiyya, don't take me with you. Who knows, if there's a fight I'll be blamed for provoking it. I stay miles away from quarrels.

Meanwhile, Mitthua came running. Bajrangi asked – Where were you sleeping?

Mitthu – In Pandaji's veranda. Arey, this is my hut that's burning. Who burnt it?

Thakurdeen – You have been awake for so long, didn't you hear the singing and dancing?

Mitthu – Has Bhairo burnt it? All right, rascal, I'll straighten you.

After all of them had returned to their homes, Mitthua slowly went towards Bhairo's shop. The gathering had dispersed. There was darkness all around. It was a winter night, not a leaf stirred. Cow-dung cakes were burning at the door of the shop. The fire never goes out at a toddy shop; even a Parsi priest probably doesn't guard the fire so carefully. Mitthua picked up a burning cow-dung cake and threw it on the thatched roof of the shop. When the roof caught fire, Mitthua dashed to Pandaji's veranda and pretended to sleep with his face covered, as if he didn't know anything. In a short while the flames began to rage, the muhalla was illuminated, the birds flew away from the trees to escape, the branches of the trees began to shake, the water of the pond became golden, and the knots of the bamboos began to splutter loudly. Lanka burned for half an hour but this entire noise was more like the weeping of a forest. The shop was at a distance from the basti. Bhairo was senseless with intoxication, the old woman was tired dancing. Who else was there at this time to go and put out the fire? It finished its work unobstructed. The pitchers broke; toddy flowed. When the fire abated somewhat, several dogs came there to rest.

When Bhairo got up at dawn he couldn't see the shop. There was a distance of two furlongs between the shop and his house but since there were no trees, the shop could be seen clearly. He was surprised, where had the shop gone? He went ahead and saw a heap of ashes. The dust disappeared from beneath his feet. He ran. Besides toddy, there was money from the sales as well in the shop. The dhol and the cymbals were also kept there. Everything had been burnt to ashes. The muhalla-valas used to go to the pond to wash up. They all reached there. The shop was on the road. The travellers also stood there. A crowd had gathered.

Bhairo (*Crying*) – I've been reduced to dust.

Thakurdeen – It's God's leela. He showed one spectacle there and this spectacle here. Praise be to you, Maharaj!

Bajrangi – It must be a mechanic's mischief. Why, Bhairo, was there enmity against anyone?

Bhairo – Against whom is there not enmity? There's enmity against the whole muhalla. I know whose mischief it is. I'll see to it that he's imprisoned. I've taken care of one of them, now it's the turn of the other.

Jagdhar enjoyed himself from a distance. He didn't come near for fear that the situation would worsen if Bhairo said something. Never in his life had he experienced such heartfelt joy. Meanwhile, several labourers came from the mill. The black mechanic said – Bhai, whether anybody agrees or not, I can only say that the blind man has the blessings of a deity.

Thakurdeen – Of course he does. I've always said that. All his enemies have been humiliated.

Bhairo – I know who his deity is. Let the thanedar come, I'll tell you who he is.

Bajrangi (*Fuming*) – This is how you think when it's your turn. Wasn't it a hut that was burnt first? A brick will always be answered with a stone. The well is waiting for the one who digs a ditch for somebody else. When you set that hut on fire did you think that Soordas doesn't have anybody of his own?

Bhairo – Did I set his hut on fire?

Bajrangi – Who else did it?

Bhairo – You are a liar.

Thakurdeen – Bhairo, why are you being arrogant? Whether you set it on fire or one of your friends did, it's the same thing. God has avenged that, so why are you crying?

Bhairo – I'll take care of everybody.

Thakurdeen – Nobody here is afraid of you.

Bhairo left chewing his lips. Human nature is so mysterious. We don't scruple at all to harm others but our blood begins to boil when we ourselves are harmed.

32

WHEN INDRADUTT LEFT AFTER HEARING THE JUDGEMENT ON Soordas's case, he met Prabhu Sevak on the way and they both began to talk.

Indradutt – Do you think Soordas is innocent?

Prabhu – Completely innocent. I'm convinced of his saintliness today. Until the judgement was announced I was sure that the blind man had seduced the woman but his last words cast a kind of spell. I'm thinking of writing a poem on this topic.

Indradutt – It's not enough merely to write a poem. Raja sahib will have to be humiliated. He shouldn't have the satisfaction of making the blind man grind the millstone. He probably thinks that the blind man won't be able to give the money. They have both been fined 300 rupees; somehow we have to pay the penalty today. When Soordas is released from jail, his procession should be taken out in the city. We'll need 200 rupees more for that. Altogether, 500 rupees should be sufficient. How much will you give?

Prabhu – Write what you think appropriate.

Indradutt – Can you give fifty rupees without difficulty?

Prabhu – How much have you written against your name?

Indradutt – I can't give more than ten rupees. I'll take 100 rupees from Rani Jahnavi. Kunwar sahib will give at least ten. I'll make up the rest by asking others. It's possible that Dr Ganguly will give the entire amount himself and we won't need to ask anybody else.

Prabhu – We'll also get something from Soordas's muhalla-valas.

Indradutt – The whole city knows him, we can get 2000 to 4000 rupees for him but I don't want to trouble other people for such a small amount.

As they went ahead while they talked, they saw Indu coming on her phaeton. She stopped when she saw Indradutt and asked – When did you return? You didn't come to see me!

Indradutt – You are in the sky and I'm in the underworld, what can we talk about?

Indu – Come and sit down, there's a lot I want to talk to you about.

Indradutt sat on the phaeton. Prabhu took out a fifty-rupee note from his pocket and putting it quietly in Indradutt's pocket, went on to the club.

Indradutt – Tell your friends too.

Prabhu– No bhai, I can't do this. I don't know how to ask! Even if somebody wants to give something, he'll tighten his fist as soon as he sees my face.

Indradutt (*To Indu*) – There was quite a spectacle here today.

Indu – I enjoyed it as if it were a play. What do you think about Soordas?

Indradutt – He seems to me to be a straightforward, truthful, simple man.

Indu – That's it, that's what I think too. I think there has been an injustice done to him. I thought him to be guilty when I heard the judgement but his appeal changed my mind. I used to think that he was deceitful and crafty, a dyed jackal. He had vilified us so much during those days. I had begun to hate him since then. I wanted to teach him a lesson. But I realized today that I was mistaken about his character. He's firm about his convictions, fearless, detached and truthful, he won't be suppressed by anyone.

Indradutt – Then will you transform this sympathy into action? We want to make a collection to pay the penalty. Will you also contribute to this noble deed?

Indu (*Smiling*) – I think lip sympathy is enough.

Indradutt – My belief that there's no ethical force in our rais will be strengthened if you also talk like this. Our raavs and rais have been helping the authorities in every proper and improper action, that's why the public no longer trusts them. It thinks them to be its enemies and not its friends. I don't want you to be counted among those rais. I have thought you to be different from them at least until now.

Indu (*Gravely*) – Indradutt, you know why I'm doing this. Raja sahib will be so distressed when he gets to know! I don't want to do anything without his knowledge.

Indradutt – I haven't yet discussed this topic with raja sahib. But I'm sure that his views will be the same as ours. He has given a legal judgement right now. His heart must have made the right decision. Perhaps I may have given the same judgement as he has if I had been in the seat of justice. But that would only have been a legal decision, not that of my conscience. I'm not intimate with him otherwise I would have managed to get something from him as well. There was no way that he could have escaped.

Indu – Perhaps your conjecture about raja sahib is correct. I'll ask him today.

Indradutt – Ask, but I doubt that raja sahib will open up that easily.

Indu – You doubt and I'm sure. But I know that in normal circumstances our views are similar. That's why I won't give you the trouble of making you wait. Take this—it's my humble gift.

Indu took out a sovereign and gave it to Indradutt.

Indradutt – I have misgivings about accepting this.

Indu – Why?

Indradutt – Because raja sahib's views may be different.

Indu looked up proudly and said – That doesn't matter.

Indradutt – Yes, now you have spoken like a rani. This sovereign is a memorial to Soordas's moral victory. Many thanks! Now give me permission to leave. I have to make several rounds. I don't yet want to let go of whatever I can get besides the penalty.

Indradutt wanted to get down to leave when Indu took out another sovereign from her pocket and said – Take this, it may reduce your rounds.

Indradutt put the sovereign in his pocket and left delighted. But Indu was a little worried. She thought – raja sahib is sure to rebuke me if he really thinks that Soordas is guilty. Well, let it be, I don't want to be dominated so much. My duty is to give in to him for the right actions. I have every right to disagree with him if he oppresses the public for his mistaken views. I'm a human being first—a wife, mother, sister, daughter later.

Absorbed in these thoughts, Indu met Mr John Sevak and his wife. John Sevak took off his hat. Mrs Sevak said – We were going to your place. We hadn't met for a long time, so we wanted to meet you. Just as well that we found you on the way.

Indu – No, you didn't find me. Look, I'm going. You can go where you want to.

John Sevak – I always believe in *compromise*.* There's a park ahead. There'll also be a band today, we can go and sit there.

Indu – That *compromise* is not neutral, but all right.

They alighted at the park and sat down on the chairs. Indu asked – Have you received any letter from Sophia?

Mrs Sevak – She's dead for me. She won't find a man like Mr Clark. She kept evading while she was here. She has joined the rebels there. I don't know what's in her fate. I'll always regret that the match with Clark didn't come through.

John Sevak – I have told you thousands of times that she won't marry anyone. She hasn't been made for married life. She's an idealist and idealists always dream of bliss, they never obtain it. If she ever does get married it will be to Kunwar Vinay Singh.

Mrs Sevak – Don't take Kunwar Vinay Singh's name in my presence. Forgive me, Rani Indu, but I don't like such incompatible and unnatural marriages.

John Sevak – But such incompatible and unnatural marriages do happen sometimes.

Mrs Sevak – I'm telling you, and Rani Indu you are a witness, that Sophie will never marry Vinay Singh.

John Sevak – What do you think about this, Rani Indu? Tell us frankly.

Indu – I think Lady Sevak is right. It doesn't matter how much Vinay may love Sophia, he'll never disdain mataji so much. There's no unhappier woman in the world today than mataji. It seems that she has no hope left in life. She is constantly preoccupied. She frowns with anger if anyone mentions Vinay even by mistake. She has taken down Vinay's portrait from her room and has had the door of his room shut. She never goes there herself nor does she let anybody else go, and mentioning Miss Sophia's name is like pinching her. Pitaji is also no longer interested in the society of volunteers. He seems to have become indifferent to social work. Aha! I left home at a very

---

* The italicized words are in English in the original.

auspicious moment today. Dr Ganguly is coming here. Well, doctor sahib, when did you return from Shimla?

Dr Ganguly – It had become cold. They have all decamped from there now. I had just gone to see your mataji. She's very distressed by Kunwar Vinay Singh's plight.

John Sevak – This time you created a stir in the Council.*

Dr Ganguly – Yes, if you think that it's work to give speeches, to raise questions, to argue, you can praise me as much as you want, but for me it's not work, it's like sawing water. Work is that which benefits the country and the people. I haven't done any such work. I don't like being there now. To begin with, people don't unite, and even if they do, the government rejects our proposals. Our effort is wasted. It's a children's game. I had hoped a lot from the new constitution but after three or four years of experience I've realized that it doesn't achieve anything. We are where we used to be. The expenditure on the military continues to increase; if misgivings are expressed about it the government says you shouldn't talk like this. A few lakhs are increased on every item when the budget is made. When I insist, the Council cuts that unnecessary expenditure to please me. The members are delighted—we have won, we have won. Ask, what have you won? What can you win? You don't have the means of winning, so how can you win? There's some economizing if I press a lot, but it's our brothers who are harmed. For example, we have cut five lakhs from the police department this time. But it's not the pay or allowances of the higher officials that have been reduced. It's the pay of the poor chowkidars, constables, thanedars that will be cut and the posts reduced. That's why I'm afraid of raising the issue of economy because it's our brothers whose throats are cut. The entire Council insisted that twenty lakhs should be sanctioned to help the people who have suffered because of the Bengal floods; the entire Council kept insisting that Mr Clark should be transferred from Udaipur, but the government didn't consent. The Council can't do anything. It can't pluck even one leaf. Those who form the Council can also destroy it. God gives life and he also kills. The government forms the Council so it is in the

---

* The Council of State set up as a result of the Government of India Act of 1919.

government's power. The country will benefit if the Council is formed by the people. Everybody knows that, but it's better to do something than to do nothing. Death is death, and to remain lying on the cot is also death, but there's no hope in one situation and some hope in the other. That's the only difference.

Indu teased him – Why do you go there if you know that it's futile? Can't you do anything by remaining outside?

Dr Ganguly (*Laughing*) – That's just it, Indu Rani, I'm lying on the cot, I can't move, I can't eat but, baba, I'll run away if I see Yamraj! I'll cry, Maharaj, give me a few more days. I've spent my life in the Council, I can't think of any other way now.

Indu – I would prefer to die than to live such a life. At least there'll be hope of a better life in the future.

Dr Ganguly (*Laughing*) – If anyone tells me that I'll return to this country after dying and will again be in the Council, I'll tell Yamraj, 'Baba, hurry up', but nobody says that.

John Sevak – I thought I'd stand for the new elections from the business chamber.

Dr Ganguly – Which party will you represent?

John Sevak – I don't have a party and I won't have one. I'll stand with the aim of protecting swadeshi business. I'll try to see that foreign goods are heavily taxed; our business will never prosper unless we follow this policy.

Dr Ganguly – What will you do about England?

John Sevak – It should also be treated like the other countries. I'm strongly opposed to being subjected to England's economic slavery.

Dr Ganguly (*Looking at his watch*) – That's very good, you should stand. I have to go alone from here now. Then the two of us will go together. All right, I'll leave now. I have to meet several people.

After Dr Ganguly had left, John Sevak also returned home. When Indu reached home, raja sahib asked – Where have you been?

Indu – I met Dr Ganguly and Mr John Sevak on the way, so we talked.

Mahendra – Why didn't you bring Ganguly with you?

Indu – He was in a hurry. This blind man was marvellous today.

Mahendra – He's a villain. Anyone who doesn't know his nature is sure to be deceived by him. Nobody could have thought of a better way to prove his innocence. It's a miracle. It has to be acknowledged that he understands human nature very well. Although he's illiterate himself, he made so many educated and thoughtful people his devotees today. People are collecting a donation to pay his penalty. I hear they also want to take out a procession. But I'm fully convinced that he has seduced that woman and I regret that I didn't give a harsher punishment.

Indu – In that case, you didn't give a donation either?

Mahendra – You say such absurd things sometimes. How could I give a donation and slap my own face?

Indu – But I did. I . . .

Mahendra – You were wrong to have given it.

Indu – How was I to know that . . .

Mahendra – Don't talk nonsense. Have you told them to keep your name secret?

Indu – No, I haven't said anything.

Mahendra – Then there's no greater fool than you in the world. You must have given Indradutt the money. Indradutt is otherwise a very courteous and generous youth and I respect him from my heart. But he'll take this opportunity to collect money from others by using your name. Just think carefully, what will people say? It's a pity! You should realize that I'm exercising infinite patience by not banging my head against the wall at this moment. I have always been humiliated because of you and this action of yours is a black mark on my face that can never be effaced.

Mahendra Kumar lay down on the armchair and gazed at the ceiling. He may or may not have exercised infinite patience by not banging his head against the wall, but Indu certainly exercised infinite patience in hiding her feelings. 'I wanted to tell him that I'm not your slave, it seems incredible that there can be such a being who is not moved by such a pitiful appeal.' But she was afraid of the matter getting out of hand. She wanted to leave the room and to trample the cruel destiny that seemed bent on destroying her peace and to show it that its cruellest blows can be opposed by patience and tolerance. But just as she walked towards the door, Mahendra Kumar sat upright and said, 'Where are you going? Do you now hate the sight of my face? I want to ask you frankly, why do you act in such an unrestrained way? I have told you so many times not to do anything without asking me on matters that concern me. Yes, you are free to do what you want about your personal affairs but why does my entreating not have any effect on you? Have you vowed to rest only after disgracing me, reducing my honour to dust and trampling my esteem?'

Indu pleaded – For God's sake, don't compel me to say anything just now. I don't want to argue about whether or not I made a mistake. I admit that I definitely made a mistake. I'm prepared to atone for it. If you are still not satisfied, then here, I'll sit down. You can say whatever you want to for as long as you like, I won't raise my head.

But anger is very cruel. It wants to see whether each and every sentence has found its mark or not, it can't bear silence. The power of silence is limitless. People may have the deadliest weapon in their arsenals but silence is the mantra that can render it powerless. Silence is invincible before it. Mahendra Kumar was annoyed and said, 'That means that I suffer from the disease of talkativeness which sometimes attacks me?'

Indu – This is what you say.

Indu made the mistake of not keeping her vow. Anger got another whip. Mahendra glared and said – You are saying this, not I. After all, what's the matter? I'm asking you out of curiosity, why do you repeatedly act in such ways that I'm criticized and become a laughing stock, my honour and esteem are reduced to dust, and I can't show my face anywhere? I know that you don't act like this out of obstinacy. I'll even go so far as to say that you try to obey my orders. But despite that, what's the reason for this censure? Could it be that we were enemies in our previous births, or that Providence has tied you to my strings to destroy my desires and ambitions? I often wonder about this but I can't fathom the mystery.

Indu – I can't guarantee that it can be kept a secret. Yes, if you wish, I can give Indradutt strict instructions that my name should not be revealed.

Mahendra – Why are you talking so childishly? You should have understood the motives with which this donation is being collected; its aim is to show disrespect for my judgement and to dig at the roots of my fame. If I scold my servant and you stroke his back, what else can I gather except that you want to vilify me? The donation will of course be collected, I don't have the right to stop it—when I don't have any control over you, what can I say about anybody else? But I won't allow the procession. I'll order it to be stopped. I won't hesitate to take the help of the army if I see people being overzealous.

Indu – Do what you think is proper. Why tell me all this?

Mahendra – I'm telling you because you are also one of the devotees of that blind man. Who can say that you haven't decided to take deeksha from him? After all Raidas Bhagat also has devotees among the higher castes.*

Indu – I don't think that deeksha is a means of salvation and I'll probably never take deeksha. Yes, you may think him to be as bad as you like, but unfortunately I'm fully convinced that Soordas is innocent. If this is devotion to him, I'm definitely his devotee.

Mahendra – You won't join the procession tomorrow, will you?

Indu – I did want to go, but now I won't because of you. I can't see a naked sword hanging over me.

Mahendra – That's good. Thank you very much for this.

Indu went to her room and lay down. She was very disturbed. She thought over what raja sahib had said for a long time, then said to herself – God, this life is unbearable. Either make him liberal or take me away from this world. I don't know where Indradutt is right now. Why don't I send him a message forbidding him to reveal my name? I unnecessarily told raja sahib that I had given a donation. How did I know this would happen?

She promptly rang the bell, the servant came in and stood there. Indu wrote the message – Dear Indra, don't talk about my donation to anyone, or I'll be very upset. I'm writing these words because I'm very helpless.

Giving the message to the servant, she asked – Do you know Indradutt-babu's house?

Servant – It's somewhere in the city, isn't it? I'll ask someone.

Indu – Perhaps it will take more than a lifetime to find his address in the city.

Servant – Give me the letter, I'll find the address.

Indu – Take a tonga, the work is urgent.

---

* Raidas Bhagat: Also known as Ravidas, a poet-saint of the fifteenth century who belonged to the chamaar community.

Servant – My legs are no less than a tonga. Do I walk slower than any wretched tonga?

Indu – Go to my house from the bazaar chowk. You'll find him there without fail. Have you seen Indradutt? Do you recognize him?

Servant – If I see somebody once, I don't forget him all my life. I have seen Inder-babu hundreds of times.

Indu – Don't show this letter to anybody.

Servant – How will anybody see it, won't I blind him first?

Indu gave the message and the servant left. She then lay down and began to think over the same things – I'm being insulted because of him. What will Indra think? That raja sahib must have scolded me, isn't it? He scolds me whenever he likes, as if I'm a maidservant. I don't have the freedom to do anything. He has the right to do what he wants; I'm forced to act according to his wishes. It's such a wretched state.

She got up hastily and rang the bell. The maidservant came in. Indu said – Go and see, has Bheekha left? I gave him a message, go and ask him for it. I won't send it now. Send somebody after him on a cycle if he has left. He'll be somewhere near the chowk.

The maidservant left and returned after a short while with Bheekha. Bheekha said – I would not have been found at home had I not left in a second.

Indu – You have done something for which you should pay a penalty because the letter was so urgent and you were still in the house. But it's for the best. That message won't be sent now, give it to me.

Indu took the message and tore it. Then she opened today's newspaper. The first headline was – 'Shastriji's important speech'. Indu threw down the paper. 'This gentleman has become more famous than the devil. Wherever you look, there's Shastri. One may admire such a man's ability but he can't be respected. As soon as I hear Shastriji's name, I'm reminded of him [Raja Mahendra]. Somebody who harasses because of the slightest difference, who'll turn his wife out of the house if there's a little too much salt in the daal, who is completely insensitive to other people's feelings and not at all concerned about the impact that his words will have on others, what kind of a man is he? Perhaps he'll tell me tomorrow not to go to my father's house, it's as if he has bought me.'

The next day she ordered a gharry and was about to leave the house, wearing a shawl. Mahendra Kumar was walking in the garden. This was his daily routine. When he saw Indu leaving, he asked – Where are you going this early in the morning?

Indu said, looking the other way – I'm going to obey your orders. I'll take back the money from Indradutt.

Mahendra – Indu, I'm telling you, you'll drive me crazy.

Indu – You want to make me dance like a puppet, now here and now there.

Indradutt could be seen approaching. Indu rushed towards him as if to greet him. Reaching the gate, she said – Indradutt, tell me the truth, you haven't discussed my donation with anybody?

Indradutt was disconcerted, like somebody who has given a shopkeeper a rupee instead of a paisa. He said – You didn't tell me not to.

Indu – You're lying, I had told you.

Indradutt – Indu Rani, I remember very well that you didn't tell me not to. Yes, I should have used my own intelligence. That's certainly my mistake.

Indu (*Softly*) – Can you at least tell Mahendra that I didn't discuss him with anybody? You'll do me a great favour. I'm in a deep moral dilemma.

Indu's eyes filled with tears as she said this. Indradutt sensed the atmosphere. He said – Yes, I will, for your sake.

Indradutt promptly went to meet raja sahib. Indu went into the house.

Mahendra Kumar – Well, mahashaya, why have you taken this trouble?

Indradutt – It's no trouble for me, I have come to give you trouble. Forgive me. Although it's against the rules, I beg you to accept the penalty for Soordas and Subhagi from me right now and order their release. The court will open only later. I'll consider this a special favour from you.

Mahendra Kumar – Yes, it is against the rules but I have to be considerate to you. Give the money to the muneem, I'll write the orders for the release. How much money have you collected?

Indradutt – I just approached a few selected gentlemen in the evening. There are about 500 rupees.

Mahendra Kumar – Then you're an expert at this art. Seeing Indu Rani's name, even those who wouldn't have given anything otherwise must have done so.

Indradutt – I have far more respect than this for Indu Rani's name. I would have brought 5000 rupees, not 500 had I shown her name.

Mahendra Kumar – If that's true, then you have protected my honour.

Indradutt – I want to make another request to you. Some people want to take Soordas home with respect. It's possible that a few hundred spectators might gather there. I want your permission for this.

Mahendra Kumar – I can't give you permission to take out a procession. There's danger of a breach of peace.

Indradutt – I assure you that not a leaf will stir.

Mahendra Kumar – That's impossible.

Indradutt – I can give a surety for this.

Mahendra Kumar – That can't be done.

Indradutt realized it was now futile to plead with raja sahib. He gave the money to the muneem and went to the tonga. Suddenly raja sahib asked – So there'll be no procession?

Indradutt – There will be. I can't stop it even if I want to.

Indradutt went from there inform his friends. It took hours to make arrangements for the procession. As soon as he had left, raja sahib rang up the daroga and told him that Soordas and Subhagi should be released and taken home in a closed gharry. When Indradutt reached the jail with a vehicle, band and other things, he found that the cage was empty; the bird had flown. He was left wringing his hands. He immediately went to Pandeypur. He saw Soordas under a neem tree sitting beside a heap of ashes. Subhagi was standing on one side with her head bowed. Jagdhar and several other men gathered there as soon as they saw Indradutt.

Indradutt – Soordas, you were in a great hurry. People there had prepared to take out your procession. Raja sahib has won the game. Tell me now what should be done with the money that had been collected for the expenses of the procession?

Soordas – It's just as well that I came here quietly. Otherwise I would have had to wander around the whole city. Are processions taken out of great men or of blind beggars? You people gave the penalty and freed me, isn't that dharma enough?

Indradutt – Achcha, tell me, what should be done with this money? Should I give it to you?

Soordas – How much money is there?

Indradutt – About 300 rupees.

Soordas – That's enough. Bhairo's shop can easily be built with that.

Jagdhar felt annoyed. He said – Think of your own hut first.

Soordas – I can stay under this tree, or in Pandaji's veranda.

Jagdhar – The person whose shop was burnt will get it built, why do you worry?

Soordas – It was burnt because of me.

Jagdhar – Your house has also been burnt.

Soordas – That will also be built, but later. Bhairo will lose such a lot if the shop is not built. My begging won't stop even for a day.

Jagdhar – Too much praise also spoils a man. People began to sing the praises of your goodness so you thought that you should do something that will get you even more praise. You shouldn't dance like this to other people's clapping.

Indradutt – Soordas, let these people blabber. You are wise; don't leave the side of wisdom. I'm leaving this money with you, do what you want with it.

When Indradutt had left, Subhagi said to Soordas – Don't even talk about getting his shop built.

Soordas – His shop will be built before my house. Who wants to bear the disgrace that Soordas got Bhairo's shop burnt? I'm convinced that one of us has burnt it.

Subhagi – It doesn't matter how much you give in to him, he'll always be your enemy. A dog's tail can never be straightened.

Soordas – I'll ask you when both of you come together again.

Subhagi – May God kill me but not show me his face again.

Soordas – I'm telling you, one day you'll be the devi of Bhairo's home.

Soordas took the money and went towards Bhairo's house. Bhairo had wanted to file a report but he was afraid of the matter of Soordas's hut coming up. What answer would he give then? He had resolved to go several times but had not yet done so. Meanwhile, he was taken aback when he saw Soordas coming. He said, surprised – Arey, have you given the penalty?

The old woman said – Beta, he definitely has the blessing of a devata, otherwise how could he have escaped from there?

Soordas said – Bhairo, God is my witness that I don't know who burnt your shop. You may think me to be as vile as you like but this would never have happened with my knowledge. Yes, I can say that it's the work of some well-wisher of mine.

Bhairo – First tell me how you've been released from there. I'm very surprised.

Soordas – By God's wish. Some dharmatmas of the city collected a donation and paid the penalty and there are also 300 rupees left which they have given me. I've come here to tell you to take this money and get your shop built so that you don't suffer any loss. I've brought all the money.

Bhairo looked at him astonished, like a man who sees pearls raining from the sky wondering whether to gather them or not, is there a mystery about them, is there a poisonous insect hidden in them, will something disastrous happen to me if I collect them? The question arose in his mind, 'Has this blind man really come to give me the money or is he taunting me? I should sound him out.' He said, 'You keep your money, nobody starves for it here. We don't accept water from an enemy even if we are dying of thirst.'

Soordas – Where is there any enmity between us? I don't think of anybody as my enemy. Why should there be enmity when life is so short? You haven't done me any wrong. If I had been in your place and had thought that you had run away with my wife I would have done what you have done. Who doesn't value his honour? The man for whom his honour is not dear to him should be counted among beasts and not men. I'm telling you the truth, I took this money only for you, otherwise the shade of the tree was enough for me. I know that you still doubt me but the misunderstanding between us will be cleared sometime or the other. Take this money and with God's name get the shop built. If it's not enough, then the God who has helped so much will help even more.

Bhairo got a glimpse of generosity and goodness in these sentences. Truth generates trust. He said softening – Come, sit. Smoke chillum. I'll understand if we talk a little. I can't guess what's in your heart. Nobody is good to an enemy, why are you being so kind to me?

Soordas – Where have you been my enemy? You did what was your dharma. All night in custody I kept wondering why you were after me. I haven't harmed you. Then I realized that you haven't harmed me. This is your dharma. There's often bloodshed because of a woman. What was wrong if you filed a complaint? Bas, my one request to you is that just as the panch yesterday said that I was innocent in the full court, you should also remove this misunderstanding about me from your heart. May I suffer even more if I have harmed you in any way! Yes, there's one thing that I can't do. I can't turn Subhagi out of my house. I'm afraid of what her plight will be if she doesn't have a shelter. If she stays with me, who knows, you may take her back some day.

Bhairo's wicked heart was moved by this inner purity. For the first time today he believed in Soordas's good intentions. He thought, 'Why would he talk to me like this if he were not sincere? He has nothing to fear from me. I've done whatever I could. The whole city is with him. They all paid his penalty. They also gave hundreds of rupees on top of that. The muhalla is also again in awe of him. He can easily ruin me if he wants to. If he were not sincere, he could now have lived comfortably with Subhagi. He's blind, he's a cripple, he begs, but he commands so much respect that even eminent men welcome him. I'm so vile and base; I cheat and deceive day and night for money. Is there any sin that I have not committed? I burnt this poor man's house, not once but twice, I stole his money twice. But he goes on being good to me. I had so many doubts about Subhagi. Who could have stopped him from keeping Subhagi with him openly if his intentions were not good? And especially now that there's no fear of the court.' He said to Soordas, 'Soordas, forgive me for all the harm that I have done you. God will punish me if I harm you from today. Don't give me this money, I have money. This too is yours. I'll get a shop built. I don't have any doubts about Subhagi either. I'm telling you, with God as my witness, I'll never speak harshly to her again. I was mistaken until now. Subhagi won't refuse to come to my place if you tell her to, will she?

Soordas – She's willing to, she's only afraid that you'll beat her again.

Bhairo – Soorey, I understand her now. I'm not fit for her. She should have married a dharmatma. (*Softly*) I'm telling you today, the first time too I was the one who had burnt your house and stolen your money.

Soordas – Forget those things, Bhairo. I know everything. Who in the world can say that I'm Gangajal. The greatest sadhus and sanyasis are trapped in the delusion of maya, not to speak of people like us. Our greatest mistake is that we don't know how to play the game as a game. If anybody wins the game by cheating, what has he won? We should play so that our gaze is on victory but we are not afraid of defeat and we don't lose our honour. We shouldn't swagger so much when we win and think that now we'll never lose. This winning and losing is a part of life. Yes, I want to give you some advice. Why don't you leave the toddy shop and earn your living in some other way?

Bhairo – I'll do what you tell me to. This is a bad occupation. I'm in the company of gamblers, thieves and badmash people day and night. I listen to their talk and learn their ways. Now I've realized that this occupation has ruined me. Tell me, what should I do?

Soordas – Why don't you get into the business of wood? It's not bad. Lots of outsiders come here these days; there'll be good sales. Get a stockade built where you had the toddy shop and begin the wood business with this money.

Bhairo – That's a very good idea. But keep this money with you. There's no knowing my mind. I may do something bad with it. A man like me should only get enough food to fill half his belly. Once I have money I'll be crazed with some other obsession.

Soordas – I have neither house nor home. Where will I keep it?

Bhairo – Get your house built with this.

Soordas – Get my house built when you earn some profit from your wood shop.

Bhairo – Persuade Subhagi.

Soordas – I will.

Soordas left. When Bhairo reached home, the old woman said – He had come to make up with you, isn't it?

Bhairo – Why wouldn't he want to make up? I'm a big laat, after all. You can't think of anything else in your old age. He's not a man, he's a sadhu.

33

THE FACTORY WAS ALMOST READY. THE MACHINES WERE NOW BEING installed. To start with, the labourers and mechanics used to stay in the mill's verandas, they'd cook under the trees and sleep there, but when their numbers increased they began to take houses in the muhalla to live in. Pandeypur was a small basti, it didn't have so many houses, with the result that the muhalla-valas began to keep the outsiders in their homes out of greed for the rent. Somebody would draw a curtain to make a wall, somebody would build a hut and live there, and somebody would give the house to tenants. Bhairo had opened a wood shop. He began to stay there with his mother and had rented out his house. Thakurdeen put up a bamboo screen in front of his shop and made do there; an overseer made himself comfortable in his house. Jagdhar was the greediest among them; he rented out his entire house and subsisted in a straw thatch. There would be a baraat constantly staying in Nayakram's veranda. Greed overtook people to such an extent that even Bajrangi rented out a part of his house. But Soordas didn't take in anybody; he lived in his new house with Subhagi, which had been built with Indu's secret donation. Subhagi was still not willing to live with Bhairo. But the frequency of Bhairo's comings and goings at Soordas's house increased.

The machines had not yet been installed in the factory but it was expanding day by day. The remaining five bighas of Soordas's land had also been occupied by the mill by the same article of the law. Soordas could only wring his hands when he heard about it. He regretted that he had not made a bargain with John sahib who had been prepared to give 5000 rupees. Now he'd get a few hundred at the most. It seemed futile to him to start another movement. What could he achieve now when he had not been able to attain anything earlier? He had been afraid that this would happen and it had happened.

It was afternoon. Soordas was lying under the tree dozing when a chaprasi from the tehseel arrived and called out to him and gave him an order. Soordas realized that this was definitely something to do with the land. He took the order to the mill to get it read by one of the babus. But how could the babus decipher the simple language of the court? Nobody could tell him anything. He was returning defeated when Prabhu Sevak saw him. He promptly called Soordas to his room and read the order. It was written – Come to the tehseel and collect 1000 rupees as compensation for your land.

Soordas – It's only 1000?

Prabhu – Yes, that's what is written.

Soordas – Then I won't go to take the money. Sahib had said he would give 5000, but there's only 1000; about 150 rupees or more will go in bribes. Sarkar's treasury is empty; it will now become full.

Prabhu – If you don't take the money, it will be confiscated. Sarkar is always on the lookout for ways to rob the public's money, some on the pretext of tax, some on the pretext of wages, and some on one pretext or the other.

Soordas – It belongs to the poor, so the market price should be given. First they took the land by force, then they give the price that they want. This is not justice.

Prabhu – Sarkar hasn't come here to do justice, bhai, it has come to rule. Does it get anything by doing justice? There was a time when justice was thought to be the foundation of rule. Times have changed. Now it is the rule of business, and for the person who doesn't accept this rule, it's like aiming cannons at stars. What can you do? If you file a case in the civil court, sarkar's servants are sitting there too on the seat of justice.

Soordas – I won't take anything. When the raja is unrighteous, how can the lives of the public be safe?

Prabhu – What's the use of that? If you are getting 1000, take it. It's best to catch hold of the loincloth of the ghost who is running away.

Indradutt then arrived and said – I'm decamping today; I'm going to Rajputana.

Prabhu – You are going uselessly. First there's the scorching heat, and then the situation there is very dangerous. You'll unnecessarily get caught somewhere.

Indradutt – Bas, I just want to meet Vinay once. I want to find out how such a change, no, such a transformation, has come about in his nature, character and behaviour.

Prabhu – There must be some mystery. He's not one to be tempted. I'm his supreme devotee. If he wavers, I'll think righteousness has disappeared from the world.

Indradutt – Don't say that, Prabhu, human nature is very complex. I'm so angry at Vinay's transformation that I'll shoot him if I find him. But at least it's gratifying that his leaving won't make any difference to our organization. You know what assiduous efforts we made for the welfare of the people of Bengal. We couldn't get even a grain for ourselves for several days.

Soordas – Bhaiyya, who are these people who provide for the poor like this?

Indradutt – Arey Soordas! You are standing here in a corner. I didn't see you. Tell me, everything is all right, isn't it?

Soordas – It's all God's mercy. Whom were you talking about just now?

Indradutt – About my companions. Kunwar Bharat Singh has gathered some young men and has formed a society. He has also donated some land for its expenses. We are around 100 people right now. Our supreme dharma and vow is to serve the country as well as we can. Some of us have gone to Rajputana and some to Punjab, where the army of the government has fired at the public.

Soordas – Bhaiyya, this is very meritorious work. One should have a darshan of such mahatmas. So bhaiyya, you must be raising donations also?

Indradutt – Yes, people give donations if they want to. But we ourselves don't go around asking.

Soordas – Will you keep me if I go with you? I just live here filling my belly. I'll become a man if I stay with you.

Indradutt to Prabhu (*In English*) – He's such a simple man. Although he's a living image of service and sacrifice, he's untouched by arrogance; he doesn't attach any value to his noble deeds. Philanthropy is not an ambition with him; it's a part of his character.

Soordas said again – I can't do anything else, I'm illiterate, I'm ignorant, but if you tell me to sit by somebody's pillow I can sway the pankha for him, I can carry around anything that's loaded on my back.

Indradutt – What you do normally is far greater than what we people do on special occasions. To be good to enemies is not inferior to taking care of the sick.

Soordas's face lit up, like that of a poet being praised by a connoisseur. He said – Bhaiyya, why are you talking about me? What dharma and meritorious work can somebody do who begs for alms to fill his belly? I'll say something if you don't mind. I'm being bold but with your permission, I'll gift the money I have got as compensation to your society.

Indradutt – What money?

Prabhu – This is a very long story. It's enough to know that he has been given a compensation of 1000 rupees for the land that papa took from him with Raja Mahendra Kumar's help. This mill is being built from the wealth of that loot.

Indradutt – You didn't try and stop your papa?

Prabhu – I swear by God, Sophie and I both tried very hard to stop papa, but you know his nature, he doesn't listen to anybody if he's obsessed by something.

Indradutt – I would have fought with my father, regardless of whether the mill was built or whether it went to hell! In such a situation it was your duty at least to dissociate yourself from the mill. It's the duty of a son to obey his father, I believe that, but the son is not bound to follow his father if the father is unjust; each long word of your compositions drips with ethical beauty, you take such flights that even Harishchandra and Husain would be defeated,* but it seems that all your energy is spent only in using words, there's nothing left for action. The fact is that you are not even worth the dust of your compositions. You are a lion only when it comes to words. Soordas, we don't take donations from poor people like you. Our donors are the rich.

Soordas – Bhaiyya, if you don't take it, some thief will. What do I need money for? By your mercy I can get enough grain to fill my belly, the hut has been built for me to live in, what else do I need? It's much better to use it for some good work than for it to be stolen by a thief. Have this much mercy on me.

---

* Husain: The Prophet's grandson, revered as a martyr who fought tyranny; was killed and beheaded in the battle of Karbala in 680.
For Harishchandra, see chapter 27, p. 336.

Indradutt – If you want to give then get a well dug. Your name will be remembered for a long time.

Soordas – Bhaiyya, I'm not hungry for fame. Don't make excuses, take this money and give it to your society. I'll be rid of this burden.

Prabhu (*In English*) – Friend, take his money, or he won't be at peace. To call this compassion divine is to insult it. My imagination can't even reach that far. There are such people in the world. And there are people like us who throw a morsel from our full platters and the next day we rush to see our names in the papers. We would shoot the editor if he didn't publish this news in bold letters. He's a pure soul.

Indradutt – I'll take the money if this is your wish, but on the condition that you'll inform us if you need anything. I think that soon your hut will become a pilgrimage place for devotees and people will come for your darshan.

Soordas – Then I'll go and get the money today.

Indradutt – Don't go alone, otherwise those dogs of the court will give you a lot of trouble. I'll go with you.

Soordas – Now I have a request for you also, sahib. Why don't you get houses built for the workers of the factory? They are scattered in the whole basti and create a racket every day. Earlier, nobody teased the women in our muhalla, there weren't so many thefts, nor such bold gambling, nor such drunken rows. The women don't leave their houses to fill water until the workers reach here for work. There's such a din at night that one can't sleep. If you try to reason with anybody, he's ready to fight.

Soordas was silent after saying this. He wondered if he had exaggerated too much. Indradutt looked scornfully at Prabhu and said – Bhai, this is not good. Tell your papa to make these arrangements soon. What's happened to all your principles? You are just sitting there watching all this and not doing anything.

Prabhu – I have hated this work from the very beginning. I don't like it nor am I suited for it. The bliss of heaven for me is to build a small hut on the slopes of a mountain by the bank of a stream and live there. There'll be no worry about this world or the next one. There'll be nobody to cry for me or to laugh at me. This is the highest ideal of my life. But I don't have the self-restraint and the enterprise needed to attain it. Well, the truth is that I haven't thought about this. It doesn't make any difference if I come here or not. I come only out of consideration for papa. I spend most of the time wondering how to be released from this imprisonment. I'll speak to papa today.

Indradutt – Yes, speak to him today. Shall I speak to him if you feel embarrassed?

Prabhu – Of course not, what's there to be embarrassed about? I'll be able to impress him even more. Papa will think that now he's interested in the work, at least he has said something. This is the complaint he has against me, that I don't say anything.

When Indradutt left, Soordas accompanied him a long way asking about the society for social service. He returned only when Indradutt repeatedly requested him to. Indradutt remained standing there, watching that meek being limping and vanishing into the shadows of the trees swayed by the breeze. Perhaps he wanted to decide whether he was a god or a human being.

34

PRABHU SEVAK BROUGHT UP THE TOPIC OF HOUSING AS SOON AS HE reached home. John Sevak was delighted that he had at last begun to take interest in the factory. He said – Yes, it's very important to get the houses built. Tell the engineers to make a plan. I'll put up the proposal before the managing committee. There's no need to make separate houses for the coolies. Long barracks can be built for ten or twelve labourers to live in each room.

Prabhu – But there must be several labourers who'll want to live there with their families.

Mrs Sevak – A town will flourish if accommodation is given to the coolies' families. Do you want to get work out of them or to habilitate them? The coolies can live in the same way as the soldiers of the army. Yes, there should be a small church and a small house for the padri.

Ishvar Sevak – May Khuda bless you, beti. I like your suggestion very much. Religious nourishment is as important for the coolies as bodily nourishment. Lord Messiah, hide me in your mantle. It's such a wonderful proposal. It has gladdened my heart. When will the day come when the coolies' hearts will be satiated by the Messiah's teachings?

John Sevak – But consider how I can put this sectarian proposal before the committee. I can't do everything alone. How will I answer the other members if they oppose it? I'm the only Christian on the committee. No, I won't put this proposal before it. You can see for yourself how religiously biased it is.

Mrs Sevak – You are unnecessarily hypercritical when it comes to religious issues. The Hindu coolies will promptly put a few bricks and stones under a tree and worship them, the Muslim coolies will also offer namaaz in the open field, so why should anybody object to a church?

Ishvar Sevak – Lord Messiah, have mercy on me. The teachings of the Bible give peace to all human beings. Nobody can object to their being spread, and even if they do, you can dismiss their argument by saying that the raja's religion is also the raja. After all the government has opened a department for religious propagation, who objects to it, and even if anyone does, who listens? I'll present this issue in the church today itself and will force the authorities to put pressure on the company. But this is your job, not mine. You should be concerned about these issues yourself. It's a pity that Mr Clark is not here right now.

Mrs Sevak – There wouldn't have been any problem had he been here.

John Sevak – I don't know how to present this proposal. If the company had decided to get a temple or a mosque built, I could have also pushed for a church. But I can't do anything until other people take the initiative, nor do I think it proper to do so.

Ishvar Sevak – Why should we follow others? We have a lamp in our hands, a stick on our shoulders, a sword at our waists, strength in our feet, why shouldn't we lead? Why should we look to others?

John Sevak thought it would be futile to argue further with his father. After eating, he sat with Prabhu until midnight making and destroying various maps—which land should be used, how much would be spent, how many houses would be built. Prabhu agreed to whatever he said. He was not interested in these things. He would look at the newspapers sometimes or turn the pages of a book or go out into the veranda. But obsession isn't very discerning. When does a speaker absorbed in the flow of his own voice notice how many people in the audience have their eyes open? Prabhu had thought of a new title and was impatient to use the brilliance of his creativity on it. New similes and adages were flowing into his mind like flowers from a stream and he was eager to collect them because they vanish forever after making an appearance just once, giving a fleeting glimpse. He was in this dilemma until midnight. He could neither sit nor get up. He even began to doze. John Sevak also thought that it was time to rest. But when Prabhu went to bed, the goddess of sleep was offended with him. He tried very hard to mollify her for some time, then he sat in front of the lamp and began to compose a poem on that same topic. In a moment he was in a different world. Unlike a villager he wasn't captivated by the razzle-dazzle of the money market. Although every object of that world was charming, fragrant, attractive and beautiful, on closer scrutiny he realized that many of them were merely gilded with gold, actually they were old or artificial! Yes, his face would brighten when he found a new jewel. The creator is always the most intelligent connoisseur of his creation. Prabhu's imagination had never soared so high. He would recite each verse after composing it and feel delighted. After completing the poem he thought, 'Let me see how much the society of poets respects it. The praise of editors doesn't have any value. Very few among them are connoisseurs of poetry. They won't accept the most beautiful poem of a new, unknown poet, but they will praise to the skies the rotten, padded stuff of the older poets. Poets are miserly in spite of being connoisseurs. They may praise the small versifiers, but they shut their ears at the very name of somebody they think of as a competitor. Kunwar sahib will surely be excited. If only Vinay were here, he would have kissed my pen. Tomorrow I'll request kunwar sahib to get my collection published. The poets of the new age can't claim to challenge me, and there's no competition between the older poets and me. Our spheres are different. Their language is graceful, there's no mistake in their prosody, you can't find any fault even if you search for it, but there's no sign of growth, no mark of originality. They keep chewing the same old morsels, there's no trace of progress in their thoughts. You may find something worthwhile after reading ten or twenty verses; even the similes are old and worn out, composed by the ancient poets. My language may not be so polished, but I haven't written a single sentence as padding. What's the use?'

Early in the morning he got ready, put the poem in his pocket, and was about to leave without having his breakfast, when John Sevak asked – Won't you have any breakfast? Where are you going this early in the morning?

Prabhu said indifferently – I'm going to kunwar sahib's.

John – In that case, do discuss yesterday's proposal with him. Nobody will have the courage to oppose it if he agrees.

Mrs Sevak – About that church?

John – Not yet, you are concerned only about your church. I have decided to get the Pandeypur basti vacated and to get the houses for the coolies built there. I can't think of a better place.

Prabhu – You didn't mention acquiring the basti last night.

John – No. Just come here and look at this map. There isn't enough land anywhere outside the basti. There's a government mental asylum on one side, Rai sahib's garden on the other, and our mill on the third. There's no other space besides the basti. And the basti is not very big after all. There are hardly fifteen to twenty or at the most thirty houses. Why shouldn't we pay compensation for them and try to acquire the land?

Prabhu – If you want to demolish the basti to get houses built for the labourers, let it be. They are subsisting somehow or the other.

John – You wouldn't have seen a single bungalow here if such bastis were to be protected. These bungalows haven't been built on barren land.

Prabhu – I prefer a hut to such a bungalow for which the houses of several poor people have to be demolished. I won't mention this topic to kunwar sahib. You can talk to him yourself.

John – This is your idleness. I won't deceive you by calling it contentment and compassion. You want all the comforts of life but you run away from the means that are essential for them. I have never seen you hate wealth and luxury in your actions. You want the best house, the best food, the best clothes but you want honey and sharbat to drip from your mouth without exerting yourself.

Prabhu – Human beings often have to act against their conscience because of custom and tradition.

John – If you are helpless because of custom and tradition for the enjoyment of your comforts, why don't the same customs make you helpless when it comes to the means of getting those comforts? I won't have the slightest objection if you scorn the present social system with your thoughts and words as much as you want. You can give speeches on this topic, write poems, compose essays, I'll read them happily and will praise you, but forget those sentiments when you enter the arena of action just as you forget sacrifice, contentment and self-restraint when you wear the best suit to go for an outing in your car.

Like so many other people who enjoyed a luxurious life, Prabhu believed in democracy in principle. But he lacked the resoluteness of that moral courage that could liberate him from the conditions of his upbringing and from the education by which he had developed mentally and spiritually. He would be happy to express the sentiments of sacrifice in the realm of ideas and was proud of them. Perhaps it never occurred to him that these sentiments could be realized in actions. He didn't have the self-restraint to sacrifice his luxuries for them. Communism was only a topic of entertainment for him; that was all. Nobody until now had criticized his conduct or had treated him as an object of ridicule, and his ideas were sufficient to put his friends in awe of his freedom of thought. Kunwar Bharat Singh's restraint and asceticism didn't affect him because Prabhu thought of him as belonging to a higher class. There's not much difference if a bag of asharfis is made of velvet or of khadi. He was so enraged by his father's ridicule that he felt as if he had been whipped. Fire may not be able to burn straw, an iron nail may not sink into the mud, glass may not break by the blow of a stone but ridicule seldom fails to enrage the heart, to pierce it and to wound it, especially when it comes from the person who can make or mar our lives. It was as if he had been bitten by a black she-snake whose bite can't even be felt. His dormant shame was awakened. He became acutely aware of his degradation. He had got ready to go to kunwar sahib's and had ordered the gharry but then he changed his mind. He returned to his room and sat down. His eyes filled with tears, not because he had been deluded for so long but at the thought that his father resented supporting him. 'After this rebuke, I should drown myself in shame if I continue to be dependent on him. I should sort out the problem of my livelihood myself. Didn't he realize that I lived luxuriously only because customs made me helpless? It's very unfair of him to taunt me in this situation. It's impossible for me to transform myself after living an artificial life for so long. Isn't it enough that these thoughts have arisen in my mind? As long as they are there, at least I won't be blinded by selfishness and hanker for wealth like others. But I'm unnecessarily being so regretful. I should be happy that papa has accomplished what thoughts and principles couldn't. I don't need to discuss anything with him now. Perhaps he won't even be distressed by my going away. He has realized full well that he can't satisfy his thirst for wealth through me. I have to decamp from here today, that's certain. I'll go and request kunwar sahib to enlist me among his volunteers. Let me enjoy that life too for a while. Let me find out whether I have any other ability or whether I can only compose poems. Now I'll wander around in the mountain ranges, go to the villages, worship the beauty of nature, every day there'll be new food, a new climate, new outings, new scenes. Which other way of life could be so enjoyable? There'll be hardships. Heat, rain, dangerous beasts, but I've never been afraid of difficulties. It's domestic wrangles that are a problem for me. One has to put up with so many insults here. To be a slave to others for one's rotis! To let one's wishes be dependent on others! A servant is so meek when he sees his master, there's so much humility and fear on his face. No, I'll learn to value my independence now.'

In the afternoon, when they were all sleeping comfortably under the fans, Prabhu quietly left and went to kunwar sahib's palace. He had wanted to change his clothes and to wear a kurta. But he had never before left the house so shabbily dressed. It perhaps requires greater moral courage to change one's apparel than to change one's views. He took only his book of poems and was ready to leave. He didn't feel the least regret or remorse. He was delighted, as if he were being released from imprisonment. 'You are welcome to your wealth. Papa thought me to be completely shameless, lacking in self-respect and engrossed in luxury, that's why he flared up over such a small thing. He'll now realize that I'm not completely dead.'

Kunwar sahib was not used to sleeping in the afternoon. He was lying on the floor thinking about something. Prabhu sat down there. Kunwar sahib didn't ask any questions – Why have you come? Why are you dejected? Even after sitting there for half an hour, Prabhu didn't have the courage to talk about himself. He couldn't think of an introduction. 'Why is this gentleman so preoccupied? Has he guessed from my appearance that I have come for a selfish reason? He used to be so delighted to see me and would rush to embrace me; today he hasn't even addressed me. This is the punishment for being dependent on others. I too left home in the afternoon when even the birds don't leave their nests. I should have come in the evening if I had to. Only somebody who is obsessed by some motive would leave the house in this scorching heat. Well, this is the first experience.' He was about to leave disappointed when Bharat Singh asked, 'Why? Why? What's the hurry? Because I didn't speak? There's no dearth of things to talk about, there's so much I want to say to you that I don't know where to begin. Do you think that Vinay made a mistake by taking the riyasat's side?

Prabhu (*Perplexed*) – This can be examined from different aspects.

Kunwar – That means he was wrong. His mother also thinks so. She's so annoyed that she doesn't want to see his face. But I think that there's no need for him to be ashamed of the policy that he has followed. Perhaps I would have done the same in his place. Even if he didn't love Sophie, the public's revolt on that occasion was enough to shake his communist principles. But since it's established that Sophia's love is in every pore of his being, his conduct is not only forgivable but completely admirable. That religion in which marrying outside the community is forbidden for fear of its being harmed is only factionalism. Religion and knowledge are one. And from this viewpoint there's only one religion in the world. Hindus, Muslims, Christians, Jews, Buddhists don't belong to that religion, they are only factions of various interests, nobody has gained anything from them except harm. If Vinay is so fortunate that he can marry Sophie, I at least won't have the slightest objection.

Prabhu – But you know that mama is as adamant about this topic as raniji.

Kunwar – The result will be that both their lives will be ruined. Both these priceless jewels will be reduced to dust.

Prabhu – I myself have become so tired of these wrangles that I have made a firm decision to leave the house. My conscience is being weakened by the communal atmosphere and the social bonds at home. I can't think of any other way except to leave. I was never very fond of business to begin with, and I have begun to hate it after so many days of experience.

Kunwar – But business is the most important part of the new culture—why are you disinterested in it?

Prabhu – Because I'm not capable of the selfishness and the manslaughter required to attain success in it. I just don't have so much enthusiasm. I'm solitary by nature and I don't want to get more involved in the struggles of life than is necessary for the full development of my art and for the inclusion of reality in it. Poets are generally solitary, but that hasn't corrupted their poetic art. Possibly they could have made their poetry even more perceptive by obtaining an extensive and thorough knowledge of life, but there's also the fear that their poetic imagination may have been paralysed had they been occupied with the struggles of life. Homer was blind, so were Soor and

Milton, but they are all shining stars of the literary sky; Tulsi, Valmiki and other great poets were beings who dwelt in huts, away from the world, but who can say that their solitude corrupted their poetic art? I don't know what my views may be in the future, but right now I'm fed up of the worship of materialism.

Kunwar – You had never before been so detached, what's the matter?

Prabhu (*Embarrassed*) – I didn't understand the complex mysteries of life earlier. But now I have realized that reality is much more complicated than I had thought it to be. Business is nothing else if not manslaughter. To think of human beings as beasts from beginning to end and to treat them brutally is its basic principle. Someone who can't do this cannot be a successful businessman. The factory is not yet ready and there's the problem of extending the land. The mechanics and labourers don't have place to live in the basti. They won't be able to subsist there when their numbers increase. That's why papa wants that according to that same article of the law Pandeypur should also be acquired and the inhabitants given compensation and evicted. Raja Mahendra Kumar is friendly with papa and the present district judge, Mr Senapati, is as friendly with the rais as Mr Clark was distant from them. Papa's proposal will be accepted without any difficulty and the muhalla-valas will forcibly be evicted. I can't bear this tyranny. I can't prevent it so I want to dissociate myself from it.

Kunwar – How much profit do you think the company will make?

Prahu – I think there'll be a profit of 25 per cent in the first year itself.

Kunwar – So have you decided to leave the factory?

Prabhu – I have made a firm decision.

Kunwar – Can your papa manage the work?

Prabhu– Papa can manage half a dozen such factories. He has a unique tenacity. The proposal for the land will be presented very soon to the managing committee. I humbly request you not to let it be accepted.

Kunwar (*Smiling*) – An old man can't learn new lessons so easily. An old parrot can't learn to read. I don't see any objection to acquiring the land by giving compensation to the people of the basti. Yes, the compensation should be adequate. Why should you bother about these problems if you are leaving the factory anyway? These are the affairs of the world, they have been happening and they'll go on happening.

Prabhu – So you won't oppose this proposal?

Kunwar – I won't oppose any proposal that will harm the factory. I have a selfish relationship with the factory; I can't be an obstacle to its progress. Yes, your leaving it is an auspicious sign for my society. You know that the chairman of the society is Dr Ganguly, but he wants to be free of this responsibility partly because of old age and partly because of the affairs of the Council. It's my heartfelt wish that you should accept it. The society is in midstream at this moment, Vinay's conduct has put it in a dangerous predicament. God has given you everything, education, intelligence, enthusiasm. You can save the society if you want to, and I'm sure that you won't disappoint me.

Prabhu's eyes filled with tears. He felt that he didn't deserve this honour. He said – I'm not capable of accepting this responsibility. I'm afraid that somebody as inexperienced and lazy as I am won't be able to further the progress of the society. It's your kindness that you think me to be so capable. It's enough for me to be in the ranks.

Kunwar sahib, encouraging him, said – From where will I get the leaders if I keep people like you in the ranks? I'm sure you'll become an expert in this work if you stay with Dr Ganguly for a few days. Courteous people always scorn their own ability, but I know you. You have a unique electric energy, much more than you are aware of. An Arabian horse can't tread in a plough; it needs a field. Your independent soul was confined in the factory; it will sprout wings when it comes out into the wide arena of the world. I had selected Vinay for this position, but I no longer trust him after seeing his present situation. I want to leave this society so well organized that it can continue its work without any obstacles. I won't be able to die in peace if this doesn't happen. I can depend on you because you are selfless. Prabhu! I have greatly misused my life. When I look back on it I can't see anything to be proud of. It's a desert where there's no trace of greenery. This society is burdened with the bad deeds of my whole life. It is the means of my atonement and the path of my moksha. My greatest ambition is that my society of volunteers should achieve something in the world. It should be devoted to service and sacrifice, and take pride in the glory of the country. When I see such people, who have nothing else except their lives, sacrificing them for the country, I want to weep because I have everything and yet I haven't done anything. The most fatal wound for me will be if this society remains merely an unsuccessful cherished desire. I'm prepared to sacrifice all I have for it. I have deposited ten lakh rupees in its account and I want to increase the sum by a lakh every year. A hundred volunteers are too few for such a vast country. There should be at least 500 men. Perhaps my ambition will be fulfilled if I live another ten years. Indradutt has all the qualities but he is rebellious by nature. That's why my mind hasn't settled on him. I earnestly request you . . .

Dr Ganguly arrived then and, seeing Prabhu, said – So you are giving a mantra to kunwar sahib here and your papa is giving lessons to Mahendra Kumar. But I have said clearly that it can't be done. It's your mill, its profit and loss will be shared by you and your shareholders, why are you turning the poor out of their houses? But nobody listens to me. I tell the bitter truth, so why should they like it? I'll raise a question about this in the Council. You people can't be unjust to others for your selfish ends. The rais of the city will be annoyed with me, but I don't care. I'll do what my conscience tells me to. If you need a different kind of person, then baba, accept my resignation. But I won't let Pandeypur be demolished.

Kunwar – This poor man is himself opposed to that proposal. There were even differences between father and son today on this issue. He has left home and doesn't want to have anything to do with the factory.

Dr Ganguly – Achcha, is that so? That's very good. Such intellectuals can't work at the mill. From where will we get men if such people work there? Prabhu! I'm old now; I'll die tomorrow. Why don't you take over my work? Our society of volunteers respects you. You can release me from this burden. An old man can do everything else, but he can't be energetic. I won't let you go now. There's so much work in the Council that I don't have time for this work. All this wouldn't have happened in Udaipur had I not been at the Council. I would have gone there and pacified everybody. After getting so much education you are going to use it to make money, chhee, chhee!

Prabhu – I've left home to join the volunteers but I'm not capable of being the leader. That position becomes only you. Let me remain among the soldiers. It will be a matter of pride for me.

Dr Ganguly (*Laughing*) – Ha-ha! It's only the incapable that work.

The capable person doesn't work; he only talks. A capable person implies a talkative one, just empty talk, the more he talks the more capable he is. He'll tell you how to do the work, which mistake was made where, but he can't work. I don't want such a capable man. We don't have work for those who just talk. I want a man who'll eat coarse food, wear coarse clothes, go around in alleys and towns, work for the welfare of the poor, help them in their difficulties. So from when will you come?

Prabhu – I'm at your service right now.

Dr Ganguly (*Smiling*) – Then your first fight will be with your father.

Prabhu – I think papa himself won't take up this proposal.

Dr Ganguly – No, no, he'll never give up. We'll have to fight him. You'll have to fight him. Our organization regards justice as supreme; justice is dearer to us than mother and father, money and wealth, name and fame. We'll give up everything else but we won't give up justice; this is our vow. You'll have to think it over carefully before coming here.

Prabhu – I have thought it over carefully.

Dr Ganguly – No, no, there's no hurry. Think it over carefully, it won't do if you come here and then run away again.

Prabhu – Now only death can part me from this society.

Dr Ganguly – Mr John Sevak will tell you, 'I don't get involved in wrangles about justice and injustice, you are my son, it's your duty to obey me,' how will you answer then? (*Laughing*) If my father had said this, I would never have told him that I wouldn't listen to him. He told me, become a barrister, so I went to England. I returned a barrister. For several years, I would go to the court and read the papers. I started studying medicine after my father's death. I didn't have the courage to tell him that I wouldn't study law.

Prabhu – It's one thing to respect one's father and another to live by one's principles. If your father had told you to go and set fire to somebody's house, would you have done so?

Dr Ganguly – No, no, never. I would never have set it on fire, even if pitaji had burnt me. But a father can't give such an order.

Rani Jahnavi entered suddenly. She was the image of grief and anger, frowning and scowling, as if a dog had touched her when she was going to do pooja after her bath. When she saw Dr Ganguly, she said – You are not tired of the Council; I'm tired of life. What I want doesn't happen, what I don't want happens. Doctor sahib, I can bear everything except my son's disreputable ways, especially such a son for whose formation no pains were spared. I wouldn't have felt so grieved if the wretch had died in the Jaswantnagar revolt.

Kunwar sahib couldn't bear to listen any longer; he got up and went out. The rani said in the same vein – How can he understand my grief? His whole life has been spent in luxury. He has never bothered about ideals when it came to self-service. Like the other rais, he was engrossed in enjoying his comforts. But I have practised severe austerities for Vinay. I have walked with him in the mountains for months together, only so that I could make him get used to hardships from his childhood. I have carefully watched over each word and each action of his so that he wouldn't acquire bad habits. If he ever got angry with a servant I have promptly made him understand. If he ever turned away from the truth I have promptly scorned him. How can he [Bharat Singh] understand my anguish?

As she said this, the rani's gaze fell on Prabhu who was standing in a corner, fiddling with books. She stopped speaking and couldn't say anything more. The harsh words that were there in her mind for Sophia remained unspoken. She only said to Dr Ganguly, 'Come and see me before you leave,' and went away.

35

IT WAS MORNING WHEN VINAY SINGH ENTERED HABITATION. HE HAD just gone a short distance when he saw an old woman approach, tapping her stick. When she saw him, she said – Beta, I'm poor. Give something if you can. It will be dharma.

Nayakram – You don't take Rama's name in the morning but you have set out to beg. It's as if you couldn't sleep at night. There's the whole day for begging.

Old woman – Beta, I'm an unhappy woman.

Nayakram – Who's happy here? I starved the whole night and suffered the growling of this lover. We can't walk straight ourselves, how can we give you money?

Old woman – Beta, I can't walk in the sunshine, my head spins. There are new troubles, bhaiyya! May God curse that vile sinner Vinay Singh. It's because of him that I have to go through all this in my old age; otherwise my son had a shop, I used to live in the house like a rani, there were servants, which comforts did we not have? You are an outsider, so you perhaps don't know that there was a revolt here. My boy didn't so much as leave the shop, but that wretch Vinay Singh gave evidence that he was also involved in the revolt. The police had been on the lookout for us for several days, but they couldn't think of a trap. They came running as soon as they got this evidence; the boy was arrested and sentenced to three years' imprisonment. There was also a penalty of 1000 rupees. Our household worth 20,000 rupees was completely destroyed. There's a bahu and children in the house, I provide for them by begging like this. I don't know for which enmity that blackguard has taken revenge.

Vinay took out a rupee from his pocket and gave it to the old woman; he looked up at the sky and sighed deeply. He had never before experienced such mental anguish.

The old woman was startled when she saw the rupee. She thought he had given it by mistake. She said – Beta, this is a rupee.

Vinay said choking – Yes, take it. I haven't given it by mistake.

The old woman went her way blessing him. When the two men walked ahead they came to a well beside which there was a peepal tree and a small temple. Nayakram thought they could wash up there. When they reached the well, they saw an old brahman sitting under the tree, chanting prayers. When he had finished, Vinay asked – Do you know where Sardar Neelkanth is these days?

Pandit (*Brusquely*) – I don't know.

Vinay – The minister of the police must be here?

Pandit – I've told you, I don't know.

Vinay – Mr Clark must be here on tour?

Pandit – I don't know anything.

Nayakram – You don't know what's going on around you while you are praying?

Pandit – Yes, I have nothing to do with anybody until my wish is fulfilled. You have uttered the names of these malechh in the morning; I don't know how the day will pass!

Nayakram – What's this wish of yours?

Pandit – To avenge my honour.

Nayakram – From whom?

Pandit – I won't take his name. He's the son of a big rais. He came from Kashi to help the poor. He devastated several homes and no one knows where he has disappeared. I'm performing this rite because of him. Half the people in the town used to be my patrons; the merchants and traders respected me. I used to teach students. My fault was that I didn't go and say salaam to the administrators. If I saw any employee doing something wrong, I would tell him so to his face. That's why the officers were hostile to me. When there was a revolt here some days ago, they accused me of rebelling against the state through that goonda from Banaras. I was punished and beaten, a penalty was imposed, my honour was reduced to dust. Now nobody in the town allows me to stand at their doorway. I've come to take Devi's refuge. I'm performing the purashcharna rite.* My tapasya will be completed the day I hear that Devi's wrath has fallen on that murderer. I'm twice-

---

* A rite with the repetition of the name of a deity accompanied by burnt offerings to obtain a purpose.

born, I don't know how to fight and wrangle. Which other weapon do I have except this?

Vinay wouldn't have felt so ashamed had he been caught coming out of a liquor shop. He now recalled this brahman's face. He remembered that he had been responsible for getting him arrested at the instigation of the police. He took out five rupees from his pocket and said to the pandit – Take this, and chant the mantra for the death of that human fiend on my behalf too. He has destroyed me as well. I'm also thirsty for his blood.

Pandit – Maharaj, may all be well with you. You'll see that there'll be worms in the enemy's body. He'll die a dog's death. The whole town is his enemy. He has escaped with his life so far because he was always surrounded by the police. But for how long? The day he leaves the house alone, Devi's wrath will fall on him. He is in this very riyasat, he hasn't left, and he can't escape and go anywhere now. His death now awaits him. How can the lament of so many suffering people be futile?

When they went further, Vinay said – Pandaji, arrange a car immediately. I'm afraid of being recognized. I have never before been so afraid for my life. I'll probably commit suicide if I come across a few more such scenes. Ah! I'm so degraded. And until now, I had thought that I hadn't done anything wrong. I had taken a vow of service; I had left home for social work. I have certainly done a lot of social work! Perhaps these people won't forget me all their lives.

Nayakram – Bhaiyya, it's human beings who make mistakes. Don't regret it now.

Vinay – Nayakram, this is not a mistake, it's ordained by God. It seems that he severely tests those who take a vow of righteousness. The status of a devotee can't be attained without succeeding in these tests. I have failed the test, failed it badly.

Nayakram had thought of going to the jail to ask after daroga sahib's welfare but when he saw that there wouldn't be an opportunity for that, he promptly went to the office of the car service. He was informed that the durbar had taken over all the cars for a week. Several friends of Mr Clark had come to play shikar. What was to be done now? Nayakram didn't know how to ride a horse and Vinay thought it improper to ride while Nayakram walked.

Nayakram – Bhaiyya, why don't you ride? It doesn't matter about me. I can walk ten kos if needed.

Vinay – I'm not dying either. The night's fatigue has gone now.

Both the men had something to eat and then left for Udaipur. Vinay had perhaps never before talked so much in his life, and that too to an uncouth villager like Nayakram. Sophie's sharp criticism now seemed to be entirely just. He said – Pandaji, I'll never show my face again if the durbar doesn't release all the prisoners who have been arrested because of my testimony. That's the only hope left for me. Go home and tell mataji how distressed I am and how deeply ashamed of my mistake.

Nayakram – Bhaiyya, if you don't go home, I won't either. I'm with you now wherever you go. We'll both put up with whatever happens.

Vinay – This is the one thing about you that I don't like. What's there in common between the two of us? I'm a sinner. I have to atone for my sins. There's no stigma on your forehead. Why are you ruining your life? I didn't know Sophia until now. I have realized today how large her heart is. I don't have any complaint against her. Yes, the only complaint I have is that she didn't think that I'm hers, or else why would she have picked on each and every thing concerning me, why would she have observed me like a spy on the slightest pretext? She knew that I would play with my life if she rejected me. Why was she so cruel to me when she knew this? Why did she forget that human beings make mistakes? Perhaps she has given me this cruel punishment thinking that I belong to her. We don't care about other people's faults; we punish only those whom we think of as ours when we see them walking on the wrong path. But we should at least be careful not to break the thread of intimacy when we punish them. It seems to me that she has turned away from me forever.

Nayakram – After all she's a Christian! She'll tie the knot with some Englishman.

Vinay – You are completely crass, you don't know how to talk properly. I think that she'll now live as a chaste woman all her life. What do you know about her? You don't understand anything, you promptly said, 'She'll tie the knot with some Englishman'. I know her somewhat. What didn't she do for me, what didn't she suffer for me? I'm so grieved when I recall her love that I want to bang my head on the rocks and give up my life. Now she's invincible; she has shut the doors of her love. I don't know what tapasya I must have done in my previous birth that I enjoyed its fruit for so many days. Even if somebody appears as a god before her now, she won't look at him. She may be a Christian by birth, but she's an Arya woman in her upbringing and actions. I have left her nowhere. I have drowned myself and have drowned her as well along with me. Now you'll see how she'll harass the riyasat. There's so much power in her words that she can destroy all traces of the riyasat in no time.

Nayakram – Yes, she is a spark of disaster.

Vinay – Again that foolish talk! I have told you so many times to take her name with respect in front of me. I don't want to hear even one improper word about her from anybody. I can't scorn her even if she pierces me with spears. Love doesn't retaliate. Love is replete with infinite forgiveness, generosity and patience.

Talking thus they reached halfway towards their destination. When they rested in the afternoon, they slept so soundly that it was evening when they woke up. They had to stay there for the night. There was a sarai, so it wasn't very difficult. Nayakram was unhappy because he couldn't get bhang for the first time in his life. He was prepared to give ten rupees instead of one for a tola of bhang, but he was destined to fast today. Defeated on all sides, he came and sat on the plinth of the well, clutching his head, as if he had just performed somebody's last rites.

Vinay said – Why are you so addicted to something that you can't stay without it even for a day? Leave it, good man, you are unnecessarily giving your life for it.

Nayakram – Bhaiyya, I can't give it up in this life, God alone knows about the next. Even when I die I'll keep a lump on my pillow, and I'll write a will that a seer of bhang should be put on my funeral pyre. There's no one to offer pinda for me after I die, but if God shows me that day, I'll tell my sons to be sure to offer a lump of bhang along with the pinda. It's only the addict who knows how enjoyable it is.

Nayakram didn't enjoy his food, he couldn't sleep, his body ached. He abused the people of the sarai in his anger and rushed to beat them. He scolded the bania for not giving clean sugar. He wrangled with the halvai because he gave bad mithai, 'Just wait and see what I'll do to you. I'll go straightaway and tell sardar sahib. Rascal, you'll see that I'll get your shop looted. My name is Nayakram. Don't you know? There's a stink of oil here.' The halvai fell at his feet but he didn't listen. He even managed to get twenty-five rupees out of him by threatening him. But Vinay had the money returned before they left, though he did warn the halvai not to make such bad mithai and not to sell things cooked in oil at the price of ghee.

They reached Udaipur by ten the next morning. The first man they saw was sardar sahib. He was coming from the durbar on a tamtam. He stopped the horse as soon as he saw Vinay and asked – Where are you going?

Vinay said – I was coming here.

Sardar – You couldn't get a car? Yes, you couldn't have got one. Then why didn't you phone? A conveyance could have been sent from here. You have unnecessarily taken so much trouble.

Vinay – I'm used to walking, there wasn't much trouble. I want to meet you today, alone. When can you meet me?

Sardar – I don't have to fix a time for you. You can come whenever you like, in fact, stay there too.

Vinay – All right.

Sardar sahib whipped the horse and left. He couldn't ask Vinay to sit with him because he would have had to ask Nayakram too. Vinay took a tonga and reached sardar sahib's house in a short while.

Sardar sahib asked – There was no news of you for several days. Where are your companions? Have you discovered anything about Mrs Clark?

Vinay – My companions have been left behind but we couldn't find Mrs Clark. All the effort was futile. But I have discovered where Veerpaal Singh is. I have also seen his house. But we couldn't find Mrs Clark.

Sardar sahib said surprised – What are you saying? The information that I have received says that you met Mrs Clark and that I should now beware of you. See, I'll show you this letter.

Sardar sahib went to the table and brought a letter written on thick brown paper, which he gave Vinay.

This was the first time in his life that Vinay had taken refuge in a lie. He flushed and then turned pale. He didn't know how to carry on. Nayakram was sitting on the floor. He understood that Vinay was perplexed. Nayakram was experienced in telling lies and inventing stories. He said, 'Kunwar sahib, just give it to me, whose letter is it?'

Vinay – Indradutt's.

Nayakram – Oho! It's that madman's letter! It's that lad isn't it, who used to come to the society for social service and sing there? His parents had turned him out of the house. Sarkar, he's crazy. He keeps doing these absurd things.

Sardar – No, this can't be a madman's style of writing. He's very intelligent. There's no doubt about it. I have been getting letters from him continuously for several days. He sometimes threatens me and sometimes preaches ethics to me. But he says whatever he wants to courteously. There's not a single impolite or unrestrained word. If it is the same Indradutt whom you also know then it's even more surprising. It's possible that it's somebody else writing under his name. He doesn't seem to me to be somebody with an ordinary education.

Vinay was as disconcerted as a servant caught opening his master's box. He was furious with himself. 'Why did I tell a lie? Where was the need for me to have hidden it? But what's Indradutt's purpose in writing this letter? Does he want to vilify me?'

Nayakram – It must be somebody else. The purpose is to incite the officials here against kunwar sahib. Why, bhaiyya, was there any scholar in the society?

Vinay – They were all scholars, who's a fool among them? Indradutt is highly educated. But I didn't know that he harboured so much rancour against me.

Vinay looked at sardar sahib with eyes full of shame. The lie became fiercer every moment and the darkness of falsehood thickened.

Then he said, embarrassed – Sardar sahib, forgive me. I lied to you. Every word in this letter is true. I did meet Mrs Clark. I wanted to keep it a secret from you because I had promised her that I would. She's very comfortable there, so much so that she didn't come with me despite my entreaties.

Sardar sahib said indifferently – Promises are not very important in politics. I'll have to be wary of you now. You would have spared no pains to deceive me had this letter not informed me of everything. Do you know how many threats we are getting from the government on this issue? You can say that our efficiency depends on Mrs Clark's safe return. Anyway, what's the matter? Why didn't Mrs Clark come? Did the rascals prevent her?

Vinay – Veerpaal Singh had gladly wanted to send her. This is the only means by which he can save his life. But she herself was not prepared to come.

Sardar – She's not angry with Mr Clark, is she?

Vinay – That's possible. Mr Clark was inebriated on the day of the revolt. Perhaps that's why she's annoyed with him. I can't be sure. Yes, after meeting her it has become clear that we took several unjust actions in suppressing the people of Jaswantnagar. We had suspected that the rebels had either imprisoned Mrs Clark or had killed her. We adopted a policy of repression only on this suspicion. We ended up beating everybody with the same stick. But neither of the two suspicions was correct. Mrs Clark is alive and well. She herself doesn't want to return. The people of Jaswantnagar unnecessarily became the victims of our wrath and I plead with you fervently that those poor people should be shown mercy. The sword is hanging over the heads of hundreds of innocent people.

Sardar sahib didn't knowingly want to be unjust to anybody, but he didn't have the courage to acknowledge his mistake. It's not so difficult to be just as it is to end injustice. He had been afraid only of the unfavourable view of the government after Sophia's disappearance. But the discovery of her whereabouts was like beating the drum of his inability and cruelty in the whole country. It was easy to please the government by pleasing Mr Clark, but the public couldn't be silenced that easily.

Sardar sahib said, somewhat embarrassed – I can believe that Mrs Clark is alive. But let alone you, even if Brahma were to come and tell me that she's happy there and doesn't want to return, I won't believe it. It's childish. One can't be so indifferent to one's home as to want to stay with enemies. The rebels must have forced Mrs Clark to say this. They won't let her go until we release all the prisoners. This is the strategy of victors and I can't accept it. Mrs Clark is being subjected to the severest tortures and she has made this recommendation to you to escape from them. It's nothing else but that.

Vinay – I don't agree. Mrs Clark seemed very happy. Somebody who is oppressed can never be so unafraid.

Sardar – This is the fault of your vision. I wouldn't believe Mrs Clark even if she were to come herself and tell me that she was very comfortable. You don't know with what spells these people can terrorize even those who would give their lives for their freedom, to the extent that the prisoner speaks their language and obeys them even after escaping from their clutches. I was once a police officer. I'm telling you the truth, there were so many political prosecutions when I made several important people, who had taken staunch vows, admit to crimes that they could never have imagined. Veerpaal Singh is more skilled on this subject than we are.

Vinay – Sardar sahib, even if I were to believe for a short while that Mrs Clark has said all this to me under pressure, when I reflect with a calm mind I'm still convinced that we shouldn't have been so ruthless in this repression. Those accused should be shown some leniency now.

Sardar – Leniency is a sign of defeat in politics. I'm not prepared to show leniency even if I were to believe that Mrs Clark is comfortable and free there, and that we have severely oppressed the people of Jaswantnagar. To be lenient is to announce one's weakness and error. Do you know what the result of leniency will be? The rebels will be encouraged, they'll lose their fear of the riyasat, and it can't survive without fear. The foundation of the administration of a state is not justice but fear. The state will be destroyed if you remove fear, and then even Arjun's bravery and Yudhishthir's justice won't be able to protect it. It's better for 100 or 200 innocent people to remain in jail than for the state to be destroyed. But why should I believe that those rebels are innocent? For several armed people to have gathered together proves that they had gone there with the intention of rebelling.

Vinay – But those who were not with them are innocent.

Sardar – Never, it was their duty to have forewarned the authorities. You are helping the thief if you don't try to awaken the people in the house when you see him breaking in. Apathy is often more dangerous than a crime.

Vinay – At least release those who were arrested on my testimony.

Sardar – That's impossible.

Vinay – I'm making this humble request not as an administrative policy but on the basis of compassion and humanity.

Sardar – I've told you, bhaijaan, that it's impossible. You are not considering the consequences.

Vinay – But the consequences of not accepting my request will also not be good. You are making the problem more complicated.

Sardar – I'm not afraid of an open revolt. I'm afraid of social workers and well-wishers of the public, and the public here is fed up of them. It will be a long time before the public begins to trust them again.

Vinay – You have greatly deceived me if it is with this intention that you have used me to harm the public, but I'm warning you that if you don't accept my request there'll be such a revolution in the riyasat that it will shake its foundations. I'll go from here to Mr Clark and make the same request. If he doesn't listen I'll present the same proposal to His Highness. If he also doesn't listen, there'll be no greater enemy of the riyasat than I.

Vinay stood up and, taking Nayakram along, went to Mr Clark's bungalow. Mr Clark had returned just then after seeing off his hunting friends and was resting. The orderly told Vinay that sahib was working. Vinay walked around in the garden for a while. When sahib didn't send for him even after half an hour he barged straight into Mr Clark's room. Clark sat up immediately when he saw Vinay and said, 'Come come, I was thinking of you. Tell me, what's the news? You must have discovered Sophia's whereabouts?'

Vinay – Yes, I have.

Vinay told the same story to Clark that he had told sardar sahib and made the same request.

Clark – Why didn't Miss Sophie come with you?

Vinay – I don't know, but there's no discomfort for her there.

Clark – Then what have you found that's new? I had thought that your coming would throw some light on this issue. Look, this is Sophia's letter. It came today, I can't show it to you but I can say that if she were to come before me right now I wouldn't hesitate for a moment to shoot her with my pistol. I've realized now that devoutness is another name for deceit and guile. Her piety has greatly deceived me. Perhaps nobody has ever been so greatly deceived. I had thought that piety generated sensitivity but I was mistaken. I was enchanted by her devoutness. I had been disappointed with the flirtatious women of England. When I saw Sophia's simple nature and religious inclination

I thought that I had obtained the object that I had desired. I ignored my own society and began to visit her and finally I proposed to her. Sophia accepted, but she wanted to postpone marriage for a while. How could I have known what was in her heart? I agreed. That's how she came here with me; in fact you can say that it was she who brought me here. The world thinks that we were married, not at all. We were not even engaged. The secret has been revealed now that she's an agent of the Bolsheviks. Her Bolshevik inclinations drip from each word of hers. By pretending love, she had wanted to discover the internal intentions of the British. She has achieved this aim. She used me to get her work done and then rejected me. Vinay Singh, you can't imagine how much I loved her. Such deviousness beneath this incomparable treasure of beauty! She has threatened me that she will publish everything that she has learnt about British society during this time for the amusement of the Indians. Why shouldn't I myself reveal what she wants to? The British want to keep India as a part of their empire until infinity. Conservative or liberal, radical or labour, nationalist or socialist, all of them harbour the same ideal. I want to make it clear before Sophie does that you shouldn't be deceived by the radical and the labour leaders. Whatever the faults of the Conservative Party, it is fearless and unafraid of bitter truths. The radical and the labour parties make optimistic promises to support their noble and bright principles that they don't have the courage to put into action. Sovereignty isn't something to be sacrificed. The history of the world ends on just this one word, 'love of sovereignty'. Human nature is the same as it had been at the beginning of creation. The British as a race have never been renowned for sacrifice, for giving their lives for high ideals. All of us—I'm Labour—are imperialists. The difference is only in the policy that the various parties adopt to establish sovereignty over this country. Somebody is a devotee of stern discipline, somebody of sympathy, somebody of achieving the goal by flattering and cajoling. That's all, actually there is no policy, there's only an objective, and that is to make our sovereignty ever more firm and lasting. I have been threatened with the revelation of this confidential secret. Had I not received this letter, I would have remained blindfolded, and what wouldn't I have done for Sophie! But it has opened my eyes and I can't help you now. In fact, I request you also to help the riyasat in crushing this Bolshevik rebellion. It's difficult to imagine how fierce it can become in the hands of such an intelligent, hard-working and determined woman like Sophie.

Vinay left disappointed and thought that it would now be futile to go to Maharaja Sahib. He'd say bluntly, 'What can I do when the minister and the Agent can't do anything?' But he couldn't help himself and ordered the tonga-vala to go to the palace.

Nayakram – What was he chit-chatting about? Did he agree?

Vinay – Why would we need to go to Maharaja Sahib if he had agreed?

Nayakrak – If he asks for 1000 or 2000 rupees, why don't you give it? Officers may be big or small but they are all greedy.

Vinay – You are talking like a madman. The British would have left this country a long time ago if they had these faults. They also take bribes, they are not gods; the British who had first come here were out and out dacoits, but they never benefit themselves if it harms their rule. Even if they take a bribe it will only be if it's not at the expense of their rule.

Nayakram was quiet. The tonga was going towards the palace. They passed several roads, schools, hospitals. All of them had English names. They even came across a park that was adorned with the name of a British agent. It seemed as if this was not an Indian city but a British camp.

When the tonga reached the palace, Vinay got down and went to the maharaja's private secretary. He was English. Shaking Vinay's hand, he said – Maharaja Sahib is at his pooja. He sat down at it at 11 a.m. and will get up at 4 p.m. Do you people worship for such a long time?

Vinay – There are worshippers among us who are absorbed in profound meditation for several days. That part of the pooja in which the Supreme Being or the other gods are entreated for prosperity and welfare is over soon, but the part that is devoted to self-purification through yoga practices is very beautiful.

Secretary – The raja with whom I worked earlier used to do pooja from the morning until 2 p.m.; then he would eat and go to sleep at 4 p.m. He would sit down again for pooja at 9 p.m. and get up at two in the night. He would go out for an hour at sunset. But I think that such a long pooja is unnatural. It's neither worship nor a practice for self-purification, it's just a kind of idleness.

Vinay was getting so agitated that he didn't reply to this aspersion. He thought, 'What should I do if Maharaja Sahib also gives a blunt answer? The blood of so many innocent people is on my hands, and if Sophie starts a campaign of secret killings, their blood will be on my head too.' He was so disturbed by this thought that he lay down on an armchair with a sigh and shut his eyes. He would say his evening prayers daily in any case, but for the first time today he prayed to God for mercy. He had been awake all night and was tired after the whole day, so he dozed off. It was 4 p.m. when he woke up. He asked the secretary, 'His Highness must have got up from his pooja now?'

Secretary – You slept for a long time.

He then said through the telephone – Kunwar Vinay Singh wants to meet His Highness.

The reply came in a second – Let him come.

Vinay entered the maharaja's special reception room. There was no decoration except for pictures of gods hanging on the walls. A white sheet was spread on the carpet on the floor. Maharaja Sahib was sitting on a cushion. There was only a silk sheet on his body and a necklace of tulsi beads around his neck. Saintliness was reflected on his face. As soon as he saw Vinay, he said, 'Come, you've taken a long time. Have you discovered anything about Mr Clark's mem?'

Vinay – Yes, she's at Veerpaal's house and very comfortable there. Actually she's not married to Mr Clark, she's only engaged to him. She doesn't want to return to him. She says she's very comfortable there and that's what I think too.

Maharaja – Hari-Hari! You've told me something very strange! She doesn't want to return to him! I've understood; they have all bewitched her. Shiva-Shiva! She doesn't want to return to him.

Vinay – Now consider this. She is alive and well there and here we have imprisoned so many innocent people, destroyed so many homes and inflicted physical punishment on so many.

Maharaja – Shiva-Shiva! It's such a terrible disaster.

Vinay – We have mistakenly oppressed the poor in ways that their recollection makes the hair stand on end. Maharaj is right, it's a terrible disaster. There'll be a hue and cry among the public as soon as people get to know about it. That's why the proper thing to do is to admit our mistake and release all the prisoners.

Maharaja – Hari-Hari, how can this be done, beta? Do rajas ever make a mistake? Shiva-Shiva! The raja is an incarnation of God. Hari-Hari! Once he says something, he can't erase it. Shiva-Shiva! The raja's word is the writing of Brahma, it can't be erased, Hari-Hari!

Vinay – The glory that's there in accepting one's mistake is absent in immortalizing injustice. It's forgiveness that becomes a king. Orders should be given for the release of the prisoners; the money taken as penalty should be returned and money given to compensate those who were given physical punishment. Your fame will be immortal if you do this, people will sing your praises and bless you lavishly.

Maharaja – Shiva-Shiva! Beta, you don't understand the stratagems of politics. A thunderbolt will fall on the riyasat if we release even one prisoner. The government will say, 'What's his intention in hiding the mem? He's perhaps infatuated with her; that's why he first pretended to punish the rebels and now he's releasing them.' Shiva-Shiva! The riyasat will be reduced to dust; it will vanish into the underworld. Nobody will ask if it's truth or lies. It won't be discussed anywhere. Hari-Hari! Our plight is even worse than that of ordinary criminals. They are at least given a chance to clear themselves, an article of the law is applied to them and they are punished according to it. Who asks us for clarifications, which court of justice do we have? Hari-Hari! There's no law for us, and no article. We are accused of any crime that they want and given any punishment that they want. There's no appeal anywhere, nor any complaint. Rajas are in any case notorious for their sensuality, how long does it take to make this accusation against them? It will be said, 'You have hidden Clark's extremely beautiful mem in your harem and have spread a rumour that she has been kidnapped.' Hari-Hari! Shiva-Shiva! I hear she's a beautiful woman, a piece of the moon, an apsara. Beta, don't put this stigma on me at this age. Even old age can't save us from such vile accusations. It's notorious that rajas are in the habit of taking liquor and other things so they remain lusty and virile throughout their lives. Shiva-Shiva! This is not to rule; it's a punishment for our karma. 'He who has a bad name is half hanged.' Shiva-Shiva! Nothing can be done now. It's nothing extraordinary for a hundred or fifty innocent people to remain in jail. They get food and clothes there. The condition of the prisons is very good now. New kurtas are given. The food is also good. Yes, I can do this much for your sake, families that don't have anybody left to protect them or those who have been impoverished because of the penalty that they have had to pay can be helped secretly. Hari-Hari! You haven't yet gone to see Clark, have you?

Vinay – I did, I'm coming from there.

Maharaja (*Anxiously*) – You haven't told him that memsahib is very comfortable there and doesn't want to return?

Vinay – I did tell him, there's nothing to hide. It will at least reassure him.

Maharaja (*Slapping his thigh with his hand*) – You have ruined everything. Hari-Hari! You have destroyed everything. Shiva-Shiva! You have lit the fire, why have you come to me now? Shiva-Shiva! Clark will say, there must be some mystery if the prisoner is comfortable in the prison. He's sure to say it. It's natural to say it. My bad days have come, Shiva-Shiva! How will I answer this accusation? Bhagwan! You have put me in grave danger. This is called childishness. What good news did you rush there to give? First you incited the public and set the riyasat on fire and now you have struck this blow. Fool! You should have told Clark that the mem was being subjected to several hardships and torments. Oh! Shiva-Shiva!

Suddenly the private secretary said on the phone – Mr Clark is coming.

The maharaja stood up and said – Yamdoot has come, he has come. Is anybody there? Bring my coat and trousers. You go, Vinay. Go away from the riyasat. Don't show me your face again. Bring my turban quickly. Remove the spittoon from here.

Vinay felt contempt for the maharaja. 'Such degradation,' he thought, 'such cowardice! It's better to drown than to rule like this.' When he came out, Nayakram asked, 'How did it go?'

Vinay – He's mortally afraid, as if he's about to lose his life. He's so scared, as if Mr Clark is a lion that will devour him the moment he arrives. I couldn't live in such a situation even for a day.

Nayakram – Bhaiyya, I think we should return home. For how long will you exhaust yourself in this mess?

Vinay (*With tears in his eyes*) – Pandaji, with what face will I return home? I'm not worthy of going home. Mataji won't see my face. I had left to serve the country and am returning after ruining hundreds of families. There's nothing left for me except to drown myself. I don't belong anywhere. I've realized, Nayakram, that I can't do anything, I can't do anybody any good; I was born only to sow poison. I'm a snake that can't do anything else except bite. What right does a vile creature like me have, who is cursed in the entire region, for whose harm rites are practised, to burden the world with his existence? I'm the object of the lamentations of so many helpless people today. The longer I live the more I'll increase the burden of my sins. If I were to die suddenly at this moment I'll think that God has saved me.

Immersed in this self-reproach, Vinay reached the house that the riyasat had given him to stay in. The servants rushed around as soon as they saw Vinay, somebody drew water, somebody began to sweep the floor, somebody began to wash the utensils. Vinay got down from the tonga and went to the reception room. As soon as he entered, he saw an envelope on the table. Vinay's heart began to beat faster. It was a letter from Rani Jahnavi. He didn't have the courage to open it. A mother receiving a telegram from her sick son in a foreign country would not have been so apprehensive. Picking up the envelope he thought, 'What else can there be in this except censure of me? What Indradutt had said about me must be repeated here in sharp words.' He put down the envelope as it was and thought, 'What should I do now? Why don't I stand in the bazaar here and inform the public that the durbar is being unjust to it? But right now the suffering public needs help, from where will the money come? Should I write to pitaji to send as much money as he can? If it comes, I'll distribute it among the orphans. No, I should meet the Viceroy first and tell him about the actual situation here. It's possible that he may pressurize the durbar and get the prisoners released. That seems best. I should leave everything now and meet the Viceroy.'

He began to prepare for the journey but the recollection of raniji's letter made him as anxious as if a naked sword were hanging over his head. He couldn't hold back any more. He opened the letter and began to read:

Vinay, several months ago I was proud to be your mother, but now I sink with shame to call you my son. What were you, and what have you become? And one doesn't know what you'll become if the same situation continues. You wouldn't have been in this world today had I known that you would make me bow down my head like this. You cruel one! Were you born from my womb for this? Did I make you drink my heart's blood for this? A painter painting a picture immediately erases it when he realizes that his feelings have not been expressed in it. I also want to obliterate you in the same way. I have created you. I have given you this body. The soul may have come from anywhere but the body is mine. I want you to return it to me. If you have any self-respect give me back what's in your custody. I'm grieved at your being alive. Why shouldn't I remove the thorn that pains my heart if I can? Will you fulfil this last desire of mine or will you reduce it to dust like my other desires? I still don't think you to be so shameless, or else I would have come myself and removed that object from your heart which is the root of your folly. Don't you know that there's something in the world that's dearer than a son? That's self-esteem. Even if I had a hundred sons like you I would have sacrificed them all to protect it. You'll think that I'm crazed with anger. This is not anger but the lament of my anguish. A weak creature like you cannot imagine the grief, disappointment and shame of a mother who can write such cruel words. I won't write more. It's futile to make you understand. What purpose can the lesson of one letter serve when the education of a lifetime has been unsuccessful? I now have only two wishes left—I wish to God not to give a child like you to one's worst enemy; and to you I wish that you'll end the cruel play of this life of yours.

Vinay didn't cry when he read this letter, he was neither angry nor remorseful. His eyes lit up with the exhilaration of pride, there was a flushed radiance on his face like that of an intrepid Rajput whose face glows when he hears the lord of the poets recite tales of the bravery of his ancestors – Mata, praise be to you. The heroic souls of the heroic women of Rajputana, seated in heaven, must be feeling proud of your idealism. I wasn't aware of your transcendental heroism until now. You have made all the wise women of India proud. Devi! I'm ashamed of calling myself your son. Yes, I'm not worthy of being your son. I bow my head before your decision. If I had a hundred lives I would have sacrificed them all to protect your self-esteem. I haven't yet become so shameless; but not like this. I want to give you the satisfaction that your son may not know how to live but he knows how to die. Why the delay now? I have done everything in life that I shouldn't have done. What better opportunity could there be to end it than this? This forehead will suffer agony at your feet just once. It's possible that I may get your sacred blessings at the very end of my life. Perhaps you may utter these elevating words, 'This is what I had expected of you, you didn't know how to live, but you know how to die.' If even at the end of my life I hear you say the two words, 'Dear son,' my soul will be at peace and be happy even in hell. If only God had given me wings, I would have flown and come to you.

Vinay looked out. The sun god had hidden his pale face in the shelter of the mountains like a shamed being. Nayakram was sitting cross-legged grinding bhang. He didn't ask the servants to do this work. He'd say, 'This is also an art, it's not haldi and masala that can be ground by all and sundry. You have to use your intelligence, only then does it become booti.' He hadn't made it yesterday. Completely engrossed, he ground the bhang and sang a few chaupais that he remembered from the Ramayana when Vinay called him.

Nayakram – What is it, bhaiyya? I'm making wonderful booti. You've never had it before. Have some today, all your fatigue will disappear.

Vinay – All right, let the booti be for the time being. There's a letter from ammaji, we have to go home, get a tonga.

Nayakram – Bhaiyya, everything you do is impetuous. If we have to go home we'll go comfortably tomorrow. I'll strain the booti and then prepare the food. You must have eaten food cooked in several Kashmiri kitchens; savour my cooking also today.

Vinay – I'll savour your cooking now only after reaching home.

Nayakram – Mataji must have called you?

Vinay – Yes, very soon.

Nayakram – All right, let the booti be prepared. The train leaves at nine at night.

Vinay – It will soon be nine. It must already be seven.

Nayakram – Get the baggage packed meanwhile, I'll quickly make it. I'm not fated to have the happiness of being carefree enough to make booti.

Vinay – No baggage will go with us. I didn't bring any from home. We have to give the key of the house to sardar sahib when we leave.

Nayakram – And all these things?

Vinay – I've said that I won't take anything.

Nayakram – Bhaiyya, you don't take anything, but I'm definitely taking this shawl and box. People will fall senseless wherever I go when I wear this shawl.

Vinay – What will you do with such a murderous thing the very sight of which will kill? Don't touch anything that belongs here; go.

Cursing fate, when Nayakram left the house he spent an hour settling the fare of the gharry. Finally, when this complicated problem couldn't be solved, he brought one forcibly. The tonga-vala came grumbling, 'They are all rulers after all; the wretched animal should also get something for his belly. No mother's brat ever realizes that I'll die doing unpaid labour, what will I eat myself, what will I feed the animal, what will I give my family! On top of that they have fixed the tariff and hung it in every alley. Bas, it's only the tonga-valas who loot everybody, all the other staff and employees are washed clean in milk. Haul boxes, beg and eat, but never ply a tonga.'

Vinay sat on the tonga as soon as it arrived but how could Nayakram leave his half-ground booti? He quickly ground and sieved it and then drank it, chewed tobacco, tied his turban in front of the mirror, said Rama-Rama to the men and went out, looking at the shawl covetously. The tonga moved. Sardar sahib's house was on the way. Nayakram gave the key to the gateman and they reached the station by 8 p.m. Nayakram thought that they wouldn't get anything to eat on the way and they couldn't eat on the train, so he ran to get some puris and water and sat down to eat. Vinay said he wasn't hungry. He was standing looking at the train timetable—When would this train reach Ajmer? Which train could they catch in Delhi? All of a sudden he saw an old woman wailing. Two or three men were supporting her. She came and sat next to Vinay. Vinay discovered that her son was the daroga of the Jaswantnagar jail; somebody had killed him in broad daylight. The news had just come and the grief-stricken mother was going to Jaswantnagar. The fares that the motor-valas were asking were too high, that's why she was going by train. She would get down on the way and get a bullock cart. She had only one son; the poor thing was not destined even to see his face.

Vinay was deeply grieved; the daroga had been a very straightforward man. He was very kind to the prisoners. What enmity could anybody have towards him? He immediately suspected that this was also the cruel work of Veerpaal Singh's followers. Sophie hadn't given an empty threat. It seemed that she had been able to gather the instruments for the secret killings. 'God! How vast is the arena of my wicked deeds? The crime of these killings is on my head, not on Sophie's. A woman as altruistic, sensible and pious as Sophie has resorted to murder only because of my weakness. God! Is there no end to my torments? I'll go again to Sophia. I'll definitely go, and falling at her feet, I'll say humbly, devi, I have been punished for my sins, now put an end to this play, or I'll give up my life in front of you. But where will I find Sophie? Who'll take me to that inaccessible fort?'

When the train arrived, Vinay made the old woman sit in his compartment. Nayakram went to a different one because he couldn't have been playful with the other passengers in Vinay's presence. The train started. The police sepoys could be seen pacing about at every station today. The durbar had made this special arrangement for the protection of the travellers. No travellers could be seen boarding the train at any station. The rebels had looted several jagirdars.

The train suddenly stopped at a short distance before the fifth station. There was no station there. Several men could be heard talking below the line. Then somebody opened the door of Vinay's compartment. Vinay first wanted to stop the newcomer; his communism was transformed into selfishness the moment he boarded a train. He even suspected that it could be a dacoit but when he looked closely he saw that they were a woman's hands. He moved away and in a moment the woman boarded the train. Vinay recognized her as soon as he saw her; it was Miss Sophia. The train started again as soon as she boarded.

The colour faded from Sophia's face when she saw Vinay. She wanted to get down but the train had started. She kept standing, at a loss for a second. She couldn't meet Vinay's eyes. She then sat down next to the old woman and looked out of the window. Both of them sat silently for a while; nobody had the courage to speak.

The old woman asked – Where are you going, beti?

Sophia – I have to go very far.

Old woman – From where have you come?

Sophia – There's a village nearby. I'm coming from there.

Old woman – Did you get the train stopped?

Sophia – There are dacoities at the stations these days. That's why I got the train stopped in the middle.

Old woman – There's nobody with you? How will you go alone?

Sophia – God is there, if not a human being.

Old woman – Who knows if there's a God? It seems to me that there's no creator, that's why there are dacoities and murders in broad daylight. The dacoits killed my son yesterday. (*Crying*) He was like a cow, a cow. He never answered me back. The prisoners of the jail used to bless him. He never tormented a good person. This thunderbolt fell on him, so how can I say that there's a God?

Sophia – Was the jailor of Jaswantnagar your son?

Old woman – Yes, beti, I had only this one son whom God has taken away.

The old woman began to sob. Sophie's face became wan, like that of a patient about to die. She sat for a while trying to suppress a surge of pity. Then she put her head out of the window and sobbed bitterly. Her wicked revenge stood naked before her eyes.

Sophie cried, hiding her face, for half an hour. Even the station arrived at which the old woman wanted to get down. Vinay took down her luggage when she alighted and reassuring her, said goodbye to her.

Vinay had not yet got back on to the train when Sophie got down, stood in front of the old woman and said – Mata, I'm your son's murderer. Give me whatever punishment you want. I'm standing before you.

The old woman said, surprised – Are you the demoness who has gathered the dacoits to fight the durbar? No, it can't be you. You look like the image of pity and compassion.

Sophie – Yes, mata, I'm that demoness.

Old woman – As you have sown, so you will reap. What else can I say to you? May your days also be spent weeping, like mine.

The engine's whistle blew. Sophie stood speechless, motionless. The train started. Sophie was still standing. Vinay jumped down from the train, caught hold of Sophia's hand, made her get on and then got on himself with great difficulty. He would have been left there had there been a moment's delay.

Sophia (*Remorsefully*) – Vinay, you may or may not believe me, but I'm telling you the truth, I didn't give Veerpaal permission for even one murder. I tried my best to stop his murderous inclinations but this group is now bent on revenge. Nobody listened to me. That's why I'm leaving now. I don't know what I said to you that night in my anger, but God alone knows how deeply I regret it. On reflecting with a calm mind I have realized that we ourselves are to blame if we continuously kill others or are killed by them in times of disaster. This condition can't be permanent. Human beings are peaceful by nature. And then if the repressive policy of the government can provoke the weak public to take revenge, won't a strong government have recourse to an even more ruthless policy? But I'm talking to you as if you are a family member. I've forgotten that you belong to the party of the loyalists of the government. But have this much mercy on me, don't hand me over to the police. I had arranged to stop the train on the way and to board it only to escape the police. I suspect that even now you are looking for me.

Vinay's eyes filled with tears. He said, annoyed – Sophia, you have the right to think me to be as degraded and base as you want, but a day will come when you'll regret what you have said and you'll realize how unfair you have been to me. But just reflect with a calm mind. Didn't you adopt the same strategy at home before coming here, when you heard the news of my arrest? The only difference was that I destroyed others, but you were prepared to destroy yourself. I thought that your strategy was forgivable, that it was aapaddharma.* You thought that my course of action was unforgivable and struck the cruellest blows that you could. But it's the same thing. You couldn't have been as startled and grieved to see me helping the police as I was when I saw you with Mr Clark. Even now you are adopting, or at least you have adopted, the same policy of retaliation towards me. And you still don't have mercy on me. The mental torture that I have

---

* The action (dharma) decreed to be performed only in situations of extreme distress and emergencies.

suffered and am still suffering because of your rebukes is unbearable for me. And you have sprinkled more salt on top of that. You'll shed tears of blood for this cruelty. Well!

Vinay choked as he said this. He couldn't speak after that. Sophie's eyes filled with tears of infinite love as she said – Come, let's be friends. Forgive those deeds of mine.

Vinay said, controlling his voice – Have I said anything? Say whatever you want to if you are not yet satisfied. There's no companion in bad times. After leaving you, only I know how much I pleaded with the authorities, with Mr Clark, even with Maharaja Sahib to release the prisoners. But nobody listened. I was disappointed from all sides.

Sophia – I knew this. Where are you going now?

Vinay – To hell.

Sophia – Take me also with you.

Vinay – There's heaven for you.

He said, after a moment – I'm going home. Ammaji has called me. She's eager to see me.

Sophia – Indradutt said she's very angry with you . . .

Vinay took out raniji's letter from his pocket and gave it to Sophia, looking the other way. Perhaps he thought that she's so withdrawn from me and I'm forcibly rushing towards her. Sophia tore the letter and threw it out of the window. Beside herself with love, she said, 'I won't let you go. God knows I won't let you go. I'll go myself to raniji in your place and tell her, I'm your culprit . . .' Her voice choked. She put her head on Vinay's shoulder and began to sob. When she was quieter, she said, 'Promise me you won't go. You can't go. You can't go for the sake of dharma and justice. Tell me, do you promise?'

There was so much pity, entreaty, humility and request in those tearful eyes!

Vinay said – No, Sophie, let me go. You know mataji very well. If I don't go, she'll think that I'm a shameless coward and one doesn't know what she may do in this agitated state.

Sophia – No, Vinay, don't torture me like this. Have mercy for God's sake. I'll go to raniji and cry, I'll fall at her feet, I'll wash away the rancour that she has for you in her heart with my tears. I'm sure that I'll be able to reawaken her love for her son. Her heart is a receptacle of compassion. When I fall at her feet and say, 'Amma! Your son is my master, forgive him for my sake,' she won't reject me. She'll get up infuriated and leave, but she'll send for me in a moment and will lovingly embrace me. I'll beg her for your life, and then I'll beg her for you. A mother's heart can never be so hard. Perhaps she's now regretting having written this letter and hoping that it hasn't reached. Promise me.

Vinay had never before heard words so saturated with love and devotion. His life now seemed successful to him. 'Ah! Sophie still loves me. She has forgiven me.' The life that had seemed so desolate, arid and inanimate was now radiant with birds and beasts, water and rivers, flowers and creepers. The doors of happiness had opened and melodies of sweet music, a glimpse of lit lamps, and a waft of fragrant breeze emanating from within enraptured the heart. Vinay was enchanted by this beautiful scene. It is the joys of life that are its sorrows. The jewels of life are detachment and despair. Our pristine desires, our chaste services, our propitious imaginings germinate and flourish only in the soil of misfortune.

Vinay said, agitated – Sophie, let me go to ammaji just once. I promise you that until she doesn't clearly say . . .

Sophie put her arms around Vinay's neck and said – No, no, I don't trust you. You can't protect yourself alone. You have courage, self-respect, principles, but not patience. I used to think that you were necessary for me but now I think that I'm necessary for you. Vinay, why are you looking at the floor? Look at me. I'm ashamed of the harsh things that I said to you. God is my witness; I'm sincerely repentant. Forget those things. Love is as forgiving as it is idealistic. Promise me. If you try to get rid of me and go away . . . you'll never find Sophie again.

Vinay said, ecstatic with love – I won't go if that's your wish.

Sophia – Then we'll get down at the next station.

Vinay – No, let's go to Banaras first. You go to ammaji. If she forgives me . . .

Sophia – Vinay, let's not go to Banaras just now. Let your heart be calm and your mind rest for a few days. And after all, what right does raniji have over you? You are mine, by all those laws that have been created by God and by human beings, you are mine. I don't want a favour, I want my right. We'll get down at the next station and then we'll think about what to do and where to go.

Vinay (*Embarrassed*) – How will we subsist? All that I have is with Nayakram. He's in a different compartment. He'll also come with us if he gets to know.

Sophia – That's nothing to worry about. Let Nayakram go. Love can be happy even in jungles.

The train was sawing its way through mountains and forts in the dark night. Nothing was visible outside except mountain ranges rushing past. Vinay was looking at the flight of the stars, Sophie was looking out to see if there were any villages nearby.

Meanwhile, they reached a station. Sophie opened the door and they both got down quietly, like a pair of birds flying from the nest in search of grain. They are not worried that there may be a hunter ahead or birds of prey or the farmer's catapult. They are both absorbed in their thoughts, gazing at the flourishing fields swaying with grain. But nobody knows if they are destined to reach there.

36

PLEASED WITH TAHIR ALI'S HARD WORK AND HONESTY, MR JOHN
Sevak had fixed a commission on the hides for him. This increased
his income as well as his influence among the mill labourers. The
overseer and the junior clerks respected him but his expenditure
also increased a great deal with his income. He could make do with
torn shoes when people of his status had not been around, he would
bargain and make purchases in the bazaar himself, he would even
draw the water sometimes. There was nobody to laugh at him. Now
he had to live more grandly in the presence of the mill staff and he
felt embarrassed to do heavy work with his own hands. So he perforce
had to employ an old woman servant. The expenses on paan-ilaichi
multiplied. On top of that, he often had to entertain. People don't
expect to be entertained by somebody who lives alone. They know
that the party will be insipid. But those with families can't escape.
Somebody would say, 'Khan sahib, get zarde cooked today. My tongue
has become thick, eating roti-daal for so many days.' Tahir would be
forced to reply, 'Haan-haan, I'll get them cooked today.' Had there
been only one woman at home, he could have made an excuse that
she was unwell, but here there were three, not one. And then Tahir
was not stingy with food. He was happy to entertain his friends. In
short, he suffered crippling losses as a result of living well. He didn't
have an iota of credit in the bazaar, he had become so notorious as a
swindler that nobody trusted him with a dhela worth of goods, so he
would survive by borrowing money from friends. The bazaar-valas
despaired and gave up making their claims; they realized that he didn't
have anything, so what could he give? A debt in writing is eternal. A
debt based on promises is lifeless and transitory. One is an Arabian
horse that can't tolerate being spurred; it will put an end either to the
rider or to itself. The other is a packhorse driven not by its feet but
by whips, if the whip breaks or if the hand of the rider stops and the
packhorse collapses, it can't get up again.

However, if matters had been confined only to entertaining friends, Tahir would have managed somehow to make two ends meet. The problem was that his younger brother, Mahir, had got admission into the police-training school in Moradabad. As soon as he received his pay, Tahir would have to shut his eyes and send half of it to Moradabad. Tahir was afraid of the expenditure but both his mothers made it difficult for him to live at home with their taunts. They were very keen that Mahir should enter the police and become a daroga. Poor Tahir wandered around the bungalows of the authorities for months together; he went hither-thither, gave presents here and gifts there, got recommendations from somebody and letters from someone else. Finally Mr John Sevak's recommendation worked. All these hurdles were crossed. The last one was the medical examination. Recommendations and flattery didn't work here. Thirty-two rupees for the civil surgeon, sixteen rupees for the assistant surgeon, and eight rupees for the clerks and peons—the total sum added up to fifty-six rupees. From where would this money come? Disappointed from all sides, Tahir went to Kulsoom and said, 'If you have any jewellery give it to me, I'll soon have it redeemed.' She flared up and banged the box in front of him, saying, 'I don't hanker for jewellery, all my desires have been fulfilled. It's enough if I can keep getting roti-daal. Your jewellery is in front of you, do what you want.' For a while, Tahir was so embarrassed that he couldn't look up. Then he looked at the box. There wasn't anything from which he could get a fourth of the sum that he needed. Yes, the work could be done if the things were trashed. Embarrassed, he took out everything, put it all in his handkerchief, and came out wondering how to take the things away, when the maidservant came. Tahir thought, 'Why don't I get the money through her? Maidservants are experts at this work.' He called her softly and confided this problem in her. The old woman said, 'Miyaan, this is not such a big thing. The things have to be deposited, nobody is asking for charity. I'll bring you the money; don't worry.' Zainab saw her as she was leaving with the bundle of jewellery. She called her and said, 'Where will you go around carrying it? I'll ask Mahir to get the money. A friend of his is a moneylender.' The maidservant gave her the bundle. After a couple of hours, Zainab herself gave fifty-six rupees. This was how the difficult problem was resolved. Mahir left for Moradabad to study. It was very difficult to meet the household expenses after sending him half the pay. They would have to fast sometimes. Mahir was not satisfied with only half the pay. He would sometimes write and ask for money for clothes or he would want a suit for playing tennis. As a result, Tahir had to send him something from his commission as well.

One morning, after fasting for the whole night, Zainab asked him – Have you thought about the money today, or is it going to be roza again?

Tahir said annoyed – From where can I get it? Didn't I send the money that I had got as commission to Moradabad in front of you? I write again and again, telling him to spend thriftily, I'm very hard up, but that hazrat says, here every boy gets hundreds from home and spends lavishly; I can't economize more than this. If this is the situation there and such is the plight here, from where can I get the money? I don't have any friend left either from whom I can borrow something.

Zainab – Do you hear what he's saying, Raqiya? He thinks he's obliging me by paying the expenses of the boy. How does it concern me if you send him the expenses or call him back? We can't fill our bellies here by his studying there. He's your brother, whether you educate him or not, how is it a favour to me?

Tahir – Then you tell me from where to get the money.

Zainab – Men have a thousand hands. Did your abbajaan get only ten rupees or more? They were increased to twenty rupees only a few days before his death. Did he provide for the household or not? It never came to starvation. Coarse or fine, it was sure to be available at least twice a day. You were educated, you got married, clothes came. By the mercy of Khuda, jewellery was also made according to our means. He never asked me from where to get the money. After all, he'd get it from somewhere or the other.

Tahir – There's every kind of scope in the police department. What's there over here? A few pieces of meat, measured gravy.

Zainab – Had I been in your place, I'd have shown you how to rain gold even in this job. There are hundreds of chamaars. Won't they all bring a pile of wood each if you ask them? Vegetables must be growing on their thatches. Why don't you ask them to pluck and bring some? You also have the right to increase or reduce the price of the hides. Nobody's sitting here watching you. How will it matter if you write a quarter to ten instead of ten? Don't you just have thumb impressions put on the receipts? Does the impression go around crying that it's ten or a quarter to ten? And now you have established your trust. Sahib can't have any suspicion. After all, shouldn't you also gain from this trust or will you go on filling other people's bellies all your life? Even now you probably have hundreds of rupees with you as ready cash. Take out as much as you need now. Put it back when you get money in your hands. You need only to balance the daily income and expenditure, don't you? What's so great about it? You didn't pay for the hides today but you will tomorrow, what's there to be anxious about that? The chamaar won't go and complain anywhere. That's what everyone does, and that's how the world functions. People should become fakirs if they want to maintain their honour.

Raqiya – Behen, where's the honour? That's how the world functions.

Tahir – Bhai, that's up to those who function like that. My soul is destroyed by these stratagems. I can't touch what's in my custody. After all, I have to show my face to Khuda. It's his wish; he can keep us alive or kill us.

Zainab – Vaah, you despicable man! I'll sacrifice my life for your honour! Your honour should remain intact, even if people in the house are dying of starvation. You want them all to blacken their faces and go away. That's all. A man is concerned only about his wife and children. The bazaar is available for them. There's starvation only for us. Their starvation is just pretence.

Tahir, stunned by this false accusation, said – Why are you exasperating me, ammijaan! Khuda is my witness if I have got a dhela worth of anything for the children. That was never my nature, it is not, and it won't be. But it's your wish—think what you like.

Raqiya – Both the children suffered all night, 'Amma, roti, amma, roti!' Ask them, should amma herself become a roti! If nothing else, your children go to the overseer's house and eat something there. Here they can only eat my life.

Zainab – You have the right to feed or not feed your children. There's nobody to examine your accounts. You can give them sheermaal or starve them. Our children can't get anything except dry rotis cooked in the house. There's no vali here who can survive by starving. Go and arrange something.

When he came out, Tahir was deeply worried for some time. For the first time today, he was rash enough to touch the money in his custody. He first looked around to see if anyone was standing there, then he gently opened the iron box. He would otherwise open and shut that box hundreds of times during the day, but now his hands were trembling frantically. Finally he took out the money and closed the safe. He threw it in front of Zainab and went out without saying anything. He tried to justify himself, 'If Khuda had wanted my honour to remain intact, why would he have burdened me with the responsibility of so many people? He should have also given me the strength to bear this burden. I can starve myself but I can't force others. It won't be fair if Khuda thinks that I should be punished in this helpless situation.' This argument gave him some comfort. But John Sevak was not a man who would accept it. Tahir began to wonder which chamaar was the wealthiest and wouldn't complain and whine if he wasn't given the money today. 'No, it wouldn't be right to stop the payment of somebody who is well-off, well-off people are unafraid. Who knows, he may tell somebody. The payment of the simplest and poorest should be stopped. There's nothing to be afraid of in this. I'll call him quietly and get his thumb impression. He won't have the courage to tell anyone.' From that day on, he would take out the money from the cash when he needed it and replace it later. Gradually he was less worried about replacing the money. There began to be a deficit in the cash. He was emboldened. In fact, within six months, 150 rupees had been spent from the cash.

Tahir was now constantly worried about this matter being discovered. He would flatter the chamaars. He wanted to think of a way by which this deficit wouldn't be discovered. But he didn't have the courage to manipulate the accounts book. He didn't tell anybody in the house about this. He just prayed to Khuda for Mahir's return. 'He'll get 100 rupees a month. I'll pay back the money in two months. Meanwhile, I'll be saved if sahib doesn't examine the accounts.'

He was determined not to take out any more money, no matter what might happen. But he had to take out twenty-five rupees again in the seventh month. Mahir was now about to complete the year. There were just a few days left. He thought, 'After all, I've been burdened with these expenses because of him. I'll hand over the house to him as soon as he comes. I'll say, bhai, I've taken care of it all this while. I spent as much as I could on your education, I've got you a job. Now give me some relief from this worry for a few days. If only this matter could be hidden until his return, I could shake my tail and escape.' Earlier, he would go to sahib for such needs. He now made it a point to meet him at least once a day. He wanted to allay suspicion by these meetings. We stick more closely to the very thing that we are afraid will collide with us. Kulsoom frequently asked him from where he had got so much money. She would try to explain, 'Look, don't taint your intentions. It's not so bad to live in want and difficulty as to be a sinner before Khuda.' But Tahir would just change the topic and distract her.

One morning, when Tahir went to the office after offering namaaz, he saw a chamaar standing there, weeping. He asked him what the matter was. The chamaar said, 'What can I say, Khan sahib, my wife passed away in the night. Now I have to perform her last rites. Give me my dues, I've come running, I don't have money even for the shroud.' Tahir did not have enough money in the cash. He had dispatched some goods from the station yesterday; the money had been spent in paying the excise. He was going to sahib today to present the accounts and to get money. He had to pay this chamaar for several hides. He couldn't make excuses. He brought a few rupees and gave them to him.

The chamaar said – Huzoor, this isn't enough even for the shroud. The dead woman won't return, so I should at least perform her last rites generously. Give me all the money that's due to me. The corpse won't be taken away from the doorway until there are at least ten bottles of liquor.

Tahir – There's no money just now, take it some other time.

Chamaar – Vaah, Khan sahib, vaah! It's been months since you took my thumb impression and now you say take it some other time. If you don't give it now, will you give it to me in heaven after I die? You should have given me some help yourself, instead you are holding back my money.

Tahir brought a few more rupees. The chamaar flung them on the ground and said – You are trying to revive the she-mouse with spit!

I'm not asking you for a loan and you are making this cut, as if you are paying from your own house.

Tahir Ali – It's not possible for me to give you more than this right now.

The chamaar was quite straightforward, but he became suspicious and flared up.

Suddenly Mr John Sevak arrived. He was irritated today. Prabhu's rebellion had disoriented him somewhat. On seeing this wrangle, he said sharply – Why don't you give his money? I had given you strict instructions to clear the accounts of all the men each day. Why do you keep any balance? Don't you have money in the cash?

Tahir was rather nervous when he went to get the money so that sahib was immediately suspicious. He picked up the register and examined the accounts. They were clear. This chamaar had been paid his dues. His thumb impression was there. Then why this balance? Meanwhile, several chamaars arrived. Seeing that chamaar getting money they thought that the accounts were being cleared today. They said, 'Sarkar, we should also get our dues.'

Sahib flung the register on the ground and shouted – What's this rigmarole? Why haven't these people been paid when receipts have been taken from them?

Tahir couldn't think of anything else so he fell at sahib's feet and began to weep. Only a very seasoned housebreaker can remain sitting and staring in the hole that he has made in the wall.

The chamaars, sensing the situation, said – Sarkar, there's nothing due to us, we are asking for today's money. We had kept the goods here a short while ago. Khan sahib was offering namaaz then.

When sahib picked up the register, he saw a faint sign against some names. He realized that this hazrat was the one who had taken the money. He asked a chamaar who was coming from the bazaar, smoking a cigarette – What's your name?

Chamaar – Chunkoo.

Sahib – How much money is due to you?

Several chamaars gestured to him with their hands to say 'nothing'. Chunkoo didn't understand. He said – There were seventeen rupees earlier, nine rupees for today.

Sahib entered his name in his notebook. He didn't say a word to

Tahir. Where was the need for rebukes and scolding when he could be punished legally? He locked the office, double-locked the safe, put the keys in his pocket, all the registers on the phaeton, and got on to it. Tahir Ali didn't have the courage to plead. His speech was paralysed. He stood stunned. The chowdhary of the chamaars reassured him, 'Why are you afraid, Khan sahib, not a hair of your head will be harmed. We'll say that we have been paid. Why, you Chunkooa, you are so stupid, you couldn't understand the hint?'

Chunkoo (*Embarrassed*) – Chowdhary, God knows, if I had got the least hint I wouldn't have mentioned the money.

Chowdhary – Change your testimony; say that you didn't remember the account orally.

Chunkoo didn't reply. To change his testimony would be to put his finger into a snake's mouth. Tahir was not at all comforted by these words. He was regretful, not because he had spent the money but because he had put signs against the names. 'Matters wouldn't have come to this if I had entered them on a separate sheet of paper. Now it's up to Khuda. Sahib is not somebody who will forgive.' He didn't know what to do and was very nervous.

Chowdhary – Khan sahib, it won't do now to sit and do nothing. This sahib is a cruel and merciless executioner. Collect the money quickly. Do you remember the total amount?

Tahir – I'm not worried about the money but about the stigma. How was I to know that this disaster would happen today or wouldn't I have prepared myself? Do you know, some worker or the other in the factory is always after me for a loan? For how many of them should I make excuses? And then one can't even make excuses out of pity for them. I take out the money and give it. This is the punishment for that decency. There must be at least 150 rupees; in fact there may even be 200.

Chowdhary – Should official money be spent like this? Whether you have spent it or lent it, it's the same thing. Will those people give the money?

Tahir – Nobody's that honest. Somebody will say I'll give it after I get my wages. Somebody will make excuses. I don't know what to do.

Chowdhary – There must be money at home?

Tahir – Of course there must be a few hundred rupees but you know that women's money is dearer to them than their lives. What will happen now is Khuda's wish.

Tahir then thought of going to some of his friends, hoping that they would help him on hearing about his situation, but instead of going anywhere he offered namaaz under a tree. He didn't hope for help from anywhere.

The chowdhary said to the chamaars – Bhaiyyon, our munshiji is in trouble. His life can be saved if all of you help a little. Sahib won't merely take back his money but also somebody's life. Think that you haven't taken any intoxicant today.

The chowdhary began to collect the money from the chamaars. Tahir's friends quietly hid themselves when they heard about his plight, afraid that he would ask for something. But people came to watch the spectacle when the daroga came to make enquiries in the third pahar and arrested Tahir. There was wailing in the house. Kulsoom went to Zainab and said, 'There you are, now your wish has been fulfilled.'

Zainab – Why are you annoyed with me, begum? It's your wishes that may or may not have been fulfilled. I didn't tell him to go and rob somebody's house. You may have lived riotously, here we don't know about anything except roti-daal.

Kulsoom didn't have a kauri even for her shroud; Zainab had money but she thought that arousing resentment was sufficient. Kulsoom was not sympathetic to Tahir at this moment. She was angry with him, like somebody annoyed with her child for having cut his finger with a knife.

It was getting on to evening. The daroga sent for an ikka for Tahir. Four constables accompanied him on it. The daroga knew that he was Mahir's brother so he had some respect for him. As they left he said, 'If you want to say anything to anyone at home, you can go ahead. The women must be anxious, go and reassure them.' But Tahir said, 'I don't want to say anything to anyone.' He didn't want to show his face to Kulsoom, whom he had deliberately devastated and was leaving without any support. Kulsoom was standing at the door. Her anger was turning to grief at every moment so that when the ikka started, she fell back unconscious. The children ran after the ikka crying, 'Abba, abba.' The daroga distracted them by giving each of them a four-anna coin for mithai. While Tahir was arrested, the chowdhary of the chamaars took the money to Mr Sevak shortly before nightfall.

Sahib said, 'Give this money to his family so that they can subsist on it. The matter is now in the hands of the police; I can't do anything.'

Chowdhary – Huzoor, human beings make mistakes. He has served you for so many days; huzoor should have some mercy on him. He has a very large family, sarkar! They will all die of starvation.

John Sevak – I know all this, undoubtedly his expenses were heavy. That's why I gave him a commission on the goods. I know that he has done what he has because of his helplessness, but poison will work like poison no matter with what intention it's eaten, it can never become nectar. Deceit is not less murderous than poison. Give this money to his family. I don't have anything against Khan sahib, but I can't leave my dharma. To forgive a sin is to commit a sin.

The chowdhary returned disappointed. The case began the next day. Tahir was found guilty. He couldn't give an explanation to clear himself. He was sentenced for six months.

When Tahir was going towards the jail with the constables, he saw Mahir coming on a tonga. He was delighted and tears poured down from his eyes. He thought, 'Mahir has rushed here to meet me. Perhaps he has arrived just today and was restless on hearing this news.' When the tonga came close, he began to weep loudly. Mahir looked at him once, but there was no salaam or greeting, he didn't stop the tonga, nor did he look that way again, he turned his face away as if he hadn't seen anything. The tonga went past Tahir. A deep sigh arose from his heart. Once again he wept loudly. The first weeping was the sound of joy, the second the lament of grief, those were drops of tears, these were drops of blood.

But his agony subsided in a moment – Mahir probably didn't see me. He did look towards me but he must have been lost in some thought. It does happen that when we are absorbed in some thought we don't see what's in front of us nor do we hear what's said close by. This must be the reason. It was just as well that he didn't see me otherwise I would have been happy but he would have been distressed.

When Mahir reached home, his younger brothers clung to him. Both Tahir's children also came running, and began to jump around saying, 'Mahir chacha has come, Mahir chacha has come.' Kulsoom also came out weeping. After salaams and greetings, Mahir went to his mother, who embraced him.

Mahir – I wouldn't have come here if I hadn't got your letter. It's only after the exams that one can enjoy oneself; there are matches sometimes, or outings and mushairas. What's this folly that bhai sahib had thought of?

Zainab – How could begum sahib's requests have been fulfilled otherwise? Jewels are needed, zarda is needed, zari is needed—from where would all this have come? On top of that, she says that it's we who have ruined him. Just ask, how could there have been an expense of fifty-six taka on roti-daal alone? I couldn't oil my hair for months on end. We have to spend our own money if we want to eat paan. And then there are so many taunts on top of that.

Mahir – When I saw him going to the jail while coming from the station, I was so ashamed that I didn't speak to him and didn't even greet him. After all, wouldn't people have said, 'His brother is going to prison'? I turned my face and came away. Bhaiyya began to cry. My heart was also wrung, I wanted to hug him but I felt embarrassed. A thanedar is not an ordinary person. He is ranked among the authorities. I'll be disgraced if I don't keep this in mind.

Zainab – He has been sentenced for six months.

Mahir – It was a big crime but perhaps the judge had mercy.

Zainab – He must have shown some consideration to your abba, otherwise he wouldn't have got off with less than three years.

Mahir – He has put a stigma on the family. He has reduced the prestige of our elders to dust.

Zainab – One hopes to Khuda that no man will read the kalma of a woman and be servile to her.

Meanwhile, the maidservant brought some mithai. Mahir gave a piece each to Zahir and Zabir. They showed them off to Sabir and Naseema. Both of them also came running. Zainab said, 'Go, why don't you play? Why are you hanging over my head? From where have these starving lads come? It's difficult to put anything into one's mouth because of these people. They hang over our heads like evil spirits. They eat day and night but are still unsatisfied.'

Raqiya – What else will the children of a worthless mother be?

Mahir gave a piece of mithai each to both of them as well. Then he said – How will we subsist? Bhabhi has some money, doesn't she?

Zainab – How can she not? It's for this money that she has sent her husband to jail. Let me see what arrangements she makes. Why should anybody here bother to ask?

Mahir – I don't know how long it will take me to get a place here. It could take a month or two months. Don't harass me until then.

Zainab – Don't worry about this, beta. She'll take care of herself. Khuda is our protector as well. If she goes to sleep after eating pulao, we'll also somehow manage to get dry rotis.

When it was evening, Zainab said to the maidservant – Go and ask begum sahib if anything is to be bought or if there's going to be mourning today.

The maidservant returned and said – She's sitting there and crying. She says whoever is hungry can eat; she doesn't want to eat.

Zainab – See! I told you that you'll get a blunt answer. She knows that the boy has come from outside but she won't part with the money. She'll get food from the bazaar for herself and her children; others may eat or die for all she cares. Anyway, she's welcome to her sweet morsels; Allah is our maalik too.

Ever since Kulsoom had heard that Tahir had been sentenced for six months, there was darkness before her eyes. She had flared up when she heard the maidservant's message. She had said – Tell them to cook and eat, I'm not hungry. If they pity the children, they can give them a few morsels as well.

It was this sentence that the maidservant had interpreted, making nonsense out of sense.

It was nine at night. Kulsoom saw that the stove had been lit. The fragrance of spices wafted around, the sound of the seasoning being roasted could also be heard, but when nobody came to call her children, she sat down and wailed. She realized that the family had deserted her and that she was now an orphan. She didn't have anybody in the world. Both the children went to sleep crying. She also remained lying at the foot of their bed. 'God! Two children, and I don't have even a worthless kauri, this is the state of the people in the family, how will this boat reach the shore?'

When Mahir sat down to eat, he asked the maidservant – Has bhabhi sent for something from the bazaar?

Zainab – Won't her secret be revealed if she gets it through the maidservant? By the grace of Khuda, Sabir is mature now. He brings the goods secretly, and he's such a wily rascal that he doesn't open his mouth no matter how much you cajole him.

Mahir – Go ask, we shouldn't eat and go to sleep while that poor thing keeps a roza.

Zainab – She's not that simple. She can make fools of us. Yes, it's my duty to ask, so I will.

Raqiya – Saalan and roti, how will she eat just that? She needs zarda and sheermaal.

The next day, when both the children entered the kitchen, Zainab stared at them so sternly that they left crying. Kulsoom could no longer control herself. She got up infuriated and going to the kitchen, said to the maidservant, 'Why didn't you give food to the children? Have you changed so soon? We have been reduced to dust because of this household and my children have to suffer pangs of hunger, did nobody have any pity?'

The maidservant said – Why are you flaring up at me? Who am I? I do what I'm told to.

Zainab (*From her room*) – If you have been reduced to dust, who has filled their houses here? There was some relationship between us until yesterday; you have broken even that. We could eat something only when we got some goods on loan from the bania. The boy had travelled a hundred kos and you didn't even ask after him. For how long can we go on singing your praises?

From that day rotis were scarce for Kulsoom. Mahir would sometimes go to the baker's shop with both his brothers and eat there, or he would be the guest of a close friend. The maidservant would cook something secretly in her own kitchen for Zainab and Raqiya. The stove wouldn't be lit at home. Naseema and Sabir would leave the house early in the morning. They would eat if somebody gave them anything. They were as afraid of Zainab and Raqiya as a mouse is of a cat. They wouldn't go to Mahir either. Children recognize their enemies and friends only too well. They were hungry now not for love but for pity. As for Kulsoom, sorrow was enough for her. She knew how to stitch and sew, she could have fended for herself by her sewing but she didn't do anything out of spite. She wanted to blacken Mahir's face, she wanted the world to see her plight and to spit on him. She was now angry with Tahir too. 'You were capable only of grinding the millstone in the jail. Your eyes will be opened now. You were afraid of the world laughing at you. The world is not laughing at anyone now. People here enjoy sweet morsels and sleep sweetly. The world is not bothered about anyone so that even falsehood puts these self-seeking people to shame. Why should anybody be so concerned that they'll laugh at somebody? People must be thinking that this is the right punishment for the foolish, who give their lives for their honour.'

A month went by like this. Subhagi came one day with vegetables for Kulsoom. This was the work that she was doing these days. On seeing Kulsoom's face, she said – Bahuji, you can't be recognized now. Will you give up your life fretting like this? The disaster has happened, how will fretting help? The proverb goes, you'll let everything be lost if you remain sitting when the storm comes. Who will bring up the children if you are not there? The world becomes blind so soon. Poor Khan sahib slaved for these people, now nobody cares. The talk in every house is that these people should not have behaved like this. How will they face God?

Kulsoom – Their hands have been blackened now in plastering the stove.

Subhagi – Bahu, people may not say anything to their faces, but they are all spitting at them. The poor tiny children wander around helplessly; my heart breaks when I see them. Yesterday, chowdhary gave Mahir miyaan a good scolding.

Kulsoom was very comforted by this talk. 'The world spits at them, it criticizes them, but what can anyone do if these shameless people are not embarrassed?' She asked, 'What about?'

Before Subhagi could reply, the chowdhary called out from outside. Subhagi went and asked him – What do you want?

Chowdhary – I want to say something to bahuji. Let her stand behind the curtain.

It was afternoon. There was silence in the house. Zainab and Raqiya had gone to the mazaar of an aulia to offer sheerni. Kulsoom stood behind the curtain.

Chowdhary – Bahuji, I've wanted to come for a long time but I didn't get the chance. I would see Mahir miyaan sitting here and go back. Yesterday he said to me, 'Give me the money that you have collected to help bhaiyya; bhabhi has asked for it.' I said, I won't give it until I ask bahuji myself.' He flared up at that and started abusing, 'I'll take care of you; I'll send you to prison.' I told him, 'Go, do what you want.' So what are your orders now? All the money is still with me, should I give it to you? I came to know only today that these people have deceived you.

Kulsoom – Khuda will reward you for this goodness. But return this money to those to whom it belongs. I don't need it.

Chowdhary – Nobody will take it back.

Kulsoom – Then keep it with you.

Chowdhary – Why don't you take it? We are not doing you a favour. We have earned a lot because of Khan sahib, any other munshi would have taken thousands of rupees as a gift. Think of this as a gift to him.

The chowdhary tried hard to persuade her, but Kulsoom didn't take the money. She wanted to show Mahir, 'I have spurned with my foot the money at which you had leapt like a dog. No matter how worthless I may be, at least I have some respect left; you are a man but you are shameless.'

As he left, the chowdhary said to Subhagi – This is how big people act. She may be reduced to bits, but she won't stretch out her hand before anybody. There would have been no difference between big and small if that had not been so. Greatness doesn't come with wealth but with dharma.

Kulsoom felt proud of herself at refusing the money. For the first time today she was also proud of Tahir – This is true respect, that the world praises you behind your back. It's better to die than to live with the shame of all and sundry insulting you to your face. People may try their best to wipe out the favours that he has done but the world gives justice after all. Clerks are punished every day. Nobody asks after their families, rather people taunt them. His good reputation has made me feel very proud today.

Subhagi – Bahu, I've seen many women, but there must be few as brave as you. May God take away your troubles!

As she was going, she left several guavas for the children.

Kulsoom said – I don't have money.

Subhagi left, smiling.

37

PRABHU SEVAK WAS A VERY ENTHUSIASTIC MAN. THERE WAS NEW LIFE in the society for social service because of him. The numbers increased daily. Those who had become passive and indifferent began to work with a new zeal. Prabhu's courtesy and sensitivity attracted everybody. Along with that his character now displayed a conscientiousness that he himself had not expected. Almost everybody among the volunteers was educated and thoughtful. They wanted to plan a new strategy for the progress of the work. This was not an army of uneducated soldiers that considered the leader's order to be divine utterance. It was an educated army that weighed and debated it and was not prepared to accept until convinced. Prabhu began to apply himself to this difficult task with great intelligence.

The work of this society had been social until now. Helping travellers during fairs and festivals, rescuing those afflicted by floods and downpours, alleviating the suffering of those distressed by famines and droughts—these were its principal concerns. Prabhu widened the sphere of its activities and gave it a political form. Although he didn't make a new proposal or even discuss any changes, gradually new ideas began to spread because of his influence.

Prabhu was a very sensitive man, but this sensitivity was transformed into violence whenever he saw anybody oppressing the poor. He would promptly be prepared to fight on behalf of the grass-cutters if he saw a sepoy snatching their grass. It seemed rather futile to him to protect the public from divinely ordained disasters. He kept a special eye on the tyranny of the powerful. He was always on the lookout for employees who took bribes, tyrannical zamindars, selfish authorities. The result was that this society's influence was established within a few days. Its office became a refuge for the weak and the afflicted. Prabhu would keep inciting the weak to take revenge. He would say that until the public learnt to protect itself, even God couldn't save it from tyranny. His conviction was, 'We must first protect our self-respect. We have become cowardly and submissive, we silently tolerate arrogance and harm; such beings can't get happiness even in heaven. It's necessary for us to become fearless and courageous, to face dangers, to learn how to die. We can't learn how to live until we learn how to die.' It was far easier for Prabhu to become the target of a bullet while protecting the weak than to sit by the pillow of a patient to fan him or to distribute food and money to those afflicted by famine. His companions too were more interested in this kind of courageous service. Some people wanted to go even further. They thought that it was the duty of the volunteers to spread unrest among the public. Indradutt was the leader of this group and Prabhu had to act with a great deal of intelligence to pacify him.

However, as the fame of the volunteers spread, the suspicions of the authorities also increased. Kunwar sahib was afraid that the government would now repress this society. A rumour also spread within a few days that the authorities were considering seizing kunwar sahib's riyasat. Kunwar sahib was a fearless man but he was shaken when he heard this rumour. He didn't want to enjoy the comfort of wealth but he couldn't renounce his attachment to it. He got much more joy from philanthropy than from luxurious living. There was prestige as well as glory in philanthropy; what joy would remain in life without that prestige? He would repeatedly try and make Prabhu understand. 'Bhai! Work discreetly. Avoid the authorities. Why do such things that will make the authorities suspicious of you? Is the sphere of philanthropy not enough for you that you want to engage in the problems of politics?' But Prabhu wouldn't pay any attention to his advice, he would threaten, 'I'll resign. What do we care about the authorities? Let them do what they want, they don't consult us, so why should we conform to their wishes? We won't waver from our chosen path. Let the authorities do what they want. What's it worth if we keep the society alive by losing our self-respect? To conform to their wishes implies that we should just eat, fight court cases, think of harming each other and sleep. There is a constant opposition between our aims and those of the rulers. They are suspicious of our welfare and their suspicions are natural in these circumstances. If we remain afraid like this, it won't matter whether we exist or not.'

One day, it came to an altercation between the two men. The officers of the revenue department had arbitrarily raised the land tax in some region. This raise was being opposed in councils, newspapers and political meetings. Prabhu thought that they should go and tell the concerned people to let the land lie fallow for a year. Kunwar sahib said that this would be openly to confront the authorities.

Prabhu – It would be better for you to leave the society to its fate if you are so afraid. You want to cross the river sitting in two boats; this is impossible. I didn't trust the rais earlier and now I despair of them.

Kunwar – Why do you count me among the rais when you know very well that I don't care about the riyasat? But no work can be carried on without money. I don't want to see this society disintegrating like other national organizations for lack of money.

Prabhu– I won't regret sacrificing the largest property for my principles.

Kunwar – Nor would I, if the property were mine. But this property is that of my heirs and I don't have the right to perform its funeral rites without their consent. I don't want my children to bear the consequences of my karma.

Prabhu – This is an old argument of the rais. They hide their devotion to wealth behind this curtain. It would be better for you to leave this society if you are afraid that our actions will harm your property.

Kunwar sahib said, worried – Prabhu, you don't know how weak the roots of this society still are. I'm afraid that it won't withstand the acute gaze of the authorities even for a second. Both of us have the same aim; I also want what you want. But I'm old, I want to go at a slow pace; you are young, you want to run. I too don't want to become the receptacle of the favours of the rulers. I had decided long ago that our destiny is in our own hands; we have to look after our own welfare, it's futile to expect sympathy or help from others. But our society should at least survive. I don't want to perform its last rites by gifting it to the suspicion of the authorities.

Prabhu didn't reply. He was afraid of the matter getting out of hand. He decided inwardly that he would dissociate kunwar sahib from the society if he objected too much. The question of wealth was not so complicated that a blow should be struck at the core of the society. Indradutt also gave the same advice. 'We should dissociate

kunwar sahib. We are not here to distribute medicines and to carry
fodder for cattle to the regions afflicted by famine. That too is our
work, we don't deny it, but I don't think it's that important. This is
the time for destruction; the time for construction will come later.
The world has never been desolated by plagues, famines and floods
and it never will be.'

Eventually, the situation came to the point that both these men
wouldn't take kunwar sahib's advice but would make decisions among
themselves. Incidents of tyranny from all around were reported daily
to the office. At some places, in fact, people were prepared to pay huge
amounts to get the help of this society. This created confidence that
the society could stand on its own feet; it didn't need a permanent
fund. There would never be lack of money if there were enthusiastic
workers. As this fact was established, people became dissatisfied with
kunwar sahib's authority.

Prabhu's compositions these days were replete with revolutionary
sentiments. Ideas of nationalism, conflict and battle dripped from
every verse. He wrote a poem titled 'Boat' which could justly be
considered an incomparable jewel in the world of poetry. People would
read it and feel remorseful. In the very first verse, the traveller had
asked, 'Why boatman, will the boat sink or will it reach the shore?'
The boatman had replied, 'Traveller, the boat will sink because that's
why this doubt has arisen in your mind.' There was no assembly,
conference or society at which this poem was not read. There was a
furore in the literary world.

Prabhu's power increased daily in the society for social service.
Practically all the members respected him and were prepared to risk
their lives to follow his ideals. They were all saturated in the same
colour, intoxicated with the liquor of nationalism, unconcerned about
wealth or home and family. They would eat plain food, wear coarse
clothes, spend the night sleeping on the floor, they didn't need a home,
they would sometimes lie under a tree and sometimes in a hut. Lofty
and pure devotion to the country surged in their hearts.

The society's excellent organization was being discussed in the whole
country. Prabhu was among the most respected and popular leaders
of the country. So much fame at such a young age! People would be
surprised. National assemblies from several places began to invite

him. People would be enthralled by his speeches wherever he went.

There was a function of the national assembly in Poona. Prabhu received an invitation. He promptly handed his responsibilities to Indradutt and left with the intention of touring the provinces in the south. Elaborate preparations were made to welcome him in Poona. This city was also a centre of the society for social service and its leader was a very resolute man, who had obtained a degree in engineering from Berlin and had joined this society for three years. He was very influential in the town. He was at the station with the members of his group. Prabhu was delighted at seeing this pomp and splendour. He thought, 'This is the influence of my leadership. Where did they have this enthusiasm, this fearlessness, this awakening? I'm the one who has spread it. I hope now that I'll be able to achieve something if I stay alive.' Ha pride!

In the evening, when he stood on the stage in the huge pavilion, he was ecstatic at seeing thousands of spectators gazing at him respectfully. European women too were present in the gallery. The Governor had also come. They all wanted to see how miraculous would be the voice of somebody in whose pen there was so much magic.

Prabhu's speech began. He didn't need to be introduced. He began a philosophical analysis of governance. What is governance? Why is it necessary? What are the rules for complying with it? In which circumstances is it the duty of the public to disregard it? What are its merits and defects? He explained these questions with great learning and extreme fearlessness. If anybody could make such a complex and profound subject simple, comprehensible and entertaining, it was Prabhu. But governance is also one of those important objects in the world that can't stand the heat of analysis and debate. Its discussion is destructive for it; it's better for the veil of ignorance to remain over it. Prabhu had raised that veil—the lines of armies vanished from sight, the huge mansions of law courts toppled, the signs of power and supremacy began to disappear, bold and bright letters proclaimed—the best governance is the end of governance. But as soon as he uttered the words, 'Our country is devoid of governance. The difference between subjection and obedience is one of boundaries,' there was the sound of a pistol shot, the bullet went past Prabhu's ear and hit the wall behind him. It was night, so nobody knew who had struck this blow. It was suspected that it was a European's mischief. People ran towards the galleries. Suddenly Prabhu said loudly, 'I forgive the person who has struck this blow on me. He can make me a target again if he wants to. Nobody has the right to avenge this on my behalf. I have come here to spread my views, not to return attacks with counter-attacks.'

A voice came from somewhere – This is a shining proof of the necessity of governance.

The assembly dispersed. The Europeans left through the back door. Armed police arrived outside.

The next evening there was a telegram for Prabhu – The managing committee of the society for social service disapproves of your speech and requests you to return, otherwise it won't be responsible for your speeches.

Prabhu tore the telegram into pieces and crushing them under his feet said to himself – Rascal, coward, dyed jackal. He boasts of nationalism; he'll serve the country! One speech has transformed him. He wants to dip his finger in blood to have his name written together with martyrs. He thinks that service to the country is a child's game. It's not a child's game, it's putting your finger into the snake's mouth; it's a trial of strength with a lion. Why do you make this pretence if your life and property are so dear to you? Go, the country won't suffer without patriots like you.

He immediately sent a reply to the telegram – I think it's demeaning for me to be subservient to the managing committee. I have nothing to do with it.

Another letter arrived after half an hour with the seal of the government on it:

My dear Sevak,

I can't tell you how much benefit and enjoyment I got from your speech yesterday. I'm not exaggerating when I say that I haven't heard such a scholarly and fundamental analysis of governance anywhere until now. Rules have silenced me, but I respect your sentiments and views and pray to God that the day may soon come when we can understand the essence of governance and can conform to its highest principles. There's only one person who couldn't tolerate your candid talk and I have to accept with deep sorrow and shame that he is European. On behalf of European society, I want to express my grief and contempt for this cowardly and inhuman attack. I assure you that the entire European society has heartfelt sympathy for you. If I can discover the whereabouts of that fiend (he can't be found since yesterday), nobody will be happier than I to inform you.

Yours,
F. Wilson

Prabhu reread the letter. There was a tingling in his heart. He put it away carefully in his box. He would certainly have read it out had anybody else been there. He began to walk in the room intoxicated with pride. 'This is the liberalism, large-heartedness and appreciation of merit of races that are enlightened. They have enjoyed independence, they have made sacrifices for it and know its importance. How can somebody whose entire life has been spent in flattery and dependence on others understand the importance of independence? We become such devotees of God when we are about to die. Bharat Singh would also have turned in that direction and chanted Rama's name; it was Vinay Singh who turned him this way. It was his influence. Vinay, you are needed now, greatly needed, where are you? Come and see the plight of the field sown by you. Its protectors are becoming its destroyers.'

38

SOPHIA AND VINAY STAYED AT THE STATION ALL NIGHT. IN THE morning, they went to a nearby village, a small basti of Bhils. Sophia liked it very much. The basti lay in the shade of a mountain, a stream flowed at its feet singing a sweet raga. The Bhils' tiny huts, on which creepers were spread, seemed as beautiful as the toys of apsaras. They decided to stay in that village until they could decide what to do, where to go, where to stay. They even found a place easily in one of the huts. The hospitality of the Bhils is famous, and both these people were used to bearing hunger and thirst, heat and cold. They ate anything, rough and coarse, that was available; they weren't addicted to tea and butter, jam and fruit. A simple and virtuous life was their ideal. They didn't have any difficulty there. Only a Bhilni lived in this hut. Her son was a servant in the army. The old woman gladly looked after them. They made it known that they belonged to Delhi and had come here for a change of climate. The villagers had a great deal of respect and regard for them.

But despite so much isolation and independence, they seldom met each other; they were both suspicious for some reason. There was no rancour between them; they were both deeply in love. Both of them were anxious, restless and impatient but the strength of ethical bonds didn't allow them to meet. The investigation of genuine dharma had liberated Sophie from communal narrowness. She believed that different doctrines were different names for the same truth. She was no longer angry with or opposed to anybody. The restlessness that had frustrated her religious principles for several months had disappeared. Now she believed only in humanity. And though Vinay's thoughts were not so liberal and worldly attachment was not worth more than a philosophical theory for him, his traditional social codes concealed themselves before Sophie's liberalism. Actually they had been united spiritually and there was no real obstacle to their physical union but despite all this they remained apart, they would never sit together when they were alone. They were now suspicious of themselves. The time for promises was over; it was now time to write. Promises don't cut the tongue. Writing can cut the hand.

But though writing may cut the hand, nothing can be finalized without it. A few differences, a slight lack of restraint can cancel the agreement. That's why both of them wanted to end this situation of uncertainty. But how? They couldn't understand this. Who would start the topic? Perhaps some obstacle would arise in the course of the discussion. Vinay's proximity was enough for Sophia. She saw him daily, she shared his happiness and anger, she believed that he was hers. She didn't want anything more. Vinay wandered around in the nearby countryside every day. A woman would get him to write a letter to her son or her husband who was in a foreign region, he would give medicines to patients, or he would have to become a mediator in personal quarrels. He would leave at dawn and return at night. This was his daily routine. Sophia would light the lamp and wait for him. She would make him wash his hands and feet and eat when he returned, fondly listen to the events of the day, and then they would go to sleep in their own rooms where Vinay would find his bed of grass ready. There would be a handi of water by his pillow. Sophia was satisfied with this. She would have considered herself to be fortunate if she could be sure that her entire life would be spent in this way. This was the blissful dream of her life. But Vinay was not so resolute nor was he such an ascetic. He was not satisfied with only a spiritual union. Sophia's incomparable beauty, the divine charm of her speech, her extraordinary figure would agitate his erotic imagination. He had lost her once because he had been trapped in intrigues. He didn't want to go through that test again. His mind could never be at peace as long as this possibility was there.

They would get newspapers, magazines, books, etc. sent at the address of the railway station so that they were aware of what was going on in the world. They had also become rather attached to the Bhils and had no desire to leave this place to go elsewhere. They were both apprehensive of what their plight could be if they left this safe place and of the turmoil that they might have to face. They prized this peaceful hut as their good fortune. Sophia trusted Vinay. She was unaware of her power to attract.

A year went by in this way. Sophia was sitting in front of the stove reading a book after giving Vinay something to eat. She would sometimes mark an 'X' with a pencil at significant points, sometimes she would put a question mark and at some places she would draw a line. Vinay was apprehensive that this absorption was a sign of the dwindling of her love. 'She's so engrossed in reading that she won't even look up.' He dressed up to go out. There was a cold wind, but there were no clothes for the winter and a blanket was not enough. He came close to the stove languidly and sat down on a maanchi, a four-legged cane stool. Sophia's eyes were fixed on the book. Vinay's lustful gaze, finding the opportunity, began to dwell unobstructed at the lustre of her lovely appearance. Sophia suddenly looked up and found Vinay gazing at her attentively. She lowered her eyes shyly and said, 'It's very cold today. Where will you go? Sit, I'll read out some portions of this book to you. It's a book very well worth studying.' She then looked towards the courtyard; the Bhilni had disappeared. She had probably gone to gather wood and wouldn't return before ten now. Sophia was rather worried.

Vinay said eagerly – No, Sophie, I won't go anywhere today. I want to talk to you. Shut the book and put it away. I yearn to talk to you even though I'm living with you.

He tried to snatch the book from Sophia's hands. Sophia resolutely held on to it and said – Stop, stop! What are you doing? This is the mischief that I don't like now. Sit, I'll tell you the views of this French philosopher. Look, he has analysed religion so liberally.

Vinay – No, ask your philosopher today for a break of ten minutes and listen to the things that I have to say which are fluttering restlessly to come out like a bird trapped in a cage. After all, is there a limit to this banishment of mine in the forest or must I always only dream of happiness in life?

Sophia – This writer's views are far more entertaining than any answer that I can give you. I have several doubts about them. An exchange of views may resolve them.

Vinay – No, shut the book and put it away. I've come today determined to make the journey. I won't let you go without taking a promise from you. Are you still testing me?

Sophia shut the book and put it away and said with affectionate

earnestness – I have cast myself at your feet. What else do you want
from me?

Vinay – I would have been satisfied with the worship of your
love had I been a god but after all I'm also a slave to desires, a paltry
human being. I'm not satisfied with what I have. I want more; I want
everything. Don't you still understand what I mean? I'm not content
with merely seeing the bird on my parapet; I want to see it going into
my cage. Shall I express this more frankly? I'm a complete voluptuary,
I'm not satiated by the fragrance alone.

Sophia – Vinay, don't compel me now. I'm yours. I couldn't say
what I'm saying to you now with greater genuineness and sincerity
in a temple, a church or before a havan-kund. I was yours even when
I had rejected you. But forgive me, I'll never do anything that will
result in your being insulted, dishonoured or criticized. This restraint
of mine is not for myself but for you. There's no obstacle for spiritual
union, but the approval of one's relations and the rules of society are
essential for social rituals, otherwise they become a matter of shame.
My soul will never forgive me if you become the object of your parents'
wrath, especially of your venerable mother, because of me, and if they
think of you as a stigma on the dynasty along with me. I can't even
imagine what punishment raniji will give you, and especially me, for
this disobedience. She is a sati, a devi, one doesn't know what disaster
may befall because of her wrath. I have realized how degraded I am in
her eyes, and she has also given you the severest punishment that was
in her power. In this situation, it won't be surprising if she commits
suicide in her anger when she comes to know that we are bound not
only by love but also by rituals. You are perhaps prepared to accept
all those obstacles and difficulties now, but I don't think that external
rituals are that important.

Vinay said dejectedly – Sophie, what else can this mean except that
my life will be spent in dreaming of bliss?

Sophia – No, Vinay, I'm not so dejected. I still hope that sometime
or the other I'll get raniji to forgive my crime as well as yours, and then
we'll get married with her blessings. Both raniji's favour and disfavour
remain within limits. We have experienced one limit. If God wills
it, we'll soon experience the other. I earnestly plead with you not to
bring up this topic again, otherwise I'll have to find another refuge.

Vinay said softly – When will the day come, when either ammaji won't exist or I won't ?

Then he covered himself with the blanket, took a stick and went out, like a farmer leaving the mahajan's house after listening to his rebukes.

The days again went by as before. Vinay would be very dejected and gloomy. As far as possible he would wander around outside the house, and if he returned, he would eat and leave again. If he didn't have to go anywhere he would go and sit by the bank of the river and watch the play of the water for hours together. He would sometimes make paper boats and float them and would chase them up to the point where they would sink into the water. He began to suspect that Sophia still didn't trust him. 'She loves me but she doubts my moral strength.'

He was sitting by the river one day when the old Bhilni came to fill water. When she saw him sitting there she put down her pitcher and said, 'Why, maalik, why are you sitting here alone? Won't maalkin be anxious at home? I see her weeping a lot. Have you said anything to her? I never see the two of you laughing and talking together.'

Vinay said – What can I do, mata? Her illness is that she is offended with me. She has been suffering from this illness for years.

Bhilni – Then, beta, I'll cure this. I'll give her such a root that she won't be at peace without you even for a moment.

Vinay – Does such a root exist?

The old woman said with simple wisdom – Beta, there are such roots that you can bind fire as well as water, make a corpse come alive, kill a plaintiff while he's at home. Yes, you need the knowledge. Your Bhil was very skilled. He used to visit the raja's durbar. He was the one who told me about a few plants. Beta, each plant is cheap at a lakh.

Vinay – Where do I have so much money?

Bhilni – No, beta, what can I take from you? You are an inhabitant of Bisunathpuri.* I have had your darshan, that's enough for me. Send a little Gangajal for me when you go there. The old woman will be saturated. You didn't tell me earlier or I'd have given you that root. I feel very sad when I see your quarrels.

In the evening, when Sophia was cooking, the Bhilni brought a root

* Vishwanathpuri: Banaras; the city of Vishwanath, Lord of the Universe (a title given to Shiva).

and gave it to Vinay. She said, 'Beta, keep it carefully, you won't get it even for a lakh of rupees. This knowledge has now disappeared. Soak it daily in your blood for fifteen days and dry it. Then cut a leaf at a time from it and give its smoke to maalkin. Tie the ones that remain after fifteen days in her jooda. Then see what happens. If God wishes it, you yourself will get tired of her. She'll be after you like a shadow.' Then she whispered a mantra in Vinay's ear, which was a collection of several meaningless words, and told him to chant it five times when soaking the root in his blood and then to blow it on the root.

Vinay was not superstitious; he didn't have an iota of belief in mantras and tantras. But he knew from hearsay that among the lower castes such tantric practices were very widespread, and that sometimes they had astonishing results. His conjecture was that there was no intrinsic power in these practices; if there were any results it was because of the weak minds of fools. What effect could they possibly have on those who were educated and generally sceptical, and who didn't accept even the existence of God? Despite that he decided to obtain this magical power. He didn't hope for any results; he only wanted to test it.

But what if this root could really produce some miracle? That would be wonderful! He was delighted at the very thought. 'Sophia will be mine. Then there'll be something special in her love.'

When the auspicious day came, he went to the river, had a bath, and cutting his finger with a knife, soaked the root in its blood. Then he kept it on a high rock and covered it with stones. He did this continuously for fifteen days. It was so cold that the hands and feet would become numb and water would freeze in the utensils. But Vinay would go and bathe daily. Sophia had never before seen him to be so dutiful. She'd say, 'Don't bathe so early in the morning, you might catch a cold, even the people of the jungle sit before their lighted stoves all day, one can't even show one's face outside, let the sun come out.' But Vinay would smile and say, 'If I fall ill, you'll at least come and sit near me.' Several fingers of his were bruised, but he would hide these bruises.

Vinay's gaze was on each thing, each movement of Sophia's. He wanted to see whether his rituals were effective or not, but no evident result was visible. He noticed a slight change in Sophia's behaviour on the fifteenth day. Perhaps he wouldn't have noticed it at any other time but his perception had become very acute these days. When he was about to leave the house, Sophie came out for some unknown reason and accompanied him for several furlongs talking to him. She returned when Vinay made repeated pleas. Vinay thought that it was the effect of that ritual.

The ritual of giving the smoke was to begin from today. Vinay was very worried 'How can I perform this ritual? It is against civility, courtesy and decency to go to Sophie's room alone. If she wakes up and sees me, she'll think that I'm so base. Perhaps she'll hate me forever. Even if she doesn't wake up, what kind of decency would it be for a man to enter a young woman's room? One doesn't know in what state she'll be lying there. It's possible that her hair will be dishevelled and the cover may have slipped. My motives will then become so despicable. I have become so morally degraded.'

He was preoccupied with these restless thoughts all day but as soon as it was evening, he went to the potter's house, brought a mud cup and kept it carefully. A strange thing about human character is that we often do things that we don't want to. Some secret inspiration makes us act against our wishes.

At midnight, Vinay went to the door of Sophie's room carrying fire in the cup and the blood-soaked root in his hand. A blanket served as a curtain. How could there be doors in a hut? He stood near the blanket and listened carefully. Sophie was sleeping soundly. He entered the room trembling and soaked in perspiration. Sophie was lying there blissfully asleep in the dim light of the lamp as if a sweet fantasy was nestling in her mind. There was terror in Vinay's heart. He stood spellbound for several moments but with self-control, as if he was in the temple of a devi. Beauty awakens reverence in enlightened hearts and desires cease. Vinay gazed worshipfully at Sophie for some time. Then he slowly sat down, broke a piece from the root, put it in the cup and slid it towards Sophie's pillow. In a moment the whole room was redolent with the fragrance of the root. Where could this aroma be found in amber or in incense? There was such a stimulating energy in the smoke that Vinay's heart became restless. As soon as the smoke disappeared, Vinay took out the ashes of the root from the cup. He sprinkled them on Sophia according to the instructions of the Bhilni and left the room. But he was repentant for several hours after returning to his room. He tried repeatedly to wound his moral sentiments and to arouse hatred for himself in his heart by calling this action deceit and the murder of virtue. Before going to sleep, he decided that he would end this ritual today. Throughout the next day he was irritable, dejected and anxious. As the night approached he was apprehensive that he would practise that ritual again. He called two or three Bhils and made them sleep near him. He ate very late so that he could fall asleep as soon as he went to bed. When he got up after eating, Sophie came and sat next to him. This was the first time that she had sat with him and talked at night. Today's newspapers had published the speech that Prabhu Sevak had given in Poona. Sophie read it out aloud, full of pride. She said, 'Look, he was such a pleasure-loving man, always obsessed with good clothes and luxurious things. He has changed so much. I had thought that he would never do anything and his whole life would be spent in self-service. The human heart is so complex. It's surprising to see this sacrifice and devotion.'

Vinay – I'm not worried now that Prabhu has become the steersman of this society. Dr Ganguly would have just turned it into a group for distributing medicines. I don't trust pitaji, and Indradutt is uncouth. A more capable man than Prabhu couldn't have been found. Had he been here, I'd have taken on his misfortunes on myself. His help is providential and I'm now optimistic that our devoted efforts won't be unsuccessful.

The Bhils could be heard snoring. When Sophie got up to leave, she looked at Vinay with glances in which there was something else besides love; sultry desire could be glimpsed in them. There was an attraction in them that shook Vinay from head to foot. When she left, he picked up a book and began to read it. But he became increasingly more nervous as the time for the ritual approached. It seemed as if somebody was forcibly pushing him. When he was convinced that Sophia had gone to sleep, he got up quietly, put the fire in the cup, and started off. He was even more afraid than he had been a day before. At one moment he even thought of flinging down the cup. But just a second later, he entered Sophie's room. Today he didn't even raise his eyes. He bowed his head, lit the smoke, scattered the ash and left. He saw Sophia's beautiful face as he left. It seemed as if she was smiling. His heart missed a beat. His whole body began to tingle. 'God! My honour is in your hands today. I hope she hasn't seen me!' With lightning speed, he came to his room, put out the lamp, and fell down on the bed. His heart continued to beat fast for several hours.

In this way, Vinay performed this ritual with great difficulty for five days, and he noticed a distinct change in Sophia within this short time, to the extent that on the fifth day she wandered around with him in the huts of the Bhils. Instead of the grave worry in her eyes, there was now a glimpse of a restless desire and the gleam of a sweet smile on her lips. That night after eating she sat down next to him and began reading the newspapers and while doing so, she put her head on Vinay's lap and taking his hands in hers said, 'Tell me the truth, Vinay, if I ask you something will you tell me? Tell me truthfully, you don't wish to get rid of this nuisance? I'm telling you, I can't be got rid of while I'm alive, nor will I leave you. You too can't escape from me. There's no way that I'll let you go. I'll go wherever you go, I'll remain as a garland around your neck.'

As she said this, she let go of Vinay's hands and put her arms around his neck.

Vinay felt that his feet had left the ground and he was floating on waves. A strange apprehension made his heart tremble, as if he had awakened the lioness while playing. Pretending to be unaware, he freed himself from Sophie's embrace and said, 'Sophie!'

Sophia was startled, as if she had been asleep. Then she sat up and said – It seems to me that I was yours in my previous birth, and even before that, since the beginning of time. I seem to remember a dream that you and I lived in a hut by the river. Really!

Vinay asked apprehensively – How are you feeling?

Sophia – Nothing has happened to me. I'm recalling my previous birth. I seem to remember that you had left me alone in the hut and had gone to a foreign country in your boat and I would sit by the bank of the river every day waiting for you, but you didn't return.

Vinay – Sophie, I'm afraid you aren't well. It's now late at night, go and sleep.

Sophia – I don't feel like going from here today. Are you feeling sleepy? Then sleep, I'll sit here. I'll go when you fall asleep.

She said again after a moment – I don't know why I'm afraid that you'll leave me and go away. Tell me the truth—will you leave me?

Vinay – Sophie, now we won't be separated until infinity.

Sophia – I know that you are not so cruel. I won't be afraid of raniji. I'll tell her frankly that Vinay is mine.

Vinay's plight was like that of a hungry man with a full platter before him, impatient with hunger, intestines shrivelling and darkness before the eyes, but unable to partake of it because food had first to be offered to some god. He had no doubt that Sophie's agitation was the result of that ritual. He was amazed at the root's power. He was ashamed of his action but, more than that, he was afraid—not of his soul, not of God, but of Sophie. 'When Sophie comes to know—the intoxication will wear off sometime—she'll ask me the cause and I won't be able to hide it. What will she say then?'

Sophie left when eventually the fire in the stove was extinguished and she began to feel cold. It was also time for the ritual. But Vinay didn't have the courage today. He had wanted to test it and had done so. He now had abiding faith in tantric practices.

As soon as Sophia lay down on the bed, she had the illusion that Rani Jahnavi was standing in front of her, glaring. She took out her head from the blanket and thought, annoyed at her psychological weakness, 'What has happened to me these days? Why do I have so many doubts? Why is my heart overcast with an apprehension of harm every day? As if I can't think. Why is Vinay withdrawn from me these days? Perhaps he's afraid that raniji may put a curse on him or commit suicide. The earlier ardour and impatience are no longer there in his love. The rani is ruining my life.'

She went to sleep preoccupied with these restless thoughts and saw that raniji was actually standing in front of her, glaring angrily, saying, 'Vinay is mine. He's my son, I have given birth to him, I have brought him up, why do you want to snatch him from me? If you snatch him from me and put a stigma on my dynasty, I'll kill you both with this sword.'

Sophie was afraid when she saw the gleam of the sword. She screamed and woke up. Her whole body trembled like grass. She strengthened her resolve and got up, went to Vinay's room and clung to him. Vinay was about to doze off. He raised his head, startled.

Sophia – Vinay, Vinay, wake up, I'm afraid.

Vinay promptly got down from the bed and asked – What is it, Sophie?

Sophia – I just saw raniji in my room. She's still standing there.

Vinay – Sophie, calm down. You have seen a dream. There's nothing to be afraid of.

Sophia – It wasn't a dream, Vinay, I saw raniji herself.

Vinay – How could she have come here? She's not just air.

Sophia – You don't know these things, Vinay! Every being has two bodies—one gross, the other subtle. They are both similar, the only difference is that the subtle body is much more subtle than the gross one. It is invisible in ordinary circumstances, but in profound meditation or sleep it becomes a substitute for the gross body. Raniji's subtle body most certainly came here.

Both of them stayed up the whole night.

Sophia was restless without Vinay even for a moment. She was not only mentally agitated but also eager for sensual pleasure. Her mind was now daily obsessed with those fantasies and emotions, the topics to which she had been averse even in her imagination, the things that had brought a blush to her face as soon as she thought of them. She was surprised that she was so immersed in desire. But when, fantasizing about sensuous pleasure, she would enter the area restricted only for marriage, that same image of raniji, blazing with anger, would stand before her and she would run out of the room, startled. She spent ten or twelve days like this. Even the plight of a plaintiff standing with a sword over his head would not have been so agonizing!

One day, she came to Vinay anxiously and said – Vinay, I'm going to Banaras. I'm in great danger. Raniji won't leave me in peace here. I might lose my life if I stay on; I'm sure some ritual has been performed on me. I've never been so agitated before. It seems I'm not the same but somebody else. I'll go and fall at raniji's feet. I'll make her forgive my crime and obtain you with her permission. I can't obtain you without her wish. And it won't be well if I do so forcibly. Vinay, I didn't imagine even in my dreams that I'd be so impatient for you. My heart was never so weak and so possessed by desire.

Vinay (*Worried*) – I'm sure that your mind will be calm in a few days.

Sophia – No, Vinay, never. Raniji has sacrificed you for a high ideal. The enjoyment of a life that has been sacrificed is harmful. I'll beg her for alms.

Vinay – Then I'll also go with you.

Sophia – No. For God's sake, don't say this. I won't take you before raniji.

Vinay – I'll never let you go alone in this condition. I'll leave you there and return.

Sophia – Promise me that you won't go to raniji without asking me.

Vinay – Yes, Sophie, this is acceptable. I promise.

Sophia – My heart still doesn't consent. I'm afraid that you might go to raniji in a fit of frenzy. Why don't you stay here? I'll write to you daily and return as soon as I can.

Vinay gave her permission to go alone to comfort her, but how could he consent to Sophia going on such a long journey in this agitated condition? He thought that he would go and sit in another compartment unnoticed by her. He had very little hope of their returning. When the Bhils came to know that they were going, they brought several gifts to see them off. There was a heap of deer hides, baghnakhas* and several kinds of roots and plants. One of the Bhils presented a bow. Both Sophia and Vinay had fallen in love with this place. The simple, natural, honest lives of the inhabitants appealed to them so much that they were deeply pained at leaving them. The Bhils were weeping and saying, 'Come back soon, don't forget us.' The old Bhilni wouldn't let go of them. All of them accompanied them to the station. But when the train arrived and it was time to part from Vinay, Sophia clung to him and began to cry. Vinay wanted to get away so that he could go and sit in another compartment, but she wouldn't let go of him. As if it was the final separation. When the whistle of the train blew she said, with her heart aching, 'Vinay, how will I live for so many days? I'll die weeping. God, what should I do?'

Vinay – Sophie, don't be anxious, I'll go with you.

Sophia – No, no, for God's sake don't. I'll go alone.

Vinay boarded the train. A little while after the train had started, Sophia said – I would probably not have reached home if you hadn't

---

* Necklaces made of tiger claws.

come. It seemed as if I was dying. Tell me the truth, Vinay, have you cast a spell on me? Why have I become so impetuous?

Vinay (*Embarrassed*) – I don't know, Sophie. I did perform a ritual. I don't know if it was a spell or something else.

Sophia – Is that true?

Vinay – Yes, absolutely true. I was afraid that your love had cooled and that you would test me again.

Sophie put her arm around Vinay's neck and said – You are a great trickster. Remove your magic! Why are you tormenting me?

Vinay – What can I say? I didn't learn how to remove it, that was a mistake.

Sophia – Then why don't you teach me the same mantra? I won't be able to remove it and nor will you. (*After a moment*) No, I won't make you senseless. One of us at least should remain in our senses. It will be a disaster if we are both intoxicated. All right, tell me, what ritual did you perform?

Vinay took the root from his pocket and showing it to her said – I gave you its smoke.

Sophia – When I was asleep, then?

Vinay (*Embarrassed*) – Yes, Sophie, then.

Sophia – You are very stubborn. All right, now give me this root. I'll also perform this ritual when I see your love cooling.

She took the root. After a while she asked – Tell me, where will you stay? I won't let you go to raniji.

Vinay – I don't have any friends now. They must all be unhappy with me. I'll go to Nayakram's house. You can meet me there. He must have reached home by now.

Sophia – He might go and tell.

Vinay – No, he may be dim-witted but he's not a traitor.

Sophia – All right. Let's see if we'll get a boon from raniji or death.

39

IT WAS EVENING WHEN THE JOURNEY ENDED ON THE THIRD DAY.
Sophia and Vinay got off the train, afraid of meeting some
acquaintance. Sophia thought of going to Seva Bhavan (Vinay's
house) but she was very nervous today. She didn't know how raniji
would greet her. She regretted having come, not knowing what would
happen. Now she remembered her rural life. It had been so peaceful
and simple, there was no difficulty or obstacle, no rancour or hostility
against anybody. Comforting her, Vinay said, 'Be resolute, don't be at
all afraid, recount the events with complete truth, without the slightest
exaggeration, there shouldn't be the least entreaty. Don't utter a word
pleading for mercy. I don't want to save my life by playing down or
exaggerating matters. I want justice, pure justice. If she is uncivil to you
or attacks you with harsh words, don't stay there even for a moment.
Come and tell me everything in the morning. Or if you say so, I'll
also come with you.'

Sophie didn't agree to take Vinay with her. Vinay went towards
Pandeypur and she left for Seva Bhavan. The tonga-vala said, 'Miss
sahib, did you go away somewhere? I'm seeing you after a long time.'
Sophie's heart began to beat fast. She said, 'When did you see me?
I've come to this city for the first time.'

The tonga-vala said – There was a miss sahib here, just like you,
who was Sevak sahib's daughter. I thought it was you.

Sophia – I'm not a Christian.

She got down from the tonga when she reached Seva Bhavan. She
didn't want raniji to get any inkling of her arrival before she met her.
With her bag in hand, she went to the porch and told the durbaan –
Go and tell raniji that Miss Sophia wants to meet her.

The durbaan knew her. He got up, salaamed and said – Huzoor,
go in, there's no need to inform her. I have got your darshan after a
long time.

Sophia – I'm fine standing here. Go and inform her.

Durbaan – Sarkar, you know her temperament. She'll be annoyed that I haven't brought you with me and ask why I have come to inform her.

Sophia – Listen to a few things for my sake.

When the durbaan went in, Sophia's heart began to beat as fast as if a leaf was trembling. The colour waxed and waned on her face. She was apprehensive that rani sahiba would come there enraged or send a message, 'Go away, I won't meet you!' 'But I won't leave without seeing her at least once, even if she reproaches me a thousand times.'

Not even a minute had passed by when raniji came to the door wearing a shawl. She broke down and embraced her, like a mother embracing her daughter who had returned from her sasural. Tears rained from her eyes. She said in a choked voice – Why are you standing here, beti, why didn't you come in? I waited for you every day. My heart yearned to meet you. I kept hoping that you'd come but you didn't. I went to the station several times for no reason hoping to see you. I would pray to God every day to let me meet you once. Come; come in. Forget the harsh words that I had said to you. (*To the durbaan*) Pick up this bag. Tell the maidservant to clean Miss Sophie's old room. Beti, I don't have the courage to look towards your room, my heart is overwhelmed with grief.

She held Sophia's hand, took her to her own room, made her sit on a cushion next to her and said – My wish has been fulfilled today. My heart was restless because I wanted to meet you.

Sophia's heart, aching with worry, was overwhelmed by this abundance of unconditional love. She could only say – I also longed for your darshan. I have come to beg you for mercy.

Rani – Beti, you are a devi, there was a veil over my mind. I didn't recognize you. I know, beti, I've heard everything. I didn't know that your soul is so pure. Ah! If only I had known earlier!

Raniji then sobbed bitterly. She said, when she was calm again –Had I known earlier, my heart would have been at peace in this house. Ah! I have done Vinay a grave injustice. You don't know, beti, when you . . . (*Thinking*) His name was Veerpaal Singh, wasn't it? Yes, when you reproached Vinay in his house that night, he was deeply ashamed and ran around asking the authorities to have mercy on the prisoners. For days together he would remain scorned, without food and water, he would weep the whole night, he'd go to the deewan sometimes, or to the agent, or to the chief of the police, or to the maharaja. But he lost despite his pleas and entreaties. Nobody listened. Nobody had mercy on the condition of the prisoners. Poor Vinay returned defeated to the place where he was staying when he got my letter. Hai! (*Crying*) Sophie, it was not a letter but a cup of poison that I made him drink with my own hands; it was a dagger that I took to his throat. I had written, 'You are not worthy to be called my son, don't show me your face.' I don't know how many other harsh things I wrote. My heart breaks when I remember. As soon as he received my letter, he was ready to come here with Nayakram without a word to anybody. Nayakram was with him for several stations. Then Pandaji fell asleep. And when he woke up, Vinay couldn't be found on the train. He searched the whole train and then went to Udaipur. He got down at every station on the way to make enquiries but couldn't discover anything. Beti, this is the story of this unfortunate woman. I'm a murderer. I'm the most unfortunate woman in the world. I don't know what happened to Vinay; there's no news. He had a great deal of self-respect, beti, he was very true to his word. My words wounded him. My beloved darling never experienced any happiness. His whole life was spent in tapasya.

The rani began to weep again. Sophie was also crying. But there was such a great difference in both their emotions! The rani's tears were those of unhappiness, grief and despair. Sophie's were those of rejoicing and elation.

After a moment, raniji asked – Beti, had he become very thin when you saw him in prison?

Sophia – Yes, he couldn't be recognized.

Rani – He didn't know how the rebels had treated you. That's all, this made him vengeful. Sit comfortably, beti, this is your home now. You are now Vinay's reflection for me. Tell me, where were you all these days? Indradutt said that you had left just three or four days after you had spurned Vinay. Where did you stay all this while? It must be more than a year now.

Sophia was ecstatic. She wanted to tell the whole story immediately and to pacify the mother's anguished grief. But she was afraid that raniji's religious pride would reawaken. She wasn't worried about Vinay now but apprehensive for herself. We worship stones when we can't get our god. So why should we worship them when we do get him? She said, 'How can I tell you where I was? I wandered here and there. And where was there any refuge? I'd repent my mistake and weep. I returned here dejected.'

Raniji – You unnecessarily went through so many difficulties. Wasn't this your home? Don't mind, beti, you have been unjust to Vinay, as much as I have been. He was even more hurt by you, because whatever he did was for your welfare. I could never have been so cruel to somebody dear to me. You must be repenting your mistake now. We are both unfortunate. Ah! Vinay didn't get happiness anywhere. You are very hard-hearted. Just imagine, if you had got news that the dacoits had captured Vinay and had killed him, what would your plight have been? Perhaps you would also have become ruthless. This is human nature. But it's no use repenting now; I myself repent every day. We now have to take up the work that was most important to him in his life. You have suffered great difficulties for him—insult, shame, punishment—you have suffered all this. Now take up his work. Think of it as the aim of your life. You wouldn't know that Prabhu Sevak had become the manager of this society for a few days. He is the right kind of man to do the work. Within a few days, he had searched the whole country and had gathered 500 volunteers. He opened branches in big cities and collected a lot of money. I was delighted that the society for which Vinay had sacrificed his life was flourishing. But I don't know what God had willed. There were differences between Prabhu and kunwar sahib. Prabhu was taking the society in exactly the same direction that Vinay had wanted. Kunwar sahib and his best friend Dr Ganguly wanted to take it in a different direction. Eventually, Prabhu resigned. The society is unstable since then, one doesn't know if it will survive or end. There's a strange change in kunwar sahib. He's now cautious with the authorities. It was rumoured that the government would seize his entire property. To allay this mistrust of the authorities, he published his opposition to Prabhu's activities. This was the main reason for their differences. It's not yet two months but the binding has disintegrated. Hundreds of volunteers were disappointed and have returned to their own occupations. There must be barely 200 people left. Come, beti, your room must have been cleaned by now. I'll get your food ready and then talk to you at leisure. (*To the maharajin*)

You recognize her, don't you? She was my guest then, now she is my bahu. Go, prepare some new dishes for her. Ah! If only Vinay were here today, I'd have given her to him with my own hands, I'd have married them. There's a provision for this in the Shastras.

Sophia was strongly tempted to reveal the secret. It was on the tip of her tongue but then she stopped.

Suddenly there was a hue and cry – Lala sahib has come! Lala sahib has come. Bhaiyya Vinay has come. The servants rushed from all directions, the maidservants left their work and ran. In a moment, Vinay stepped into the room. The rani looked him up and down, as if making sure that this was her Vinay and not somebody else, or perhaps she wanted to see if there were marks of any blows. Then she got up and said, 'Beta, you have come after a long time! Come, let me embrace you.' But Vinay promptly put his head at her feet. Raniji couldn't think of anything in the flow of her tears, nor could she utter anything in the surge of her love. Bending down, she tried to hold Vinay's head and make him get up. It was such a heavenly union of devotion and parental love.

But Vinay had not forgotten the rani's words. When he saw his mother, he ardently wanted to sacrifice himself at her feet. There was a compelling desire to end his life at her feet, to show that though he had committed a crime, he was not totally shameless, and that if he didn't know how to live at least he knew how to die. He looked all around. There was a sword hanging on the wall in front. With a lightning flash, he took it down and drawing it said, 'Amma, I'm not worthy of being called your son, but obeying your last wishes I'll repent all my infamy. Give me your blessings.'

Sophia screamed and clung to Vinay. Jahnavi rushed and caught his hand and said – Vinay, God is my witness, I have forgiven you long ago. Leave the sword. Sophie, snatch the sword from his hand, help me.

Vinay's face was radiant, his eyes were red like beerbahuti. He realized how easy it was to slit one's neck with a sword. Sophia caught hold of his fist with both hands and looking tearfully at him said, 'Vinay, have mercy on me.'

Her gaze was so tender, so humble that Vinay's heart melted. His grasp loosened. Sophia took the sword and hung it on the wall. Meanwhile, Kunwar Bharat Singh came in and embraced Vinay, saying, 'You are unrecognizable, your moustache has grown so long. Why are you so thin? Were you ill?'

Vinay – No, I wasn't ill. I'm not so thin either. I'll get fat now, eating mataji's delicacies.

Kunwar – Why are you standing far away, Sophia? Come, let me embrace you too. I thought of you every day. Vinay was lucky to get a beautiful woman like you. Such a beautiful woman can't be found in the world, I don't know about heaven. It's a good coincidence that you have both come on the same day. Beti, I recommend Vinay to you. The scolding that you gave him has made poor Nayakram so afraid of women that he has rejected the engagement that had been arranged for him. He longed for a woman all his life, but now he doesn't even mention her name. He says, 'They are a faithless lot. The one for whom Bhaiyya Vinay suffered infamy and risked his life has turned away from him. I'll catch hold of my ears, I'll die but I won't marry.' Give me your hand, Vinay. Sophie, if you take this hand I'll be reassured that your misunderstandings have been cleared. Jahnavi, let's go out, let them placate each other. They must want to make so many reproaches and be eager to talk to each other. It's a very auspicious day today.

When they were alone, Sophie asked – How did you come so soon?

Vinay (*Embarrassed*) – Sophie, I was ashamed of sitting there hiding my face. To hide for fear of your life is for cowards. Let mataji do what she wishes. Nayakram kept saying, let miss sahib return but I couldn't wait.

Sophia – Well, it's good that you came. Mataji wept profusely talking about you. She's not offended with you now.

Vinay – Didn't she say anything to you?

Sophia – She embraced me so eagerly that I was taken aback. This is the influence of those harsh words that I had spoken to you. No matter how much a mother may scold her son, she can't bear it if anyone else even looks at him sternly. My injustice awakened her sense of justice.

Vinay – We left at a very auspicious moment.

Sophia – Yes, Vinay, it has gone well so far. God knows what will happen now.

Vinay – We have suffered our share of sorrow.

Sophia (*Apprehensively*) – I hope to God that it's so.

But Sophia could apprehend the shadow of misfortune in her inner being. She couldn't express it but she was dejected. It's possible that this was the result of regret at going against her lifelong religious upbringing, or that she thought of it as the excessive downpour that is the precursor of a drought. We can't say, but when Sophia went to sleep at night after eating, there was a burden on her mind.

40

THERE WAS VERY LITTLE WORK LEFT FOR THE MILL TO BE READY. Gharries loaded with tobacco kept coming from outside. Farmers were being given advances of money for sowing tobacco. The Governor had been requested to perform the inaugural ceremony and he had even accepted. The date had been decided. That's why work was being done with great enthusiasm to complete the construction by then. No work was to be left incomplete. It would be delightful if a cigar made at this factory could be presented at the party. Mr John Sevak was zealously occupied with these preparations from morning to evening. In fact, double wages were being paid to get the work done even at night. Permanent houses had been built around the mill. Labourers had built huts on either side of the road and in the nearby fields. In fact, only rows of huts could be seen on both sides of the road for a mile. There was a great deal of bustle. Shopkeepers had also put up their thatches. Shops selling paan, mithai, grain, gur, ghee, saag, vegetables and narcotics had opened. It seemed there had been an invasion here.

The mill's foreign labourers, who needed to have no fear of the community and no respect for relatives, worked at the mill all day and drank liquor and toddy at night. There was gambling every day. Even prostitutes reach such places. Here too, a small brothel had begun to flourish. The old bazaar of Pandeypur had begun to slow down. Mitthua, Gheesoo, Vidyadhar would often come here and gamble. Gheesoo would come on the pretext of selling milk, Vidyadhar on the excuse of finding a job and Mitthua to give them company. There would be a great deal of revelry until ten or eleven at night. Somebody would eat chaat, somebody would stand in front of the paan shop and somebody would joke with prostitutes. There was a continuous flow of obscene merriment and banter, shameful exchanges of flirtatious glances and lustful blandishments. Where did Pandeypur have such interesting things? The boys didn't have the courage to stand in front of the toddy shop for fear of being seen by somebody in the family. The youths didn't dare to harass a woman, afraid that she would report it at home, since they all interacted with each other in Pandeypur. Where were those impediments here? Each individual was free. He was not afraid of anybody nor was he embarrassed. There was nobody to ridicule anybody else. The three young men were told not to go there or to return as soon as they had finished their work, but youth is crazy, who listens to anybody? The worst plight was Bajrangi's. Gheesoo would make off with a rupee or eight annas every day. If questioned, he would be annoyed and ask, 'Am I a thief?'

One day, Bajrangi said to Soordas – Soorey, the boys are being ruined. They are at the brothel all the time. Gheesooa never had the habit of stealing. He has now become so nimble that he finds the money even if I put it away as carefully as possible.

Jagdhar was sitting with Soordas. On hearing this he said – I'm in the same state, bhai! I educated Vidyadhar, with great difficulty I took him up to middle school. I'd remain hungry, the family would long for clothes but he was not denied anything. I hoped that he would earn a little money, my old age would be taken care of, the household would be managed, he would raise my prestige in the community. And now he goes there every day to gamble. He makes the excuse that he goes to learn some work from a babu. I hear that he's having an affair with a woman. Several labourers from the factory had come to me looking for him. They'll beat him up if they find him. They too are that woman's lovers. I pleaded with them and saw them off. We have been ruined because of the opening of this factory. There's some profit of course, there's an income of a few paise. I couldn't sell even one khoncha earlier, now I can sell three, but what's the use of this gold that deafens the ears.

Bajrangi – It would have been all right as long as he only gambled, our Gheesoo has gone astray. Don't you see how his appearance has been ruined? His body had developed so well. I had hoped that he would win wrestling bouts, no vigorous youth in the wrestling arena is a match for him, but he's wasting away day by day ever since he has become addicted to the brothel. You had seen dada, hadn't you? Nobody for ten-five kos around could shake hands with him. He could crack a betel nut at a pinch. Even I won several wrestling bouts in my youth. You saw how I punched that Punjabi and won 500 rupees as a prize and became famous far and wide in the newspapers. No mother's bold brat ever made my back bite the dust. So what was the reason? I was a true celibate. My moustache had sprouted but I hadn't seen a woman's face until then. Even after I was married I didn't pay attention to the woman in my obsession with hard work and exercise. It's on that strength that I can still claim I can take the wind out of the sails of five or ten if I confront them. But this lad has sunk the boat. Ghoorey Ustaad said that he doesn't have any strength, he starts panting like a buffalo after just a couple of bouts.

Soordas – I'm a blind man. What do I know about the pranks of these boys? But Subhagi says that Mitthua's ways are not good. He earns a rupee or ten annas daily ever since he has become a coolie at the station, but I can take an oath if he gives even a paisa at home. He eats at my expense and spends whatever he gets on drinking.

Jagdhar – You suffer from a false sense of shame. Why don't you throw him out of the house? He'll know the cost of atta–daal when he has to fend for himself. It's different if he's one's own son, but can brothers and nephews ever become one's own?

Soordas – I have brought him up like a son. My heart doesn't consent.

Jagdhar – He won't become yours even if you try to make him so.

Meanwhile, Thakurdeen had also come. When he heard Jagdhar he said – Has God written in your karma that you should sow only thorns, you can't think of anybody's welfare?

Soordas – Let him do what he wants, but I can't eat and sleep myself and not bother about him.

Thakurdeen – Before saying anything, people should consider whether the person hearing it will like it or not. Should he now abandon the boy whom he has brought up since childhood, better than people would bring up their own sons?

Jamuni – Whatever these kalyugi boys don't do is a mercy. Subhagi has played with Gheesoo in her lap, his milk teeth have not yet broken, and today he's flirting with her. There's no respect now for anybody, small or big. Subhagi has a good figure, otherwise if she had had children they would have been older than Gheesoo.

While this talk was going on here, the three boys were sitting in Nayakram's veranda making plans. Gheesoo said – Subhagi is killing me.

I want to embrace her when I see her. She takes my life when she walks, swaying with the basket of vegetables on her head. She's very wicked.

Vidyadhar – You are a dimwit. You are not educated, how will you understand? A lover never admits that she's willing. You should guess from her eyes. The more she's offended, the more she's willing at heart. Had you been educated, you would have known how coy women are.

Mitthua – Subhagi would also be angry with me earlier, she wouldn't come into my clutches, she wouldn't even listen to me, but one day I plucked up my courage, caught hold of her wrist and said 'I won't leave you now. I have to die one day, so I'll die at your hands. I'm dying as it is, if I die at your hands I'll go straight to heaven.' First she was angry and started abusing, then she said, 'Let me go, it'll be a calamity if anybody sees, I'm your bua.' But I didn't pay any attention. And then she came into my clutches from that day.

Mitthua was adept at fabricating imaginary tales of his victories in love. Though illiterate, he had surpassed Vidyadhar at gossiping. He would colour his fantasies in such a way that his friends would believe his yarns. Gheesoo said, 'What should I do? I don't have the courage. I'm afraid there'll be a calamity if she makes a noise. How did you dare?'

Vidyadhar – You are an illiterate fool. The beloved tests her lover to see if he has some courage or if he is just a dandy. A woman loves only somebody who is bold, fearless and ready to jump into the fire.

Gheesoo – Are you ready?

Vidyadhar – Yes, right now.

Mitthua – But be careful. Dada sleeps at the doorway under the neem tree.

Gheesoo – That's nothing to be afraid of. I'll give him one push and he'll fall down far away.

The three of them, bantering and planning the moves of this conspiracy, went towards the coolie bazaar. They drank liquor and stayed there until 10 or 11 p.m., listening to music. There is never any lack of music for toneless ears in taverns. When the three of them returned completely drunk, Gheesoo said, 'So it's finally decided? Let it be resolved today, whether it's heads or tails.'

It was past midnight. The chowkidar had finished his watch and had left. Gheesoo and Vidyadhar came to Soordas's door.

Gheesoo – You go first, I'm standing here.

Vidyadhar – No, you go, you are an ignorant villager. You won't be able to cover up if anyone sees us.

Liquor had made Gheesoo lose control over himself. He wanted to show that he was not as weak as people thought him to be. He went into the hut and caught hold of Subhagi's arm. Subhagi got up with a start and said loudly, 'Who is it? Go away.'

Gheesoo – Quiet, quiet, it's me.

Subhagi – Thief! Thief!

Soordas woke up. He wanted to go into the hut when somebody caught hold of him. He asked, scolding, who is it? When he didn't get a reply, he too caught hold of that man's hand and screamed – Thief! Thief! On hearing these voices, the people of the muhalla picked up their sticks and came out. Bajrangi asked, 'Where has he gone? Where . . .?' Subhagi said, 'I'm holding on to him.' Soordas said, 'I'm holding on to another.' When people came, they saw that Subhagi was holding on to Gheesoo inside and Soordas was holding on to Vidyadhar outside. Mitthua was standing at Nayakram's door, he ran as soon as he heard the uproar. The whole muhalla broke loose in a moment. Very few people come out to catch a thief, but they all reach to give a few kicks when he has been caught. But when they reached there they saw that there was neither a thief nor the thief's brother, but boys from their own muhalla.

A woman – Such are the times that there's no concern for village or home, whose honour will be safe?

Thakurdeen – Such lads should be beheaded.

Nayakram – Quiet, Thakurdeen, this is something to cry about, not be angry over!

Jagdhar, Bajrangi, Jamuni were standing with their heads bowed, they couldn't utter a word. Bajrangi was so enraged that he wanted to throttle Gheesoo. Seeing this crowd and uproar several constables also reached there. A fine game had been trapped, their fists would be warmed now. They promptly caught hold of the wrists of both the young men. Jamuni said weeping, 'These boys will blacken our faces. They should be punished for six months each, only then will their eyes be opened. I was tired of trying to make him understand, beta, don't go on the wrong path, but who listens? Now go and grind the millstone. It would have been better for me to have been barren.'

Nayakram – All right, now go to your homes. Jamadar, they are boys, leave them, let's go now.

Jamadar – Don't say that, Pandaji, if kotval sahib gets to know, he'll think that we have taken something to let them go.

Nayakram – What do you say, Soorey, shouldn't these people leave now?

Thakurdeen – Yes, what else? Boys make mistakes. What they did was bad, but now let them go, what has happened has happened.

Soordas – Who am I to let them go? It's for the kotval, the deputy, the officers to let them go.

Bajrangi – Soorey, God knows, if I didn't fear for my life I would have chewed this villain alive.

Soordas – It's now in the hands of the authorities. They can let them go or punish them.

Bajrangi – Nothing will happen if you don't do anything. We'll persuade the jamadars.

Soordas – So, bhaiyya, it's clear that I won't rest until I have made a report to sarkar, even if the whole muhalla becomes my enemy.

Bajrangi – Is this what's going to happen, Soordas? You won't have any consideration for village or home, tola or muhalla? The boys have made a mistake, but what's to be gained by spoiling their lives?

Jagdhar – Subhagi isn't a devi either. The whole muhalla is familiar with her ways ever since she left Bhairo. Nobody goes into somebody's home without a previous understanding!

Soordas – So why are you telling me all this, bhai? Subhagi may be a devi or a common prostitute, that's her concern. I have caught thieves in my house, I'll surely inform the thana about this, if the people at the thana don't listen, I'll tell the officers. Boys are boys if they follow the path of boys; they are hooligans if they follow the path of hooligans. Do the badmash have horns and tails?

Bajrangi – Soorey, I'm telling you, there'll be bloodshed.

Soordas – So what? Who's there to weep for me?

Nayakram thought it futile to remain there. Why should he spoil his sleep? As he left, Jagdhar said – Pandaji, what will happen here if you also leave?

Nayakram replied – Bhai, Soordas won't listen, no matter how hard you try. I have tried, I'll try again, but nothing will happen. Forget about Gheesoo and Vidya, Soordas wouldn't have spared even Mitthua. He's a stubborn man.

Jagdhar – He's not such a rich seth that he can do what he wants. Come and speak to him sternly.

Nayakram returned and told Soordas – Soorey, sometimes one has to show some regard for village and home. What will you get by spoiling the boys' lives?

Soordas – Pandaji, you have also begun to talk like the others? Is there any justice in the world or not? Is a woman's honour worth nothing? Subhagi is poor, she's a weak woman, she fills her belly by working. Does that mean that anybody who wants to can ruin her honour? Can anyone think that she's a common prostitute?

The whole muhalla was united, even the two chowkidars sided with the muhalla-valas. One of them said – The woman herself is a common prostitute.

The second – The people of the muhalla can digest blood if they want to, this is not such a great crime.

The first – How will the crime be proved if there's no witness?

Soordas – There won't be any witness only if I die. She's a prostitute?

Chowkidar – Of course she's a prostitute. We have seen her not once but hundreds of times selling vegetables and laughing.

Soordas – So selling vegetables in the bazaar and laughing is the work of a prostitute?

Chowkidar – Arey, you'll only go up to the thana! After all, you'll have to report it to us there.

Nayakram – All right, let him report. I'll take care of it. Darogaji is not a stranger.

Soordas – Yes, let darogaji do what he wants, crime and sin are with him.

Nayakram – I'm telling you, you won't be able to live in the muhalla.

Soordas – I'll live here as long as I'm alive, I'll see what happens after I die.

Somebody would threaten Soordas, somebody else would try to persuade him. Only those people remained who wanted to suppress the matter. Those who were in favour of taking it further returned home because they couldn't say anything for fear of Bajrangi and

Nayakram. No one had the courage to take on the enmity of these two men. But Soordas was so adamant that there was no way he could be persuaded. It was finally decided that he should be allowed to go and file the report in the thana. They would persuade the thanedar himself and part with a few rupees.

Nayakram – Arey, that lala is the thanedar, isn't he? I'll fix him in no time. He's an old acquaintance of mine.

Jagdhar – Pandaji, I don't have any money. How will my life be saved?

Nayakram – I too have returned from a foreign country. My hand is empty. Go and arrange the money from somewhere.

Jagdhar – I had thought Soorey to be my well-wisher. I have always helped him in need. I took on Bhairo's enmity because of him. Despite that, he's not with me.

Nayakram – He doesn't belong to anybody and nobody belongs to him. Go and look, get at least twenty-five rupees from somewhere.

Jagdhar – Whom can I ask for money? Who will trust me?

Nayakram – Arey, go and ask Vidya's amma for some ornament. Save your life just now, you can redeem it later.

Jagdhar began to make excuses – She won't give even a ring; she won't give money even for my shroud when I die.

He began to cry as he said this. Nayakram had pity on him and promised to give the money.

When Soordas left for the thana in the morning, Bajrangi said – Soorey, death is playing over your head, go!

Jamuni clung to Soorey's feet and said, weeping – Soorey, we never thought that you'll become our enemy.

Bajrangi said – He's mean, what else! We go on taking care of him. We never let him go to sleep hungry. We have never forsaken him in sickness or in health. We have never let him go empty-handed whenever he has come to ask for milk. This is the return for all that goodness. It's true, the blind have no mercy—for the sake of a paasi's wife!

Nayakram rushed to the thana and narrated the entire incident to the thanedar. He said – The deal is fifty, neither less nor more. Don't write the report.

The daroga said – Pandaji, when you are involved in it fifty or a hundred don't matter but if the blind man comes to know that the report has not been written, he'll go straight to deputy sahib. Then I'll be in trouble. He's a very ruthless officer, in fact he's the sworn enemy of the police. The blind man is not a customer to be easily persuaded. When he could torment the Raja of Chataari and make him chew gram with his nose, what do others matter! Bas, all that can be done is that you shouldn't let anybody testify when I come to investigate. The matter will be dismissed if there's no proof. I can only do this much, that I won't force anybody to testify and will also trim the accounts of the witnesses.

Darogaji came the next evening to make enquiries. All the people of the muhalla gathered there but whoever was asked just said 'I don't know anything, I didn't hear anybody's cry of "thief, thief"' or 'I didn't see anybody at Soordas's door, I was asleep at home with the door shut'. Even Thakurdeen said bluntly – Sahib, I don't know anything.

The daroga said angrily to Soordas – You are making a false report, badmash.

Soordas – The report isn't false, it's true.

Daroga – Do you think I'll believe you? Is there any witness?

Soordas addressed the muhalla-valas and said – Yaaron, don't be afraid to tell the truth. Being friendly and kind doesn't mean that a woman's honour should be ruined and people should cover it up; somebody's house should be robbed and people should hide it. Nobody's honour will be safe if this remains the state of affairs. God has given everyone betis—think of them. A woman's honour is not a laughing matter. Heads are chopped off, rivers of blood flow because of it. I won't ask anyone else, Thakurdeen, you are God-fearing, you were the first to come, what did you see here? Weren't Subhagi and I both holding on to Gheesoo's and Vidyadhar's hands? Look, don't try to please people, nobody will go with you when you die. Tell the truth about what you saw.

Thakurdeen was indeed a God-fearing man. He was afraid when he heard all this and said – I don't know anything about theft or dacoity, this is what I have already said, I can't go back on my words. Yes, when I came Subhagi and you were holding on to both the boys and shouting.

Soordas – Had I caught hold of them and brought them from their homes?

Thakurdeen – God only knows that. Yes, I did hear the cry of 'thief, thief'.

Soordas – Achcha, now I'm asking you, jamadar, hadn't you also come? Speak, was there a gathering here or not?

When the chowkidar saw Thakurdeen being won over, he was afraid that the blind man would win over a few more people and he would be exposed. He said – Yes, of course there was a gathering.

Soordas – Was Subhagi holding on to Gheesoo or not? Was I holding on to Vidyadhar or not?

Chowkidar – We didn't see any theft.

Soordas – Were we holding on to both the boys or not?

Chowkidar – Yes, you were holding on to them, but we didn't see any theft.

Soordas – Darogaji, do you now have the testimony or should I give you some more? Naked, corrupt people don't live here, this is a basti of decent people. Tell me, shall I get Bajrangi to speak, should I get Gheesoo himself to speak? Nobody will tell a lie. Kindness has its own place and love has its own. Nobody will ruin his next world for kindness and love.

Bajrangi realized it wouldn't be possible to save his son, so why ruin his honour? He came and stood before the daroga and said – Darogaji, Soorey is right. People should suffer the results of their actions. Why should we spoil our next world? Why would our faces have been blackened had the boy not been so worthless? For how long can I protect him when he has gone astray? His eyes will be opened if he is punished.

The atmosphere changed. There was a line of witnesses in a second. Both the accused were arrested. The trial was held, they were both sentenced for three months each. Bajrangi and Jagdhar had been Soordas's devotees. Nayakram's task had been to make everybody sing Soordas's praises. Now all three became his enemies. Twice before too he had rebelled against the muhalla, but on both those occasions there hadn't been such a blow because of him, this time he had committed a serious crime. Whenever Jamuni saw him she would leave all her work and curse him. It was difficult for Subhagi to leave the house. Even Mitthua deserted him. Now he would spend the night at the station. The plight of his companions had opened his eyes. Nayakram was so angry that he stopped going by Soordas's door and would take a roundabout way. Only Bhairo remained his companion. Yes, sometimes Thakurdeen, avoiding other people, would come and ask about his welfare. In fact, even Dayagiri began to avoid him because he was afraid that people would think that he was Soordas's friend and stop giving him dakshina and alms.

Truth has few friends, far fewer than enemies.

41

THE EXPERIENCE AND KNOWLEDGE THAT PRABHU SEVAK HAD gained after staying three years in America and spending thousands of rupees, Mr John Sevak had acquired in as many months by his association with him. More than that, unlike Prabhu, he was not satisfied with following the prescribed path blindly; he looked ahead and behind, left and right. There's a narrowness in specialists that limits their horizon. They don't have a wider perspective on any subject independently; rules, principles and customary behaviour don't allow them a wide-ranging vision. The vaidya searches for medicines for every disease in texts; he's merely a servant of diagnostics, a slave to symptoms; he doesn't know that even Luqmaan* didn't have medicines for several diseases. Common sense may not be very acute but it's not narrow either. It can reflect widely on every subject without getting entangled with trivia. That's why the defence minister sitting in the ministry can rule over the army chief. John Sevak was not in the least worried after his separation from Prabhu. He began to work with double the enthusiasm. He was a practical man. When the need arose, he could run the wheels of an engine as easily as he wrote the office accounts. Earlier he would cast a cursory glance at the mill, now he went there regularly and punctually. He would often eat there and return home only in the evening, sometimes as late as 9 or 10 p.m. He wanted to show Prabhu that he had not taken up this work on the basis of Prabhu's strength alone; the day dawns even without the crow's cry. The basis of his love of wealth was not love for his children.

---

* Luqmaan (also known as Luqmaan the Wise and Luqmaan al-Hakeem) for whom the Surat Luqmaan the thirty-first sura (chapter) of the Quran was named. He was believed to be from Africa. He chose the gift of wisdom over prophethood from an angel sent by Allah. Subsequently, he was enslaved and sold by Arab raiders who invaded Africa. His owner, impressed by his wisdom, decreed that Luqmaan be freed after his death.

It was the most important part of his existence, the main source of the current of his life. All other affairs of the world were subsumed in it.

The problem of getting houses built for the labourers and craftsmen had still not been solved. Although John Sevak had increased his interaction with the district magistrate, he was very apprehensive of the Raja Sahib of Chataari. Raja sahib had become so notorious because he had once ignored public opinion that now even the hope of a much more important victory than that couldn't provoke him to suffer those wounds again. The mill was functioning at great speed, but not having houses for the labourers was the biggest obstacle in the way of its progress. John Sevak was preoccupied with this dilemma.

By coincidence, there was such a reversal in circumstances that this difficult problem was solved without any special effort. Prabhu's non-cooperation achieved what perhaps even his cooperation could not have done.

Ever since Sophia and Vinay had returned, the society for social service was progressing rapidly. The pace of its politics became more intense and extreme day by day. This time, kunwar sahib couldn't allay the suspicions of the authorities as easily as he had done earlier. The problem had now become much more serious. It had not been difficult to force Prabhu to resign; it was much more difficult to turn Vinay out of the house and to leave him at the mercy of the authorities. There was no doubt that kunwar sahib was a fearless man, steeped in love for the country, independent, without desire, and reflective. His life was so simple and virtuous that people thought him to be the image of sacrifice. He didn't need a large property for a luxurious life. But he was not prepared openly to become the object of the wrath of the authorities. He could give all he had for the welfare of the country but in such a way that the means of that welfare would remain in his hands. He didn't have the ability for that self-sacrifice which obliterates oneself disinterestedly and selflessly. He was convinced that they could be much more useful by staying in the background than by coming into the open. Vinay thought differently. He would say, 'Why should we murder our spiritual freedom for the sake of property? We should be masters of our property, not its slaves. What's the use of this tapasya if we can't abstain from wealth? This is a shameless crime. After all, this is the abstention for which we are striving.' Kunwar sahib would reply,

'We are not the masters of this property but its guardians. It's there only in custody for the coming generations. What right do we have to snatch this comfort and happiness from the prospective children who are its heirs? It's quite possible that they may not be so idealistic, or that they may not need to be self-sacrificing because of changed circumstances. It's also possible that they may not have those innate qualities that regard wealth as worthless.' It was with such arguments that he would try unsuccessfully to propitiate Vinay. The fact was that having enjoyed the comfort and prestige of ostentation all his life he couldn't accept the true meaning of abstention. He didn't want children; he wanted children for his wealth. Their place was secondary to that of wealth. He hated having to please the authorities; he thought it demeaning to consent to everything that the rulers wanted but he believed that it was folly to fall in their eyes and to rankle in their hearts, to the extent that they would be eager to become enemies. There was only one way by which kunwar sahib could bring Vinay to the right path, and that was his marriage to Sophia. By binding him in these chains, he wanted to pacify Vinay's rebelliousness but if there was any delay now it was because of Sophia. Sophia was still afraid that though the rani was now very kind to her she still didn't like this relationship. Her fear was not baseless either. The rani could and did love Sophia, she could and did respect her. But she didn't value sacrifice and thoughtfulness in her daughter-in-law as much as she esteemed modesty, simplicity, shyness and the prestige of the dynasty. She didn't want a sanyasini daughter-in-law who would renounce the world, but a daughter-in-law who would participate in it. But she never expressed her deepest feelings even by mistake. Nor did she want these thoughts to come to her mind; she thought that it would be ingratitude.

Kunwar sahib was in a dilemma for several days. How could the marriage be arranged without discussing it with John Sevak? Eventually, against his wishes, he went to see him one day. It was evening. John Sevak had just returned from the mill and was pondering over something, with the scheme for the houses of the labourers in front of him. As soon as he saw kunwar sahib, he got up and shook hands with great alacrity.

Sitting down on a chair kunwar sahib said – What have you decided about Vinay and Sophia's marriage? You are my friend as well as

Sophia's father and, on the basis of both these relations, I have the right to tell you not to delay in this matter.

John – You can take whatever service you want from me on the basis of friendship but (*gravely*) I don't have any right to take a decision on the basis of being Sophia's father. She has deprived me of this right. Otherwise, she has been here for so many days, couldn't she have come here even once? She has snatched this right from us.

Meanwhile, Mrs Sevak arrived too. On hearing her husband, she said – I'll die but I won't see her face. We don't have anything to do with her now.

Kunwar – You are being unfair to her. She has not left the house even for a day since she has come. The reason for this is embarrassment, nothing else. Perhaps she's afraid that she won't know what to say if she goes out and meets an old acquaintance. Imagine for a little while that one of us was in her place, how would we feel? She deserves to be forgiven. It will be my misfortune if you people are alienated from her. There shouldn't be any delay in the marriage now.

Mrs Sevak – I hope Khuda won't show us that day. She's dead for me. I have read her fatiha, I have cried over her name as much as I could.

Kunwar – You are doing an injustice to my riyasat. Marriage is the means of quelling Vinay's rebellion.

John – I would advise you to hand over the riyasat to the court of wards. The government will gladly accept your proposal and all its doubts about you will be removed. Kunwar Vinay Singh's political rebellion will then not have any effect at all on the riyasat and though this arrangement will seem disagreeable to you now, Vinay will be grateful to you and think of you as a sincere well-wisher when his views become mature after some time. Yes, I'll request you fully to fortify yourself before intervening in this matter. All your efforts will be in vain if there's any hesitation on your part; instead of allaying the suspicions of the government you will increase them even more.

Kunwar – I'm willing to do anything to protect the property. All I want is that Vinay should not have to face any financial difficulty. That's all. I don't want anything for myself.

John – You can't do anything openly for Kunwar Vinay Singh. Yes, what can be done is that you can give him as much as you think proper from your allowance.

Kunwar – All right, suppose Vinay progresses even further on this path, then?

John – Then he'll have no right over the riyasat.

Kunwar – But will his children have this right?

John – Certainly.

Kunwar – Will the government clearly accept this?

John – There's no reason why it shouldn't.

Kunwar – I hope Vinay's children won't have to suffer the consequences of his actions; won't the government seize the riyasat permanently? This has happened in a couple of places. Look at Berar for instance.*

John – One can't tell if something special were to happen. But this has never been the policy of the government. Forget about Berar. That's such a large province that it can cause political difficulties if it joins a riyasat.

Kunwar – So should I send a telegram to Dr Ganguly tomorrow and ask him to return from Shimla?

John – You can call him if you want to. I think that we should make a draft here and send it to him or I can go myself and get everything finalized according to your wishes.

Kunwar sahib thanked him and returned home. All night he was in a dilemma, wondering whether to tell Vinay and Jahnavi about this decision. He knew their answer. He didn't expect the slightest sympathy from them, only their scorn and opposition. 'What's the use of telling them? Right now Vinay has some fear. He will become even bolder when he hears of this situation.' Eventually he decided that there was no point in telling them now since there was the possibility of obstacles coming in the way. There would be enough time for discussion later, after the work had been finalized.

John Sevak didn't want the grass to grow under his feet. The next day, he had an application written by a barrister and showed it to kunwar sahib. He sent that paper to Dr Ganguly on the same day. Dr Ganguly liked this proposal very much and came himself from Shimla. He consulted kunwar sahib and they both went to meet the

---

* The Marathi-speaking Berar region of the Hyderabad princely state was annexed to the Central Provinces in 1903 by the British.

Governor of the province. What objection could the Governor have, especially when there was not even a kauri of debt on the riyasat? The officers began to examine the accounts of the riyasat and within a month the government had obtained authority over it. Kunwar sahib spoke very little to Vinay these days out of shame and embarrassment, he was seldom at home, and he averted his eyes to avoid this topic. On the day when all the conditions had been accepted, kunwar sahib couldn't restrain himself and he said to Vinay, 'The government now has authority over the riyasat.'

Vinay (*Startled*) – Has it been seized?

Kunwar – No, I have entrusted it to the court of wards.

He then described the conditions and said humbly – Forgive me, I didn't consult you about this.

Vinay – I'm not at all unhappy about that, but you have unnecessarily put yourself in the government's hands. Your status is now only that of a stipend holder, whose stipend can be stopped any time.

Kunwar – You are to be blamed for that.

Vinay – Such a situation would not have arisen if you had asked my advice before taking this decision. I would have given a declaration that I'll dissociate myself from the riyasat for the rest of my life. You could have published it and pleased the rulers.

Kunwar (*Thinking*) – Even in that situation, there could have been a suspicion that I'm helping you secretly. What other means did I have of removing this suspicion?

Vinay – Then I would have left this house and not had anything to do with you. Even now it would be best if you could get this arrangement cancelled. I'm not saying this from my point of view but from yours. I'll find some way of subsisting.

Kunwar (*Tearfully*) – Vinay, don't say such harsh things to me. I deserve to be the object of your sympathy and compassion not of your scorn. I know that we can't be liberated only by social service. I'm also aware that we can't even do social service independently. Any scheme that awakens in the country an awareness of its condition and arouses the sentiments of brotherhood and nationalism can't be free of suspicion. Knowing all this I entered the arena of service. But I didn't know that the society would take this form in such a short time and that this would be the result! I thought I would continue to run it unobtrusively; I didn't realize that I would have to sacrifice all that is mine in return—and not only mine but also that of prospective children. I admit that I don't have the ability to make such a great sacrifice.

Vinay didn't reply. He was not worried about Sophie or himself but about the functioning of the society. From where would the money come? They had never needed to beg for alms. He didn't have the talent for collecting money from the public. There was an expenditure of at least 5000 rupees a month. A separate organization would be needed to collect so much money. He now realized that money and wealth were not such insignificant things; 5000 rupees a month, 60,000 rupees a year—a permanent fund of twelve lakh rupees would be needed. His mind wouldn't work. Jahnavi had some personal wealth but she didn't want to give that, and now it was even more important to protect it because she didn't want to make Vinay a pauper.

It was the third pahar. Both Vinay and Indradutt were preoccupied with anxiety about money. Suddenly Sophia came and said – Shall I give a solution?

Indradutt – Should we go and beg for alms?

Sophia – Why don't we put up a play? We have actors, we can get some curtains made, I'll also help in making the curtains.

Vinay – It's a good suggestion, but you'll have to be the heroine.

Sophia – Indu rani will play the heroine, I'll take the part of a maidservant.

Indradutt – All right, which play should be put up? Bhattji's *Durgavati*?

Vinay – I like Prasad's *Ajaatshatru* very much.

Sophia – I liked *Karbala* very much. It has a good blend of both the rasas, veer and karuna.*

---

* Badrinath Bhatt (1881–1932). His play *Durgavati* is about Rani Durgavati, a contemporary of Rana Pratap. She fought against Akbar and became part of the folklore of Madhya Pradesh.

Jaishankar Prasad (1889–1937). His play *Ajaatshatru* (1922) is set during the time of the Buddha, who reconciles the differences among the kingdoms of Magadha, Kosambi and Kosal by advocating non-violence. Ajaatshatru, the

Meanwhile, the postman arrived and gave Vinay a sealed registered envelope. Prabhu Sevak's seal was on the envelope. It had come from London.

Vinay – All right, what do you think this contains?

Sophia – There won't be money, whatever else it may contain. How can that poor man have any money? It must be difficult for him to pay the hotel expenses there.

Vinay – And I say that there can't be anything else except money.

Indradutt – Never. It must be a new composition.

Vinay – Then why did it need to be registered?

Indradutt – Wouldn't he have got it insured had it been money?

Vinay – I'm telling you; you can bet on it.

Indradutt – I have only five rupees; it's a bet of five-five.

Vinay – Not this. If there's money in it, I'll ride on your neck from here to the other end of the room. If not, then you'll ride on mine. All right?

Indradutt – Accepted, open the envelope.

There was a cheque in the envelope for 10,000 rupees, drawn on the Bank of London. Vinay was delighted. He said – Didn't I say so? I have studied the science of palmistry. Come, bring your neck.

Indradutt – Stop, stop, will you break my neck? Just read the letter, what's written in it, where is he, what is he doing? You are only concerned about fixing your ride.

Vinay – No way, this can't be. You'll have to give a ride. I'm not responsible for your neck breaking or remaining intact. You are not weak or thin; you are quite a giant.

---

eponymous hero of the play, is the son of Bimbisar, emperor of Magadha. These historical plays attempt to construct India's past to inspire a sense of nationalism.

Karbala by Premchand was first published in the Devanagari script in November1924. It is a tribute to the martyrs of Karbala and an attempt at reconciling Hindu–Muslim relations, showing Hindus fighting together with Muslims in the battle against tyranny. Although the play was published a few months after the Hindi draft of *Rangbhoomi* had been completed in August 1924, Premchand obviously had it in mind while writing the novel.

Veer and karuna: the sentiments or rasas of heroism and compassion.

Indradutt – Bhai, don't cast the evil eye on a Mangal. I'm now only two maunds and thirty-five seers. I weighed over three maunds before going to Rajputana.

Vinay – Well, don't delay, stand with your neck bowed.

Indradutt – Sophia, save me. You were the one who first said that there would be no money in it. I just repeated that when I heard you.

Sophia – I don't want to get involved in your squabbles. It's between you and him.

She then began to read the letter:

Dear friends,
I don't know to whom I'm writing this letter. I don't know who the manager is these days. But I still have the same love for the society for social service that I had earlier. I think it's my duty to serve it. You must be keen to know about my welfare. I was in Poona when the Governor sent for me to meet him. We discussed literature for a long time. He's a true connoisseur. Such savants are seldom found in our country. Except Vinay (I have no news of him), I haven't found anybody as sensitive to poetry. There was such genuine sympathy! It's because of the Governor's inspiration that I came here, and there has been a continuous flow of hospitality ever since I've come. Actually it's only the enlightened nations that know how to respect talent. They are very generous, liberal and affectionate people. I have now come to venerate this race and I'm convinced that it can never harm us. I was invited by a university yesterday. I have never before seen such a gathering of people who love literature! I was captivated by the affection and the hospitality of the women. There was a banquet at the India Office a couple of days ago. The literary society has invited me today. The Liberal Association will give a party tomorrow. It's the Parsi Society's turn the next day. On the same day, there will be a party on behalf of the Union Club. I had never hoped even in my dreams that I'll become an important person in such a short time. I'm not a critic of fame and respect. What other prize can talented people hope for except this? Now I know for what I have come to this world and what the goal of my life is. I was under an illusion

until now. The mission of my life will now be to bind the East and the West with love, to end their mutual conflicts and to awaken the sentiments of equality in both. I'll take this vow. At some time in the past the East had shown the West the path of dharma; it will now speak the message of love to the West and show it the path of love. The first collection of my poems will soon be published by the Macmillan Company. The Governor will write the introduction for those poems. The publishers have given me 40,000 rupees for this collection. I had wanted to present the entire amount to my beloved society but I'm also thinking of visiting America. So please accept whatever I have sent. I have fulfilled my duty, so I don't expect any thanks. Yes, I do think it's necessary to request you to follow the high ideals of service, and detaching yourselves from political conditions, to make the propagation of 'vasudhaiv kutumbakam'* your goal. You'll get reports of my speeches in the newspapers here. You'll see how much my political views have changed. I'm not a nationalist now but a universalist, the whole world is my country; my friendship is with all human beings, and effacing geographical and national boundaries is the purpose of my life. Pray that I'll return safe from America.

Your sincere friend,
Prabhu Sevak

Sophia put the letter on the table and said gravely – This can have both meanings—spiritual elevation or degradation. I think it's degradation.

Vinay – Why? Why not elevation?

Sophia – Because Prabhu's soul loves luxuries. He has never been stable. A person who is so elated by prestige will become just as dejected if he is scorned.

Vinay – That's not true. I may also have been elated in the same way. It's completely natural. What recognition did he get here? He would have remained unknown until his death.

---

* The whole world is one family.

Indradutt – Let him be famous since he's of no use to us now. Nobody has ever benefited by such universalists and never will. If nobody is one's own, how can there be anyone who is a stranger?

Sophia – Universalism has been the ruin of so many of our poets, it will also be his.* It's all the same for us whether he's here or not, in fact I now fear harm from him. I'll go just now and reply to this letter.

Sophia went to her room taking the letter with her. Vinay said – What should I do? Should I return the money?

Indradutt – Why should you return the money? He hasn't put any conditions. He has only given friendly advice and it's very good advice. That's our purpose too. The only difference is that he is preaching friendship without equality while we consider equality to be essential for friendship.

Vinay – Why don't you say that friendship is based on equality?

Indradutt – Sophia devi will really take him to task.

Vinay – All right, I'll keep the money for the time being, we'll see about it later.

Indradutt – Our work can be accomplished if we get a few more such friends.

Vinay – What do you think of Sophia's suggestion of putting up a play?

Indradutt – What's there to ask? People will be taken aback when they see her acting.

Vinay – Would you have liked her to be on the stage had you been in my place?

Indradutt – Not professionally, but I would perhaps not object to her being on the stage for philanthropy.

Vinay – Then you are far more liberal than I am. I don't like it in any circumstances. Yes, tell me, Sophia seems rather downcast these days. She has said very pessimistic things to me. She's afraid that the riyasat is in this situation because of her. Mataji dotes on her but Sophia runs far away from her. She talks about those spiritual things again, whose meaning I haven't understood till today—I don't want

---

* Perhaps a reference to Rabindranath Tagore's propagation of universal brotherhood, of which Premchand was critical.

to be the chain binding your feet, your love is enough for me, and goodness knows what else. And my predicament is that I'm restless if I don't see her for an hour.

Meanwhile, they heard the sound of a car and Indu arrived in a moment.

Indradutt – Come, Indu rani, come. We were waiting for you.

Indu – You are a liar, there was no discussion about me, you are worried about money.

Indradutt – So it seems that you have brought something. Let's have it, actually we were very worried.

Indu – You are asking me? Knowing my situation? I have learnt my lesson forever after giving a donation once. (*To Vinay*) Where's Sophia? Has ammaji consented now?

Vinay – How can one know what's in somebody's heart?

Indu – I think that even if ammaji consents, you still won't get Sophie. You'll feel distressed if I say this, but it's better to be prepared for a blow than for it to fall suddenly on one's head.

Vinay said, holding back his tears – This is what I think too.

Indu – Sophie came to meet me yesterday. What she said made her cry and made me also cry. She's in a dharmic dilemma. She doesn't want to disappoint you, nor does she want to displease mataji. I don't know why she still suspects that mataji doesn't want to accept her as her daughter-in-law. I think it's only her illusion, she herself doesn't understand the mystery of her own heart. She's not a woman, but merely a fantasy, full of emotions and desires. You can savour her but not experience her; you can't see her tangibly. A poet can't express his deepest emotions. Speech doesn't have that ability. Sophia is that innermost emotion of the poet.

Indradutt – And all that you are saying is also merely poetic fantasy. Sophia is neither a poetic fantasy nor a secret mystery; she is neither a goddess nor a god, neither an apsara nor a fairy. She is a woman like other women with the same emotions and thoughts. Have you people made any preparations for the marriage; have you ever said anything to indicate that you are eager about it? So if you people yourselves are indifferent, why should she go around discussing it? I'm an uncouth man. No matter how much she may love Vinay, she'll never talk about marriage herself. You people want something that can never happen.

That's why she has found this strategy of protecting her modesty. Begin the preparations, we can complain about her if she has any objection then. She uses these strategies to protect her honour when she sees you people wavering.

Indu – Don't ever say that, even by mistake, or she won't even stay in this house.

Meanwhile, they saw Sophia coming with the letter that she had written to Prabhu. Indu changed the topic and said – You people probably don't know yet, Mr Sevak has got Pandeypur.

Sophia asked, embracing Indu – What will papa do with the village?

Indu – Don't you know yet? That muhalla will be dug up and thrown away and houses for the mill's labourers will be built there.

Indradutt – Has raja sahib consented? He has forgotten so soon. It will be difficult for him to live in the city now.

Indu – It was the order of the government, how could he not consent?

Indradutt – Sahib has run very fast. He has cast a mantra even on the government.

Indu – Why, didn't he manage to put such a big riyasat under the government's authority? Hasn't he maimed a traitorous raja? Hasn't he dug the foundations of a revolutionary organization? Would he have let off the government after doing it so many favours? It's as if he's not a clever businessman but some raja or thakur. The best part of it is that the company has subjugated most of the members of the board by giving a profit of 25 per cent.

Vinay – Raja sahib should have resigned. That would have been better than taking on such a big responsibility.

Indu – He must have thought about it before consenting. I hear that the people of Pandeypur aren't willing to leave their houses.

Indradutt – And they shouldn't be.

Sophia – We should go there and see what's happening. But what if I see papa! No, I won't go, you people go.

The three of them left for Pandeypur.

42

IF THE COURT GAVE BOTH THE YOUNG MEN RIGOROUS PUNISHMENT, the public didn't punish Soordas less rigorously. All of them spat at him. Let alone the muhalla-valas, even the villagers nearby would hurl a few taunts. 'He begs for alms but he thinks so much of himself. A few good men have encouraged him and he has become so arrogant that his feet don't touch the ground.' Soordas was so ashamed that it was difficult for him to leave his home. One good result of all this was that Bajrangi's and Jagdhar's anger was pacified. Bajrangi thought, 'Why should I beat him now? His face has already been blackened.' Jagdhar didn't have the courage to do anything alone. The second result was that Subhagi agreed to return to Bhairo's house. She realized that she couldn't escape these blasts without some shelter. Soordas's shelter was only that of a bamboo screen.

One day Soordas was lamenting the bigotry and immorality of the world when Subhagi said – Bhaiyya, you are facing a squall on all sides because of me, Bajrangi and Jagdhar are both bent on killing you, so take me now to my own house to stop this. All that will happen is that he'll beat me. What can I do? I'll bear it. At least I'll escape this disgrace.

Bhairo had just been waiting and was delighted; he came and fetched Subhagi with great respect. Subhagi fell at the old woman's feet and wept profusely. The old woman picked her up and embraced her. The poor thing couldn't see now. There was nobody to sit at the shop when Bhairo went anywhere and people would just take away the wood in the dark. She could somehow cook the food but it was difficult to put up with the loss resulting from this snatching and pinching. Subhagi would now be there to look after the house. As for Bhairo, there was not an iota of deceit in his heart now. He had more faith in Soordas than perhaps in any devata. He now repented his earlier ways and loudly sang Soordas's praises.

Soordas had been free of household worries all these days—he would get cooked rotis, the utensils would be washed, the house would be swept. He was now burdened with the old problems again. Mitthua stayed at the station. The punishment given to Gheesoo and Vidyadhar had opened his eyes. 'I swear, I'll never go near gambling and charas now!' He would eat parched grain that he got from the bazaar and would stay in the veranda of the station. Who could be bothered walking three or four miles a day? He was not at all worried about how Soordas would be coping; it didn't occur to him to ask, 'Now that I'm grown up, do I have a duty towards him or not? After all, why did he bring me up as his own son?' Soordas went to the station himself several times and told him to return home in the evenings 'Should I still continue to beg for alms?' But Mitthua was not in the least concerned. On one occasion, he said bluntly, 'I can't cope myself, from where can I get anything for you? What tapasya did you do for me? You just gave me a morsel of roti, you didn't give it to the dog so you gave it to me. Did I ask you to feed me? Why didn't you leave me? Do the boys who don't have mothers and fathers die? Just as you gave me a morsel, I could have got many such morsels.' Soordas was so heartbroken by these words that he never asked Mitthua to return home again.

Sophia had met Soordas several times. She wouldn't go anywhere else but she would be sure to take time off to meet Soordas. She would come at a time when she wouldn't have to confront Sevakji. She always brought a gift for Soordas whenever she came. She had heard his entire story from Indradutt—his appealing to the public in the court, not keeping the money that had been collected for him but giving it to someone else, donating the money that he had received for the land from the government—she had become even more devoted to him after that. The craving for religion among the ignorant is appeased by worshipping bricks and stones, the devotion of the educated by serving the siddhas. Every frenzied person seems to them to be some rishi from a previous birth. They listen to his abuses, wash his unclean utensils, even wash his dusty feet and drink the water as nectar. It seems to them that a divine soul resides in their bodies. Sophia had begun to have this kind of devotion for Soordas. She once brought some oranges and apples for him. Soordas brought them home, but he didn't eat them himself, he thought of Mitthua and forgot Mitthua's harsh words. He took them to the station in the morning and gave them to him. On one occasion, Indu had also come with Sophie. It was winter. Soordas was standing there shivering. Indu gave him the blanket with which she had covered her feet. Soordas liked it so much that he couldn't use it himself. 'I'm an old beggar, where will I go covering myself with this blanket? Who will then give me alms? I merely lie down on the ground at night, I stand at the roadside all day, what will I do with it?' He went and gave it to Mitthua. There was still so much love on his side, but Mitthua was so selfish that he wouldn't even ask Soordas if he had eaten. Soordas thought that he was just a boy; these were the days for him to enjoy himself. 'He doesn't care for me but at least he himself lives comfortably. He's mine, so some day he'll be useful.'

It was an evening in the month of Phagun. A woman was returning after selling grass. The labourers had just finished their work. They were bored, having stood in front of the wheels all day, and were eager for entertainment. As soon as they saw the grass-cutter, they hurled a volley of obscene kabir* at her. This offended Soordas.

He said – Yaaron, why are you soiling your speech? This poor thing is just going her way and you won't leave her alone. She must also be somebody's bahu or beti.

One labourer – Go and beg, that's what is written in your karma. Why is your nani dying if we sing?

Soordas – Nobody is stopping you from singing.

Labourer – Are we using sticks?

Soordas – Why are you harassing this woman?

Labourer – Why should you mind it? Is she your behen or your beti?

Soordas – She's my behen and my beti; so what if she's mine or some other brother's?

Before he had completed the last sentence, one of the labourers quietly pulled his leg from behind. The poor thing had been standing unaware. He fell so hard on his face on the stones in front that two of his teeth broke, his chest was hurt, his lips were cut, and he fainted. He remained lying there unconscious for fifteen to twenty minutes. No labourer came anywhere near him, they all went their way. By

---

* Obscene songs sung at Holi.

coincidence, Nayakram was coming from the city just then. When he saw Soordas on the road, he was startled and wondered what the matter could be. 'Has somebody beaten him up? Who else would have so much courage except Bajrangi? It was wrong. No matter what else, Soordas is true to his dharma.' He felt pity for Soordas. When he came close and shook him, Soordas regained consciousness, he got up, held Nayakram's hand and began walking with his stick in his other hand.

Nayakram asked – Has anybody beaten you, Soorey? There's blood flowing from your mouth.

Soordas – No bhaiyya, I stumbled and fell.

Nayakram – Don't hide. Tell me if Bajrangi or Jagdhar have beaten you. I'm not a brahman if I don't have them sent in for a year each.

Soordas – No bhaiyya, nobody beat me. Why should I tell a lie about anybody?

Nayakram – Has anybody from the mill beaten you? They harass wayfarers a lot. I tell them that I'll get them looted and will burn their huts. Tell me, who has done this? You have never before stumbled and fallen. Your whole body is soaked with blood.

Soordas didn't name anyone. He knew that Nayakram wouldn't be afraid of killing in his anger. The whole muhalla came running when he reached home. 'Hai! Hai! Who is the enemy who has beaten up the blind man? Just look, his face is so swollen.' People made Soordas lie down on the bedding. Bhairo came running, Bajrangi lit the fire, Soordas was massaged with opium and oil. All of them softened towards him. The only person who was happy was Jagdhar. He said to Jamuni, 'God has avenged us. We were patient, but God is the one who gives justice.'

Jamuni said, flaring up – Be quiet, who do you think you are, trying to be the tail of justice? We shouldn't laugh even at our enemies when they are in trouble; he's not our enemy. He'll give his life for the truth, whether anybody likes it or not. If anyone of us were to fall ill today, you'd see if he stays up the whole night or not. How can there be any enmity towards such a man?

Jagdhar was ashamed.

Soordas was not in a condition to leave the house for fifteen days. His mouth bled for several days. Subhagi would sit by his side the whole day. Bhairo would sleep there at night. Jamuni would bring hot milk at the crack of dawn and make him drink it with her own hands. Bajrangi brought medicines from the bazaar. If there was someone who did not come to see him, it was Mitthua. Somebody went to him three times, but Mitthua didn't have the courage even to come and ask about his welfare, let alone look after him. He was afraid that he would have to give something if he went there because of what people would say. He had now tasted money. Even Soordas was compelled to say, 'It's only self-interest that matters. The father died when he was tiny. I supported the mother and the son, when the mother died I brought him up as my own son and became a father myself, I would sleep his sleep and remain awake when he slept, today he earns a few paise so he doesn't care about me. Well, God is there for me as well. Let him be happy wherever he is. He has his temperament; I have mine. He may not be concerned about me but I am concerned about him. How can I forget that I have brought him up as my own son?'

Pandeypur's fate was being decided while Soordas was lying on the sickbed. One morning Raja Mahendra Kumar, Mr John Sevak, an officer for making an assessment of the property, some police officers and a daroga arrived in Pandeypur. Raja sahib assembled the inhabitants and explained, 'Sarkar needs the muhalla for some special government work. It has decided that you people will be given an appropriate price and the land will be taken from you, this is the order of laat sahib. An officer sahib has been appointed for making the estimate. His court will be held here from tomorrow. He will make an assessment of the prices of all the houses and you will get due compensation. If you have any petitions and complaints, tell him. You have to vacate your houses within three months from today; you'll get the compensation later. If anybody doesn't vacate his house within this period, the money for his compensation will be appropriated and he will forcibly be thrown out of his house. If anybody puts obstructions in the way, the police will prosecute him and he will be punished. Sarkar is not giving you unnecessary trouble; it needs this land urgently. I'm only carrying out sarkar's orders.'

The villagers had already got news about this but had been consoling themselves, thinking that nobody knew whether this information was correct or not. As the delay lengthened, their lazy souls became complacent. Somebody hoped that he would somehow save his house by negotiating with the officers, somebody was concerned about protecting himself by giving something or the other, somebody had decided to make excuses, somebody was sitting quietly thinking that nobody knew what was going to happen so why worry now, we'll see about it when it happens. Despite that, it was as if a thunderbolt had fallen when people suddenly heard the order. All of them stood with folded hands before raja sahib and said, 'Sarkar, so many generations have lived here, where will we go if sarkar throws us out now? We could somehow squeeze in somewhere if there were just a few of us, where will the whole muhalla go if it is uprooted? Just as sarkar is throwing us out, let it also tell us where to go.'

Raja sahib – Even I deeply regret this, and I had even objected on your behalf to sarkar, but sarkar says, 'Our work can't be done without this land.' I have sincere sympathy for you, but I'm helpless, I can't do anything, it's sarkar's orders, I have to follow them.

Nobody had the courage to reply to this. People kept nudging each other to ask the rate of compensation but nobody moved. Nayakram was usually quite a smooth operator but he too was silent on this occasion. He thought it futile to discuss anything with raja sahib and was thinking of ways of getting the estimate increased by the officer. It seemed easier to get the work done by giving him something. All of them remembered Soordas in this calamity. 'Had he been here, he would surely have pleaded for us. Nobody else has so much courage.' Several people rushed to Soordas and gave him the news.

Soordas – Everyone else is there, what can I do? Why doesn't Nayakram come to the forefront? He bellows so much otherwise, why doesn't he open his mouth now? Is he there to show his clout only in the muhalla?

Thakurdeen – We have seen them all. Curd has set in their mouths. It needs courage and intelligence to talk to the officers.

Shivsevak bania – I tremble from head to foot when I stand in front of them. I don't know how people can talk to the officers. I'm scared out of my wits if they scold me even a little.

Jhingur teli – Officers have a lot of power. One loses one's wits in front of them.

Soordas – I can't even get up. How can I go even if I want to?

Soordas had started moving about with the help of his stick, but now he wanted to assert his pride. The dhobi doesn't mount a donkey just because he's told to.

Thakurdeen – What's so difficult about that? We'll carry you.

Soordas – Bhai, you will all do what you want to, why do you want me to be mocked? My plight will be like everybody else's. What will happen is God's will.

Thakurdeen pleaded a lot but Soordas didn't consent to go with them. This angered Thakurdeen. He usually spoke bluntly. He said – All right, don't go. Do you think that morning won't come if the cock doesn't crow? You have become so arrogant just because a few people have sung your praises. It's true, the crow doesn't become a crane just by being washed.

The authorities left by eight. People now went to Nayakram's house and held a panchayat to decide what to do.

Jamuni – You people will just go on blabbering, nobody else can do anything. Why don't you go to Soordas and consult him? See what he says.

Bajrangi – Why don't you go then? I'm not the only one concerned.

Jamuni – Then go and sit at home. What will we get by gossiping uselessly?

Bhairo – Bajrangi, this is no time for bravado. Let us all go to Soordas. He's sure to find some way.

Thakurdeen – I'll never go to his door now. I was tired of pleading but he didn't get up. He has started thinking too much of himself.

Jagdhar – Is Soordas a devata that he can change the order of the officers?

Thakurdeen – I was ready to carry him in my lap.

Bajrangi – It's only pride and nothing else because more people didn't go to him. Why didn't he face the officers? He's not dying after all.

Jamuni – Why should he have come? He'll be in the bad books of the officers, and if you do what you want to here, he's the one who'll be humiliated.

Bhairo – You are right, if the plaintiff is slow, why should the witness be active? First go and ask what he advises. Accept it if it's worth accepting, don't if it's not. Yes, we'll have to be firm about what we decide. You shouldn't say something and then escape, so that while the leader thinks his men are behind him, they have all fled home.

Bajrangi – Come Pandaji, let's go and ask.

Nayakram – He'll say, let's go to burra sahib; if we don't get a hearing there, let's go to Paraagraj to laat sahib. Do you have the courage to do that?

Jagdhar – Bhaiyya is right, maharaj. Nobody opened his mouth here, who'll go to laat sahib?

Jamuni – Why don't you go at least once? At least see what he advises.

Nayakram – I'm ready, come.

Thakurdeen – I won't go, whoever wants to go can go.

Jagdhar – Then why should the rest of us be so concerned?

Bajrangi – We'll be in the same situation as everybody else.

The panchayat continued for an hour but nobody went to Soordas. The needle of collective action moves like the loading of a cart. You go, I'll come, this was the clamour that went on. People went home after that. Bhairo went to see Soordas in the evening.

Soordas – What happened today?

Bhairo – What could happen? There was blabbering for an hour. And then people went home.

Soordas – Nothing was decided about what's to be done?

Bhairo – We'll have to leave, what else? Why, Soorey, will nobody listen?

Soordas – The person who should listen to us is also the one who is making us leave. A third person would have listened had he been there.

Bhairo – It's the death of me. I have thousands of maunds of wood, where will I lug it? Where else will I get so much land that I can set up another wood store?

Soordas – It's death for everybody. Where will Bajrangi get so much land that fifteen to twenty animals can live there and so can he? And even if he does get it he'll have to pay so much rent that he'll be bankrupt. See, Mitthua hasn't come even today. If I get to know that he's ill I wouldn't wait for a moment, I'd run like a dog, even if he doesn't talk to me. Those for whom one ruins one's life turn away when times are difficult.

Bhairo – All right, tell me, what will you do, have you thought of anything?

Soordas – Why do you ask me? I had land; I have lost it. I'll get a few rupees at the most for the hut. How does it matter if I get them or not? I'll remain here as long as nobody tells me to go. If somebody catches hold of my hand and forces me out, I'll go and sit outside. If he makes me get up from there I'll come back and stay here. I'll die where I was born. I won't leave my hut as long as I'm alive. They can take what they want after I die. I have lost the land of my forefathers, this is the only token left, I'm not going to leave it. I'll also die along with it.

Bhairo – Soorey, nobody here has so much courage.

Soordas – That's why I didn't say anything. Just think, it's such injustice that we who have been living here for seventy generations should be thrown out and others should come and live here. This is our home; we can't leave it because somebody tells us to. They can make us leave by force, not by law. You have the power, so you can beat us. If we had it, we could have beaten you. This is not justice. Sarkar has the strength to beat us; we at least have the strength to die if we don't have any other strength.

Bhairo repeated these views to the others. Jagdhar said – See, this is his advice. Not only will we lose our homes, we'll also lose our lives.

Thakurdeen – This must be Soordas's doing. He doesn't have a master in front or a tether behind, so what if he dies? Who will look after our families if we die?

Bajrangi – You need a heart to die. What will we do with the houses when we ourselves are dead?

Nayakram – We have seen many such people who are ready to die; he didn't even come out of the house and he says he'll die!

Bhairo – Don't say anything about him, Pandaji, it's a question of what one wants.

The assessment officer began to hold his court in one of the rooms in the mill from the next day. A munshi began to make a list of the names of the inhabitants of the muhalla, whether the houses were mud or brick, new or old, their length, width, etc. The patwari and the munshi went from house to house. Nayakram was the mukhia, the village headman. It was necessary for him to be with them. Everybody's fate at this time was in the hands of this trimurti.* Nayakram was rising

---

* Triad of Brahma, Vishnu and Shiva.

fast. He began to act as a broker. He'd tell people, 'We'll have to leave after all, where's the harm if a small loss can help in increasing the compensation?' His fist was being warmed without his doing anything, so why let it go? The gist of it was that the basis of the status of the houses was the gift that was offered to this trimurti. Nayakram played shikar behind the bamboo screen. He earned fame as well as wealth. Bhairo's big house and the field in front were shrunk and the area reduced, the trimurti had not been worshipped here. Jagdhar's small house was expanded. Pleased with his gift, the trimurti had loosened the ropes; the area increased. Thakurdeen thought that it would be easier to please Shivji rather than these devatas. That didn't require any greater expense than a lota of water. He began to offer water twice a day. But right now it was the trimurti that held sway, Shivji couldn't do anything. The trimurti proved that his small house was mud and not brick. Let alone pleasing the devatas, Bajrangi had succeeded in offending them, but Jamuni managed to mend matters with her good sense. Munshiji was enamoured of one of her female calves; he had set his heart on her. Bajrangi thought animals to be dearer than life; he flared up. Nayakram said, 'Bajrangi, you'll regret it.' Bajrangi retorted, 'I don't care if I don't get a kauri as compensation but I won't give the calf.' Finally Jamuni, who was adept at bargaining, took him aside and explained. 'Do we have any shelter for the animals? Where will you wander around with them? If we can gain a hundred rupees by giving a calf, why don't we do so? Several more such calves will be born, give it and get rid of this misfortune on your head.' Bajrangi finally agreed after her persuasion.

The trimurti ruled for fifteen days. The assessment officer would come from home at noon, smoke a few cigars in his room, read the newspapers, and return home at 1 or 2 p.m. He began to examine the list when it was ready. Then the inhabitants were summoned. The officer read out each one's assessment. It was trickery from the very outset. Bhairo said, 'Huzoor, come and see our house—is it bigger or is Jagdhar's? He's getting 400 rupees and I'm getting 300 rupees. I should get 600 rupees on this basis.'

Thakurdeen, who was short-tempered, said bluntly – Sahib, the assessment has not been made on any basis. Those who have given sweets have prospered; those who have depended on God have been castrated. Yet you are not going to the site to investigate so that the assessment can be done properly; you are razing the throats of the poor.

The officer said angrily – We kept the mukhia of your village on your behalf. The assessment has been made on his advice. Nothing can be done now.

Thakurdeen – Those who claim to be ours loot us even more.

Officer – Nothing can be done now.

Soordas's hut had been assessed at one rupee, Nayakram's house for a full 10,000 rupees! People said – This is the plight of the village and the family! They are our blood relations and yet they cut our throats. And then they arrogantly claim that they are not greedy for money. He's a panda who cheats pilgrims, after all. That's why this has happened. He has turned away from us just because he has got a little power. Had he been a thanedar, he would not have let people stay in their houses. That's why it's said that the bald don't have nails.

Mr Senapati had become the district magistrate after Mr Clark. He trembled if he had to spend the government's money and would make do with a dhela instead of a paisa. He was afraid of being disgraced. He didn't have the self-confidence of the English officers. The English can't be suspected of favouritism, they are fearless and independent. Mr Senapati suspected that the compensations had been decided too leniently. He thought that half the sum was sufficient. The file of the case was now sent to the provincial government for approval. It was again examined there. Three months passed in this way, and Mr John Sevak arrived with the police superintendent, Daroga Mahir Ali, and some labourers to get the muhalla vacated. People said that they had still not received any money. John Sevak replied, 'We are not concerned about your money; take it from whoever will give it to you. The government has promised us that it will get the muhalla vacated on 1 May, and if anybody tells us that it's not 1 May today we'll go back.' People were very restless now. 'What are the intentions of sarkar? Will we be thrown out without compensation? We'll have to leave our homes and we won't even get compensation. This is death without our dying. We could have at least built houses somewhere if we had been given the money; where will we go empty-handed? First there are orders that four annas should be given instead of a rupee, and this is the situation on top of that! We don't know if sarkar has changed its intentions or if the middlemen have taken the money.'

Mahir – Say whatever you want to the district officer. The houses will be vacated today.

Bajrangi – How can the houses be vacated? Is it a highway robbery? The officer who had given the earlier order has also given this one.

Mahir – I'm telling you, load your bedding and boxes and get moving. Why are you making me angry? You've had it if Mr Hunter's anger is aroused.*

Nayakram – Darogaji, give us a few days. We'll get the money after all, these poor things are not wrong when they ask where they'll wander around without money.

John Sevak had gone with the superintendent to visit the mill; tea had been arranged there, so it was Mahir who ruled here. He said – Pandaji, you can hoodwink other people. I have known you for a long time and I recognize each pore of your being. The houses will be vacated today and only today.

Suddenly, two children came there playing, they were both barefoot, wearing torn clothes, but cheerful. As soon as they saw Mahir they ran towards him crying, 'Chacha! Chacha!' They were Sabir and Naseema. Kulsoom had rented a small house for a rupee in this muhalla after John Sevak had got the godown vacated. The poor thing eked out her difficult days in this small house. When Mahir saw the children he said, somewhat abashed, 'Run away, why have you come here?' He was embarrassed inwardly because people would say, 'They are his nephew and niece and they are so hard up, he doesn't take care of them.'

Nayakram gave both the children two paise each and said – Go and eat mithai. He's not your chacha.

Naseema – Hoon! Of course he's chacha, don't I recognize him?

Nayakram – Had he been your chacha, wouldn't he have picked you up in his lap and got mithai for you? You are forgetting.

Mahir (*Annoyed*) – Pandaji, why are you concerned about these unnecessary things? Whether they are my nephew and niece or not, it's none of your business. Who are you to interfere in someone's personal affairs? Run Sabir, Naseema run, or the sepoy will catch you.

---

* Mahir's ironic reference to the hunter used by the British to whip Indians.

Both the children looked unbelievingly at Mahir and ran away. On the way Naseema said – He's like chacha, why Sabir, he's chacha isn't he?

Sabir – Who else is he otherwise?

Naseema – Then why did he make us run away?

Sabir – He used to love us when abba was here. Abba used to feed everybody, but he isn't here now.

Naseema – Abba doesn't feed amma now. But she loves us even more than she used to earlier. She didn't give us money earlier, now she even gives us money.

Sabir – That's because she's our amma.

The children had left. Darogaji gave the order – Throw away the baggage and vacate the houses immediately. These people need to be kicked; they won't listen to words.

Two constables forced themselves into Bajrangi's house and began to throw out all the utensils. Bajrangi was standing outside, furious, chewing his lips. Jamuni was running helter-skelter in the house, picking up handis and taking them outside, or collecting the utensils that had been thrown out. She wouldn't shut her mouth for even a second. 'They behead us and build factories, they'll destroy the world and fill their houses. Even God isn't destroying such sinners; who knows where he is sleeping! Hai! Hai! They have flung down Gheesooa's clubs and broken them.'

Bajrangi picked up the broken clubs and going to a sepoy said – Jamadar, what did you get by breaking these clubs? They could have been of some use if you had picked them up unbroken. It's just as well that you are wearing a red turban, otherwise today . . .

He hadn't completed what he was saying when both the sepoys began beating him with sticks. Bajrangi couldn't control himself now, he leapt and caught hold of one sepoy's neck with one hand and the other sepoy's with his other one, throttling them so hard that their eyes popped out. When Jamuni saw that there would be a disaster, she went crying to Bajrangi and said, 'I swear to you by God, don't fight with anybody. Let it be, let it be. Why are you becoming your own enemy?'

Bajrangi – You go and sit. If I'm hanged you can go to your maika. I'm determined to take their lives.

Jamuni – I swear to you by Gheesoo, you'll eat my flesh if you don't let go of these two and go away from here.

Bajrangi let go of both sepoys but they ran to Mahir as soon as they were free and returned with several more sepoys. But Jamuni had already taken Bajrangi to the stack. When the sepoys couldn't find the lion they began to beat the lion's den, they broke everything in the house. If they saw something they could use, they just swiped it. This play was going on in the other houses as well. There was looting everywhere. Somebody bolted the door from inside; somebody escaped from the back with his family. It was as if the sepoys had been given orders to loot and plunder rather than to get the houses vacated. They wouldn't give anybody time to collect their utensils and belongings. Nayakram's house was also attacked. Mahir himself forced his way in with five sepoys. They couldn't find even a grain from a sparrow's beak there, the house had been swept; not even a broken handi could be found. The sepoys' ambitions remained unfulfilled. They had thought that they would plunder this house to their heart's content, but they had to leave disappointed and ashamed. The fact was that Nayakram had already thrown out his belongings from his house.

The sepoys began to break the locks of the houses. Somebody would be beaten up, somewhere else somebody would be running with his belongings. There was a clamour everywhere. It was a strange scene, as if there was a dacoity in broad daylight. They were all either coming out of their houses or being thrown out and were assembling on the road. There is usually a collection of troublemakers on such occasions. There was the greed for loot, somebody bore illwill towards the inhabitants, and somebody bore malice towards the police. Every moment there was fear of a breach of peace and chaos. When Mahir saw the wrath of the crowd, he promptly sent a sepoy to the police cantonment and a contingent of armed police reached by 4 p.m. Mahir was even more emboldened with the arrival of reinforcements. He ordered, 'Beat them up and chase them all away. Why are people standing there? Make them flee. If you see anybody standing here, beat him up.' Until now people were busy collecting their goods and baggage. Even if they were beaten, they quietly put up with it. How could they take on so many sepoys alone? Now all of them stood there in one place. They were becoming somewhat aware of their collective strength and, on top of that, Nayakram kept inciting them, 'Don't let them go without beating them if they come here, they won't listen until a few people's limbs are broken.' The bomb was about to explode when Indu's car arrived and Vinay, Indradutt and Indu alighted. They saw that there was a crowd of several thousand people. Some were inhabitants of the muhalla, some were wayfarers, there were some people from the nearby villages, and some labourers from the mill. Some had come only to watch the spectacle, some to sympathize with neighbours, and some jealously to enjoy this uprising. Mahir and his sepoys were trying to drive away people from the road with the zeal that those of a base nature have in oppressing others, but the crowd was surging forward instead of moving back.

Vinay went to Mahir and said – Darogaji, can't these people be given even one day's time?

Mahir – They were given three months, and it will be the same situation even if they are given three years when it comes to vacating the houses. They will never leave in a straightforward way.

Vinay – Can you do me the favour of stopping the sepoys for a while, so that I can inform the superintendent about the condition here?

Mahir – Sahib is here. Mr John Sevak had taken him to show him the mill. I don't know if he has left from there, he hasn't yet returned.

Actually sahib bahadur had not gone anywhere, he was sitting in the office with John Sevak drinking comfortably. Both the men had misunderstood the situation. They had thought that people would be in awe of them on seeing them and would be so afraid that they would run away on their own.

Vinay rushed to the mill to give sahib the news but he stopped when he saw raja sahib coming in his car. He thought, 'Now that he has come, there's no need to go to sahib, I'll go and talk to him.' But he felt embarrassed to go and meet him. 'What will I do if the public insults him? He might think that I have instigated them.' He was in this dilemma when raja sahib saw Indu's car. He flared up, and when he saw Indradutt and Vinay it was as if a fit of fever had overtaken him. 'These people are present here, so why wouldn't there be a riot? It's a mercy if something doesn't happen wherever these three great people are around.' He seldom lost his temper, but this time he couldn't control it. He said to Vinay, 'All this seems to be your doing.'

Vinay calmly said – I have just come. I was about to go to the superintendent when I saw you.

Raja – Well, you are the leader now. Will you disperse them with some magic or mantra or will I have to take some other action?

Vinay – These people have only one complaint, that they haven't yet been given the compensation. So, where can they go? How will they buy land? How will they buy material for new houses? If you can reassure them, they will themselves go away.

Raja – They are only making excuses. Actually they want to riot.

Vinay – Perhaps you won't have to resort to some other action if they are given compensation.

Raja – You are suggesting a way that will take six months; I want a path that will take only a month.

Vinay – There are thorns on that path.

Raja – That doesn't worry me. I like paths with thorns.

Vinay – Right now the condition of this crowd is like dry straw.

Raja – We'll burn the straw if it comes in our way.

They were all restless with fear, anything could happen at any moment, but in spite of that the sea of humanity kept surging towards raja sahib as if under the spell of some unknown power. The policemen also came from different directions and stood near the car. Gradually an infinite, bottomless river of human beings began to gush all around them, as if it would swallow these few men with one wave and drown this tiny bank with its flow.

Raja Mahendra Kumar had not come here to pour oil on fire but to quell it. He had received information moment by moment. He had been very worried because he felt responsible, although he had no moral responsibility. After all, what could he do if there was pressure from the provincial government? If he resigned, somebody else would obey the government's orders. In no circumstances could this disaster have been averted for the people of Pandeypur, but from the very outset he had been trying continuously to get the compensation paid to the people before they were evicted. He would give continuous reminders. His suspicions had increased as the last date approached. In fact he had even wanted some advance to be given to the inhabitants so that they could arrange their accommodation beforehand. But for some unknown reason there was a delay in approving the money. He had repeatedly told Mr Senapati to give it on his own authority in anticipation of the approval, but the district magistrate would cover his ears with his hands and say, 'I don't know what the government plans to do. I can't do anything without orders.' When the approval hadn't come even today, raja sahib sent a telegram and waited for a reply until the afternoon. Finally, he was apprehensive when he heard about this gathering and immediately rushed to the district magistrate's bungalow to ask his advice. He had hoped that the district magistrate himself would be prepared to go to the scene of the incident, but on going there, he found that sahib was ill. It was not illness but an excuse—the only way of avoiding disgrace. He said to raja sahib, 'I regret that I can't go myself. You go and do whatever you think proper to pacify the rebellion.'

Mahendra Kumar was now very anxious, it seemed as if there was no way of saving his own life. 'I won't be anywhere if there's bloodshed. I'll be held responsible for everything. I have already become notorious. It's the end of my public life today. I'm being killed when I'm innocent. It seems that Saturn is governing me in such a way that I act against my own wishes, as if I have no control over myself. My getting involved in the affair of this land has become poisonous for me. Ever since then there have been problems that have ruined my ambitions. Let alone lamenting for fame, name, respect, it's difficult for me to show my face anywhere.'

He had returned home to take Indu's advice and to see what she would have to say. But Indu wasn't there. When he asked, he was told that she had gone out.

Raja sahib's state at this time was like that of a miser who sees his wealth being looted in front of his eyes but who can't say anything because he is afraid that the secret of his being wealthy will be revealed. All of a sudden he thought of something – Why don't I give the money for the compensation myself? The money won't go anywhere. I'll take it back when the approval comes. It's a question of a few days, and it will have such a good effect on the public. It's only 70,000 rupees. And it's not necessary to give the entire sum today. I'll give some today and some tomorrow, the approval is sure to come by then. People will feel reassured when they start getting the money, they won't be afraid that the government will seize it. I'm sorry that I didn't think of this earlier, otherwise this problem wouldn't have arisen.

He immediately wrote a cheque for 20,000 rupees, drawn on the Imperial Bank. It was very late so he wrote a letter to the manager of the bank requesting him not to delay the payment otherwise there was fear of a breach of peace. It was 5 p.m. when the man returned with the money from the bank. Raja sahib promptly took the car and reached Pandeypur. These were the good intentions with which he had come, but he was enraged when he saw Vinay and Indu there. He thought, 'I'll tell the people, take the money from those on whose strength you are dancing, and I'll write to the government that the people are ready to rebel, their money should be seized.' It was in this rage that he had spoken those words to Vinay, which have been narrated above. But when he saw that the surge of the crowd was swelling, people's faces were distorted with anger, armed police had mounted bayonets, and a few stones were also being thrown, his plight became that of a person who is intoxicated with fear. He promptly stood on the car and said, screaming loudly, 'Friends, calm down. You won't get anything by rioting like this. I have brought the money, you'll get your compensation now. The government hasn't yet sent its approval but you can take your money from me if you want. Your rebellion over such a small matter is highly improper. I know that it's not your fault; you have prepared yourselves for this mischief because you have been misled by somebody. But I won't let you jump into these flames of rebellion prepared by your well-wishers. Take it, this is your money. All the men should come by turn and get their names written, give their thumb impressions, take the money and go home quietly.

One man said – You have seized our houses.

Raja – It won't take you long to find houses if you have money. We won't hesitate to give you any help that we can. This crowd should disperse immediately now, otherwise there will be a delay in getting the money.

The crowd that was becoming fierce and impenetrable, like gathering clouds, broke up like flocks of cotton wool as soon as this announcement was heard. Nobody knew where people had vanished. Only those who had to get money remained. This was a shining example of how timely intelligence can so easily resolve a hovering calamity. One inappropriate word, one harsh sentence could have made the situation uncontrollable.

The patwari began to read the list of names. Raja sahib distributed the money with his own hands. An individual would take the money, put his thumb impression, and then two sepoys would accompany him to get the house vacated.

This was what people said as they returned after getting the money:

A Musalman – This raja is a big villain, sarkar had sent the money, but he has suppressed it. He would have digested it himself if we had not agitated.

A second – He must have thought, I'll get the houses vacated; I'll then return the money to sarkar and so become noble.

A brahman contradicted this – What are you blabbering? The poor thing has given his own money.

A third – You have the hide of a cow, what do you know about these tricks? Go and read your books and swindle money.

A fourth – They must have all consulted each other earlier. They would have shared the money among themselves; we would have been left on bamboo frames.

A munshiji – How will he please sarkar if he doesn't do even this much? He should have fought with sarkar on behalf of the people, but he is a fawning donkey. The pressure of sarkar is only an excuse.

A fifth – So you should realize that the poor things wouldn't have got even a kauri had we not reached. Who gives and who gets once the houses are vacated? If they had gone to ask for money, they would have been beaten by the chaprasis and thrown out.

It's very difficult to win the public's trust after it has been lost. This was the gift that raja sahib was being given by the public's durbar.

It was evening. Only four or five people could get the money by the time it was dark. Raja sahib distributed it until 9 p.m. by the light of the lamp. Nayakram then said – Sarkar, it's very late. If it can't be done now, leave it till tomorrow.

Raja sahib was also tired, the public too didn't see any difficulty in getting the money now, so the work was postponed until the next day. The armed police camped there in case people assembled again.

Raja sahib came again at 10 a.m. the next day. Vinay and Indradutt also reached there together with several volunteers. The list of names was opened. Soordas was the first to be summoned. He came tapping his stick and stood before raja sahib.

Raja sahib looked him over from head to foot and said – The compensation for your house is only one rupee, take it and vacate the house.

Soordas – What's this money?

Raja – You don't even know yet that sarkar has taken your house. It's the compensation for that.

Soordas – I didn't tell anybody to sell my house.

Raja – Other people are also vacating their houses.

Soordas – Give it to the people who are prepared to leave. Let my hut be. I'll remain here and wish for huzoor's welfare.

Raja – It's not a question of what you want, it's sarkar's orders. Sarkar needs this land. How can it be that the other houses are pulled down and your hut should remain?

Soordas – Sarkar doesn't lack land. The whole country is there. Its work won't stop by leaving a poor man's hut.

Raja – You are arguing unnecessarily, take this rupee, put your thumb impression, and go to the hut and take out your belongings.

Soordas – What will sarkar do with the money? Will a temple be built here? Will a pond be dug? Will a dharmashala be built? Tell me.

Raja – I don't know anything about this.

Soordas – Of course you know, the world knows, every child knows. Houses will be built for the factory labourers. How will I gain if they are built so that I should leave my home and go away? The gain will be sahib's. The public will be ruined. I won't leave my hut for such work. Yes, if it had been some work for dharma, I would have been the first to give my hut. You have the right to use force, you can order the policemen, how long does it take to set straw on fire? But this is not justice. In ancient times when a raja began getting his garden made, an old woman's hut came in the way. The raja called her and said, 'Give me this hut and I'll give you as much money as you want, I'll get a house built wherever you want.' The old woman said, 'Let my hut be. When the world sees that there's the old woman's hut in a corner of your garden, it will praise you for your dharma and justice. The garden's wall will be crooked for a few feet, but your name will be immortal forever because of it.' The raja left the old woman's hut. Is sarkar's dharma to take care of the public or to ruin its homes and to destroy it?

Raja sahib (*Annoyed*) – I haven't come to argue with you, I have come to obey official orders.

Soordas – Huzoor, how can I dare to argue with you? But don't destroy me. This hut is the only mark left of my forefathers; let it remain.

Where did raja sahib have the time to argue for hours with each individual? He gave orders for the next man to be called.

When Indradutt saw that Soordas was still standing there, refusing to move, he was afraid that raja sahib might give orders to the policemen to push him away. Indradutt quietly took Soordas's hand and taking him aside said – Soorey, this is injustice, but what can you do? You'll have to leave the hut. Take whatever you can get. I'm afraid of raja sahib being humiliated, or I wouldn't have told you to take it.

Several people surrounded these men. People's curiosity is aroused on such occasions. What happened? What happened? What was his answer? Everybody is curious about these questions. Soordas said tearfully, his voice trembling with anger – Bhaiyya, even you are telling me to take the rupee? This factory has crushed me. The land of my forefathers was ten bighas, that's already gone, now this hut is also being snatched from me. The world is the name for this illusion and attachment. I won't come to live in this hut when I'm liberated from it. But I can't leave my home as long as I'm alive. It's my home, I won't give it. Yes, anybody can take it by force if they want to.

Indradutt – Nobody is using force. These houses are being vacated by law. Sarkar has the right to take any house or land that it needs for official work.

Soordas – There may be such a law, I know only the law of dharma. You can make any law that you want by force. There's nobody here to catch hold of sarkar's hand. Its advisers are also seths and mahajans after all.

Indradutt went to raja sahib and said – It would be best if you postponed the affair of the blind man. He's an ignorant villager, he doesn't understand, he just goes on singing his own tune.

Raja sahib looked angrily at Indradutt and said – He's not an ignorant villager, he's a seasoned rascal. He can teach the law to both of us. He's a beggar, but he's stubborn. I'll get his hut pulled down.

Soordas heard the last words of this sentence. He said – Why should you get the hut pulled down? It would be better if you have me killed with a bullet.

Soordas then left, tapping his stick. Raja sahib was enraged by his insolence. It's very difficult for prestige to forget itself, especially when it is insulted in front of others. He called Mahir Ali and said – Pull down his hut immediately.

Daroga Mahir Ali went forth, with unarmed and armed police and a group of labourers, as if he were going to attack a fort. A crowd of people also followed him. Raja sahib lost his wits when he saw the attitude of these people. There was fear of a rebellion. It didn't seem as easy to pull down the hut as he had thought it would be. He regretted having given this order to Mahir Ali. 'The hut would have fallen anyway once the muhalla became a field; Soordas is not a ghost who could have remained there alone. I tried to kill an ant with a sword. Mahir Ali is a short-tempered man, and the attitudes of these men have also changed. The public forgets itself when it is enraged; it laughs at death. There's sure to be a rebellion if Mahir Ali acts impetuously. All the blame will fall on my head. This blind man is drowning already, he'll make me drown with him as well. He's really after me.' But at this time he was in the position of an officer. He couldn't take back the order. He was far more afraid of a stigma on his own honour than on that of the government. The only way left now was not letting the public go towards the hut. The superintendent had just returned from the mill, riding a horse and smoking a cigar. Raja sahib went to him and said, 'These men should be stopped.'

He said – Let it be, there's no harm, there'll be a shikar.

'There'll be fierce killing.'

'We are ready for it.'

The colour waned from Vinay's face. He couldn't go forward nor could he go back. Deeply tormented, he said – Indra, I'm in a great dilemma.

Indradutt said – There's no doubt about it.

'It's difficult to control the public.'

'You go, I'll see to it. It's not proper for you to stay here.'

'You'll go alone?'

'There's nothing to worry about.'

'Why don't you come with me as well? We have now done our duty.'

'You go. I don't have the dilemma that you do. I'm not afraid of the honour and dishonour of somebody dear to me.'

Vinay stood there, restless and transfixed, like a woman who has been turned out of the house. When Indradutt left him and went ahead, the crowd of people had stopped at the turning of the lane that went to Soordas's hut. Five sepoys were standing there with bayonets. To move a step forward meant taking the point of the bayonet on the chest. There was a wall of bayonets in front.

Indradutt stood on the plinth of a well and said loudly – Bhaiyyon! Think about it, what do you want? Will you fight with the police for this hut? Will you shed your blood and that of your brothers? This hut is very expensive at that price. If you want to save it then request these people in uniform, with bayonets, who are standing in front of you like yamdoots. And although they are apparently your enemies, there's not one of them whose heart is not with you, who thinks that it is in his interest to pull down the hut of a helpless, weak, blind man. They are all good people with families, who have left their homes to protect your lives and property on low wages.

One man – Do they protect our lives and property or sarkar's clout and power?

Indradutt – It's the same thing. It's essential to protect sarkar's clout and power to protect your lives and property. The wages they get are less than those of a labourer . . .

A question – Don't they take money from buggy-valas and ikka-valas?

A second question – Don't they get thefts done? Don't they encourage gambling? Don't they take bribes?

Indradutt – All this is because they don't get the wages that they should. They are also human beings like you and me, they too have pity and discrimination, they too think it base to raise their hands on the weak. They do what they have to because they are helpless. Tell them to have mercy on the blind man and to save his hut. (*To the policemen*) Why friends, should we hope for this mercy from you? What will you do with these people?

Indradutt tried to arouse sympathy among the public for the policemen on one side, and on the other he tried to awaken the innate compassion of the policemen. The havaldar was standing behind the bayonets. He said, 'Protect our livelihood and then do what you want. Don't go this way.'

Indradutt – So you'll destroy so many people for the sake of your livelihood? These poor people have also come to protect a meek human being. Will the God who takes care of you here let you starve somewhere else? Arey! Who is throwing stones? Remember, you have come here to protect justice, not to riot. Don't disgrace yourselves with such base blows. Don't raise your hands, even if there's a volley of bullets shot at you . . .

Indradutt didn't get an opportunity to say anything. When the superintendent saw the crowd of people at the turning of the lane, he went there galloping on his horse. When he heard Indradutt's voice he scolded – Drive him away. Drive away all these men from here immediately. Go away immediately, all of you, or I'll shoot.

The crowd didn't move a jot.

'Go away immediately, or I'll fire!'

Not a single man moved from his place.

The superintendent ordered them to leave a third time.

The crowd remained calm, grave and still.

Orders were given to open fire, the policemen took up their rifles. Meanwhile, raja sahib came panicking and said, '*For God's sake, Mr Brown, spare me!*' But the orders had been given. The flood surged, there was smoke from the mouths of the rifles, the dreadful sound of dhain-dhain and several people fainted and fell down. There was a volley of stones from the crowd. A few branches had fallen but the tree was still standing.

Orders were given to fire again. This time raja sahib pleaded earnestly, '*Mr Brown, these shots are piercing my heart!*' But the order had already been given, there was a second flood, several men fell again. Branches fell, but the tree stood firm.

Orders were given to fire a third time. Raja sahib said tearfully, in an anguished voice, '*Mr Brown, now I am done for!*'* The flood surged, several men fell, Indradutt with them. The bullet pierced his breast and passed through it. The trunk of the tree had fallen.

---

* The italicized sentences are in English in the original.

There was a stampede in the crowd. People began to run, falling on each other, crushing each other. Somebody hid behind a tree, somebody pushed himself into someone's house, somebody hid in the ditches on the roadside, but the majority of the people came away from there and stood on the road.

Nayakram said to Vinay Singh – Bhaiyya, why are you standing here? Indradutt has been shot.

Vinay was still standing apathetically. As soon as he heard the news it was as if he had been shot. He ran headlong and came and stood in front of the bayonets at the entrance of the lane. As soon as they saw him those who were running away stopped, those who were hiding came out of their hiding places. 'What are we worth when there are such people who have all the comforts of the world and are ready to die?' This is what people thought. The wall that had been falling rose again. The superintendent gritted his teeth and gave orders to fire a fourth time. But what was this? No sepoy fired, the havaldar flung down the rifles, the sepoys also put down their rifles along with him. The havaldar said, 'Huzoor has the right, do what you want, but we cannot shoot now. We are also human beings, not murderers.'

Brown – You'll be court-martialled.

Havaldar – Let it happen.

Brown – You traitors!

Havaldar – We took up service to protect our brothers, not to cut their throats.

After that, all of them turned back and went towards Soordas's hut. They were accompanied by thousands of people shouting cries of victory. Vinay was ahead of them. Both raja sahib and Brown remained standing, rather lost. The incident that was happening in front of them was heralding a new age in the history of the police that was against tradition, against human nature, against ethics. That the old servants of the government, many of whom had spent the major part of their lives in suppressing the public, should walk on so insolently! That they should be prepared to sacrifice all they had, including their lives! Raja sahib had so far been trembling because of the burden of his responsibility but now he was afraid that these people would fall upon him. Brown was on his horse, whipping people with his hunter, trying to drive them away, and raja sahib was looking for a place in which to hide, but nobody even glanced at him. They were all running towards Soordas's hut at a volatile pace, shouting cries of victory. When they reached there, they saw hundreds of people surrounding the hut. Mahir Ali was standing with his men under the neem tree waiting for a new contingent of armed police; he didn't have the courage to penetrate this formation and go near the hut. Nayakram was standing in the forefront with his club on his shoulder. In the middle of this formation, at the doorway of the hut, Soordas was sitting with his head bowed, as if he was a living, radiant image of fortitude, spiritual strength, and calm.

As soon as he saw Vinay, Nayakram said – Bhaiyya, now don't worry about anything. I'll manage. There was a misunderstanding between Soordas and me for months, we weren't even on talking terms, but today I'm amazed at his courageous heart. Such spirit in a blind cripple! The rest of us are merely carrying this burden of mud for show . . .

Vinay – Indradutt's death is a disaster.

Nayakram – Bhaiyya, don't despair; this must be God's will.

Vinay – He has died such a brave death.

Nayakram – I was standing there watching; there wasn't a wrinkle on his brow.

Vinay – I didn't know that it would come to this; or I would have jumped in first. He could have managed the society for social service alone; I can't manage it. He was so courageous. He never thought about difficulties; he was always ready to jump into the fire. It's just as well that he was not married.

Nayakram – His family tried so hard to persuade him, but he refused once and then never said yes.

Vinay – A woman's life has been saved.

Nayakram – What are you saying, bhaiyya? Had he been married, he wouldn't have faced the bullets so fearlessly. What will the plight of his poor mother and father be?

Vinay – They'll die weeping, what else?

Nayakram – It's just as well that there are several brothers who are the family's strength.

Vinay – Let's see what the plight of these policemen will be. The army will come by tomorrow. We should be concerned about these poor people.

Nayakram – What can you do, bhaiyya? They'll be court-martialled. Where will they escape?

Vinay – That's what we need to tell them, that they shouldn't run away, they shouldn't be afraid to accept the glory for what they have done. The havaldar will be hanged.

When both the men came near the hut, the havaldar said, 'Kunwar sahib, I'm sure to be court-martialled, take care of my family.' He began to wail loudly.

Several people assembled there and said – Kunwar sahib, start a collection. Havaldar, you are a true warrior who doesn't raise his hand on the weak.

Vinay – Havaldar, we won't hesitate to do what we can. You have protected our honour today.

Havaldar – I'm not worried about living or dying, I'll have to die some day, there can't be a better death than to die serving one's brothers. Blessings on you, you have renounced comfort and luxury to protect the unfortunate.

Vinay – Those of your men who need employment can find a place with us.

Havaldar – Let's see, who's saved and who dies.

Raja sahib fled in his car as soon as he got the opportunity. Mr Brown went to consult the district magistrate about army assistance. Mahir Ali and his sepoys stayed on there. It was dark; the public also left one by one. Suddenly Soordas came and asked – Where is kunwarji? Dharmavatar, why are you taking so much trouble over an arm's length of land? So many people have lost their lives today because of me, I didn't know that a mountain would be made out of a mustard seed, or I would have set this hut on fire with my own hands and gone away somewhere after blackening my face. What did I need? I would have just stayed wherever I begged. Bhaiyya, I can't bear it that so many homes should be destroyed because of my hut. You can do what you like after I die.

Vinay – It's not your hut; it's our national temple. We can't sit quietly when we see spades striking it.

Soordas – The spade will first strike my body and then my house.

Vinay – And if it's set on fire?

Soordas – Then my funeral pyre will have been prepared. Bhaiyya,

I say to you and to all my brothers with folded hands that if any mother's lap has been made desolate because of me, or if any sister of mine has become a widow, I'll set this hut on fire and die burning.

Vinay said to Nayakram – What now?

Nayakram – He's true to his word, he's sure to do what he says.

Vinay – Then let it remain like this. Let's see what happens tomorrow. We'll think of what to do when we see what they have decided. Let's go now and emancipate our heroes. They are our national martyrs, their funerals should be held with pomp and grandeur.

By 9 p.m., nine biers and three coffins were raised. Indradutt's bier was in the front, and those of the other heroes behind it. The coffins were taken to the cemetery. About 10,000 people walked behind the biers, barefoot, with heads bowed. The crowd swelled at every step. People came running from all directions. But there were no signs of grief or pain on anybody's face. There were no tears in any eyes, no sound of anguish from any throat. On the contrary, people's hearts were elated with pride; their eyes were intoxicated with patriotism. The public would not have stepped back at this time even if cannons had been mounted on the way. There was no sound of grief, no victory song, but a transcendental silence—emotional, flowing, rapturous.

They passed Raja Mahendra Singh's palace on the way. Raja sahib was watching this scene from the terrace. A group of armed guards was standing at the gate with mounted bayonets. As soon as the biers passed in front of the gate, a woman emerged from inside and joined the flow of people. It was Indu. Nobody noticed her. There was a garland of roses in her hands that she had woven herself. She went forward with it and going to Indradutt's bier, offered it with her teardrops. Vinay saw her. He said, 'Indu!' Indu looked at him tearfully and didn't say anything; she couldn't say anything.

Gangey! Perhaps your eyes have never beheld such a moving spectacle. You have seen the bravest of the brave, who could have made lions turn back, being reduced to ashes; the greatest of majestic kings, at whose roar even the dikpaal* would tremble with fear, have mingled with ashes before your eyes; the greatest of mighty warriors have been immersed in funeral pyres here. Somebody was a votary of sacrificial

---

* The guardian deities of the ten points of the compass.

acts and fame, somebody of expanding his empire, somebody of envy and greed. So many sages, ascetics, yogis, pandits have mounted the funeral pyre before your eyes. Tell the truth, was your heart ever so rapturous with joy? Had your waves ever raised their heads like this? Everybody dies for themselves, some for this world, some for the next. The people who have come in your lap today are those who were selfless, who sacrificed themselves to protect sacred, pure justice.

And have you ever seen such a condolence meeting, of which each constituent was replete with brotherly love, patriotism and devotion to heroism?

The flames burnt all night, as if the souls of the heroes were seated on a plane of fire, ascending to heaven.

The golden rays of dawn began to embrace the pyres. This was the blessing of the sun god.

Only a few people remained when it was time to return. The women returned singing songs of heroism. Rani Jahnavi was in the forefront, Sophie, Indu and several other women followed her. The sound of their melodious music, saturated in the rasa of heroism, was dancing on the rays of light of the dawn, like love dancing on the strings of the heart.

43

SOPHIA'S RELIGIOUS VIEWS, HER CONDUCT, LIFESTYLE, EDUCATION and upbringing were all such that a Hindu woman could hate. But the experience of so many days had resolved all raniji's doubts. Sophia had not yet been initiated into the Hindu dharma, but her conduct was in full conformity with Hindu dharma and Hindu society. Jahnavi didn't have the least doubt about it now. If she had any doubt left, it was that Vinay would forget his objective once he was engrossed in matrimonial love. But by taking on the burden of leadership in this rebellion Vinay had proved that this apprehension was baseless. Raniji was now busy with preparations for the marriage. Kunwar sahib had already consented but it was necessary to get Sophia's mother's approval. Indu couldn't have any objection. Raniji was not worried about the approval or disapproval of the other relations. So she went to Mr Sevak's house one day to finalize this alliance. Mr Sevak was happy but Mrs Sevak was adamant. In her view, an Indian could never have the respect that a European could, no matter how powerful he was. She knew that the most ordinary European was esteemed more than the greatest raja here. Prabhu had chosen the path to Europe; he didn't even write letters home now. Sophia had now chosen this path. All Mrs Sevak's ambitions were dampened. She flared up at Jahnavi's request and said, 'It's Sophia's happiness that matters, if she's happy then it's all the same whether I give my approval or not. I'm a mother, I can only utter good wishes for my child, I can't wish her harm, but forgive me, I can't participate in the marriage ceremony. I'm trying to restrain myself not to curse Sophia, but it's better that such a girl, who has defamed the family and turned against her religion, should die.'

Raniji didn't have the courage to say anything else. When she returned home she sent for a learned pandit and fixed the auspicious date for the ceremonies for Sophia's dharma initiation and her wedding.

While Rani Jahnavi was making elaborate preparations for these ceremonies, the revolution at Pandeypur was growing fiercer by the day. They had all received their compensation now, although the approval had still not come and Raja Mahendra Kumar had to give all the claimants money from his own pocket, but labourers couldn't be found to pull down these houses. No labourer would come at even double or triple the wages. The authorities called labourers from other parts of the district, but they ran away at night when they saw the situation here. The authorities then gave huge incentives to the government guards and the peons of the tehseel to persuade them to continue the work but when hundreds of young men, many from high families, stood with folded hands and requested, 'Bhaiyyon, for God's sake don't strike with the spades, and if you do have to, strike them first on our necks,' they were all transformed. They didn't return to work from the next day. Vinay and his fellow volunteers were busy these days, leading this satyagraha.

Soordas would sit like a statue at the door of the hut from morning to evening. The havaldar and his sepoys were being prosecuted in the court. Armed police had been summoned from another district for the protection of the site of the incident. These sepoys paced about in the field opposite the hut twenty-four hours of the day, with bayonets mounted. As many as a thousand to two thousand people from the city were present all the time. If somebody left, someone else came to replace him. There was an uninterrupted flow of people coming and going. The volunteers were also ensconced in Nayakram's vacant veranda in case there was a disturbance. Raja sahib and the police superintendent made it a point to come at least twice a day each, but for some reason they wouldn't give orders to pull down the hut. They were not so afraid of an uprising by the public as of the disobedience of the police. All the authorities were terrified because of the havaldar's behaviour. The provincial government was informed daily about the condition here. The government also gave an assurance that a regiment of Gurkhas would soon be sent. The hopes of the authorities now depended entirely on the Gurkhas, whose loyalty to the government they completely trusted. Vinay usually stayed there all day. There was now a naked sword between him and raja sahib. Raja sahib would turn his face away with hatred whenever he saw Vinay. In his eyes Vinay was the sutradhaar, the puppet-master, and Soordas merely the puppet.

As Rani Jahnavi prepared for the wedding and the date of the ceremonies approached, Sophia's heart was filled with an unknown fear, an imperceptible apprehension, an ominous foreboding. She was afraid that perhaps their married life wouldn't be happy for they would both get to know each other's faults. For Vinay, Sophie was an immutable, impeccable, divine goddess accomplished in all the qualities. Sophie didn't have so much faith in Vinay. Her investigations into reality had made her aware of the shortcomings of human character. She had seen the greatest mahatmas, rishis, sages, scholars, yogis and seers, who had conquered themselves with their severe ascetic practices and meditation, slip on the smooth, but scum-covered surface of the world. She knew that though it's very difficult for men with self-restraint to slip, once they do so, they can't recover—their frustrated passions, caged desires, suppressed inclinations flow powerfully in the opposite direction. The man who walks on the ground can rise again if he falls, but who can stop the man who soars in the sky if he falls? There's no hope for him, no solution. Sophia was afraid that she would have to suffer this unpleasant experience and to face that situation. 'Possibly some shortcoming of mine may be revealed, which will make me fall in Vinay's eyes, and he may begin to be disrespectful towards me.' This was the most powerful, the most despairing apprehension. 'Ah! What will my plight be then? There are so many married couples in the world. Would they be satisfied with their first choice if they had the right to choose a second time?'

Sophie was constantly immersed in these doubts. Vinay would come to her frequently; he would want to talk to her, to ask her advice about the situation in Pandeypur, but seeing her indifference, he didn't wish to do anything.

Worry is the root of illness. Sophie would be so obsessed with worry that she wouldn't emerge from her room for days together; she ate very little and often went without food. It was as if a lamp were burning in her heart, but in whom could she confide? She couldn't say a word on this topic to Vinay, for she knew that the result would be disastrous. She didn't know what Vinay would do in a state of despair. Eventually, her delicate sensibility couldn't bear this fire of agony. To begin with, she'd get a headache, gradually there was a violent onset of fever.

But as soon as Sophie fell ill, she couldn't bear to be parted from

Vinay even for a moment. A weak person can fall deeply in love even with his walking stick. We desire affection when we are ill. Sophia, who would earlier seek a hole in which to hide whenever Vinay came to her room, for fear that he would begin to talk about love, and tremble at the desire in his eyes, his sweet smile, and his gentle laughter, like a patient who is afraid when he sees the choicest food before him in case he eats something unwholesome, would now look incessantly at the door, waiting for Vinay. She now didn't want him to go anywhere but to sit with her. Vinay stayed with her most of the time. He left the responsibility of Pandeypur to his companions and became engrossed in taking care of her. Sophie would be very calm when he stayed with her. She would put her weak hand on Vinay's thigh and gaze at his face with childish desire. If she saw Vinay going anywhere, she would be restless and request him to sit down with pleading eyes.

There was now a marked difference in Rani Jahnavi's behaviour too. She couldn't express it clearly, but she would try to stop Vinay from participating in the Pandeypur satyagraha through gestures. Indradutt's murder had made her very apprehensive. She was afraid that the final spectacle of that massacre would be far fiercer than that. And, most important, as soon as the wedding was fixed, Vinay's enthusiasm also began to wane. He now enjoyed sitting with Sophia, talking to her reassuringly and listening to her loving conversation. Sophia's secret pleading had strengthened the surge of his love. We are first human beings and patriots after that. We can't ignore our human desires for the sake of our love for the country. This is unnatural. Grief for the death of one's own son is far greater than a disaster that befalls the country. Personal pain is piercing, national grief disheartening. We weep at our personal grief and worry at national grief.

Vinay was returning one morning after getting medicine from the doctor (despite there being good vaidyas, he had more faith in Western medicine), when kunwar sahib sent for him. Vinay had not gone to see him for several months. He felt a constant resentment. Vinay made Sophie drink the medicine, and then went to meet kunwar sahib who was pacing about in his room. He said as soon as he saw Vinay – You never come now!

Vinay said indifferently – I don't have the time. You also didn't remember me. Perhaps your time is wasted if I come.

Kunwar sahib didn't heed this sarcasm and said – I want to consult you about a dilemma. Sit carefully, you won't be let off soon.

Vinay – Go ahead, I'm listening.

Kunwar sahib said in deep perplexity – The government has given orders that your name from the riyasat . . .

Kunwar sahib began weeping as he said this. After a while, the surge of tenderness subsided a little. He said – I humbly request you to dissociate yourself openly from the society for social service and to advertise this intention in the newspapers. Only you can imagine how ashamed and grieved I am to make this request, but circumstances have made me helpless. I'm not telling you by any means to plead with anybody, to bow your head before anybody, no. I myself have hated this and still do. But accept my request to protect your land and property. I had thought that it would be enough to hand over the riyasat to the government. But the authorities don't think this to be adequate. In these circumstances, I have only two solutions—either you should dissociate yourself from these movements on your own or at least not play a prominent role in them, or I should give a declaration disinheriting you from the riyasat. It's supremely important that this property should be protected for future children. The second solution is as difficult for me as the first is for you. What's your decision on this issue?

Vinay said haughtily – I don't want to make property the chain binding my feet. There's no need for any condition if the property is ours. It's not property if it is somebody else's and your right is subservient to his favours. Property is not necessary for genuine esteem and respect, sacrifice and service are enough for that.

Bharat Singh – Beta, I'm not discussing property with you right now, I only want to see it from a practical point of view. I agree that to some extent property is an obstacle in the way of our actual independence, but there's also a brighter side to it—freedom from the cares of a livelihood and that position of respect and esteem which requires extraordinary sacrifice and service to attain, but which can be obtained here on its own without any effort. All I want from you is that you shouldn't have any visible association with this society, you can help it as much as you like unobtrusively. Just protect yourself from the clutches of the law.

Vinay – That's to say I should even read the newspapers secretively, with the door shut so that nobody gets an inkling. Any work that needs to be carried out behind a curtain, no matter how sacred its goal, is insulting. In more explicit words, I don't object even to call it theft. This life of mistrust and suspicion ridicules man's highest qualities. That much independence is essential for me in word and action which can protect our self-respect. I can't express my views more frankly on this issue.

Kunwar sahib looked tearfully at Vinay. There was so much entreaty, humility and anguish in his eyes. Then he said – Consent at least to this much for my sake.

Vinay – I can sacrifice myself at your feet, but I can't kill my independence.

Vinay wanted to leave after saying this when kunwar sahib asked – You probably don't have any money?

Vinay – I'm not worried about money.

Kunwar – Take this with you, for my sake.

He pushed a bundle of notes towards Vinay. Vinay couldn't refuse. He pitied kunwar sahib. When he left the room with the notes, kunwar sahib fell on the chair, tormented with anguish and despair. The world became dark for him.

Vinay's self-respect had incited him to sacrifice the riyasat but now there was a new problem facing him. This was anxiety about a livelihood. He was not particularly worried about the society for social service, the country was responsible for it, and it was not something to be ashamed of to beg for social work. He was convinced that a permanent fund could be collected if efforts were made, but what was to be done about a livelihood? The problem was that a livelihood for him was not merely a question of meeting his daily needs but also one of protecting the traditions of his dynasty. He had not until now realized the gravity of this issue. So far he merely had to wish for something. He was now anxious since he was confronted with this problem in all its clarity. It was possible that even now his parents' love would free him of this anxiety for some time, but the mansion of his life couldn't be built on this weak foundation. And then how could his self-respect tolerate that he should make his parents atone for his love of principles and devotion to ideals? This was nothing but shame, sheer cowardice. He had no right to burden his parents with the responsibility of his life. He didn't mention this meeting even to his mother; he continued to drown and to sink inwardly. And then, he was not worried only about himself; Sophia had also become a part of his life. That's why this issue was all the more inflammatory. 'No doubt Sophie will bear the greatest hardships of life with me, but is it right to give her this severe punishment for the sake of love? Should her love be put through such a difficult test?' He was preoccupied with these worries all day. This problem seemed insoluble to him. The question of a livelihood had not been given the slightest attention in his education. Only a few days earlier, this question didn't have any significance for him. He was used to putting up with difficulties himself and had thought that he would take a lifelong vow of service. But his plans had been transformed because of Sophia. The things that earlier had no value for him now seemed most essential. Love is especially interested in fantasies of luxury. It can't dream of sorrow and poverty. Vinay wanted to keep Sophia like a queen, he wanted to give her all those comforts that had been invented for luxurious living, but circumstances had become such that all these high ambitions were reduced to dust. Only a thorny expanse of troubles and poverty was visible all around. In this mentally agitated state, he would sometimes go to Sophia or to his room, somewhat preoccupied, sad, dejected, lifeless, listless, as if he had returned after losing a high goal. Frightening pieces of news were coming from Pandeypur—the commissioner came today, today the Gurkha regiment arrived, the Gurkhas have begun to pull down the houses today and they beat up those who protested, today the police began to arrest the social workers, ten of them had been caught, twenty have been caught today, orders have been given today to fix barbed wire from the road to Soordas's hut, nobody can go there. Vinay would listen to such news and writhe like a wingless bird.

A week went by like this and Sophie's health began to improve. There was enough strength in her legs so that she could falteringly walk in the garden, she became interested in food, the aura of good health was reflected on her face. Vinay's devoted care had won her over completely. The doubts that used to arise in her mind earlier were allayed. Devoted care had strengthened the bond of love even more. She wanted to express this gratitude not with words but with self-sacrifice. When she saw Vinay dejected, she'd say, 'Why are you so worried about me? I'm not hungry for your prosperity and your property, which won't give me an opportunity to take care of you and will make you unfeeling. I would prefer you to be poor instead.' As she felt better she began to think that people were perhaps maligning her because Vinay didn't go to Pandeypur for her sake. 'He doesn't participate in this battle which is his duty, he has lit the fire and is standing far away watching the spectacle.' But even when these thoughts came to her mind she didn't want Vinay to go to Pandeypur.

Indu came one day to see her. She was very depressed and aloof. She had lost so much faith in her husband that she had not spoken with him for weeks, in fact she didn't hesitate to criticize him openly. He too didn't speak to her. In the course of their conversation, she said to Vinay – The desire to please the authorities destroyed him, love of wealth destroyed pitaji, will love destroy you too? Why, Sophie, you don't release him from prison even for a moment? If this is his plight now what's going to happen after the wedding? He'll then probably be oblivious to the world; he'll just be intoxicated like a bee drinking the nectar of your love.

Sophia was very embarrassed; she couldn't give an answer. Her suspicion was confirmed that she was thought to be the reason for Vinay's apathy. But could it be that Vinay was using her illness as a pretext to dissociate himself from the battle because he wanted to protect his property? This base thought forcibly arose in her mind. She wanted to remove it from her heart, just as we turn our faces away from something contemptible. But it was necessary to remove this accusation from her mind. She said embarrassed, 'I have never stopped him.'

Indu – There are several ways of stopping.

Sophia – All right, then I'm saying this in front of you, I have no objection to his going there, in fact I think it's a matter of pride for both of us. By the grace of God and by Vinay's efforts I'm all right now, and I want to assure him that I'll have no problem if he goes. I'll go myself in a few days.

Indu looked at Vinay emboldened – So, now there's no obstacle for you? All the work will be done systematically if you are there and it's possible that the authorities will soon have to come to an agreement. I don't want anybody else to get the credit for that.

But when Vinay was still not goaded, Sophia was convinced that the reason for this apathy may not be desire for wealth, but it was definitely not love. 'Why is he letting me be ridiculed when he knows that I'm being criticized because of his dissociation? This is an excuse for a drowsy person to remain idle. He had already begun to cry. There's now grit in his eyes. I haven't caught hold of his feet. Now he doesn't even mention Pandeypur, as if nothing is happening there.' She also tried to instigate Vinay to go there, though not directly but indirectly. But he again avoided it. Actually Vinay now felt embarrassed to go after being indifferent all these days. He was afraid that people would ridicule him. 'You hid because you were afraid, why did you let your personal worries become a thorn in the way of your duty? I could have gone with Sophie's consent, she would never have stopped me. Sophie has this one big fault that even if I do something in her interest, she scrutinizes it like a ruthless critic. She herself may not give a straw for her duty because of her love, but I can't move even a jot from my ideal.' Now he realized that it was his weakness, his cowardice and his shirking that had made him hide his face behind Sophie's illness, otherwise his place was in the first rank of soldiers. He wished that something would happen so that he could wipe out this shame and wash this stigma. He hoped that news would come of some severe misfortune from another province so that he could recover his honour there. Sophia now didn't like his proximity to her all the time. When we recover, we don't even touch the stick with whose support we totter during our illness. Even a mother wants her child to go and play for some time. Sophia's heart still didn't want Vinay to stray from her sight, her face would blossom like a flower as soon as she saw him, her eyes would be intoxicated with love, but her discriminating intelligence would immediately remind her of her duty. She wanted to be cruel and not talk to Vinay when he came near her so that he would leave on his own, but this was merely her good intention. She couldn't be so cruel and heartless. She was afraid that he'd be offended. 'He might think that I'm capricious and selfish, that I was the image of love during my illness, and now my tongue aches even if I have to talk to him.' Sophie! Your heart is immersed in love, your mind in glory and fame. And there is a constant conflict between the two.

It was two months since the battle had started. The problem was becoming fiercer by the day. Not satisfied with capturing and arresting the volunteers, the Gurkhas now began to torture them physically, they would insult them and instil fear in them by their inhuman actions. But nobody had the courage to shoot the blind man or to set his hut on fire. They were not afraid of a revolution, the fiercest rebellion couldn't make them afraid, the fear was that of a massacre, they didn't know how many poor people would die, how much turmoil there might be. Even a heart of stone trembles at least once at the thought of carnage.

This matter was being discussed in the whole city, in every alley, in every home. Thousands of citizens arrived there every day, not merely to watch the spectacle but to get a darshan of that hermitage and its blind inhabitant, and to do whatever they could if the occasion arose. The arrest of the social workers fuelled their enthusiasm even more. There seemed to be a wave of self-sacrifice.

It was the third pahar. A man emerged beating a drum and making a proclamation. Vinay sent a servant to find out what was happening. He returned and said – It is sarkar's order that from today nobody from the city should go to Pandeypur, sarkar won't be responsible for the safety of his life.

Vinay (*Anxiously*) – There's going to be a new attack today.

Sophia – It seems like that.

Vinay – Perhaps the government has decided to end this battle.

Sophia – It seems so.

Vinay – There'll be fierce carnage.

Sophia – It's bound to happen.

Suddenly a volunteer came and greeted Vinay and said – The route there has been closed today. Mr Clark has returned from Rajputana as the district magistrate. Mr Senapati has been suspended.

Vinay – Really! Mr Clark has come? When did he come?

Volunteer – He has taken charge today. It is said that the government has especially appointed him for this task.

Vinay – How many men do you have there?

Volunteer – About fifty.

Vinay began to reflect about something. After several minutes, the volunteer asked him – Do you want to give any special orders?

Vinay said, looking down – Don't unnecessarily jump into the fire and stop the public from taking that road as far as possible.

Volunteer – Will you also come?

Vinay (*Somewhat annoyed*) – I'll see.

After the volunteer had left, Vinay was immersed in grief for some time. The problem was whether to go or not to go. He began to debate both sides of the issue. 'What will I do by going? The authorities are sure to do what they want. There's no hope of an agreement now. But it's so shameful that the people of the city are eager to go there and I, who had started this battle, am sitting here, hiding my face. My remaining ensconced here will be a lifelong disgrace for me, my plight will be worse than Mahendra Kumar's. People will think me a coward. It will be the end of my public life in a way.

'But it's quite possible that bullets will be fired today. They are sure to be fired. Who knows what will happen? To whom will Sophia belong? Ah! I have unnecessarily awakened this sentiment in the public. The blind man's hut would have been pulled down and the whole story would have ended there. I planted the flag of satyagraha, I awakened the snake, I poked my finger into the lion's mouth.'

Reproaching himself, he thought – Why have I become such a coward today? Am I afraid of death? I have to die one day. Will the country be bereft if I die? Am I the only steersman? Is there no other mother of heroes in the country?

Sophia kept staring at his face for some time. She got up suddenly and said – I'm going there.

Vinay said, anxious with fear – It's rashness to go there today. Haven't you heard, there's a curfew everywhere?

Sophia – Nobody will stop women.

Vinay caught hold of Sophia's hand and said lovingly and humbly – Dearest, listen to me, don't go today. The signs aren't good. There's going to be some disaster.

Sophia – That's why I want to go. If fear is an obstruction for others, why should it be so for me as well?

Vinay – Clark's coming is unfortunate.

Sophia – That's why I want to go even more. I'm sure that he won't do anything diabolical in my presence. He still has that much decency.

Sophia then went to her room and carefully put her old pistol in her pocket. She had already ordered the gharry to be prepared. It was ready when she came out. She peeped into Vinay's room, he wasn't there. She then stood at the door for some time, some unknown apprehension, some inauspicious premonition made her heart restless. She wanted to return to her room when she saw kunwar sahib coming. Sophie was afraid that he might ask something, so she quickly got on to the gharry and ordered the coachman to drive it fast. But when it had gone some distance she began to wonder where Vinay had gone. 'Has he gone ahead before me, seeing my impatience?' She regretted having unnecessarily insisted on going there. 'Vinay didn't want to go. He has gone because of my insistence. God! Please protect him. Clark is already jealous of him, suppose there's a rebellion? I had thought Vinay to be a shirker. It was so presumptuous of me. This is the second time that I have accused him falsely. Perhaps I still haven't understood him. He's a brave soul. It's my meanness that I often doubt him. His life would have been so untainted, so bright had I not become a thorn in his path. I'm his weakness; I'm the one to have put a stigma on him! I hope to God he hasn't gone there. It's better if he doesn't go. How can I find out if he has gone there or not? Let me go and see.'

She ordered the coachman to drive faster. Vinay had gone to the office and was writing the accounts of the income and expenditure of the society for social service. He was very dejected. There was despair on his face. He would frequently look all around him with anguished anxiety and then write the accounts again. He didn't know whether he would return or not, that's why he thought it important to balance the accounts accurately. After completing the accounts he looked up prayerfully, then he came out, picked up his bicycle and began to ride it fast, looking back at the palace, the garden, and the giant trees with such longing as if he would never see them again, as if this was the last time that he would see them.

After he had gone some distance, he saw Sophia going. Had he met her, perhaps Sophie would have returned with him, but he was obsessed with the desire of reaching before Sophie. As soon as the turning came, he turned his cycle and took a different path. The result was that Sophia had still not arrived when he reached the site of the battle. Vinay saw that hundreds of small gable tents stood in place of the houses that had been pulled down and Gurkhas were pacing all around. There was no scope for anybody to enter. Thousands of people were standing around, like spectators standing in a circle to watch a grand play. In the middle, Soordas's hut was stationary like a stage. Soordas was standing with his stick in front of the hut, like a sutradhaar, waiting to start the play. They were all so absorbed in watching the scene that nobody noticed Vinay. The volunteers had reached the hut at night. Vinay decided to stand there too.

Suddenly somebody behind him caught his hand and pulled him. He was startled, and saw that it was Sophia. The colour had waned from her face. She asked anxiously – When did you come?

Vinay – How could I have left you alone?

Sophia – I'm very frightened. These cannons have been mounted.

Vinay had not seen the cannons. Actually there were three cannons with their mouths facing the hut, as if demons had entered the playground.

Vinay – Perhaps they have decided to end the satyagraha today.

Sophia – I came here unnecessarily. Take me home.

For the first time that day, Sophia experienced the weaker side of love. She had never before been so agitated with fear for Vinay's safety. She knew that Vinay's duty, honour and virtue lay in remaining here. But knowing this, she wanted to take him away. She was not in the least worried about herself. She seemed to have forgotten all about herself.

Vinay – Yes, it's dangerous for you to stay here. I had warned you but you didn't listen.

Sophia wanted to catch hold of Vinay's hand and make him sit on the phaeton when suddenly Indu's car arrived. She got down and going to Sophia, said – Why, Sophie, are you leaving?

Sophia pretended – No, I'm not going, I just want to move back a little.

Indu's arrival had never before seemed so unwelcome to Sophie. Vinay too didn't like it. He said – Why have you come?

Indu – Because your bhai sahib had forbidden me to come through a letter.

Vinay – The situation is very delicate today. Our endurance and courage will be tried severely.

Indu – This is what your bhai sahib wrote in the letter.

Vinay – Look at Clark. He's whipping people so ruthlessly with his hunter. But nobody is willing to move. The public's restraint and endurance have reached a breaking point today. Nobody can tell what's going to happen when.

Vinay realized today how firm and resolute the ordinary public could be. Every individual seemed ready to carry his life in his hands. Meanwhile, Nayakram arrived and seeing Vinay, asked surprised – How have you forgotten your way here today, bhaiyya?

There was such sarcasm, scorn and ridicule in this question that Vinay squirmed. Changing the topic, he said – Clark is so ruthless.

Nayakram removed the towel and showed Vinay his back. There was a blue, bloody line drawn from neck to waist, as if he had been scratched by a pointed nail. Vinay asked – How did you get this wound?

Nayakram – I have just been whipped by his hunter. I'll see to him if I survive today. I was so enraged that I wanted to catch hold of his leg and drag him down, but I was afraid that everybody would be scorched if there's firing. You have stopped coming here. The snare of a woman's attraction is very arduous.

Sophia heard the last sentence of this conversation. She said – Thank God that you were not caught in this snare.

Sophia's innuendo delighted Nayakram. All his anger vanished. He said – Bhaiyya, answer miss sahib. I know the answer but I can't bring myself to tell it. Yes, how?

Vinay – Why, you yourself had decided that you wouldn't go near women; they are very unfaithful. It was on the day that I was going to Udaipur after listening to Sophia's scornful rejection.

Nayakram (*Embarrassed*) – Vaah bhaiyya! You have foisted this on my head!

Vinay – What else can I say? Why should I be embarrassed to tell the truth? It's a problem if they are pleased and a problem if they are angry.

Nayakram – That's it, bhaiyya, you have said what's in my heart. This is exactly how it is. It's the men who are defeated on all sides. It's a problem if they are pleased, and an even bigger problem if they are angry!

Sophia – If women are such a calamity, why do men constantly suffer them? You see them all running after them. Are all the men in the world fools? Does nobody have any intelligence?

Nayakram – Bhaiyya, miss sahib has rolled the stone to me. It's true, if woman is such a big calamity, why are people bewildered by her? Why don't they learn from somebody else's misfortune? Say, bhaiyya, do you have an answer?

Vinay – Of course I have an answer. You are one of those who has learned from my misfortune. There must be so many others like you.

Nayakram (*Laughing*) – Bhaiyya, you have again foisted it on my head. This isn't a proper answer.

Vinay – The proper one is that which you had given as you came, that the snare of a woman's attraction is very arduous.

Human beings are naturally fun-loving. They can think of laughing even in such distress, even those who are about to be hanged have been known to laugh. While this conversation was going on here, Mr Clark reached, galloping on his horse, driving away people and crushing them. His gaze fell on Sophie. It was as if an arrow had pierced him. He took off his hat and said – Is this the same play, or have you started another one?

The sentence was a cruel one, more piercing than a lancet, harder than a stone. Mr Clark had crammed all his disappointment, sorrow, distrust and anger in these few words.

Sophia promptly replied – No, it's absolutely new. Those who were friends then are enemies now.

Clark flared up, understanding the sarcasm. He said – You are being unfair. I haven't deviated from my policy by even a jot.

Sophia – Is it the same thing first to give shelter to somebody and then to raise your sword against him? You have come running from Rajputana to raise your sword on the neck of the same blind man for whom you had opposed the rais, become notorious, and suffered punishment. Are they both the same thing?

Clark – Yes, Miss Sevak. They are both the same thing. We have come here to rule, not to follow our emotions or personal views. We efface our personalities from the moment we get down from the ship. There's only one cherished goal for our justice, our sympathy, our good wishes. Our first and last aim is to rule.

Mr Clark's target was not so much Sophie as Vinay. He was indirectly threatening Vinay. In forthright words, his meaning was that we are not anybody's friends, we have come here to rule, and we'll root out anybody who is an obstacle in our way.

Sophia said – Unjust rule is not rule; it's war.

Clark – You have called a spade a spade. We have some decency. All right, I'll see you again.

He then spurred his horse. Sophia said loudly – No, don't ever come, I don't want to see you.

The sky was getting overcast. It was evening before its time. Clark had just left when Mr Sevak's car arrived. Hundreds of people rushed towards him as soon as he got down. The public is subjugated by rulers; awareness of their power curbs it. It loses its self-restraint where there is no fear of that power. Although Mr Sevak was a receptacle of the the rulers' favours, he was not a ruler himself. John Sevak ran for his life towards the Gurkhas' camp but he stumbled and fell. Mr Clark, who was on his horse, saw him running. When he saw him fall he thought that the public had attacked him. He promptly sent a party of Gurkhas for his protection. The public also got infuriated—mice were ready to fight the cat. Soordas had been standing quietly until now. When he heard this tumult, he was afraid and said to Bhairo, who didn't leave him even for a moment, 'Bhaiyya, just lift me on to your shoulder, let me try and persuade the people once more. Why don't they go away from here? I have said this hundreds of times; nobody listens. If there's firing there'll be an even bigger massacre today than there was the other day.'

Bhairo lifted Soordas on to his shoulder. Soordas's head became the span of a hand higher in this crowd of people. People rushed from different directions to hear him speak. Worship of heroes is a natural characteristic of the public. It seemed as if a blind Greek god was standing in the midst of his devotees.

Soordas looked at the crowd with his lustreless eyes and said – Bhaiyyon, go to your homes. I'm requesting you with folded hands to go home. Where's the point of assembling here and annoying the authorities? If death comes to me, you people will just remain standing and I'll die. If death doesn't come to me, I'll escape, protecting myself from the mouths of the cannons. Actually you people haven't come to help me but to show your enmity. You have turned the thoughts of mercy and dharma that would have come to the minds of the authorities, of the army, of the police, into anger by assembling here.

I would have shown the authorities how a meek, blind man can turn back the army, stop the mouth of the cannon, bend the edge of the sword. I wanted to fight on the strength of dharma . . .

He couldn't say anything after that. When Mr Clark saw him standing and saying something, he thought, 'The blind man is inciting the public to rebel.' He was convinced that as long as this soul was alive, the movement of the bodies wouldn't stop. That's why it was necessary to destroy this soul. If the outlet was stopped, the flow of water would stop as well. He was waiting for an opportunity to transform this conviction into action, but there was always a crowd of people surrounding Soordas, so Clark couldn't find it. He found it when he saw Soordas's raised head. This was the golden chance that could end this battle. He knew what would happen after that. The public would get excited and rain stones, set houses on fire, loot government offices. He had sufficient power to quell these uprisings. The root mantra was removing the blind man from the battlefield—this was the epicentre of life, the source of the movement. He took out his pistol from his pocket and fired it at Soordas. The aim was unerring. The arrow pierced the target. The bullet hit Soordas's shoulder, his head dangled, blood began to flow. Bhairo couldn't hold on to him; he fell on to the ground. Spiritual strength couldn't counteract brute strength.

Sophia saw Mr Clark taking out the pistol from his pocket and aiming at Soordas. When she saw Soordas falling, she understood that the murderer had fulfilled his cherished desire. She was standing on the phaeton; she jumped down and rushed towards the site of the murder, like a mother running after her child when she sees a vehicle approaching him. Vinay ran after her to stop her, he kept saying, 'Sophie! For God's sake, don't go there, have pity on me. Look, the Gurkhas are getting their rifles ready. Hai! You won't listen.' He caught hold of her hand and pulled her towards himself. But Sophia freed it with a jerk and began to run again. She couldn't think of anything else, she was not afraid of bullets or of bayonets. People automatically moved back from her path as she ran. There was a wall of Gurkhas in front, but they also moved back when they saw Sophia. Mr Clark had given strict instructions beforehand that no soldier should harass women. Vinay couldn't penetrate this wall. The fluid object could go through the gap, but not the solid one.

When Sophia reached there, she saw that blood was flowing from Soordas's shoulder, his limbs had become inert, his face had become colourless, but his eyes were open, and the light of complete peace, content, and calm emanated from them, there was forgiveness in them and no sign of anger. Sophia immediately took out her handkerchief and stopped the flow of blood. She said in a trembling voice, 'He should be sent to the hospital. There's life in him yet, it's possible that he may be saved.' Bhairo picked him up in his lap. Sophia brought him to her gharry, made him lie down on it, sat on it herself, and ordered the coachman to go to the hospital.

The public was frenzied with despair and anger. 'We will also sacrifice ourselves here.' Nobody was conscious enough to realize that they would be harming themselves and not anyone else by this sacrifice. When the child is fractious, he knows that his mother will protect him. There was no mother here to protect these fractious beings. But the door of reflection is shut in anger. The boundless ocean of that crowd of people swelled towards the Gurkhas. The volunteers nervously ran helter-skelter, but their persuasion had no effect on anybody. People ran around collecting bricks, pebbles and stones. How could there be a shortage of rubble in ruins? Soon there were heaps of stones at several places.

Vinay realized that there would soon be a disaster. Several lives would be in danger in a moment. He promptly climbed a fallen wall and said – Friends, this is not an occasion for anger or for revenge, it's an occasion to enjoy and to celebrate the victory of truth.

One man said – Arey! This is Kunwar Vinay Singh.

A second – It really is an occasion to enjoy, so go and celebrate, congratulations on your wedding.

A third – You have come here to weep over the corpses after the field has been cleared. Go! Enjoy yourself in the bedroom. Why are you taking this trouble?

Vinay – Yes, it's an occasion to celebrate because even now there's so much extraordinary spiritual strength in our fallen, downtrodden, afflicted country that a helpless, maimed, blind beggar can confront the powerful authorities with such heroism.

One man sarcastically said – Rajas and rais can't do what a helpless blind man can.

A second – Go and sleep in your palace. It's getting late. Let us unfortunate beings die.

A third – What reward will you get from sarkar?

A fourth – It was you who had taken the durbar's side in Rajputana and had thrown the public into the fire.

Vinay – Bhaiyyon! There'll be time enough to criticize me. Although I couldn't support you here for some special reasons, God knows, my sympathy is with you. I wasn't negligent towards you even for a moment.

One man – Yaaron, why are you blabbering here? Let's go and be slaughtered if you have the courage.

A second – This is not the time to give speeches. Today we have to show how heroically we can give our lives for justice.

A third – Go and stand in front of the Gurkhas. Nobody should step back. Make a heap of your corpses here. Leave your families to God.

A fourth – He can't bring himself to go forward and throw a challenge to make the blood of cowards boil. He's trying to make us understand, as if we can't see that the army is standing with loaded rifles and will massacre us in one surge.

A fifth – Bhai, the lives of us poor people are cheap. Had we been sons of the rais, we could have also stood and watched the spectacle from afar.

A sixth – Tell him to go and drown himself in a handful of water. We don't need his sermons. He wants to become a martyr by putting blood on his finger.

These insulting, sarcastic, bitter words pierced Vinay's heart like an arrow. 'Ha, misfortune! This is the result of my lifelong devotion to service, my sacrifice and my restraint! This is the reward for sacrificing all I have at the altar of the service of the country and depriving myself even of rotis! Will the stigma of the riyasat never be effaced from my forehead?' He forgot, 'I have come here to protect the public; the Gurkhas are in front. The moment I move from here there will be a diabolic massacre. My main duty is to stop them till the last moment. It doesn't matter if they have taunted me, insulted me, put a stigma, spoken harsh words. I'm guilty, even if I'm not I should act with restraint.' He forgot all these things. A prudent person acts according to circumstances. He submits where he needs to submit, he is angry where there is need to be angry. He is not happy or unhappy at the thought of honour or dishonour. He constantly has his goal in sight and moves towards it at an uninterrupted and irrepressible pace. But simple, honourable, sincere souls are like clouds that satiate the earth when the wind is favourable but scatter when its force is unfavourable. For the politic person his goal is everything, the soul has no value before it. For honourable people, their strength of character is paramount. They can't tolerate attacks on their character. It is far more important for them to prove their innocence than to attain their goal. Vinay's gentle appearance became resplendent, his eyes blazed. He stopped the path of the public like somebody frenzied and said, 'Do you want to see how the sons of the rais lay down their lives? Look!'

He took out the loaded pistol from his pocket, pointed the barrel at his chest, and by the time people rushed, fell to the ground. The corpse began to writhe. All the cherished desires of the heart ended in a flow of blood. It began to rain simultaneously. As if the souls residing in heaven were raining flowers.

The thread of life is so delicate. Is it not more delicate than a flower that bears the blasts of the wind and doesn't wither? Is it not more delicate than the creepers that bear the gusts of the hard trees and remain clinging to them? Is it not more delicate than the bubbles of water that float on the waves and don't burst? Which other object in the world is so delicate, so unstable, so insubstantial, for whom one innuendo, one harsh word, one precept is cruel, unbearable, wounding? And this is the foundation on which so many grand, magnificent, huge mansions are built!

The public was stunned, as if there was darkness all around. Its rage was transformed into compassion. People came running from all sides to sanctify their eyes by getting Vinay's darshan, to shed a few tears on his corpse. The person who had been a traitor, selfish and lustful, became like a devata, the image of sacrifice, the beloved of the country, the star of the public's eyes. Those who had reached the Gurkhas also turned back. Tears were raining from thousands of grief-stricken eyes and were mingling with the drops from the clouds to satiate the earth. Each heart was torn with grief, each heart was reproaching itself and repenting—Ah! This is the sinful doing of our sarcastic arrows, the piercing shafts of our words. We are his executioners, this murder is on our heads. Hai! He was such a heroic soul, so steadfast, so grave, so progressive, so honourable, so self-respecting, such a sincere worker for the poor, and such a true devotee of justice, who had thought such a big riyasat to be worth a straw, and we vile people have murdered him, we didn't understand him!

One of them said weeping – I hope to Khuda my tongue gets burnt. I was the one who had taunted him by congratulating him on his marriage.

Another said – Friends, sacrifice yourselves on this corpse, annihilate yourselves, fall at his feet and die.

Saying this, he drew his sword from his waist, slit his throat with it and began to writhe there.

A third said, beating his head – His face is so resplendent. Ha! How could I have known that my sarcastic words would become thunderbolts!

A fourth – This wound will always remain green in our hearts, we'll never forget this godly image. How bravely he sacrificed his life, like somebody taking out a paisa and throwing it in front of a beggar. It is only princes who have these qualities. If they know how to live they also know how to die. This is the mark of a rais, that he will sacrifice his life to keep his word.

It was dark and raining heavily. The raindrops would be light at times and then begin to fall heavily again, like somebody crying who takes a breath when he is tired and then begins weeping again. The earth had hidden its face in water, the mother had covered her face with her aanchal and was weeping. There were frequent blasts of broken walls falling, as if somebody was beating his breast, dham-dham. Lightning would crackle from moment to moment, as if the creatures of heaven were shrieking. The tragic news spread all around within moments. Indu was with Mr John Sevak. She fainted and fell down as soon as she heard the news.

A sheet had been stretched over Vinay's corpse. His face still blossomed like a flower in the light of the lamp. The spectators would come, weep, and then stand in the condolence assembly. Some would put garlands of flowers. This is the way heroes die. Desires are not chains around their necks. They are not worried about who will laugh and who will cry after them. They are not afraid about who will manage after them. These are only excuses for those who cling to the world. Heroes are liberated souls. They are free as long as they live, and they are free when they die.

Why should we give importance to this tragic incident? When tears flowed from the eyes of strangers and their hearts sighed, what can be said about the near and dear ones? Nayakram had gone to the hospital with Soordas. He had just returned when he saw this spectacle. He took a deep breath, put his head on Vinay's feet and began to sob inconsolably. When he calmed down a little, he went to give the news to Sophia, who was still at the hospital.

Nayakram ran all the way but when he reached Sophia, his voice was so choked that he couldn't utter a word. He merely looked at her and began to sob. There was a sharp pain in Sophia's heart. Nayakram had just left and had now returned post-haste. There was surely some inauspicious news. She asked, 'What is it, Pandaji?' Her voice too choked as she said this.

Nayakram's sobs became a lament. Sophia ran and held his hand and asked, her voice trembling with frenzy, 'Is Vinay . . .?' As she said this, she left the hospital, overwhelmed by grief, and went to Pandeypur. Nayakram went ahead, showing the lantern. The rain had united water and land. The trees on the roadside, immersed in water, indicated the road. Sophia's grief was transformed into self-mortification. 'Hai! I'm a murderess. Why doesn't a thunderbolt fall from the sky and burn me to cinders? Why doesn't a snake emerge from the earth and bite me? Why doesn't the earth part and swallow me? Hai! Had I not gone there today, he would also not have gone. How did I know that providence was taking me towards total destruction! I was angry with him at heart, I was also suspicious that he was afraid! Ah! All this has happened because of me, I'm the cause of my own devastation! I have destroyed myself with my own hands! Hai! I couldn't attain the ideal of his love.'

Then she thought – Perhaps the news is false. He may have been hurt and has lost consciousness. Ah! If only I could sanctify my heart once with the nectar of his words! No, no, he is alive, God can't commit such an atrocity on me. I have never hurt anybody; I have never distrusted Him so why would He give me such a dire punishment!

A deep dread overcame Sophia as she reached the battlefield. She sat down on a milestone by the roadside. 'How can I go there? How will I see him, how will I touch him?' The picture of his death was painted before her eyes; his dead body was lying on the earth wrapped in blood and dust! She had seen him well and alive. How could she see him in this decrepit state? She felt a powerful desire to fall at his feet and give up her life as soon as she reached there. 'What happiness can there be for me now in the world? Hai! How will I bear this cruel bereavement? I have destroyed my life, I have sacrificed such a jewel of a man to the diabolic cruelty of dharma.'

Although she knew that Vinay had died, she still had the mistaken hope that perhaps he had only fainted. She suddenly saw a car coming from behind, piercing the water. In that bright light the parted waters seemed as if they were being attacked from both sides by aquatic creatures. The car came close and stopped. It was Rani Jahnavi. When she saw Sophia she said, 'Beti, why are you sitting here? Come with me. Couldn't you get a gharry?'

Sophia screamed and clung to the rani. But there were no tears in the rani's eyes, no sign of grief on her face. Her eyes were intoxicated with pride; there was an aura of victory on her face. Embracing Sophia she said – Why are you crying, beti? For Vinay? Tears are not shed at the death of heroes, ragas of festivity are sung. If I had diamonds and jewels, I would have offered them on his body. I'm not grieved at his death. I would have been grieved if he had saved his life and escaped. This was my lifelong ambition, a very old one. From the time when I was young and had read the stories of self-sacrifice made by heroic Rajputs and Rajputanis, this desire had germinated that God should give me also a son who would play with death like those heroes, who would sacrifice his life for the country and for the welfare of the community, who would bring glory to his dynasty. That desire has been fulfilled. Today I'm the mother of a brave son. Why are you crying? This will grieve his soul. You have read the sacred texts. Does man ever die? The atma is immortal. Even Parmatma can't destroy it. Death is only an indication of rebirth, the path to a higher life. Vinay will again come to the world, his fame will spread even more widely. What kind of a death is it when the family cries? That's just rubbing the heels. A heroic death is that when strangers cry and the family celebrates. A glorious death is far superior to a glorious life. There's the apprehension of a base death in a glorious life, how can there be this fear in a glorious death? No creature is glorious unless his death is also glorious. Look, we have reached. There's such catastrophic rain, such dense darkness! In spite of that thousands of people are raining tears on his corpse—is this an occasion to weep?

The car stopped. People dispersed when they saw Sophia and Jahnavi. Indu ran and clung to her mother. Tears fell from thousands of eyes. Jahnavi took Vinay's head in her lap, embraced and kissed him, and said, looking proudly at the condolence assembly – This youth, who sacrificed his life for Vinay, is greater than Vinay. What did you say? He's a Musalman! In the field of action there's no difference between Hindu and Musalman, they are both in the same boat, if they drown, they will both drown; if they are saved, they will both be saved. I'll build a mazaar for this brave soul here. Who will dig and throw away the mazaar of a martyr, who can be so base and vile? He was a true martyr. Why are you people crying? For Vinay? There are so many young men among you, so many people with families. I'll say to the youth – Go and learn how to sacrifice your lives like Vinay. The world is not just a place for filling one's belly. The eyes of the country are on you; you have to liberate it. Don't get trapped in the snare of domesticity until you can do some good for the country. See how Vinay is laughing! I remember the time when he was a child. This is how he used to laugh. I never saw him crying. It's such an extraordinary smile. Did he give his life for wealth? His home was filled with wealth, he never so much as looked at it. He didn't sleep on a bed for years, he didn't wear shoes, he didn't eat his fill. Just look at the calluses on his feet. He was an ascetic, a sadhu, you people should also become such sadhus. I request those with families, don't make your dear children bullocks at the grindstone, don't make them slaves of domesticity. Give them such an education that they'll live not as the slaves of life, but as its masters. This is the education that this brave soul has given you. Do you know that he was about to get married? This sweet child was about to be his bride. Has anybody ever seen such enviable beauty, such ethereal loveliness? Ranis could draw water in front of her! No pandit can open his mouth in front of her when it comes to knowledge. Saraswati resides on her tongue, she's the light of the house. Ask her how much Vinay loved her. But what happened? When the occasion arose he broke the bond of love like a weak thread, he didn't let it become a stigma on his face, he didn't sacrifice his ideals for it. Dear ones! Don't sacrifice your youth, your souls, your ambitions for the sake of your bellies. Indu beti, why are you crying? Who else has such a brother?

A fire had been blazing within Indu for a long time. She thought that her husband was the root cause of all these troubles. The fire had been in her heart so far; it erupted now. She was not aware of what she was saying in the presence of all these people, she shut her eyes to propriety and said – Mataji, the stigma of this murder is on my head. I won't see that person's face now, who succeeded in taking my brave brother's life, and that too only for his self-interest.

Rani Jahnavi said sharply – Are you talking about Mahendra? I'll throttle you if you ever talk like that in my presence again. Will you make him your slave? You are a woman and you don't want anybody to hold your hand. Being a man, why wouldn't he want that as well? Why should he look at the world only through your eyes, hasn't God given him eyes? Why should he make you the accountant of his profit and loss, hasn't God given him intelligence? In your opinion, in my opinion, in the opinion of all those who are standing here, the path on which we are walking is a good one; he thinks that it is dangerous, full of beasts of prey. Why take offence at it? If you don't like his ways, try to like them. He's your husband, there's no better path for you than to serve him.

It was 10 p.m. People were waiting for Kunwar Bharat Singh. When the clock sounded 10 p.m., Rani Jahnavi said – Don't wait for him, he won't come, and he can't come. He is one of those fathers who lives for his son, dies for his son, and makes plans for his son. There must be darkness in his eyes, the whole world must be desolate for him, he must be lying unconscious. It's possible that his life has ended. His dharma, his karma, his life, his death, his religion, his world, they all depended on this jewel of a son. He has nothing to support him now, there's no aim, no meaning in his life. He will never come; he can't come. Come, let me perform my last duty for Vinay; I had rocked him in the cradle with these hands; let me now make him lie down on the pyre with them. I used to make him eat with these hands; let me make him drink Gangajal with them.

44

IT WAS NINE O'CLOCK THE NEXT MORNING WHEN THEY RETURNED from the Ganga. A crowd of thousands of people, narrow, slushy alleys, flowers raining at every step, the patriotic music of the society for social service—it was morning by the time they reached the Ganga. While returning, Jahnavi said – Come, let's go and see Soordas, we don't know if he's dead or alive; I hear that the wound was very deep.

When Sophia and Jahnavi reached the hospital, they saw Soordas lying on a cot in the veranda. Bhairo was standing at the foot of the bed and Subhagi was sitting by the pillow, fanning him with a pankha. Jahnavi asked the doctor – How is he? Is there any hope of his surviving?

The doctor said, 'Any other man would have been dead by now if he had received this wound. His tolerance is amazing. We have to give chloroform to the other men when we use the lancet, we had to make an incision that was two inches deep and two inches wide on his shoulder, but he refused the chloroform. The bullet has been removed, but we don't know if he'll survive.' One night's terrible grief had wasted away Sophia so much that it was difficult to recognize her, as if a flower had withered. Her pace slow, her face sad, her eyes dimmed, as if she was wandering about not in the existent world but in that of reflection. Her eyes had wept as much as they could, now each pore was weeping. She went to Soordas and asked, 'Soordas, how are you feeling? Rani Jahnavi has come.'

Soordas – What good fortune! I'm well.

Jahnavi – Is there a lot of pain?

Soordas – There's no pain. I fell down playing and am hurt, I'll get well. What's happened there? Has the hut been saved or not?

Sophia – It hasn't gone yet, but perhaps it won't remain any longer. We have come after entrusting Vinay to Ganga's lap.

Soordas said feebly – It's God's will; this is the dharma of heroes. The true hero is the one who gives his life for the poor.

585

Jahnavi – You are a sadhu. Tell God that Vinay should be reborn in this country.

Soordas – That's how it will be, mataji, that's how it will be. Great men will now be born only in our country. Devatas go wherever there is injustice and unrighteousness. Their samskara pull them there. My heart says that a mahatma will soon be born in this country . . .!

The doctor came and said – Raniji, I deeply regret to have to tell you not to talk to Soordas, otherwise his condition will deteriorate because of the strain. The most important consideration in such a situation is that the patient shouldn't become weak.

As soon as the patients and the staff came to know that Vinay Singh's mataji had come, all of them gathered for her darshan. Many of them smeared their foreheads with the dust of her feet. Jahnavi's heart swelled with pride when she saw this esteem. She was about to leave after cheerfully giving her blessings to everybody when Sophia said – Mataji, if you give me permission I'll stay here. Soordas's condition is worrying. The philosophical wisdom in his conversation is a premonition of death. I have never heard him speak with such spiritual wisdom when he was conscious.

The rani embraced Sophia and gladly gave her permission. Actually Sophia didn't want to return to Seva Bhavan. Each thing there, the flowers and the leaves, even the air, would remind her of Vinay. She was tormented at the very thought of living without Vinay in the palace where she had lived with him. After the rani left, Sophia took a morha and sat next to Soordas's bed. Soordas's eyes were shut, but there was a captivating peace on his face. Sophia realized today that real beauty is peace of mind.

Sophia sat there the whole day. Without water and food, disconsolate, she was dreaming of happy memories, and when her eyes filled with tears, she would go aside and wipe them with her handkerchief. The most piercing pain for her now was that she had not fulfilled any of Vinay's desires, she had not satisfied any of his wishes, she had deprived him. The memory of his love twisted her heart and tormented her.

It was evening. Sophia was sitting before the lamp narrating the Lord Messiah's life to Soordas. Soordas was so engrossed as if he was in no pain whatsoever. Suddenly Raja Mahendra Kumar arrived and held out his hand to Sophia. Sophia remained sitting. She didn't attempt to shake raja sahib's hand.

Soordas asked – Who is it, miss sahib?

Sophia said – It's Raja Mahendra Kumar.

Soordas wanted to get up respectfully, but Sophia made him lie down and said – Don't move, or the wound will reopen. Keep lying down comfortably.

Soordas – Raja sahib has come. Shouldn't I give him even this much respect? I have been so fortunate. Is there something on which to sit down?

Sophia – Yes, he has sat down on a chair.

Raja sahib asked – Soordas, how are you?

Soordas – It's God's mercy.

Raja sahib was embarrassed to utter the sentiments that he had come to express in front of Sophia. He sat silently for a while and said eventually – Soordas, I have come to ask your forgiveness for my mistakes. Had it been in my power, I would have exchanged my life for yours today.

Soordas – Sarkar, don't talk like that. You are a raja, I'm a beggar. Whatever you did was for the welfare of others. Whatever I did was because I thought it was my dharma. You have become notorious because of me, so many houses have been destroyed, even two jewels like Indradutt and Kunwar Vinay Singh have lost their lives. But what power do we have? We only play the game, victory and defeat are in God's hands. He does what he thinks is right; the motives should be right, that's all.

Raja – Soordas, who looks at motives? I have always been concerned about the welfare of the public, but today there's not a single individual in the city who doesn't think me to be debased, low, selfish, unrighteous, sinful. Let alone others, even my wife hates me. How can one not feel detached by such things? How can one not hate the world? I can't show my face anywhere now.

Soordas – Don't worry about that. Loss, profit, life, death, honour, dishonour—all are in the hands of destiny, we have been created only to play in the field. All the players play their best, they all want to win but only one of them can, so should those who are defeated lose courage? They play again, lose again, and then play again. They will win sometime or the other. Those who think that you are bad today will bow their heads before you tomorrow. Yes, the motives should be right. Won't the families of those who have lost their lives because of me think that I'm bad? Such precious people like Indradutt and Kunwar Vinay Singh, who would have done so much good for the world, have left it. Honour and dishonour are in God's hands, what power do we have here?

Raja – Ah Soordas! You don't know how distressed I am. If there are a few who think that you are bad, there are innumerable people to sing your praises, even the authorities talk about your determination and restraint. I have lost on both sides. I'm thought to be a traitor to the public as well as to the government. The authorities are foisting the crime of this entire disaster on my head. They think that I'm incapable, short-sighted and selfish. All I want to do now is to blacken my face and go away somewhere.

Soordas – No, no, raja sahib, to despair is against the dharma of players. If there's defeat today, there'll be victory some other time.

Raja – I can't believe that I will ever be respected again. Miss Sevak, you must be laughing at my weakness, but I'm very distressed.

Sophia (*Sceptically*) – The public is very forgiving. Perhaps it will respect you again if you can convince it even now that you regret this disaster.

Before the raja could reply, Soordas said – Sarkar, honour and dishonour don't come by many people making a din. True honour is within one's heart. If my heart tells me that I have done what I should have, and that it wasn't right for me to have done anything else, that's honour. If you are distressed by this slaughter, it's your dharma that you should write to laat sahib about it. If he doesn't listen, go to a higher officer, and don't rest until sarkar gives justice to the public. But if you think that what you did was your dharma, and that you didn't do anything out of greed for your self-interest, you shouldn't regret it at all.

Sophia looked down at the floor and said – It's difficult for those who side with the rulers to prove that they are free of self-interest.

Raja – Miss Sevak, I assure you most sincerely that I didn't side with the authorities to win their respect and esteem and I have never coveted a position. I myself don't know what it was that drew me to the government. Perhaps it was fear of some misfortune, or just flattery, but I had no self-interest. Perhaps I was afraid of that society's criticism, its devious aspersions and ridicule. I myself can't decide. I had believed that I could do much more for the welfare of the public by being in the good books of the government than by opposing it. But I have realized today that there's much greater fear of harm from it than hope of benefit. The path to glory and fame is the one that Soordas has taken. Soordas, give me your blessings that God will give me the courage to follow the path of truth.

Clouds were hovering in the sky. Soordas was fast asleep. He was tired after all this conversation. Subhagi brought a piece of matting and spreading it, lay down at the foot of Soordas's bed. The hospital staff left. There was silence everywhere.

Sophia was waiting for the gharry – 'It must be 10 p.m. Raniji has perhaps forgotten to send the gharry. She had promised to send it in the evening. How will I go? What's the harm? I'll stay here. What will I do there except cry? Ah! I have destroyed Vinay. He vacillated from the path of duty twice because of me, he lost his life because of me. I'll now crave to see his captivating image. I know that we'll meet again, but I don't know when.' She remembered the days in the village of the Bhils when she used to wait for him at the door at this very time, and he would come, wrapped in his blanket, bareheaded, barefoot, with a stick in his hands, and ask smiling, 'I'm not late, am I?' She remembered the day when Vinay had looked at her with ardent but despairing eyes when he left for Rajputana. Ah! She remembered the day when raniji had looked at him sharply for gazing at her, and he had bowed his head and had gone out. Sophie was overcome with grief. Just as gusts of wind stir the dust that has settled on the earth, this silent night had awakened her memories; her heart was full of them. She became restless, and getting up from the chair, began to walk. She didn't know what she wanted. 'Let me fly away somewhere, let me die, to what extent can I console myself, to what extent can I restrain myself? Now I won't console myself, I'll cry, I'll suffer to my heart's content! He who used to give his life for me should leave the world, and I should console myself that it's no use crying now! I will weep, I'll weep so much that my eyes will burst, blood from my heart will flow through them, my voice will choke. What will I do with my eyes now? What will they look upon with gratitude? What's the use of my heart's blood flowing?

Meanwhile, there was the sound of somebody's presence. Mitthua and Bhairo both came to the veranda. Mitthua said salaam to Sophie and and stood by Soordas's bed. Soordas asked startled – Who's there? Bhairo?

Mitthua – Dada, it's me.

Soordas – It's good that you have come, beta, I have now met you. Why have you taken so long?

Mitthua – What could I do, dada? I kept asking burra babu for leave since the evening, but he would give me one task after another. I saw off Down number three, then Up number one, then the parcel train arrived, I got it loaded, I've been able to come now after seeing off Down number thirty. I was better off as a coolie, I could come whenever I liked, there was nobody to stop me. I don't have time now to bathe and to eat; the babus keep making me run hither and thither. They don't have the means to keep a servant, so they get their work done for free.

Soordas – You wouldn't have come even now had I not sent for you. You don't even care that he's a blind man, I don't know how he is, let me go and find out. I've called you so that if I die you should perform my last rites, give pinda-daan with your own hands, give a feast to the community, and go to Gaya if possible. Say, will you do this much?

Bhairo – Bhaiyya, don't worry about this, your last rites will be performed with such pomp and splendour that there'll be nothing like it in the community.

Soordas – I'll get a name if it's done with pomp and splendour, but it's only what Mitthua gives that will reach me.

Mitthua – Dada, you can search me if I have even a dhela. I don't have enough to eat, what can I save?

Soordas – Arey, so you won't even perform my last rites?

Mitthua – How can I, dada, if I don't have anything?

Soordas – So you have taken away even this support. I'm not fated to gain from your earnings either when I was alive or after I'm dead.

Mitthua – Dada, now don't force me to speak, let the curtain remain. You are dying after ruining me and, on top of that, you are telling me to perform your last rites, to go to Gaya and Paraag. Did we have ten bighas of ancestral land or not? Did you get compensation worth at least two paise, four paise, for it or not? What did I get out of that? Do I have a share in the house or not? Couldn't we have got at least 100 rupees for that house if you hadn't taken on the enmity of the authorities? How did Pandaji manage to wangle 5000 rupees? Is his house worth 5000? I have planted two neem trees with my own hands at the doorway. Were they expensive even at five rupees each? You have reduced me to dust, you haven't left me anywhere. You may be good for the rest of the world, but you have taken the knife to my throat, you have slaughtered me. I also have to get engaged and marry and build a house. From where will I get so much money if I perform the last rites? I don't have any doubt about your earnings, but you wasted some, burnt some, and now you are leaving me without a shelter, there's no place even to sit. I was quiet until now; I was underage. Now even I'm grown up. I'll see how I don't get the compensation for my land. Sahib may be a lakhpati in his own house, but how can he suppress my share? I also have a share in the house. (*Peeping*) Miss sahib is standing at the gate, why doesn't she go home? And why should I be afraid even if she overhears? If sahib gives it in a straightforward way, it's all right or else I'll do what I want. I don't have two lives, but sahib will also realize that snatching somebody's right is not a joke.

Soordas was taken aback. He had never imagined even in his dreams that he would hear such cruel words from Mitthua. He was extremely distressed, especially because all this had been said at a time when he was starving for reassurance and peace, when he had hoped that his own people would sit by him and find a solution for his problems. This is the time when a man wants to hear his praises sung, when his feeble heart craves, like children, for love, esteem, care, to be fondled in somebody's lap. The person whom he had brought up as a son, for whom he had borne so many difficulties, was claiming his rights when his end had come. His eyes filled with tears. He said, 'Beta, I made a mistake in asking you to perform my last rites. Don't do anything. Let me remain without pinda-daan and water; that will be far better than your asking sahib for compensation. I didn't know that you have read so much law, or else I would have kept the accounts for each paisa.

Mitthua – I'll definitely claim my compensation. Let sahib give it, or sarkar, or a black thief, I'm concerned only with my money.

Soordas – Sarkar may perhaps give it, sahib has nothing to do with it.

Mitthua – I'll take it from sahib, let him get it from anybody he wants. If he doesn't get it for me, I'll do whatever I can. Sahib is not a laat. He can't digest my property. Why were you so concerned about him? You must have thought, after all, I don't have a son. So you just sat quietly. I won't remain silent.

Soordas – Mitthu, why are you paining my heart? What didn't I do for that land? I even gave my life for the house. What else could I have done? But just tell me, how will you get the money from sahib? You can't take it from him in the law court. He has money, and the law court belongs to those with money. Even if he loses, he'll ruin you. And then sarkar has taken your land legally. How will you challenge sarkar?

Mitthua – I have studied it all. I'll set fire, the godown will be burnt to ashes. (*Softly*) I know how to make bombs. The factory will be on fire if I plant one bomb. What can anybody do to me?

Soordas – Bhairo, have you heard what he is saying? You try to make him understand.

Bhairo – I've been trying the whole way, he just doesn't listen.

Soordas – Then I'll tell sahib to beware of him.

Mitthua – May you bear the sin of killing a cow if you tell sahib or anybody else about this. If I'm caught, you'll have to bear the sin for it. When you lived you wanted to harm me, do you want to sow thorns after dying? It's a sin to see your face.

Mitthua left, full of anger. Bhairo kept trying to stop him but he wouldn't listen. Soordas was unconscious for half an hour. The wound from this blow was severer than the bullet's. Mitthu's deviousness, the fear of its consequences, his own responsibility, his duty of cautioning sahib, this mountain-like oath, no way of escape, Soordas was lying there fettered on all sides when Mr Sevak arrived. Sophia also accompanied him from the gate. She said from afar, 'Soordas, papa has come to see you.' Actually Mr Sevak hadn't come to see Soordas, he had come to comply with the formality of condoling with Sophia. He didn't get the time all day. He had remembered when he left the mill at 9 p.m. and had gone to Seva Bhavan where he was told that Sophia was at the hospital, so he had turned the gharry in that direction. Sophia was waiting for Rani Jahnavi's gharry. She hadn't thought that papa would come. She began to cry when she saw him. Papa loves me, she had always been convinced of that, and this was a fact. Mr Sevak thought of Sophia a great deal. Although he was preoccupied with his business, he was not unconcerned about her. He was helpless because of his wife, who had full supremacy over him. He was full of tenderness when he saw Sophia crying, he embraced her and comforted her. He constantly regretted having started this factory, which had hounded him like a fatal disease. The peace of the house had been destroyed because of it, the family had been scattered, there was notoriety in the city, all the goods had been destroyed, thousands of rupees had been spent from the house, and there was no hope yet of a profit. Now the mechanics and the coolies were also leaving the work and returning to their homes. And there was a movement against the factory in the city as well as in the province. Prabhu Sevak's leaving the house burnt his heart like a lamp. No one knew Khuda's will.

Mr Sevak narrated his tale of woes to Sophia for half an hour. Finally he said – Sophie, your mama didn't like this relationship, but I had no objection. Who wouldn't think himself to be fortunate to get a son or a son-in-law like Kunwar Vinay Singh? I didn't care in the least about its being against our religion. Religion is there for our protection and welfare. If it can't give peace to the soul and comfort to the body, I would prefer to discard it like an old coat. The sooner we can get rid of the religion that binds the soul, the better it would be. I'll always regret that, explicitly and inexplicitly, I betrayed you. I would never have thought of occupying that village had I been at all aware that this issue would become so fierce and that the consequences would be so disastrous. I had thought that the villagers would oppose a little but would settle down when they were threatened. I didn't know that a battle would resound and that I would be defeated. Why was it, Sophie, that Rani Jahnavi treated me with so much courtesy and humility today? I wanted to send for you outside, but the durbaan informed raniji and she came out immediately. I was sinking with embarrassment and remorse and she was talking and laughing cheerfully. She's very large-hearted. There wasn't a trace of the earlier arrogance. Sophie, who won't grieve at Vinay Singh's untimely death, but his self-sacrifice saved hundreds of lives, otherwise the public was ready to leap into the fire. There would have been a great calamity. Mr Clark shot Soordas, but he was anxious when he saw the attitude of the public, not knowing what would happen. Vinay was a heroic soul, very courageous.

After comforting Sophia, Mr Sevak requested her to return home. Sophia said evasively – Papa, excuse me this time, Soordas's condition is very delicate. The doctor and the staff pay special attention to him if I'm here. Nobody will care about him if I'm not here. Come, just have a look. You'll be surprised at how percipient he is even in this condition and how intelligently he talks. He seems to me to be an angel in a human body.

Sevak – Will he mind if I go and see him?

Sophia – Never, papa, don't even think of it. There's not a whiff of resentment and rancour in his heart.

Soordas was agitated with remorse when both of them went in to see him. Mr Sevak asked – Soordas, how are you feeling?

Soordas – Sahib, salaam. I'm very well. I'm very fortunate. I'll become a great man in my death.

Sevak – No, no, Soordas! Don't talk like this, you'll soon be well.

Soordas (*Laughing*) – What will I do by living? I'll get Baikunth if I die now. Who knows what may happen after that? Just as there's a time for the field to be harvested, there's a time to die. The grain will rot if the field is not harvested when it's ripe; my condition will be the same. I know many people whose fame would have been sung if they had died ten years earlier; but they are being criticized today.

Sevak – You have been harmed a great deal because of me. Forgive me for that.

Soordas – You have not harmed me at all; where was there any enmity between us? You and I played on the boundaries facing each other. You tried your best; I also tried my best. The one who had to win won, and the one who had to lose lost. There's no enmity between players. Even boys are ashamed to cry while playing. There should be no feeling of rancour in a game, no matter if one is hurt or if one dies. I have no complaint against you.

Sevak – Soordas, if I could have understood this axiom, this secret of life, like you, this situation would not have arisen today. I remember you saved my factory from being burnt once. If I had been in your place, perhaps I would have poured more oil on the fire. You are an expert in this battle, Soordas, I'm a mere child in front of you.

According to popular opinion, I have won and you have lost, but I'm unhappy even though I have won, you are happy even though you have lost. Your name is being worshipped; people are burning my effigy. Despite having wealth, respect, esteem, I couldn't fight you in the open. I fought in sarkar's shelter. I deviously attacked you whenever I got the chance. I regret this.

The praises of a man on his deathbed are freely sung even by those whose entire lives have been devoted to incurring his enmity because now there's no apprehension of any harm from him.

Soordas said generously – No sahib, you have not done me any injustice. Deceit is the weapon of the weak. The strong are never base.

Sevak – Yes Soordas, it should be as you say, but it's not. I have never been ethical. I thought the world to be not a playfield but a battlefield, and trickery, deceit, secret attacks, are all used in battle. These are not the days for a dharmayuddha, a battle of righteousness.

Soordas didn't answer. He was debating whether to tell sahib about Mitthua. 'He has put me under a very difficult oath. But the best thing is to tell. The lad is obstinate and depraved, on top of that there's Gheesoo's company, he's sure to do something immoral. I can't be accused of killing just because he's put me under an oath. If he does some mischief, sahib will think that the blind man has continued his enmity even after his death.' He said, 'Sahib, I want to tell you something.'

Sevak – Tell me, you are most welcome.

Soordas briefly narrated Mitthua's unrestrained talk to Mr Sevak and said finally – My only request to you is to keep a sharp eye on him. He's not one to miss the opportunity if he gets it. You will then get angry with him and think of some way of punishing him. I don't want either of these things to happen.

Like other wealthy people, Sevak was very afraid of villains. He said apprehensively – Soordas, I'm very grateful to you because you have warned me. That's the difference between us. I would never have cautioned you like this. Even if I saw your throat being slit by somebody, I would probably not have felt any pity. Butchers can be compassionate as well as cruel. We surpass even the cruel butchers in our rage. (*To Sophia in English*) He's a very truth-loving man. Perhaps the world is not a place for such people to live in. He thinks it's his duty to save me from a hidden enemy. It's his nephew, but he would definitely have cautioned me even if it had been his son.

Sophia – I'm convinced now that education is the creation of the deceitful and nature of the noble.

John Sevak didn't like what she said. Such criticism of education was intolerable for him. He said – Soordas, tell me if I can be of any service.

Soordas – I don't have the courage to say it.

Sevak – No no, say whatever you want to unhesitatingly.

Soordas – Employ Tahir Ali again. His family is in great trouble.

Sevak – I deeply regret that I can't follow your instructions. It's against my principles to support somebody with bad intentions. I'm very sorry that I can't agree to what you say. But this is an important principle of my life, and I can't break it.

Soordas – Compassion is never opposed to principles.

Sevak – I can do this much, I can take care of Tahir Ali's family. But I can't employ him.

Soordas – As you wish. Those poor people should somehow be supported.

While this conversation was going on, Rani Jahnavi's car arrived. The rani alighted and came to Sophia. She said – Beti, forgive me, it's very late. I hope you weren't anxious? I was about to leave the house after giving food to the mendicants when kunwar sahib arrived. There was a wrangle with him during the conversation. I can't understand why human beings are so blinded by wealth in old age. Why, Mr Sevak, what's your experience?

Sevak – I have seen both kinds of characters. If Prabhu thinks that wealth is worth a straw, pitaji likes tea without sugar, plain chapatis, and dim lights. In contrast there's Dr Ganguly, whose income isn't enough for his expenses, and Raja Mahendra Kumar Singh, at whose place accounts are maintained for each dhela.

Talking thus, they reached their cars. Mr Sevak went to his bungalow and Sophia went with the rani to Seva Bhavan.

45

THE GURKHAS WERE STILL CAMPED IN PANDEYPUR. THERE WAS SMOKE all around because of the burning of their cow-dung cakes. The ruins of the basti appeared frightening in that darkness. Even now there would be a crowd of spectators during the day. There was perhaps nobody in the city who had not come here at least once during the last two or three days. This place had now become like a shaheedgaah, a place of martyrs for Muslims, and a tapobhoomi, a sacred grove of asceticism, for Hindus. People would remove their shoes when they visited the spot where Vinay Singh had put an end to the play of his life. Some devotees had also offered gifts of flowers there. The most important relics here were the traces of Soordas's hut.

Heaps of straw were still lying there. People would come and stand for hours and look at the soldiers with anger and contempt. 'These demons have trampled our honour and they are still ensconced here. What do they want to do now?' Bajrangi, Thakurdeen, Nayakram, Jagdhar, spent most of their time wandering around here even now. The memory of one's home can be forgotten only with time. Somebody would come to look for his things that had been lost, somebody to buy stones or wood, and the children were happy looking for traces of their houses. One of them would ask, all right, tell me, where was our house? A second would say, there, where the dog is lying down. A third would say, that was Bechu's house. Can't you see, that guava tree was in his courtyard? The shopkeepers too came here morning and evening and sat for hours with their heads bowed, like family members gathered around a corpse. This was my courtyard, this was my veranda, this was where I used to sit and write my accounts. Arey, my handi of ghee is lying here, the dogs must have licked it or we could have taken it with us. It was a very old handi. Arey! My old hoe is lying here. It has become so huge, swollen in the water. There were a few gentlemen who came to look for the money buried by their ancestors. There hadn't been time for them to dig their houses in the haste. 'Dada died with all his earnings from Bengal buried under his pillow, he never revealed its place. No matter how hot it was, or how many mosquitoes bit him, he would sleep only in his room. Pitaji kept trying to dig it up. He was afraid that there would be a noise. Where's the hurry? It's in the house after all, I'll take it out whenever I want to. That's what I had also thought. How did I know that this calamity would fall, else wouldn't I have dug it up earlier? How can it be found now? The one who is destined to find it will get it.'

It was evening. Nayakram, Bajrangi and some of their friends came and sat down under a tree.

Nayakram – Well, Bajrangi, could you find a house anywhere?

Bajrangi – I didn't find a house, I found stones. How will I pay so much rent if I live in the city? From where will I get the fodder? Where can I find so much space? Yes, I can manage if I too mix water in milk like the others, but how can I do this now when I haven't done it all my life? If I stay in the countryside, I'll have to build a house, I can't get land if I don't give some gift or present to the zamindar. They want 200 rupees for each biswa. I need 1000 rupees to build the house. How can I get so much money? Not even a room can be built with the compensation that has been given. I think I should sell the animals and work as a labourer in the factory. That will be the end of all the problems. The wages are good. How can I keep wandering around finding a shelter?

Jagdhar – That's what I think as well. There'll be a readymade house to live in, I can just stay there. I won't get anything to eat by staying at home. I won't wander around with my basket all day but I'll work as a labourer here.

Thakurdeen – If you people can work as labourers, go ahead. I can starve but I can't work as a labourer. This is work for shudras, trade is the work of the bais.* Why should we be responsible for losing our status? God will give us some shelter after all. Even if somebody tells me to stay here for free now, I won't. The basti becomes the abode of ghosts when it is abandoned. Don't you see, there's so much stillness here? Otherwise this place used to flourish at this time.

---

* Bais: Dialect reference to the vaishya caste.

Nayakram – What do you advise me, Bajrangi? Should I live in the countryside or in the city?

Bajrangi – Bhaiyya, you won't be able to subsist in the countryside. You'll have to move back somewhere. You have to travel to the city every day; it will be so troublesome. And then your pilgrims won't go with you to the countryside. The city was not so far from this place, that's why they all came here.

Nayakram – What's your advice, Jagdhar?

Jagdhar – Bhaiyya, I won't advise you to live in the city. The expenses will rise so much. You have to pay for mud as well as for water. You'll get a small house for forty or fifty rupees. Ten or twenty people stay with you every day. So you'll have to take a big house. The rent for that won't be less than 100 rupees. Where will you keep your cows and buffaloes? Where will you put up the pilgrims? You won't even get land for the compensation that you have received, not to speak of building a house.

Nayakram – Say, bhai Bajrangi, from where will I get 1200 rupees a year for the rent? Will I have to spend all my earnings on the rent?

Bajrangi – You'll have to buy land even in the countryside, you won't get it free. And then you don't know in which village you'll get land. So many of the nearby villages are so full that even a hut can't be built there. There's not even a courtyard at the door. If you do get the land, you'll have to get all the material to build the house from the city. How much will that cost? The wood will cost nine and the expense will be ninety. There'll be so much discomfort if you get a mud house built! It will leak, there'll be slush and maunds of garbage every day, it will have to be plastered every seventh day, who's there to do the plastering in your house? You won't be able to live in a mud house. You'll have to keep a vehicle to travel to the city. That expense won't be less than fifty rupees. You have never lived in a mud house. What do you know about termites, insects, damp? It's a complete mess. You are fond of your recreation. Paan and hemp leaves, saag and vegetables, how will you get them in the countryside? I'll say that even if your expense in the city is double that in the countryside, you should live in the city. You'll also be able to meet us there. After all, I'll have to take milk and curds to the city every day.

Nayakram – Vaah, bahadur, vaah! I'm impressed. Your match was

Bhairo, who else can stand before you? I'm convinced by what you've said. Say, Jagdhar, what do you have to say to this? Otherwise Bajrangi gets the degree. I'm willing to pay 100 rupees for the rent, who's going to take on all these problems?

Jagdhar – Bhaiyya, go to the city if you want to. I'm not fighting with Bajrangi. But the countryside is the countryside, and the city is the city. You can't even get good water in the city. You drink water from the water pipe, you lose your dharma and you don't even get the taste.

Thakurdeen – The blind man was prophetic. He knew that this factory would exile us one day. He lost his life but he didn't give his land. Had we not been tricked by this Kirantey and deserted him, sahib could have beaten his head to death but he wouldn't have succeeded.

Nayakram – There doesn't seem any hope of his surviving now. I went there today. He's in a bad state. They say that he was conscious at night. He talked for a long time with John Sevak and raja sahib, he also talked with Mitthua. They all thought that he would survive now. The Civil Surgeon himself told me that there's no danger to his life. But Soordas kept saying, you can torture me as much as you want, I won't survive. He's not allowed to talk today. Mitthua turned out to be a very bad son. It's his baseness that has taken the blind man's life. His heart was broken, or he would have lived a little longer. Such heroes are seldom found. He was not a man but a devata.

Bajrangi – You are right, bhaiyya, he was not a man but a devata. I haven't seen such a lion of a man anywhere. He didn't care about anybody when it came to the truth, even though he may have been a laat in his own house. I was angry with him because of Gheesoo, but when I think about it now, I realize that Soordas didn't do any injustice. If a villain looks at our bahus and betis with bad intentions, won't we mind it? We'll be thirsty for his blood, we'll behead him if we get a chance. What was wrong if Soorey behaved like this with us? Gheesoo's ways had become depraved. Goodness knows what outrage he would have done had he not been punished.

Thakurdeen – Either his life would have been in danger or somebody else's.

Jagdhar – Chowdhary, you can't be so truthful in the home and the village. The truth should remain hidden if it harms anyone. Everything else about Soorey was good, but this was his fault.

Thakurdeen – Look, Jagdhar, Soordas isn't here, you shouldn't criticize somebody behind his back. Even those who listen commit a sin, let alone the one who criticizes. I don't know what sin I had committed in my previous life, thieves robbed all my savings, I won't commit this sin now.

Bajrangi – Yes, Jagdhar, this isn't right. I have also gone through what you have, but I can't hear ill of Soordas.

Thakurdeen – He wouldn't talk like this if somebody were to stare at his bahu or beti.

Jagdhar – There's a difference between bahu-betis and prostitutes.

Thakurdeen – Now, just keep quiet, Jagdhar. You were the one who used to go around supporting Subhagi, and you are calling her a prostitute today. Don't you feel ashamed?

Nayakram – This is a very bad habit.

Bajrangi – If you spit on the moon, the spit falls on your face.

Jagdhar – Arey, where am I criticizing Soordas? I just utter what's in my heart when it aches. Just think! Of what use is Vidyadhar now? His education has been reduced to dust, hasn't it? Now he won't get a job with sarkar and nor will anybody else employ him. His life has been ruined. Bas, this is my sorrow, that's all, otherwise who else is there like Soordas?

Nayakram – Yes, I agree that his life has been ruined. A truth should not be uttered if it harms somebody. But everything is forgiven Soordas.

Thakurdeen – Soordas hasn't snatched his education, has he?

Jagdhar – Of what use is this education when he can't find work anywhere? It would have been useful somehow had it concerned dharma. Of what use will this education be to us now?

Nayakram – Achcha, tell me, if Soordas dies, will you come and bathe in the Ganga or not?

Jagdhar – Why won't I go and bathe in the Ganga? I'll reach before everybody else. One lends one's shoulder even to the bier of one's enemy; Soordas was not our enemy. When he didn't let off Mitthua, whom he had brought up like his own son, how would others have mattered? Let alone Mitthua, he wouldn't have let off his favourite son.

Nayakram – Come, let's go and see him.

All the four men went to see Soordas.

46

IT WAS 9 P.M. BY THE TIME THE FOUR MEN REACHED THE HOSPITAL. THE sky was asleep but the earth was awake. Bhairo was standing, fanning Soordas with a pankha. Tears fell from his eyes as soon as he saw them. Sophia was sitting on a chair by the pillow looking anxiously at Soordas. Subhagi was kindling the stove so she could warm some milk for Soordas. The faces of all three were pictures of despair. There was the silence all around which is a premonition of death.

Sophia (*Dejectedly*) – Pandaji, it's a night for grief today. His pulse can't be found for minutes together. It may be difficult for him to last the night. The movement of his body has changed.

Bhairo – He has been like this since the afternoon, he doesn't say anything and doesn't recognize anybody.

Sophia – Dr Ganguly must be about to arrive. He had sent a telegram that he was coming. While nobody has any medicine for death, it's possible that Dr Ganguly may be destined to win some glory.

Subhagi – I had called out to him in the evening; he opened his eyes but didn't say anything.

Thakurdeen – He was a very valiant man.

While this conversation was going on, a car arrived and Kunwar Bharat Singh, Dr Ganguly and Rani Jahnavi alighted. Ganguly looked at Soordas and said with a smile of despair – I wouldn't have got his darshan had I been even ten minutes late. The vimaan* has arrived. Why are you heating the milk, bhai, who'll drink it? Yamraj doesn't give time to drink milk.

Sophia (*With simplicity*) – Can't anything be done now, doctor sahib?

Dr Ganguly – A great deal can be done, Miss Sophia! I'll defeat Yamraj. The real lives of such people begin after death, when they are liberated from the samskara of the five elements. Soordas won't die

---

* Vimaan: aerial vehicle of the gods.

right now, he won't die for several days. All of us will die, somebody tomorrow, somebody the day after, but Soordas has become immortal, he has conquered time. His life had been limited by the samaskara of the five elements so far. But now it will be diffused, it will bestow enlightenment to the whole province, to the entire country, it will teach us the ideal of action, of heroism. This is not Soordas's death, Sophie, this is the expansion of the light of his life. This is how I understand it.

Dr Ganguly then took out a bottle from his pocket and poured several drops from it into Soordas's mouth. Its effect was visible immediately. A slight flush spread over his pale face. He opened his eyes, laughed, looked around with a steadfast gaze, and said in a hoarse, artificial, dry voice like that of a gramophone – Bas, bas! Why are you killing me now? You have won, I have lost. This game is in your hands, I couldn't play. You are an experienced player, you don't lose your breath, you unite the players when you play and your zest is enormous. We lose our breath and begin to pant, we don't unite the players to play, we fight with each other, we curse and abuse, we beat and hit, nobody listens to anybody else. You are an expert at playing, we are amateurs. Bas, that's the only difference. Why are you clapping? This is not the dharma of victors. Your dharma is to slap our backs. So what if we have lost? We didn't run away from the field, we didn't cry, we didn't cheat. We'll play again, just give us time to take our breath again, we'll lose again and again and learn how to play from you, and victory will be ours one day, it's sure to be.

Dr Ganguly listened to this unrestrained speech with rapt attention, as if he were listening to Brahma's utterance. Then he said reverentially – He's a very great soul. He has given an extremely beautiful description of our entire personal, social and political life in a few words.

Sophia said to Soordas – Soordas, kunwar sahib and raniji have come. Do you want to say anything?

Soordas (*Ecstatically*) – Haan, haan, haan! There's a lot that I want to say, where are they? Smear the dust of their feet on my forehead, I'll be satiated, no no, make me sit up, remove this bandage, I have finished playing, I don't need any dressing and bandaging. Which rani, Vinay Singh's mother? Kunwar sahib is his father, isn't he? Make me sit up, let me rub my eyes on their feet. My eyes will open. Put your hand on my head and bless me, mata, I'll win now. Speak! Vinay Singh and Indradutt are seated on the throne in front and are calling me. Their faces are so radiant. I'm also coming. I couldn't serve you here. I'll serve you there now. Mata and pita, brothers and friends, Soordas's Rama-Rama to all, I'm going now. Forgive whatever was done or ruined.

Rani Jahnavi went forward, and putting her head on Soordas's feet, moved with devotion, began to sob uncontrollably. Soordas's feet were wet with tears. Kunwar sahib covered his eyes with his handkerchief and stood there crying.

Soordas's face darkened again. The effect of the medicine was over. His lips were blue. His limbs were cold. Nayakram ran to get Gangajal. Jagdhar went close to Soordas and said loudly, 'Soordas, I'm Jagdhar, forgive my crime.' His voice choked with emotion as he said this.

Soordas didn't say anything, he folded both his hands, two teardrops ran down his cheeks, and the player departed the field.

The news spread everywhere within a moment. Big and small, rich and poor, women and men, old and young, came in thousands. Bareheaded, barefoot, with small towels around their necks, they all gathered on the field of the hospital. The whole city swelled there. All of them wanted to have a glimpse of this player, in whose defeat too there was the pride of victory. Somebody said he was a siddha, somebody said he was a vali, somebody called him a devata, but in reality he was a player—that player who never lost his honour, never lost courage, never stepped back. He was cheerful when he won and cheerful when he lost; if he lost, he didn't harbour a grudge against the victor, if he won he didn't ridicule the defeated. He was always ethical when he played, never cheated, never hid behind any scheming in order to attack. He was a beggar, maimed, blind, poor, he never got a bellyful of grain, never got clothes to wear on his body, but his heart was a bottomless reserve of fortitude and forgiveness, truth and courage. There was no flesh on his body, but his heart was replete with humility, virtue and compassion.

Yes, he was neither a sadhu, nor a mahatma, nor a devata, nor an angel. He was a small, feeble creature, surrounded with worries and obstacles, with defects as well as virtues. The virtues were few and the defects many. Anger, greed, attachment, pride, his character was full of these defects, but there was only one virtue. However, like those objects that become salt when they enter a salt mine, all these defects assumed the form of godly virtues when they came in contact with that supreme virtue—anger became righteous anger, greed became beatific love, attachment was transformed into moral zeal, and pride into self-respect! And what was that virtue? Love of justice, devotion to truth, philanthropy, compassion, or any other name that you want to give it. He couldn't tolerate injustice; immorality was unbearable for him.

It is futile to discuss the splendour and pomp with which the corpse was taken out. There was no band or music, no elephants and horses, but there was no dearth of eyes that wept and of mouths that sang praises. It was a big gathering. Soordas's biggest victory was that even his enemies didn't harbour enmity against him. If Sophia, Dr Ganguly, Jahnavi, Bharat Singh, Nayakram and Bhairo were present in the condolence meeting, so were Mahendra Kumar, John Sevak, Jagdhar, and even Mr Clark. A funeral pyre of sandalwood was built, on which a victory flag swayed. Who would perform the last rites? Mitthua arrived weeping exactly at that moment. What Soordas couldn't accomplish while alive, he achieved in his death.

This very spectacle of grief had been seen here some days ago at this very place. The only difference was that on that day people's hearts were aching with grief, and today they were replete with the pride of victory. That was the heroic death of a heroic soul, this was the last leela of a player. The rays of the sun fell on the funeral pyre once, there was an aura of pride in them, as if the notes of a victory song were emanating from the sky.

As they were returning, Mr Clark said to Raja Mahendra Kumar – I regret that such a good man was killed by my hands.

Raja sahib said warily – Call it good fortune, not a misfortune.

Clark – No raja sahib, it's a misfortune. We are not afraid of people like you, we are afraid of people like him who rule over the hearts of the public. The penance of ruling is that we have to kill such people in this country whom we would have considered to be godlike in England.

Sophia passed by them at this very moment. She heard this sentence and said – How I wish that these words had come from your inner being!

She moved ahead as she said this. Mr Clark was disconcerted when he heard this innuendo. He moved his horse forward and said – This is the result of the injustice that you did to me.

Sophia had gone ahead. She didn't hear these words.

The sojourners of the vault of the sky, who had emerged from the cover of the clouds, were leaving one by one. Those who had come with the corpse also left one by one. But where was Sophia to go? She was standing in this dilemma when she met Indu. She said – Indu, just stop, I'll also go with you.

47

IT WAS EVENING. THE MILL'S LABOURERS HAD BEEN LET OFF. NOWADAYS, very few labourers came to work even though they were given double the wages. There was dead silence in Pandeypur. Nothing was visible but the debris of houses. Yes, the trees still stood there as they had earlier. That tiny neem tree still indicated a trace of Soordas's house, people had gathered the straw and had taken it away. The ground was being levelled and at some places the lines for laying the foundations of the new houses had also been marked. There was only one small tiled house at the end of the basti that was still inhabited, as if all the other members of the family had died, leaving only a decrepit, disease-afflicted, old man to carry on the name. This is Kulsoom's house which, according to the promise he had given to Soordas, Mr John Sevak has not got demolished. Naseema and Sabir are playing at the door, Tahir Ali is sitting on a broken cot, his head bowed. It seems as if he hasn't had a haircut for months. His body is weak, his face withered, and his eyes protrude. His hair has become salt and pepper. The rigours of prison and worries about his home have broken his back. The passage of time has done the work of years in a few months on him. His own clothes, which had been returned to him after his release from jail, seem like cast-offs. He has come in the morning from Naini Jail and the miserable plight of his home has stunned him so much that he has no desire to get a haircut. His tears don't stop flowing despite his efforts to console himself. Even now his eyes are full of tears. He is constantly angry with Mahir Ali but all he can do is to sigh deeply. He remembers the difficulties that he had cheerfully borne for the family—all those discomforts and sacrifices, all the austerity had become worthless. 'Did I suffer all those hardships for this day? Did I water the tree of the household with my blood for this day? To eat this bitter fruit? After all, why did I go to jail? My income was enough for the maintenance of my wife and children. That household became the cause of my ruin. The wrath of Khuda! This tyranny on me! This calamity on me! I never wore new

607

shoes, for years I made do by patching my clothes, the children would hanker for mithai, my wife didn't have oil for her hair, it was not in her luck to wear bangles, we starved ourselves, let alone clothes and jewellery, the children didn't even get new clothes on Eid, I never had the means to get even a ring of iron made for my wife. Rather, I sold all her jewellery to feed them. This is the result of all that tapasya! And that too in my absence! My children were turned out of the house as if they were a stranger's, my wife had to spend the days weeping, there was no one to dry her tears, and I had embezzled for the sake of this lad? I had spent the amount in my custody for him! Was I dead? If they had kept my wife and children with respect and honour, was I that worthless that I wouldn't have tried to repay the debt of their obligation? Let them not have given milk and ghee to eat, or fine muslin to wear, they could have given dry rotis and coarse clothes, but they could have at least kept my wife and children in the house. They must be eating paan worth several rupees, and here my wife had to subsist by stitching clothes. Even John Sevak is better than them, he didn't allow the house to be pulled down, at least he came to help.

Kulsoom had indeed survived these days by stitching clothes. The women of the countryside would get kurtis stitched for themselves and caps and kurtas for their children. Some of them would give money, others grain. She didn't have any difficulty about food and clothes. Tahir Ali had not been able to provide more comfort even when he was prosperous. The only difference was that she then had her husband's shelter and now she didn't have anybody's. This absence of a shelter had made her misfortune even more unbearable. Desolation becomes more frightening in the darkness.

Tahir Ali was sitting despondently with his head bowed when Kulsoom came to the door and said – It's evening and you still haven't eaten. Come, the food is getting cold.

Tahir gazed at the ruins in front and asked – Does Mahir live in the thana or has he taken a house somewhere else?

Kulsoom – How do I know? He hasn't come here since then even as a formality. He had come one day with sepoys when these houses were being vacated. Naseema and Sabir ran to him crying chacha, chacha, but he rebuked them.

Tahir – Yes, why wouldn't he rebuke them? What are they to him?

Kulsoom – Come and eat a few morsels.

Tahir – Food and water are forbidden for me until I meet Mahir miyaan.

Kulsoom – You can meet him, he's not running away anywhere.

Tahir – I won't be comforted until I can talk to him to my heart's content.

Kulsoom – May Khuda keep him happy, we have managed to subsist somehow. Khuda sent us a livelihood on some pretext or the other. If you remain well, we'll live comfortably again, and better than before. We'll have only two people to feed before eating ourselves. Khuda will give those people the result and punishment for what they have done.

Tahir – Why would we have been in this situation had Khuda been just? He has stopped being just.

Meanwhile, an old woman came with a basket on her head and said – Bahu, I have brought some bhutte for the children. Has your miyaan returned?

Kulsoom went into the room with the old woman. She had stitched some clothes for her. They began to talk about various things.

The dark night came hastening from the east like the waves of a river. Those ruins seemed as frightening as if it were a cemetery. Both Naseema and Sabir came and sat on Tahir's lap.

Naseema – Abba, you won't leave us and go away now?

Sabir – I'll hold on to him if he goes away now. I'll see how he'll go away.

Tahir – I didn't even bring mithai for you.

Naseema – You are our abbajaan. When you weren't here, chacha made us run away from him.

Sabir – Pandaji gave us money . . . Do you remember, Naseema?

Naseema – And Soordas gave us gur to eat when we went to his hut. He used to pick me up in his lap and fondle me.

Sabir – A sahib shot him with a bullet, abba! He's dead.

Naseema – A platoon had come here, abba. We didn't come out of the house because we were so afraid. Isn't it, Sabir?

Sabir – Wouldn't the platoon-valas have taken us away if we had come out?

The children were sitting on their father's lap, chirping away, but he didn't pay attention to them. He was eager to meet Mahir. Now that he had the chance, he left, on the pretext that he would get mithai for the children. When he reached the thana, he was told that darogaji was ensconced in the bungalow with his friends. Tahir went to the bungalow. It was an octagonal straw hut, decorated with creepers and plants. Mahir had got it built to sleep there during the rains and to entertain his friends. There was a breeze on all sides. When Tahir went close to it, he saw that several worthy men were sitting there leaning against bolsters. There was a spittoon in the centre and the pervasive aroma of fragrant tobacco wafted all around. There were paan and ilaichi on a plate. Two chowkidars were standing, fanning them with pankhas. Cards were being played. There would also be merriment in between. Rancour gnawed at Tahir, as if a snake was writhing on his breast. 'These festivities are going on here, the bazaar of pleasure and luxury is brisk, while I don't even have a place to sit, I'm hard up even for rotis. My children could have been provided for with the amount that's being wasted on paan and tobacco.' He began to chew his lips in anger. His blood began to boil. Unabashed, he forced his way into the party of friends and said, crazed with anger and disgust, 'Mahir! Do you recognize who I am? Look carefully. Long hair and torn clothes have not changed me so much that I can't be recognized. Misfortune doesn't change a person's appearance. Friends, perhaps you don't know. I'm this unfaithful, deceitful, debased man's brother. What difficulties didn't I face for him? My Khuda alone knows. I sacrificed my children, my household, my honour for his sake; I did whatever was humanly possible for his mother and his brothers. I took a loan to provide for his needs and for his pleasure and education; I was unfaithful to my master's trust and went to jail. The reward for all those good deeds is that he didn't even ask after my family. He returned from Moradabad on the same day that I was sentenced. I saw him coming on the tonga, tears came to my eyes, I was delighted that my brother would now come and comfort me and take care of the family. But this ungrateful man just went straight on, he didn't even look at me, he turned his face away. After a few days, he came here with his brothers and left my children in that wilderness. There's a party and merrymaking here, and not even a lamp in my dark house there. Had Khuda been just, his wrath would have fallen on his head like lightning. But he has stopped dispensing justice. Ask this tyrant if I deserved this treatment and cruelty, was it for this day that I lived like a fakir? Shame him, blacken his face, spit on him. No, you people are his friends, you won't be able to do justice out of courtesy. I'll have to do it now. Khuda is my witness and so is his own heart that I have not even looked at him harshly until today, I have fed him and remained hungry myself, I have clothed him and remained naked myself. I don't remember when I wore new shoes or got new clothes stitched. I survived on his cast-offs. If Khuda's wrath doesn't fall on such a tyrant, it can only mean that he has stopped being just.

Tahir impetuously expressed his feelings with the velocity of the flow of a stream and before Mahir could respond, or think how to respond, or stop Tahir, he grabbed an inkpot, took out the ink, and tightly clutching Mahir's neck, smeared it on his face, then he bowed three times and salaamed him, and finally said, 'My desires have been fulfilled now, you are dead for me from today and you already think that I'm dead. Bas, this was the only relationship between us. Even that has ended today. I've got the reward and the repayment for all my troubles. Now you have the right to arrest me, to beat me, to humiliate me. I have come here to die, I'm fed up of life, the world is not a place to live in, there's so much deceit, disloyalty, rancour, malice that one can never be happy by staying alive here.'

Mahir sat stunned. But a friend of his said – Even if it's admitted that he was unfaithful . . .

Tahir – What's there to admit, sahib? I'm suffering it, it's not a matter of admitting it.

The friend – I made a mistake. He was definitely unfaithful but you are an old man, and it is indecent to rebuke him in front of the whole gathering and blacken his face.

Another friend – It's not just indecent, it's madness; such a man should be locked up in a mental asylum.

Tahir – I know, I realize that it's indecent but I'm not decent, I'm mad, I'm crazy. Decency has become tears and has streamed down from my eyes. A man can't be decent if his children beg in alleys and shops, if his wife grinds flour in the houses of neighbours to subsist, if there's nobody to ask about his welfare, if he doesn't have a house to live in, if he doesn't have clothes to wear, but that man alone can be decent who has mercilessly reduced me to this abject state. If it's decency to turn your face away from your brother who has returned from prison, then this is also decency. Why miyaan Mahir, why don't you speak? Do you remember, you would wear a new achkan and I would wear it when you cast it off? Do you remember, I used to get your torn shoes mended and wear them? Do you remember, my salary was only twenty-five rupees a month, and I used to send it all to you at Moradabad? Do you remember? Just look at me. The expenses for your tobacco would have been enough to provide for my family. No, you have forgotten everything. All right, forget it all, I'm not your brother and you are not mine. The compensation for all my troubles is this ink on your face. Here, I'm leaving, you'll never see my face again; I won't now seek your shelter on the day of hijaab. I don't have any claim on you.

Tahir then got up and went into the darkness from where he had come, like a gust of wind that comes and goes. Mahir raised his head after a long time. He promptly washed his face with soap and wiped it with a towel. Then he looked at himself in the mirror and said – You people are witnesses, I'll make him pay for this.

One friend – Aji, let it be, he seems crazy to me.

A second friend – What else is he, if not crazy? Is this how sensible people behave?

Mahir – He has always been his wife's slave; she can lead him by his nose. What can I tell you about my family troubles? Even an enemy shouldn't suffer the hardships that my brothers and my mother have suffered at my sister-in-law's hands. There wasn't even a grain to be had unless one cried for it. However, he used to show some consideration to me. He must have thought that I would be his lifelong slave if he made some outward show. How could one exist with such a woman? This hazrat was in jail and she began to starve us. I was empty-handed so I was in great trouble. You can realize that I got this place with a lot of effort or Khuda alone knows what our plight would have been. We would remain hungry day after day while mithai would be brought and eaten there. I had always respected him and this is the reward that he has given. Did you people see? I put up with so much humiliation but I didn't so much as raise my head, I didn't open my mouth, or else I could have given him one push and he would have tumbled head over heels twenty times. Even now he can be imprisoned if I take legal action, but then the world will say that I have humiliated my older brother.

A friend – Let it be, miyaan, these quarrels keep happening in homes. Get rid of the affliction of shameless women, they don't have any respect for men. Come, pick up the cards, we could have played at least one round by now.

Mahir Ali – I swear by Kalaam-e-Shareef, ammajaan gave him 2000 rupees of her own, or else how could this poor man have provided for himself and also managed the expenses of the entire household on twenty-five rupees a month?

A constable – Huzoor, it happens this way in families. Let it be, what's happened has happened. He's older, you are younger, the world will spit on him and praise you.

A friend – He came bounding in like a lion, took out the ink from the inkpot and managed to smear it! It's admirable.

Mahir Ali – Hazrat, don't make my heart burn right now. I swear by Khuda, I'm very upset.

Tahir's pace was not so agitated when he returned. He regretted having unnecessarily lost his dignity. When he returned home, Kulsoom asked – Where had you disappeared? I was tired waiting for you. The children went to sleep crying because abba had left them and had gone away again.

Tahir – I just went to meet Mahir Ali.

Kulsoom – Where was the need for the hurry? You could have met him tomorrow. Wasn't he embarrassed to see you so down and out?

Tahir – I reviled him so much that he won't forget it all his life. He couldn't even open his mouth. I blackened his face in that rage.

Kulsoom, dejected, said – You have acted very foolishly. Does one lose one's self-control like this? You haven't blackened his face, but now ink has been spread over all that you have done throughout your life. You have reduced all your good deeds to dust. What were you thinking of, after all? You were never so full of anger. Couldn't you have restrained yourself by considering that after all he's your brother? If you brought him up, which Hatim's tomb did you kick?* Chhee, chhee! If somebody does a good deed for a stranger, he throws it into

---

* Hatim: Hatim Tai lived in the sixth century CE. He was famous for his legendary generosity, as in the Arabic phrase, 'more generous than Hatim'. He also figures in *The Arabian Nights*.

the river, he doesn't go around collecting a debt. You did what you did to follow the path of Khuda since it was your duty. You didn't give a loan that you should take it back with interest! You are not worthy of showing your face anywhere, nor have you left me worthy of showing mine. The world used to laugh at him until now, even the women from the countryside would curse him. Now people will laugh at you. I don't care whether the world laughs or not. Until now he was guilty in the eyes of Khuda and Rasool,* but you are the one who is guilty now.

Tahir (*Ashamed*) – I have been foolish, but I had gone completely insane.

Kulsoom – He didn't so much as raise his head in front of the entire gathering, and you were still not embarrassed? I'll say that he's much more decent than you, otherwise it wasn't difficult for him to have humiliated you.

Tahir – I'm now afraid that he might take legal action against me.

Kulsoom – He has more humanity than you.

Kulsoom made him feel so ashamed that he wept for a long time. He got up to eat after a great deal of persuasion and then went to sleep.

He remained in his room for three days. His mind wouldn't work; he didn't know where to go, what to do, how to subsist. He went to look for a job on the fourth day but nothing worked out. Suddenly he thought of taking up the occupation of book-binding which he had learnt in jail. He made a firm decision. Kulsoom also liked the idea. 'Even if we get only a little, at least you won't be anybody's slave.' A certificate is needed only for employment; those who have been imprisoned can't find work anywhere. No certificate is needed for those in business; their work is their certificate. Tahir left this house on the fourth day. He took a small house in another muhalla of the city and began the job of book-binding.

The bindings that he makes are very beautiful and strong. There's no dearth of work, he doesn't have time even to look up. He has now employed two or three book-binders and earns two to three rupees by the evening. He had never before been so prosperous.

---

* Rasool: generally understood as the Messenger of Allah.

48

THERE WERE PEOPLE OF DIFFERENT POLITICAL SECTS ON KASHI'S municipal board. From dictatorship to democracy, every view had its followers. Wealth was still predominant; it was the rule of the mahajans and the rais. The followers of democracy were powerless. They didn't have the courage to raise their heads. Raja Mahendra Singh's awe was so powerfully established that nobody could oppose him. But Pandeypur's satyagraha had generated a new unity among the democrats. The entire blame for that disaster was being foisted on to raja sahib. There was a movement to present a resolution of no confidence against him. The movement grew stronger by the day. The democrats decided that the present situation, because of which the public had endured such hardship, should be ended. This was a very trying time for raja sahib. On the one hand, the authorities were dissatisfied with him and, on the other, this opposition group had arisen. He was in a deep dilemma. He decided to retaliate against the authorities with the help of the democrats. His political views had also changed somewhat. He now wanted to administer the municipality by taking the public along, but what could be done now? He tried to stall this resolution. He met prominent democrat leaders and assured them that he wouldn't do anything against their wishes in the future. He also tried to unite his own group. He had always looked down upon the democrats but now he was forced to beseech them. He knew that this resolution was bound to be accepted if it came up before the board. He ran around himself and also made his friends run around to get rid of this problem but all his attempts failed because of the people banished from Pandeypur who wandered around lamenting in the city. People would ask, how can we believe that he won't act so ruthlessly again? Soordas was the jewel of our city, Kunwar Vinay Singh and Indradutt were the jewels of humanity. On whose head is their blood?

Eventually this proposal did come up to the board according to

615

the given procedure. People began gathering on the grounds of the municipal board from the morning. As many as 10,000–20,000 people had collected there by the afternoon. The resolution was presented at 1 p.m. Raja sahib stood up and gave a very moving speech in his own defence; he argued that he had been helpless, anybody else in his place would have acted in the same way in that situation, there had been no other option. His last words were, 'I don't covet position or esteem, I only want to serve you, even more so now because I have to do penance which I can't do without this position, the means of doing it will be taken out of my hands. I'm as much a devotee of Soordas as anybody can be. You people perhaps don't know that I had gone to the hospital and asked his forgiveness and sincerely expressed my regret. It was Soordas's instruction that I should remain firm in my position, otherwise I had already decided to resign. Except his parents, nobody else but I can feel as much grief at Kunwar Vinay Singh's untimely death. He was my brother. His death has given me a wound that cannot be healed all my life. I was also Indradutt's intimate friend. Am I so base, so devious, so mean, so despicable that I would take the knife with my own hands to the throats of my brother and my friend? This allegation is completely unjust, it is like sprinkling salt on my wound. I am innocent before my conscience and before God. I don't want to remind you of my services, they are self-evident. You people know how much time I have spent in your service, how much hard work I have done, how unendingly industrious I have been! I don't want any leniency; I only want justice.'

The speech was very powerful, but it couldn't sway the democrats from their decision. The proposal was accepted in fifteen minutes and raja sahib announced his resignation immediately.

When he emerged from the assembly house, the public, which had not had the opportunity of listening to his speech, made such fun of him and ridiculed him so much that the poor man reached his car with great difficulty. There would definitely have been a riot had the police not been alert. Raja sahib looked back tearfully at the assembly house once and then left. His lifetime's earnings were wasted, all the glory, esteem and fame were washed away in the flow of the public's anger.

When raja sahib returned home, enraged, he saw that Indu and Sophia were both sitting there, talking. As soon as she saw him, Indu said – Miss Sophia is collecting a donation for Soordas's statue. You had also been captivated by his heroism, how much will you give?

Sophia – Indu rani has donated a thousand rupees, and less than double that amount won't become you.

Mahendra Kumar (*Frowning*) – I'll think about it and let you know.

Sophia – When should I come again?

Mahendra Kumar (*Indifferently*) – There's no need for you to come, I'll send it myself.

When Sophia looked at his face, she saw that he was frowning. She got up and left. Then raja sahib said to Indu – Why do you do such things without asking me, which result in my being completely humiliated? I'm tired of making you understand so often. I had to bite the dust today because of that blind man, the board has passed a resolution of no confidence against me today, and you have given a donation for his statue and are telling me also to give it.

Indu – How was I to know what had happened at the board? You had also said that there was no possibility of that resolution being passed.

Raja sahib – You only want to insult me, that's all.

Indu – You were singing Soordas's praises the other day. I thought there was no harm in the donation. I don't know the secret of anybody's heart. Why was the resolution passed after all?

Raja – How do I know? All I know is that it has been passed. Everything doesn't always happen according to one's wishes. The people in whom I had full confidence were the ones who betrayed me when the occasion arose, they didn't come to the board. I'm not so tolerant that I'll worship the person who is responsible for my humiliation. I'll do everything in my power to defeat this movement for a statue. I have already become notorious and I don't care if I become more so. I'll influence the government so much that the statue won't be raised at all. I may no longer have the power to do some good for the country but I do have the power to harm it, and it will increase day by day. You should also take back your donation.

Indu (*Surprised*) – I should take back the money that I have given?

Raja – Yes, there's no harm in it.

Indu – You may not think that there's any harm, but it's **very** humiliating for me.

Raja – It won't be unfair if I don't care about your humiliation just as you don't care about mine.

Indu – I don't ask you for money.

The exchange of words increased, it turned into an altercation and then to ridicule, and in a moment there was an attack of abuses. They both thought that they were in the right, that's why neither of them would submit.

Raja sahib – I don't know when the day will come when I'll be rid of you. Perhaps there's no way out now except death.

Indu – You are welcome to your fame and esteem. God is my master. I'm also fed up of life. To what extent can I be a maidservant? It's the limit now.

Raja – You'll be my maidservant! Those satis are different who give their lives for their husbands. You would give me poison if you had your way, and you are giving it, what can be worse than this?

Indu – Why are you spitting this poison? Why don't you tell me frankly to get out of the house? I know that my staying here irks you. I have known it for several days, not just from today. I realized it the day I gave the maidservant my new sari and you created a Mahabharata. I realized then that this creeper can't flourish. For as long as I lived here you never let me think that this was my home. I wasn't left in peace even if I rendered the account for every paisa. Perhaps you think that I had thought your money to be mine and so spent it as I wanted to, but I swear that I haven't touched a dhela of yours. I have married you; I haven't sold my soul.

Mahendra said, chewing his lips – Let God give every sorrow but not bad company. Let him give death instead if he wants to. It won't be against dharma even to strangle a woman like you. You should be grateful to this rule that you are living here peacefully. Had it been our rule this tongue of yours that wags like scissors would have been pulled out from the palate.

Indu – All right, be quiet now, that's enough. I haven't come here to listen to your abuses. Here, take your house, spread your legs as much as you can and sleep.

Raja – Go, at least take your presence away somehow. The mouse is better off alone if the cat lets it be!

Indu (*Muttering*) – Who is crazy about you here?

Raja (*Enraged*) – You are abusing! I'll pull out your tongue.

Indu had reached the door to leave. She turned back when she heard this threat and said, revolting like a lioness – Don't be complacent. So what if my brother is dead. My father is still there. Not a hair of your head will remain. Why would you have become so notorious in the world if you are so noble?

Indu then returned to her room. She collected whatever she had got from her maika. She separated all the things that belonged here. There was no grief, no sorrow, but a fire that was spreading in her delicate body like poison. Her face, eyes and nose were red, sparks seemed to be flying from every pore. Humiliation is incendiary.

Indu collected all her belongings and ordered her personal gharry to be prepared. Meanwhile, she paced about in the veranda. As soon as she heard the sound of the horses' hooves at the gate, she went and sat down on the gharry, she didn't even turn to look back. The house in which she had been a rani, which she had thought to be hers, where she would be at the servants' heads if there was the least bit of dirt lying around, she left that house like life leaving the body—that body which it had always protected, that body whose slightest pain would make it agitated. She didn't say anything to anybody, nor did anyone have the courage to ask her anything. After she had left, the maharajin said to Mahendra– Sarkar, I don't know where rani bahu is going.

Mahendra looked at her sharply and said – Let her go.

Maharajin – Sarkar, she has taken her boxes and caskets with her.

Mahendra – I've told you, let her go.

Maharajin – Sarkar, she seems to be offended. She couldn't have gone far, you should persuade her.

Mahendra – Don't eat my head.

When Indu reached Seva Bhavan with bag and baggage, Jahnavi said to her – You have fought and come, why?

Indu – Is there a compulsion if somebody won't let you stay in the house?

Jahnavi – Sophia told me as soon as she came that all was not well today.

Indu – I can't live there as a maidservant.

Jahnavi – Why did you give a donation without asking him?

Indu – I haven't sold my soul to anybody.

Jahnavi – The woman who humiliates her husband can't find peace either in this world or the next one.

Indu – Do you want me to go away from here as well? Don't sprinkle salt on my wound.

Jahnavi – You'll regret it. I was tired of trying to make you understand but you didn't give up your obstinacy.

Indu got up and went to Sophia's room. Her mother's words seemed like poison to her.

This dispute entered the political sphere from the matrimonial one. Mahendra Kumar was doing his utmost to oppose this movement; he would prevent people from giving donations and incite the provincial government, while Indu was busy collecting donations with Sophia. Mr Clark was still hostile to raja sahib at heart, he had not forgotten his humiliation; he didn't think it necessary to intervene in this movement, with the result that raja sahib couldn't achieve anything. Donations were briskly being collected. More than one lakh rupees was collected in a month. There was no pressure on anyone; nobody made any recommendations to anyone. This was the miracle performed by the noble efforts of the two women; no, it was the vibhuti, the glory and supernatural power, of the heroism of the martyrs, at whose memories people still wept. People would come and give on their own, more than they could afford. Mr John Sevak also voluntarily gave 1000 rupees, Indu had already donated 1000 rupees of her own; she also gave several precious ornaments, which were sold for 20,000 rupees. A snake writhed on raja sahib's breast. Whereas earlier he had opposed imperceptibly, he now opposed openly. He went to the Governor himself and incited the rais. He did everything he could, but what had to happen, happened.

Six months had passed. Soordas's statue had been built and had arrived. A famous sculptor from Poona had created it as his homage. It was proposed that it should be installed at Pandeypur. John Sevak gladly gave permission. The statue was installed where Soordas's hut had been. What other means does man have to immortalize the fame of the famous? Ashoka's memory too is immortal because of the inscriptions of his pillars. Not all can attain the stature of Valmiki and Vyasa, Homer and Firdausi.

There was a grand ceremony at Pandeypur. The citizens had left their work to participate in this festival. Rani Jahnavi installed the statue with a tender voice and tearful eyes. After that devotional songs were sung for a long time. Then there were powerful speeches by political leaders and wrestlers displayed their feats. There was a feast in the evening, touchable and untouchable both sat in the same row and ate together. This was Soordas's greatest victory. At night, a theatre group performed a play titled 'Soordas', which dramatized his character. Prabhu Sevak had written this play and had sent it from England for this occasion. The festival ended by midnight. People returned to their respective homes. There was silence there after that.

The moonlight was shimmering and, in that gleaming light, Soordas's statue was standing with one hand tapping his stick and the other spread before an invisible donor—the same weak body, ribs protruding, back bent, meekness and simplicity reflected on his face, it seemed to be Soordas incarnate. The only difference was that he had been mobile, but the statue was immobile; he could speak, this was mute; and the sculptor had carved that parental love which had not been evident in the original. It seemed as if a mendicant from heaven were requesting a boon from the gods for the welfare of the world.

Half the night was over. A man came close to the statue on a cycle. There was an instrument in his hand. For a moment, he looked at the statue from head to foot and then struck a blow at it with the same instrument. There was the sound of the cracking of a whip and the statue fell on the ground with a bang on top of the very man who had broken it. He was perhaps about to strike a second blow when the statue fell on him, he couldn't run away, he was buried under it.

People saw in the morning that it was Raja Mahendra Kumar Singh. The news spread in the entire city that raja sahib had broken Soordas's statue and had been crushed under it. As long as he had lived, he had harboured enmity against Soordas, he didn't let go of his hatred even after Soordas's death. Such jealous people also exist! God too promptly gave the fruit for that. As long as he had lived, he had looked below Soordas; even when he died, he was buried below him. Traitor to the country, enemy, hypocrite, impostor, he was discussed with these and even harsher words.

The craftsmen repaired the statue's feet and made it stand again. But the marks of that blow are still there on the feet and the face too has become distorted.

49

WHILE THE DONATION WAS BEING COLLECTED FOR SOORDAS'S statue, preparations were also being made for laying the foundation stone of the coolies' quarter. Eminent men of the city had been invited. The Governor of the province had been requested to lay the foundation stone. A garden party had been planned. The Governor was also to be given a ceremonial address. Mrs Sevak was making the preparations with her heart and soul. The bungalow was being cleaned and decorated and ornamental arched gateways were being put up. An English band had been called. Mr Clark had ordered the official staff to help Mrs Sevak and was himself running around in all directions.

A new hope had germinated in Mrs Sevak's heart now. Perhaps Vinay Singh's death might attract Sophia to Mr Clark; that's why she entertained Mr Clark even more. She had decided to go herself and bring Sophia back. 'I'll bring her back in any way that I can, if she doesn't come cheerfully I'll force her, I'll cry, I'll fall at her feet and won't leave her without bringing her back.'

Mr John Sevak was busy preparing the annual report of the company. He had chosen this occasion to announce the profits of the last year. Although the actual profit was very low, by manipulating the income and expenditure to conform to his wishes, he wanted to show a profit that was beyond expectations so that the value of the company's shares would rise and people would fall over backwards to buy them. He wanted to make up the loss by this strategy. The scribes had to work all night and Mr Sevak himself laboured much more at preparing the accounts than at preparations for the ceremony.

But Mr Ishvar Sevak, who thought that these preparations were a waste of money, didn't like them at all. He would repeatedly be infuriated; the poor old man spent the time from morning to night beating his head. Sometimes he would be enraged with his son, sometimes with his daughter-in-law, sometimes with the staff, sometimes with the servants. 'Where's the need for this five maunds of ice? Will people bathe in it? A maund would have been enough. Even half a maund would have sufficed. Where's the need for so much alcohol? Do you want to make a water channel or to kill the guests by making them drunk? What's the use if people drink so much that they are intoxicated and begin to fight each other with shoes? Burn the house or give me poison; if I'm not alive, I won't be upset. Lord Messiah! Take me in your mantle; there's no end to this disaster, where's the need for the army band? Is the Governor a child that he'll be delighted with the band, or are the rais of the city hungry for bands? What kinds of fireworks will there be? The wrath of Khuda, have they all eaten bhang? Is this a welcome for the Governor or children's play? Who'll be happy with crackers and sparklers? Admittedly there won't be crackers and sparklers, there'll be English fireworks, but hasn't the Governor seen fireworks? What's the use of doing these absurd things? Suppose a poor man's house is burnt and there's an accident, it will create a problem. Where's the need to get fruit and dried fruit, jams and mithai for the Hindustani rais? They are not so greedy. A cigarette each would have been enough for them. Yes, paan-ilaichi could also have been arranged. They won't be coming here for a feast; they'll come to hear the annual report of the company. Arey o khansama, sooar! Don't make me break your head. You only do what that madwoman (Mrs Sevak) tells you to. Do I have any intelligence or not? Do you know that grapes cost four rupees a seer? There's no need for them. Beware if grapes come here!'

The gist of it is that for several days continuously he had been feeling rather unwell because of this constant ranting. Nobody listened to him, they would all do what they wanted. When he was tired raving he would get up and go into the garden. But he would return in a short while, feeling anxious, and begin the war of words again. When John Sevak proposed, a week before the ceremony, that all the servants of the house and the peons of the factory should be given uniforms made by the Elgin Mill, Ishvar Sevak was so infuriated that he beat his head with the Bible that he was apparently reading with the help of his spectacles but actually from memory and said, 'Ya Khuda, take me away from the snare of this world.' His head was close to the wall; it banged against it with the impact of the jolt. Ninety years old, a decrepit body, you can say that though the bones were old, they just about functioned; he fell unconscious. His forehead couldn't survive this blow, his eyes popped out, his lips parted, and by the time people could call the doctor, his life had fled. God had accepted his last request, He had released him from this snare. The cause of his death can't be ascertained decisively—this blow or the conflagration of the house?

When Sophia heard this sad news, she could no longer stand on her pride. If anybody had now loved her at home, it was only Ishvar Sevak. She too respected him. She immediately wore mourning clothes and went home. Mrs Sevak ran to embrace her, and mother and daughter wept copiously by the dead body.

When the mourning feast was over at night and people went home, Mrs Sevak said to Sophia – Beti, you are staying somewhere else when you have your own home, isn't this a matter of shame and sorrow for us? Who else is the master or heir here except you? How can Prabhu be depended upon? He may or may not return. Now you are all that's there. If we have ever said harsh things to you it must have been for your own good. I'm not your enemy. Stay in your home now. There'll be no restriction on your movements, you can also visit rani sahiba, but you shouldn't live there. Khuda has fulfilled all my other desires; I would have been free from worry had you been married. We would have seen about Prabhu when he returns. Such a long mourning is not a short period; it won't be well now to lose time. I want you to get married now and all of us should then go to Mussoorie for two or three months in the summer.

Sophia said – As you wish, I'll do it.

Mrs Sevak – Of course, beti, times don't always remain the same, there's no guarantee of our lives. Your grandfather died with this wish. So should I make preparations?

Sophia – I have already told you.

Mrs Sevak – Your papa will be delighted when he gets to know. I'm not criticizing Kunwar Vinay Singh, he was a very courageous man; but, beti, it's different getting married to somebody of one's own religion.

Sophia – Yes, of course.

Mrs Sevak – So now you won't return to Rani Jahnavi's place?

Sophia – No, I won't.

Mrs Sevak – So should I tell the men to bring your things?

Sophia – Raniji will send them herself tomorrow.

Mrs Sevak cheerfully began to clean the room for the banquet.

Mr Clark was still there. He was given this good news and was elated. He went rushing to Sophia and said – Sophie, you have brought me back to life. Ah! I'm so fortunate! But tell me this once yourself. Will you keep your promise?

Sophia – I will.

There were several other people present, so Mr Clark couldn't embrace Sophia. Twirling his moustache, building castles in the air, eating imaginary sweets, he went home. Sophia couldn't be found in the morning! Enquiries were made. The gardener said, 'I didn't see her going but there was the sound of the gate being opened once when everybody was asleep here.' People thought that she must have gone to Kunwar Bharat Singh's place. A man was sent there immediately. But she couldn't be found there either. There was a great deal of panic, where had she gone?

John Sevak – Was there any quarrel between you at night?

Mrs Sevak – We were talking about the wedding. She even told me to make the preparations. She was happy when she went to sleep.

John Sevak – You misunderstood her. She had made her feelings apparent. She had warned you that she wouldn't be here tomorrow. Do you know what she meant by marriage? Self-sacrifice! She'll now get married to Vinay. What couldn't happen here will now happen in heaven. I had told you earlier that she won't get married to anybody. You scared her by talking about marriage last night. What would have happened a few days later has happened now. Cry as much as you want to now; I have already wept.

Meanwhile, Rani Jahnavi arrived; her eyes were red like beerbahuti with weeping. She gave Mr Sevak a letter and sitting down on a chair, covered her face and wept.

This was Sophia's letter; the postman had just given it. The letter said:

Respected mataji, your Sophia is leaving the world today. For whom should I remain when Vinay is no longer here? I tried to console myself all these days. I thought I would drown the memories of my grief in books and fulfil my life by doing social service. But my beloved Vinay is calling me. He doesn't have a moment's peace there without me. I'm going to meet him. This physical form is an obstacle in my way, that's why I'm leaving it behind. I'm entrusting it to Ganga's lap. My heart is ecstatic, my feet are flying, each pore of my being is delighted with bliss, I'll soon get Vinay's darshan now. Don't grieve for me; don't make futile efforts to find me. Because by the time you get this letter, Sophia's head will be at Vinay's feet. A powerful force is pulling me and the chains are breaking by themselves.

Tell mama and papa, Sophie is married, don't worry about her now.

As soon as the letter ended, Mrs Sevak said violently, like a madwoman – You are the black she-snake, the knot of poison, who has ruined my life, dug my roots with a spade, crushed my desires under your feet, trampled on my honour. You captivated my simple Sophie with your sweet words, your tricks and deception, your secret mantras, and ruined her in the end. It's because of your blandishments and encouragement that I don't know where and in which country my son is today and this has happened to my daughter. You have reduced all my ambitions to dust.

One doesn't know what else she would have said in this wave of anger but John Sevak caught hold of her hand and pulled her away. Rani Jahnavi didn't respond to these bitter, insulting words, she kept looking sympathetically at Mrs Sevak and then got up and left without saying anything.

Frost had fallen on Mrs Sevak's ambitions. From that day onwards, nobody saw her going to church, she was not seen wearing a gown and a hat, she didn't go again to the European club and she didn't participate in English parties. The next morning Father Pym and Mr Clark came to offer their condolences. Mrs Sevak berated them so severely that they left shamefacedly. The gist is that she lost her wits from that day; her mind couldn't bear such a severe blow. She is still alive, but her plight is extremely pitiable. She hates people, she laughs sometimes, or weeps, or dances, or sings. If anybody goes near her she rushes to bite them.

That leaves John Sevak. He is engrossed in his business affairs from
morning to evening with a despairing fortitude. He has no desire left
in the world, no wish, he has a selfless love for wealth, something
of that devotion that devotees have for the object of their worship.
Wealth is not the means to any end for him. It is an end in itself. He
doesn't care if it is day or night. The business is growing day by day.
It is doubtful, though, if the profits are also growing day by day. In
every alley, every shop of the country there is a glut of cigarettes and
cigars from this factory. He is now planning to start a tobacco mill
in Patna because tobacco grows abundantly in the province of Bihar.
His desire for wealth, like the passion for knowledge, is never satiated.

50

Rani Jahnavi's enthusiasm doubled after Kunwar Vinay Singh's heroic death. She became much more active than before. An extraordinary energy suffused every pore of her being. The lethargy of old age was transformed into the vigour of youth. She fortified herself and took over the administration of the society for social service. She left the women's quarters, entered the arena of action and worked with such zeal that the society attained the progress that it had never been able to so far. There had never before been such an abundance of wealth, nor had there been so many volunteers. The sphere of the society's work had also never before been so vast. The rani had donated her personal wealth to the society, to the extent that she didn't keep a single ornament for herself. When she assumed the garb of a tapasvini, she proved how conscientious women could be when the occasion arose.

Dr Ganguly's optimism was also evident in its naked form eventually. He realized that in the present situation optimism was nothing but self-deception. He made a great deal of noise in the Council against Mr Clark but it proved to be like weeping in the wilderness. Months of discussion, the continuous flow of questions, were futile. He couldn't persuade the government to censure Mr Clark. On the contrary, Mr Clark was promoted. Doctor sahib was so infuriated that he couldn't restrain himself. He severely reproached the Governor in the full assembly, to the extent that the chairman of the assembly had to ask him to sit down. He was even more enraged by this and took the chairman to task. He accused him of partisanship. The chairman then ordered him to leave the Assembly House and threatened to call the police. But even this didn't pacify Dr Ganguly's wrath. He said excitedly, 'You want to silence me with brute strength because you don't have the strength of righteousness and justice. Today I have lost the firm conviction that I have had for the last forty years that the government wants to rule us on the strength of justice. The veneer has worn off that strength of justice today, the veil has been lifted from our eyes and we are seeing the government in its naked, unveiled form. We can now clearly see that we are being ruled only to be crushed and to make us sweat, to destroy our identity, to murder our civilization and our humanity, to make us remain as bullocks at the grindstone until infinity. If anybody spoke to me like this until now, I would be ready to fight with him, I would recount the fame of Ripon, Hume and Besant, etc. in an attempt to silence him.* But now it is evident that all of them have the same goal, only the means are different.'

He couldn't speak any more after that. A police sergeant took him away from the Assembly House. The other members of the assembly also got up and left. People were initially afraid that the government would prosecute Dr Ganguly but perhaps the adjudicators had pity on his old age, especially because Dr Ganguly sent his resignation letter on the same day as soon as he reached home.

He left that very day and met Kunwar Bharat Singh on the third

---

* Lord Ripon: Governor General and Viceroy of India from 1880 to 1884. A radical Liberal, he introduced several measures such as local self-government to ensure popular participation. He set up the Indian Education Commission (1882) headed by W.W. Hunter for looking into the problems of primary and secondary education; established the Rent Commission in 1880 in response to widespread peasant unrest; repealed the Vernacular Press Act (1878) that required the editors of Indian newspapers either to give an undertaking not to publish any matter objectionable to the government or to show the proof sheets before publication for scrutiny; introduced the controversial Ilbert Bill that proposed an amendment to the existing law, allowing Indian judges and magistrates the jurisdiction of trying British subjects in criminal offences.

A.O. Hume: One of the founders of the Indian National Congress (1885). Introduced free primary and secondary education as a district officer in the Indian Civil Service; opposed the government's exploitative policies and resigned from government service.

Annie Besant: Became president of the Theosophical Society in 1908; joined the Indian National Congress; helped launch the Home Rule League in 1916 to campaign for democracy in India; elected as president of the Indian National Congress in December 1917. Premchand claimed to have based Sophia's character on her, especially in her rejection of Christianity and attraction to Hinduism.

day. Kunwar sahib said – You were never so quick-tempered, what's happened to you?

Dr Ganguly – What's happened? What's happened should have happened forty years ago. I too have become your companion now. We will both work enthusiastically for the society for social service.

Kunwar – No, doctor sahib, I regret that I can't accompany you. I don't have the same enthusiasm now. Everything has gone with Vinay. However, Jahnavi will help you. Your expulsion has removed any doubt that I had until now that the authorities are suspicious of the society for social service, and if I'm not dissociated from it I'll have to wash my hands off my property. It's now certain that slavery is written in our destiny . . .

Dr Ganguly – What makes you sure of this?

Kunwar – The circumstances, what else? Why should I lose my property when it's certain that we'll always be slaves? If the property is safe, we can still help our distressed brothers even in our wretched condition. Both our hands will be cut if we lose even that. We won't be able even to wipe the tears of those who weep.

Dr Ganguly – Aha! So, even Kunwar Vinay Singh's death couldn't break this chain of yours. I had thought that you were liberated now but I see that this chain is binding your feet just as before. You will have realized now why I don't trust wealthy men. They are slaves to their wealth. They can never enter the fight for truth. The soldier who goes to battle with a brick of gold tied round his neck can never fight. He will be anxious only about his brick. We can never achieve our goal until we sacrifice attachment. I had some suspicion until now, but even that has been removed, that a wealthy man will harm us instead of helping us. You were a pessimist earlier, now you have become a capitalist.

When Dr Ganguly got up dejectedly and went to see Jahnavi, he saw that she was ready to go somewhere. As soon as she saw him, she greeted him with a smile and said – Now you have become my colleague. I knew that some day or the other we'll definitely pull you over. Those in whom self-respect is alive don't have any place there. There's a place there only for those who are devoted to their self-interest or skilled in deceiving themselves. Will you rest here for a few days? I'm leaving by today's train for Punjab.

Dr Ganguly – The time to rest is approaching now, where's the hurry? Now I'll rest forever. I'll also go with you.

Jahnavi – What can I say? Poor Sophia is no longer alive, otherwise she would have been a great help.

Dr Ganguly – I heard the news about her there. Her life would have been difficult now. It's just as well that she's no more. She could never have been happy deprived of love. Whatever else, she was a sati, and this is the dharma of sati women. Rani Indu is well, isn't she?

Jahnavi – She was offended with Mahendra Kumar and had come away earlier. She lives here now. She is also going with me. She has decided to make a trust for the management of her riyasat and you'll be its chairman. She won't have anything to do with the riyasat.

Meanwhile, Indu came and as soon as she saw Dr Ganguly she did pranaam to him and remarked – You have come yourself, I had thought that I would come and see you after returning from Punjab.

Dr Ganguly ate something and the three of them left in the evening. There was only one flame in the hearts of all the three, one aspiration. All three of them had full faith in God.

Kunwar Bharat Singh is again living a life of luxury, the same outings and shikar, the same foibles of the rich, the same ostentation of the rais, the same pomp and splendour. The foundations of his religious belief have been uprooted. There's nothing beyond this life for him except an infinite void and the infinite sky. The world is meaningless, the other world is also meaningless, laugh and enjoy yourself as long as there's life. Who knows what will happen after death? The world has always been like this and will always remain like this. Nobody has been able to manage it well and nobody ever will. The greatest sages, the greatest metaphysicians, rishis and seers have died, and nobody has been able to fathom this mystery. We are only human beings and our job is just to live. Patriotism, worship of the universe, service, philanthropy are all delusions. It is only these thoughts now that give peace to his heart anguished with despair.

Works Cited

Works by Premchand

Premchand, *Chitthi-Patri* (Correspondence), eds. Amrit Rai and Madan Gopal. Delhi: Janvani Prakashan Pvt. Ltd., 1996. *Premchand Rachnavali* (The Collected Works of Munshi Premchand), Vol 19.

Premchand Rachnavali, Vols 7–9, ed. Ram Anand. Delhi: Janvani Prakashan Pvt. Ltd., 1996 (Articles, speeches, memories, editorials, introductions, criticism).

Secondary Sources

Anand, S., 'On Claiming Dalit Subjectivity', *Seminar* 558 (2006). Accessed online: http://www.india-seminar.com/semframe.htm

Brueck, Laura, 'The Emerging Complexity of Dalit Consciousness', *Himal Southasian*, January 2010. Accessed online: http://www.himalmag.com/the-emerging-complexity-of-Dalit-consciousness-nw3952.html

Chandra, Sudhir, 'Premchand: A Historiographic View', *Economic and Political Weekly*, 16, 15 (11 April 1981), pp. 669–75.

Chandra, Sudhir, 'Premchand and Indian Nationalism', *Modern Asian Studies*, 16, 4 (1982), pp. 601–21.

Chandra, Sudhir, *The Oppressive Present: Literature and Social Consciousness in Colonial India*. New Delhi: Oxford University Press, 1992.

Chatterjee, Partha, *The Nation and Its Fragments: Colonial and Postcolonial Histories*. Delhi: Oxford University Press, 1994.

Dalit Atrocities – 2006, Compiled by K. Samu, Human Rights Documentation, Indian Social Institute, Lodi Road, New Delhi, India. Accessed online: http://www.isidelhi.org.in/hrnews/HR_THEMATIC_ ISSUES/DALITS/Dalit 2006.pdf

Dhanagare, D.N., *Peasant Movements in India, 1920–1950*. Delhi: Oxford University Press, 1983.

Eliot, T.S., 'Goethe as the Sage', *On Poetry and Poets*. London: Faber & Faber, 1957.

Fox, Ralph, *The Colonial Policy of British Imperialism*, introduction by Ian Talbot. Oxford: Oxford University Press, 2008.

Foucault, Michel, *Power/Knowledge: Selected Interviews and Other Writings 1972–1977*, ed. Colin Gordon, trans. Colin Gordon, Leo Marshall, John Mepham, Kate Soper. New York: Pantheon Books, 1980.

Foucault, Michel, *The History of Sexuality*, Vol. 1, trans. Robert Hurley. New York: Vintage Books, 1990.

Gopal, Madan, *Munshi Premchand: A Literary Biography.* Bombay: Asia Publishing House, 1964.

Hooja, Rima, *A History of Rajasthan.* New Delhi: Rupa & Co, 2006.

Kakar, Sudhir, *The Inner World: A Psychoanalytic Study of Childhood and Society in India.* Delhi: Oxford University Press, 1982.

Masters, Brian, *Maharana – The Story of the Rulers of Udaipur.* Ahmedabad: Mapin Publishing Pvt. Ltd., 1990.

Meininger, Irmgard, *The Kingdom of Mewar.* New Delhi: D.K. Printworld [P] Ltd., 2000.

Nehru, Jawaharlal, *The Discovery of India.* Bombay: Asia Publishing House, 1969.

Pandey, Geetanjali, *Between Two Worlds: An Intellecual Biography of Premchand.* New Delhi: Manohar, 1989.

Pandey, Gyanendra, *The Construction of Communalism in Colonial North India.* Delhi: Oxford University Press, 1990.

Rai, Alok, 'Introduction To Premchand', *Rangbhumi*, trans. Christopher King. New Delhi: Oxford University Press, 2010, pp. vii–xvi.

Rai, Amrit, *Premchand: A Life*, trans. Harish Trivedi. New Delhi: People's Publishing House, 1982.

Ray, Rajat K., 'Mewar: The Breakdown of the Princely Order', *People, Princes and Paramount Power: Society and Politics in the Indian Princely States*, ed. Robin Jeffrey. Delhi: Oxford University Press, 1978, pp. 205–39.

Sarkar, Sumit, *Modern India: 1885-1947*. Delhi: Macmillan. 2002.

Sharma, Govind Narain, *Premchand: Novelist and Thinker.* Delhi: Pragati Publications, 1999.

Sharma, Ramvilas, *Premchand Aur Unka Yug* (Premchand and His Age). New Delhi and Patna: Rajkamal Prakashan, 1995.

Shivarani Devi, *Premchand: Ghar Mein* (Premchand: In the House). Banaras: Saraswati Press, 1944.

Singh, C.S.K., 'Bhils' Participation in Rajasthan in the 1920s', *Social Scientist*, 13, 4 (April 1985), pp. 31–43.

Glossary

Aaka: Master.

Aanchal: The end of the sari which goes over the shoulder.

Aapaddharma: The action (dharma) decreed to be performed only in situations of extreme distress and emergencies.

Aheer/Aheeran: A herdsman, a herdswoman.

Apsara: A celestial nymph.

Asharfi: A gold coin formerly, current worth between sixteen and twenty-five rupees.

Ashtsiddhi: The eight siddhis: supernatural powers said to be attainable by the perfection of the techniques of yoga.

Aulia: A Muslim saint or holy man.

Baati: A thick bread-cake baked on cinders.

Bacchha: Child; pejoratively, a simple, ignorant person.

Bahu: Daughter-in-law.

Baikunth: Paradise.

Baraat: The wedding procession or journey of the bridegroom to the bride's house.

Basti: A settlement or suburb.

Behen: Sister.

Beta: Son.

Beti: Daughter.

Beeda: Rolled paan leaves stuffed with areca nuts, spices etc.

Beerbahuti: Red insects that appear in the monsoons (like ladybirds).

Bhagat: A devotee, a holy and pious man; a Vaishnavite ascetic.

Bhai/Bhaiyya/Bhaiyyon/Biraadar: Brother/brothers, an informal and affectionate form of address.

Bhabhi/Bhauji/Bhaavaj: Brother's wife.

Bhog: Food offered to a deity.

Bhutte: Corn cobs.

Bigha: A measure of land area varying from five-eighths to a third or a quarter of an acre.

Biswa: A twentieth of a bigha.

Booti: A narcotic such as bhang; any medicinal plant.

Bua: Father's sister.

Burra, burre: Big; elder; older; important.

Chaadar: A light shawl; a sheet.

Chacha: Father's brother; Uncle.

Chamaar: A man belonging to the chamaar or leather-worker's community.

Charnamrit: A mixture of milk, curd, ghee, sugar and honey which is offered to a deity; the water with which the feet of an idol are washed and then given to devotees as prasad; literally, ambrosia of the feet.

Chauka: The cooking and eating area.

Chaupaal: The assembly hall of a village.

Chaupai: A quatrain (usually printed as two lines of verse, each containing sixteen metrical instants).

Chhatank: One-sixteenth of a seer, approximately two ounces; metaphorically, a tiny amount.

Chhatthi: The sixth day after the birth of a child when rituals such as naming the child are performed. 'To remember chhatthi's milk' suggests being reduced to a completely helpless and dependent state.

Chhattisi: A lewd woman who pretends to be chaste.

Chhota/Chhotey/Chhoti: Small, young.

Chhoti haaziri: Breakfast (in British India).

Choona: Lime

Chooran: Digestive powder composed of ground spices.

Dada: Paternal grandfather; also older brother; a form of address for an older man.

Dakshina/Dacchina: Remuneration given to a brahman for the performance of rituals or other religious services; donation. Also, remuneration or donation given to a guru or teacher (guru dakshina).

Darshan: Seeing or meeting a holy or a respected person, a shrine, or a deity.

Deeksha: Initiation of a disciple.

Deenbandhu: Friend of the poor.

Dharmashala: An inn or rest-house for pilgrims and travellers; an alms-house built to obtain religious merit.

Dharmavatar: Incarnation of dharma.

Dharmayuddha: Battle of righteousness.

Dhuniya: A cotton-carder.

Dikpaal: The guardian deities of the ten points of the compass.

Doha: A rhyming couplet.

Dom/Domra: Belonging to the dom community (makers of ropes, baskets etc; workers at cremation places; also, a community of singers and dancers).

Durbaan: Doorman, gatekeeper.

Fatiha: The first chapter of the Quran, read for dying Muslims; prayers for the dead; prayers in the name of, and offerings to, saints.

Farzi: The queen in chess, minister, vizier.

Gangajal: Water from the Ganga.

Ghuyien: The tuberous herb *colocasia antiquorum* (arvi, kacchu).

Gopi: Milkmaid; in mythology, any of the milkmaids who were in love with Krishna.

Gora: Fair, white-skinned; a European man.

Habshi: A black African.

Halvai: A maker and seller of sweets (mithai).

Havan-kund: A vessel of metal or clay in which oblations to fire are made.

Ikka: A small one-horse vehicle.

Janeu/Janeudhaari: The sacred thread of a brahman; those who wear the sacred thread, i.e. brahmans.

Julaha: weaver.

Kama: The god of love.

Kahaar: A carrier of palanquins or a water-drawer belonging to the kahaar community.

Kalma: The Muslim confession of faith; a word, speech; ironically, to read somebody's kalma: to be servile.

Kalyuga: Name of the last and worst of the four ages of the world according to Hindu belief — the present age, at the end of which the world will be destroyed.

Kanyadaan: The Hindu marriage rite of giving away one's daughter.

Kartik: The eighth month of the Hindu lunar year (October-November).

Kaviraj: A title for physicians in Bengal.

Kevra: The screwpine and its fragrant flower.

Khaat: Cot strung with rope.

Khanjari: Tambourine.

Khasam: Husband.

Khoncha: Baskets carried on their heads by hawkers.

Khurma: A sweet shaped like a date.

Kirantey: Christian of low social status.

Kirastaani: Christianity

Kos: Approximately two miles.

Koyal: The black cuckoo.

Kulhar: A clay cup.

Kulhiya: A small clay cup.

Lacchmi: Variation of Lakshmi, goddess of wealth; Vishnu's consort.

Laat: Governor in British India; Lord.

Leela: Play; the creative play of God in this world.

Loo: The hot wind that blows in May and June on the plains of north India.

Maalik/Maalkin: Master, mistress.

Maagh: The eleventh month of the Hindu lunar calendar (January-February).

Mahajan: Merchant; money-lender.

Maharajin: A woman cook.

Mahto: A village headman.

Maika: Mother's house; parental home of a married woman.

Malecch: a person of low birth; an outcaste; a barbarian; a sinful person.

Mandap: A temporary canopy where a wedding ceremony takes place.

Mangal: Good fortune; an auspicious event, such as a marriage; also Mars; Tuesday.

Maulsiri: A large evergreen tree and its fruit and flowers. The flowers are used in making perfume.

Mazaar: Shrine; tomb; grave.

Misrain: A woman cook belonging to the Misra or brahman community.

Morha: A stool made of cane or reed.

Muhalla: A suburb; quarter, or ward of a city or a town.

Mukhia: Chief; the village headman.

Nani: Maternal grandmother.

Naazim: An administrator.

Nadirshahi: Recalling the Persian king Nadirshah, known for his cruelty and harsh rule.

Naihar: Maternal home.

Paasi/Paasin: A toddy extractor/a woman toddy extractor or the wife of a toddy extractor.

Pahar: A unit of time of three hours. The first pahar begins at 3 a.m.

Panchayat/Panch: A village council comprising five members; panch: the members of the council.

Panda: A brahman who has the hereditary function of superintending a place of pilgrimage.

Paraat: A large, circular metal dish with a raised edge.

Paseri: A weight of five seers.

Pattal: A platter made of leaves.

Patwari: Registrar of the village land accounts.

Peer: A Muslim saint or holy man.

Phagun: The twelfth lunar month of the Hindu calendar (February-March).

Phullauri: A small puffed cake of pulses or rice (sometimes with fruit), fried in ghee or oil.

Pinda-daan: Oblation to ancestors.

Ponga: Stupid, foolish, empty.

Prasad: Food offered to a deity and later shared among devotees.

Qasba: A small town; a large village.

Ramabaan: Rama's arrow; an immediately effective or reliable medicine.

Ramdana: Amaranth seeds.

Raav/Rai: A high ranking title during British rule in India; also a prince, a chieftain.

Rais: A person of rank or status; a nobleman; a wealthy person.

Riyasat: A princely state.

Saala: Wife's brother; often a term of abuse.

Saavan: The fifth month of the Hindu lunar calendar (July-August).

Sagun: The Supreme Being seen as positively qualified or personal.

Sanjeevani: A life-giving herb.

Shara: Religious injunction of the Quran.

Samskara: Education; upbringing; influence of previous birth; purificatory ceremony or rite.

Sanyas/Sanyasi/Sanyasini: Renunciation of the world; a man or a woman who has renounced the world.

Saraswati: The goddess of speech and learning and patroness of the arts.

Sasural: The home of a girl's in-laws.

Sattu: Coarse flour made of parched grain (barley, gram etc).

Satyuga: Immemorially ancient; of uncorrupted, pristine virtue; also the first of the four ages when truth and virtue prevailed.

Sehra: A chaplet of flowers and other materials worn by a bridegroom.

Shastric: Doctrinal, pertaining to the Shastras, the ancient Indian scriptures.

Shraadh: A ceremony for the benefit of deceased ancestors and relatives.

Siddha: An ascetic of great powers and saintliness.

Siddhi: Supernatural powers said to be attainable by the perfection of the techniques of yoga.

Somrasa: The intoxicating, fermented juice of a particular plant which was drunk at Vedic rituals and offered to the gods; the drink of the gods.

Sooar: Swine.

Sootradhaar: Literally thread-holder; stage-manager or principal actor who superintends a dramatic performance and plays a leading role in the prelude; a puppet-master.

Tamolin: a paan seller's wife; a woman who sells paan.

Tamtam: A one-horse carriage.

Tap/Tapasya: Arduous ascetic practices, especially for the grant of a boon.

Tapasvi/Tapasvini: Male/female ascetic.

Tauk: Metal collar.

Teeka/Tilak: A mark on the forehead, made with saffron or sandal, as a sign of eminence or as a sectarian mark to indicate caste, status, or sect.

Tilakdhaari: Those who wear the tilak.

Trimurti: Triad of Brahma, Vishnu and Shiva.

Vaalid: Father.

Vaidya: A practitioner of Ayurvedic medicine.

Vaishnava: Follower of Vishnu.

Vazir: The queen in chess; a minister.

Vibhuti: Glory; supernatural power; ashes.

Victoria: A light, four-wheeled horse-carriage with a collapsible hood, seats for two passengers and an elevated driver's seat in front. Named after Queen Victoria.

Vilayat: A realm beyond India; England; Britain; Europe; the West. The main reference is to England during British rule in India.

Vimaan: The aerial vehicle of the gods.

Yaar/Yaaron: Friend/friends; it can also mean lover in some contexts.

Yamraj: The god of death, who judges and rules the dead.

Yamdoot: The ambassador of Yamraj.